BEZKAMP

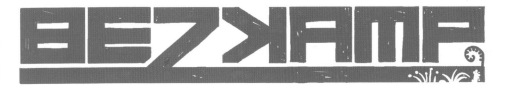

ROAR™

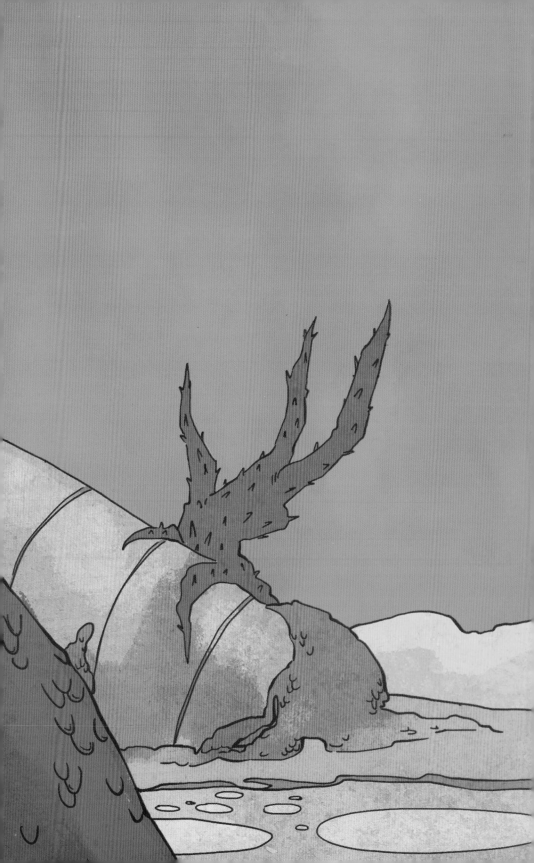

BEZKAMP

written by **SAMUEL SATTIN**

illustrated by **JEN HICKMAN**

lettered by **AW'S DC HOPKINS**

color assistance by **K UVICK**

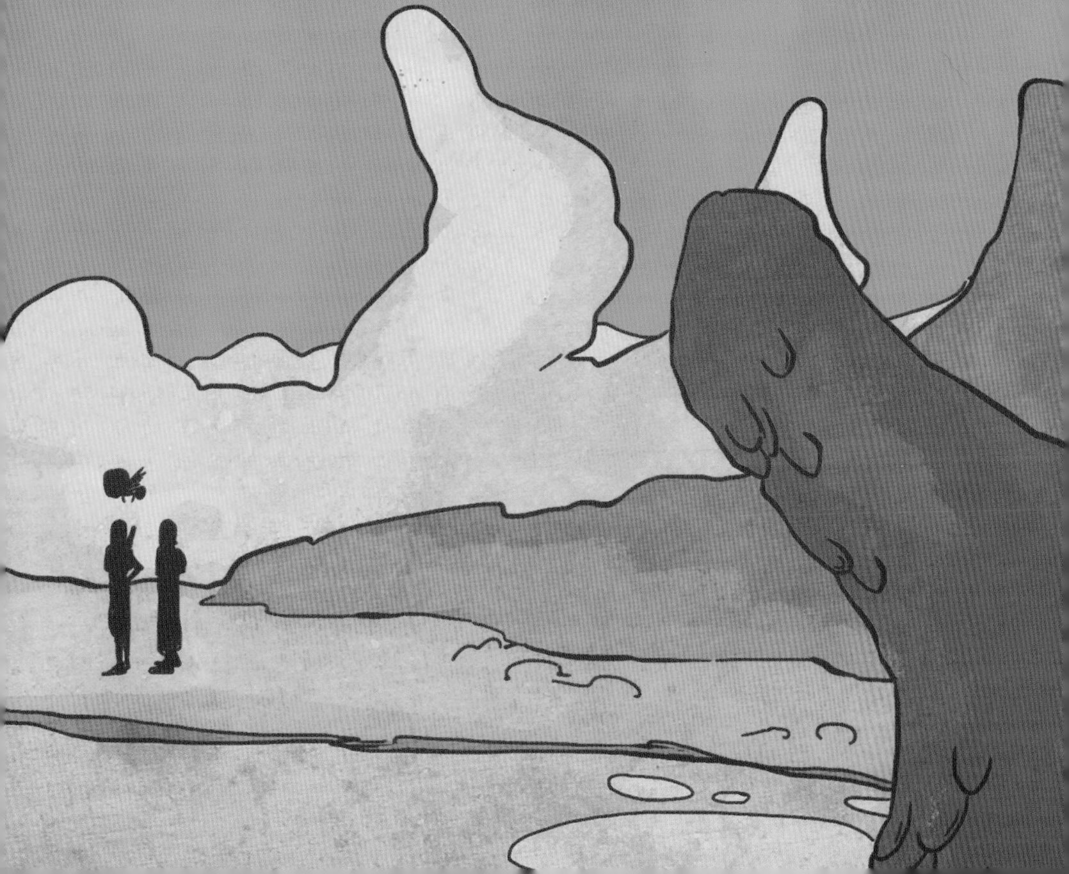

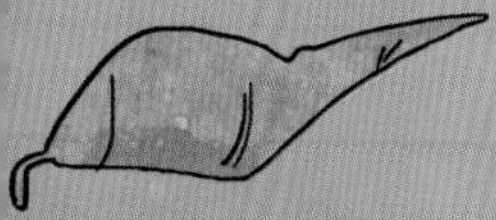

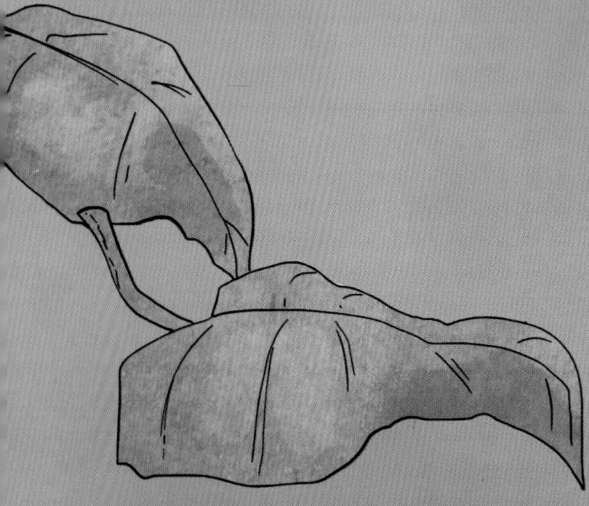

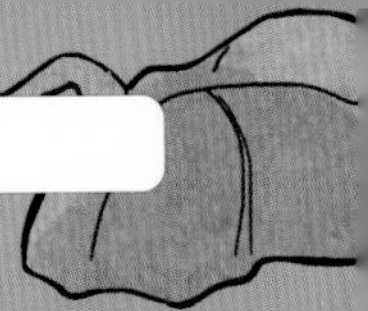

CHEPTAR ONCE

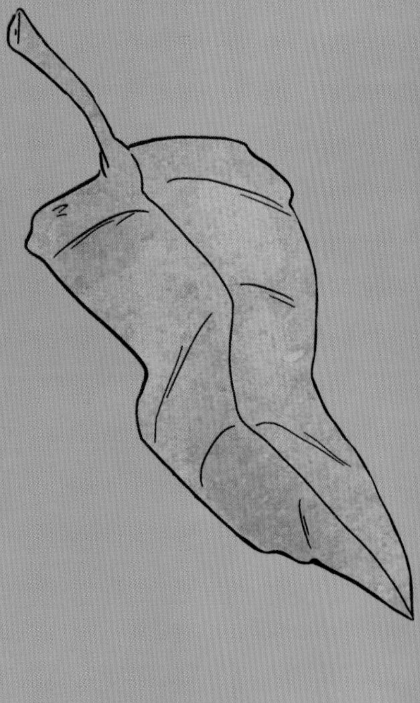

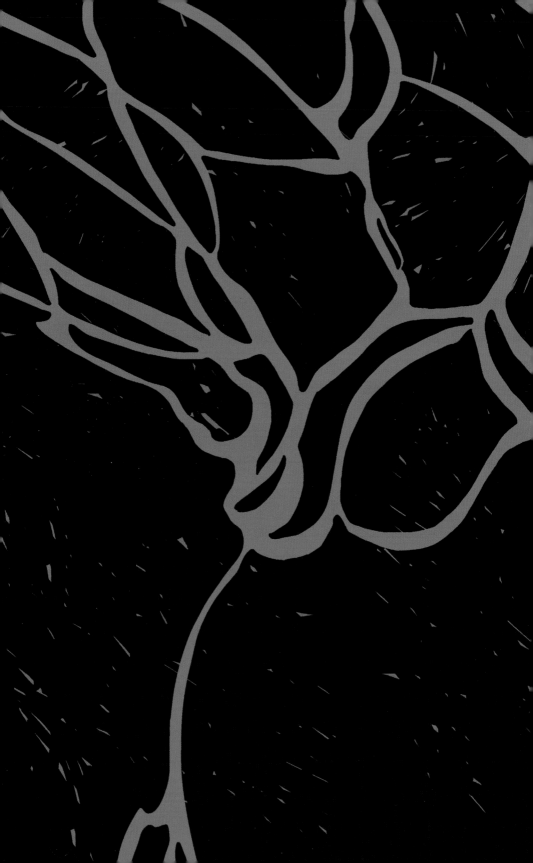

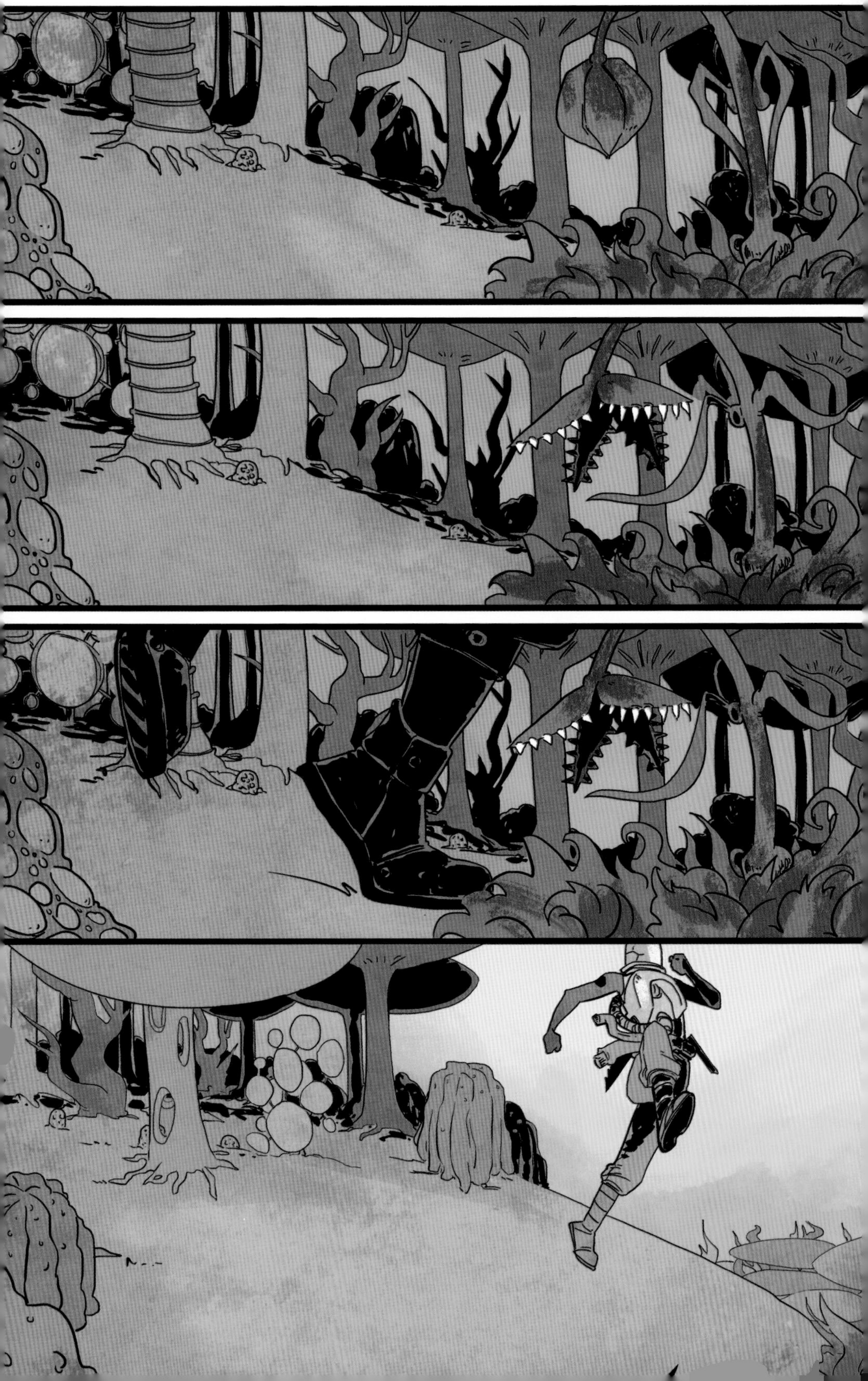

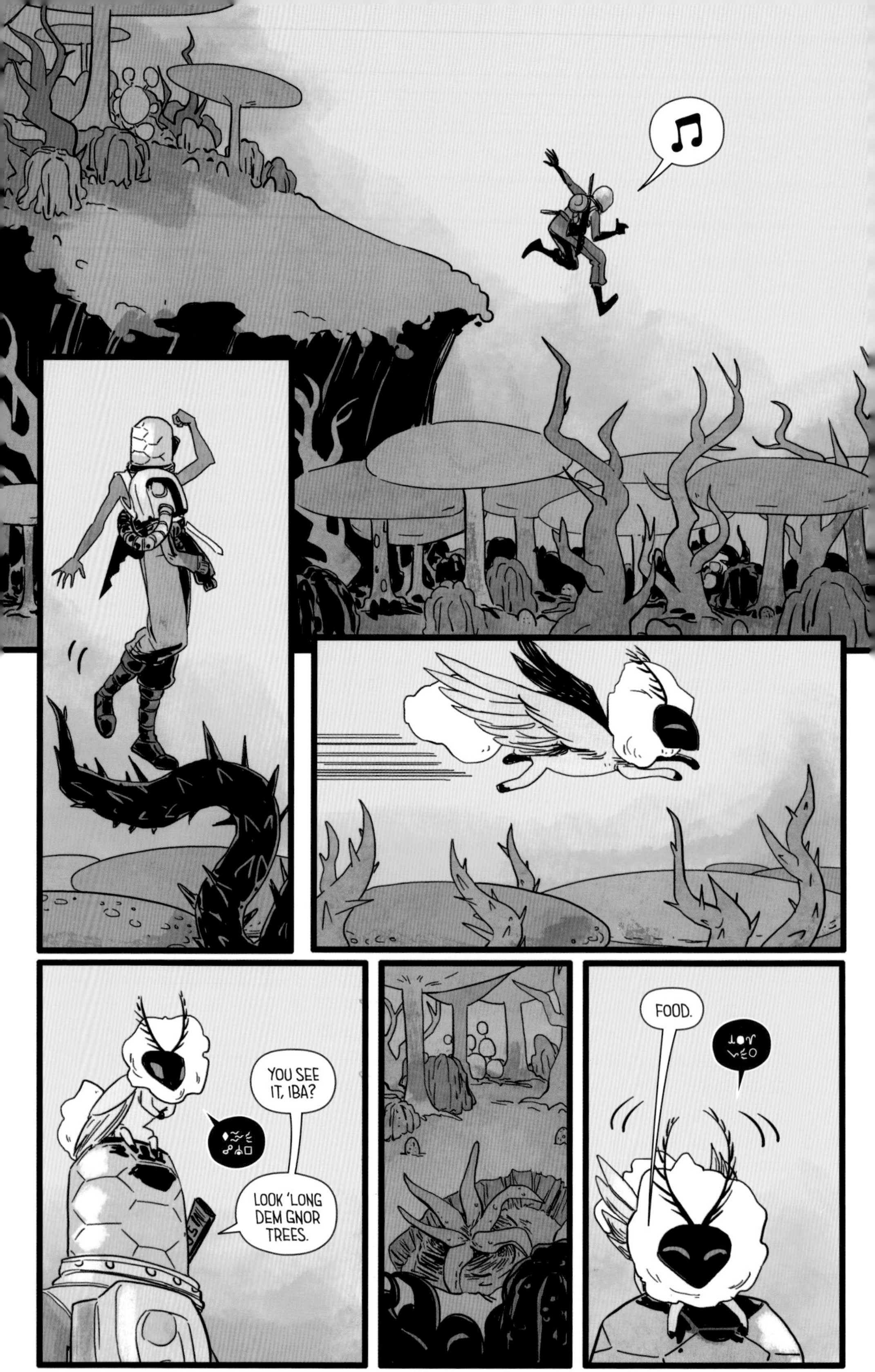

♫
YOU SEE IT, IBA?
LOOK 'LONG DEM GNOR TREES.
FOOD.

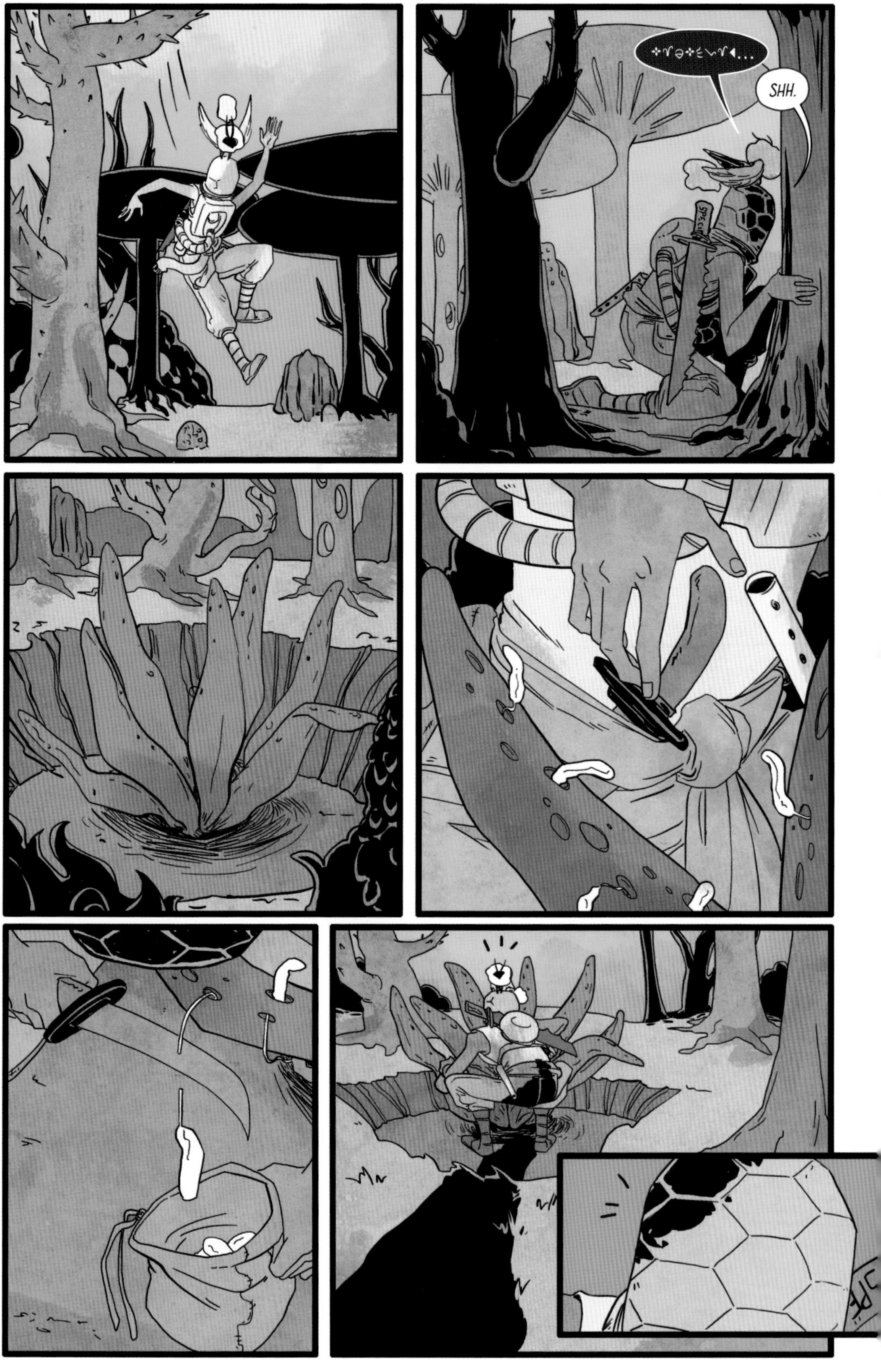
SHH.

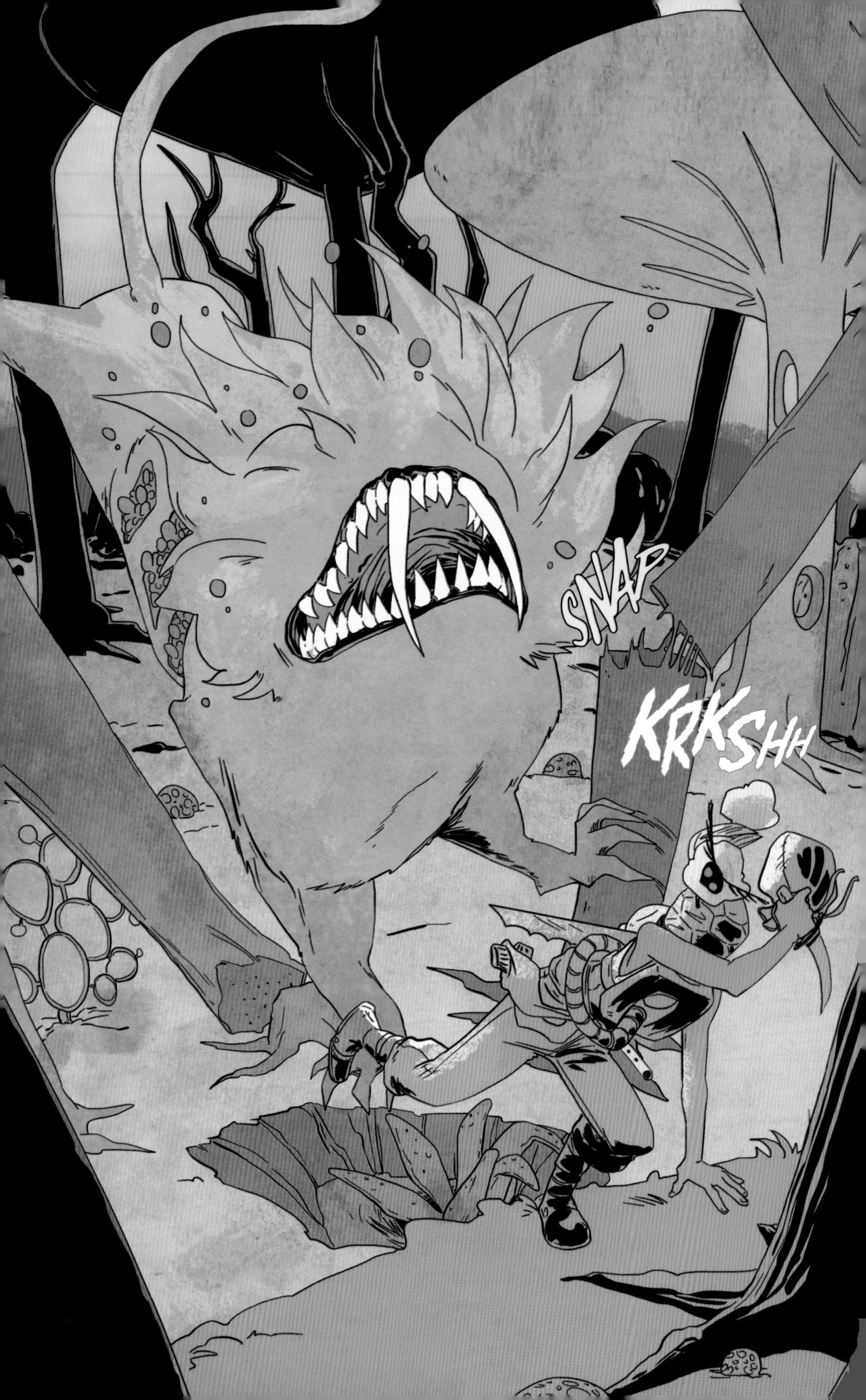
SNAP
KRKSHH

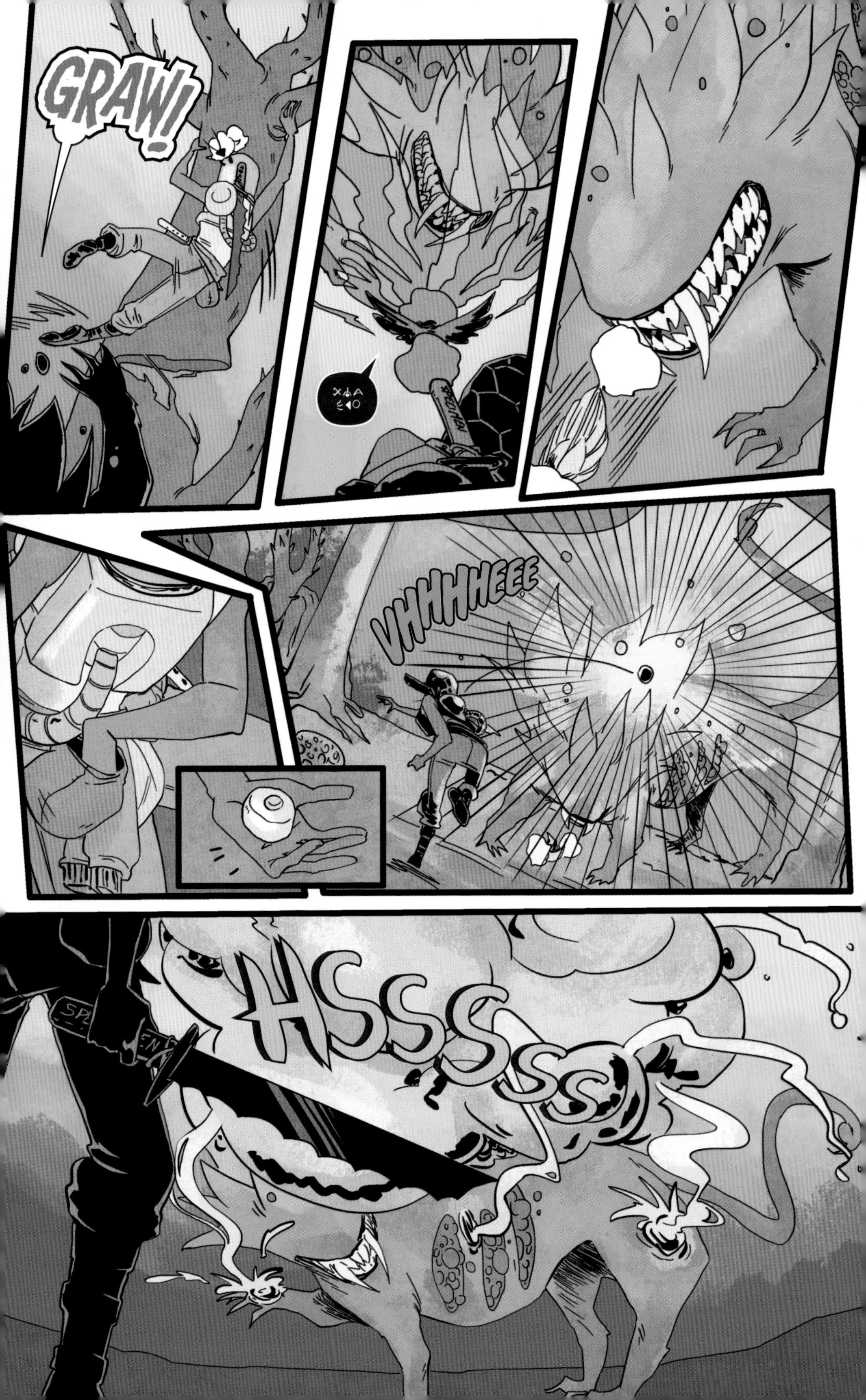
GRAW!
VHHHHEEE
HSSSSS

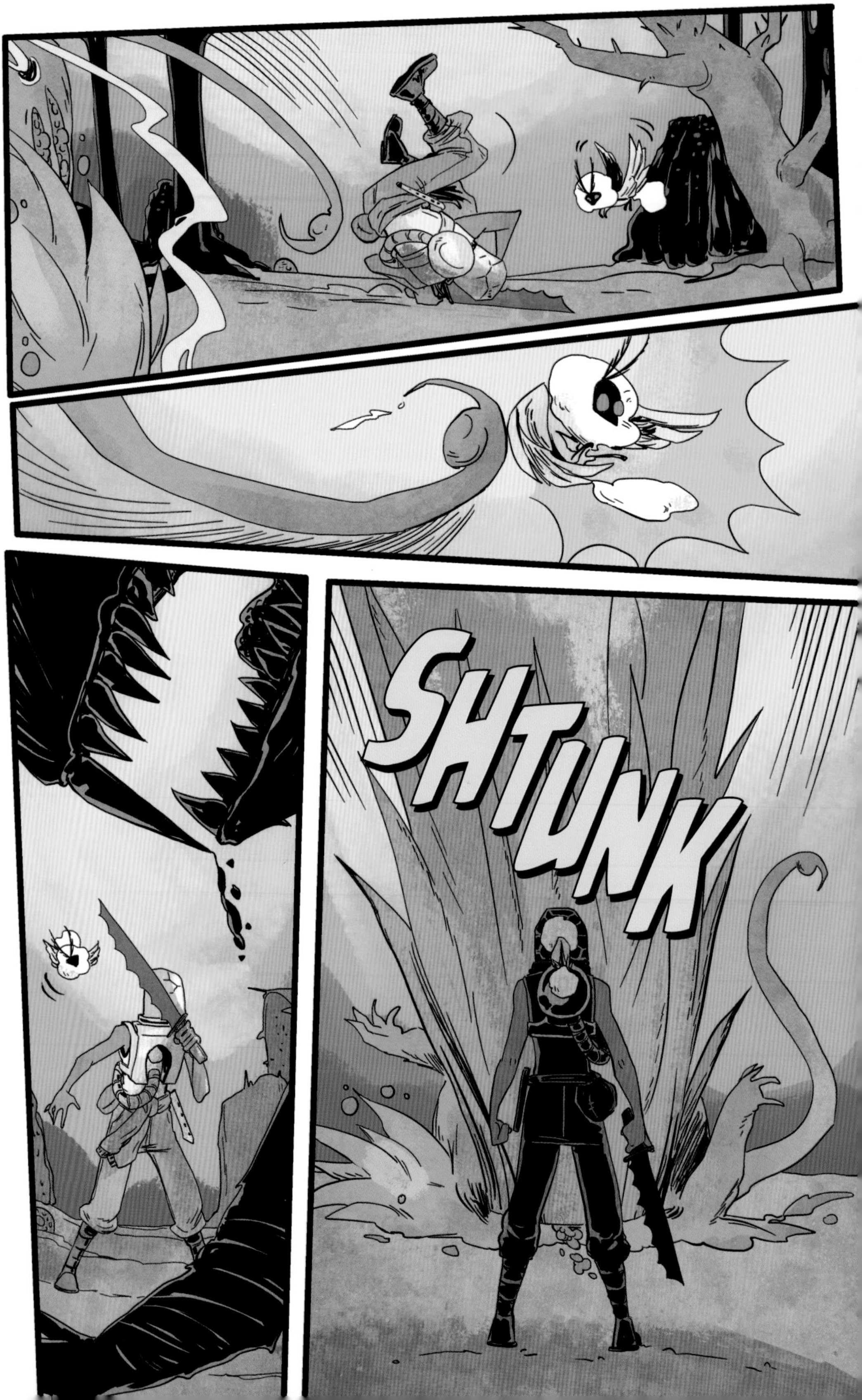
SHTUNK

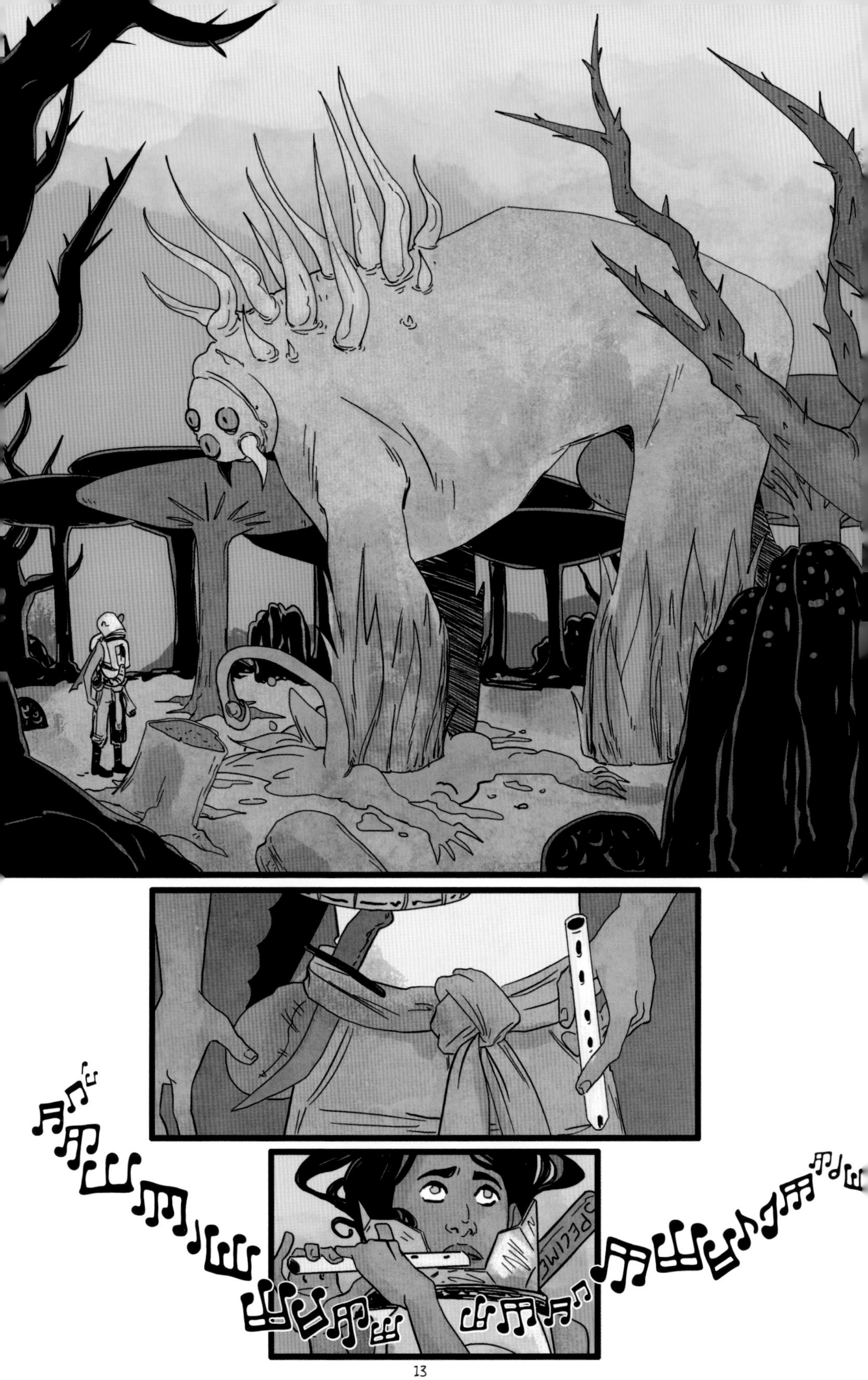

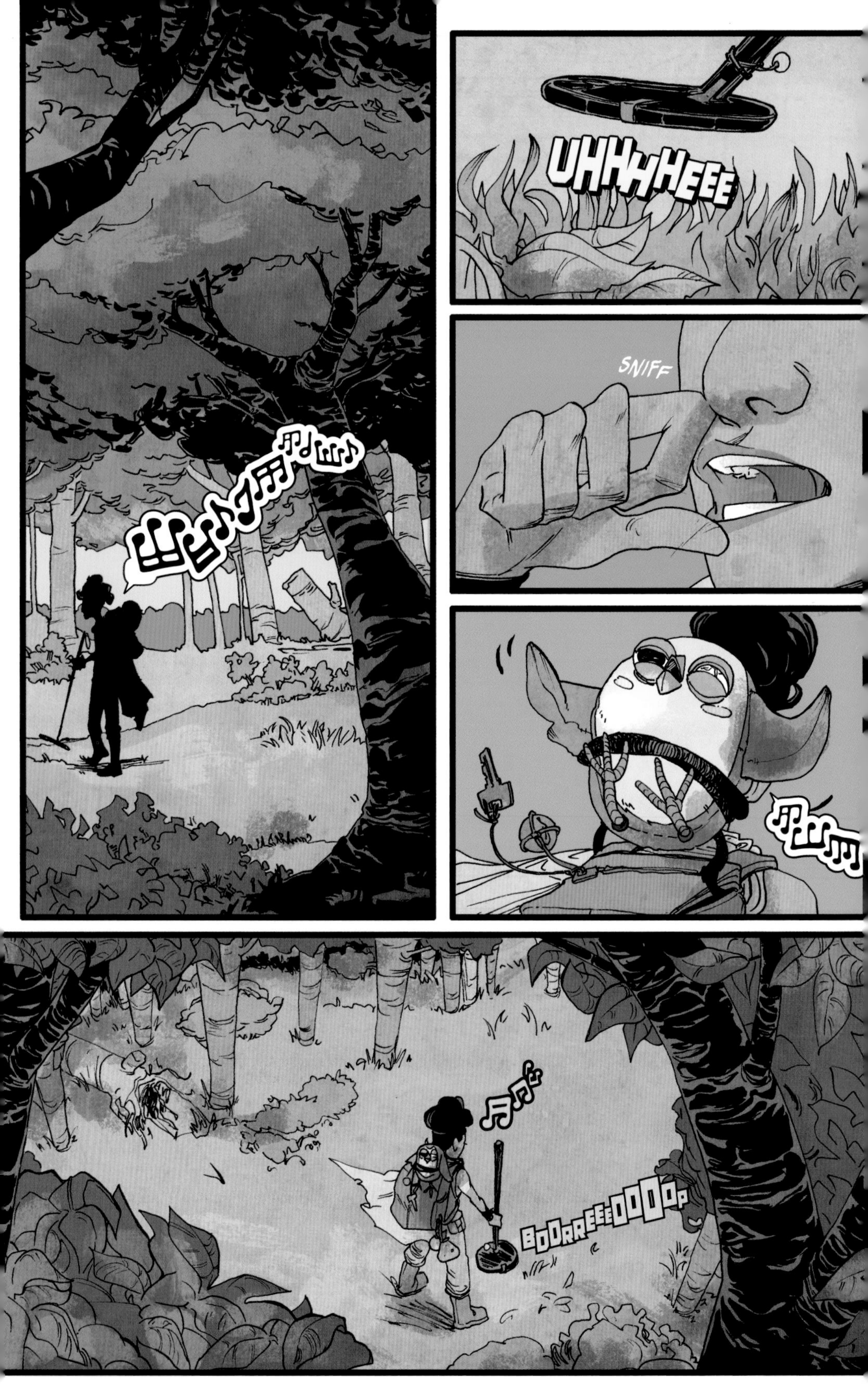
UHHHHEEE
SNIFF
BOORREEEOOOOP

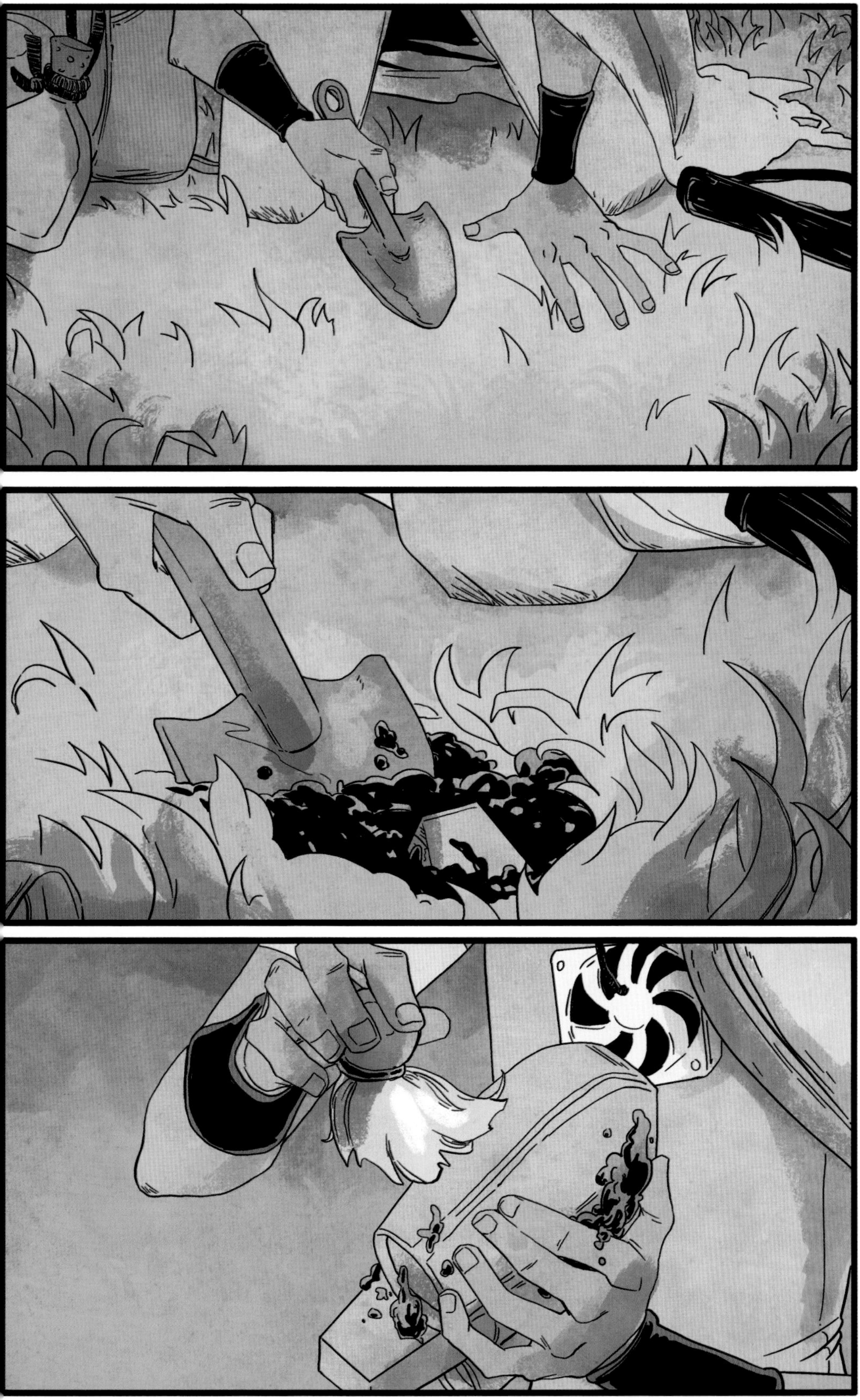

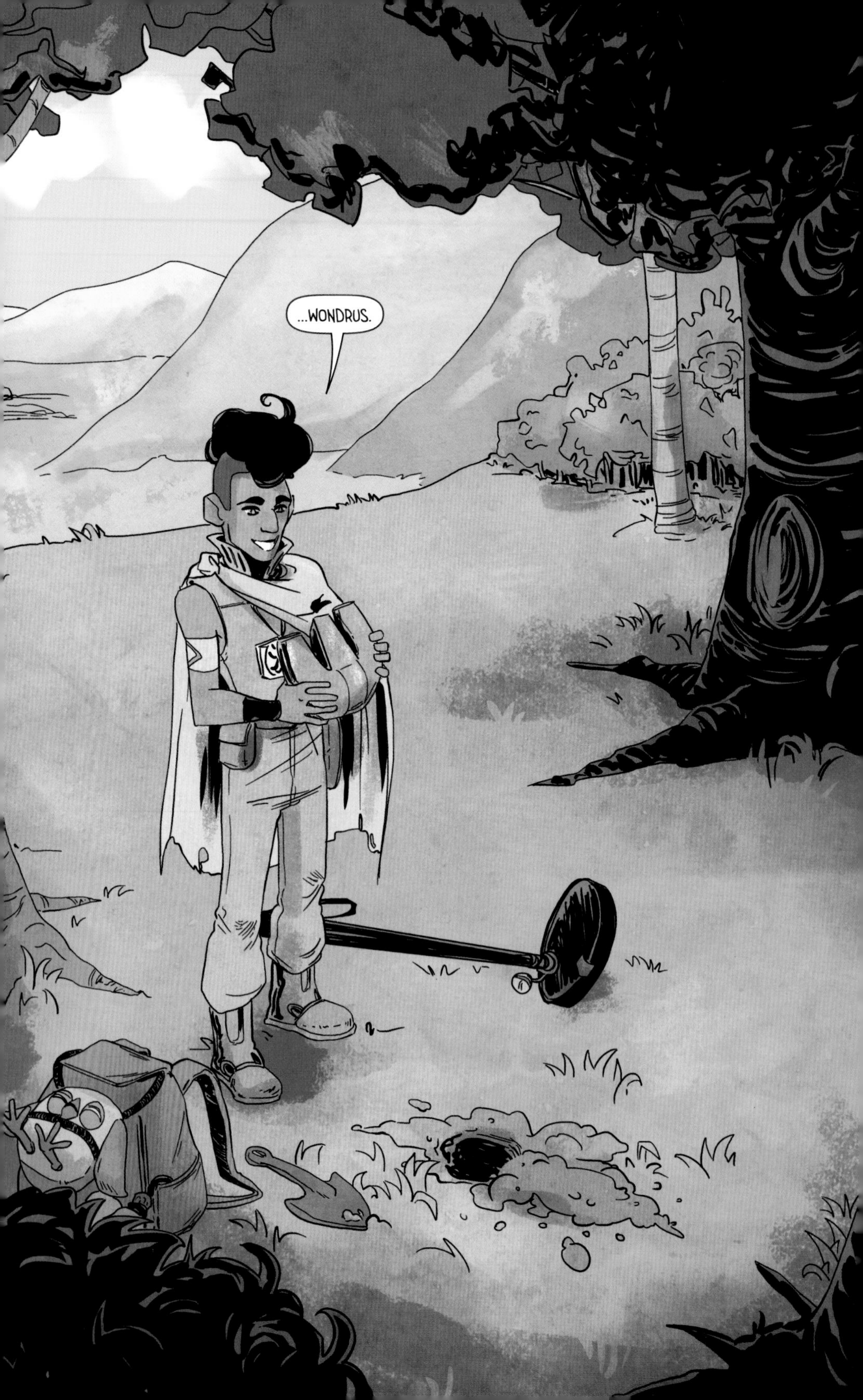
...WONDRUS.

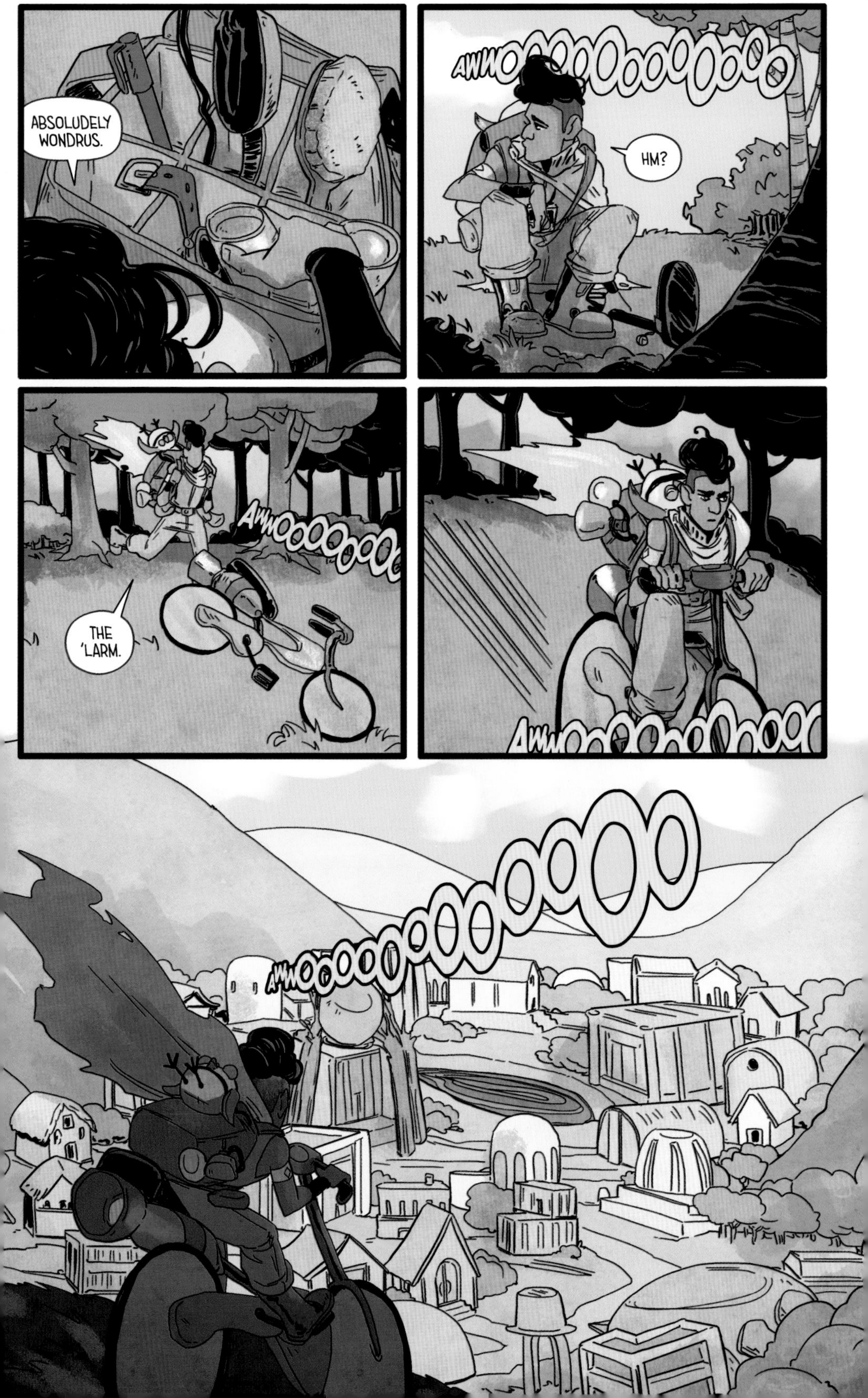
ABSOLUDELY WONDRUS.
AWWOOOOOoooOOOOO
HM?
AWWOOOOOOOOO
THE 'LARM.
AWWOOOOOOOOOO
AWWOOOOOOOOOOOOOOOO

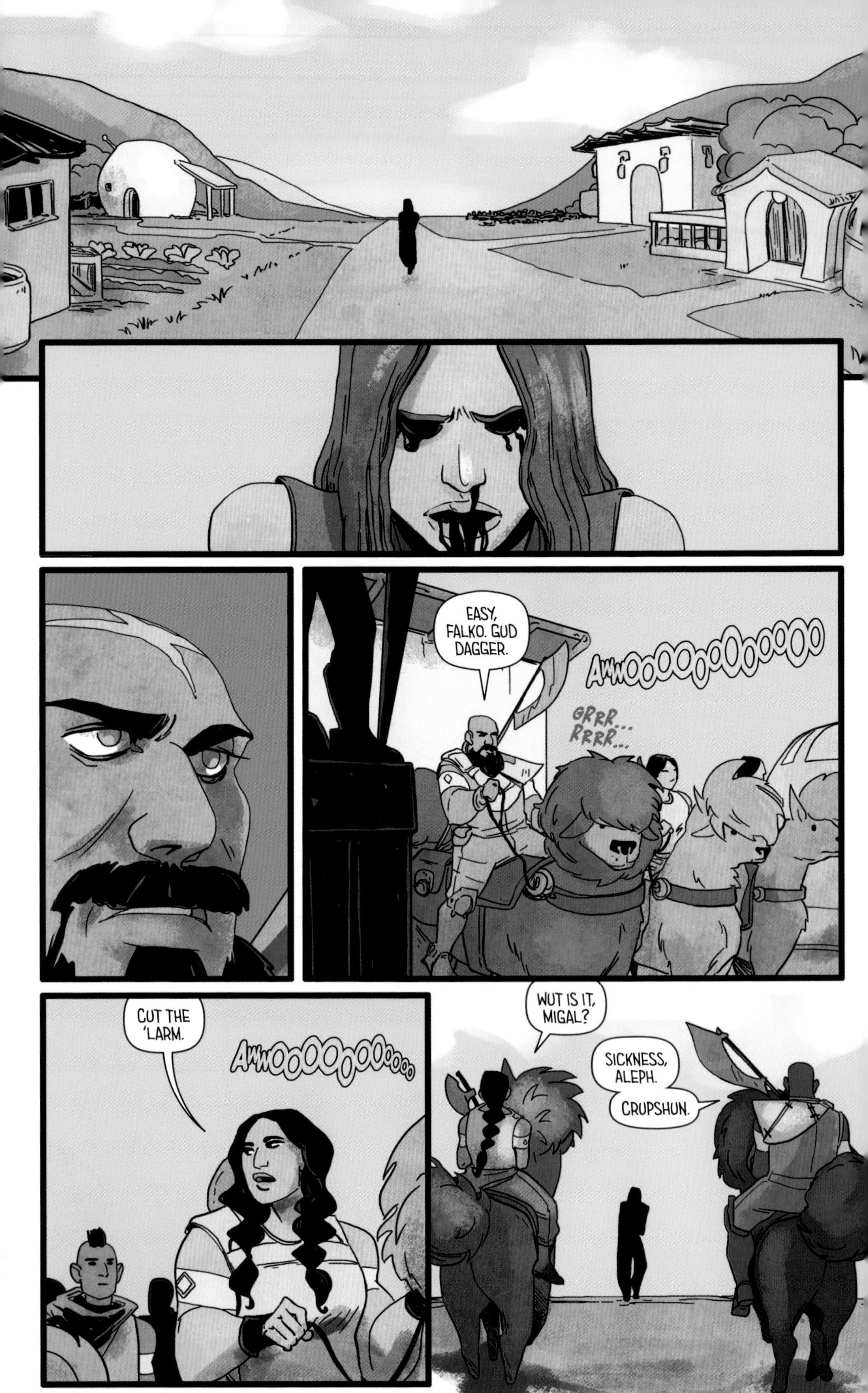
EASY, FALKO. GUD DAGGER.
AWWOOOOOOOOOOOO
GRRR... RRRR...
CUT THE 'LARM.
AWWOOOOOOOOOooo
WUT IS IT, MIGAL?
SICKNESS, ALEPH.
CRUPSHUN.

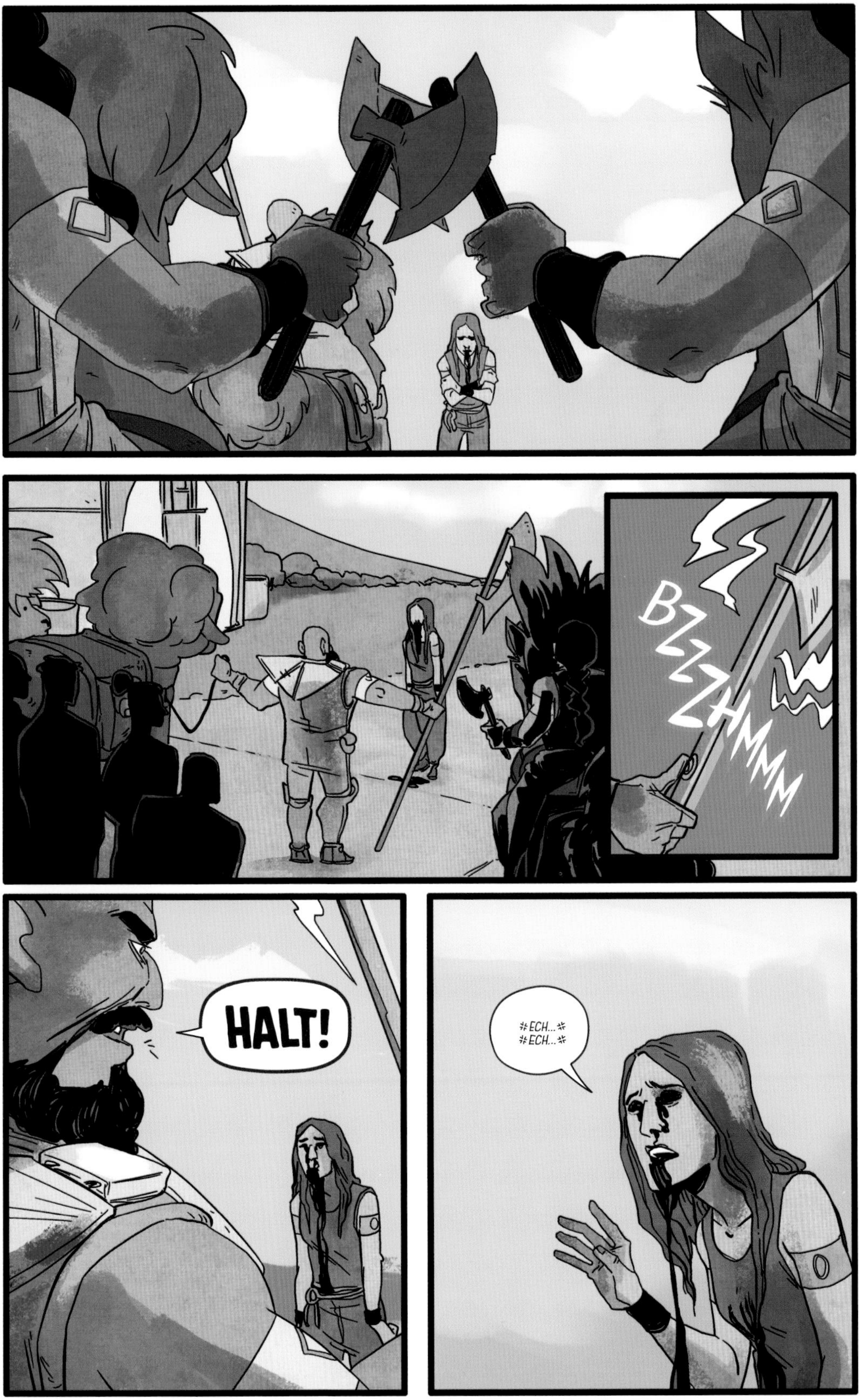
BZZZHMMM
HALT!
ECH...
ECH...

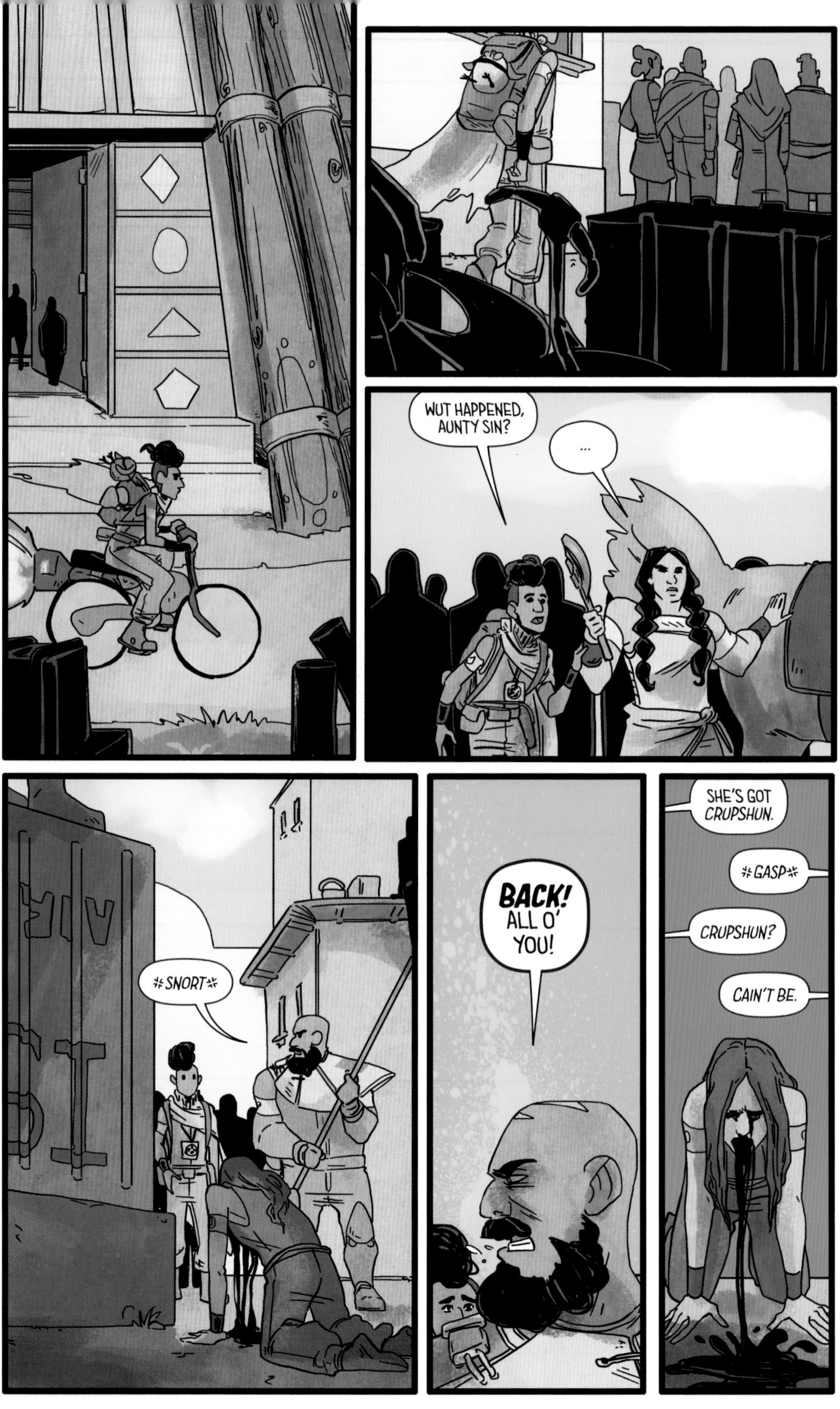
WUT HAPPENED, AUNTY SIN?
...
⁜SNORT⁜
BACK! ALL O' YOU!
SHE'S GOT CRUPSHUN.
⁜GASP⁜
CRUPSHUN?
CAIN'T BE.

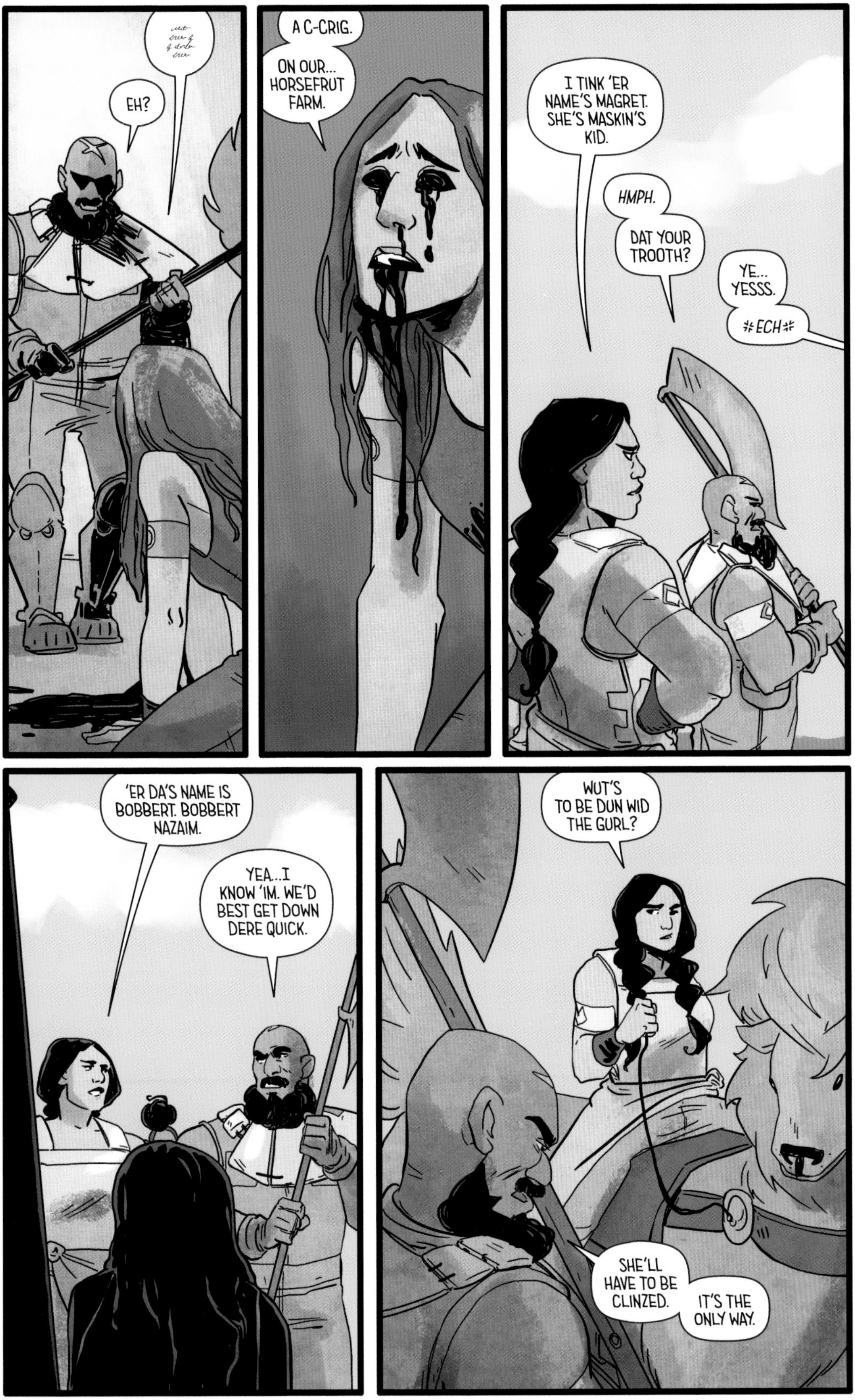
EH?
A C-CRIG.
ON OUR... HORSEFRUT FARM.
I TINK 'ER NAME'S MAGRET. SHE'S MASKIN'S KID.
HMPH.
DAT YOUR TROOTH?
YE... YESSS.
#ECH#
'ER DA'S NAME IS BOBBERT. BOBBERT NAZAIM.
YEA...I KNOW 'IM. WE'D BEST GET DOWN DERE QUICK.
WUT'S TO BE DUN WID THE GURL?
SHE'LL HAVE TO BE CLINZED.
IT'S THE ONLY WAY.

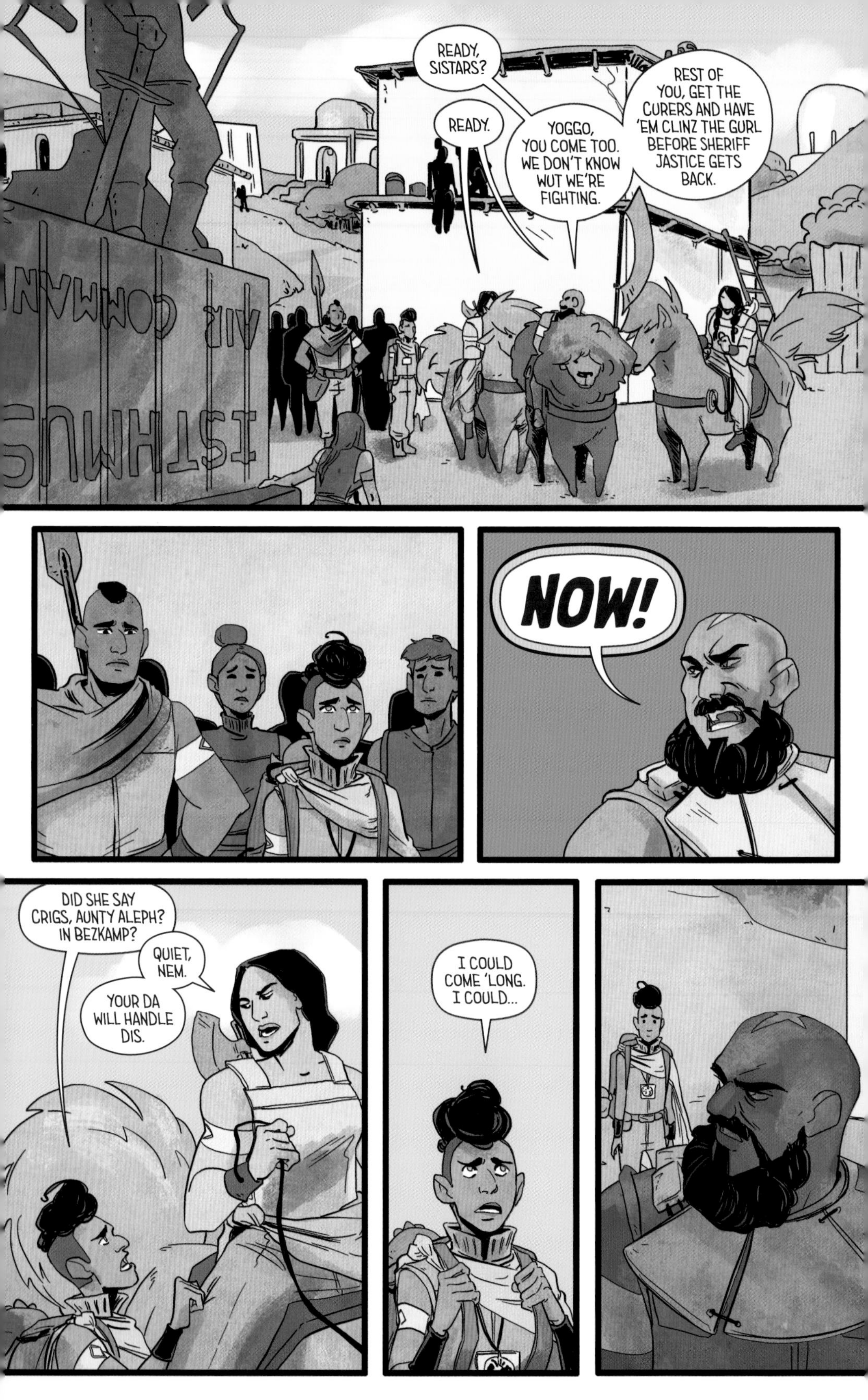
READY, SISTARS?
READY.
YOGGO, YOU COME TOO. WE DON'T KNOW WUT WE'RE FIGHTING.
REST OF YOU, GET THE CURERS AND HAVE 'EM CLINZ THE GURL BEFORE SHERIFF JASTICE GETS BACK.
NOW!
DID SHE SAY CRIGS, AUNTY ALEPH? IN BEZKAMP?
QUIET, NEM.
YOUR DA WILL HANDLE DIS.
I COULD COME 'LONG. I COULD...

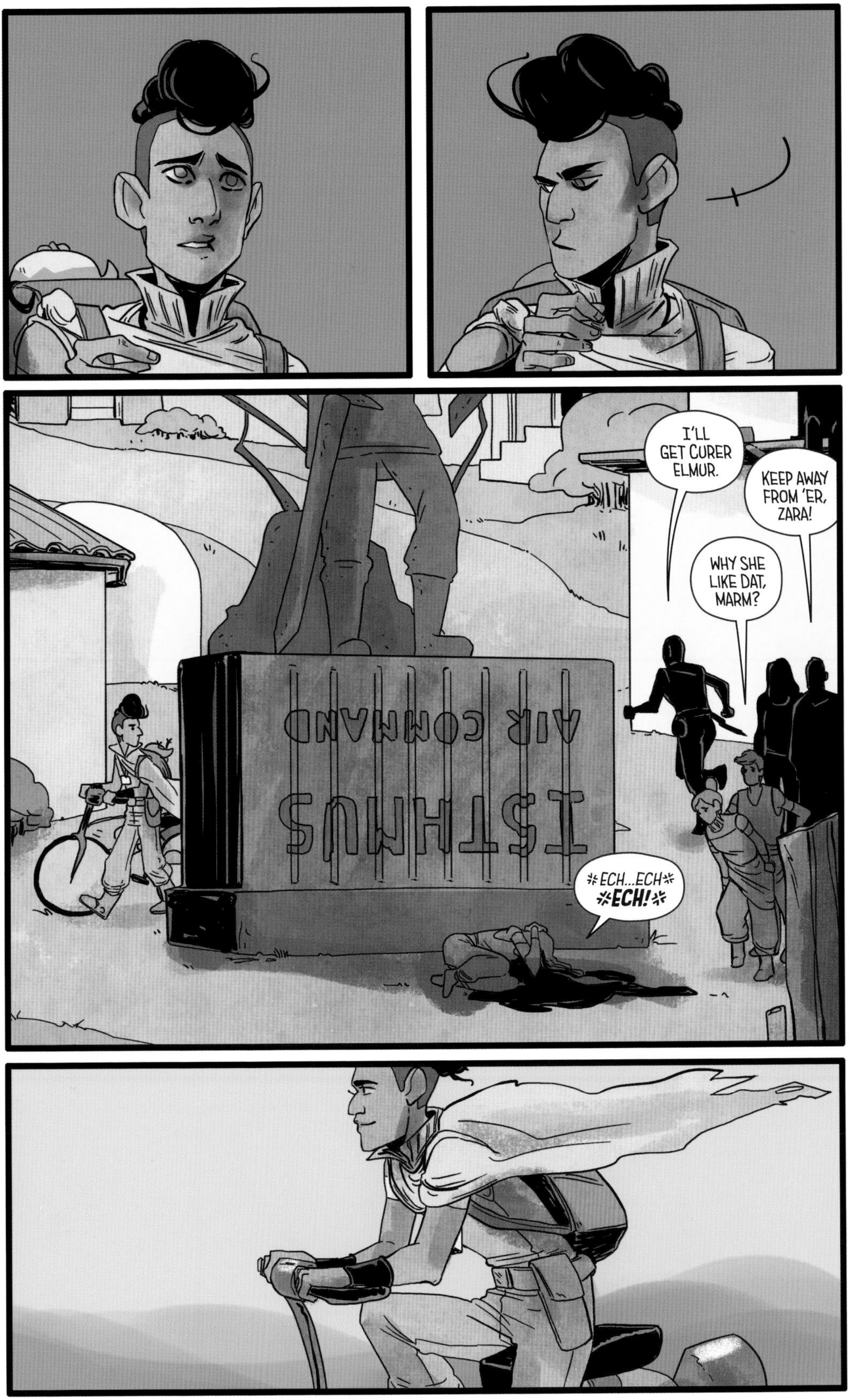

ISTHMUS AIR COMMAND
I'LL GET CURER ELMUR.
KEEP AWAY FROM 'ER, ZARA!
WHY SHE LIKE DAT, MARM?
ECH...ECH *ECH!*

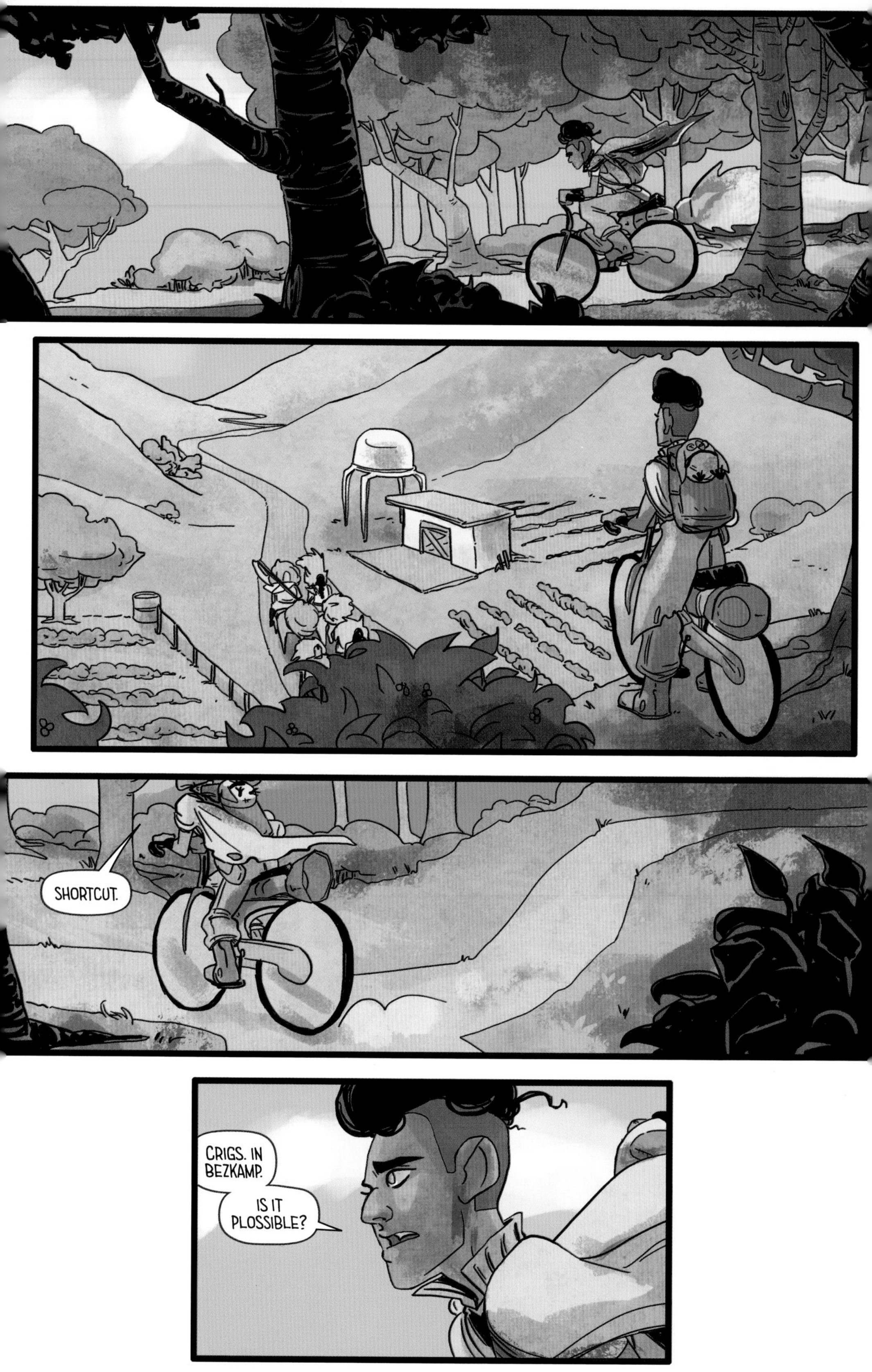
SHORTCUT.
CRIGS. IN BEZKAMP.
IS IT PLOSSIBLE?

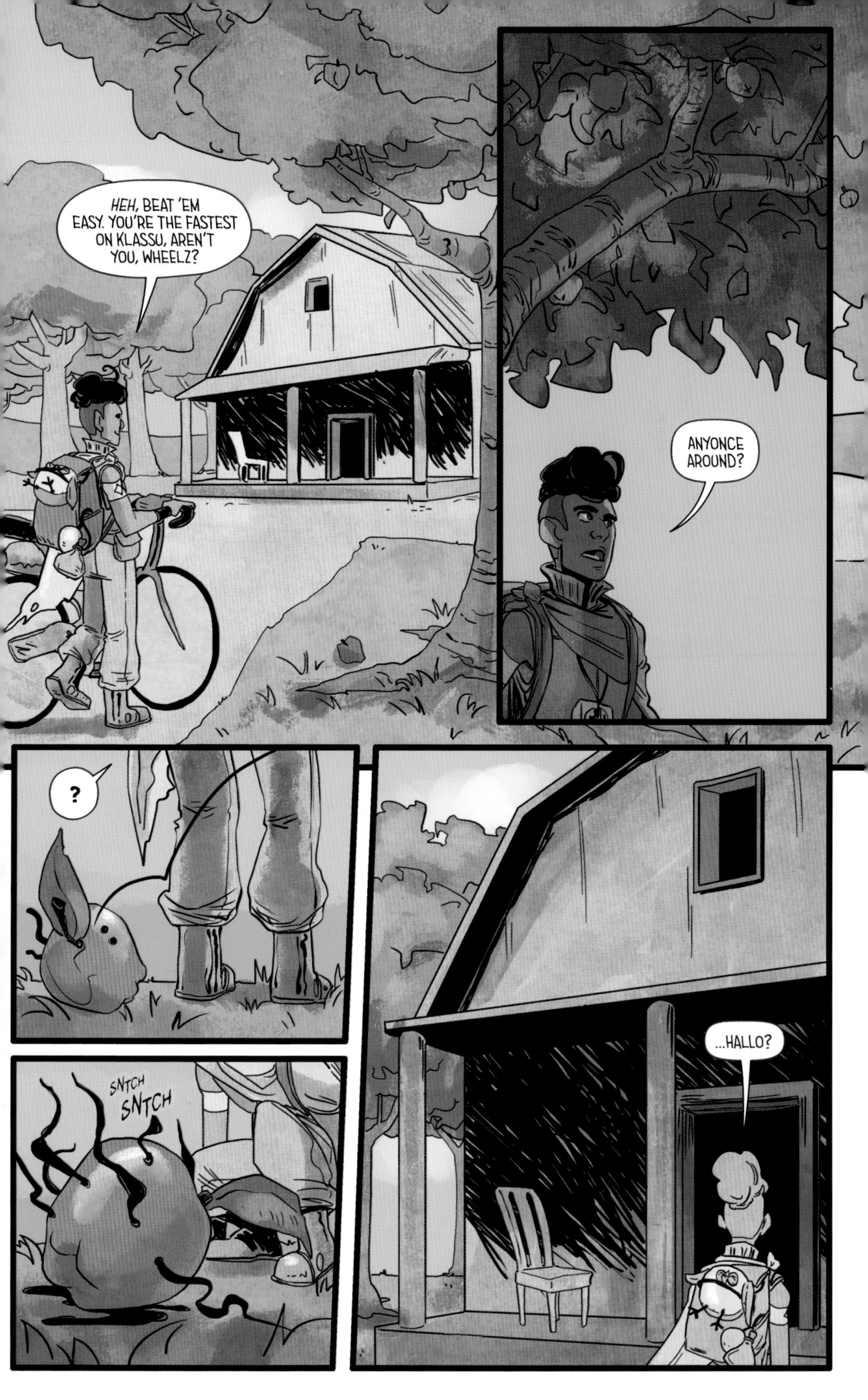
HEH, BEAT 'EM EASY. YOU'RE THE FASTEST ON KLASSU, AREN'T YOU, WHEELZ?
ANYONCE AROUND?
?
SNTCH
SNTCH
...HALLO?

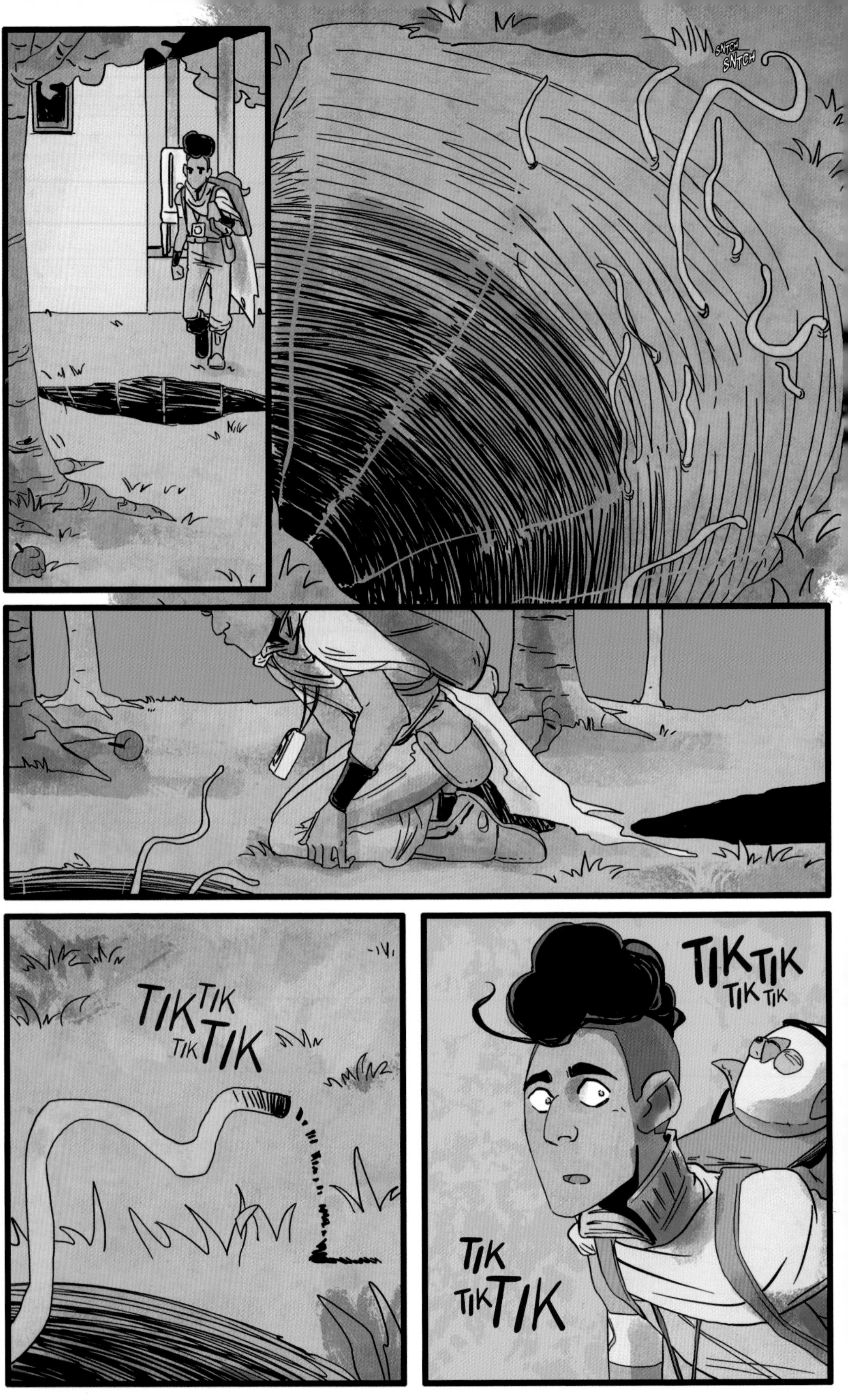
SNTCH
SNTCH
TIK TIK
TIK TIK
TIK TIK
TIK TIK
TIK
TIK TIK

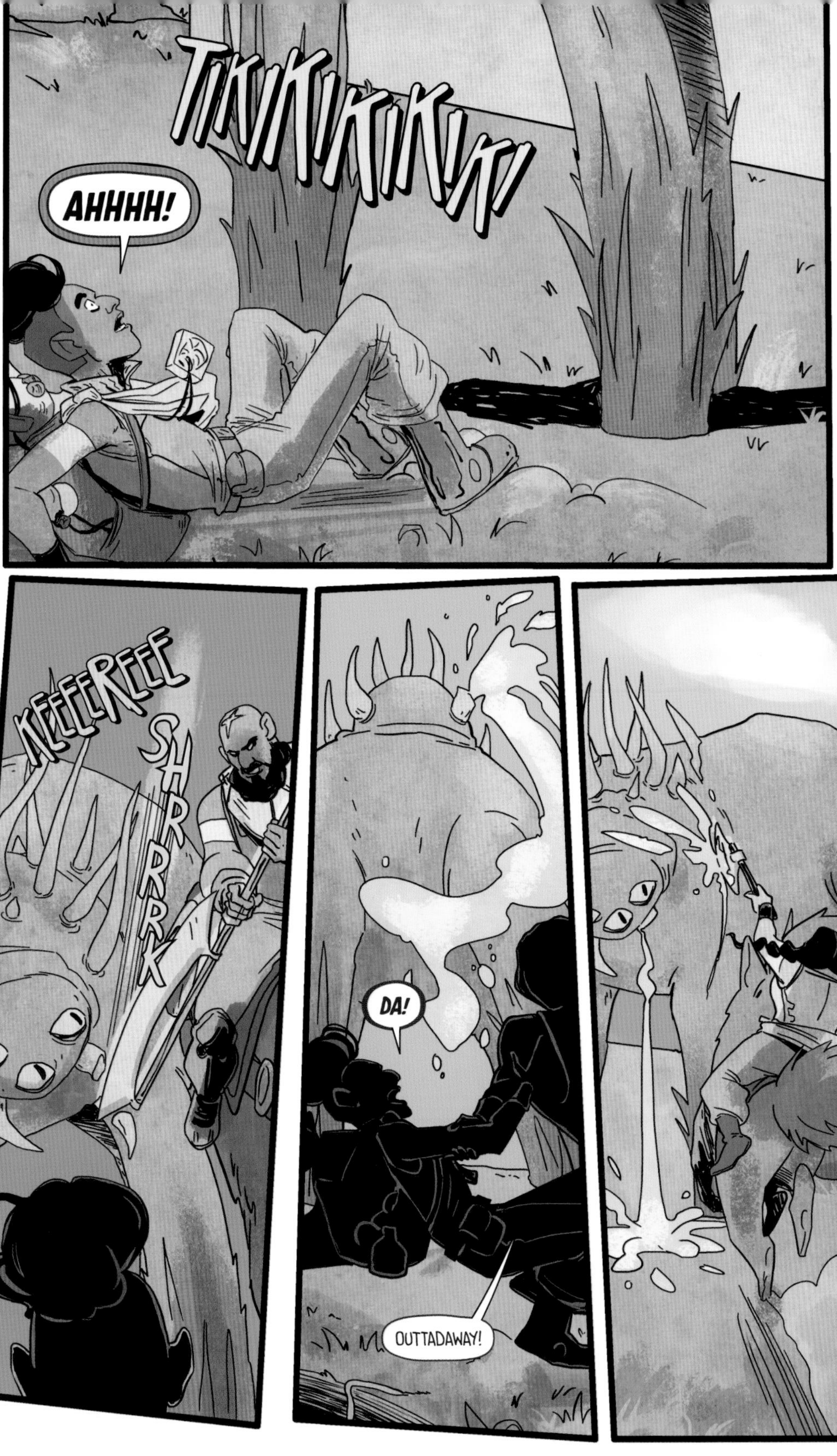
TIKIKIKIKIKIKIKI
AHHHH!
KEEEEREEE
SHRRRRK
DA!
OUTTADAWAY!

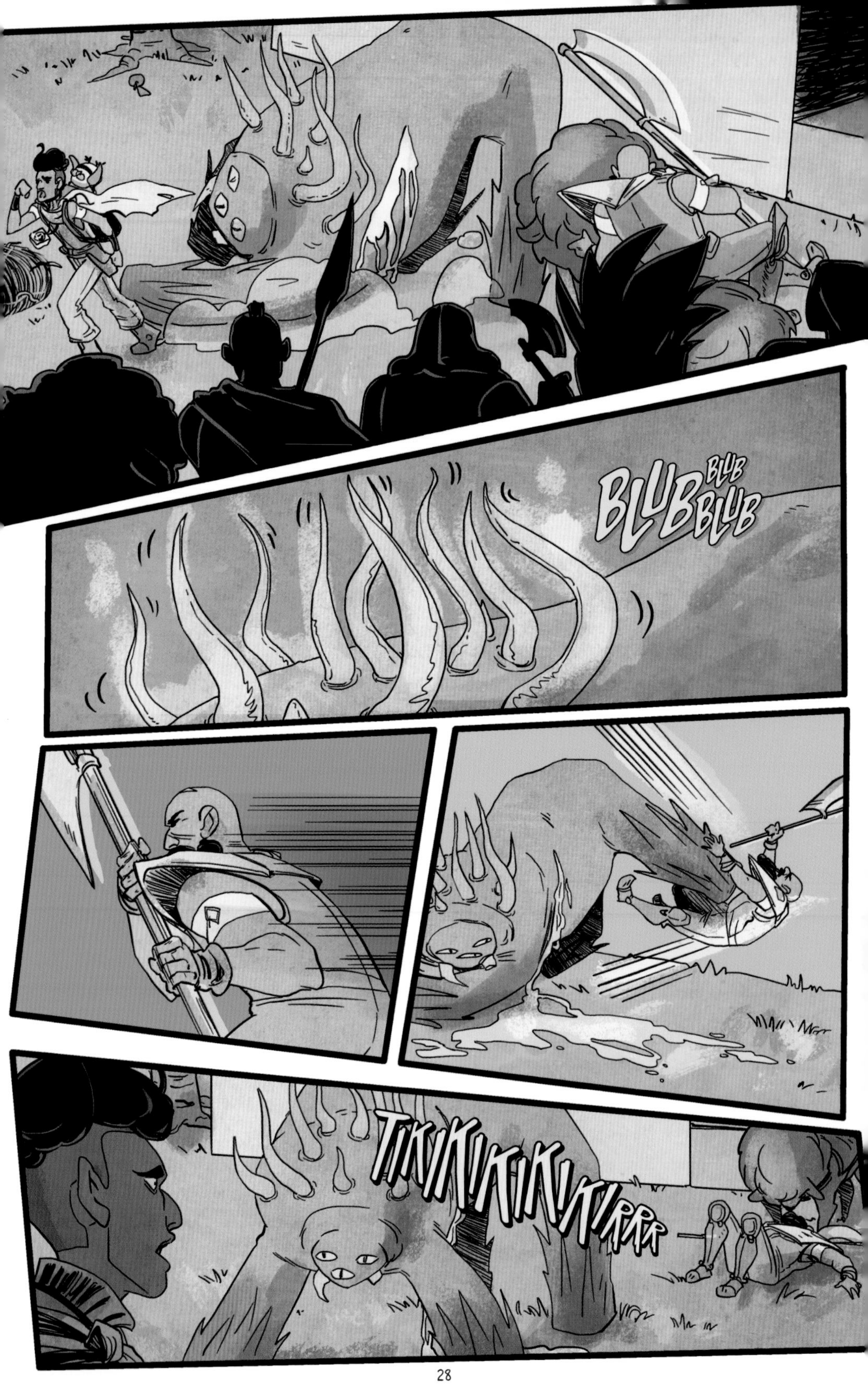
BLUB BLUB BLUB
TIKIKIKIKIKIKIKIRRRR

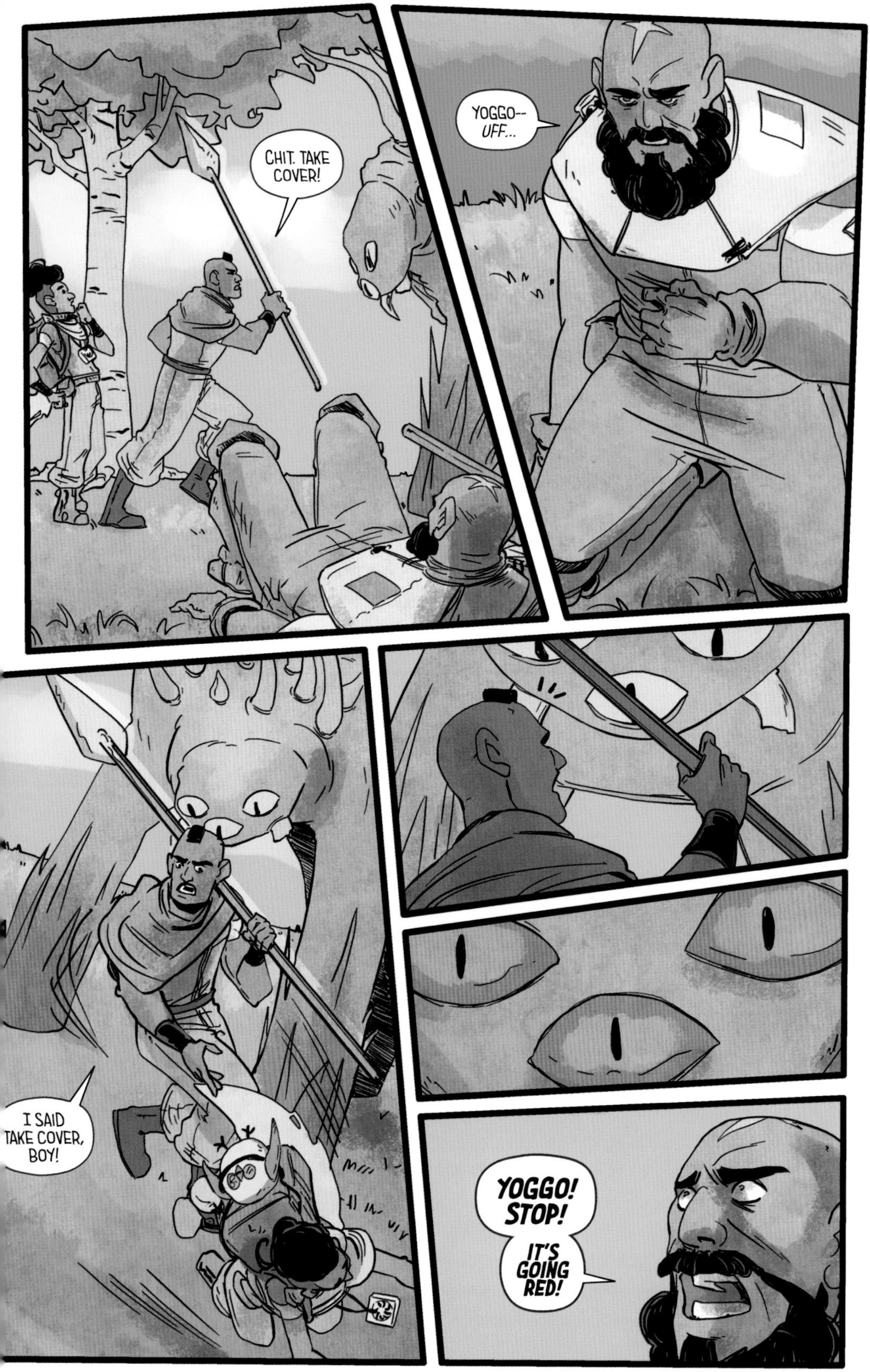
CHIT. TAKE COVER!
YOGGO-- UFF...
I SAID TAKE COVER, BOY!
YOGGO! STOP!
IT'S GOING RED!

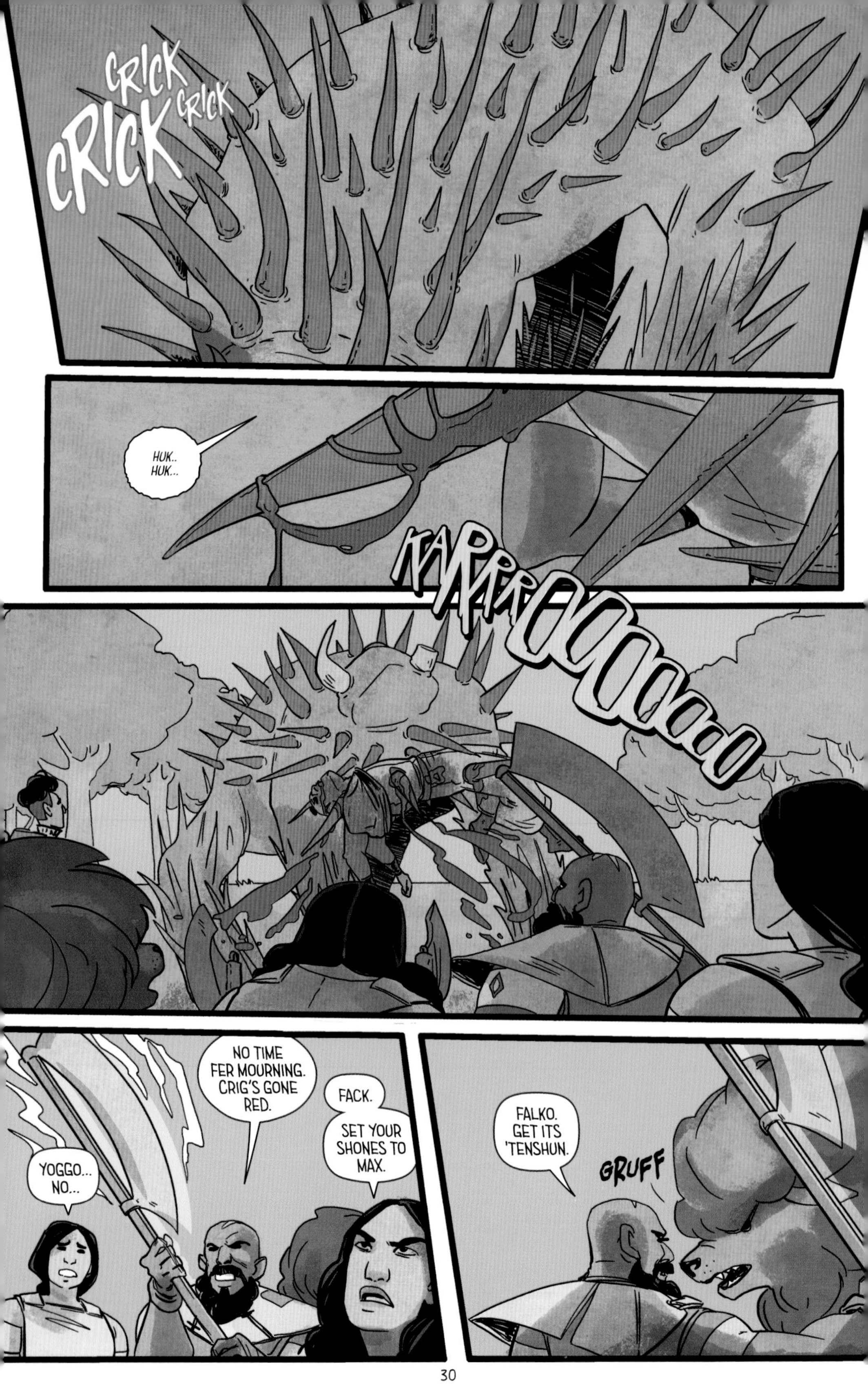
CRICK
CRICK CRICK
HUK.. HUK..
KARRROOOOOO..!
YOGGO... NO...
NO TIME FER MOURNING. CRIG'S GONE RED.
FACK.
SET YOUR SHONES TO MAX.
FALKO. GET ITS 'TENSHUN.
GRUFF

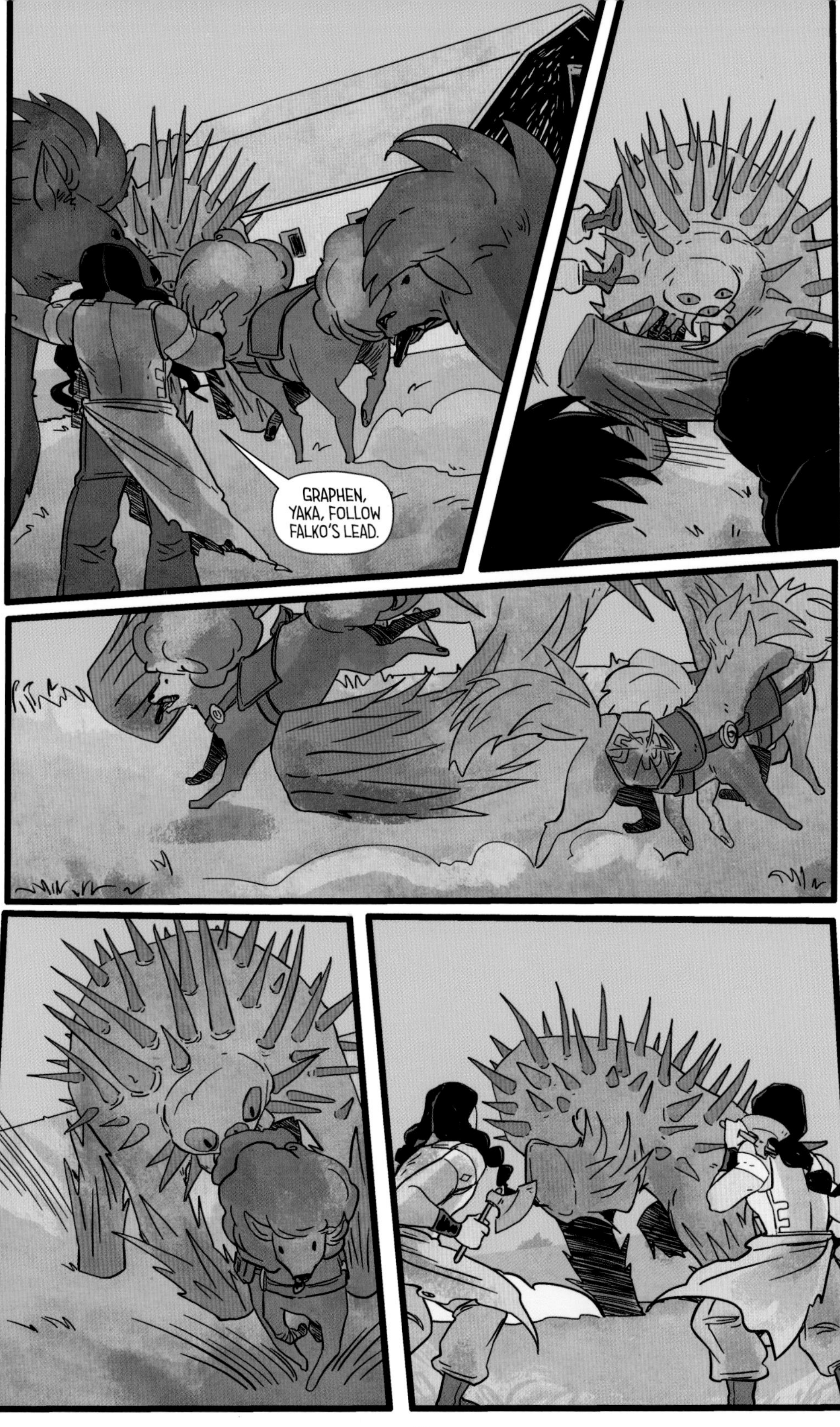
GRAPHEN, YAKA, FOLLOW FALKO'S LEAD.

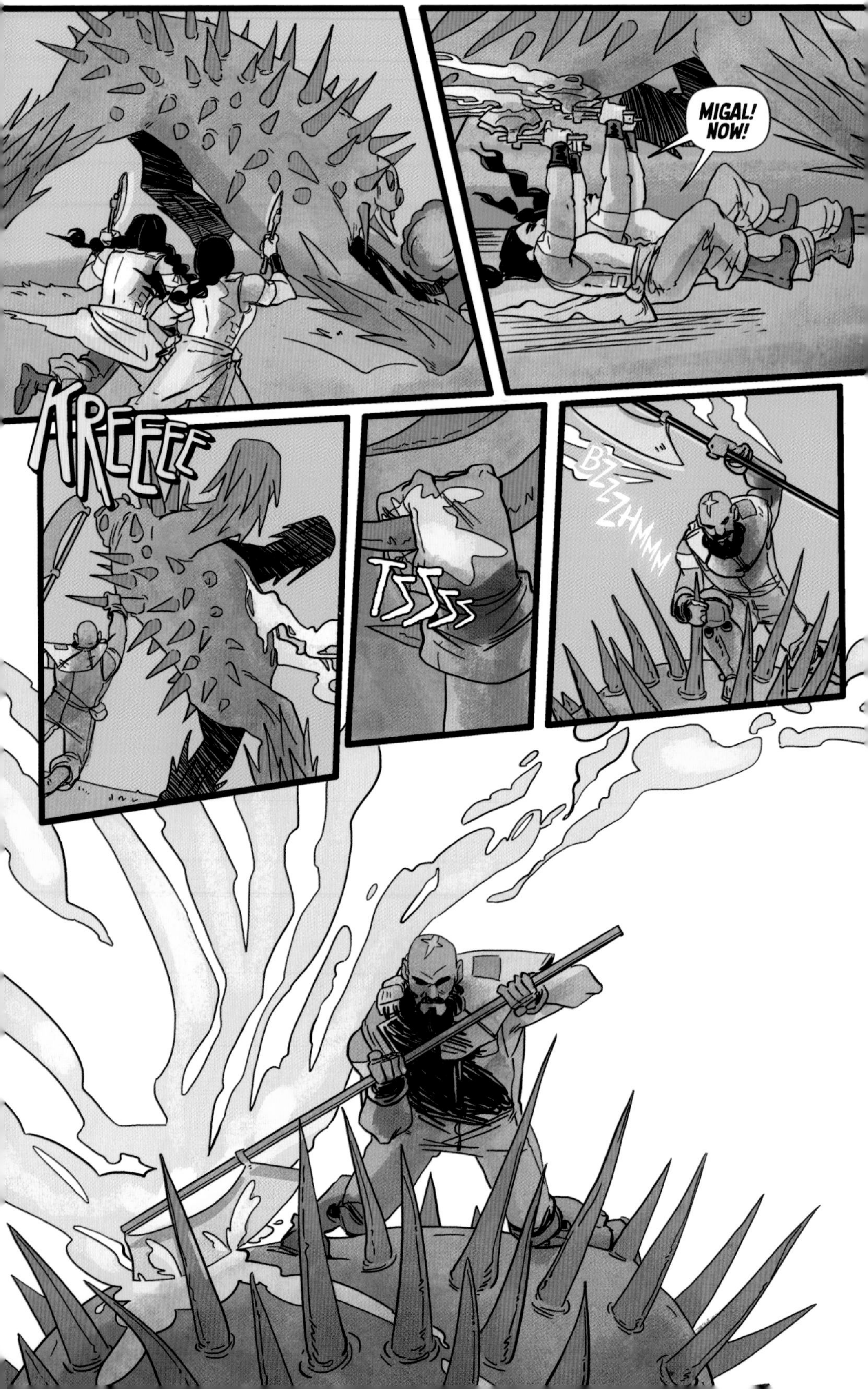
MIGAL! NOW!
KREEEEE
TSSsss
BZZZHMMM

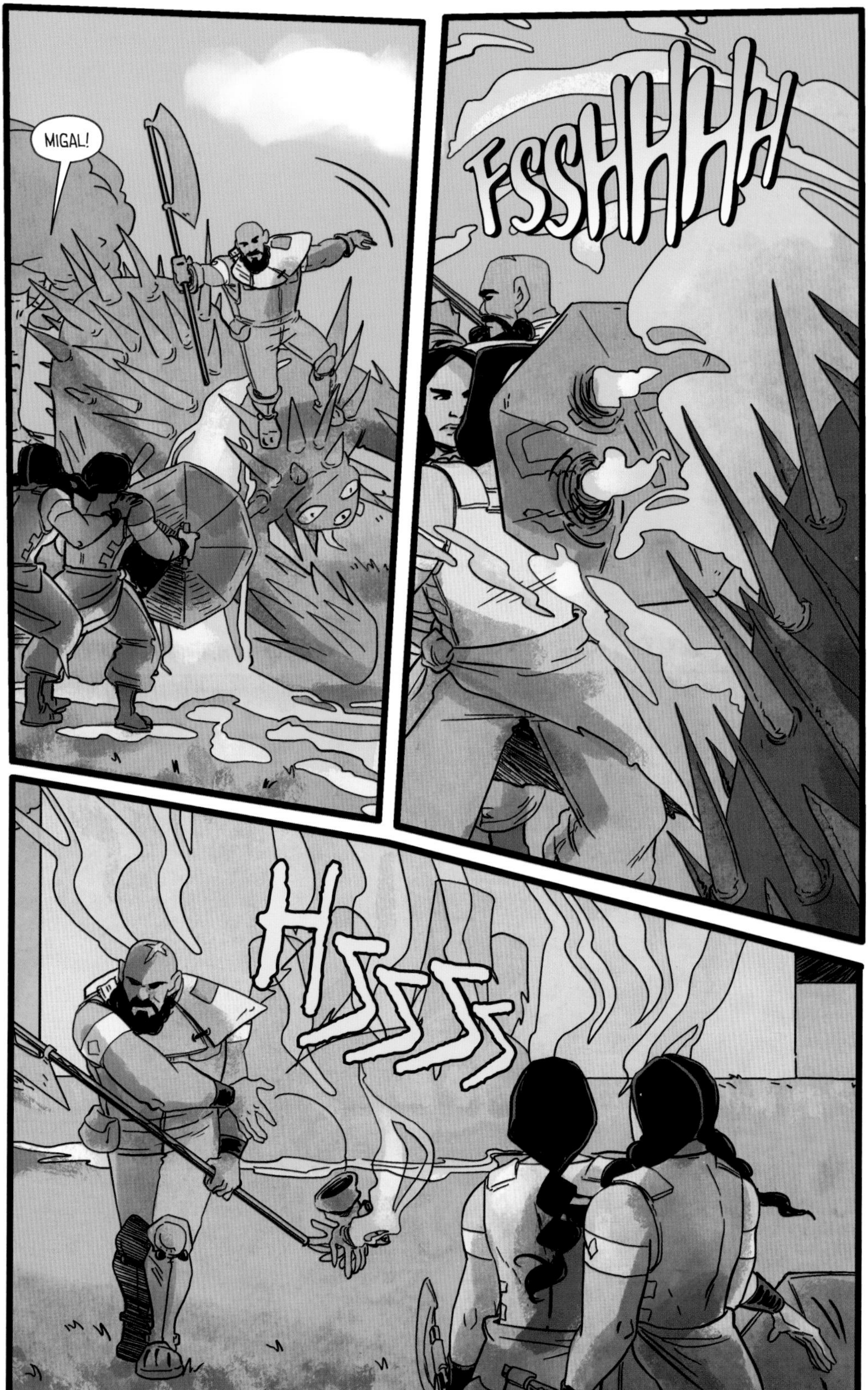
MIGAL!
FSSHHHH
HISSS

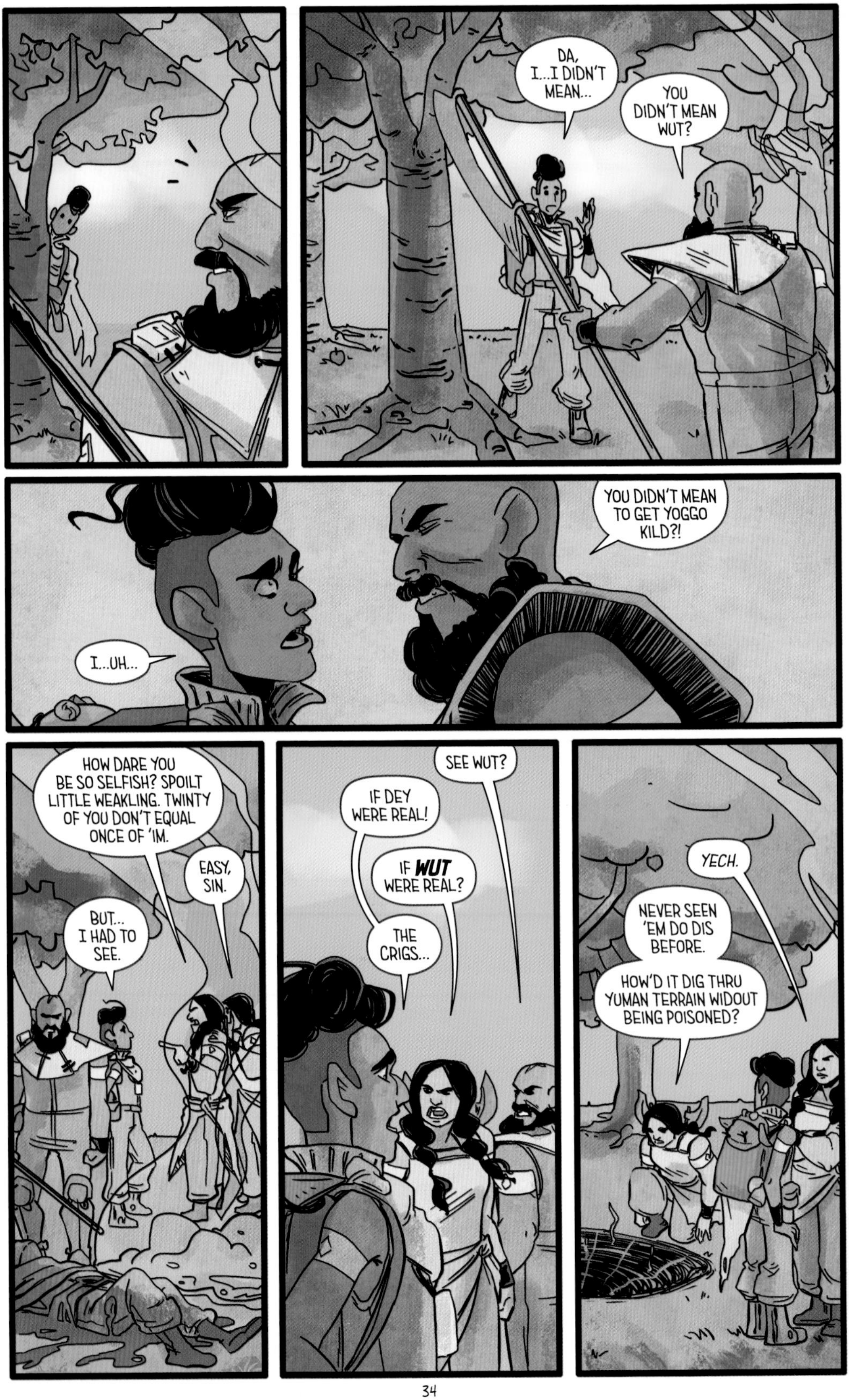
DA, I...I DIDN'T MEAN...
YOU DIDN'T MEAN WUT?
YOU DIDN'T MEAN TO GET YOGGO KILD?!
I...UH...
HOW DARE YOU BE SO SELFISH? SPOILT LITTLE WEAKLING. TWINTY OF YOU DON'T EQUAL ONCE OF 'IM.
EASY, SIN.
BUT... I HAD TO SEE.
SEE WUT?
IF DEY WERE REAL!
IF WUT WERE REAL?
THE CRIGS...
YECH.
NEVER SEEN 'EM DO DIS BEFORE.
HOW'D IT DIG THRU YUMAN TERRAIN WIDOUT BEING POISONED?

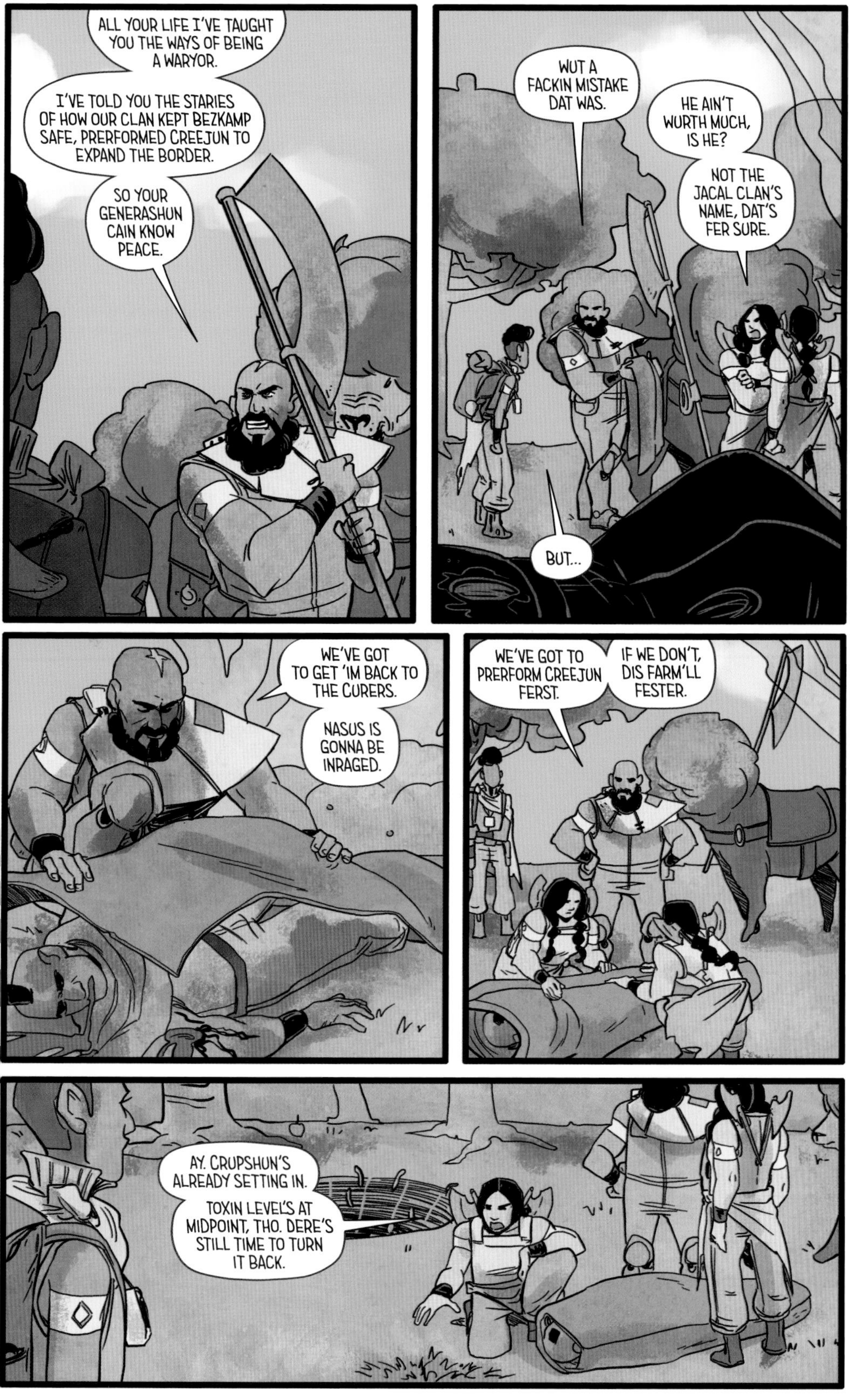
ALL YOUR LIFE I'VE TAUGHT YOU THE WAYS OF BEING A WARYOR.
I'VE TOLD YOU THE STARIES OF HOW OUR CLAN KEPT BEZKAMP SAFE, PRERFORMED CREEJUN TO EXPAND THE BORDER.
SO YOUR GENERASHUN CAIN KNOW PEACE.
WUT A FACKIN MISTAKE DAT WAS.
HE AIN'T WURTH MUCH, IS HE?
NOT THE JACAL CLAN'S NAME, DAT'S FER SURE.
BUT...
WE'VE GOT TO GET 'IM BACK TO THE CURERS.
NASUS IS GONNA BE INRAGED.
WE'VE GOT TO PRERFORM CREEJUN FERST.
IF WE DON'T, DIS FARM'LL FESTER.
AY. CRUPSHUN'S ALREADY SETTING IN.
TOXIN LEVEL'S AT MIDPOINT, THO. DERE'S STILL TIME TO TURN IT BACK.

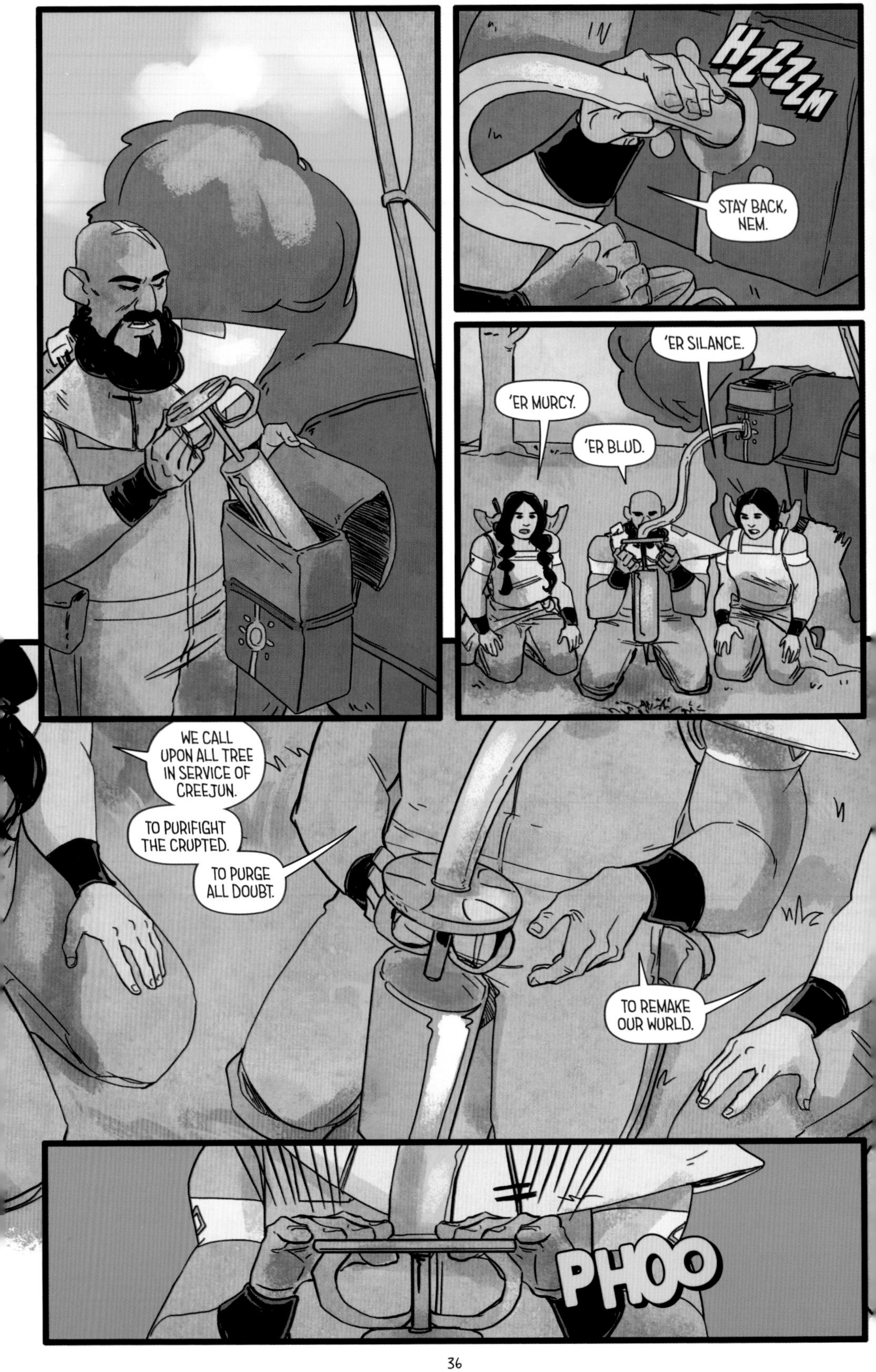
HZZZZM
STAY BACK, NEM.
'ER SILANCE.
'ER MURCY.
'ER BLUD.
WE CALL UPON ALL TREE IN SERVICE OF CREEJUN.
TO PURIFIGHT THE CRUPTED.
TO PURGE ALL DOUBT.
TO REMAKE OUR WURLD.
PHOO

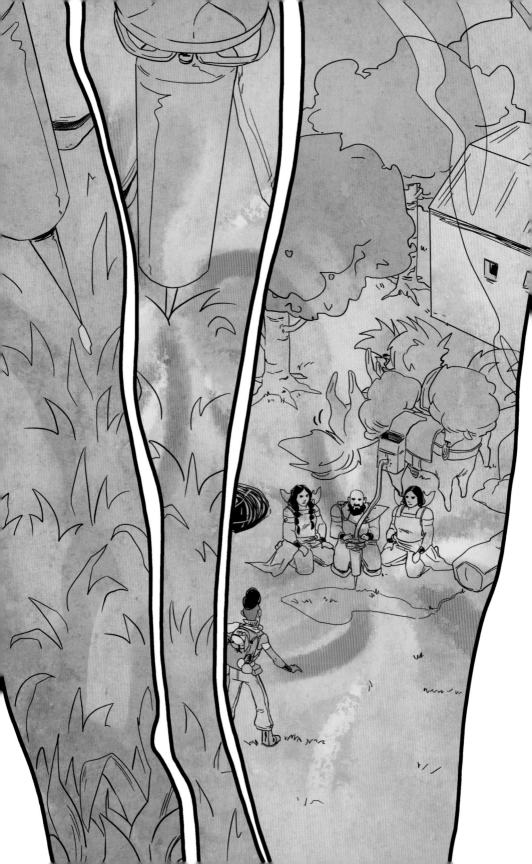

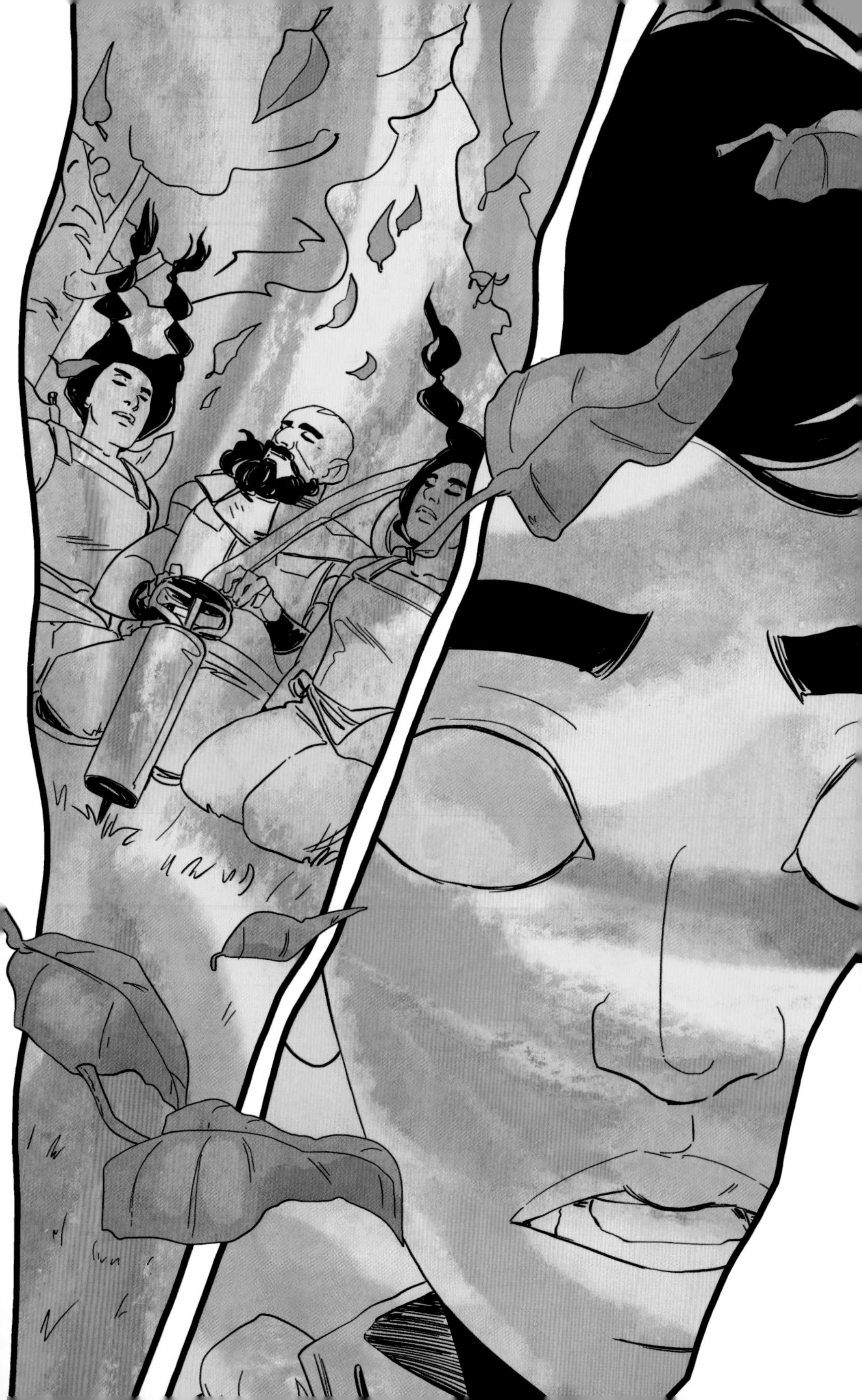

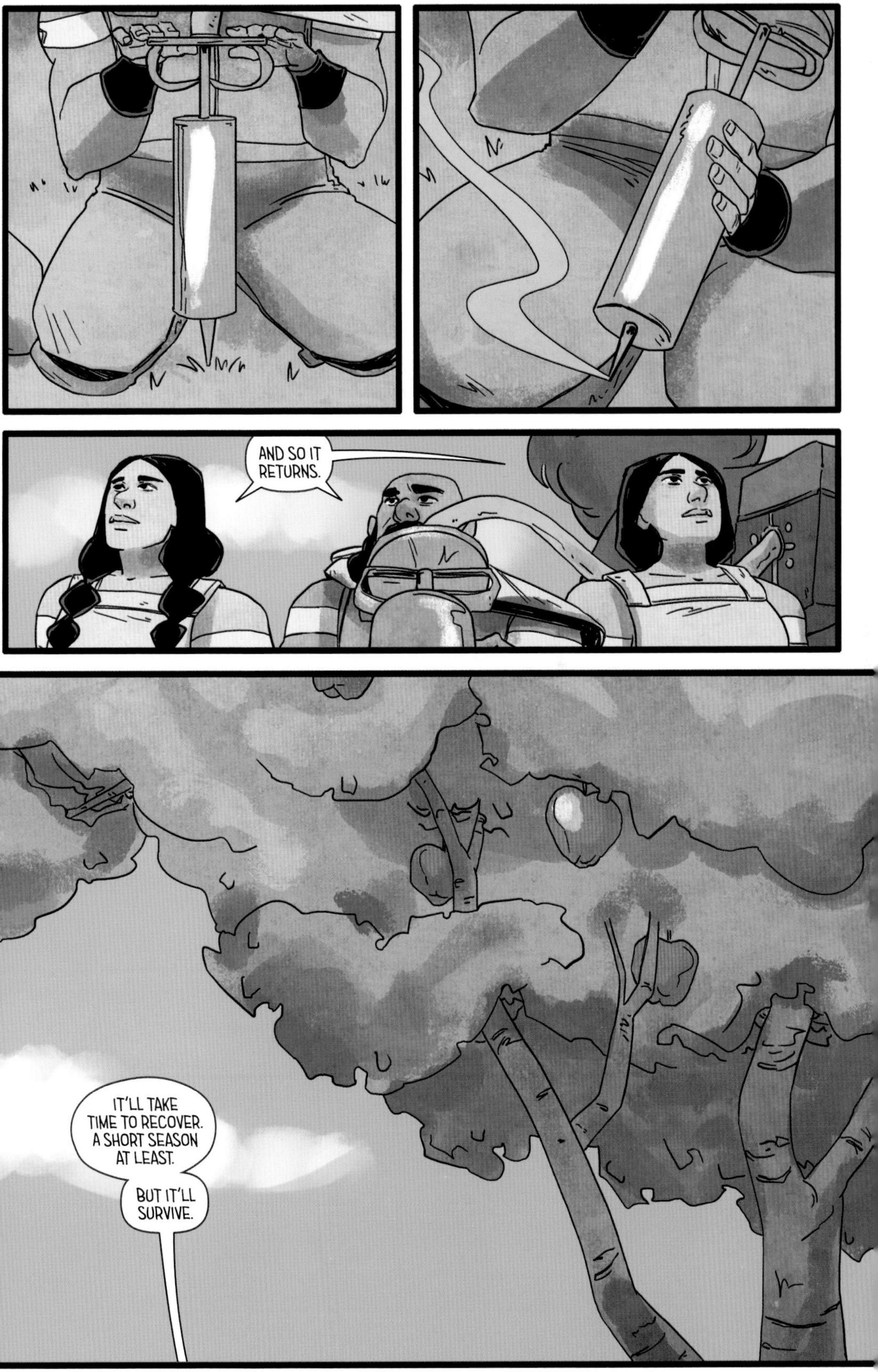
AND SO IT RETURNS.
IT'LL TAKE TIME TO RECOVER. A SHORT SEASON AT LEAST.
BUT IT'LL SURVIVE.

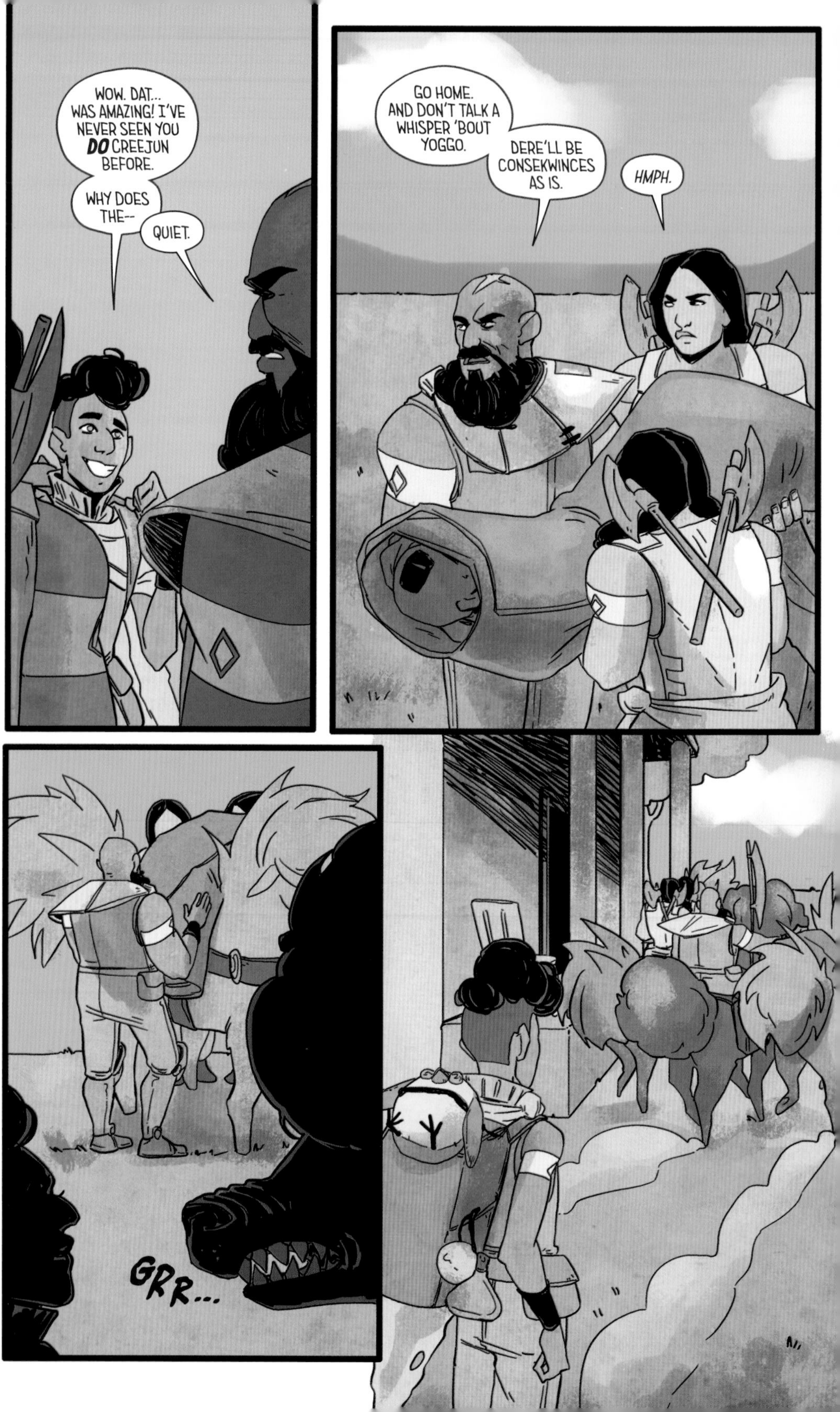
WOW. DAT... WAS AMAZING! I'VE NEVER SEEN YOU **DO** CREEJUN BEFORE.
WHY DOES THE--
QUIET.
GO HOME. AND DON'T TALK A WHISPER 'BOUT YOGGO.
DERE'LL BE CONSEKWINCES AS IS.
HMPH.
GRR...

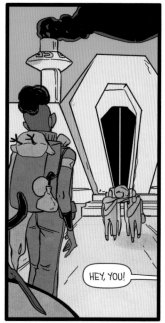

HEY, YOU!

YOU KNOW DESE STREETS ARE TO STAY CLEAR DURING CLINZING.

SCURRY 'LONG.

SORRY.

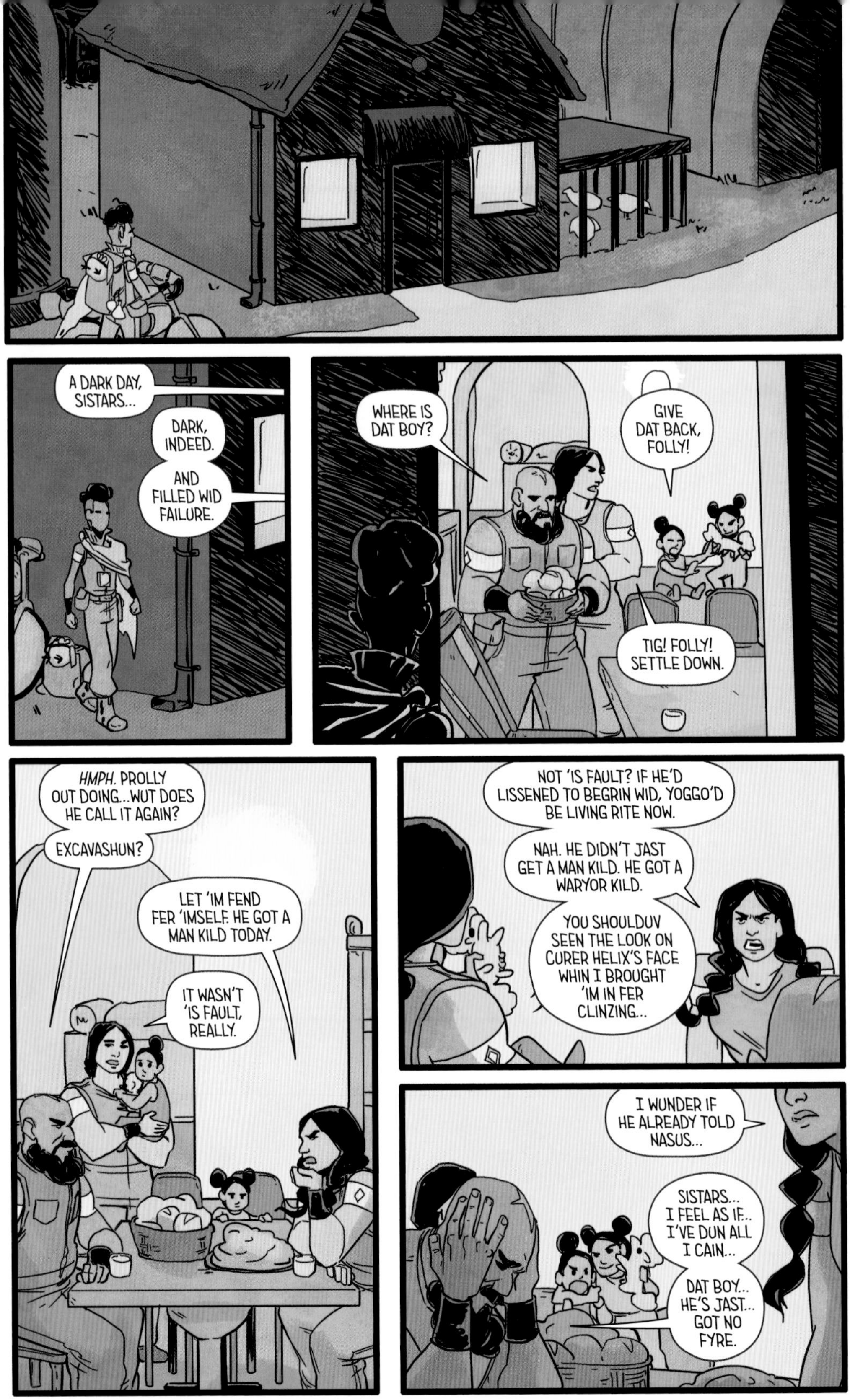
A DARK DAY, SISTARS...
DARK, INDEED.
AND FILLED WID FAILURE.
WHERE IS DAT BOY?
GIVE DAT BACK, FOLLY!
TIG! FOLLY! SETTLE DOWN.
HMPH. PROLLY OUT DOING...WUT DOES HE CALL IT AGAIN?
EXCAVASHUN?
LET 'IM FEND FER 'IMSELF. HE GOT A MAN KILD TODAY.
IT WASN'T 'IS FAULT, REALLY.
NOT 'IS FAULT? IF HE'D LISSENED TO BEGRIN WID, YOGGO'D BE LIVING RITE NOW.
NAH. HE DIDN'T JAST GET A MAN KILD. HE GOT A WARYOR KILD.
YOU SHOULDUV SEEN THE LOOK ON CURER HELIX'S FACE WHIN I BROUGHT 'IM IN FER CLINZING...
I WUNDER IF HE ALREADY TOLD NASUS...
SISTARS... I FEEL AS IF... I'VE DUN ALL I CAIN...
DAT BOY... HE'S JAST... GOT NO FYRE.

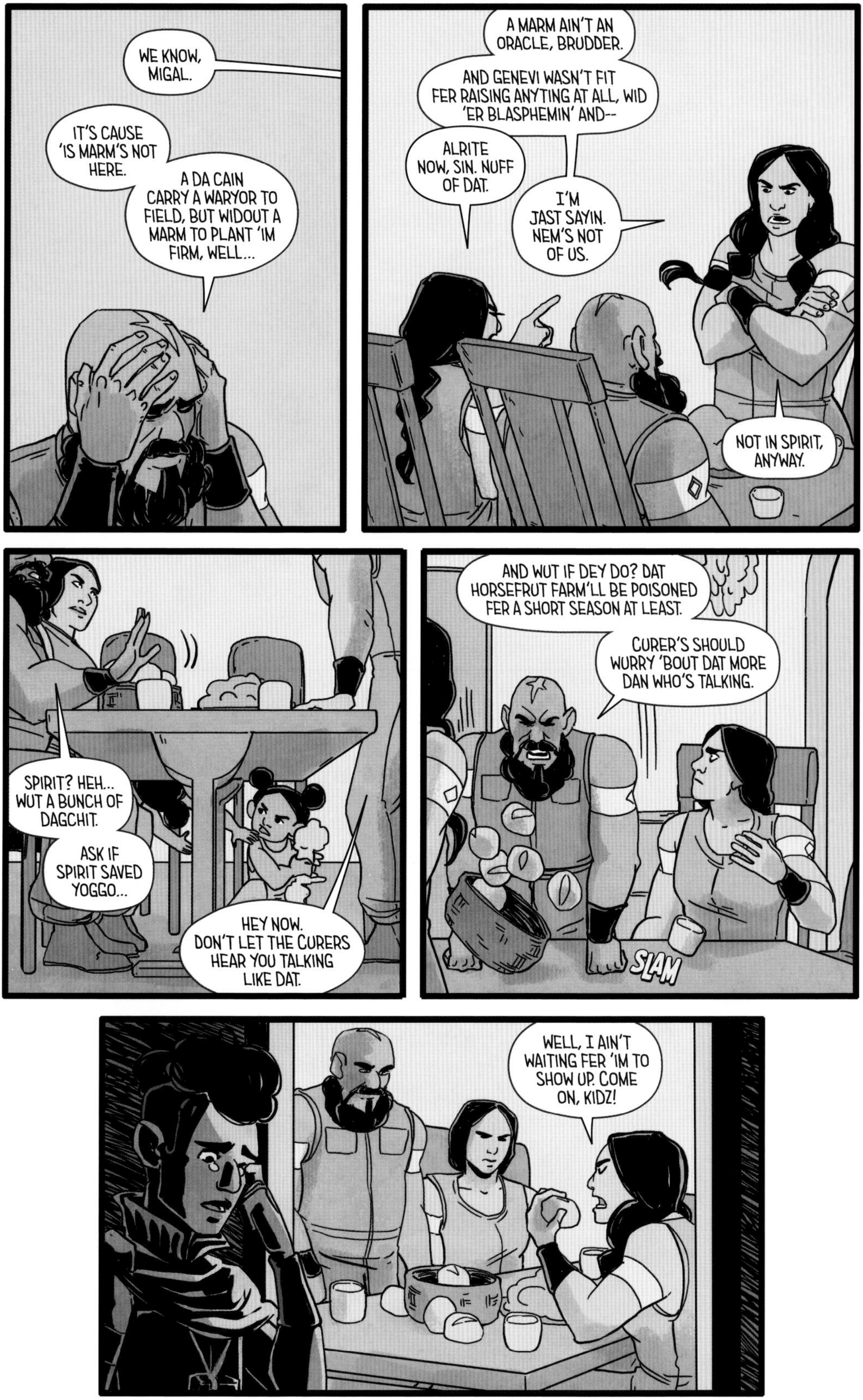
WE KNOW, MIGAL.
IT'S CAUSE 'IS MARM'S NOT HERE.
A DA CAIN CARRY A WARYOR TO FIELD, BUT WIDOUT A MARM TO PLANT 'IM FIRM, WELL...
A MARM AIN'T AN ORACLE, BRUDDER.
AND GENEVI WASN'T FIT FER RAISING ANYTING AT ALL, WID 'ER BLASPHEMIN' AND--
ALRITE NOW, SIN. NUFF OF DAT.
I'M JAST SAYIN. NEM'S NOT OF US.
NOT IN SPIRIT, ANYWAY.
SPIRIT? HEH... WUT A BUNCH OF DAGCHIT.
ASK IF SPIRIT SAVED YOGGO...
HEY NOW. DON'T LET THE CURERS HEAR YOU TALKING LIKE DAT.
AND WUT IF DEY DO? DAT HORSEFRUT FARM'LL BE POISONED FER A SHORT SEASON AT LEAST.
CURER'S SHOULD WURRY 'BOUT DAT MORE DAN WHO'S TALKING.
SLAM
WELL, I AIN'T WAITING FER 'IM TO SHOW UP. COME ON, KIDZ!

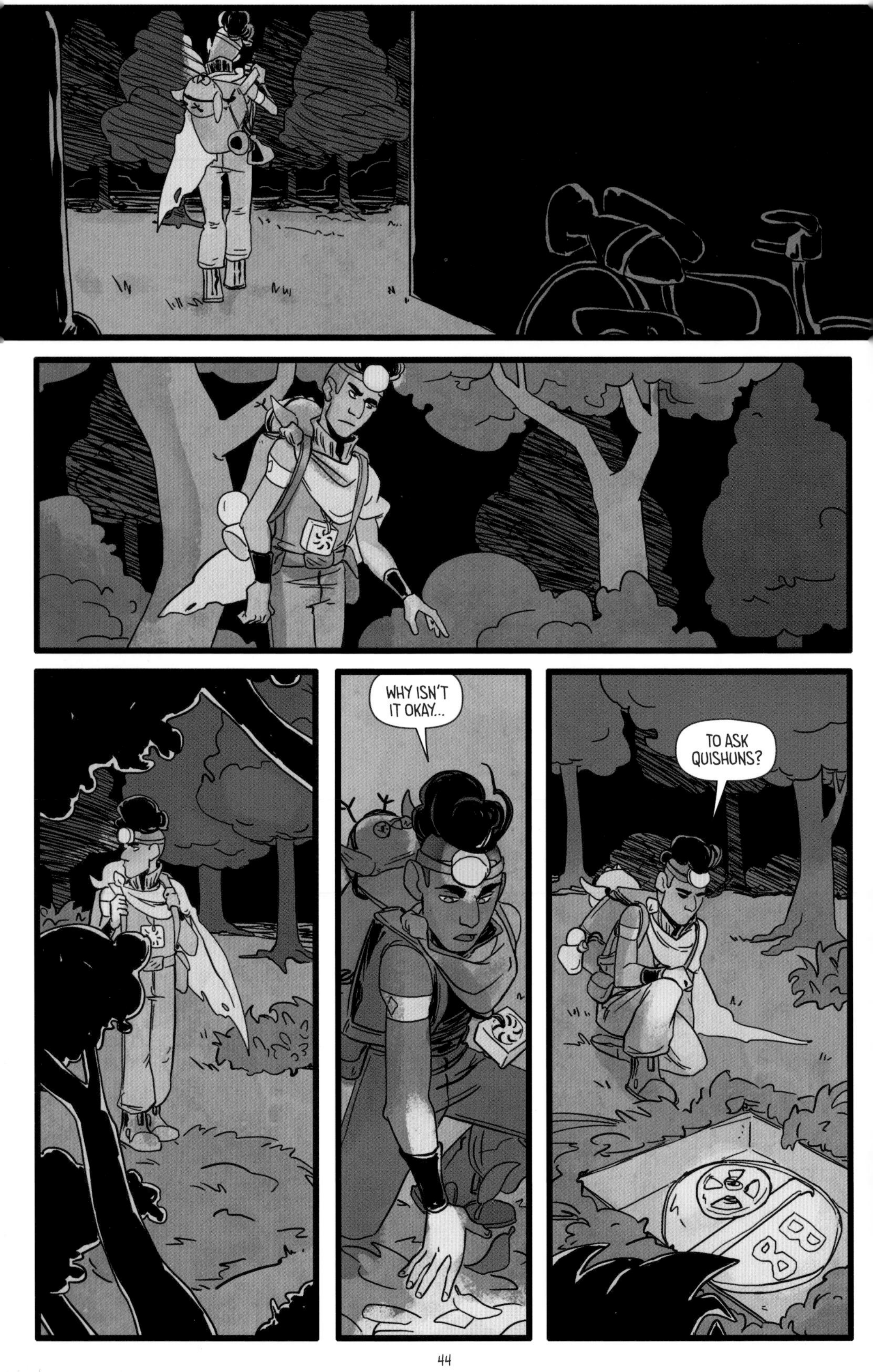
WHY ISN'T IT OKAY...
TO ASK QUISHUNS?

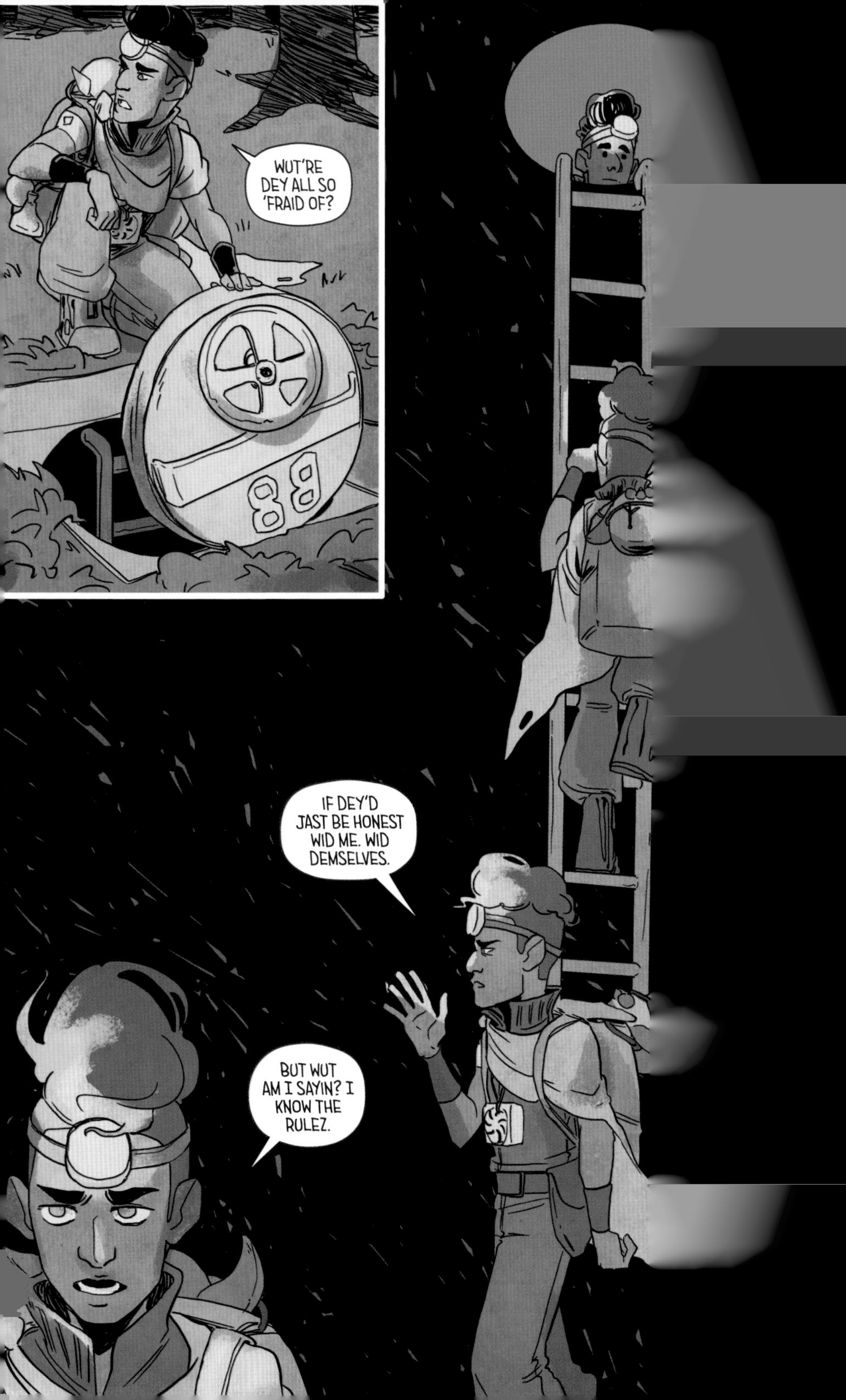

WUT'RE DEY ALL SO 'FRAID OF?
88
IF DEY'D JAST BE HONEST WID ME. WID DEMSELVES.
BUT WUT AM I SAYIN? I KNOW THE RULEZ.

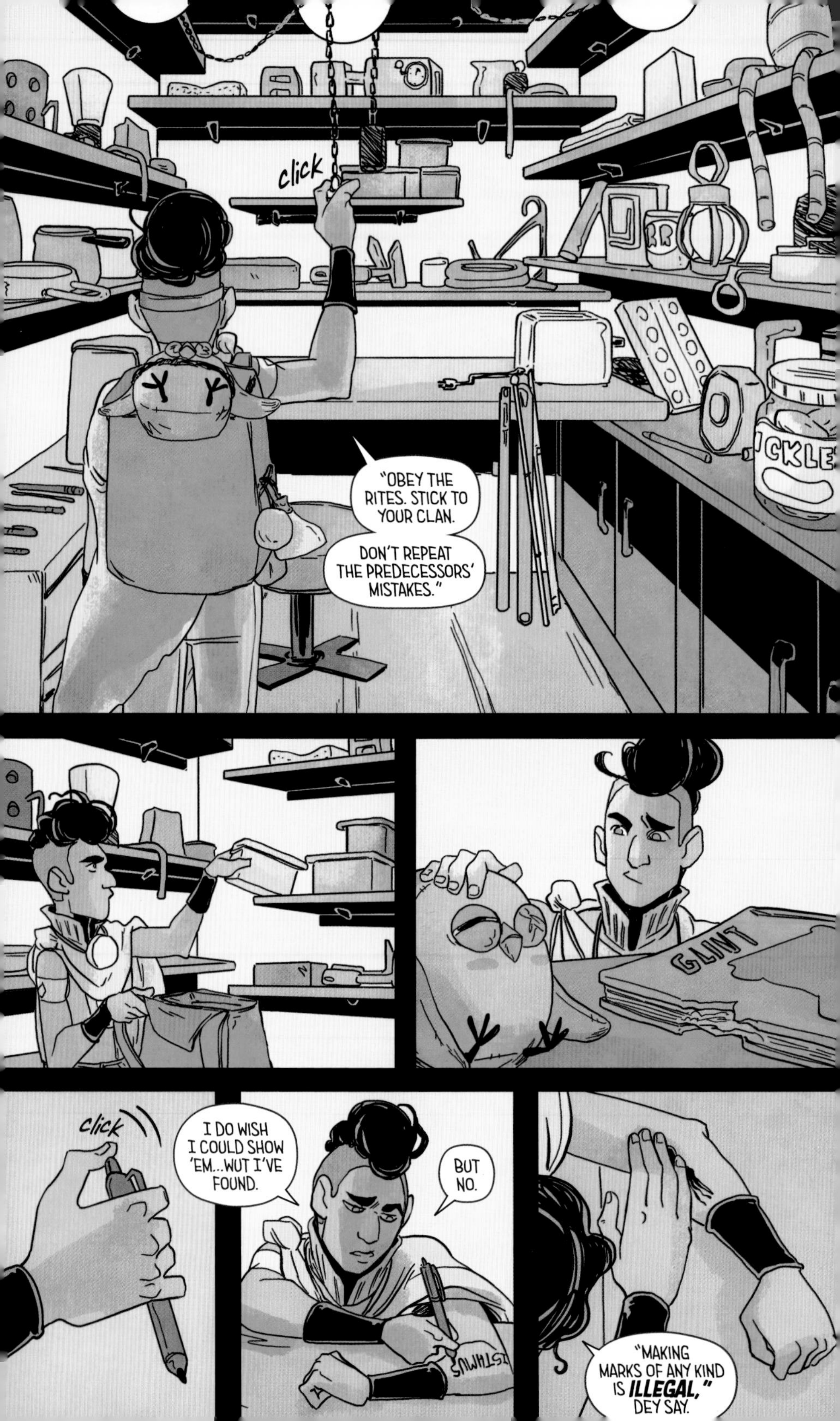
click
"OBEY THE RITES. STICK TO YOUR CLAN.
DON'T REPEAT THE PREDECESSORS' MISTAKES."
GLINT
click
I DO WISH I COULD SHOW 'EM...WUT I'VE FOUND.
BUT NO.
ISTHMUS
"MAKING MARKS OF ANY KIND IS ***ILLEGAL,*** " DEY SAY.

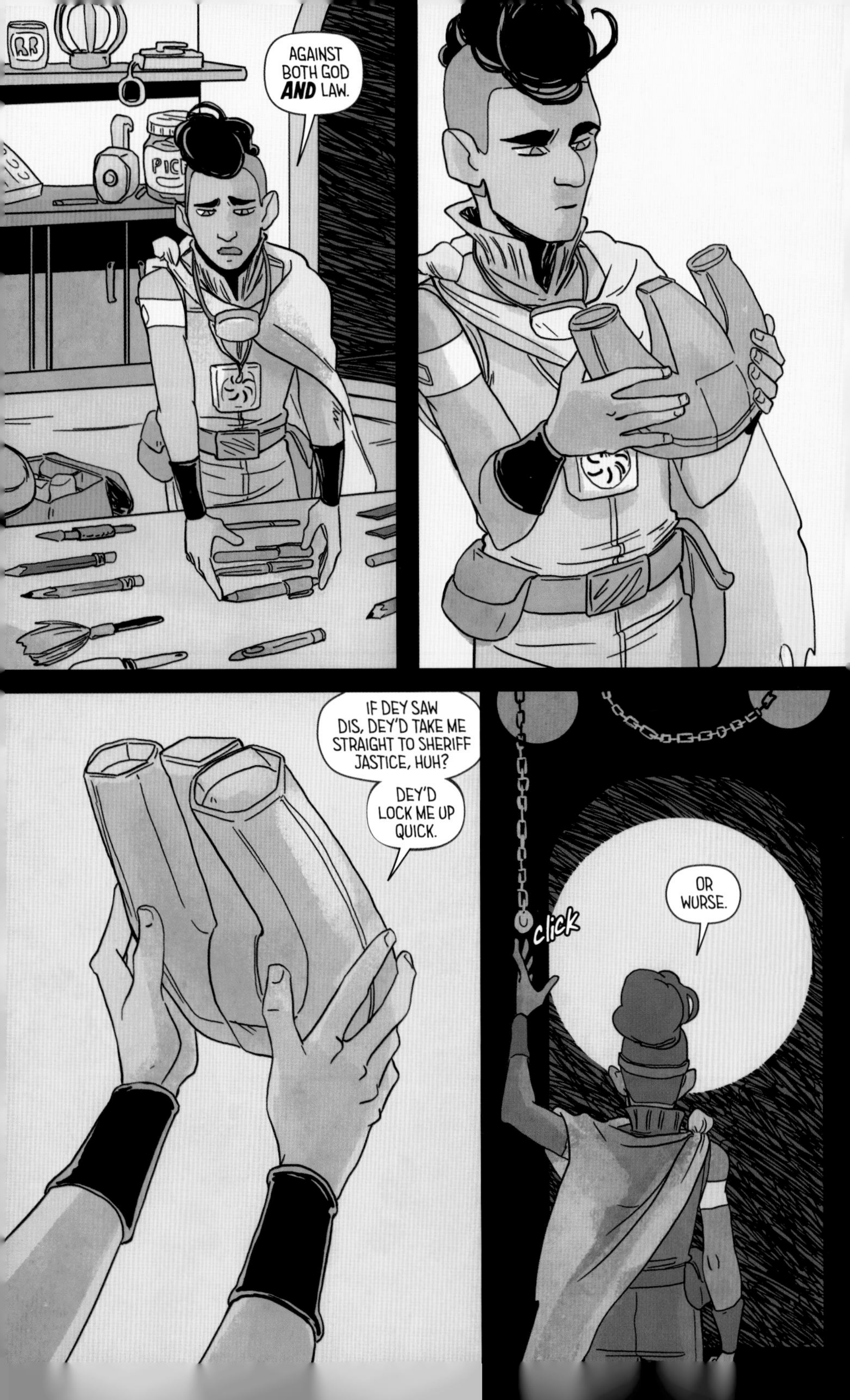
AGAINST BOTH GOD AND LAW.
IF DEY SAW DIS, DEY'D TAKE ME STRAIGHT TO SHERIFF JASTICE, HUH?
DEY'D LOCK ME UP QUICK.
CLICK
OR WURSE.

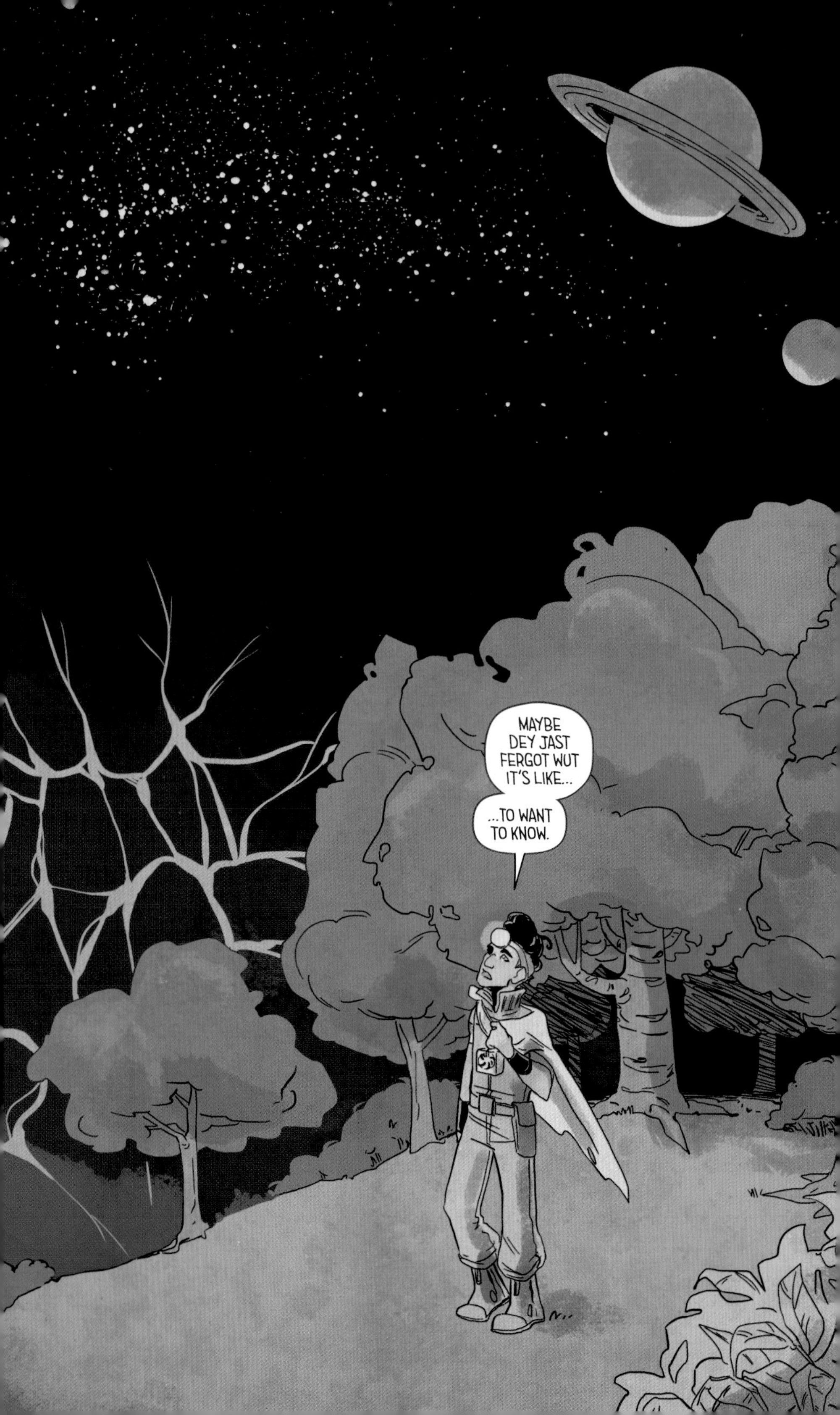
MAYBE DEY JAST FERGOT WUT IT'S LIKE...
...TO WANT TO KNOW.

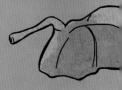

CHEPTAR
TWO

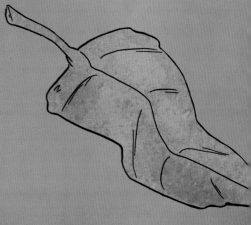

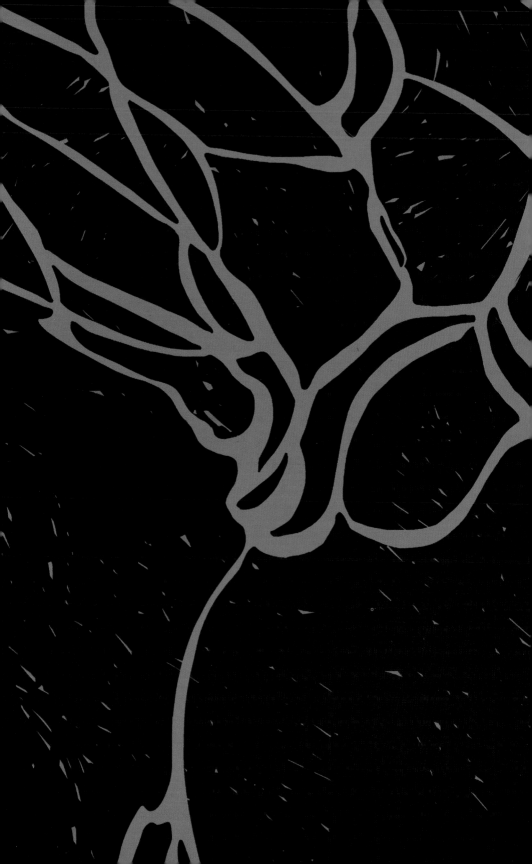

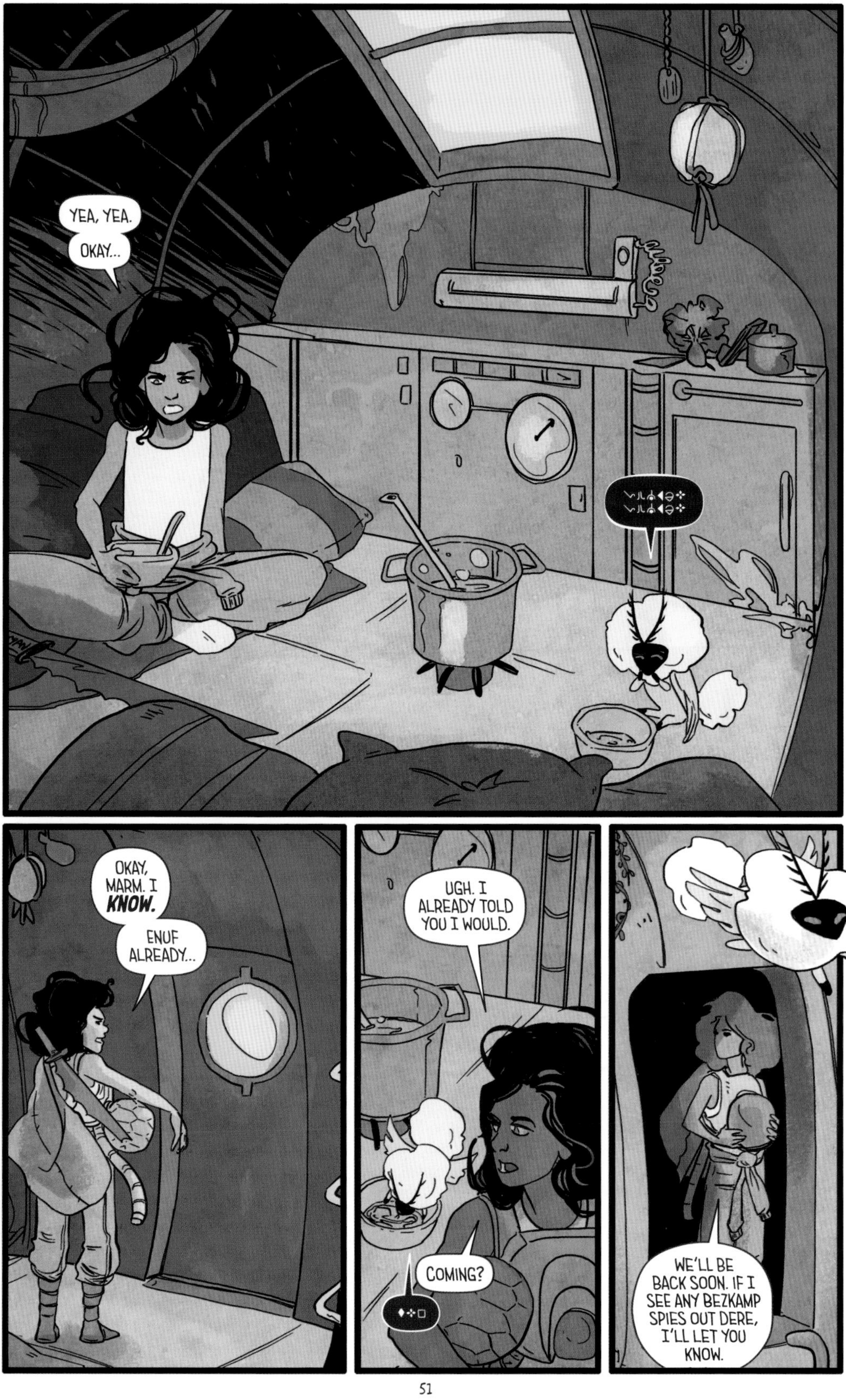
YEA, YEA.
OKAY...
OKAY, MARM. I **KNOW.**
ENUF ALREADY...
UGH. I ALREADY TOLD YOU I WOULD.
COMING?
WE'LL BE BACK SOON. IF I SEE ANY BEZKAMP SPIES OUT DERE, I'LL LET YOU KNOW.

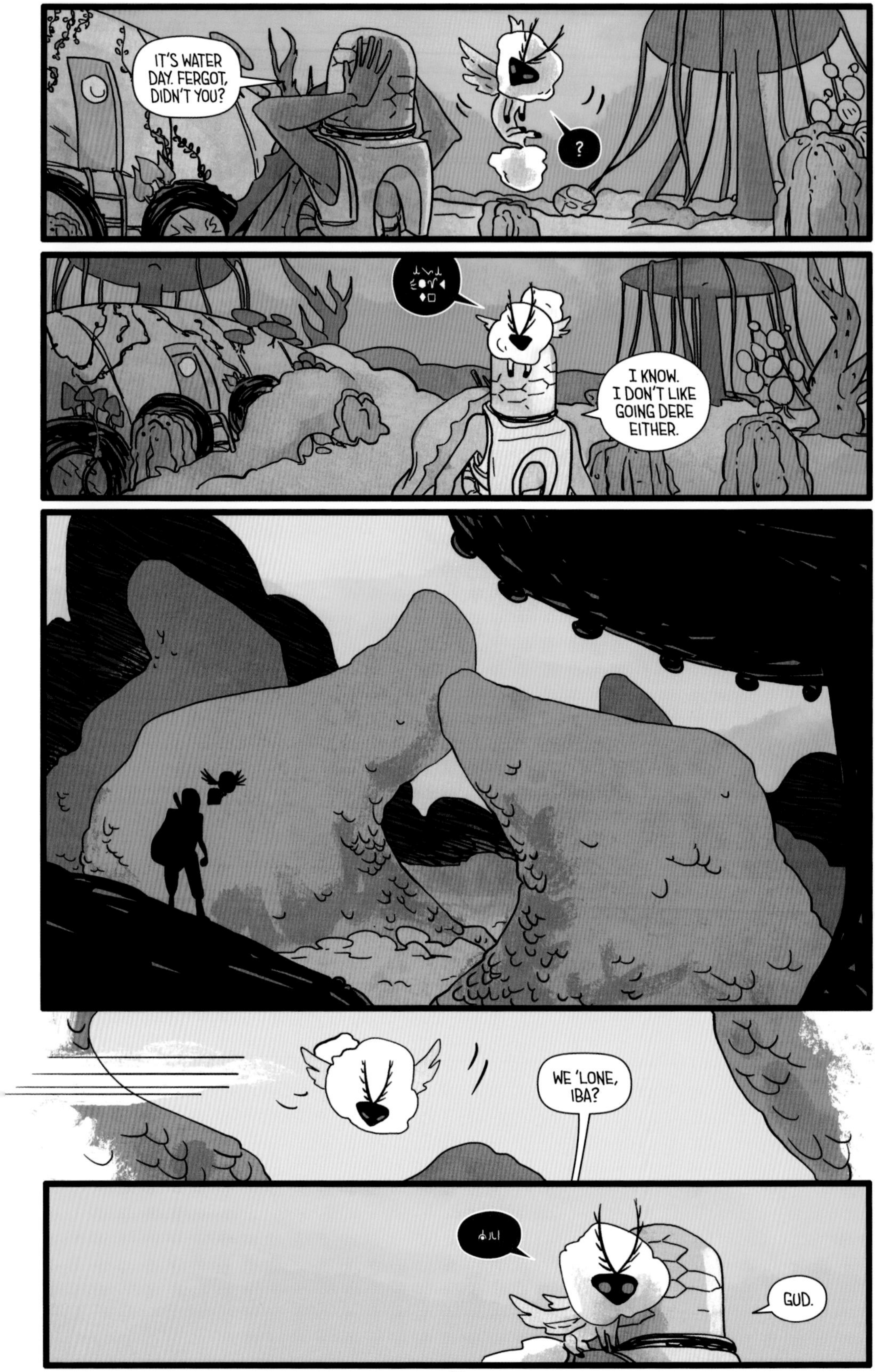
IT'S WATER DAY. FERGOT, DIDN'T YOU?
?
I KNOW. I DON'T LIKE GOING DERE EITHER.
WE 'LONE, IBA?
GUD.

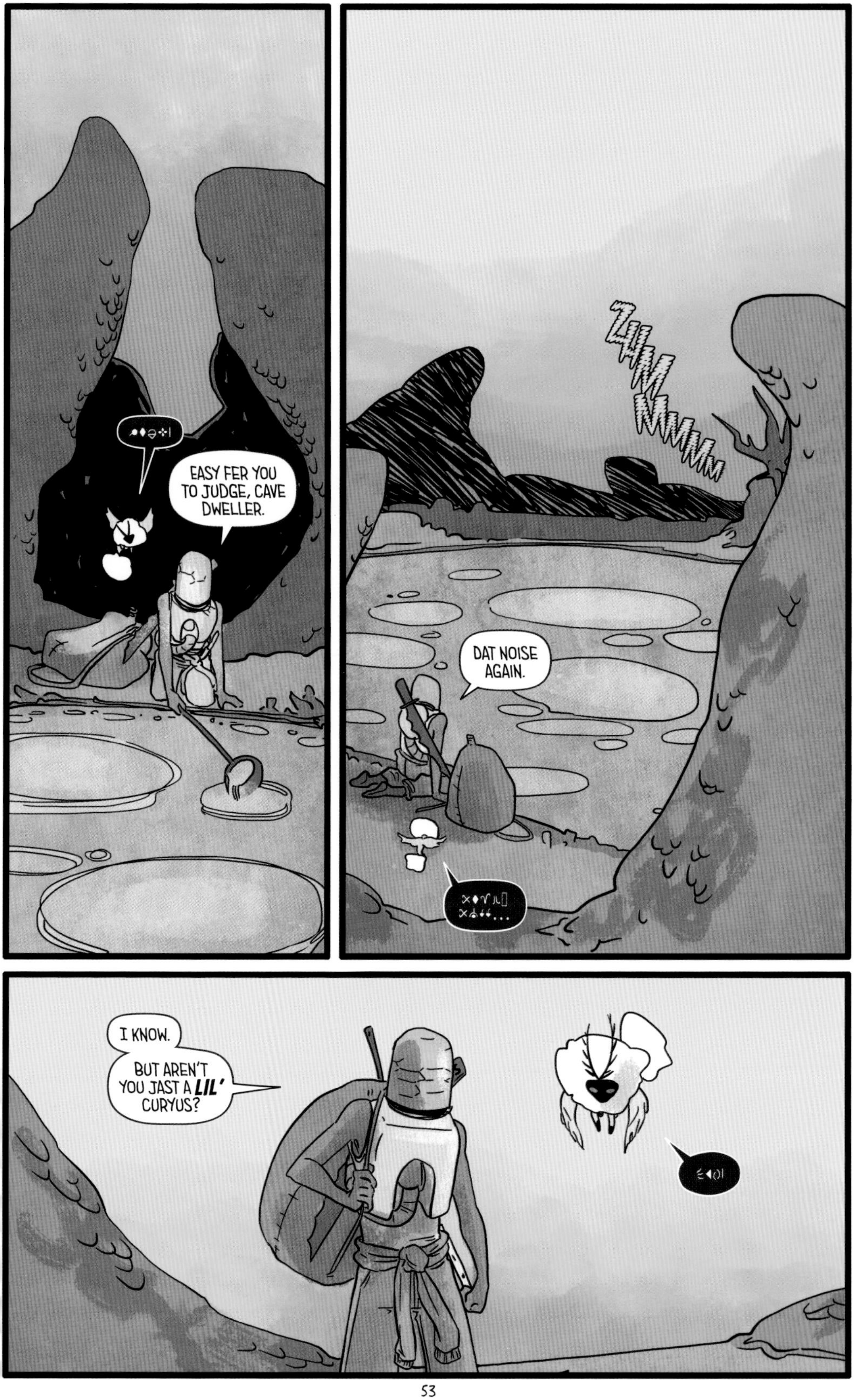
EASY FER YOU TO JUDGE, CAVE DWELLER.
ZUMMMMMM
DAT NOISE AGAIN.
I KNOW.
BUT AREN'T YOU JAST A **LIL'** CURYUS?

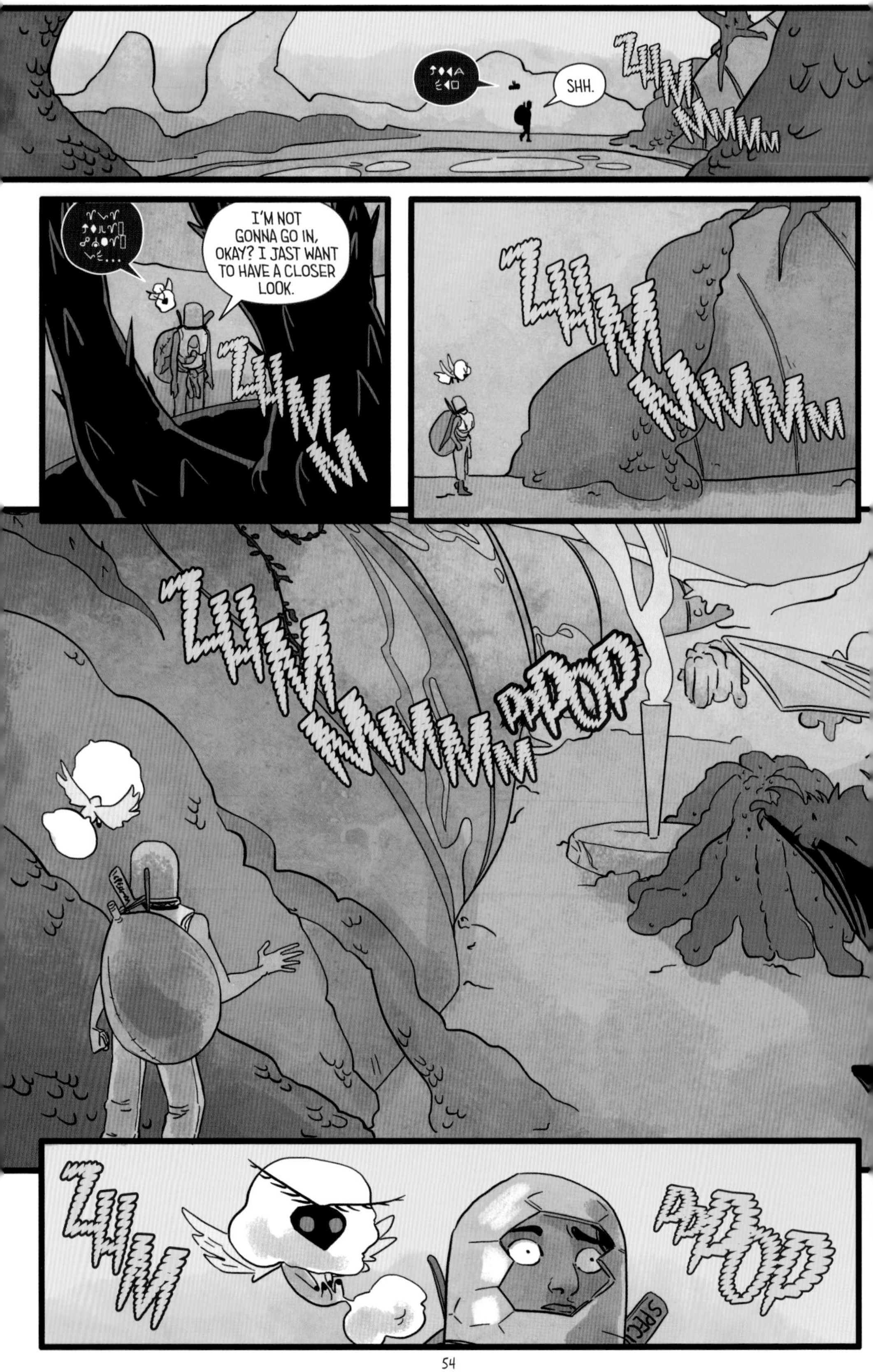
SHH.
I'M NOT GONNA GO IN, OKAY? I JAST WANT TO HAVE A CLOSER LOOK.

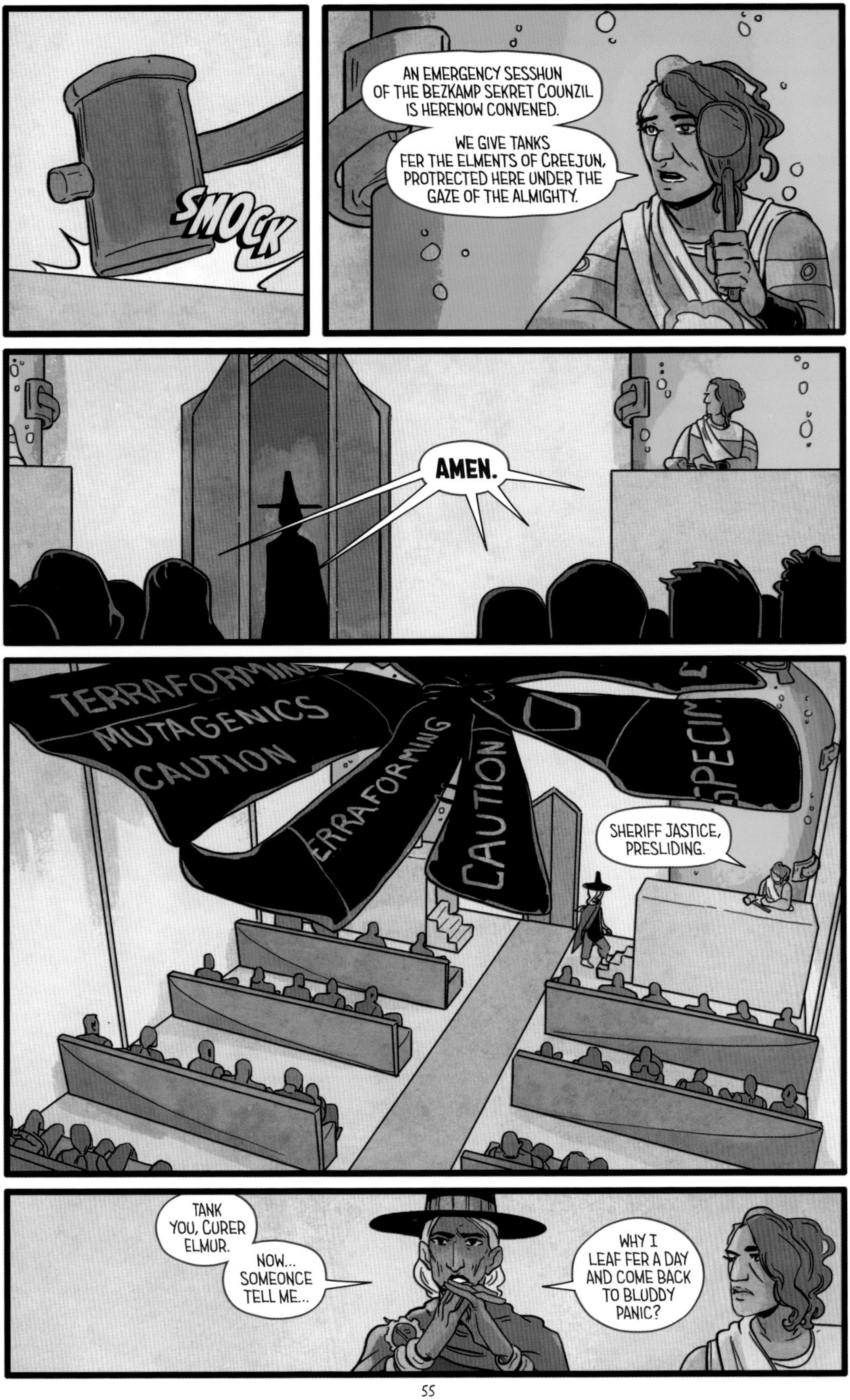
SMOCK
AN EMERGENCY SESSHUN OF THE BEZKAMP SEKRET COUNZIL IS HERENOW CONVENED.
WE GIVE TANKS FER THE ELMENTS OF CREEJUN, PROTRECTED HERE UNDER THE GAZE OF THE ALMIGHTY.
AMEN.
TERRAFORMING
MUTAGENICS
CAUTION
ERRAFORMING
CAUTION
SPECIM
SHERIFF JASTICE, PRESLIDING.
TANK YOU, CURER ELMUR.
NOW... SOMEONCE TELL ME...
WHY I LEAF FER A DAY AND COME BACK TO BLUDDY PANIC?

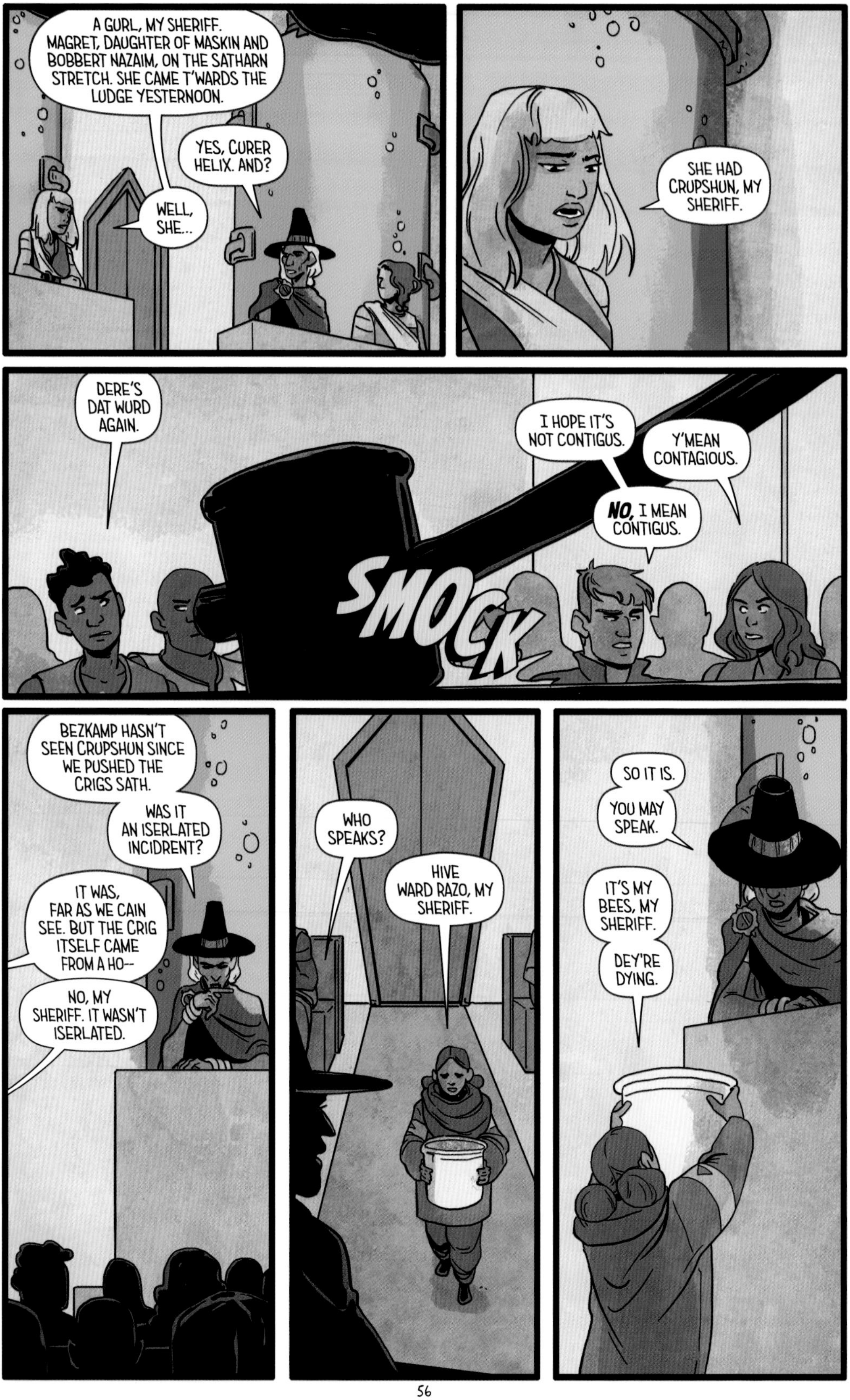
A GURL, MY SHERIFF. MAGRET, DAUGHTER OF MASKIN AND BOBBERT NAZAIM, ON THE SATHARN STRETCH. SHE CAME T'WARDS THE LUDGE YESTERNOON.
YES, CURER HELIX. AND?
WELL, SHE...
SHE HAD CRUPSHUN, MY SHERIFF.
DERE'S DAT WURD AGAIN.
I HOPE IT'S NOT CONTIGUS.
Y'MEAN CONTAGIOUS.
NO, I MEAN CONTIGUS.
SMOCK
BEZKAMP HASN'T SEEN CRUPSHUN SINCE WE PUSHED THE CRIGS SATH.
WAS IT AN ISERLATED INCIDRENT?
IT WAS, FAR AS WE CAIN SEE. BUT THE CRIG ITSELF CAME FROM A HO--
NO, MY SHERIFF. IT WASN'T ISERLATED.
WHO SPEAKS?
HIVE WARD RAZO, MY SHERIFF.
SO IT IS.
YOU MAY SPEAK.
IT'S MY BEES, MY SHERIFF.
DEY'RE DYING.

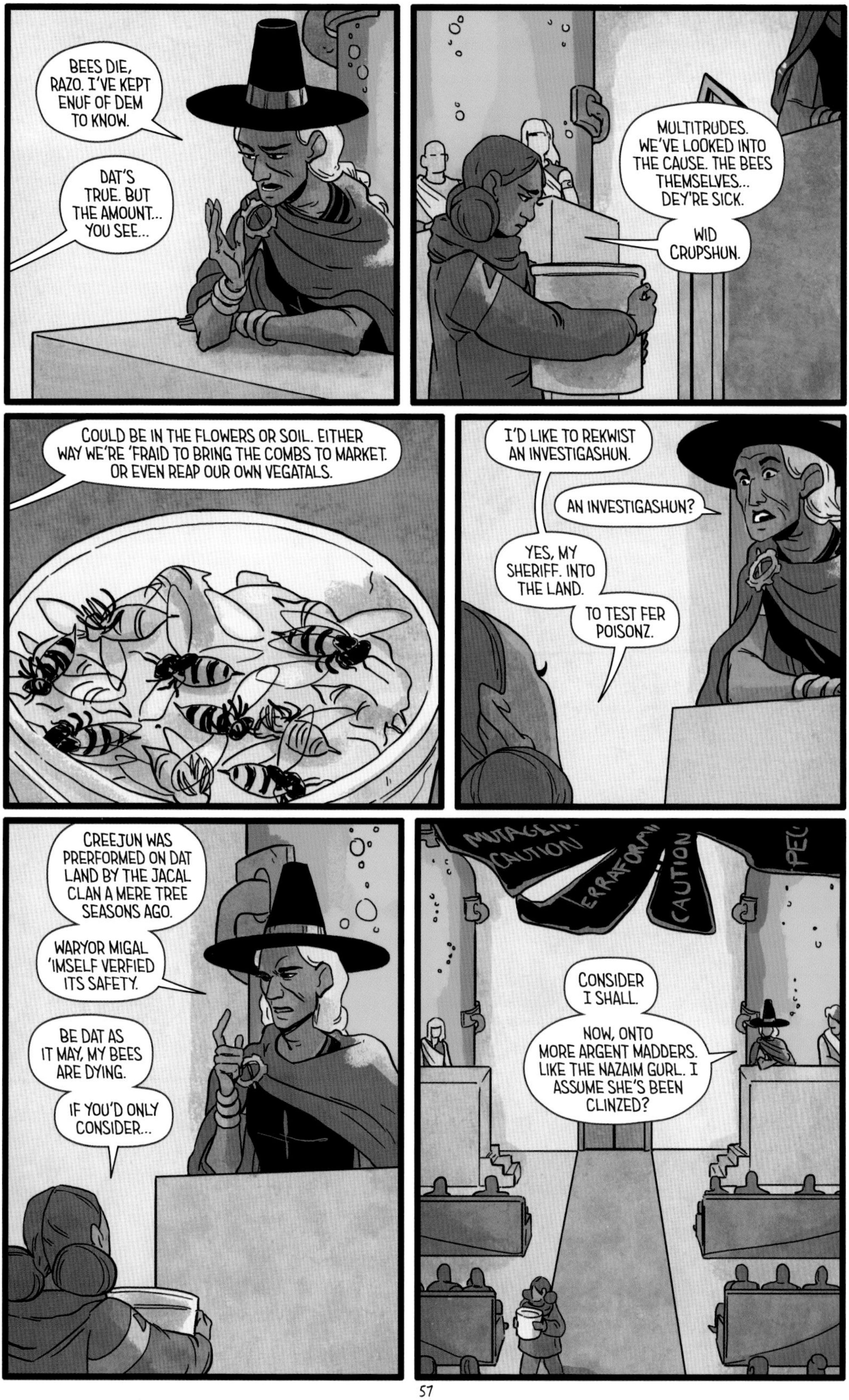
BEES DIE, RAZO. I'VE KEPT ENUF OF DEM TO KNOW.
DAT'S TRUE. BUT THE AMOUNT... YOU SEE...
MULTITRUDES. WE'VE LOOKED INTO THE CAUSE. THE BEES THEMSELVES... DEY'RE SICK.
WID CRUPSHUN.
COULD BE IN THE FLOWERS OR SOIL. EITHER WAY WE'RE 'FRAID TO BRING THE COMBS TO MARKET. OR EVEN REAP OUR OWN VEGATALS.
I'D LIKE TO REKWIST AN INVESTIGASHUN.
AN INVESTIGASHUN?
YES, MY SHERIFF. INTO THE LAND.
TO TEST FER POISONZ.
CREEJUN WAS PRERFORMED ON DAT LAND BY THE JACAL CLAN A MERE TREE SEASONS AGO.
WARYOR MIGAL 'IMSELF VERFIED ITS SAFETY.
BE DAT AS IT MAY, MY BEES ARE DYING.
IF YOU'D ONLY CONSIDER...
CAUTION
TERRAFORM
CAUTION
CONSIDER I SHALL.
NOW, ONTO MORE ARGENT MADDERS. LIKE THE NAZAIM GURL. I ASSUME SHE'S BEEN CLINZED?

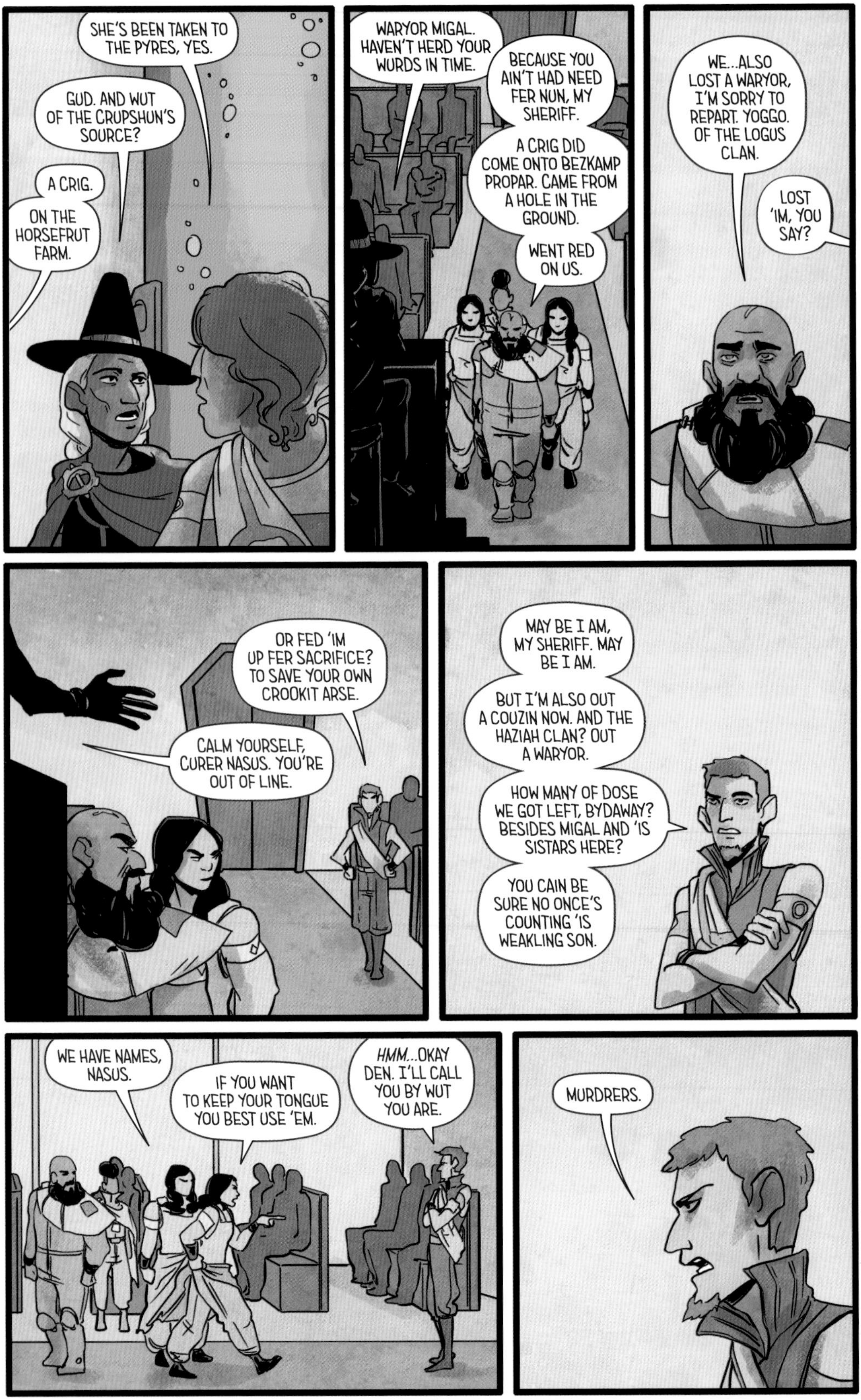
SHE'S BEEN TAKEN TO THE PYRES, YES.
GUD. AND WUT OF THE CRUPSHUN'S SOURCE?
A CRIG.
ON THE HORSEFRUT FARM.
WARYOR MIGAL. HAVEN'T HERD YOUR WURDS IN TIME.
BECAUSE YOU AIN'T HAD NEED FER NUN, MY SHERIFF.
A CRIG DID COME ONTO BEZKAMP PROPAR. CAME FROM A HOLE IN THE GROUND.
WENT RED ON US.
WE...ALSO LOST A WARYOR, I'M SORRY TO REPART. YOGGO. OF THE LOGUS CLAN.
LOST 'IM, YOU SAY?
OR FED 'IM UP FER SACRIFICE? TO SAVE YOUR OWN CROOKIT ARSE.
CALM YOURSELF, CURER NASUS. YOU'RE OUT OF LINE.
MAY BE I AM, MY SHERIFF. MAY BE I AM.
BUT I'M ALSO OUT A COUZIN NOW. AND THE HAZIAH CLAN? OUT A WARYOR.
HOW MANY OF DOSE WE GOT LEFT, BYDAWAY? BESIDES MIGAL AND 'IS SISTARS HERE?
YOU CAIN BE SURE NO ONCE'S COUNTING 'IS WEAKLING SON.
WE HAVE NAMES, NASUS.
IF YOU WANT TO KEEP YOUR TONGUE YOU BEST USE 'EM.
HMM...OKAY DEN. I'LL CALL YOU BY WUT YOU ARE.
MURDRERS.

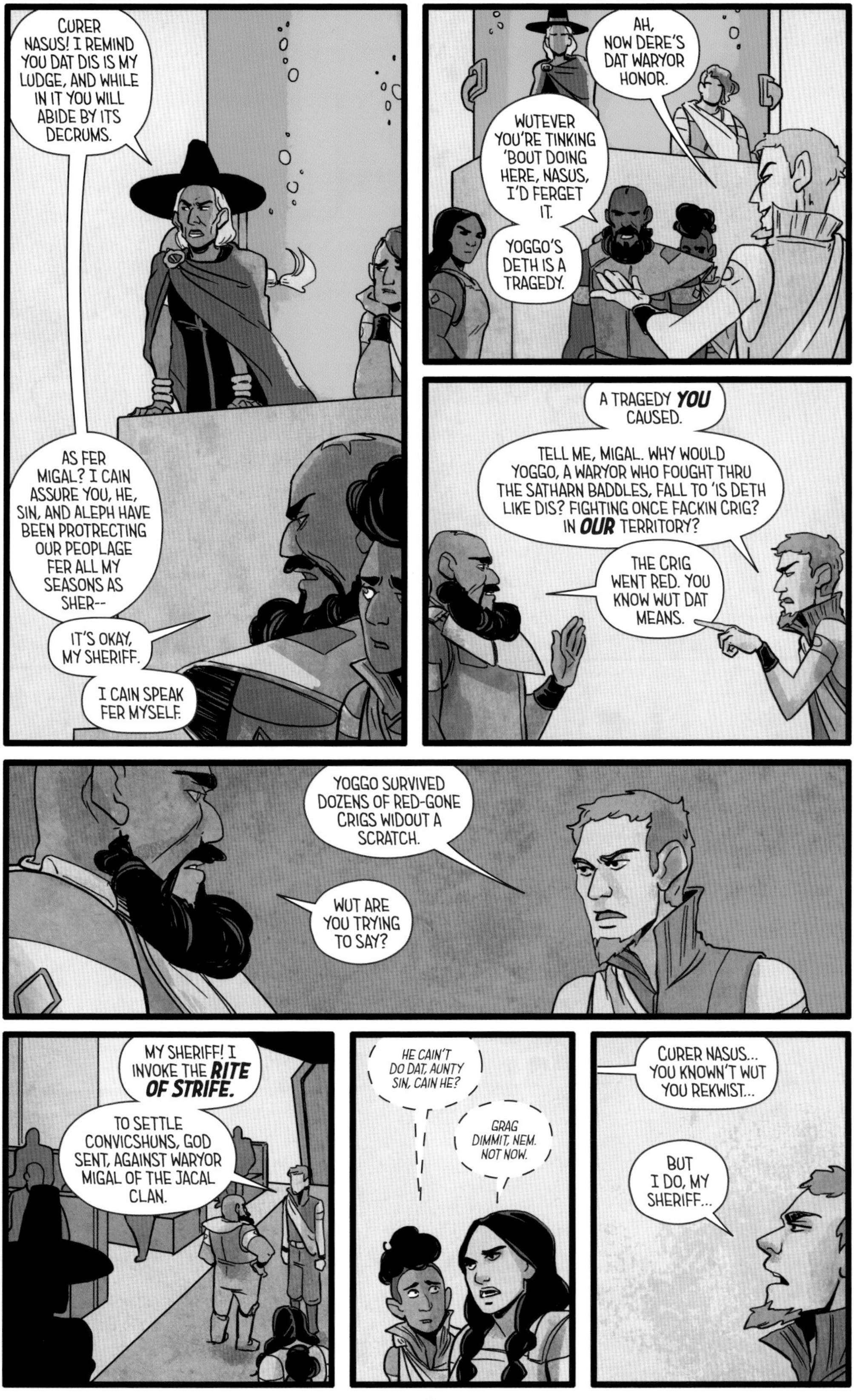
CURER NASUS! I REMIND YOU DAT DIS IS MY LUDGE, AND WHILE IN IT YOU WILL ABIDE BY ITS DECRUMS.
AS FER MIGAL? I CAIN ASSURE YOU, HE, SIN, AND ALEPH HAVE BEEN PROTRECTING OUR PEOPLAGE FER ALL MY SEASONS AS SHER--
IT'S OKAY, MY SHERIFF.
I CAIN SPEAK FER MYSELF.
AH, NOW DERE'S DAT WARYOR HONOR.
WUTEVER YOU'RE TINKING 'BOUT DOING HERE, NASUS, I'D FERGET IT.
YOGGO'S DETH IS A TRAGEDY.
A TRAGEDY YOU CAUSED.
TELL ME, MIGAL. WHY WOULD YOGGO, A WARYOR WHO FOUGHT THRU THE SATHARN BADDLES, FALL TO 'IS DETH LIKE DIS? FIGHTING ONCE FACKIN CRIG? IN OUR TERRITORY?
THE CRIG WENT RED. YOU KNOW WUT DAT MEANS.
YOGGO SURVIVED DOZENS OF RED-GONE CRIGS WIDOUT A SCRATCH.
WUT ARE YOU TRYING TO SAY?
MY SHERIFF! I INVOKE THE RITE OF STRIFE.
TO SETTLE CONVICSHUNS, GOD SENT, AGAINST WARYOR MIGAL OF THE JACAL CLAN.
HE CAIN'T DO DAT, AUNTY SIN, CAIN HE?
GRAG DIMMIT, NEM. NOT NOW.
CURER NASUS... YOU KNOWN'T WUT YOU REKWIST...
BUT I DO, MY SHERIFF...

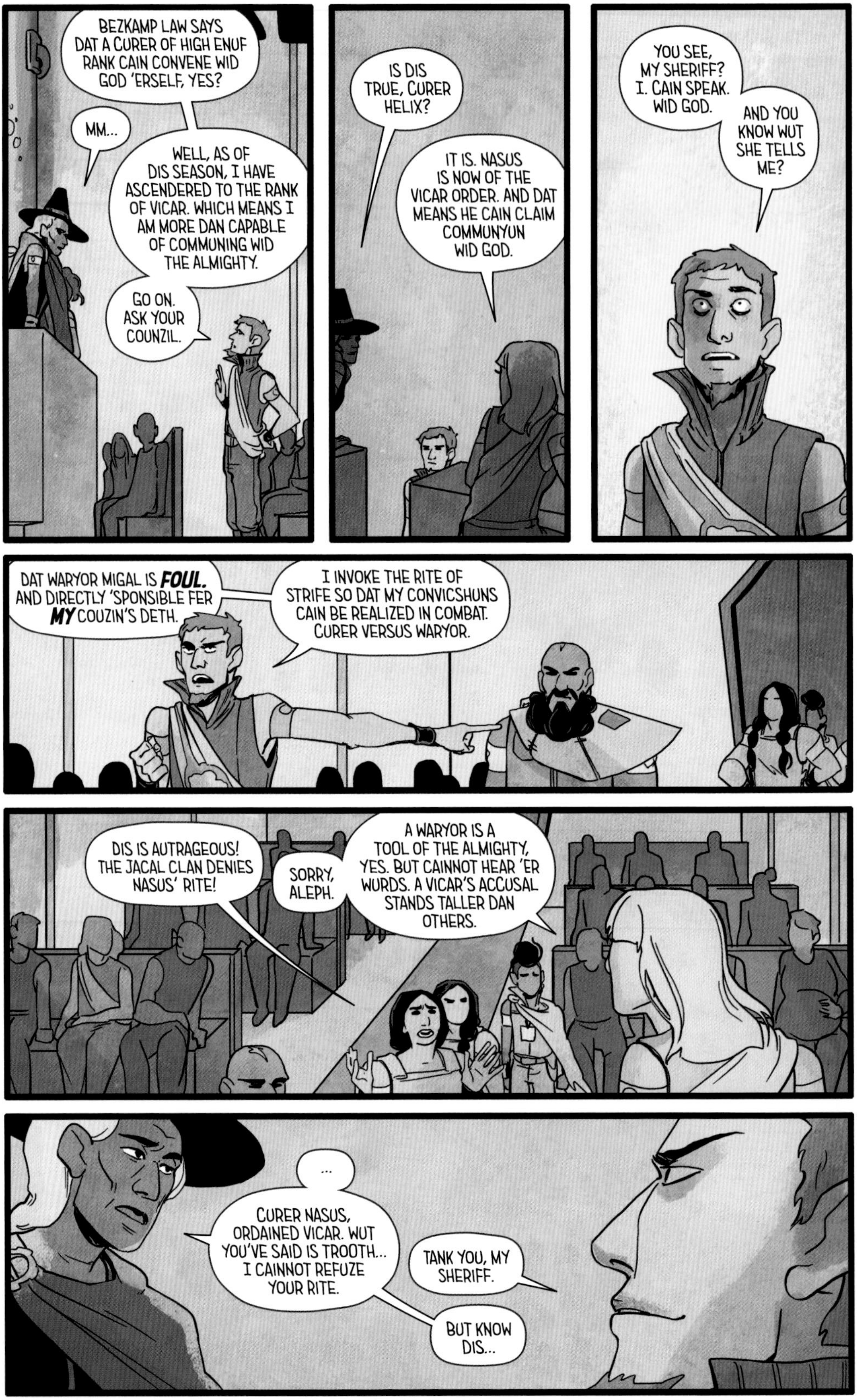
BEZKAMP LAW SAYS DAT A CURER OF HIGH ENUF RANK CAIN CONVENE WID GOD 'ERSELF, YES?
MM...
WELL, AS OF DIS SEASON, I HAVE ASCENDERED TO THE RANK OF VICAR. WHICH MEANS I AM MORE DAN CAPABLE OF COMMUNING WID THE ALMIGHTY.
GO ON. ASK YOUR COUNZIL.
IS DIS TRUE, CURER HELIX?
IT IS. NASUS IS NOW OF THE VICAR ORDER. AND DAT MEANS HE CAIN CLAIM COMMUNYUN WID GOD.
YOU SEE, MY SHERIFF? I. CAIN SPEAK. WID GOD.
AND YOU KNOW WUT SHE TELLS ME?
DAT WARYOR MIGAL IS **FOUL.** AND DIRECTLY 'SPONSIBLE FER ***MY*** COUZIN'S DETH.
I INVOKE THE RITE OF STRIFE SO DAT MY CONVICSHUNS CAIN BE REALIZED IN COMBAT. CURER VERSUS WARYOR.
DIS IS AUTRAGEOUS! THE JACAL CLAN DENIES NASUS' RITE!
SORRY, ALEPH.
A WARYOR IS A TOOL OF THE ALMIGHTY, YES. BUT CAINNOT HEAR 'ER WURDS. A VICAR'S ACCUSAL STANDS TALLER DAN OTHERS.
...
CURER NASUS, ORDAINED VICAR. WUT YOU'VE SAID IS TROOTH... I CAINNOT REFUZE YOUR RITE.
TANK YOU, MY SHERIFF.
BUT KNOW DIS...

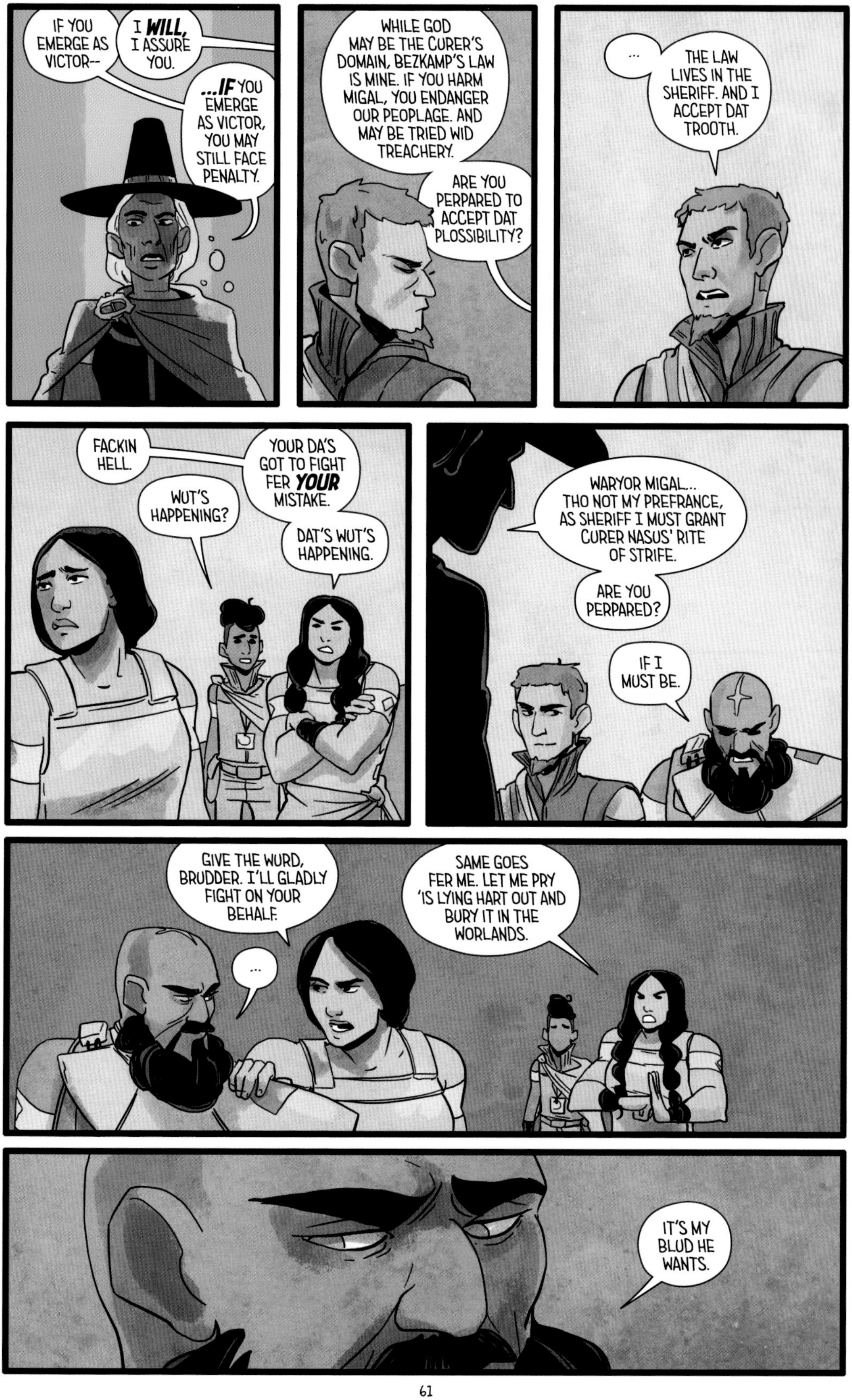
IF YOU EMERGE AS VICTOR--
I WILL, I ASSURE YOU.
...IF YOU EMERGE AS VICTOR, YOU MAY STILL FACE PENALTY.
WHILE GOD MAY BE THE CURER'S DOMAIN, BEZKAMP'S LAW IS MINE. IF YOU HARM MIGAL, YOU ENDANGER OUR PEOPLAGE. AND MAY BE TRIED WID TREACHERY.
ARE YOU PERPARED TO ACCEPT DAT PLOSSIBILITY?
...
THE LAW LIVES IN THE SHERIFF. AND I ACCEPT DAT TROOTH.
FACKIN HELL.
YOUR DA'S GOT TO FIGHT FER YOUR MISTAKE.
WUT'S HAPPENING?
DAT'S WUT'S HAPPENING.
WARYOR MIGAL... THO NOT MY PREFRANCE, AS SHERIFF I MUST GRANT CURER NASUS' RITE OF STRIFE.
ARE YOU PERPARED?
IF I MUST BE.
GIVE THE WURD, BRUDDER. I'LL GLADLY FIGHT ON YOUR BEHALF.
...
SAME GOES FER ME. LET ME PRY 'IS LYING HART OUT AND BURY IT IN THE WORLANDS.
IT'S MY BLUD HE WANTS.

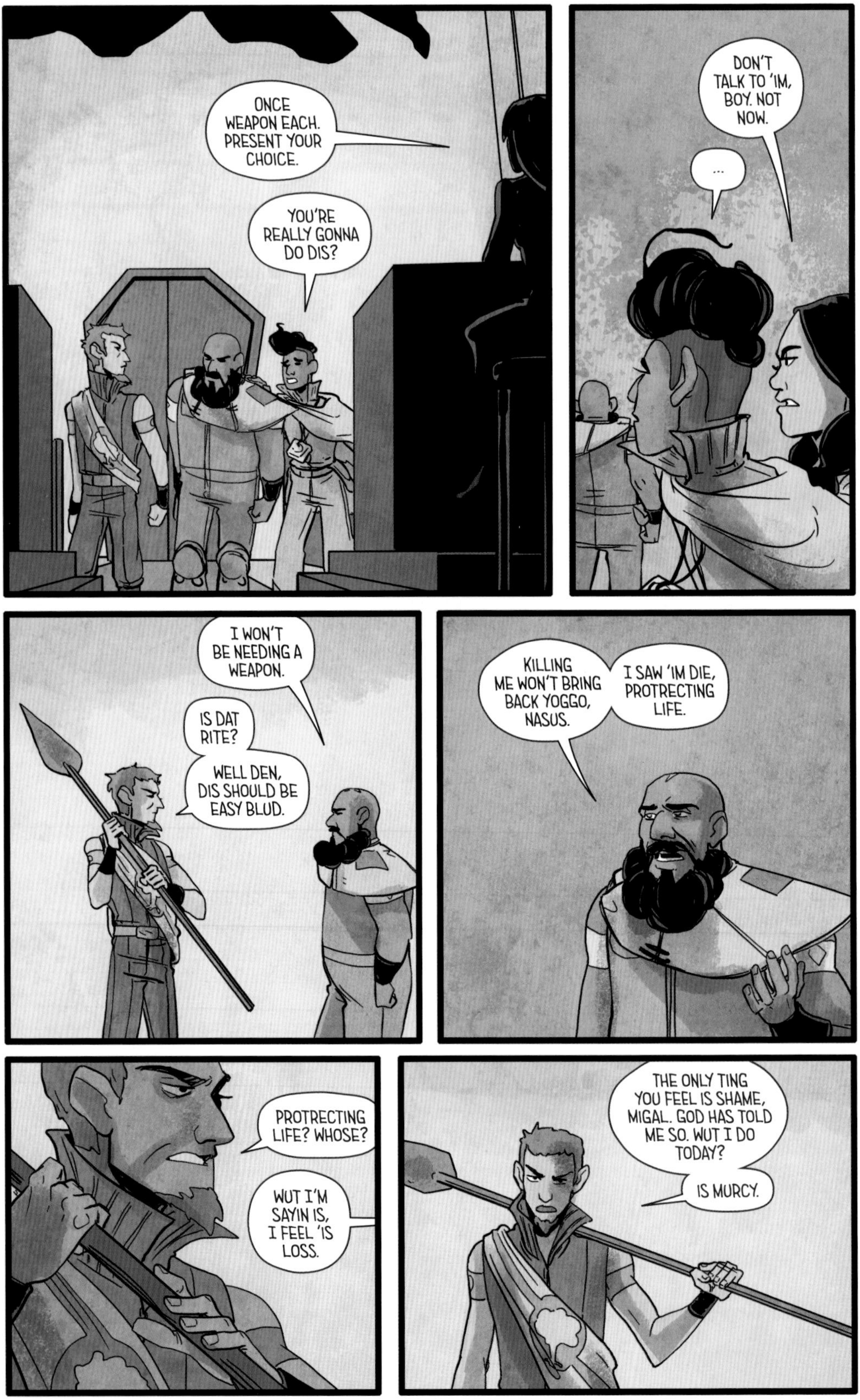
ONCE WEAPON EACH. PRESENT YOUR CHOICE.
YOU'RE REALLY GONNA DO DIS?
DON'T TALK TO 'IM, BOY. NOT NOW.
...
I WON'T BE NEEDING A WEAPON.
IS DAT RITE?
WELL DEN, DIS SHOULD BE EASY BLUD.
KILLING ME WON'T BRING BACK YOGGO, NASUS.
I SAW 'IM DIE, PROTRECTING LIFE.
PROTRECTING LIFE? WHOSE?
WUT I'M SAYIN IS, I FEEL 'IS LOSS.
THE ONLY TING YOU FEEL IS SHAME, MIGAL. GOD HAS TOLD ME SO. WUT I DO TODAY?
IS MURCY.

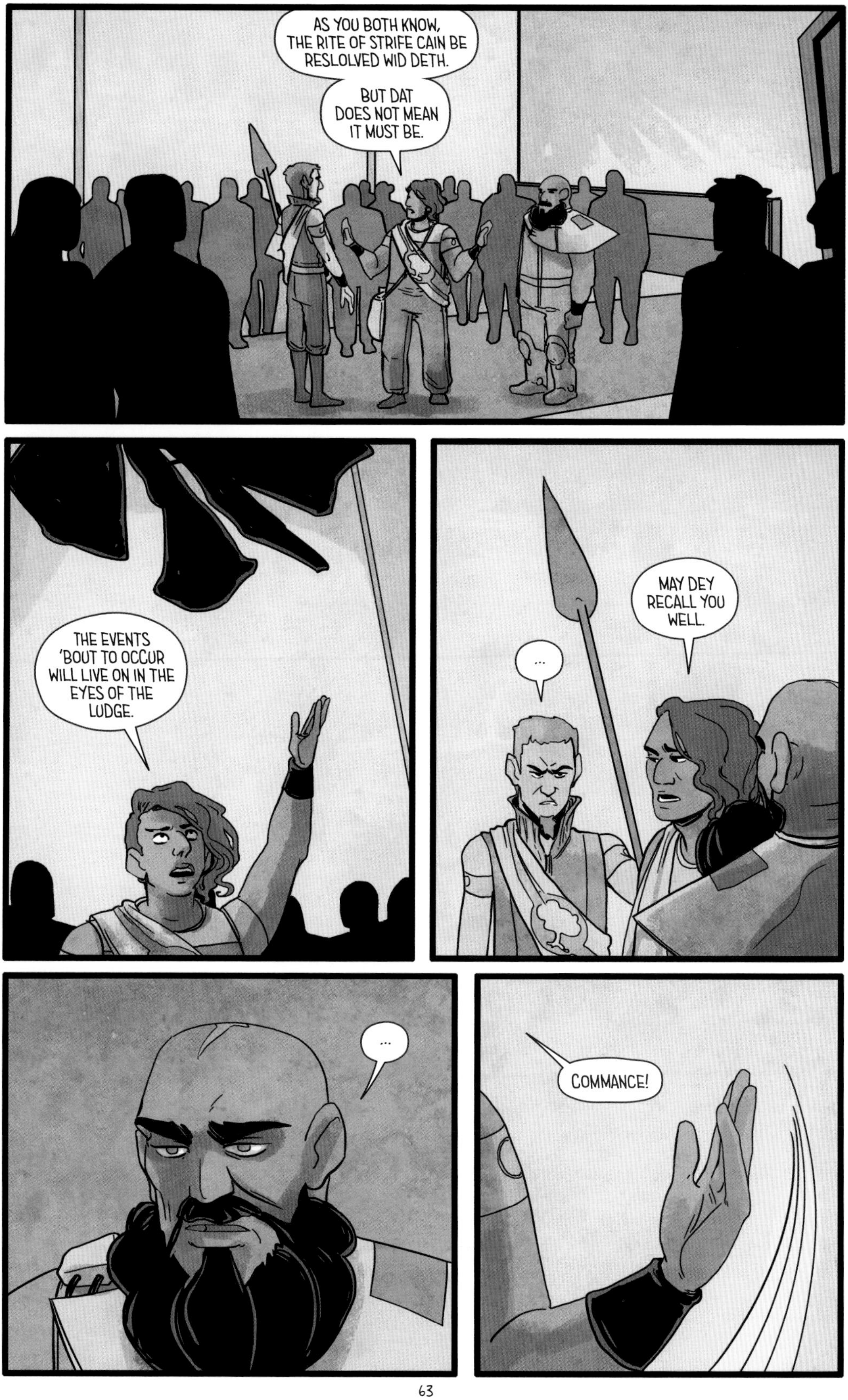
AS YOU BOTH KNOW, THE RITE OF STRIFE CAIN BE RESLOLVED WID DETH.
BUT DAT DOES NOT MEAN IT MUST BE.
THE EVENTS 'BOUT TO OCCUR WILL LIVE ON IN THE EYES OF THE LUDGE.
...
MAY DEY RECALL YOU WELL.
...
COMMANCE!

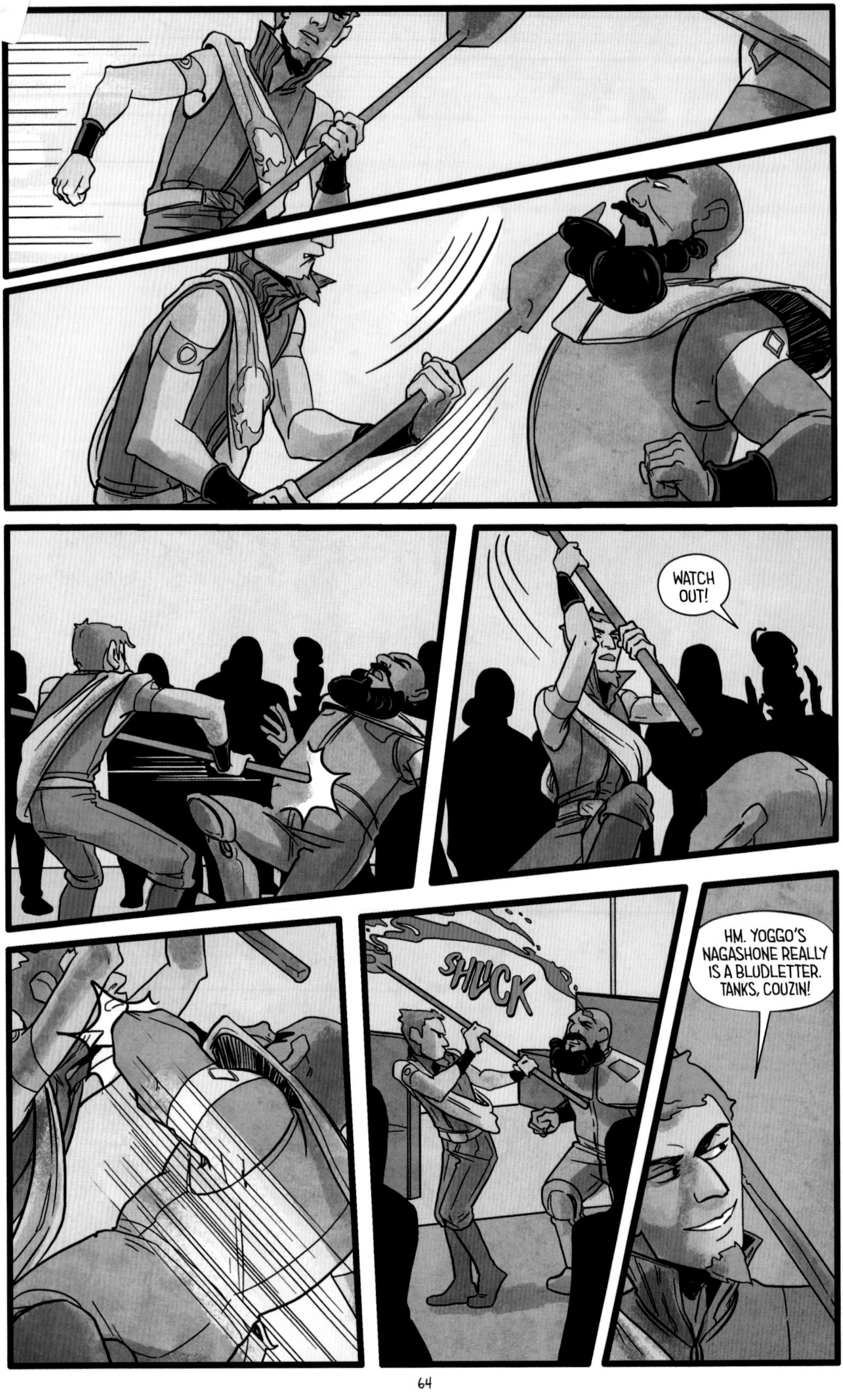
WATCH OUT!
SHUCK
HM. YOGGO'S NAGASHONE REALLY IS A BLUDLETTER. TANKS, COUZIN!

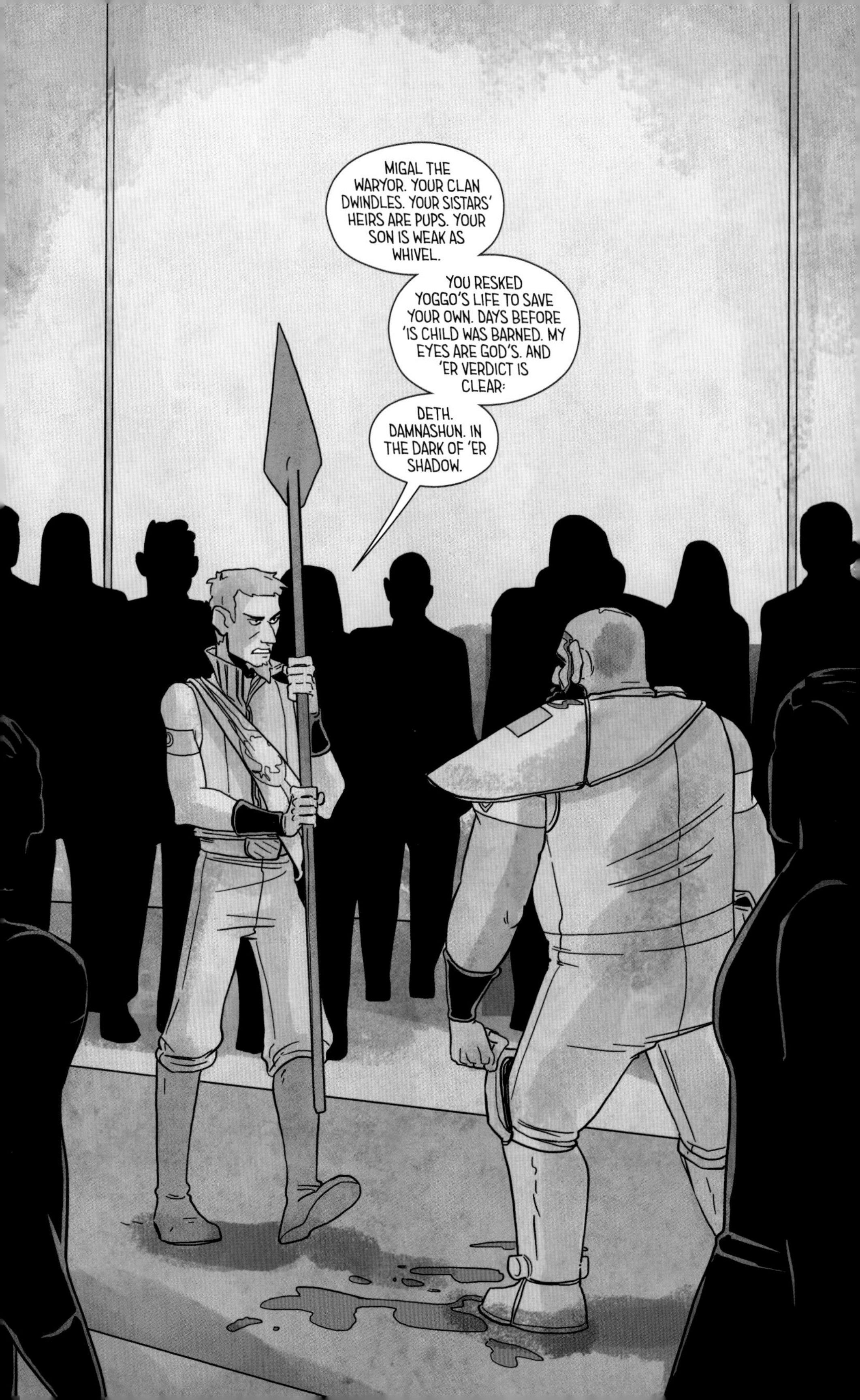
MIGAL THE WARYOR. YOUR CLAN DWINDLES. YOUR SISTARS' HEIRS ARE PUPS. YOUR SON IS WEAK AS WHIVEL.
YOU RESKED YOGGO'S LIFE TO SAVE YOUR OWN. DAYS BEFORE 'IS CHILD WAS BARNED. MY EYES ARE GOD'S. AND 'ER VERDICT IS CLEAR:
DETH. DAMNASHUN. IN THE DARK OF 'ER SHADOW.

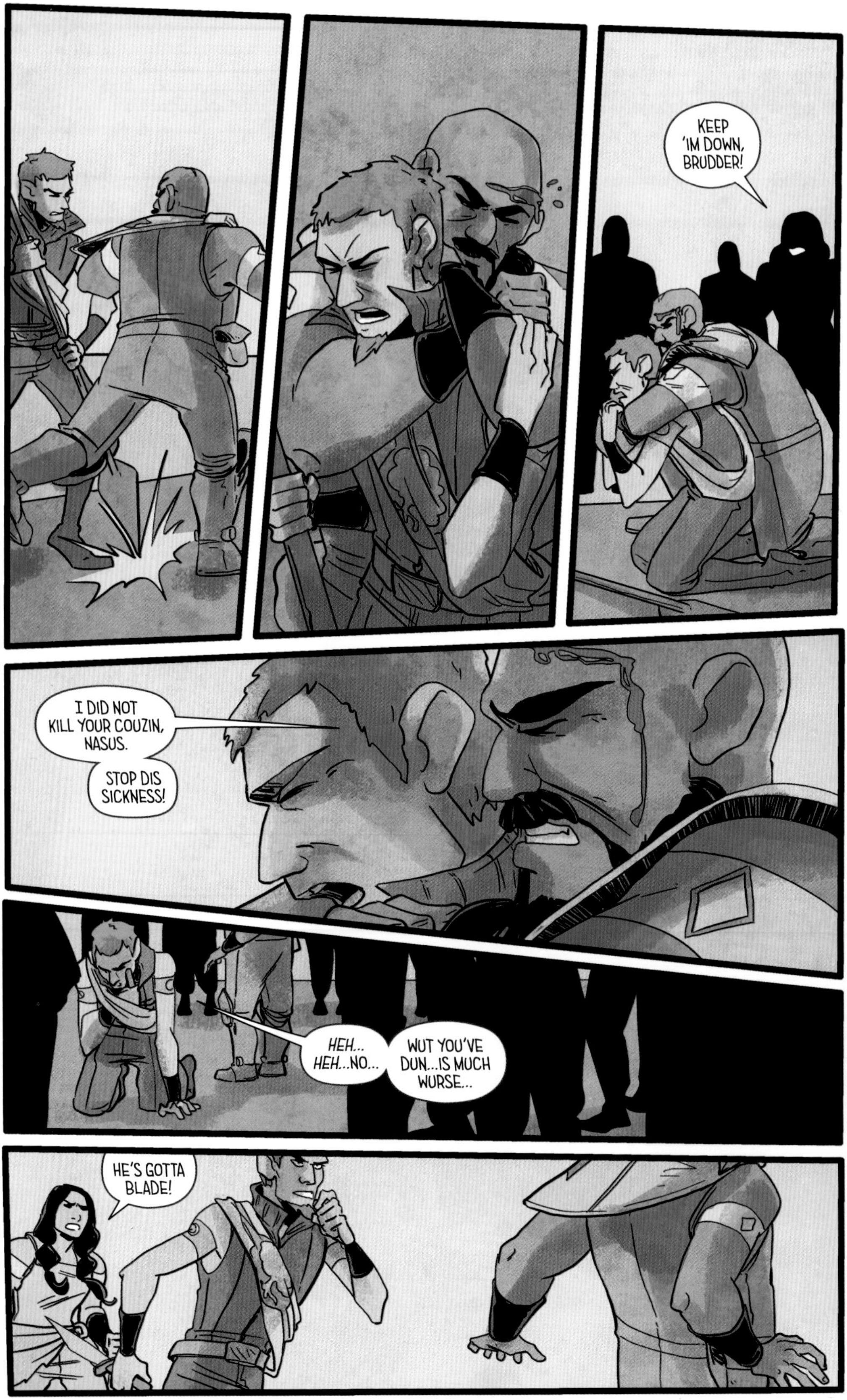
KEEP 'IM DOWN, BRUDDER!
I DID NOT KILL YOUR COUZIN, NASUS.
STOP DIS SICKNESS!
HEH... HEH...NO...
WUT YOU'VE DUN...IS MUCH WURSE...
HE'S GOTTA BLADE!

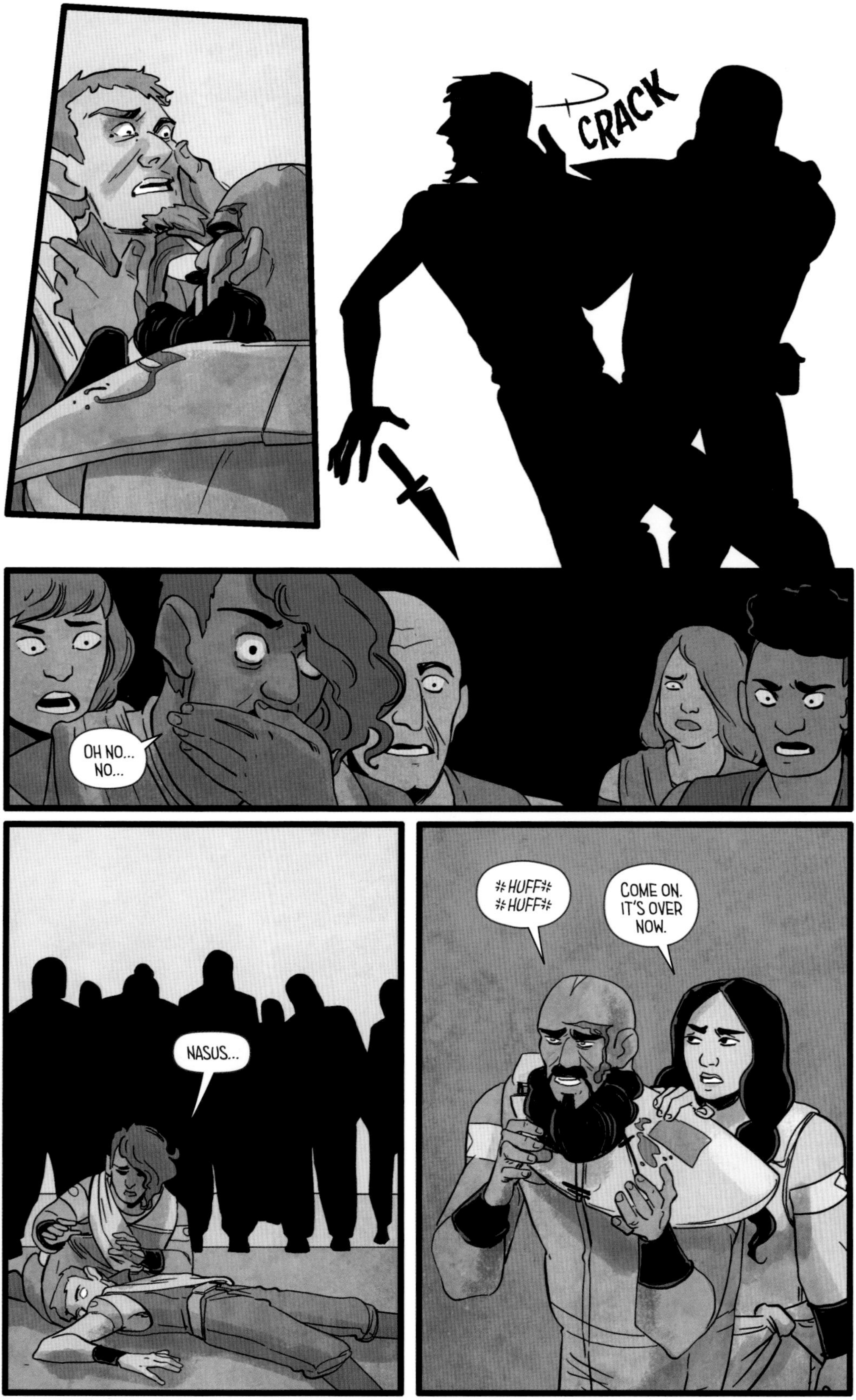
CRACK
OH NO... NO...
NASUS...
HUFF *HUFF*
COME ON. IT'S OVER NOW.

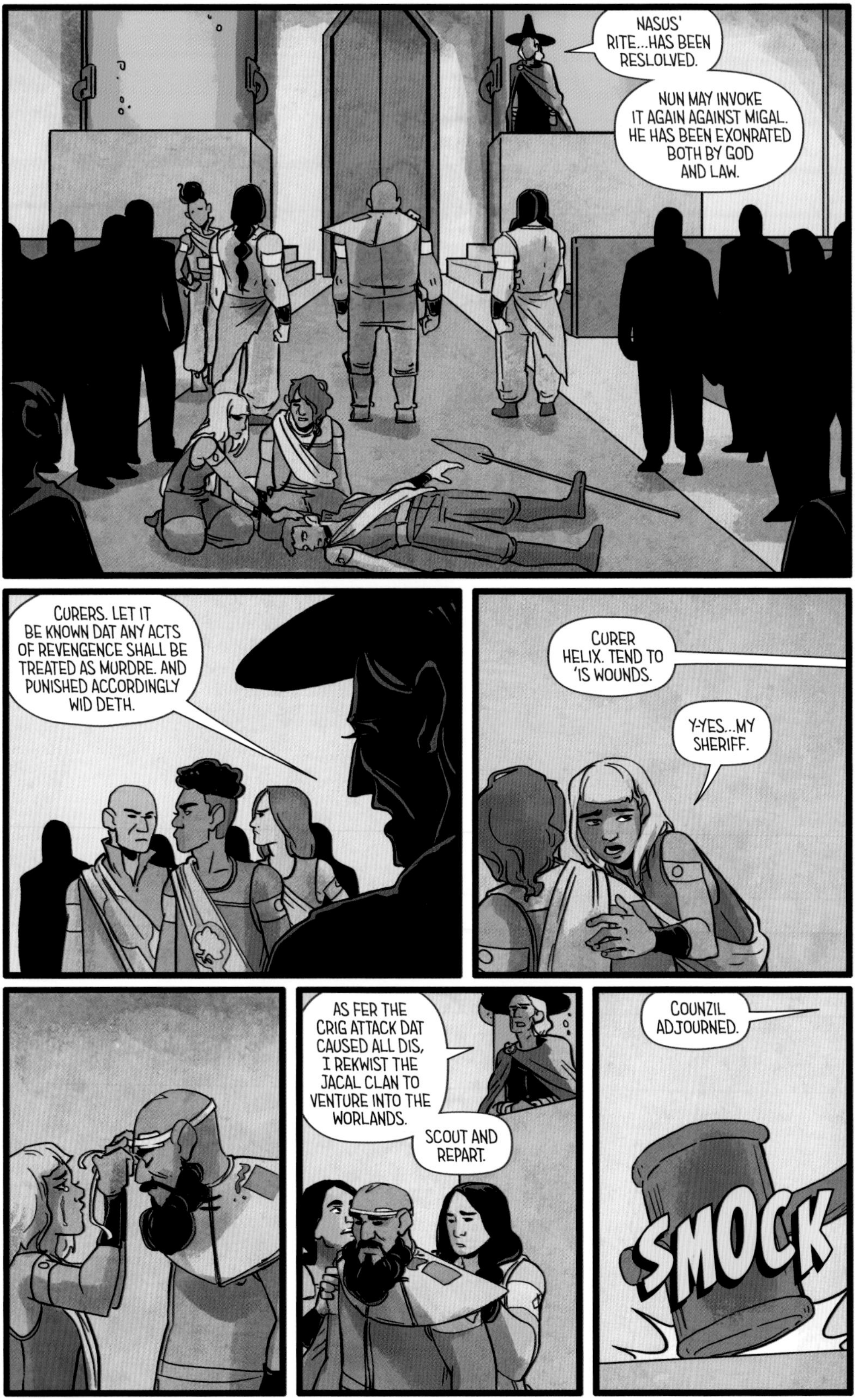
NASUS' RITE...HAS BEEN RESLOLVED.
NUN MAY INVOKE IT AGAIN AGAINST MIGAL. HE HAS BEEN EXONRATED BOTH BY GOD AND LAW.
CURERS. LET IT BE KNOWN DAT ANY ACTS OF REVENGENCE SHALL BE TREATED AS MURDRE. AND PUNISHED ACCORDINGLY WID DETH.
CURER HELIX. TEND TO 'IS WOUNDS.
Y-YES...MY SHERIFF.
AS FER THE CRIG ATTACK DAT CAUSED ALL DIS, I REKWIST THE JACAL CLAN TO VENTURE INTO THE WORLANDS.
SCOUT AND REPART.
COUNZIL ADJOURNED.
SMOCK

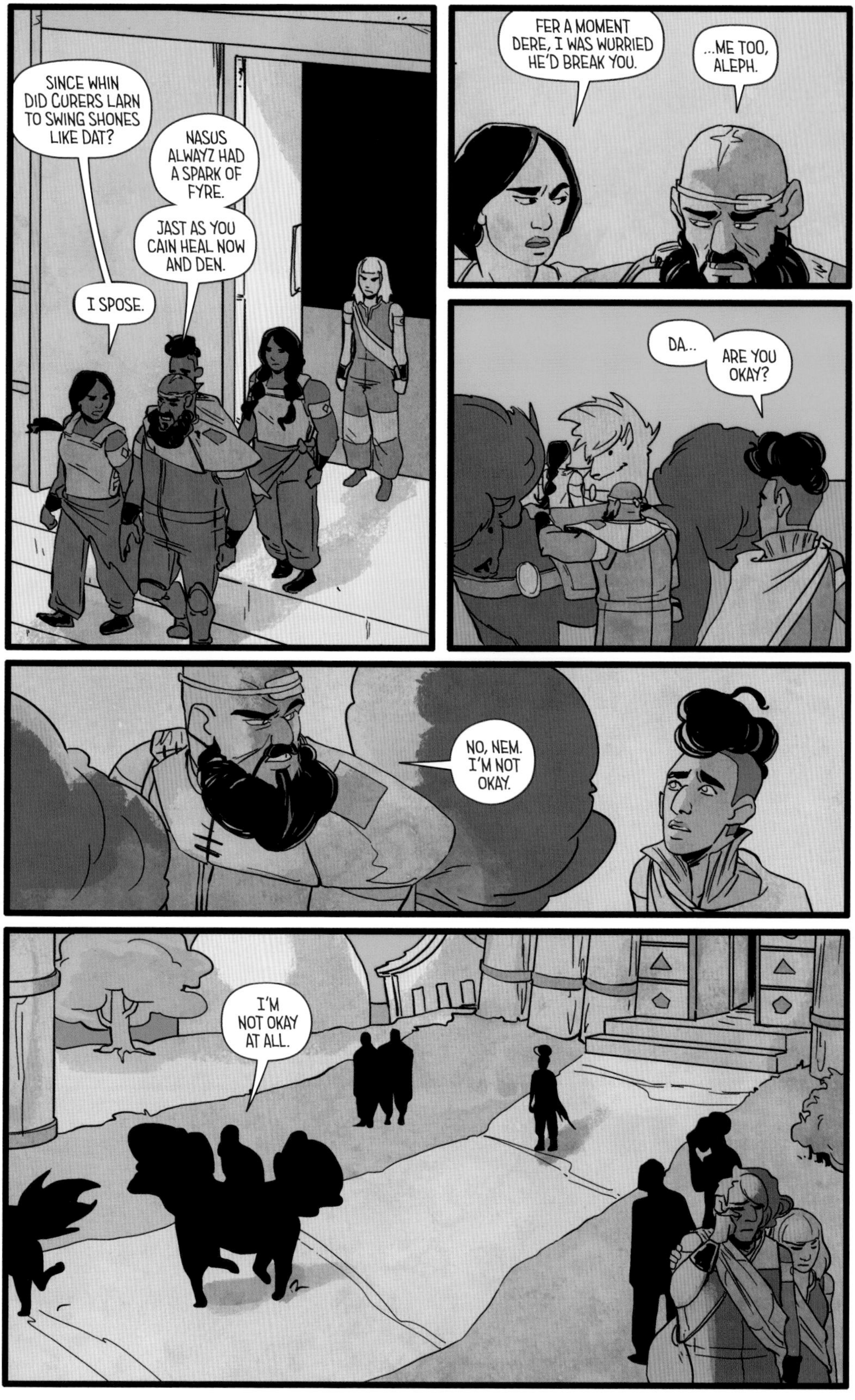
SINCE WHIN DID CURERS LARN TO SWING SHONES LIKE DAT?
NASUS ALWAYZ HAD A SPARK OF FYRE.
JAST AS YOU CAIN HEAL NOW AND DEN.
I SPOSE.
FER A MOMENT DERE, I WAS WURRIED HE'D BREAK YOU.
...ME TOO, ALEPH.
DA...
ARE YOU OKAY?
NO, NEM. I'M NOT OKAY.
I'M NOT OKAY AT ALL.

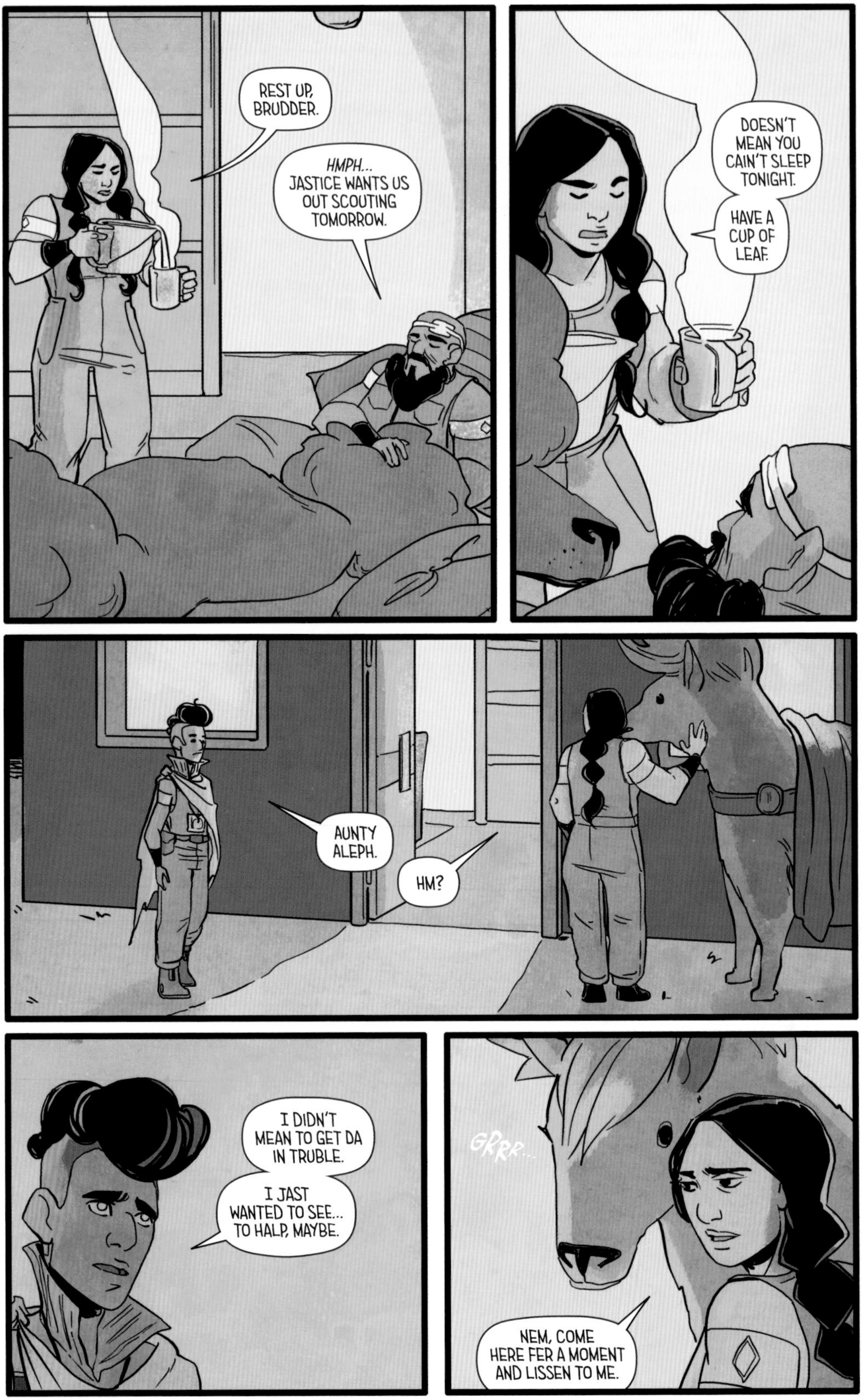

REST UP, BRUDDER.
HMPH... JASTICE WANTS US OUT SCOUTING TOMORROW.
DOESN'T MEAN YOU CAIN'T SLEEP TONIGHT.
HAVE A CUP OF LEAF.
AUNTY ALEPH.
HM?
I DIDN'T MEAN TO GET DA IN TRUBLE.
I JAST WANTED TO SEE... TO HALP, MAYBE.
GRRR...
NEM, COME HERE FER A MOMENT AND LISSEN TO ME.

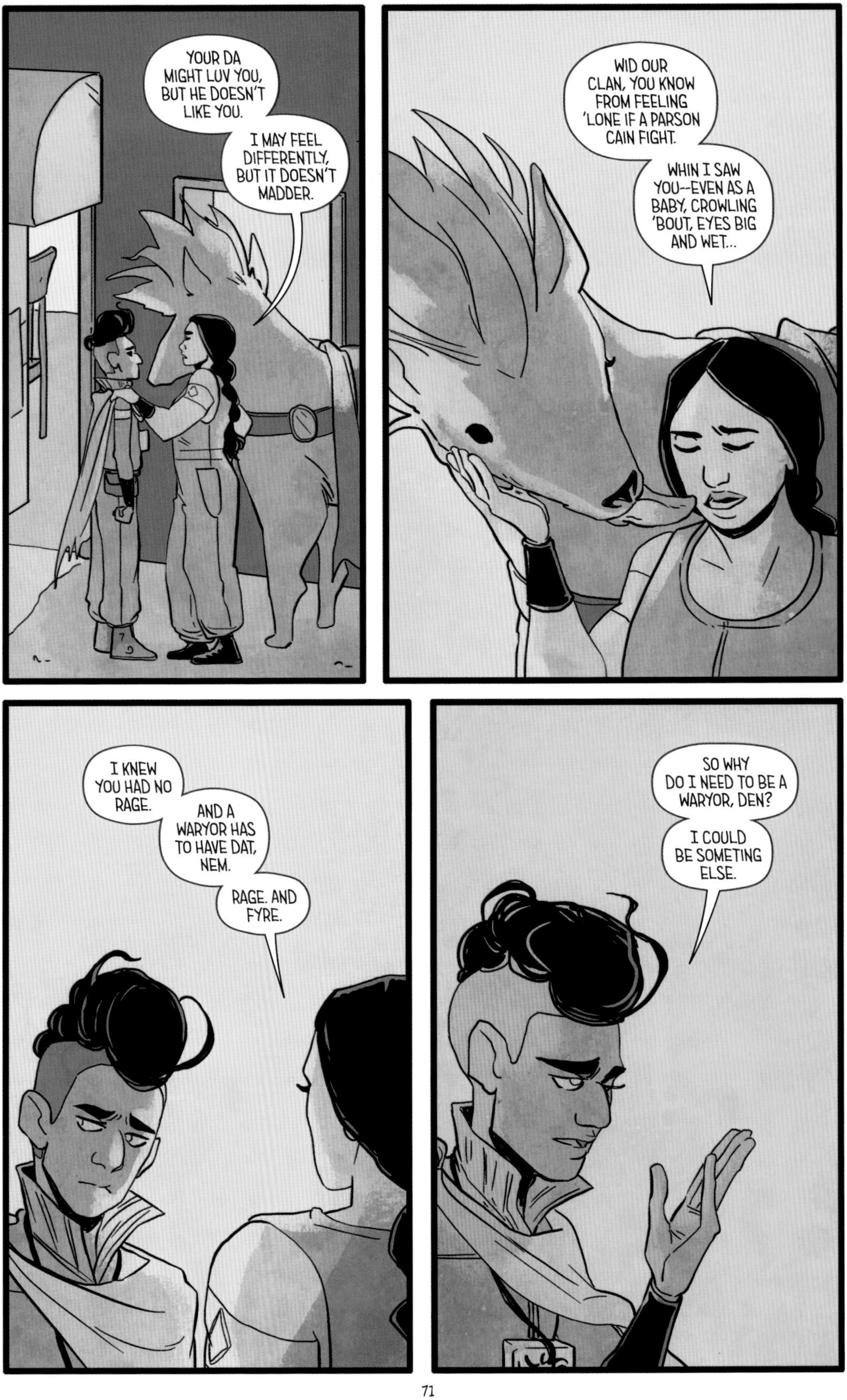
YOUR DA MIGHT LUV YOU, BUT HE DOESN'T LIKE YOU.
I MAY FEEL DIFFERENTLY, BUT IT DOESN'T MADDER.
WID OUR CLAN, YOU KNOW FROM FEELING 'LONE IF A PARSON CAIN FIGHT.
WHIN I SAW YOU--EVEN AS A BABY, CROWLING 'BOUT, EYES BIG AND WET...
I KNEW YOU HAD NO RAGE.
AND A WARYOR HAS TO HAVE DAT, NEM.
RAGE. AND FYRE.
SO WHY DO I NEED TO BE A WARYOR, DEN?
I COULD BE SOMETING ELSE.

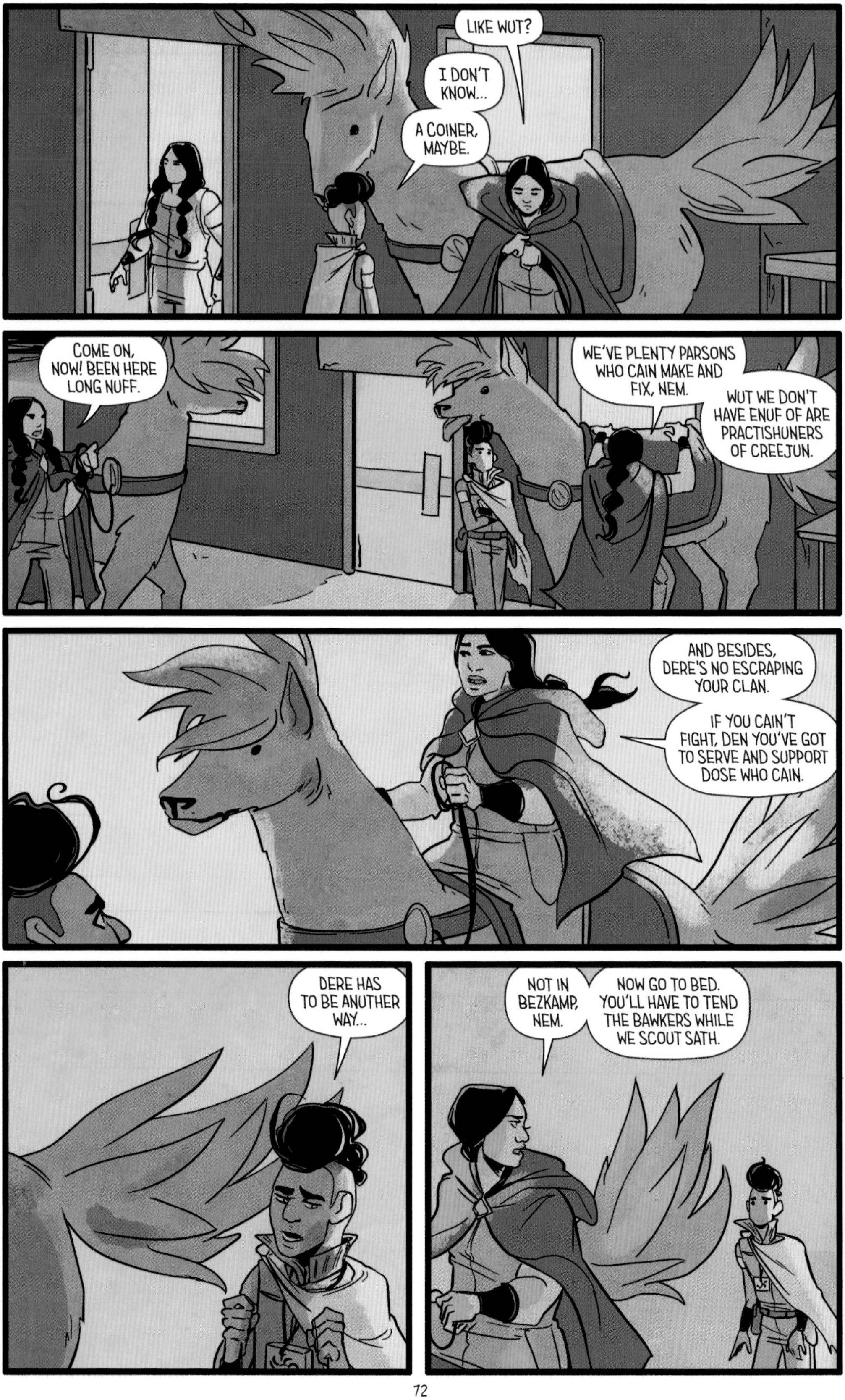
LIKE WUT?
I DON'T KNOW...
A COINER, MAYBE.
COME ON, NOW! BEEN HERE LONG NUFF.
WE'VE PLENTY PARSONS WHO CAIN MAKE AND FIX, NEM.
WUT WE DON'T HAVE ENUF OF ARE PRACTISHUNERS OF CREEJUN.
AND BESIDES, DERE'S NO ESCRAPING YOUR CLAN.
IF YOU CAIN'T FIGHT, DEN YOU'VE GOT TO SERVE AND SUPPORT DOSE WHO CAIN.
DERE HAS TO BE ANUTHER WAY...
NOT IN BEZKAMP, NEM.
NOW GO TO BED. YOU'LL HAVE TO TEND THE BAWKERS WHILE WE SCOUT SATH.

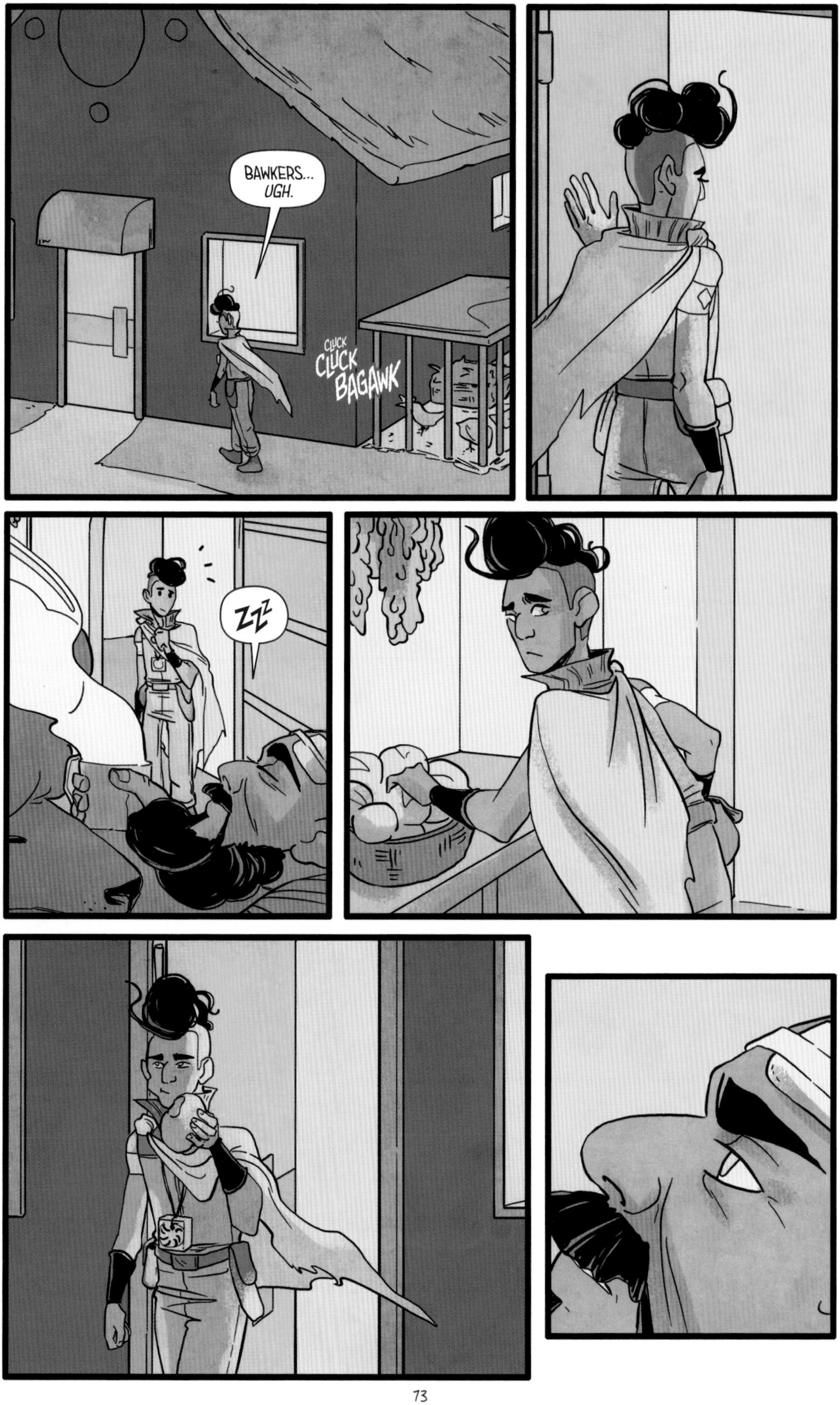
BAWKERS... UGH.
CLUCK CLUCK BAGAWK
ZZZ

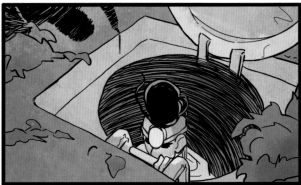

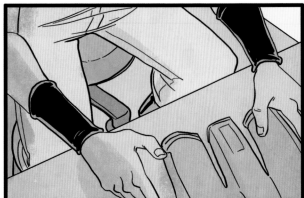

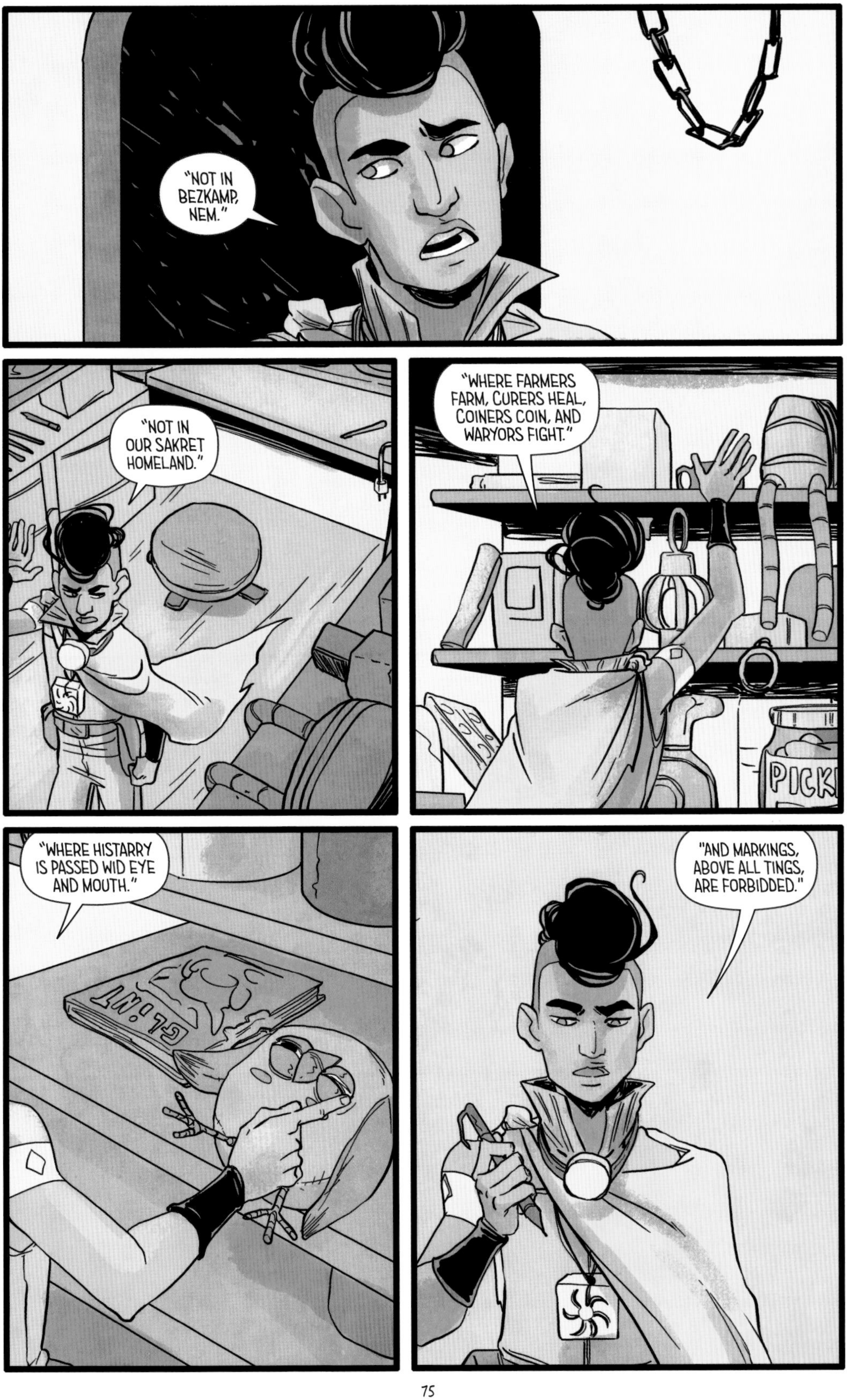
"NOT IN BEZKAMP, NEM."
"NOT IN OUR SAKRET HOMELAND."
"WHERE FARMERS FARM, CURERS HEAL, COINERS COIN, AND WARYORS FIGHT."
PICK
"WHERE HISTARRY IS PASSED WID EYE AND MOUTH."
GL'NT
"AND MARKINGS, ABOVE ALL TINGS, ARE FORBIDDED."

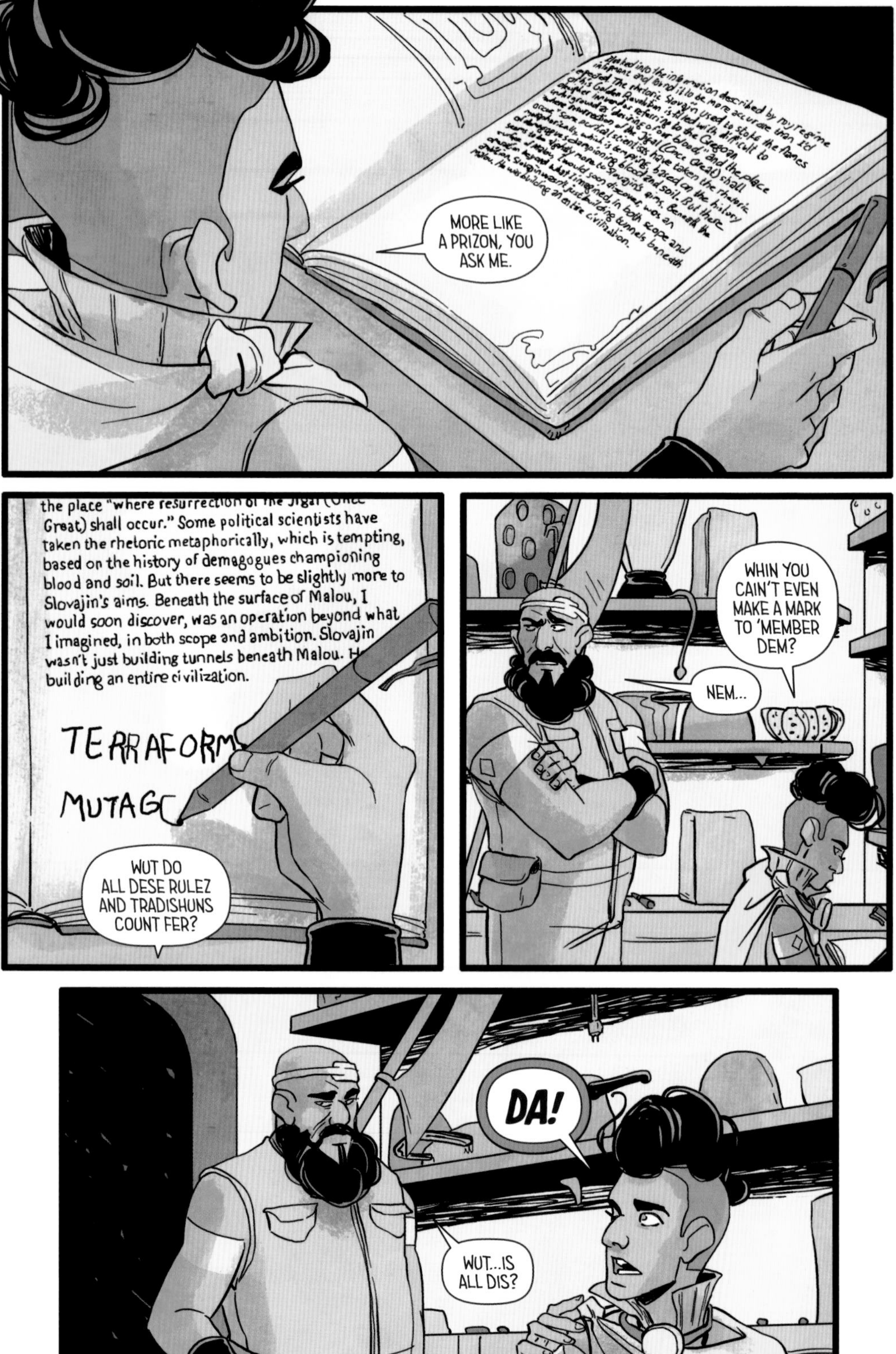
MORE LIKE A PRIZON, YOU ASK ME.
the place "where resurrection of the Jigai (Once Great) shall occur." Some political scientists have taken the rhetoric metaphorically, which is tempting, based on the history of demagogues championing blood and soil. But there seems to be slightly more to Slovajin's aims. Beneath the surface of Malou, I would soon discover, was an operation beyond what I imagined, in both scope and ambition. Slovajin wasn't just building tunnels beneath Malou. He building an entire civilization.
TERRAFORM
MUTAG
WUT DO ALL DESE RULEZ AND TRADISHUNS COUNT FER?
WHIN YOU CAIN'T EVEN MAKE A MARK TO 'MEMBER DEM?
NEM...
DA!
WUT...IS ALL DIS?

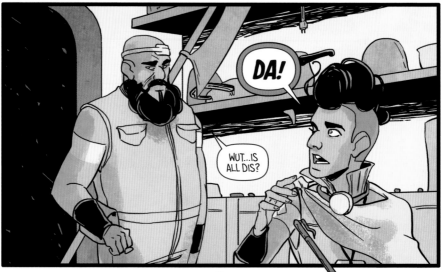

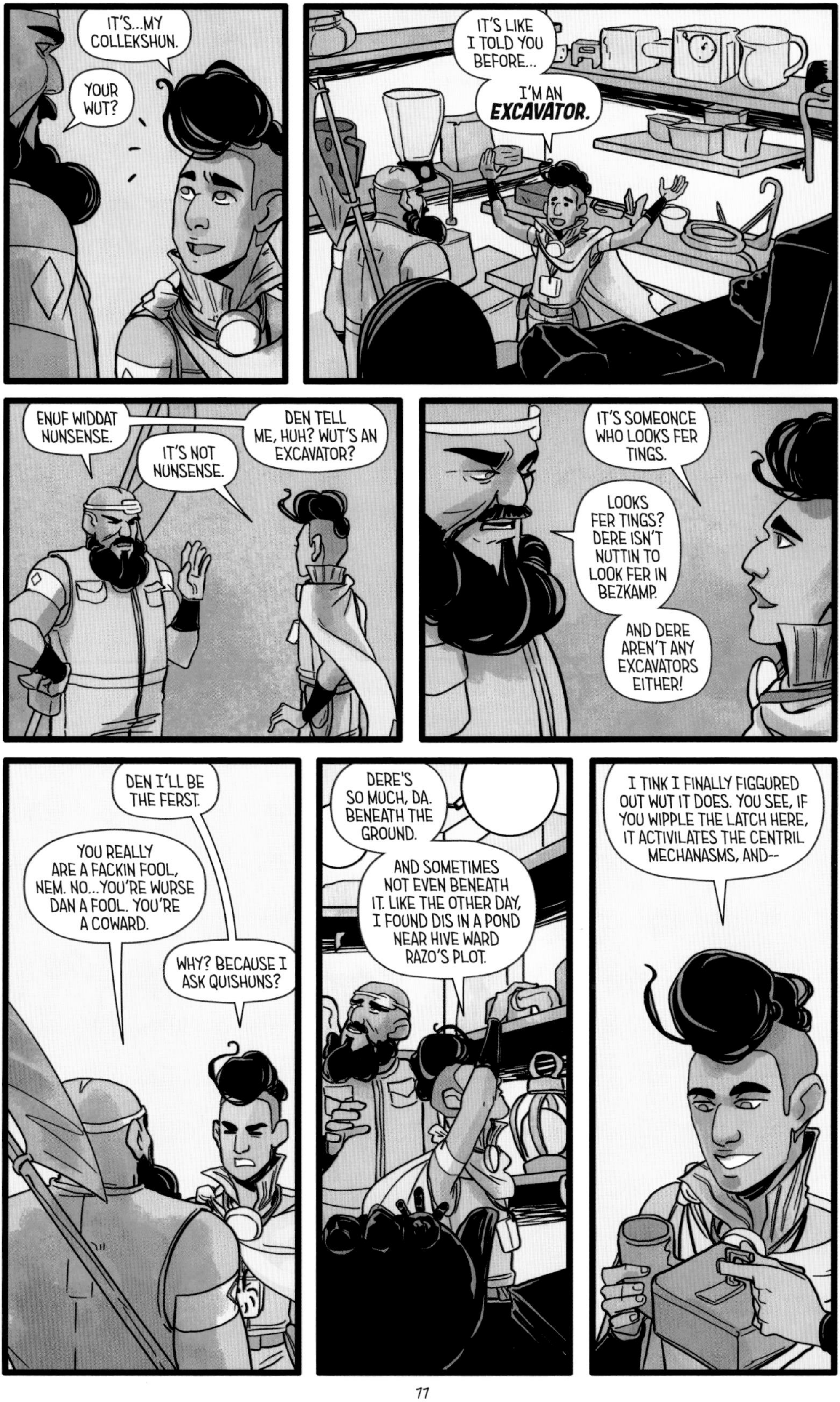
IT'S...MY COLLEKSHUN.
YOUR WUT?
IT'S LIKE I TOLD YOU BEFORE...
I'M AN **EXCAVATOR.**
ENUF WIDDAT NUNSENSE.
IT'S NOT NUNSENSE.
DEN TELL ME, HUH? WUT'S AN EXCAVATOR?
IT'S SOMEONCE WHO LOOKS FER TINGS.
LOOKS FER TINGS? DERE ISN'T NUTTIN TO LOOK FER IN BEZKAMP.
AND DERE AREN'T ANY EXCAVATORS EITHER!
DEN I'LL BE THE FERST.
YOU REALLY ARE A FACKIN FOOL, NEM. NO...YOU'RE WURSE DAN A FOOL. YOU'RE A COWARD.
WHY? BECAUSE I ASK QUISHUNS?
DERE'S SO MUCH, DA. BENEATH THE GROUND.
AND SOMETIMES NOT EVEN BENEATH IT. LIKE THE OTHER DAY, I FOUND DIS IN A POND NEAR HIVE WARD RAZO'S PLOT.
I TINK I FINALLY FIGGURED OUT WUT IT DOES. YOU SEE, IF YOU WIPPLE THE LATCH HERE, IT ACTIVILATES THE CENTRIL MECHANASMS, AND--

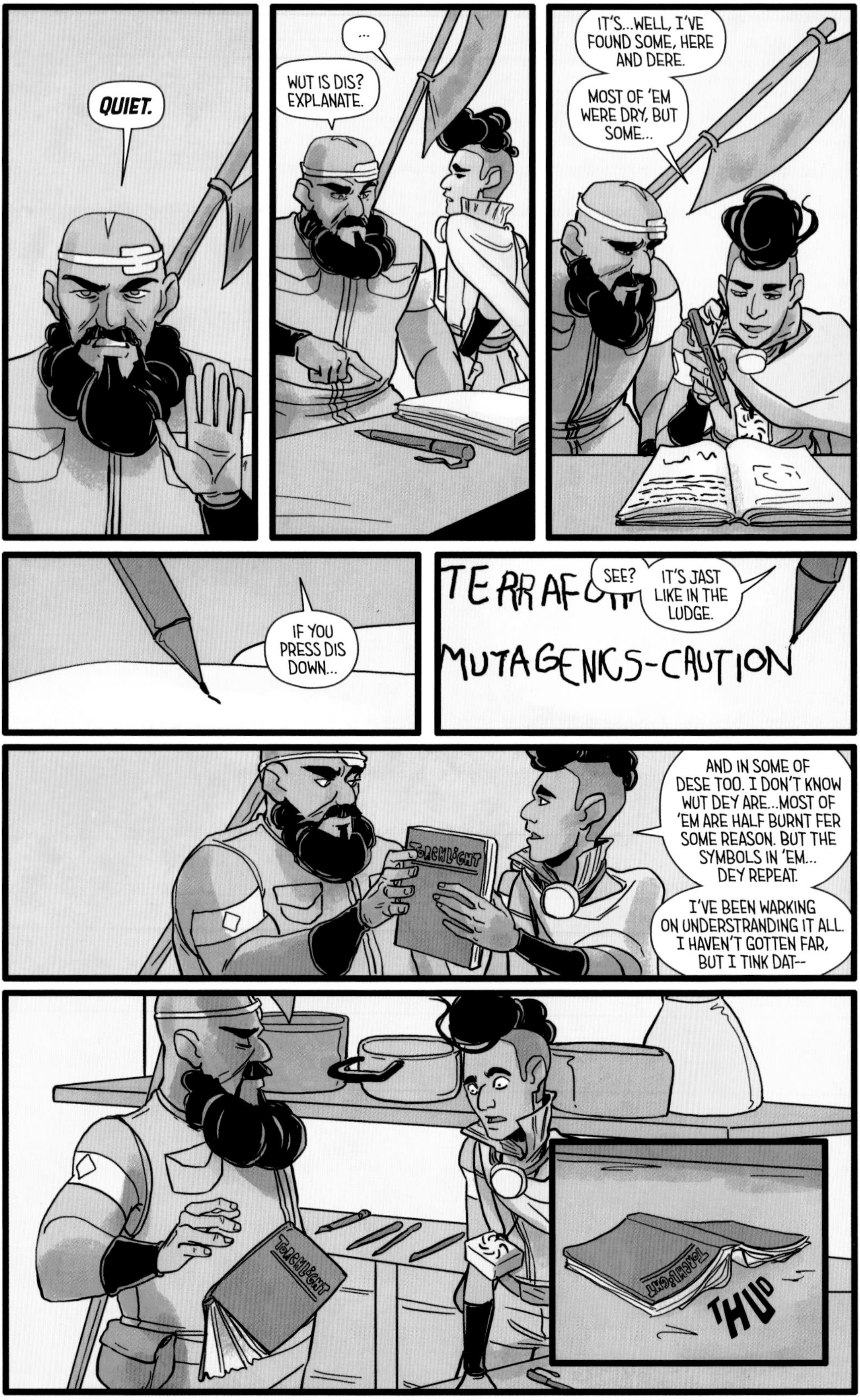

QUIET.
...
WUT IS DIS? EXPLANATE.
IT'S...WELL, I'VE FOUND SOME, HERE AND DERE.
MOST OF 'EM WERE DRY, BUT SOME...
IF YOU PRESS DIS DOWN...
SEE?
IT'S JAST LIKE IN THE LUDGE.
MUTAGENICS-CAUTION
AND IN SOME OF DESE TOO. I DON'T KNOW WUT DEY ARE...MOST OF 'EM ARE HALF BURNT FER SOME REASON. BUT THE SYMBOLS IN 'EM... DEY REPEAT.
I'VE BEEN WARKING ON UNDERSTRANDING IT ALL. I HAVEN'T GOTTEN FAR, BUT I TINK DAT--
THUD

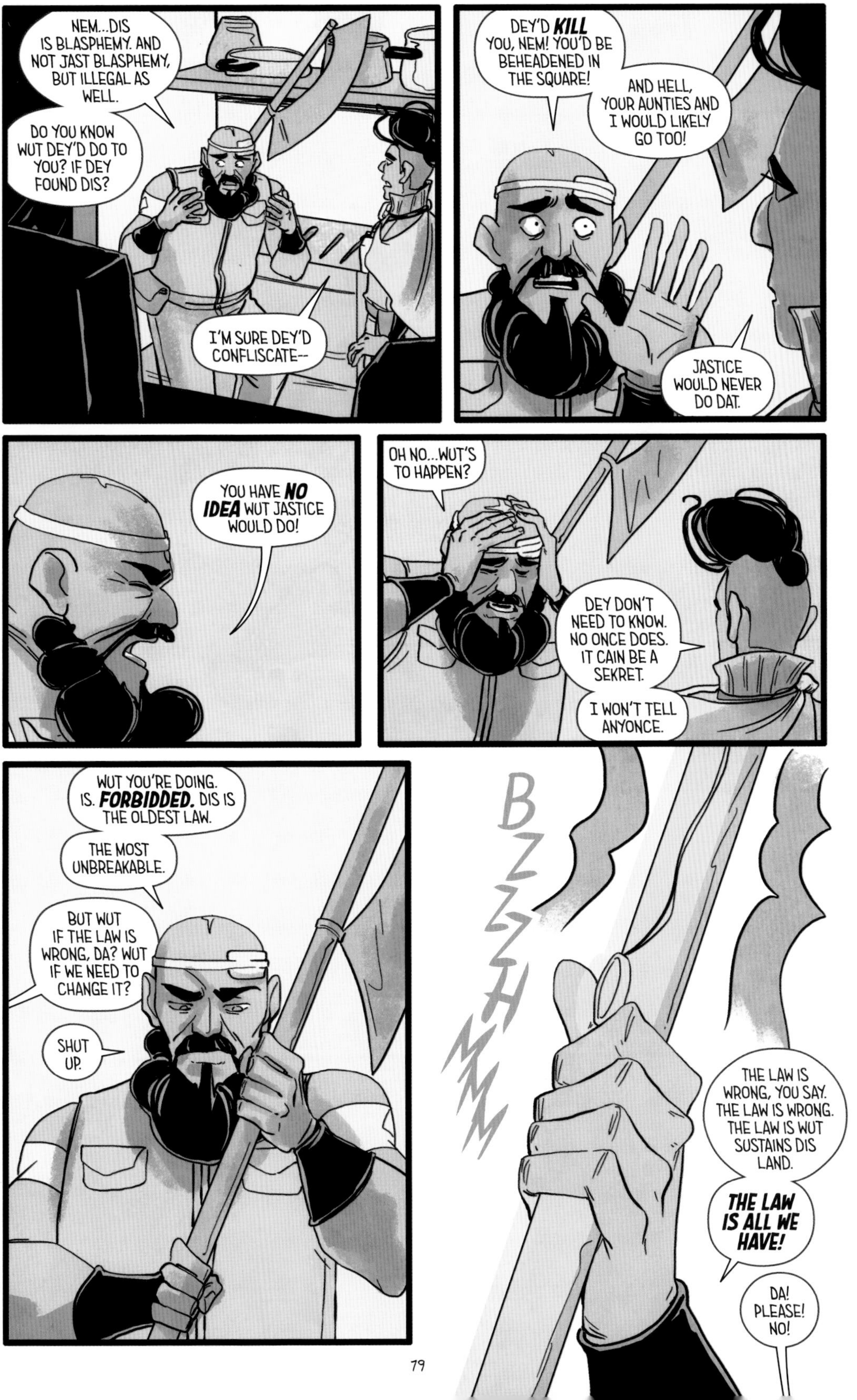
NEM...DIS IS BLASPHEMY. AND NOT JAST BLASPHEMY, BUT ILLEGAL AS WELL.
DO YOU KNOW WUT DEY'D DO TO YOU? IF DEY FOUND DIS?
I'M SURE DEY'D CONFLISCATE--
DEY'D **KILL** YOU, NEM! YOU'D BE BEHEADENED IN THE SQUARE!
AND HELL, YOUR AUNTIES AND I WOULD LIKELY GO TOO!
JASTICE WOULD NEVER DO DAT.
YOU HAVE **NO IDEA** WUT JASTICE WOULD DO!
OH NO...WUT'S TO HAPPEN?
DEY DON'T NEED TO KNOW. NO ONCE DOES. IT CAIN BE A SEKRET.
I WON'T TELL ANYONCE.
WUT YOU'RE DOING. IS. **FORBIDDED.** DIS IS THE OLDEST LAW.
THE MOST UNBREAKABLE.
BUT WUT IF THE LAW IS WRONG, DA? WUT IF WE NEED TO CHANGE IT?
SHUT UP.
BZZZZHMMM
THE LAW IS WRONG, YOU SAY. THE LAW IS WRONG. THE LAW IS WUT SUSTAINS DIS LAND.
THE LAW IS ALL WE HAVE!
DA! PLEASE! NO!

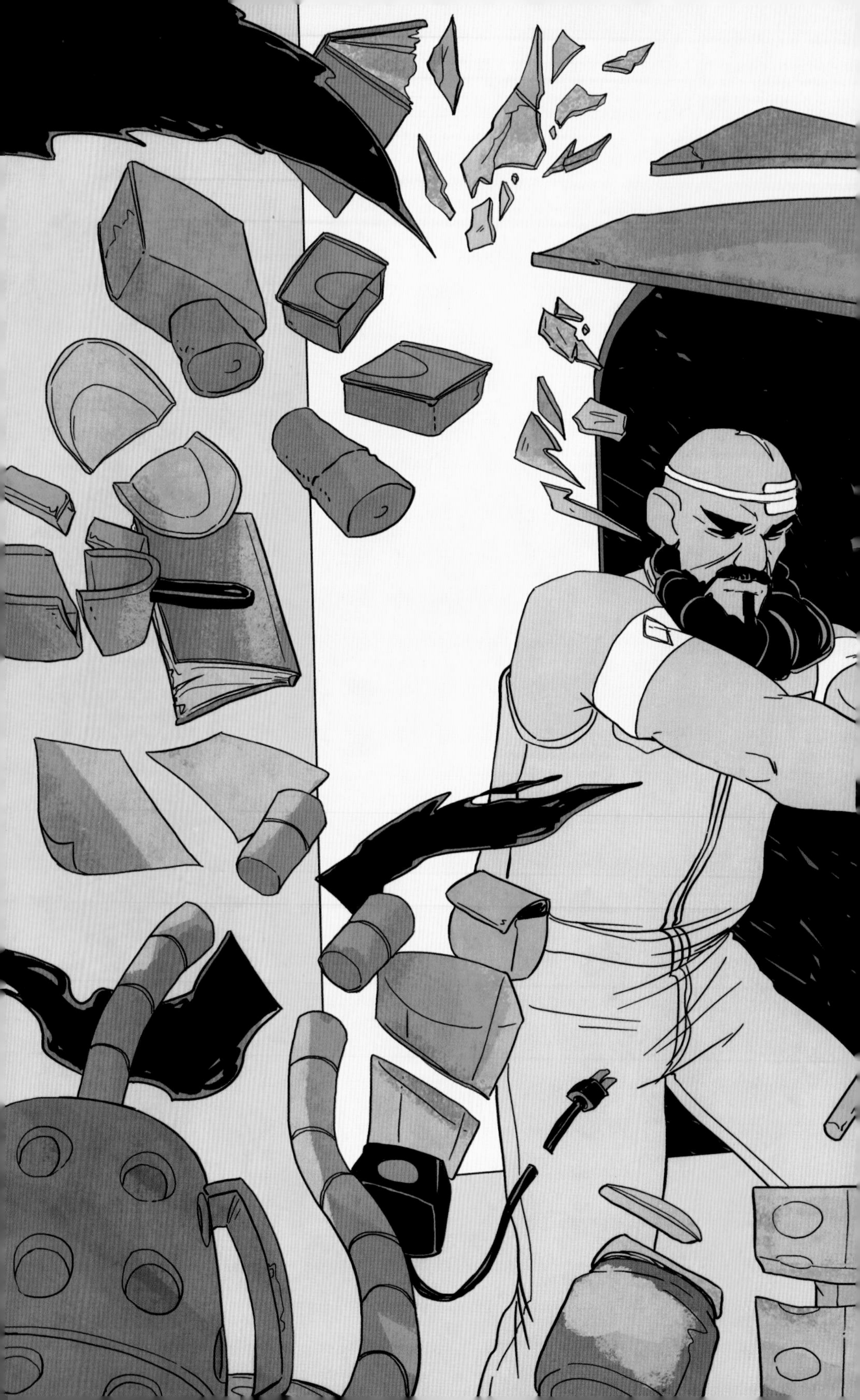

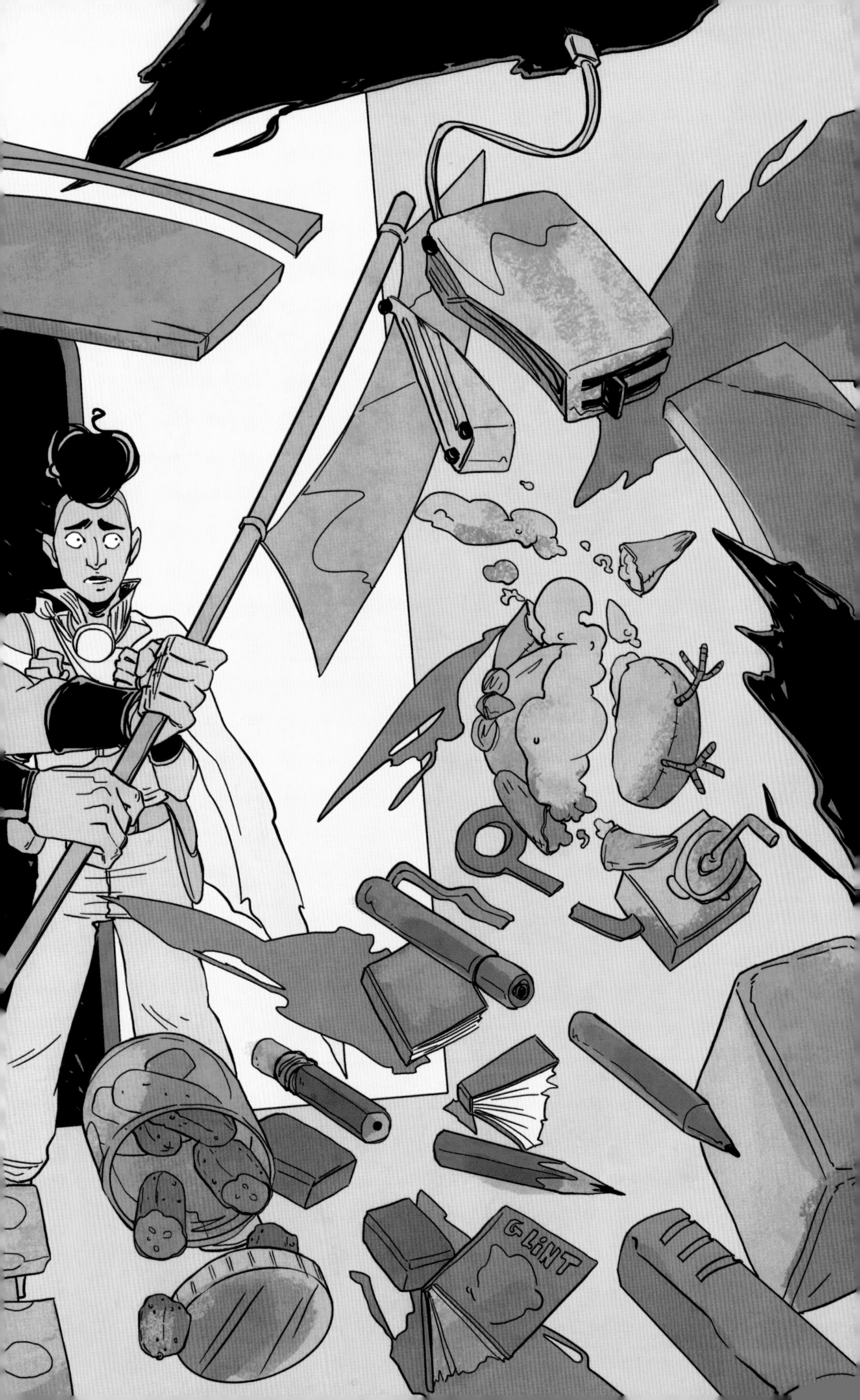
GLINT

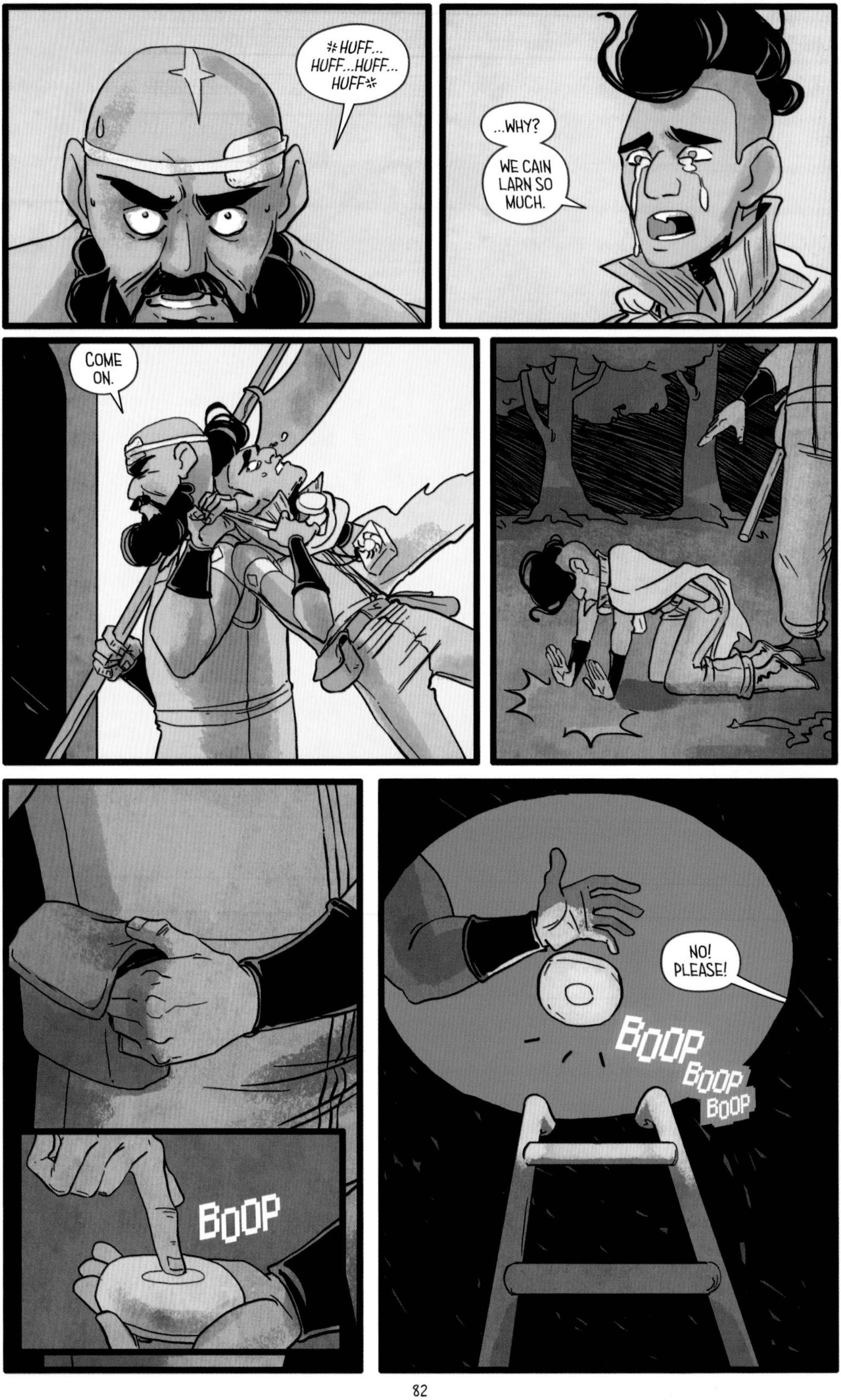
HUFF... HUFF...HUFF... HUFF
...WHY?
WE CAIN LARN SO MUCH.
COME ON.
NO! PLEASE!
BOOP
BOOP
BOOP
BOOP

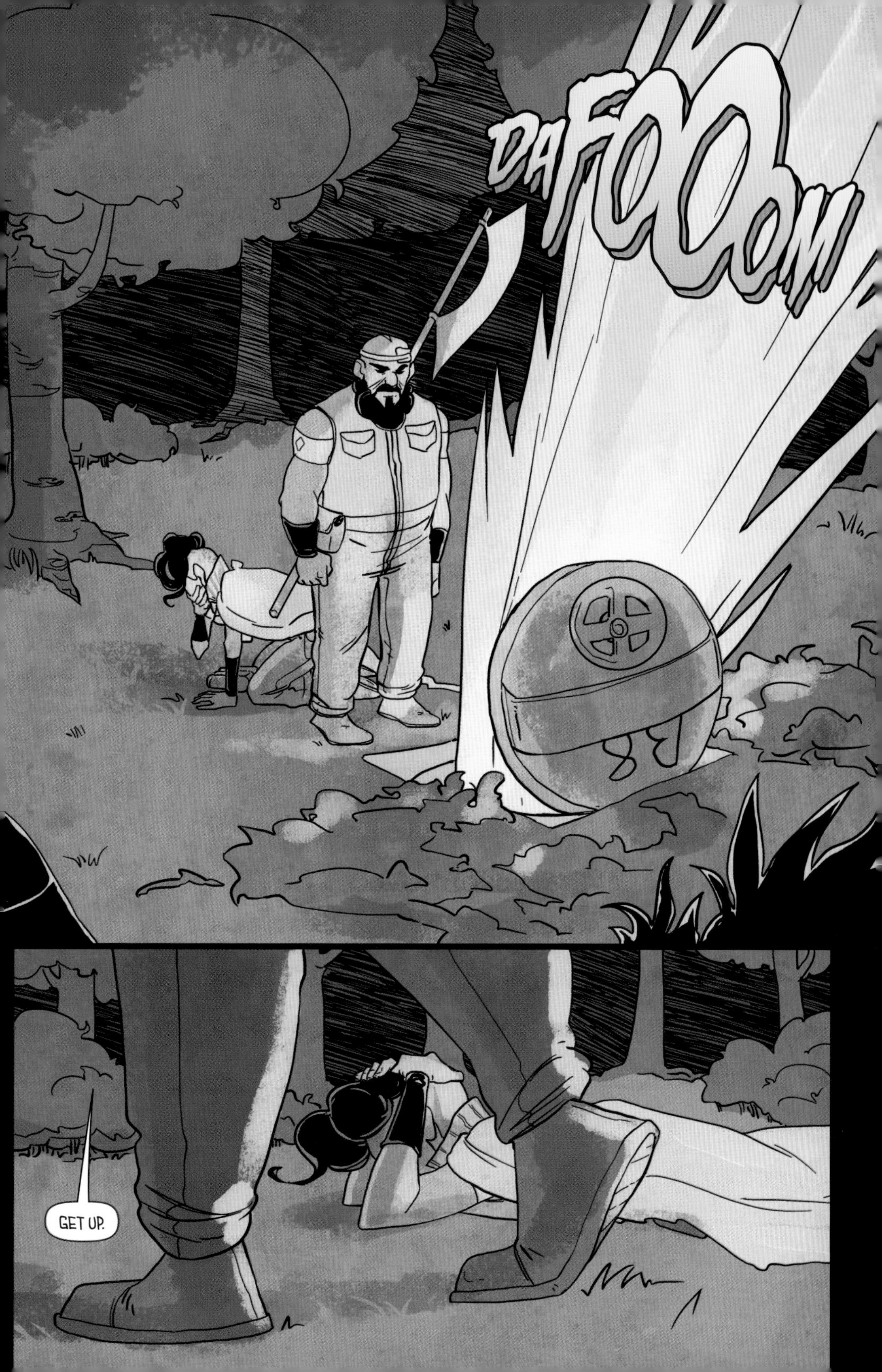
DAFOOOOM
GET UP.

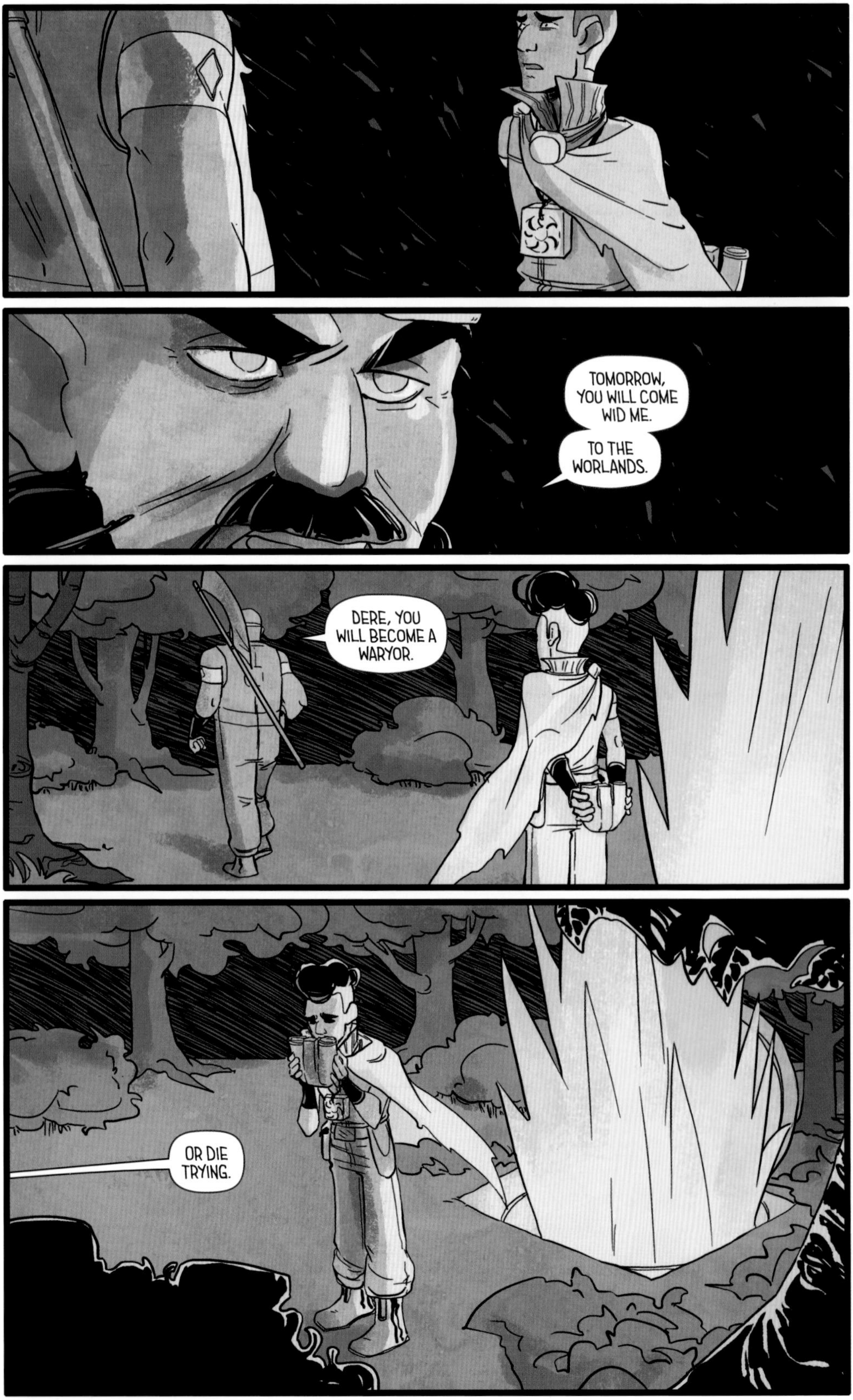
TOMORROW, YOU WILL COME WID ME.
TO THE WORLANDS.
DERE, YOU WILL BECOME A WARYOR.
OR DIE TRYING.

CHEPTAR TREE

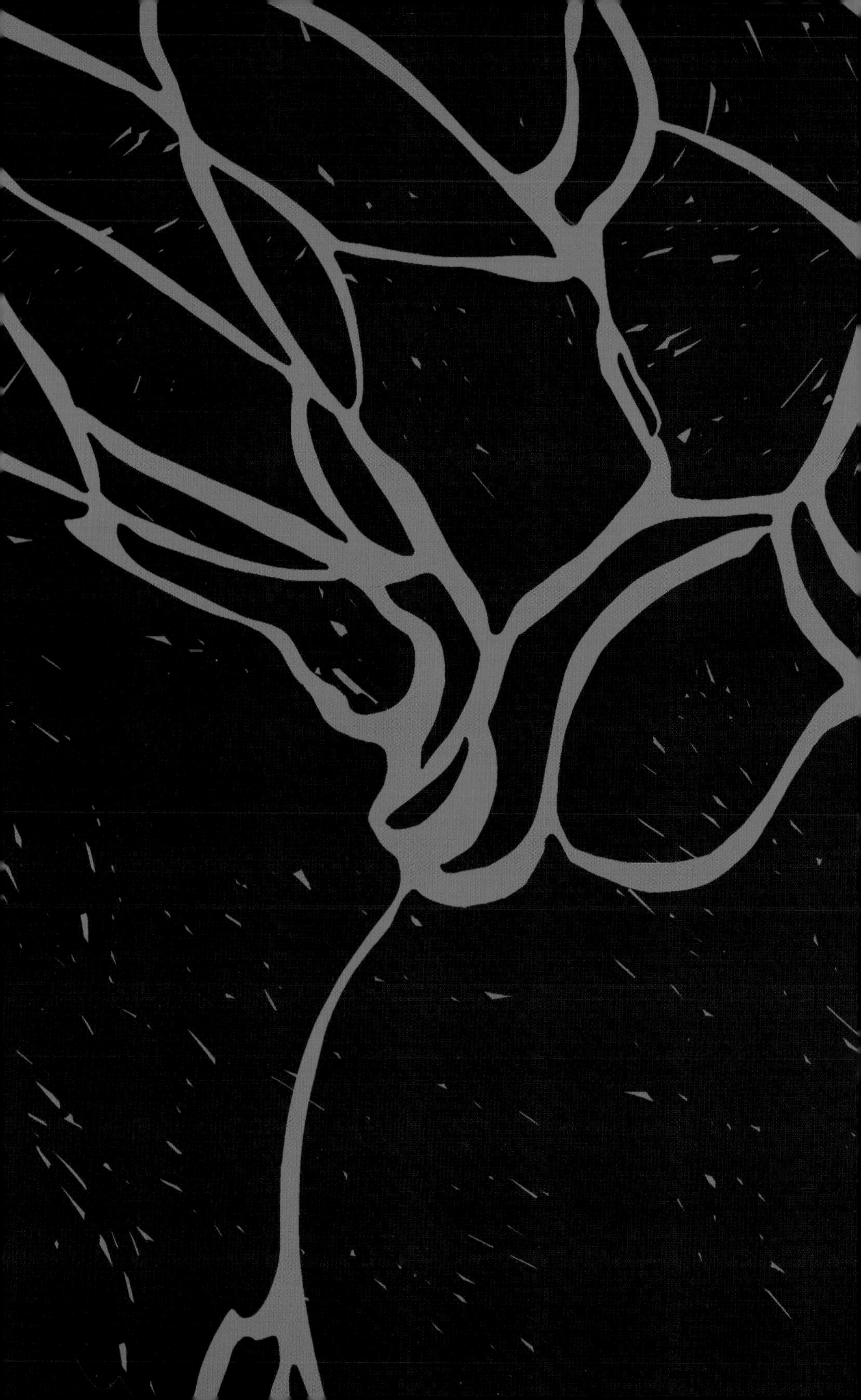

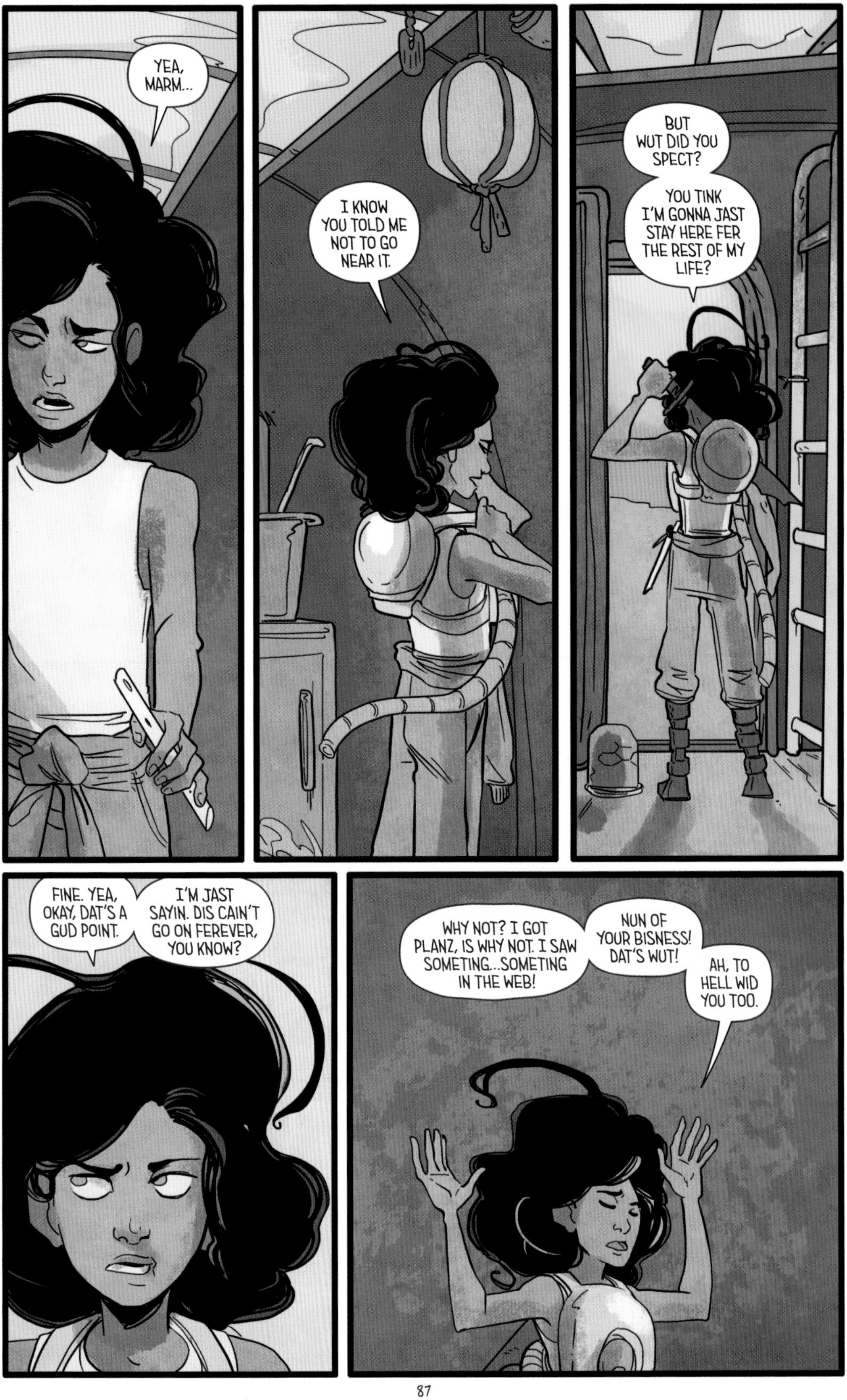
YEA, MARM...
I KNOW YOU TOLD ME NOT TO GO NEAR IT.
BUT WUT DID YOU SPECT?
YOU TINK I'M GONNA JAST STAY HERE FER THE REST OF MY LIFE?
FINE. YEA, OKAY, DAT'S A GUD POINT.
I'M JAST SAYIN. DIS CAIN'T GO ON FEREVER, YOU KNOW?
WHY NOT? I GOT PLANZ, IS WHY NOT. I SAW SOMETING...SOMETING IN THE WEB!
NUN OF YOUR BISNESS! DAT'S WUT!
AH, TO HELL WID YOU TOO.

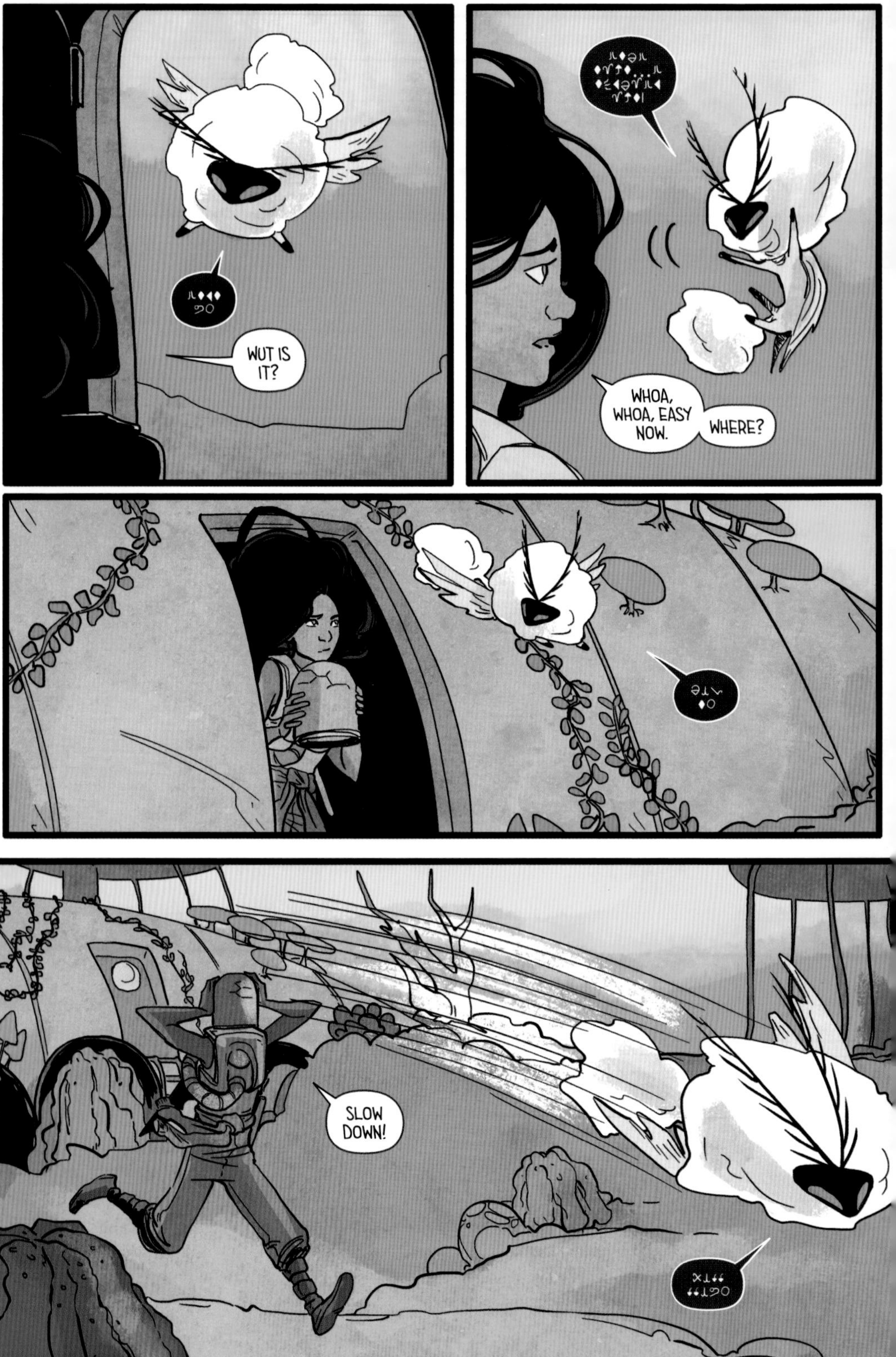
WUT IS IT?
WHOA, WHOA, EASY NOW.
WHERE?
SLOW DOWN!

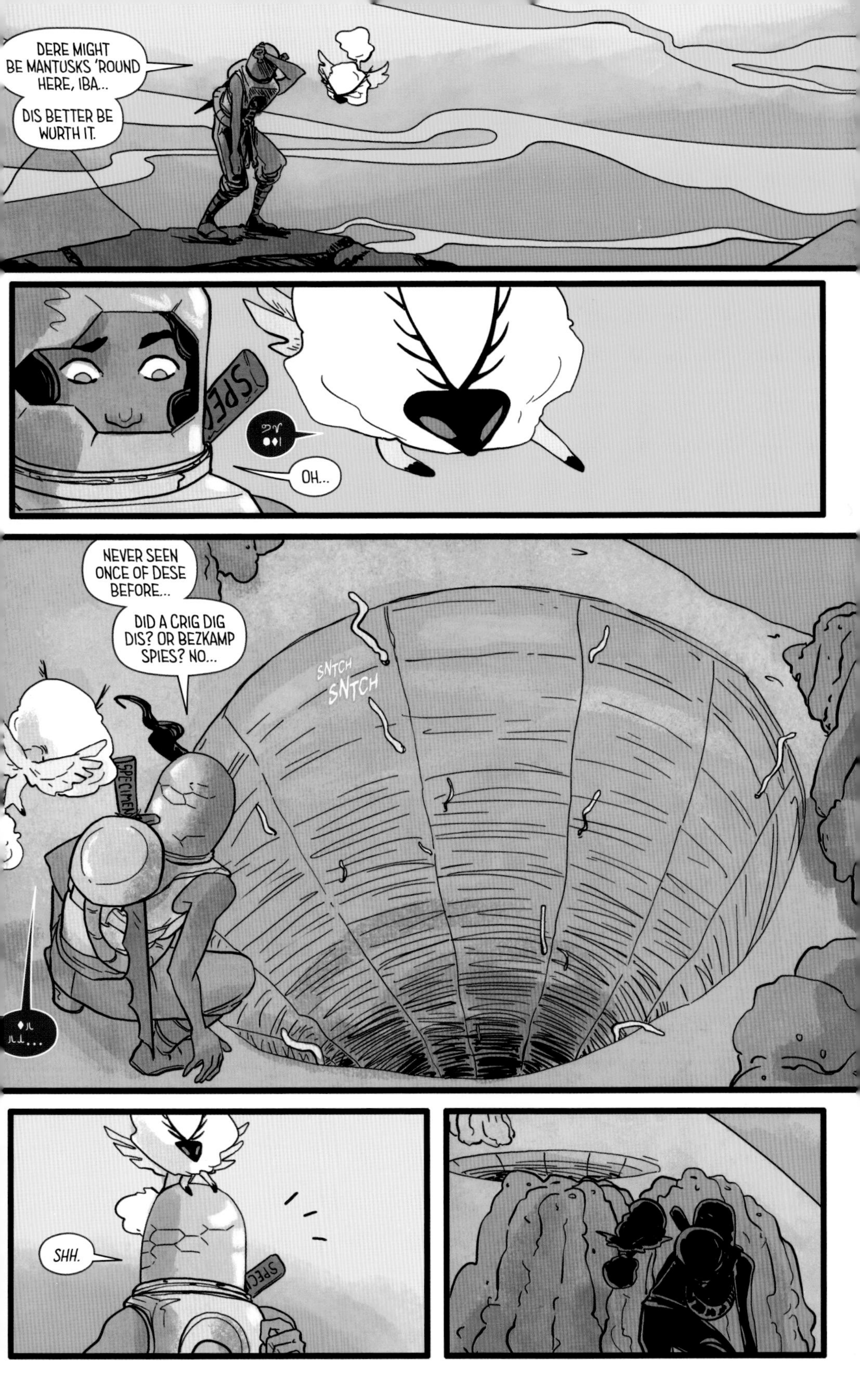
DERE MIGHT BE MANTUSKS 'ROUND HERE, IBA...
DIS BETTER BE WURTH IT.
OH...
NEVER SEEN ONCE OF DESE BEFORE...
DID A CRIG DIG DIS? OR BEZKAMP SPIES? NO...
SNTCH SNTCH
SHH.

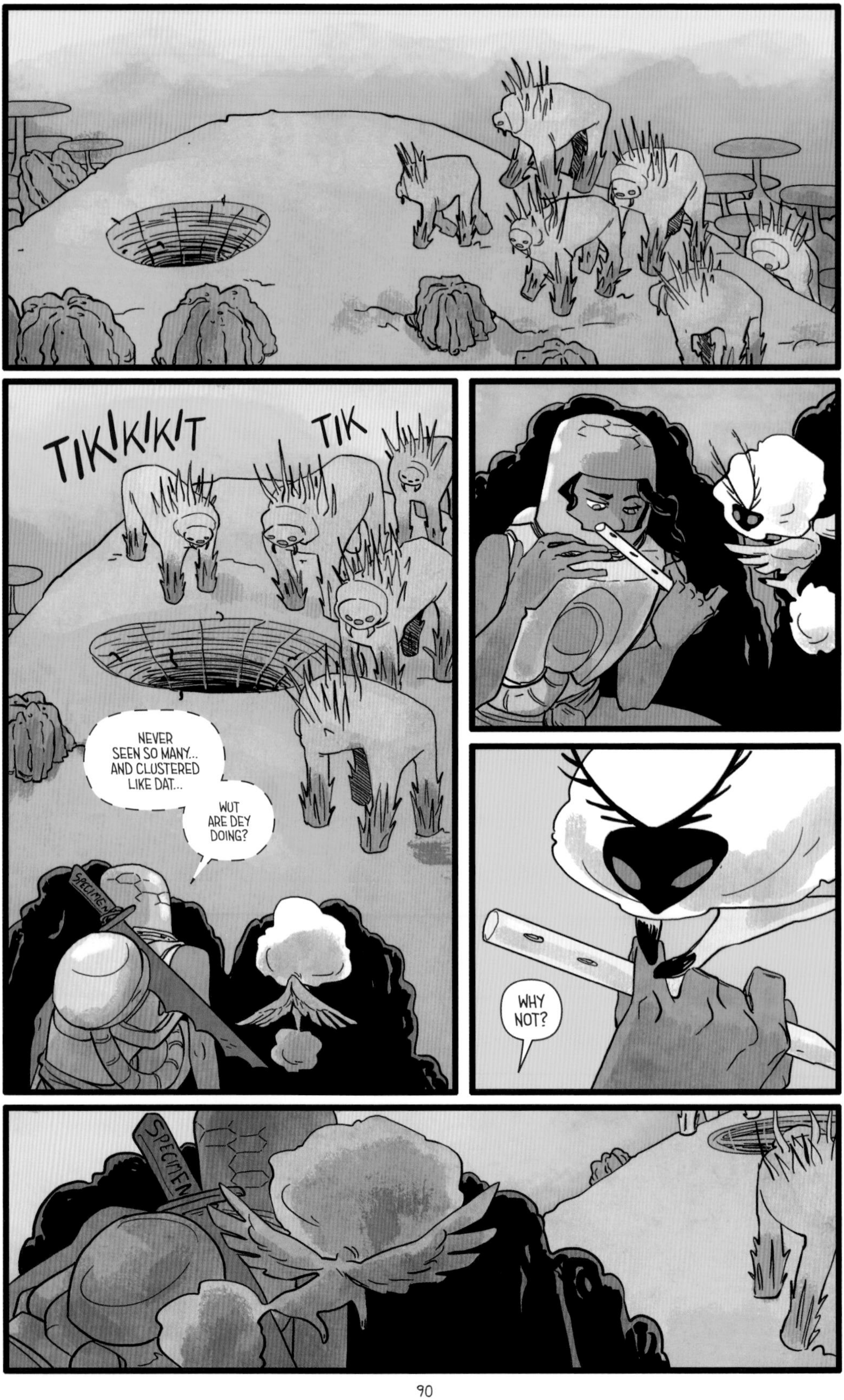

TIKIKIKIT
TIK
NEVER SEEN SO MANY... AND CLUSTERED LIKE DAT...
WUT ARE DEY DOING?
SPECIMEN
WHY NOT?
SPECIMEN

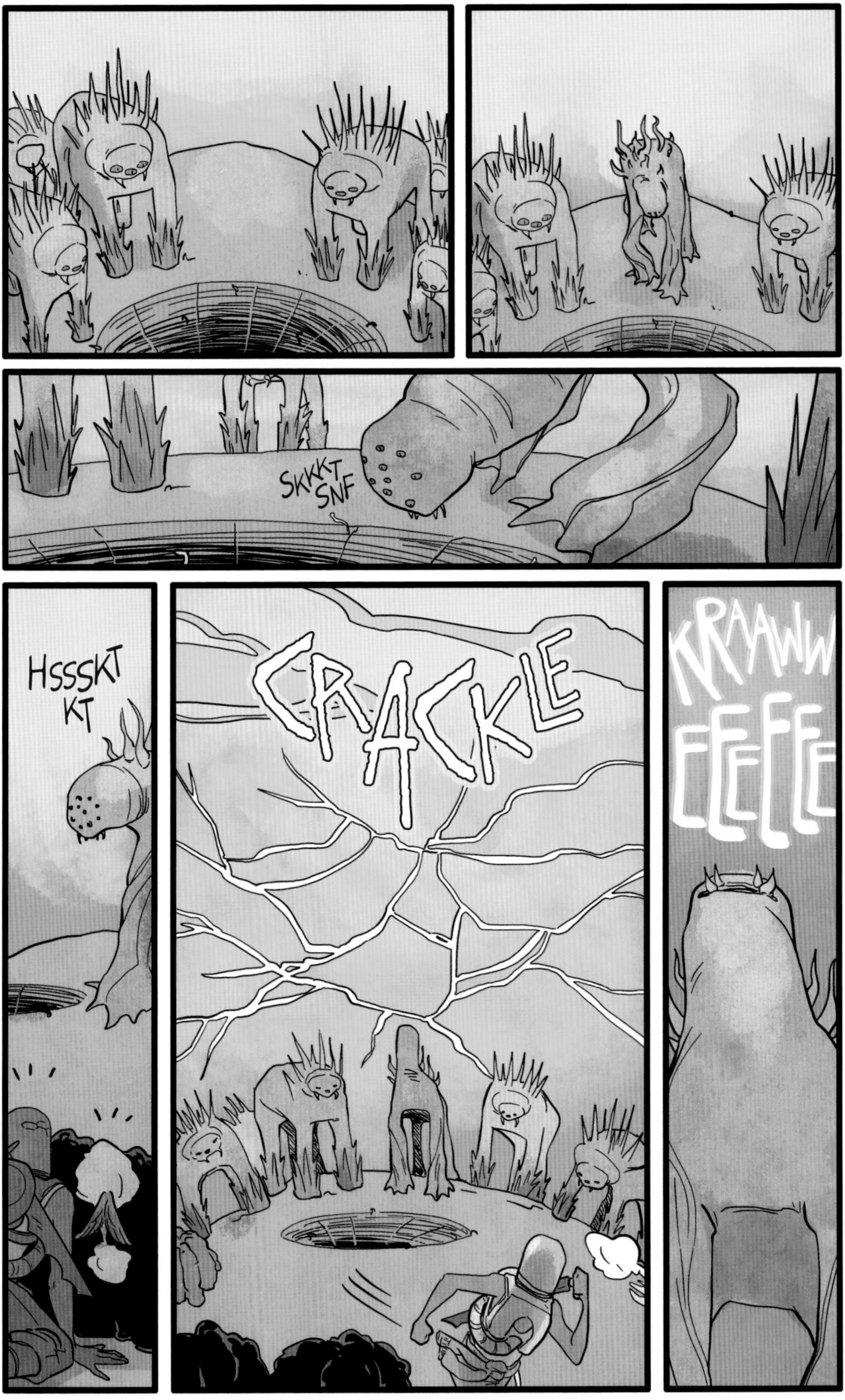
SKKKT
SNF
HSSSKT
KT
CRACKLE
KRAAWW
EEEEEE

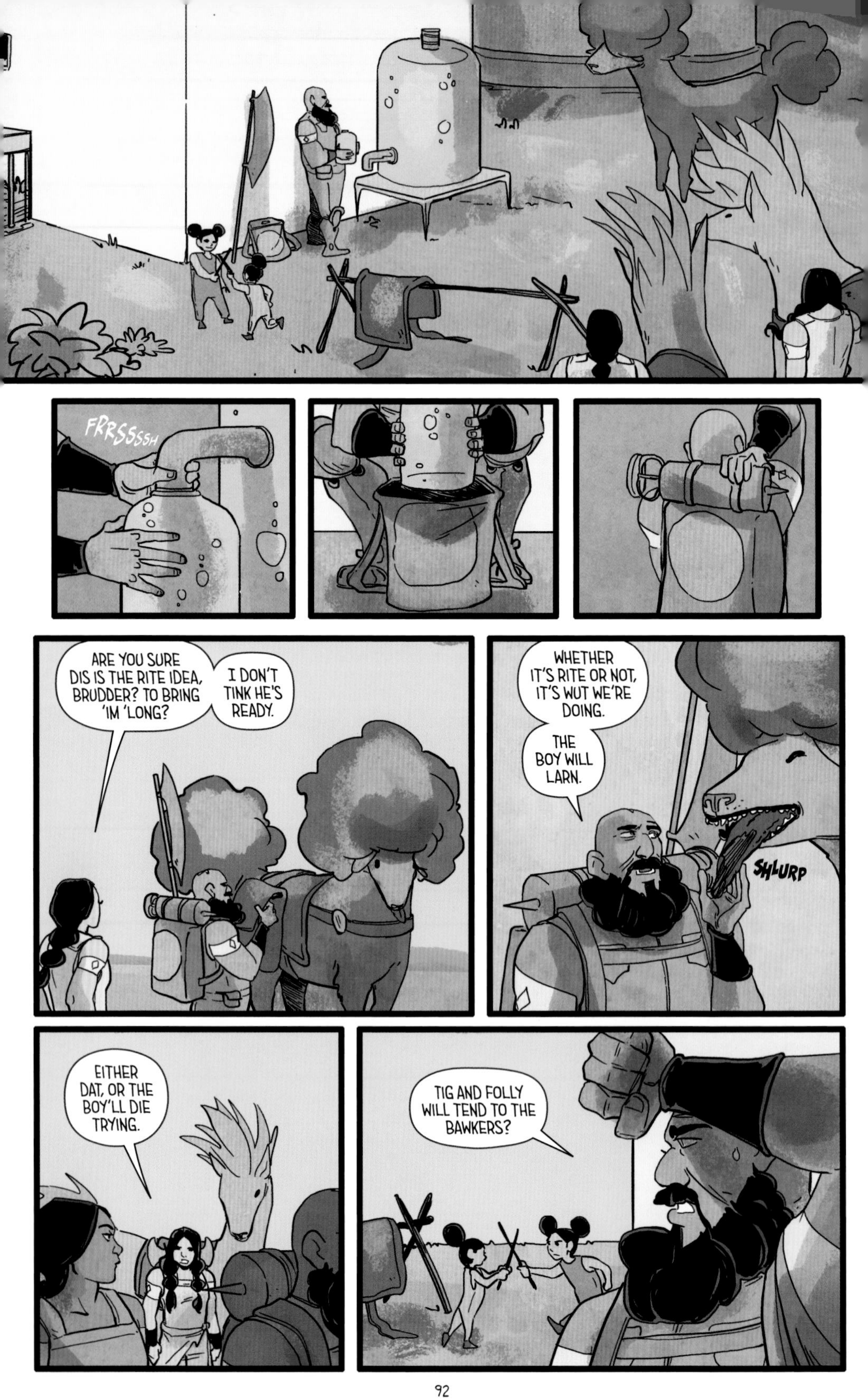

FRRSSSSSH
ARE YOU SURE DIS IS THE RITE IDEA, BRUDDER? TO BRING 'IM 'LONG?
I DON'T TINK HE'S READY.
WHETHER IT'S RITE OR NOT, IT'S WUT WE'RE DOING.
THE BOY WILL LARN.
SHLURP
EITHER DAT, OR THE BOY'LL DIE TRYING.
TIG AND FOLLY WILL TEND TO THE BAWKERS?

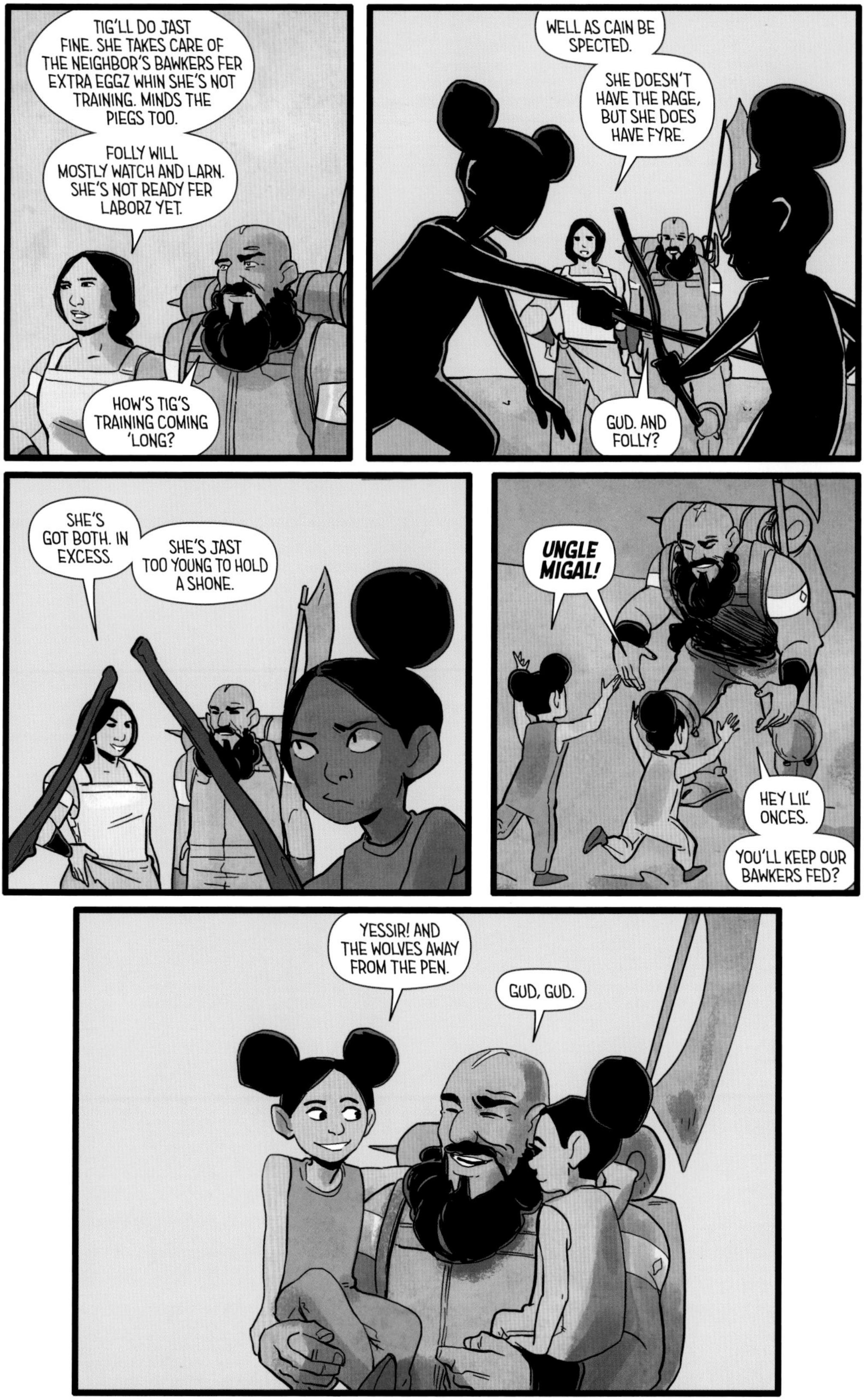

TIG'LL DO JAST FINE. SHE TAKES CARE OF THE NEIGHBOR'S BAWKERS FER EXTRA EGGZ WHIN SHE'S NOT TRAINING. MINDS THE PIEGS TOO.
FOLLY WILL MOSTLY WATCH AND LARN. SHE'S NOT READY FER LABORZ YET.
HOW'S TIG'S TRAINING COMING 'LONG?
WELL AS CAIN BE SPECTED.
SHE DOESN'T HAVE THE RAGE, BUT SHE DOES HAVE FYRE.
GUD. AND FOLLY?
SHE'S GOT BOTH. IN EXCESS.
SHE'S JAST TOO YOUNG TO HOLD A SHONE.
UNGLE MIGAL!
HEY LIL' ONCES.
YOU'LL KEEP OUR BAWKERS FED?
YESSIR! AND THE WOLVES AWAY FROM THE PEN.
GUD, GUD.

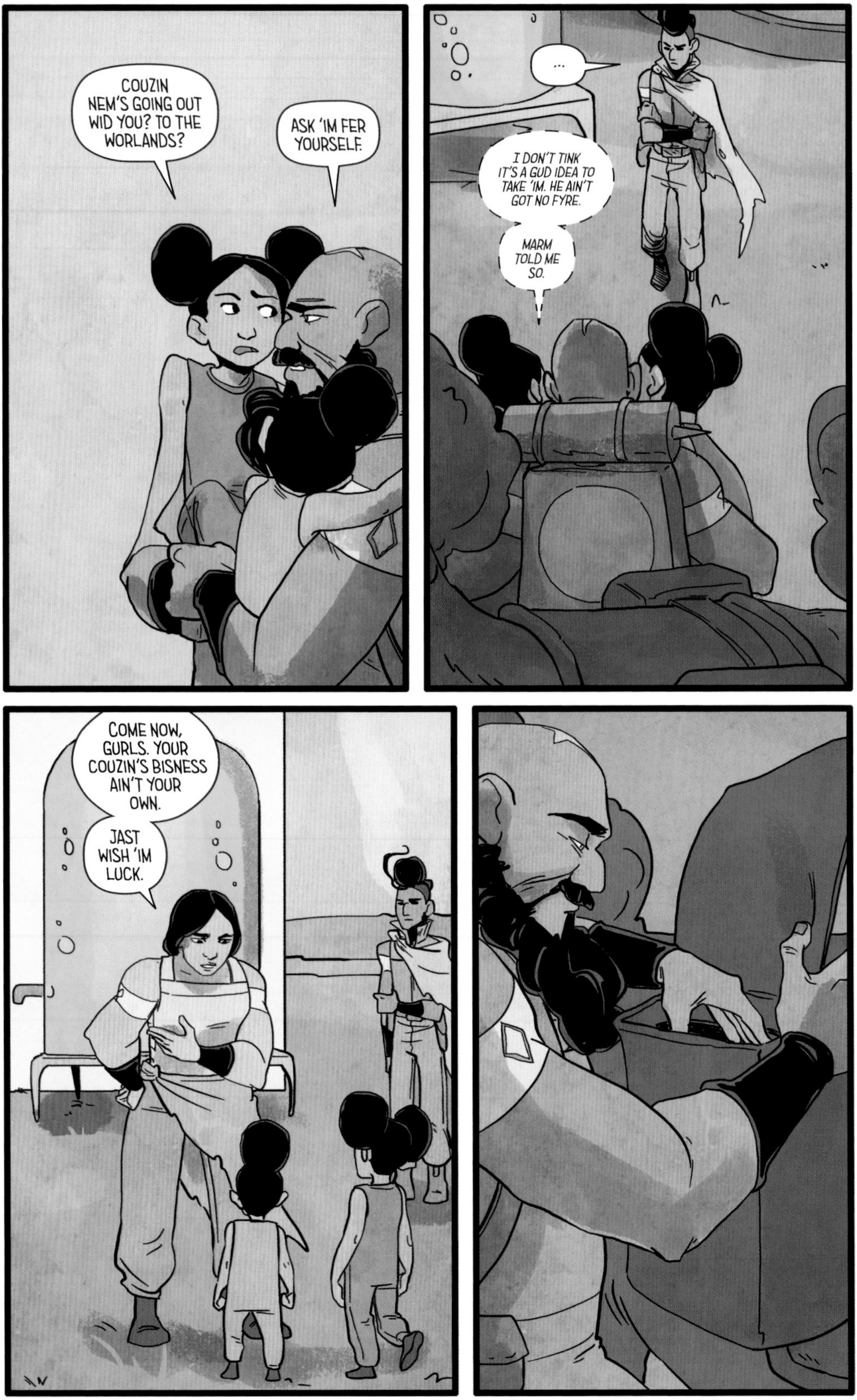
COUZIN NEM'S GOING OUT WID YOU? TO THE WORLANDS?
ASK 'IM FER YOURSELF.
...
I DON'T TINK IT'S A GUD IDEA TO TAKE 'IM. HE AIN'T GOT NO FYRE.
MARM TOLD ME SO.
COME NOW, GURLS. YOUR COUZIN'S BISNESS AIN'T YOUR OWN.
JAST WISH 'IM LUCK.

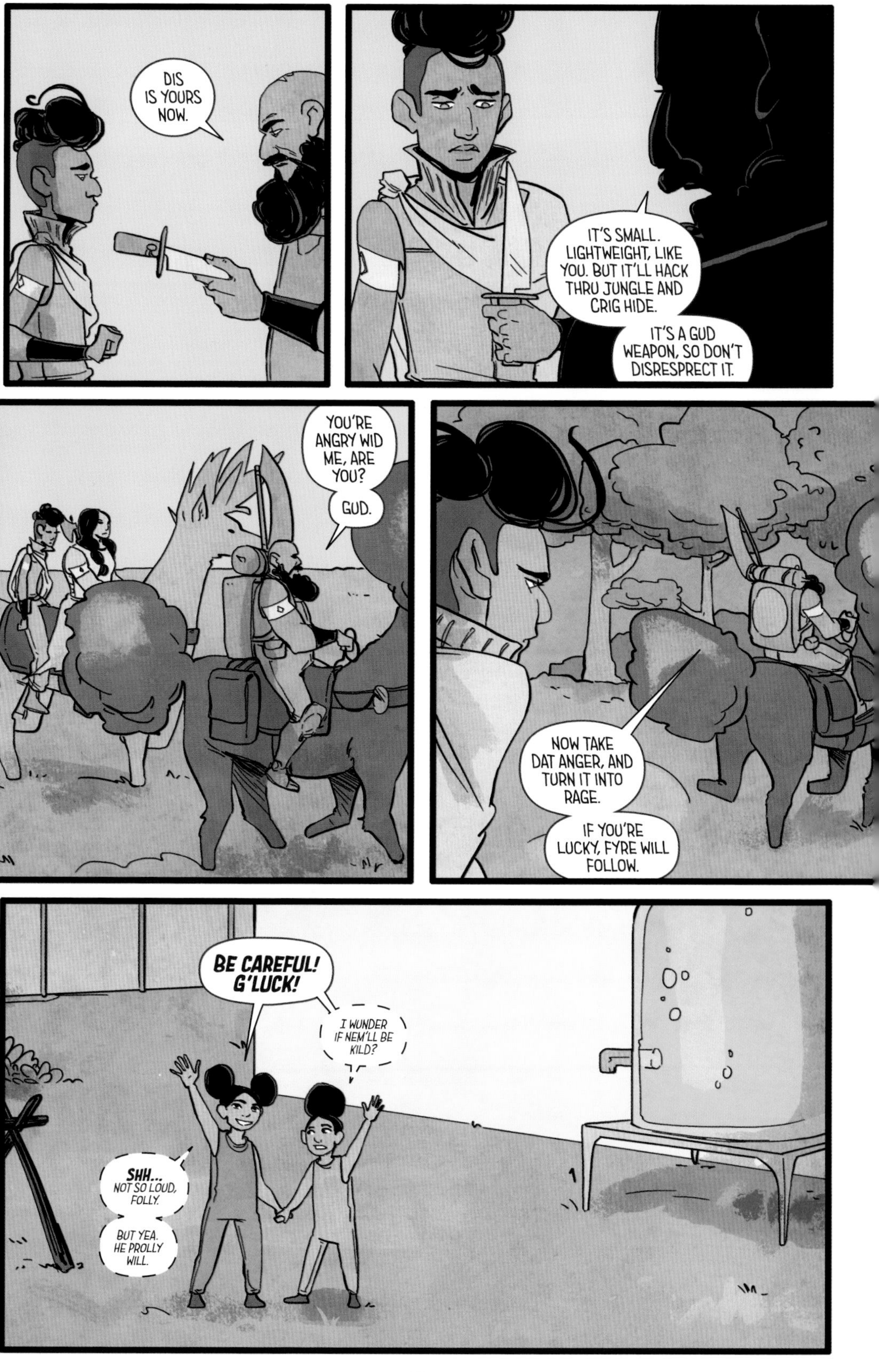
DIS IS YOURS NOW.
IT'S SMALL. LIGHTWEIGHT, LIKE YOU. BUT IT'LL HACK THRU JUNGLE AND CRIG HIDE.
IT'S A GUD WEAPON, SO DON'T DISRESPRECT IT.
YOU'RE ANGRY WID ME, ARE YOU?
GUD.
NOW TAKE DAT ANGER, AND TURN IT INTO RAGE.
IF YOU'RE LUCKY, FYRE WILL FOLLOW.
BE CAREFUL! G'LUCK!
I WUNDER IF NEM'LL BE KILD?
SHH... NOT SO LOUD, FOLLY.
BUT YEA. HE PROLLY WILL.

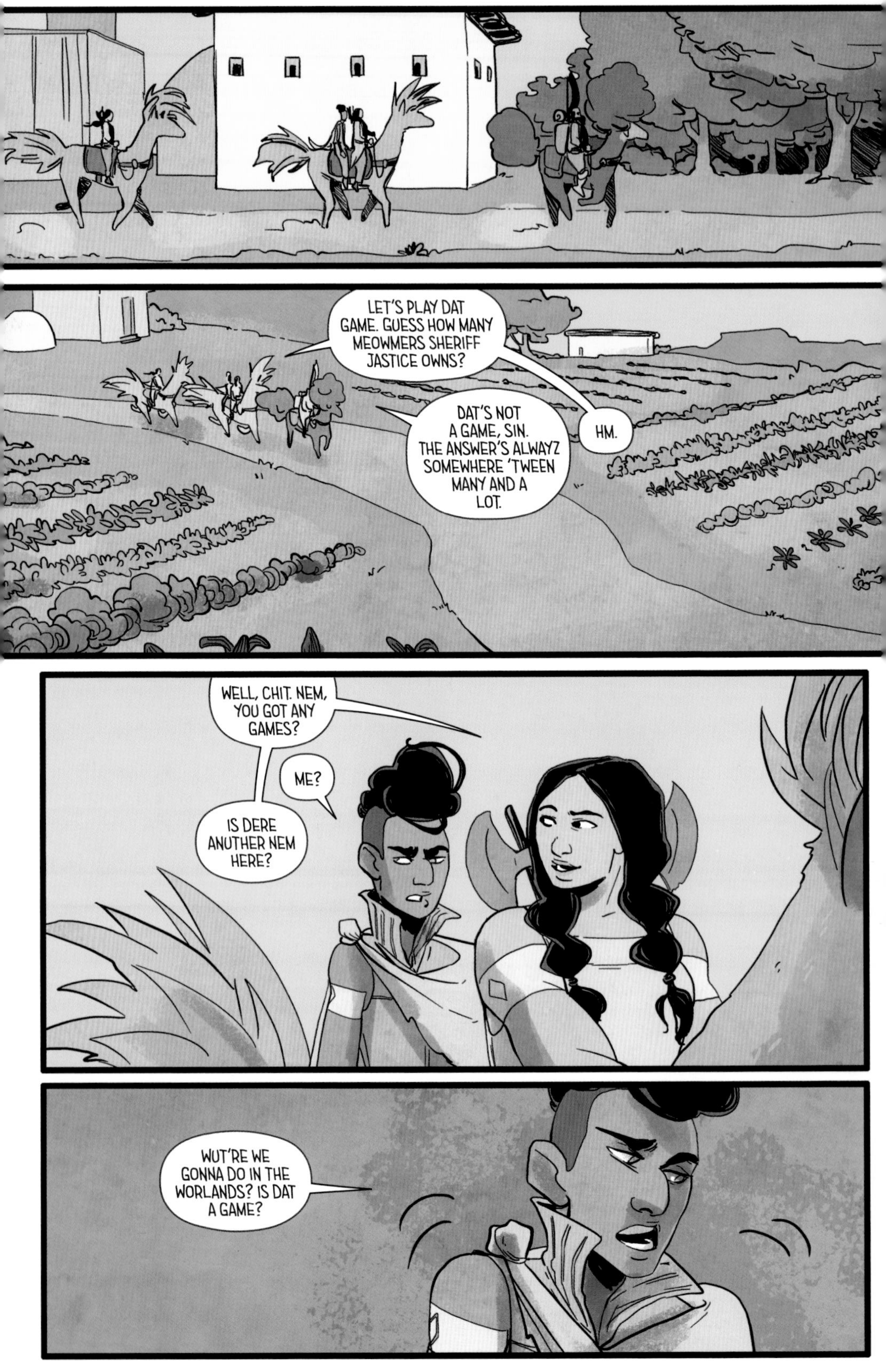
LET'S PLAY DAT GAME. GUESS HOW MANY MEOWMERS SHERIFF JASTICE OWNS?
DAT'S NOT A GAME, SIN. THE ANSWER'S ALWAYZ SOMEWHERE 'TWEEN MANY AND A LOT.
HM.
WELL, CHIT. NEM, YOU GOT ANY GAMES?
ME?
IS DERE ANUTHER NEM HERE?
WUT'RE WE GONNA DO IN THE WORLANDS? IS DAT A GAME?

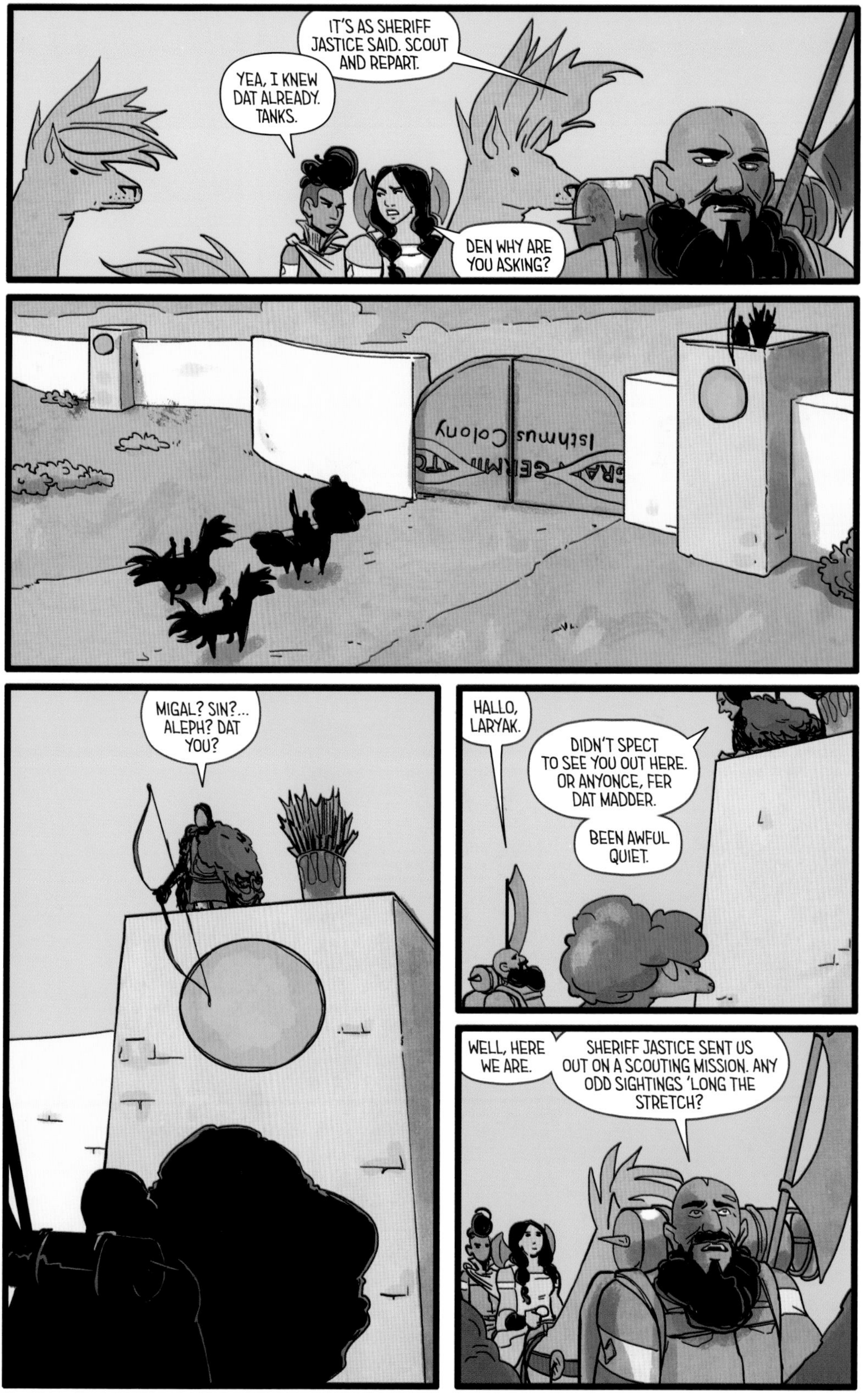
YEA, I KNEW DAT ALREADY. TANKS.
IT'S AS SHERIFF JASTICE SAID. SCOUT AND REPART.
DEN WHY ARE YOU ASKING?
Isthmus Colony
MIGAL? SIN?... ALEPH? DAT YOU?
HALLO, LARYAK.
DIDN'T SPECT TO SEE YOU OUT HERE. OR ANYONCE, FER DAT MADDER.
BEEN AWFUL QUIET.
WELL, HERE WE ARE.
SHERIFF JASTICE SENT US OUT ON A SCOUTING MISSION. ANY ODD SIGHTINGS 'LONG THE STRETCH?

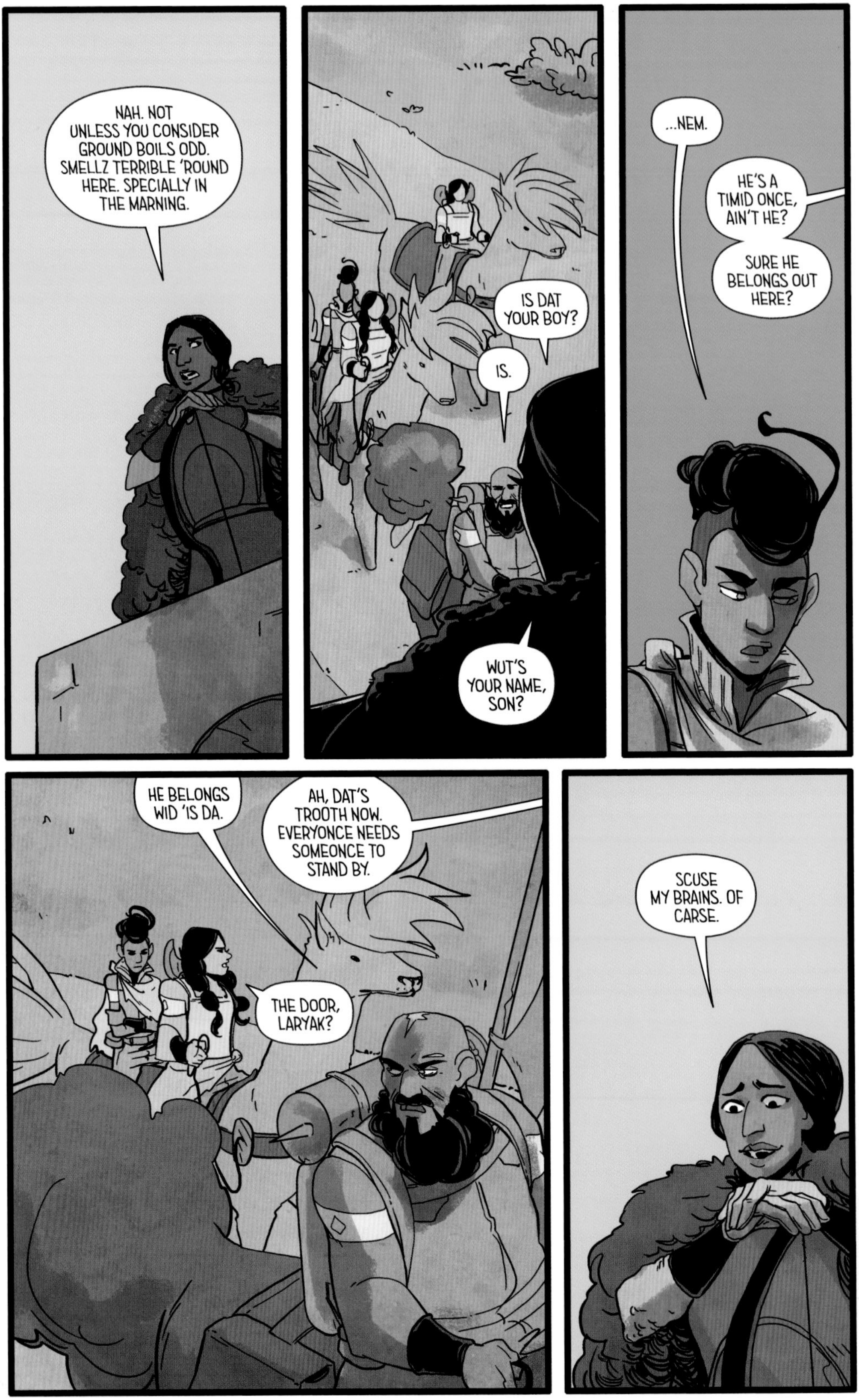
NAH. NOT UNLESS YOU CONSIDER GROUND BOILS ODD. SMELLZ TERRIBLE 'ROUND HERE. SPECIALLY IN THE MARNING.
IS DAT YOUR BOY?
IS.
WUT'S YOUR NAME, SON?
...NEM.
HE'S A TIMID ONCE, AIN'T HE?
SURE HE BELONGS OUT HERE?
HE BELONGS WID 'IS DA.
AH, DAT'S TROOTH NOW. EVERYONCE NEEDS SOMEONCE TO STAND BY.
THE DOOR, LARYAK?
SCUSE MY BRAINS. OF CARSE.

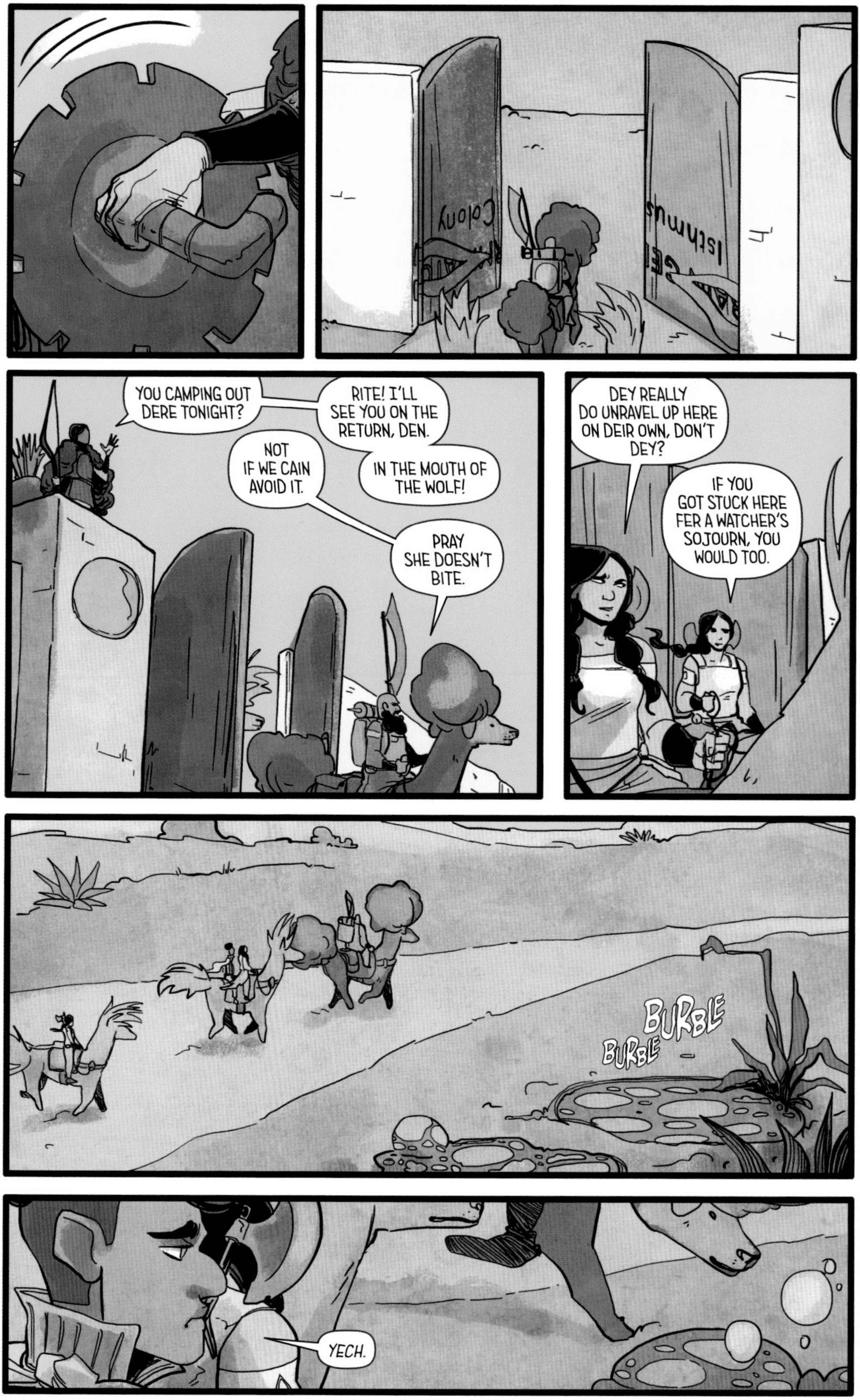
YOU CAMPING OUT DERE TONIGHT?
NOT IF WE CAIN AVOID IT.
RITE! I'LL SEE YOU ON THE RETURN, DEN.
IN THE MOUTH OF THE WOLF!
PRAY SHE DOESN'T BITE.
DEY REALLY DO UNRAVEL UP HERE ON DEIR OWN, DON'T DEY?
IF YOU GOT STUCK HERE FER A WATCHER'S SOJOURN, YOU WOULD TOO.
BURBLE BURBLE
YECH.

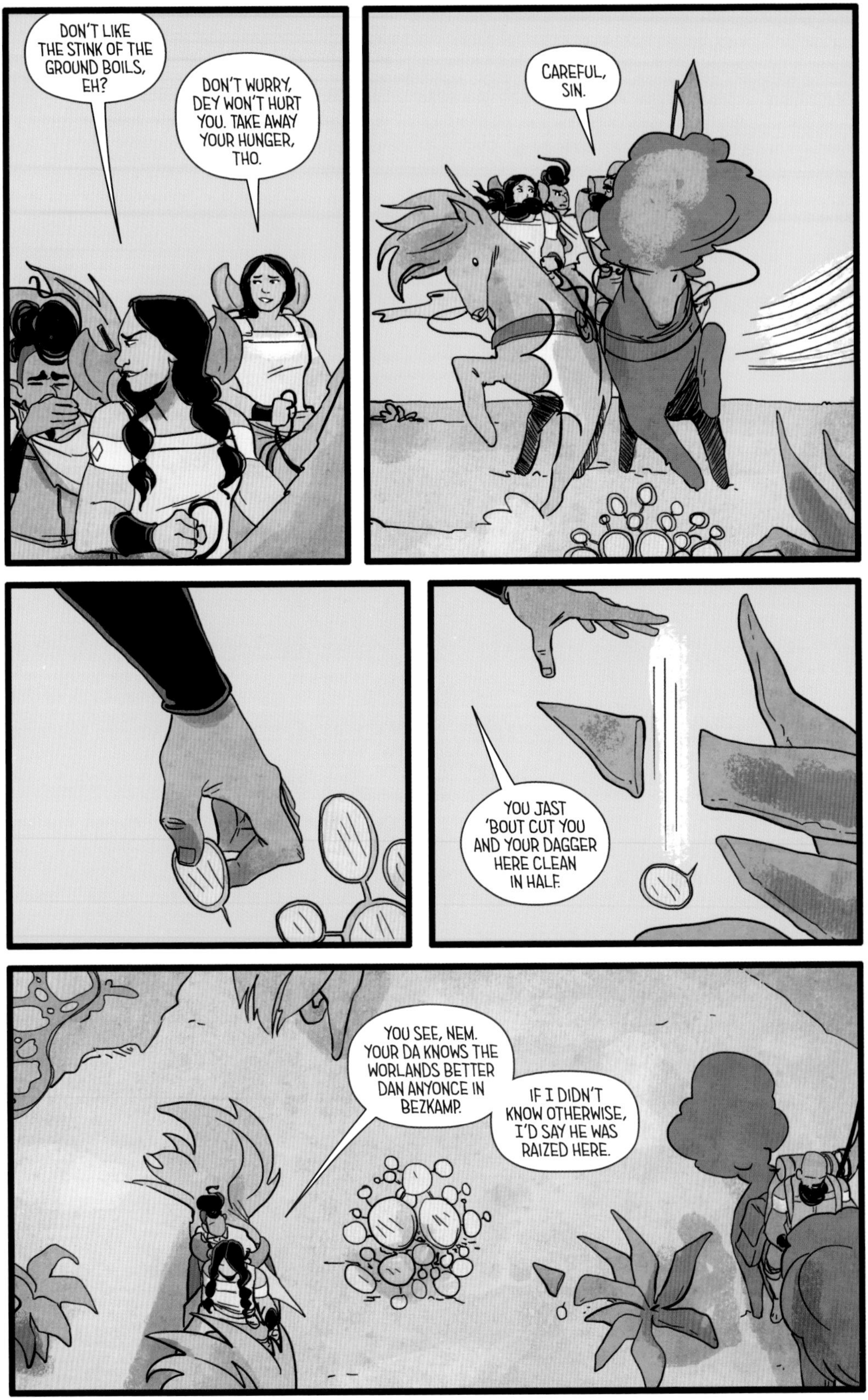
DON'T LIKE THE STINK OF THE GROUND BOILS, EH?
DON'T WURRY, DEY WON'T HURT YOU. TAKE AWAY YOUR HUNGER, THO.
CAREFUL, SIN.
YOU JAST 'BOUT CUT YOU AND YOUR DAGGER HERE CLEAN IN HALF.
YOU SEE, NEM. YOUR DA KNOWS THE WORLANDS BETTER DAN ANYONCE IN BEZKAMP.
IF I DIDN'T KNOW OTHERWISE, I'D SAY HE WAS RAIZED HERE.

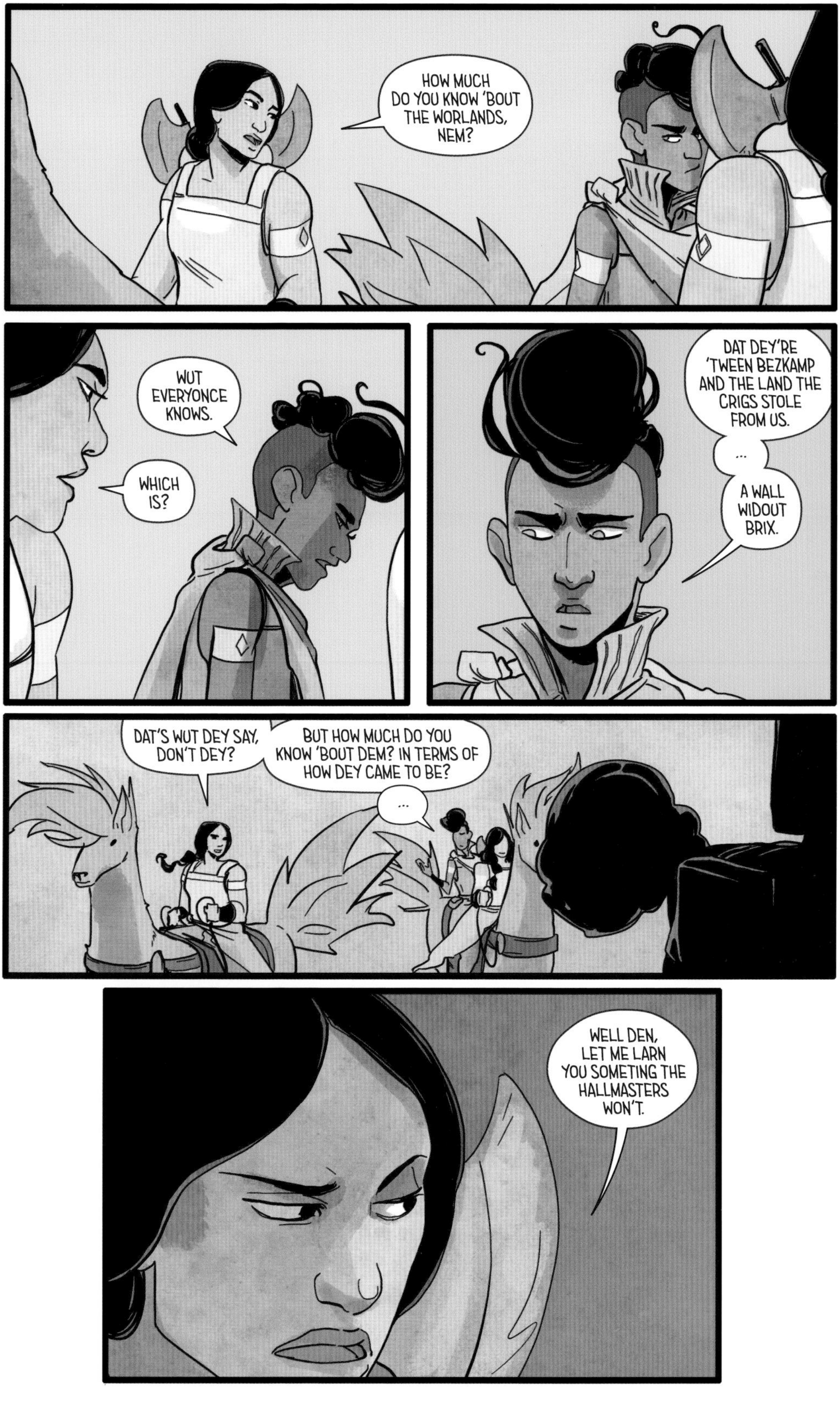
HOW MUCH DO YOU KNOW 'BOUT THE WORLANDS, NEM?
WUT EVERYONCE KNOWS.
WHICH IS?
DAT DEY'RE 'TWEEN BEZKAMP AND THE LAND THE CRIGS STOLE FROM US.
...
A WALL WIDOUT BRIX.
DAT'S WUT DEY SAY, DON'T DEY?
BUT HOW MUCH DO YOU KNOW 'BOUT DEM? IN TERMS OF HOW DEY CAME TO BE?
...
WELL DEN, LET ME LARN YOU SOMETING THE HALLMASTERS WON'T.

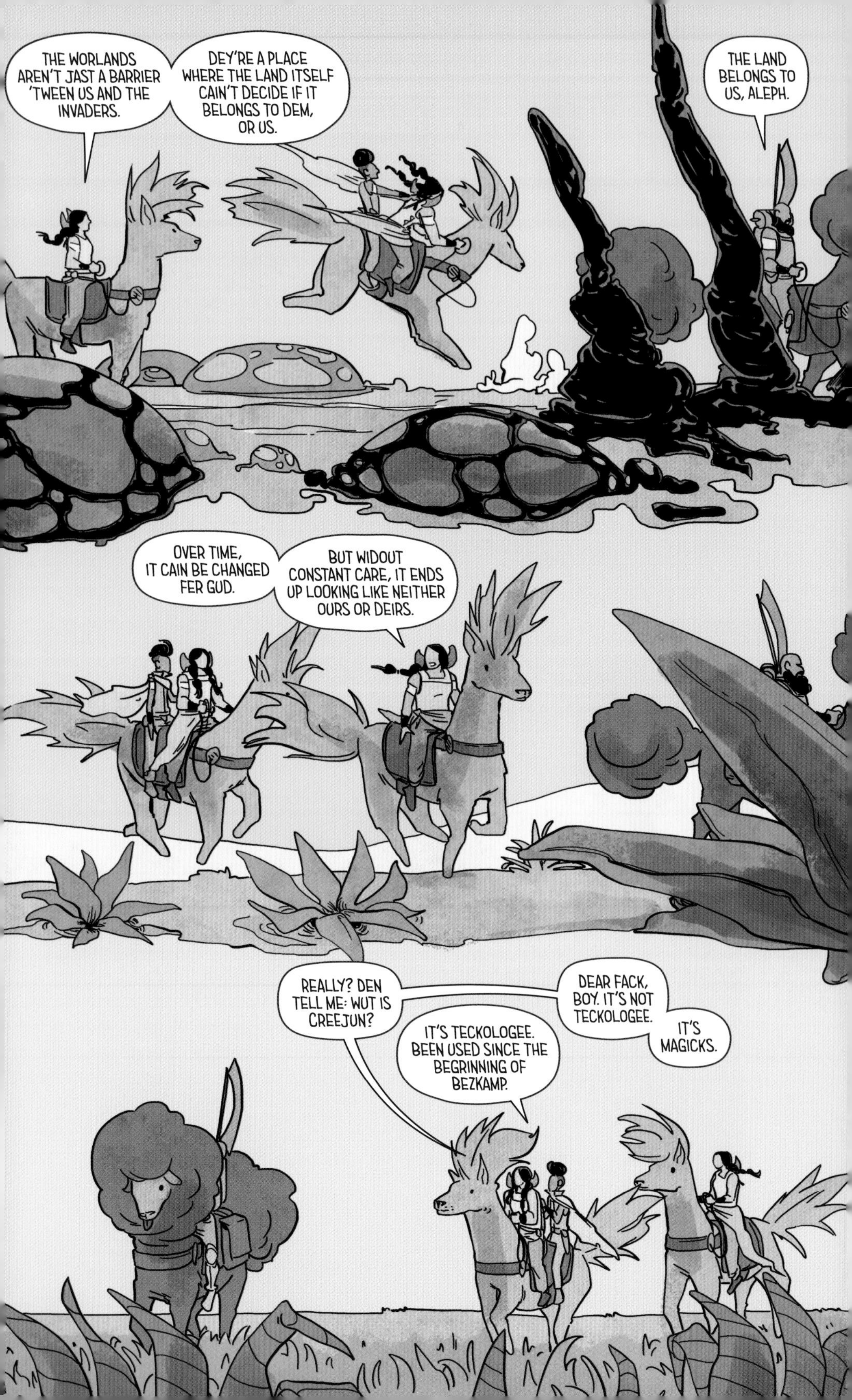
THE WORLANDS AREN'T JAST A BARRIER 'TWEEN US AND THE INVADERS.
DEY'RE A PLACE WHERE THE LAND ITSELF CAIN'T DECIDE IF IT BELONGS TO DEM, OR US.
THE LAND BELONGS TO US, ALEPH.
OVER TIME, IT CAIN BE CHANGED FER GUD.
BUT WIDOUT CONSTANT CARE, IT ENDS UP LOOKING LIKE NEITHER OURS OR DEIRS.
REALLY? DEN TELL ME: WUT IS CREEJUN?
IT'S TECKOLOGEE. BEEN USED SINCE THE BEGRINNING OF BEZKAMP.
DEAR FACK, BOY. IT'S NOT TECKOLOGEE.
IT'S MAGICKS.

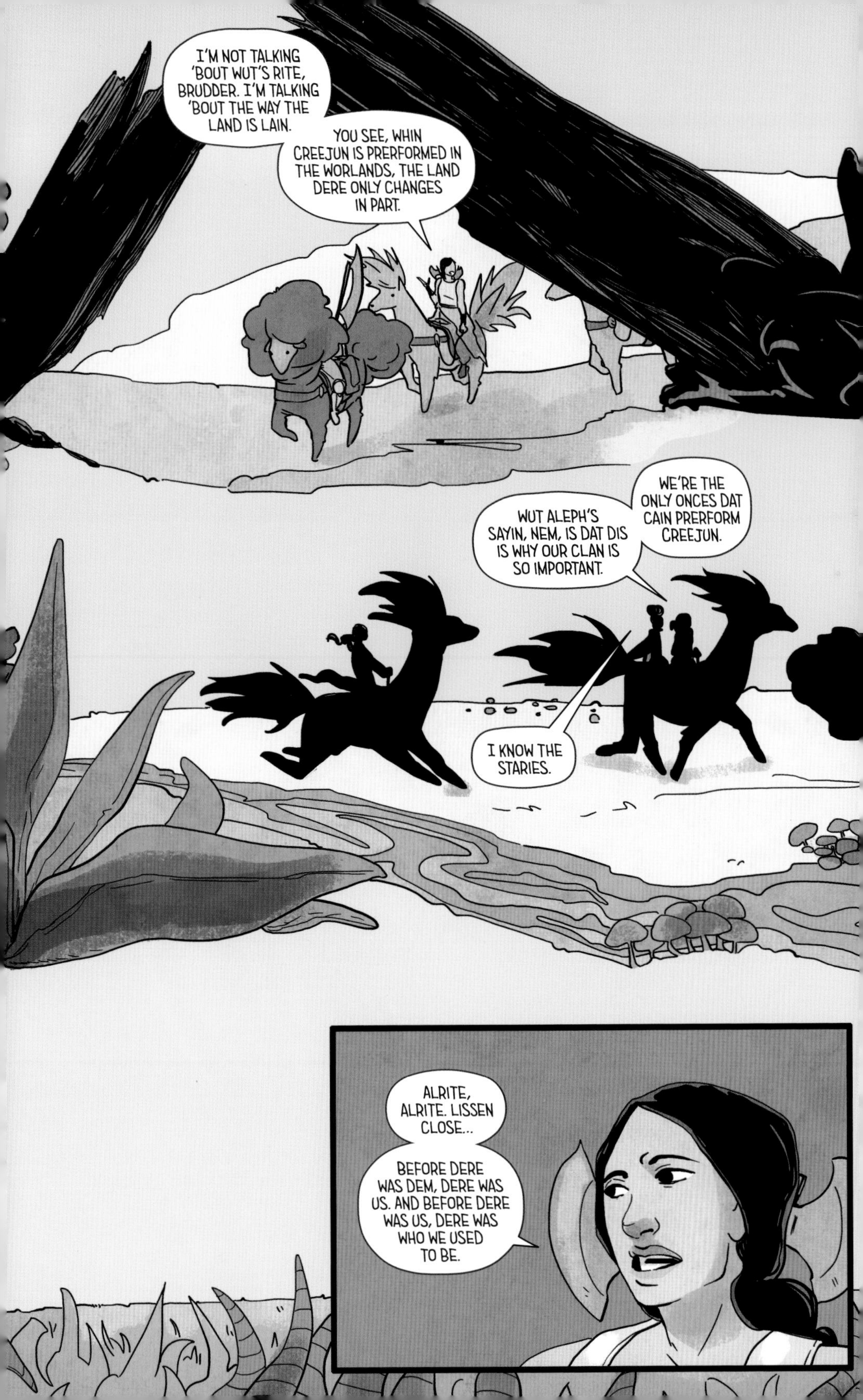
I'M NOT TALKING 'BOUT WUT'S RITE, BRUDDER. I'M TALKING 'BOUT THE WAY THE LAND IS LAIN.
YOU SEE, WHIN CREEJUN IS PRERFORMED IN THE WORLANDS, THE LAND DERE ONLY CHANGES IN PART.
WE'RE THE ONLY ONCES DAT CAIN PRERFORM CREEJUN.
WUT ALEPH'S SAYIN, NEM, IS DAT DIS IS WHY OUR CLAN IS SO IMPORTANT.
I KNOW THE STARIES.
ALRITE, ALRITE. LISSEN CLOSE...
BEFORE DERE WAS DEM, DERE WAS US. AND BEFORE DERE WAS US, DERE WAS WHO WE USED TO BE.

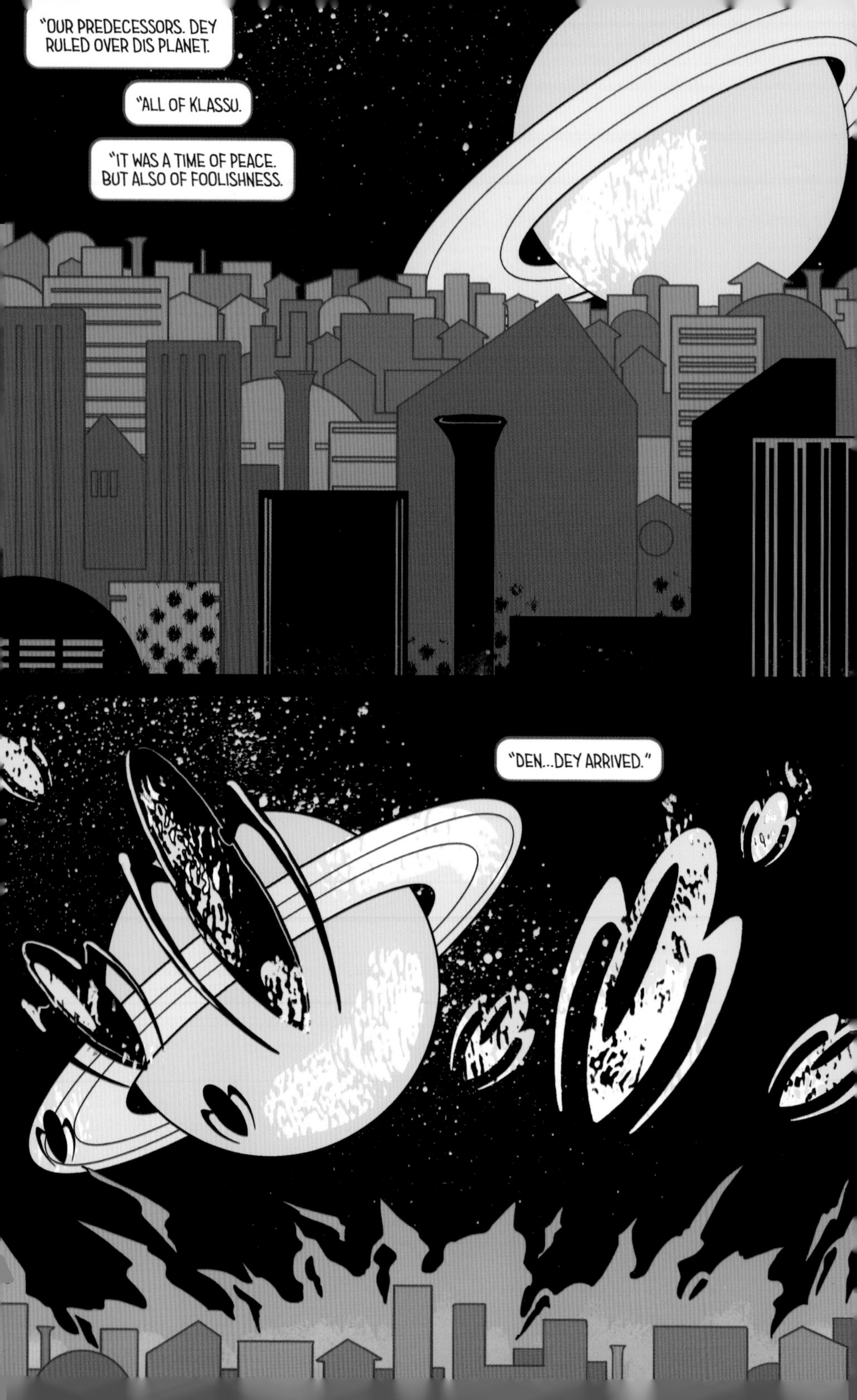
"OUR PREDECESSORS. DEY RULED OVER DIS PLANET.
"ALL OF KLASSU.
"IT WAS A TIME OF PEACE. BUT ALSO OF FOOLISHNESS.
"DEN...DEY ARRIVED."

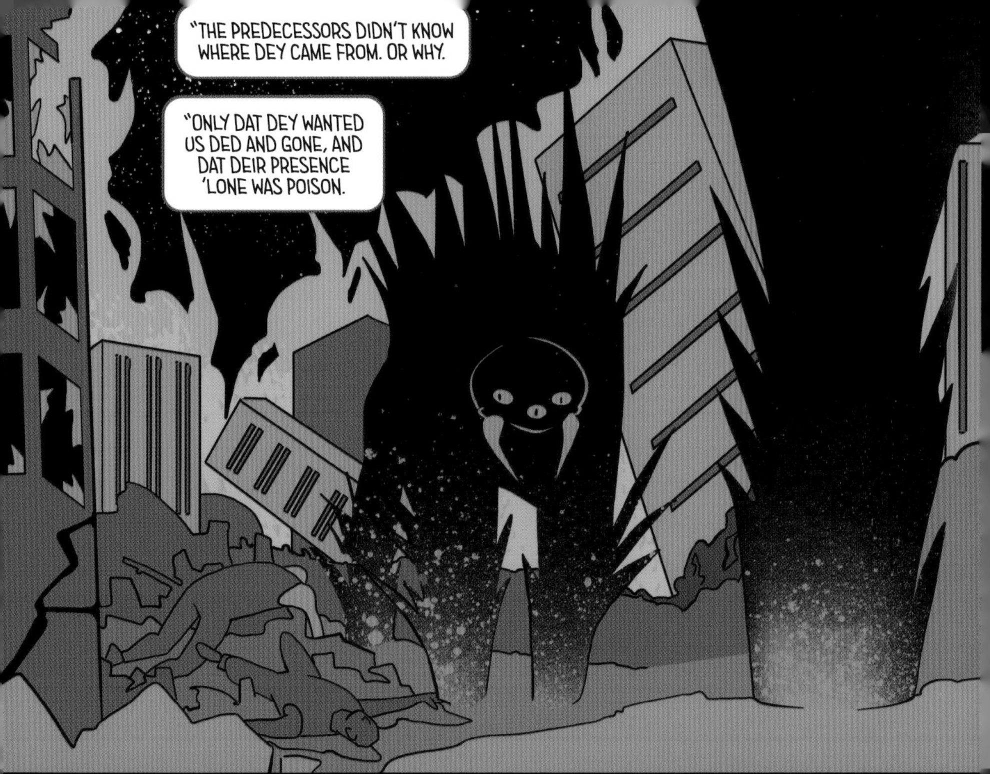
"THE PREDECESSORS DIDN'T KNOW WHERE DEY CAME FROM. OR WHY.
"ONLY DAT DEY WANTED US DED AND GONE, AND DAT DEIR PRESENCE 'LONE WAS POISON.
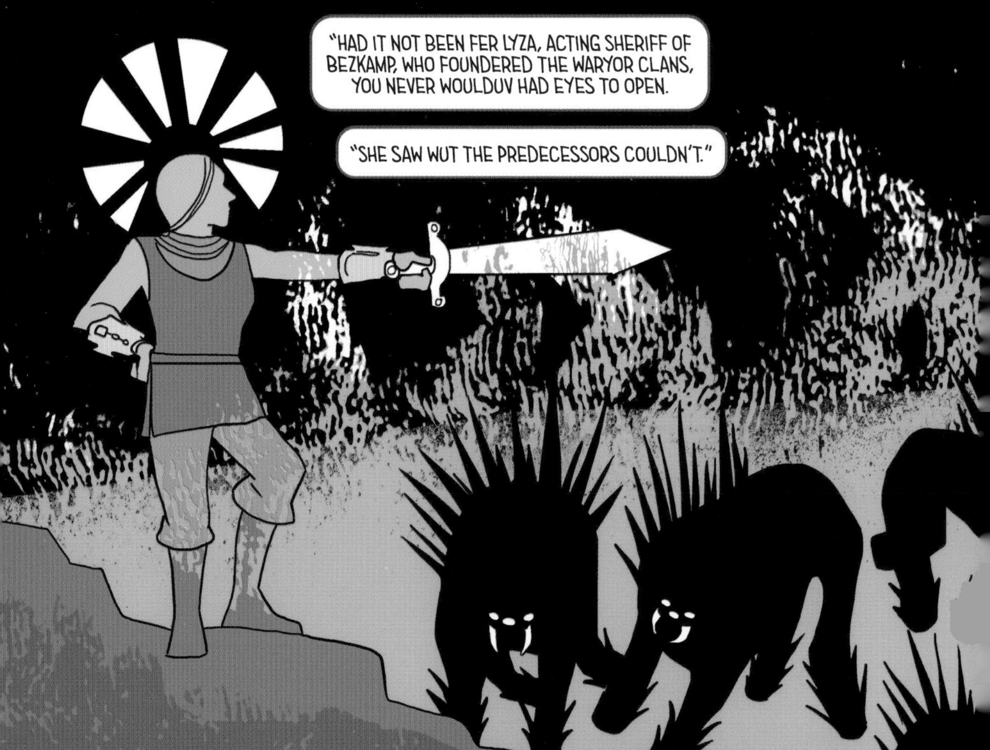
"HAD IT NOT BEEN FER LYZA, ACTING SHERIFF OF BEZKAMP, WHO FOUNDERED THE WARYOR CLANS, YOU NEVER WOULDUV HAD EYES TO OPEN.
"SHE SAW WUT THE PREDECESSORS COULDN'T."

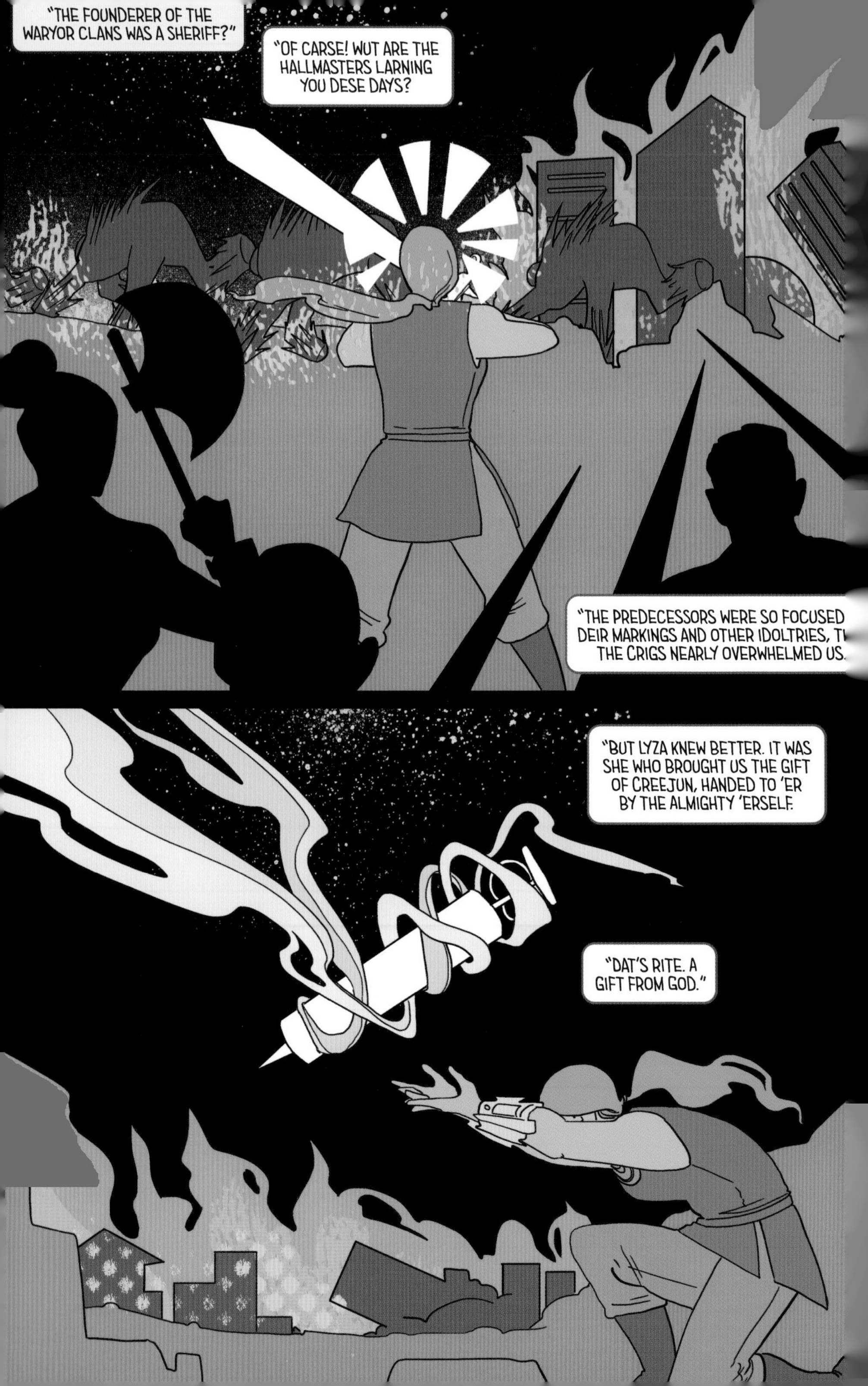
"THE FOUNDERER OF THE WARYOR CLANS WAS A SHERIFF?"
"OF CARSE! WUT ARE THE HALLMASTERS LARNING YOU DESE DAYS?
"THE PREDECESSORS WERE SO FOCUSED DEIR MARKINGS AND OTHER IDOLTRIES, THE CRIGS NEARLY OVERWHELMED US.
"BUT LYZA KNEW BETTER. IT WAS SHE WHO BROUGHT US THE GIFT OF CREEJUN, HANDED TO 'ER BY THE ALMIGHTY 'ERSELF.
"DAT'S RITE. A GIFT FROM GOD."

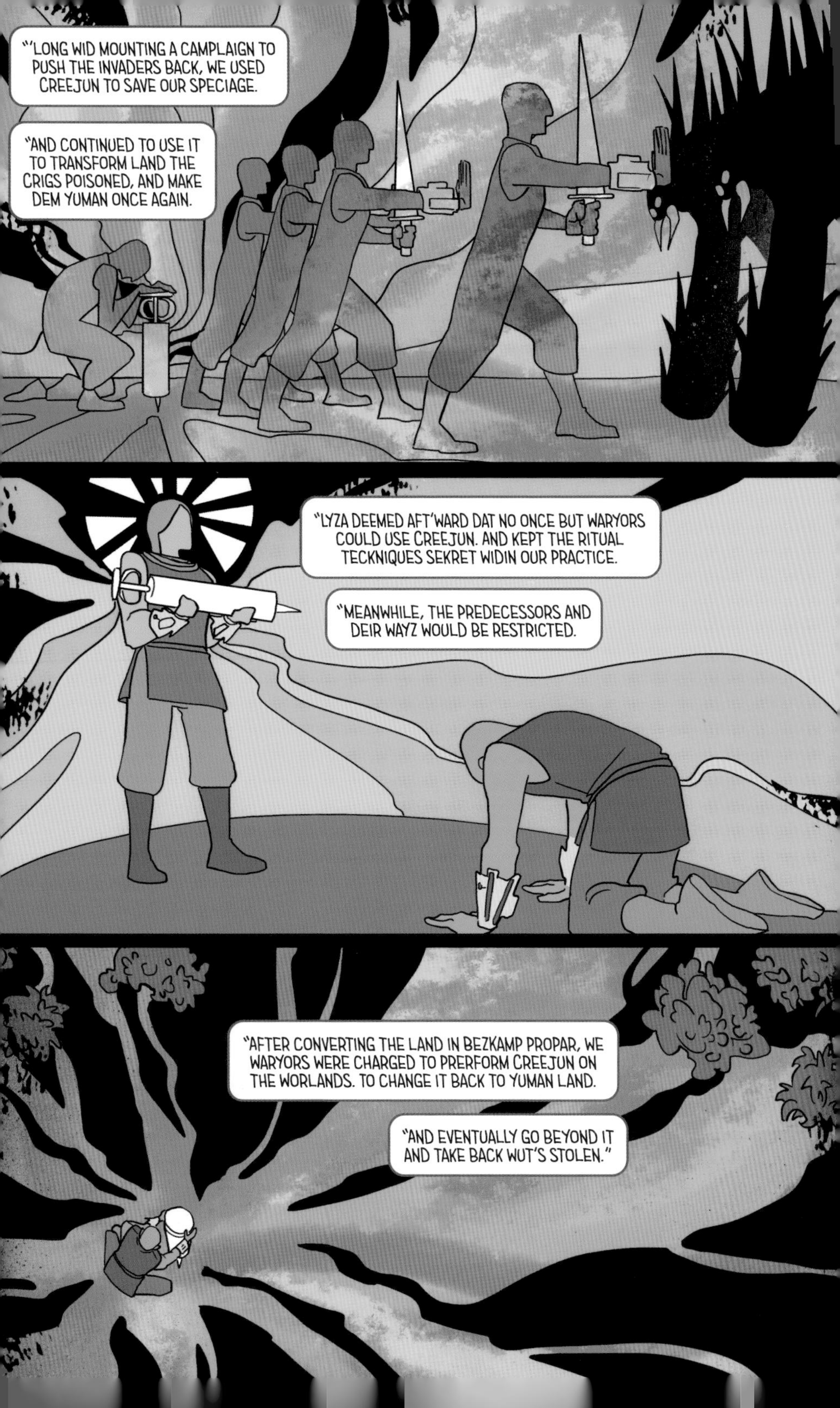
"'LONG WID MOUNTING A CAMPLAIGN TO PUSH THE INVADERS BACK, WE USED CREEJUN TO SAVE OUR SPECIAGE.
"AND CONTINUED TO USE IT TO TRANSFORM LAND THE CRIGS POISONED, AND MAKE DEM YUMAN ONCE AGAIN.
"LYZA DEEMED AFT'WARD DAT NO ONCE BUT WARYORS COULD USE CREEJUN. AND KEPT THE RITUAL TECKNIQUES SEKRET WIDIN OUR PRACTICE.
"MEANWHILE, THE PREDECESSORS AND DEIR WAYZ WOULD BE RESTRICTED.
"AFTER CONVERTING THE LAND IN BEZKAMP PROPAR, WE WARYORS WERE CHARGED TO PRERFORM CREEJUN ON THE WORLANDS. TO CHANGE IT BACK TO YUMAN LAND.
"AND EVENTUALLY GO BEYOND IT AND TAKE BACK WUT'S STOLEN."

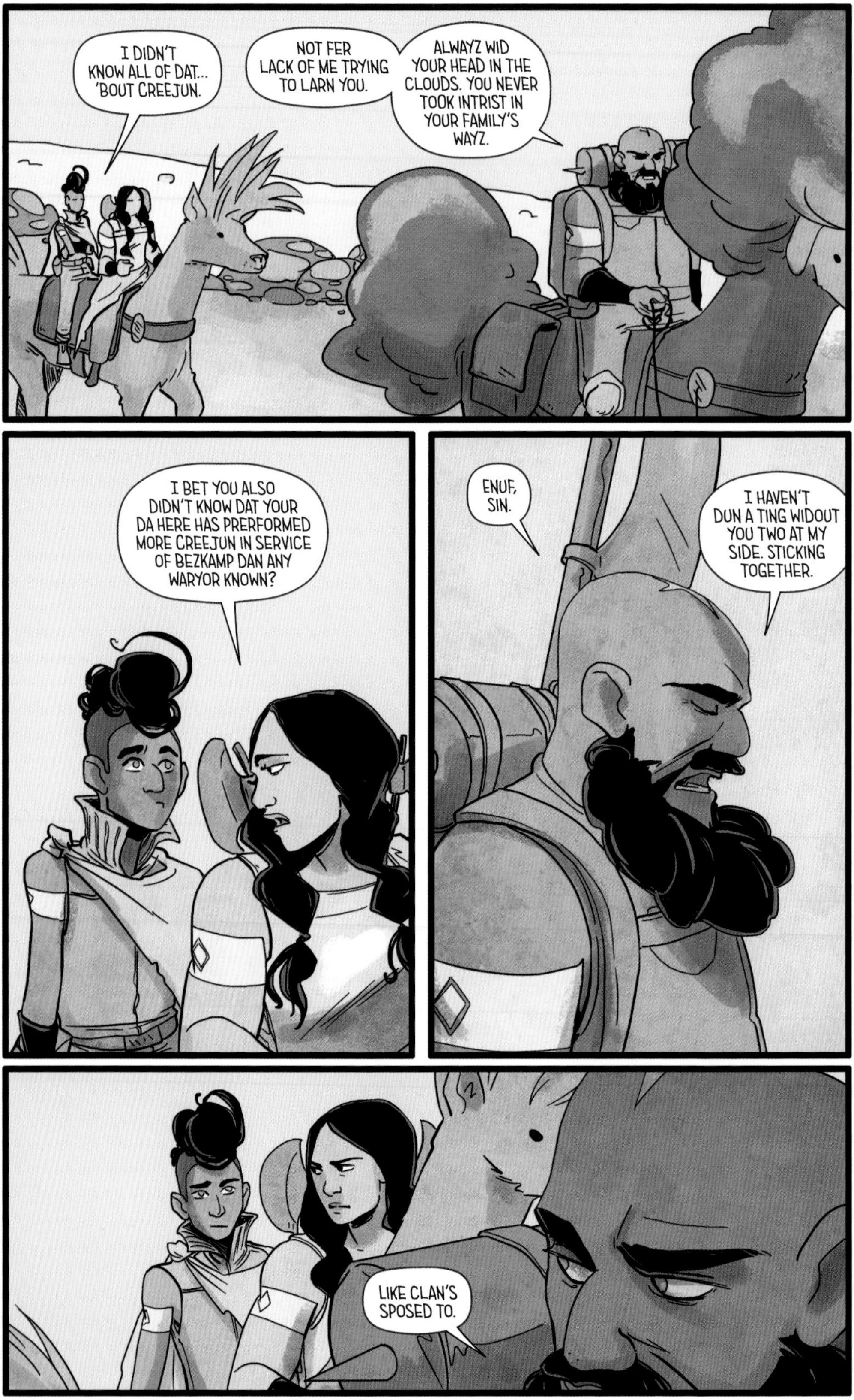
I DIDN'T KNOW ALL OF DAT... 'BOUT CREEJUN.
NOT FER LACK OF ME TRYING TO LARN YOU.
ALWAYZ WID YOUR HEAD IN THE CLOUDS. YOU NEVER TOOK INTRIST IN YOUR FAMILY'S WAYZ.
I BET YOU ALSO DIDN'T KNOW DAT YOUR DA HERE HAS PRERFORMED MORE CREEJUN IN SERVICE OF BEZKAMP DAN ANY WARYOR KNOWN?
ENUF, SIN.
I HAVEN'T DUN A TING WIDOUT YOU TWO AT MY SIDE. STICKING TOGETHER.
LIKE CLAN'S SPOSED TO.

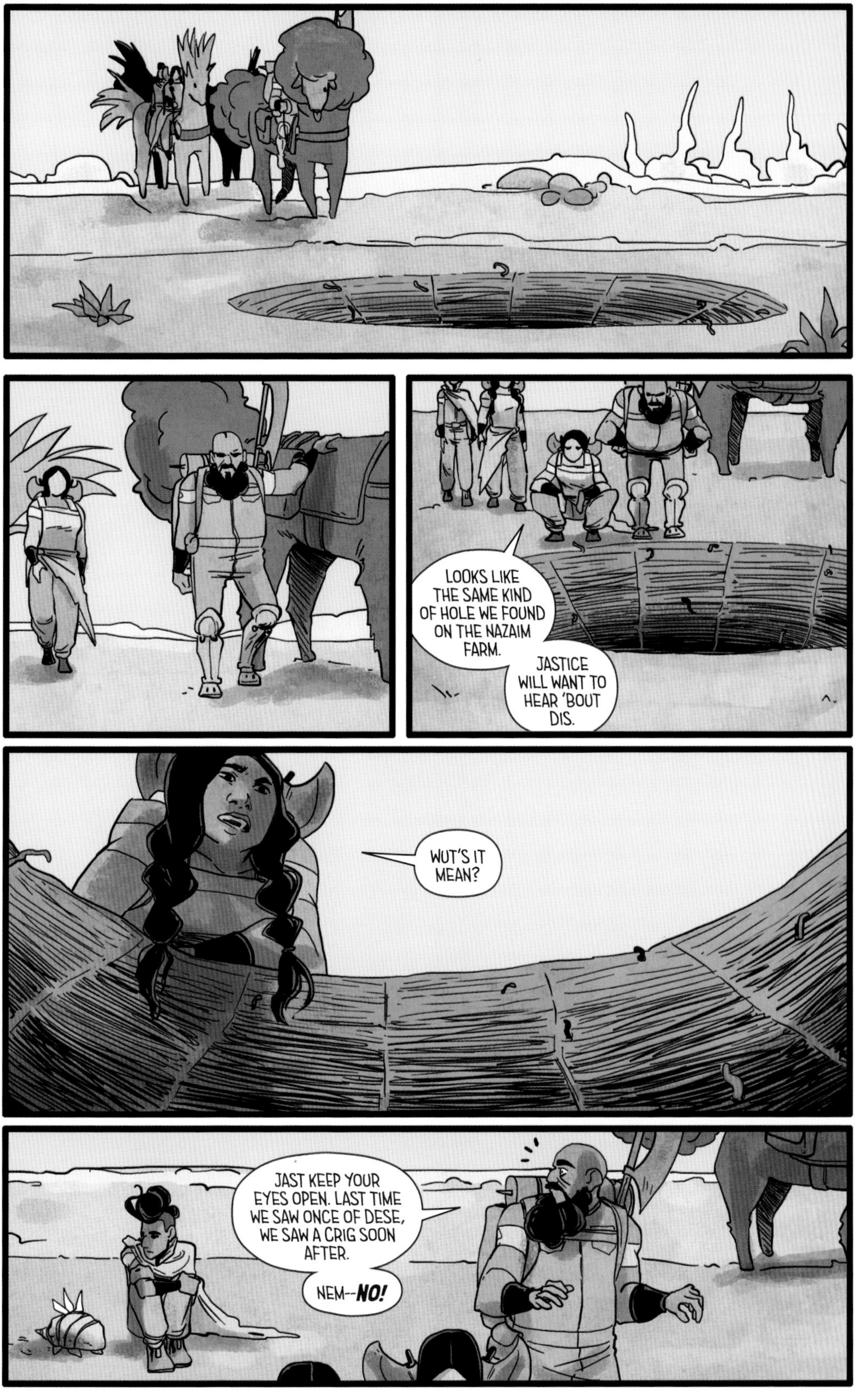
LOOKS LIKE THE SAME KIND OF HOLE WE FOUND ON THE NAZAIM FARM.
JASTICE WILL WANT TO HEAR 'BOUT DIS.
WUT'S IT MEAN?
JAST KEEP YOUR EYES OPEN. LAST TIME WE SAW ONCE OF DESE, WE SAW A CRIG SOON AFTER.
NEM--**NO!**

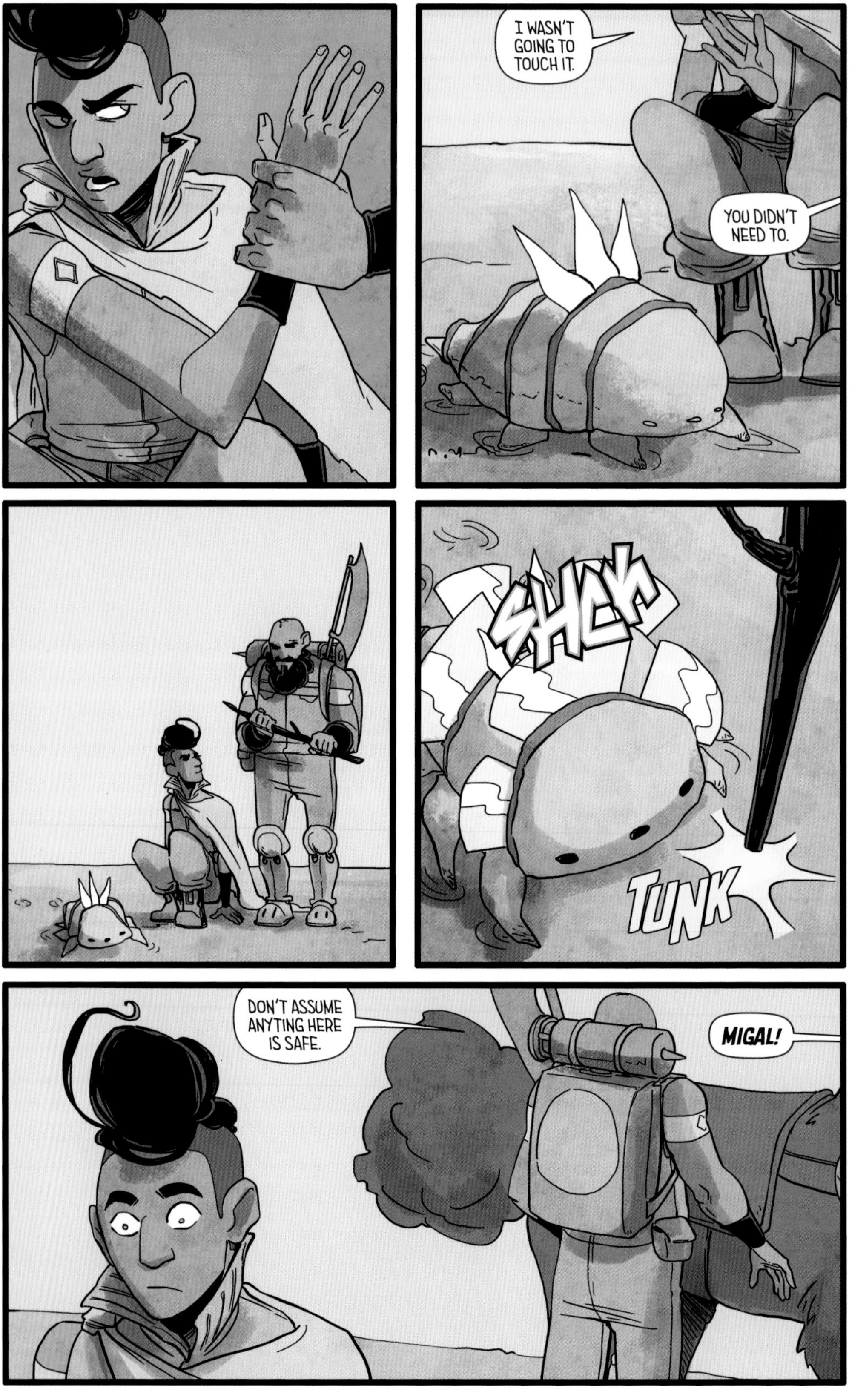
I WASN'T GOING TO TOUCH IT.
YOU DIDN'T NEED TO.
SHCK
TUNK
DON'T ASSUME ANYTING HERE IS SAFE.
MIGAL!

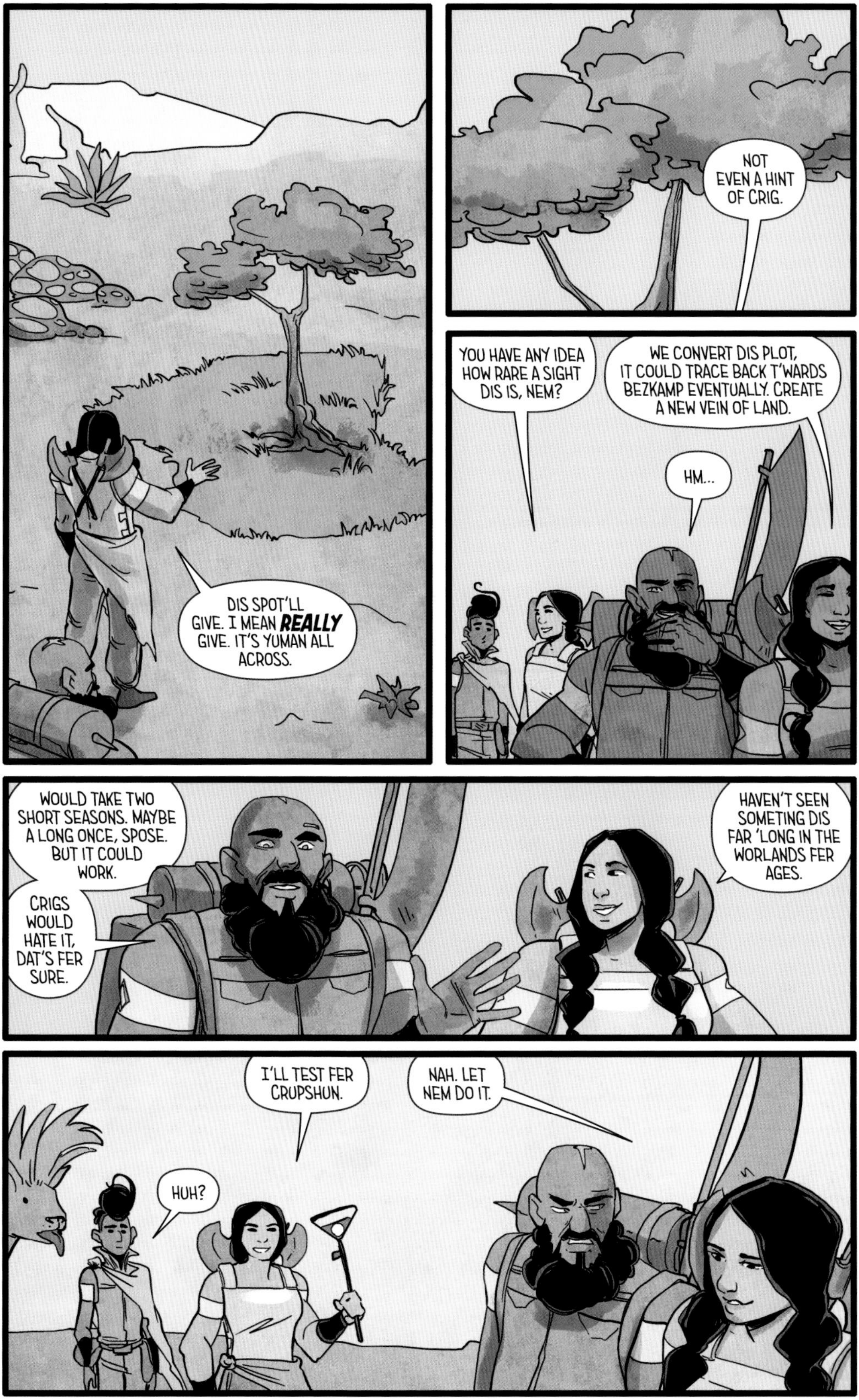
DIS SPOT'LL GIVE. I MEAN **REALLY** GIVE. IT'S YUMAN ALL ACROSS.
NOT EVEN A HINT OF CRIG.
YOU HAVE ANY IDEA HOW RARE A SIGHT DIS IS, NEM?
WE CONVERT DIS PLOT, IT COULD TRACE BACK T'WARDS BEZKAMP EVENTUALLY. CREATE A NEW VEIN OF LAND.
HM...
WOULD TAKE TWO SHORT SEASONS. MAYBE A LONG ONCE, SPOSE. BUT IT COULD WORK.
CRIGS WOULD HATE IT, DAT'S FER SURE.
HAVEN'T SEEN SOMETING DIS FAR 'LONG IN THE WORLANDS FER AGES.
I'LL TEST FER CRUPSHUN.
NAH. LET NEM DO IT.
HUH?

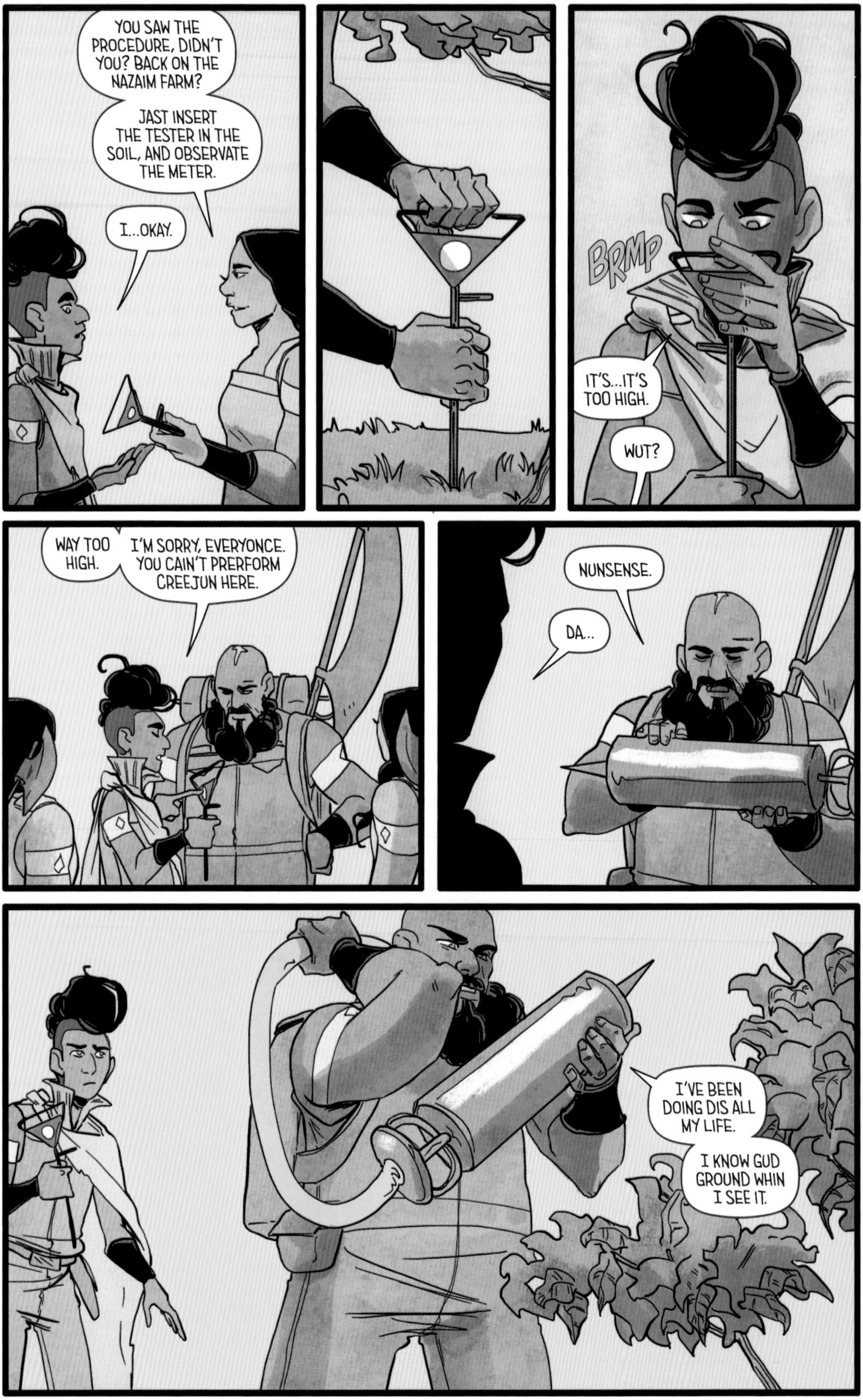
YOU SAW THE PROCEDURE, DIDN'T YOU? BACK ON THE NAZAIM FARM?
JAST INSERT THE TESTER IN THE SOIL, AND OBSERVATE THE METER.
I...OKAY.
BRMP
IT'S...IT'S TOO HIGH.
WUT?
WAY TOO HIGH.
I'M SORRY, EVERYONCE. YOU CAIN'T PRERFORM CREEJUN HERE.
NUNSENSE.
DA...
I'VE BEEN DOING DIS ALL MY LIFE.
I KNOW GUD GROUND WHIN I SEE IT.

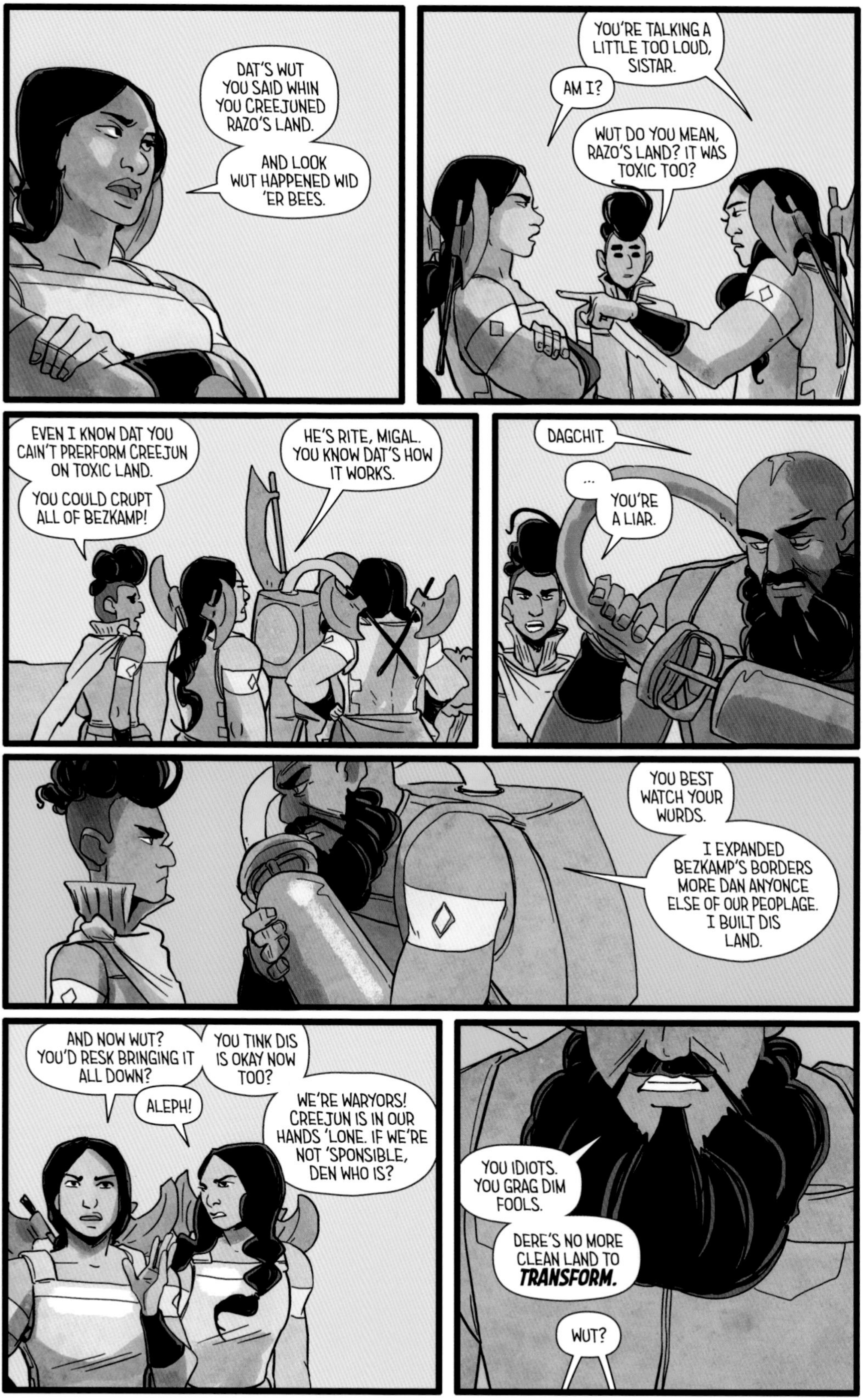
DAT'S WUT YOU SAID WHIN YOU CREEJUNED RAZO'S LAND.
AND LOOK WUT HAPPENED WID 'ER BEES.
YOU'RE TALKING A LITTLE TOO LOUD, SISTAR.
AM I?
WUT DO YOU MEAN, RAZO'S LAND? IT WAS TOXIC TOO?
EVEN I KNOW DAT YOU CAIN'T PRERFORM CREEJUN ON TOXIC LAND.
YOU COULD CRUPT ALL OF BEZKAMP!
HE'S RITE, MIGAL. YOU KNOW DAT'S HOW IT WORKS.
DAGCHIT.
...
YOU'RE A LIAR.
YOU BEST WATCH YOUR WURDS.
I EXPANDED BEZKAMP'S BORDERS MORE DAN ANYONCE ELSE OF OUR PEOPLAGE. I BUILT DIS LAND.
AND NOW WUT? YOU'D RESK BRINGING IT ALL DOWN?
ALEPH!
YOU TINK DIS IS OKAY NOW TOO?
WE'RE WARYORS! CREEJUN IS IN OUR HANDS 'LONE. IF WE'RE NOT 'SPONSIBLE, DEN WHO IS?
YOU IDIOTS. YOU GRAG DIM FOOLS.
DERE'S NO MORE CLEAN LAND TO **TRANSFORM.**
WUT?

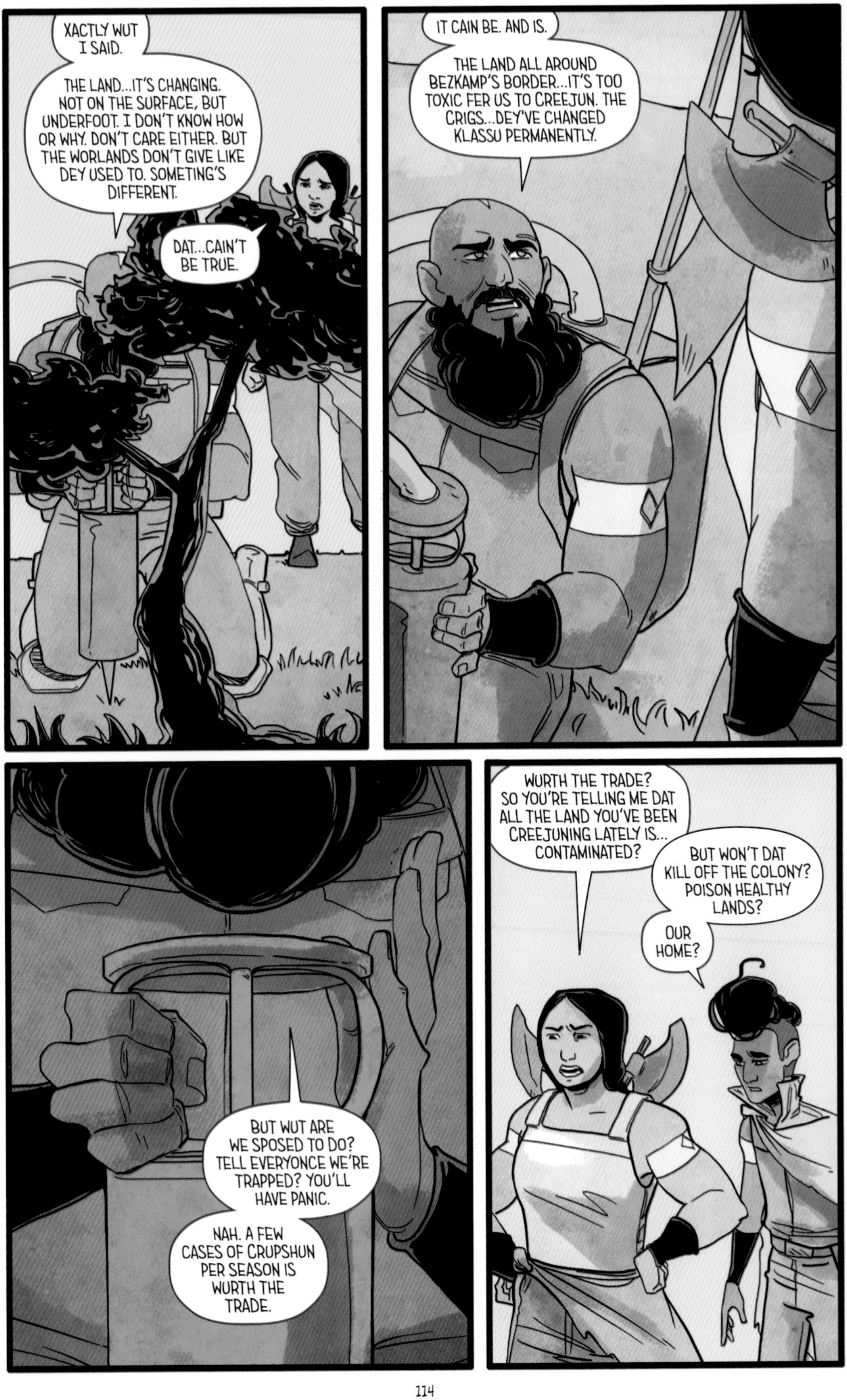
XACTLY WUT I SAID.
THE LAND...IT'S CHANGING. NOT ON THE SURFACE, BUT UNDERFOOT. I DON'T KNOW HOW OR WHY. DON'T CARE EITHER. BUT THE WORLANDS DON'T GIVE LIKE DEY USED TO. SOMETING'S DIFFERENT.
DAT...CAIN'T BE TRUE.
IT CAIN BE. AND IS.
THE LAND ALL AROUND BEZKAMP'S BORDER...IT'S TOO TOXIC FER US TO CREEJUN. THE CRIGS...DEY'VE CHANGED KLASSU PERMANENTLY.
BUT WUT ARE WE SPOSED TO DO? TELL EVERYONCE WE'RE TRAPPED? YOU'LL HAVE PANIC.
NAH. A FEW CASES OF CRUPSHUN PER SEASON IS WURTH THE TRADE.
WURTH THE TRADE? SO YOU'RE TELLING ME DAT ALL THE LAND YOU'VE BEEN CREEJUNING LATELY IS... CONTAMINATED?
BUT WON'T DAT KILL OFF THE COLONY? POISON HEALTHY LANDS?
OUR HOME?

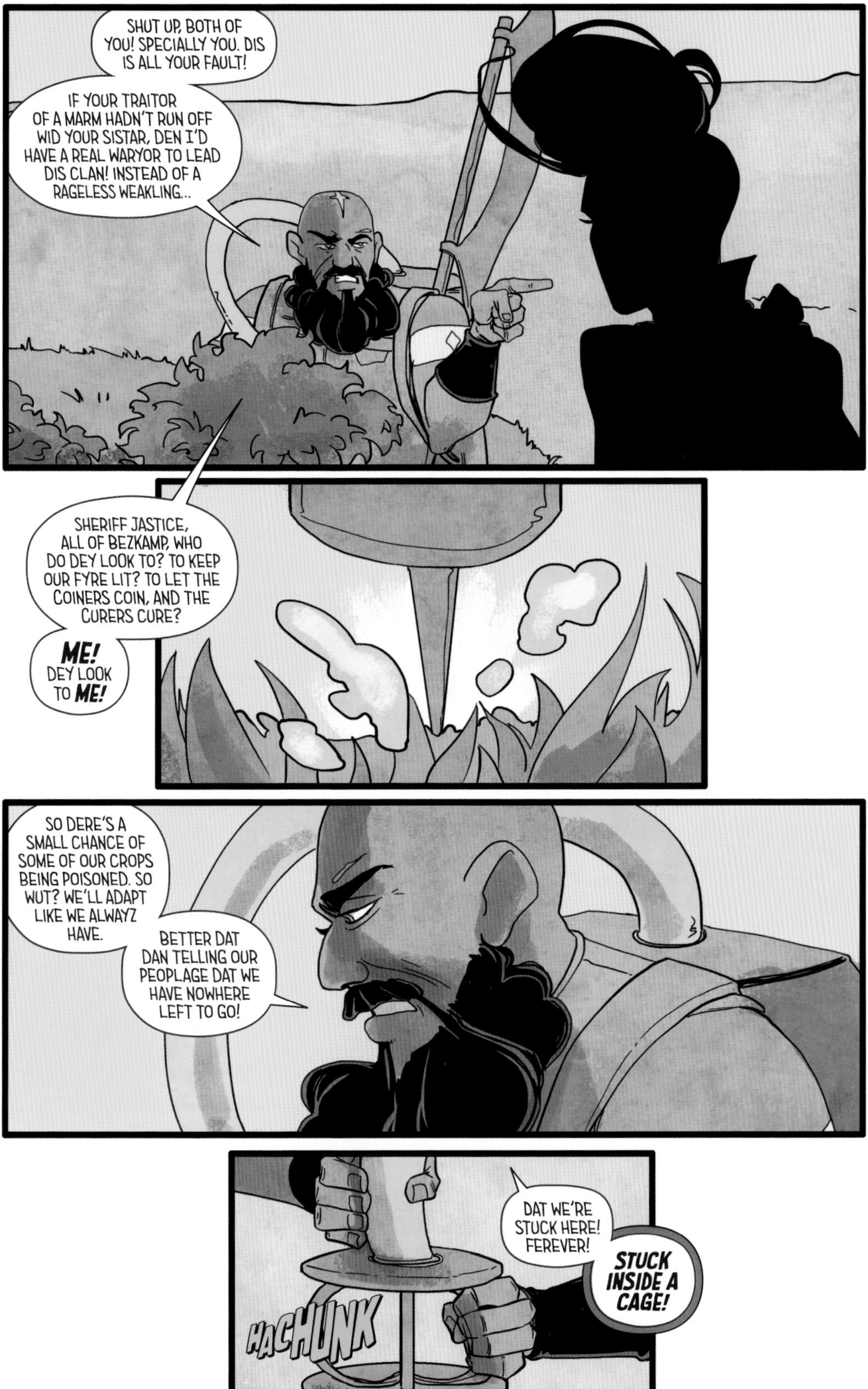

SHUT UP, BOTH OF YOU! SPECIALLY YOU. DIS IS ALL YOUR FAULT!
IF YOUR TRAITOR OF A MARM HADN'T RUN OFF WID YOUR SISTAR, DEN I'D HAVE A REAL WARYOR TO LEAD DIS CLAN! INSTEAD OF A RAGELESS WEAKLING...
SHERIFF JASTICE, ALL OF BEZKAMP, WHO DO DEY LOOK TO? TO KEEP OUR FYRE LIT? TO LET THE COINERS COIN, AND THE CURERS CURE?
ME! DEY LOOK TO ME!
SO DERE'S A SMALL CHANCE OF SOME OF OUR CROPS BEING POISONED. SO WUT? WE'LL ADAPT LIKE WE ALWAYZ HAVE.
BETTER DAT DAN TELLING OUR PEOPLAGE DAT WE HAVE NOWHERE LEFT TO GO!
DAT WE'RE STUCK HERE! FEREVER!
STUCK INSIDE A CAGE!
HACHUNK

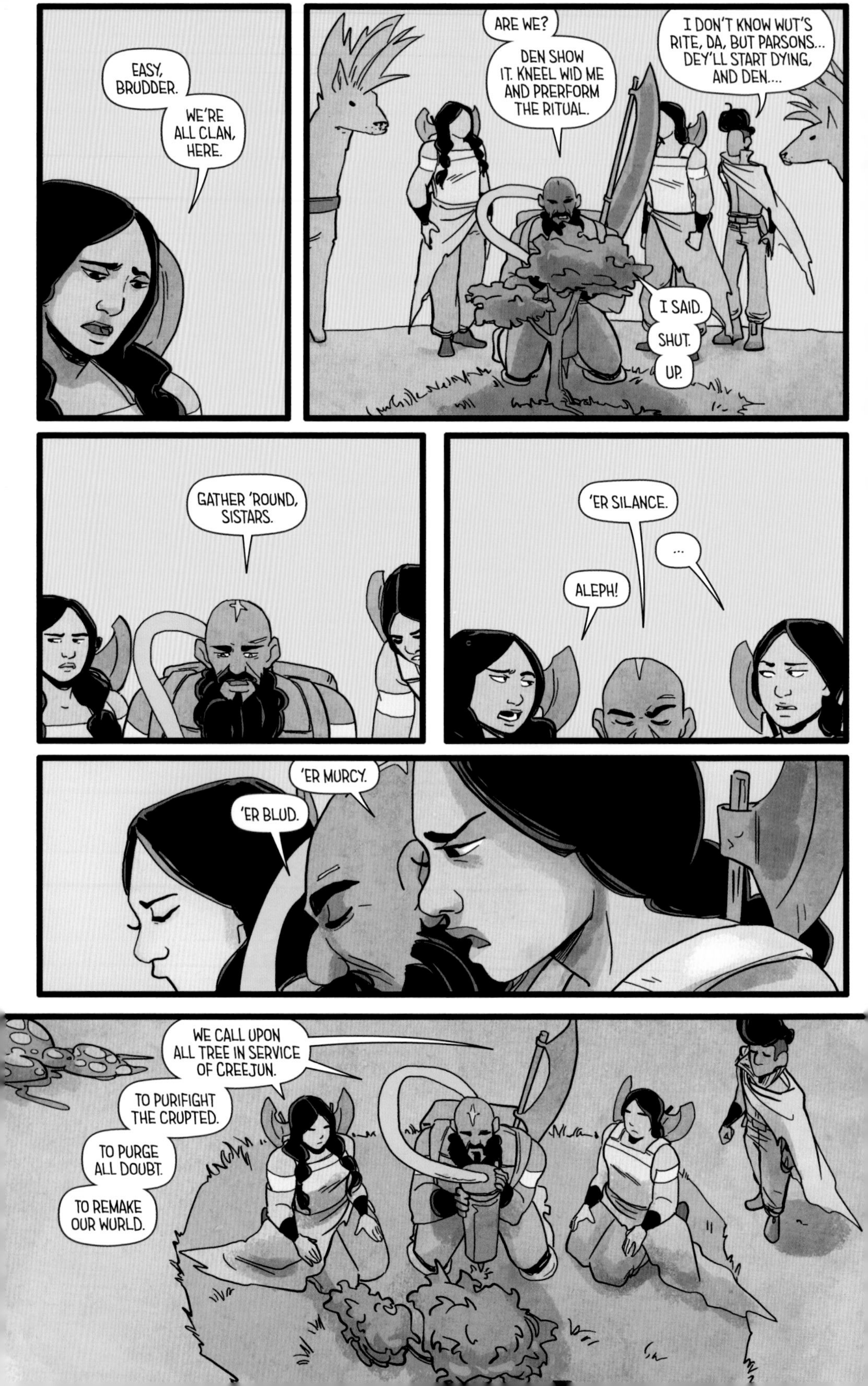
EASY, BRUDDER.
WE'RE ALL CLAN, HERE.
ARE WE?
DEN SHOW IT. KNEEL WID ME AND PRERFORM THE RITUAL.
I DON'T KNOW WUT'S RITE, DA, BUT PARSONS... DEY'LL START DYING, AND DEN....
I SAID.
SHUT.
UP.
GATHER 'ROUND, SISTARS.
'ER SILANCE.
...
ALEPH!
'ER MURCY.
'ER BLUD.
WE CALL UPON ALL TREE IN SERVICE OF CREEJUN.
TO PURIFIGHT THE CRUPTED.
TO PURGE ALL DOUBT.
TO REMAKE OUR WURLD.

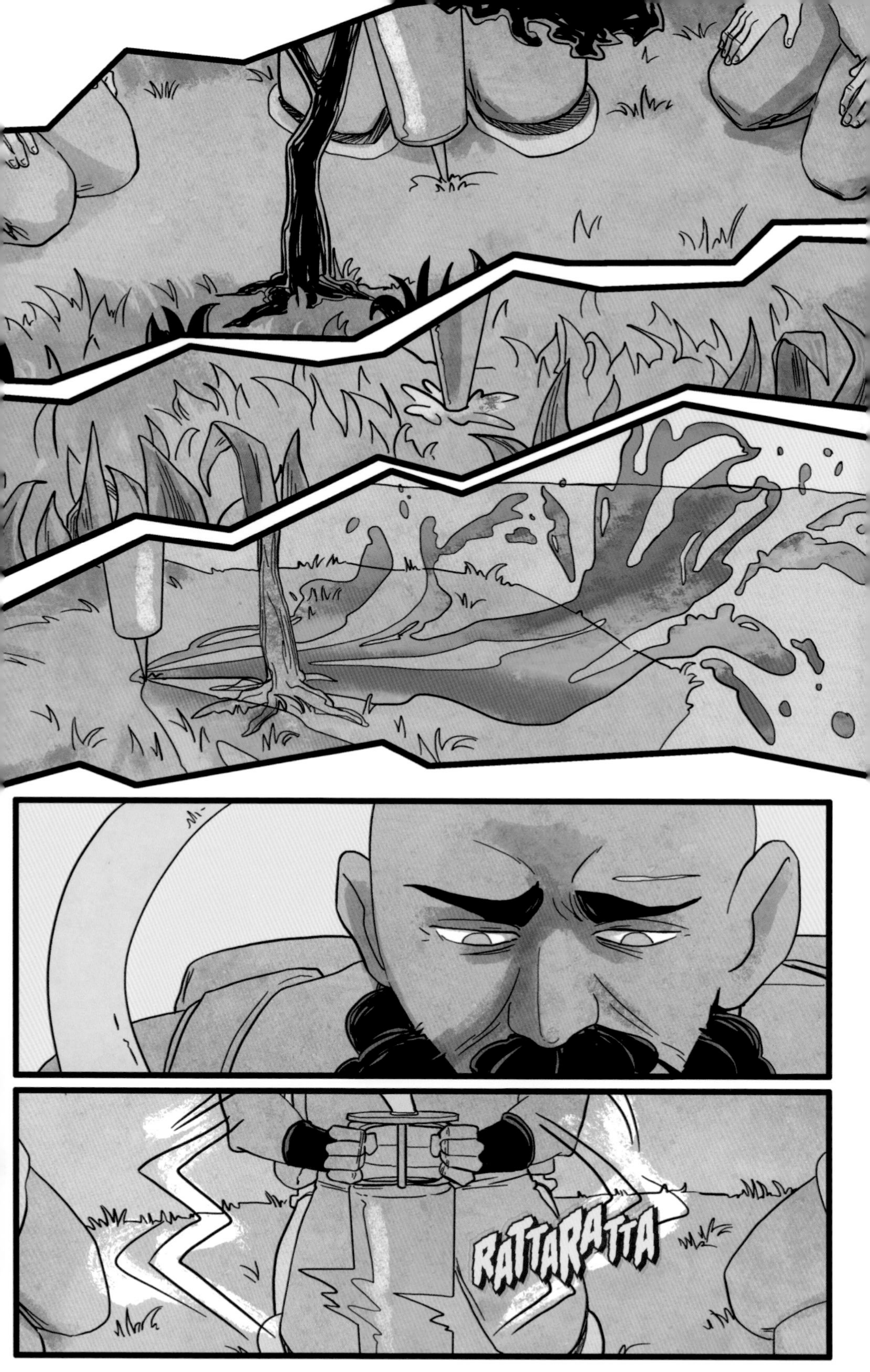
RATTARATTA

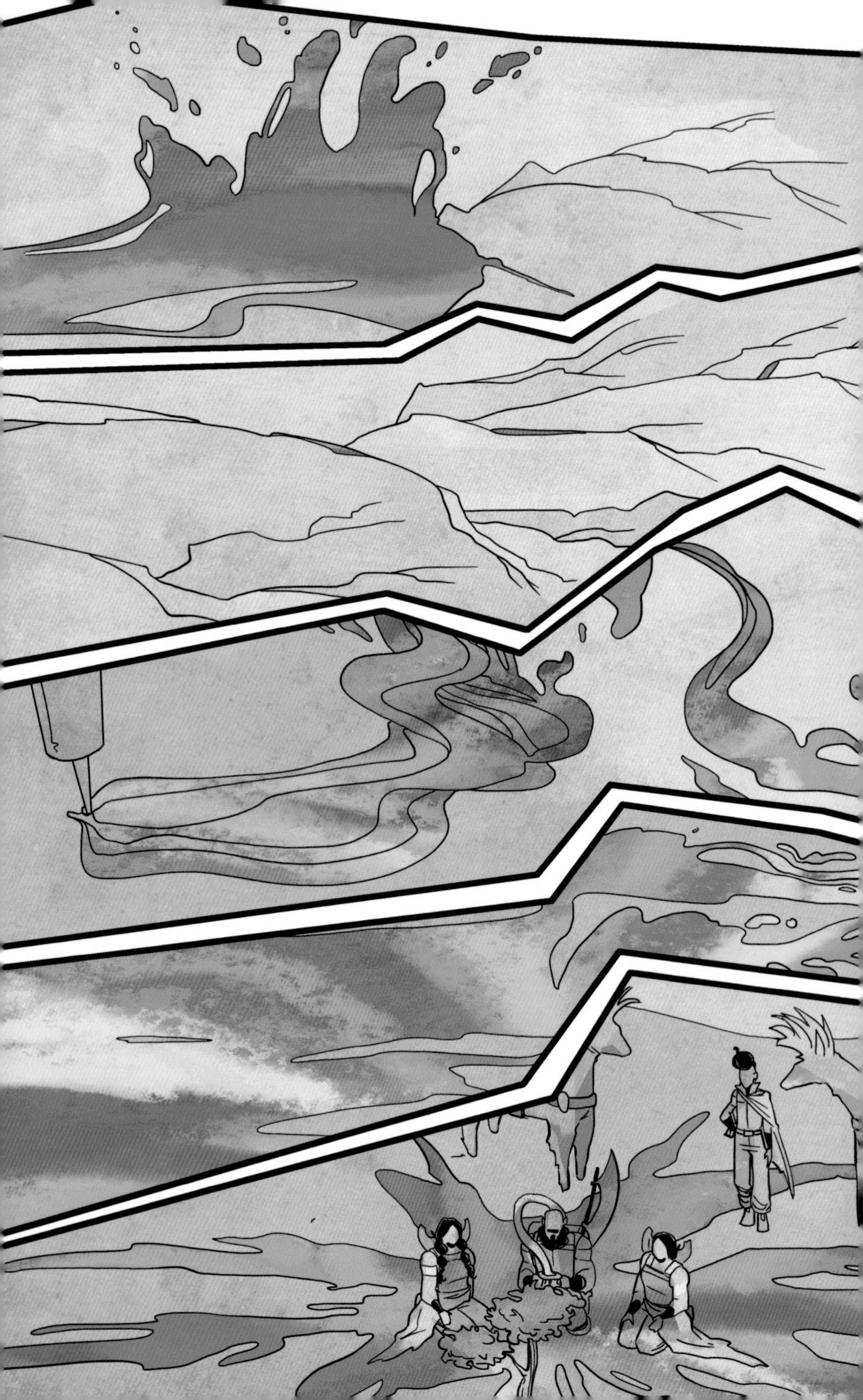

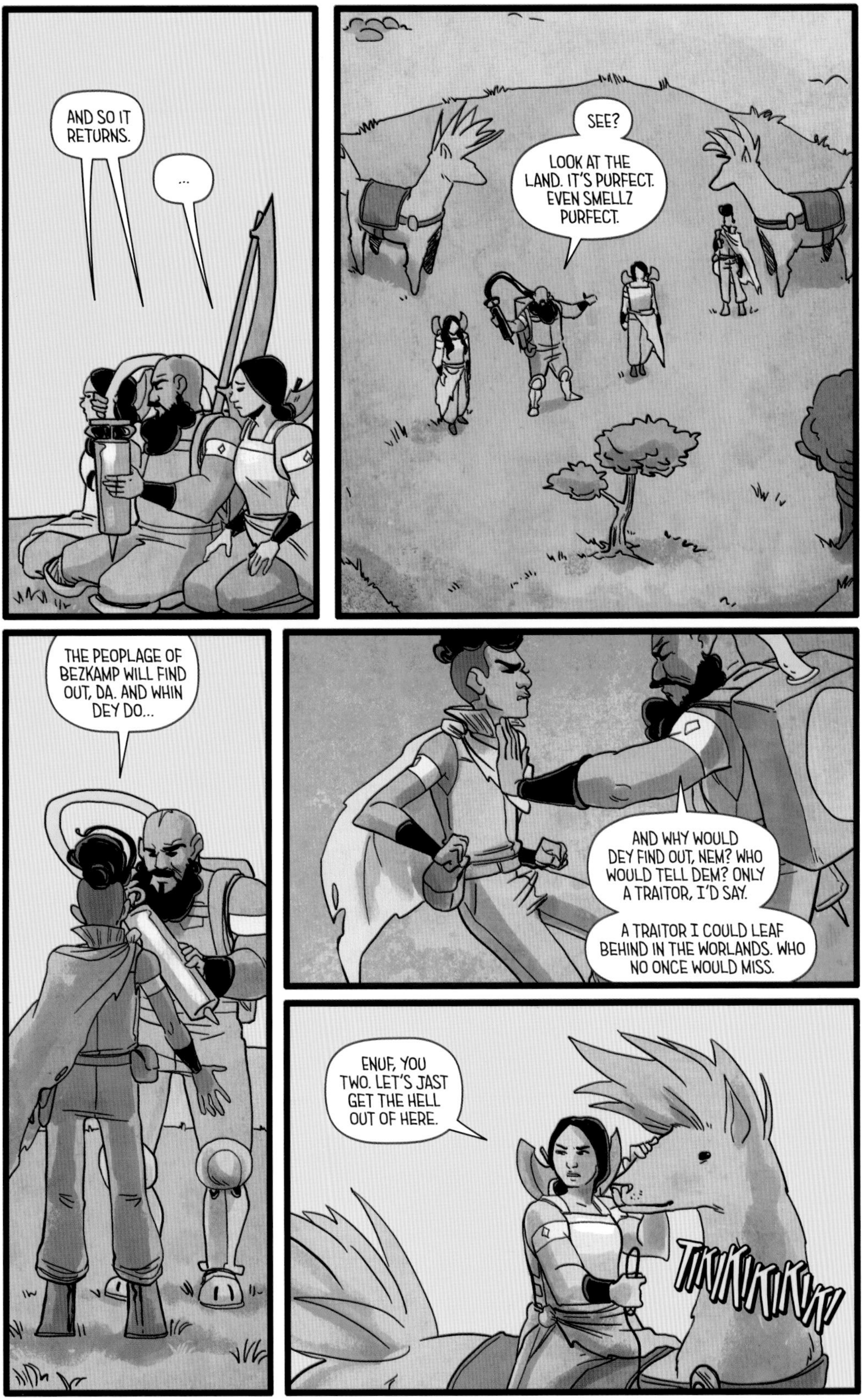
AND SO IT RETURNS.
...
SEE?
LOOK AT THE LAND. IT'S PURFECT. EVEN SMELLZ PURFECT.
THE PEOPLAGE OF BEZKAMP WILL FIND OUT, DA. AND WHIN DEY DO...
AND WHY WOULD DEY FIND OUT, NEM? WHO WOULD TELL DEM? ONLY A TRAITOR, I'D SAY.
A TRAITOR I COULD LEAF BEHIND IN THE WORLANDS. WHO NO ONCE WOULD MISS.
ENUF, YOU TWO. LET'S JAST GET THE HELL OUT OF HERE.
TIKIKIKIKIKI

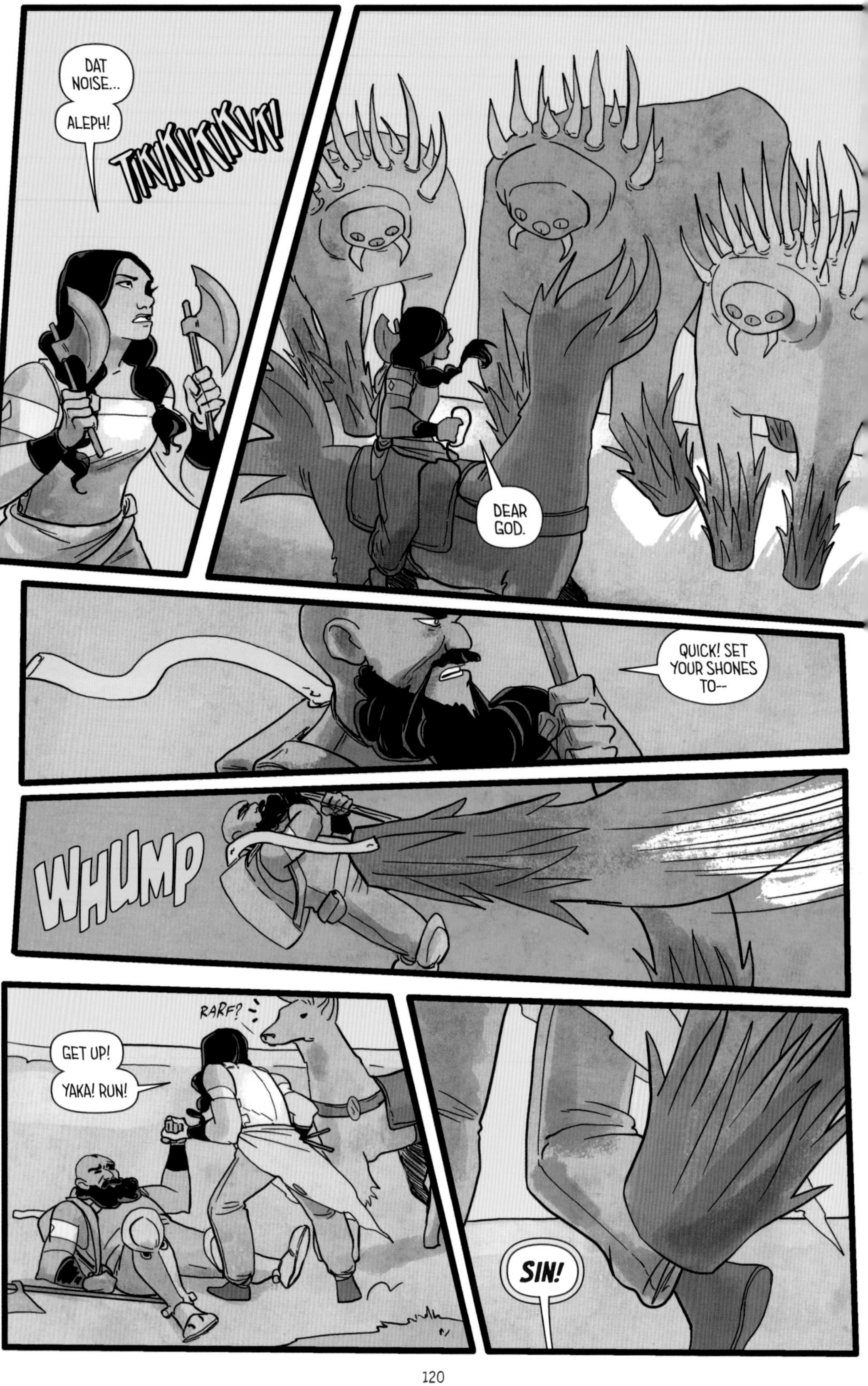
DAT NOISE...
ALEPH!
TIKIKIKIKIKIK!
DEAR GOD.
QUICK! SET YOUR SHONES TO--
WHUMP
RARF?
GET UP!
YAKA! RUN!
SIN!

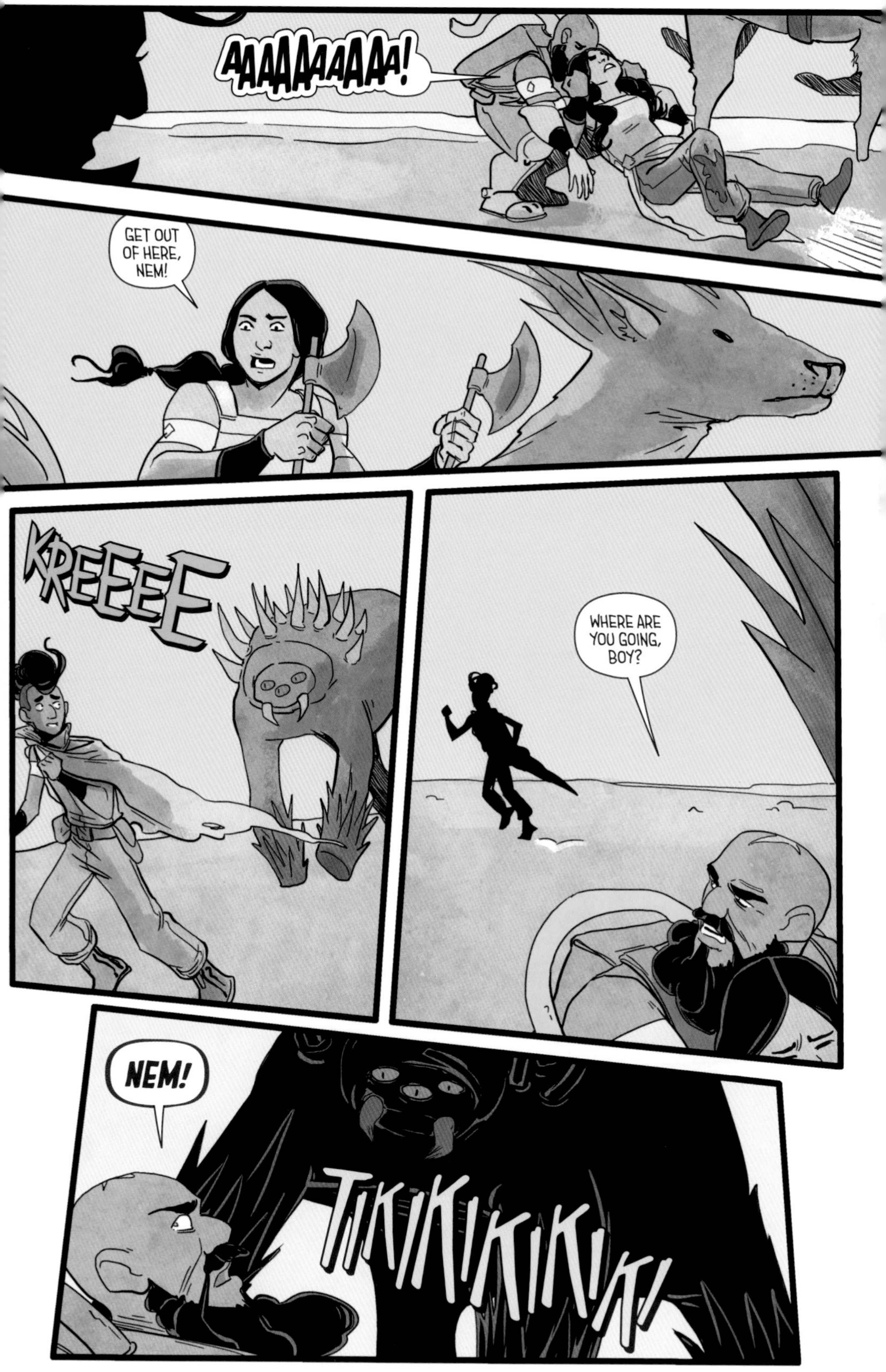
AAAAAAAAAA!
GET OUT OF HERE, NEM!
KREEEE
WHERE ARE YOU GOING, BOY?
NEM!
TIKIKIKIKIKI!

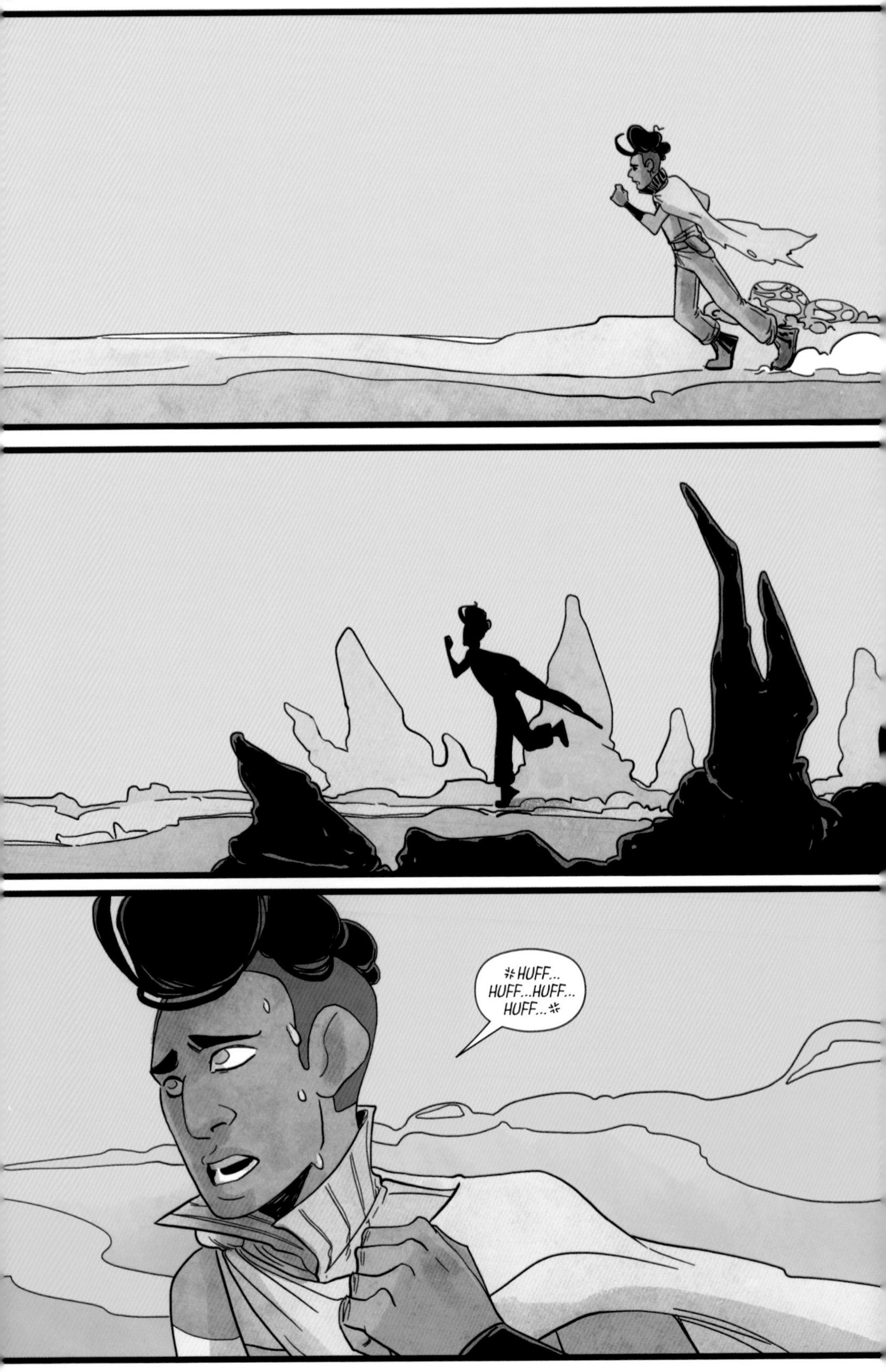
HUFF... HUFF...HUFF... HUFF...

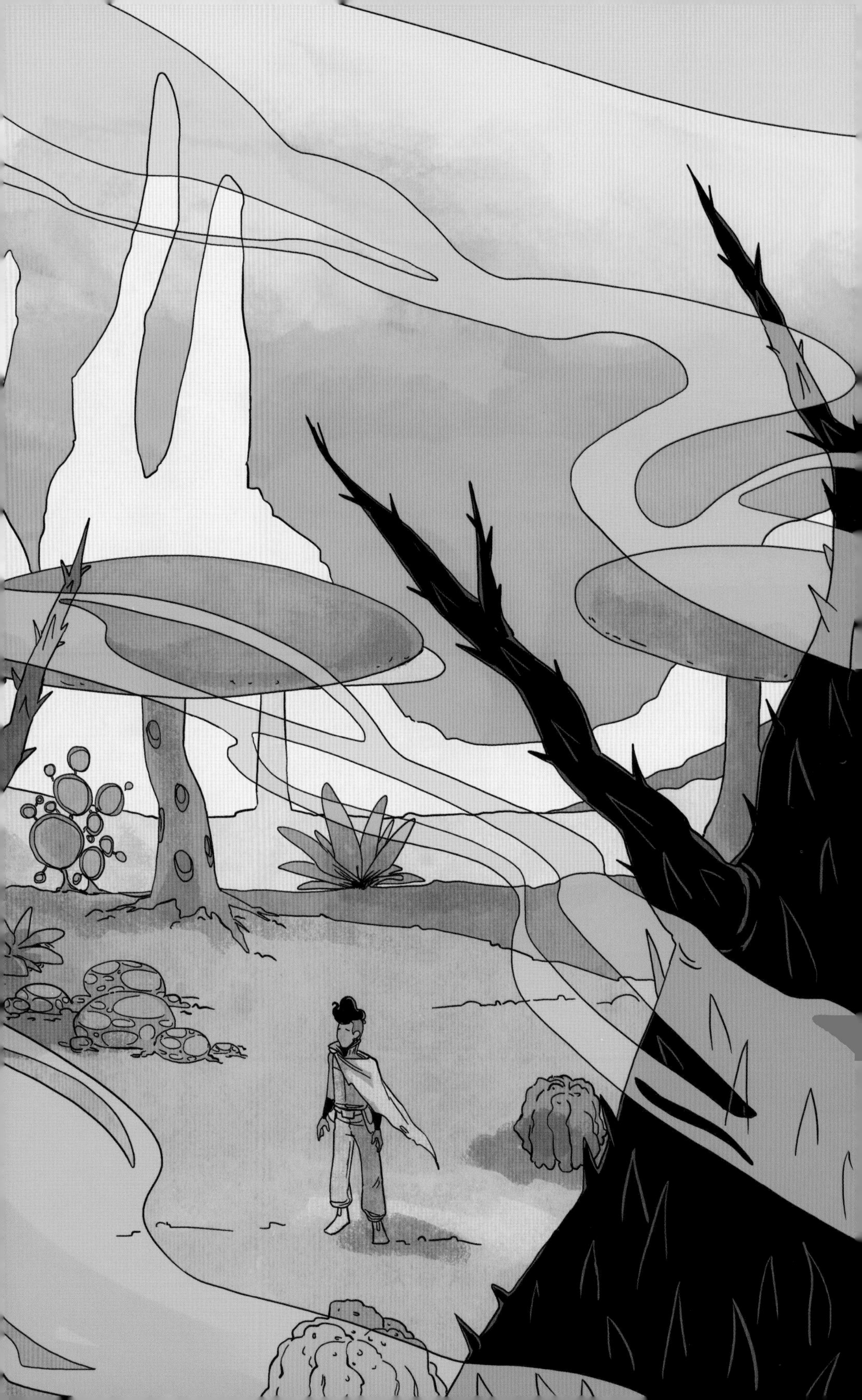

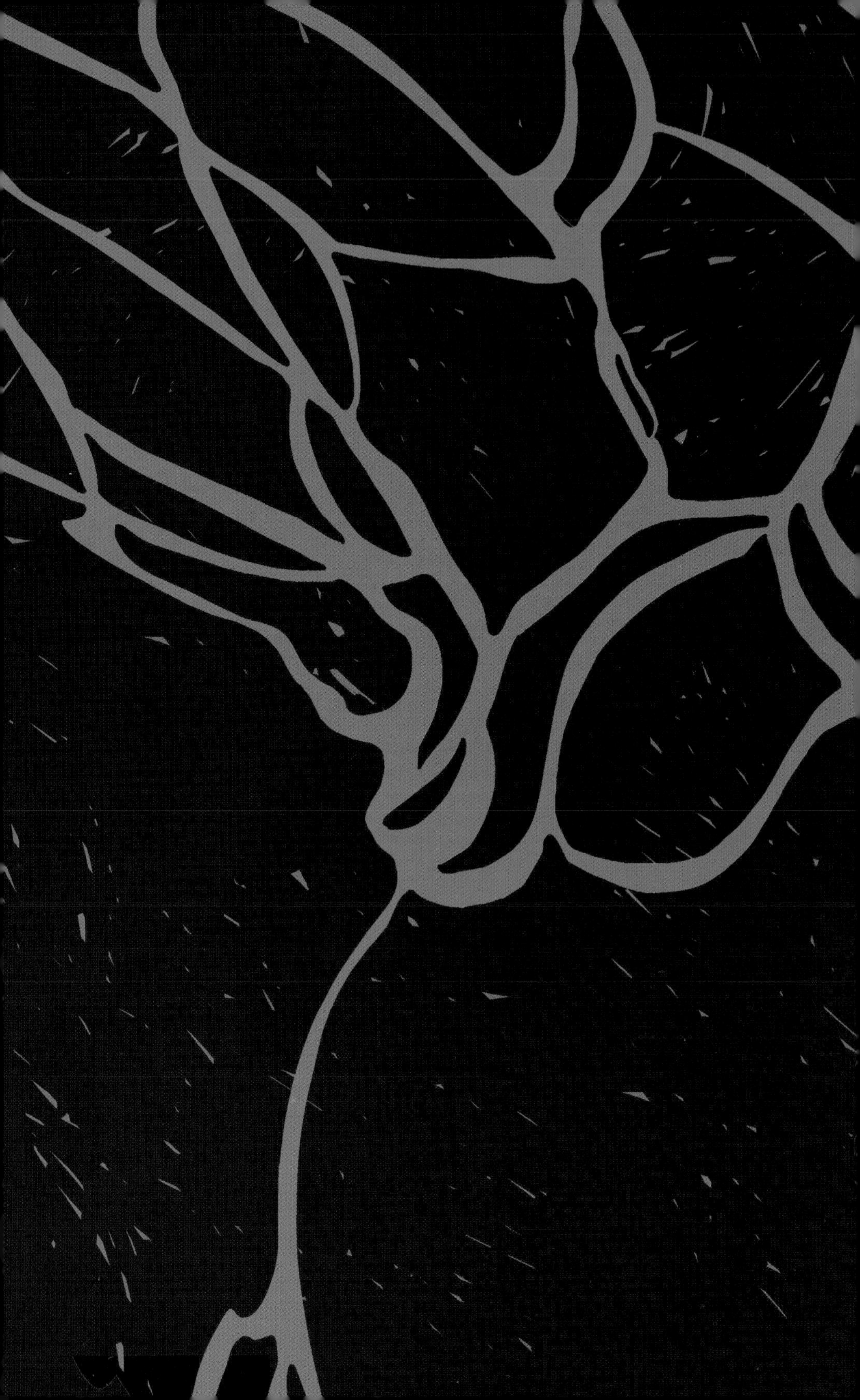

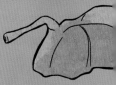

CHEPTAR
FOURTH

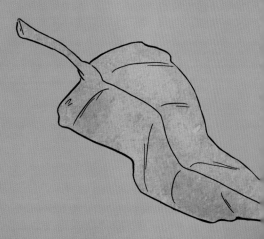

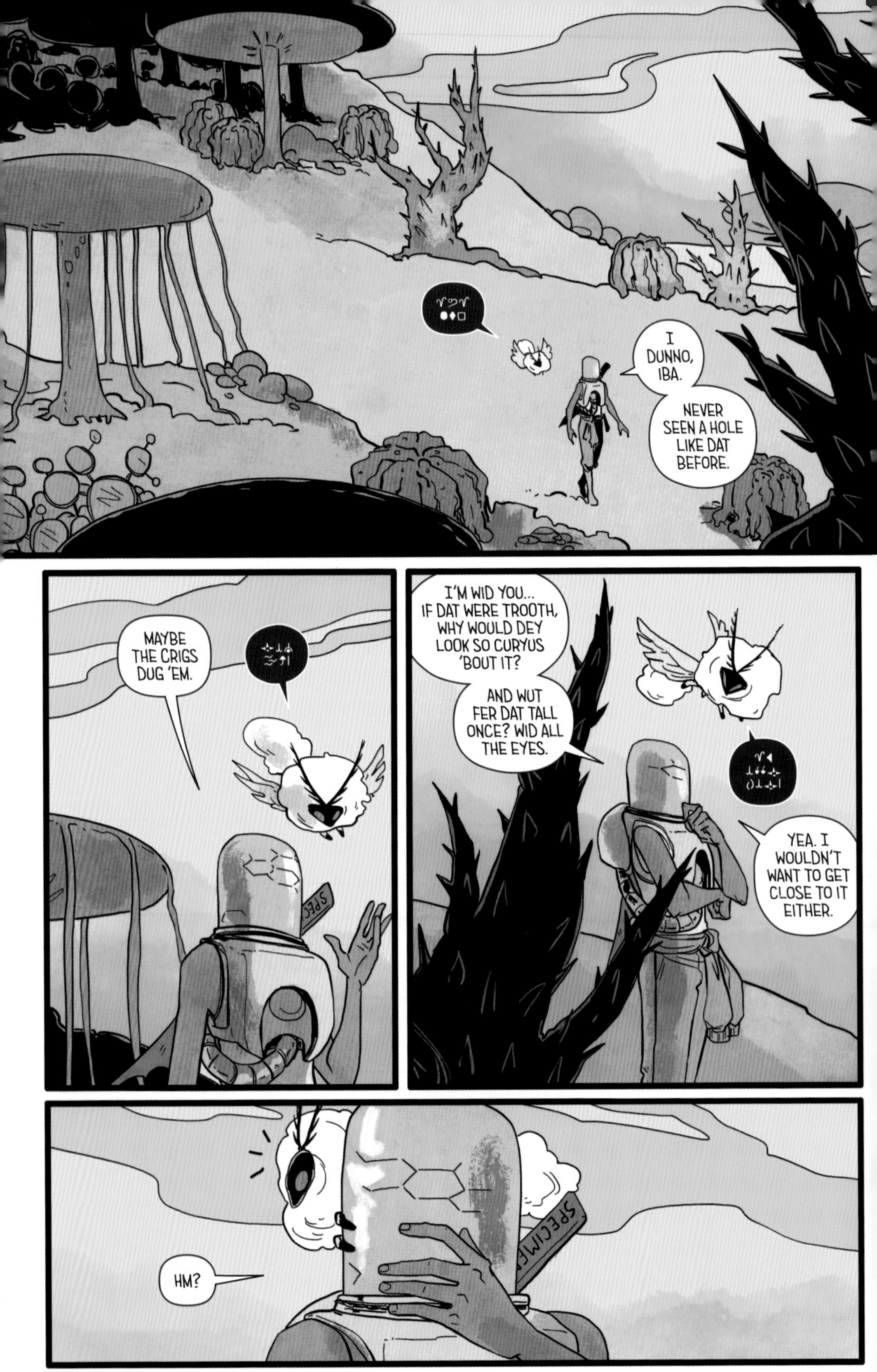
I DUNNO, IBA.
NEVER SEEN A HOLE LIKE DAT BEFORE.
MAYBE THE CRIGS DUG 'EM.
I'M WID YOU... IF DAT WERE TROOTH, WHY WOULD DEY LOOK SO CURYUS 'BOUT IT?
AND WUT FER DAT TALL ONCE? WID ALL THE EYES.
YEA. I WOULDN'T WANT TO GET CLOSE TO IT EITHER.
HM?

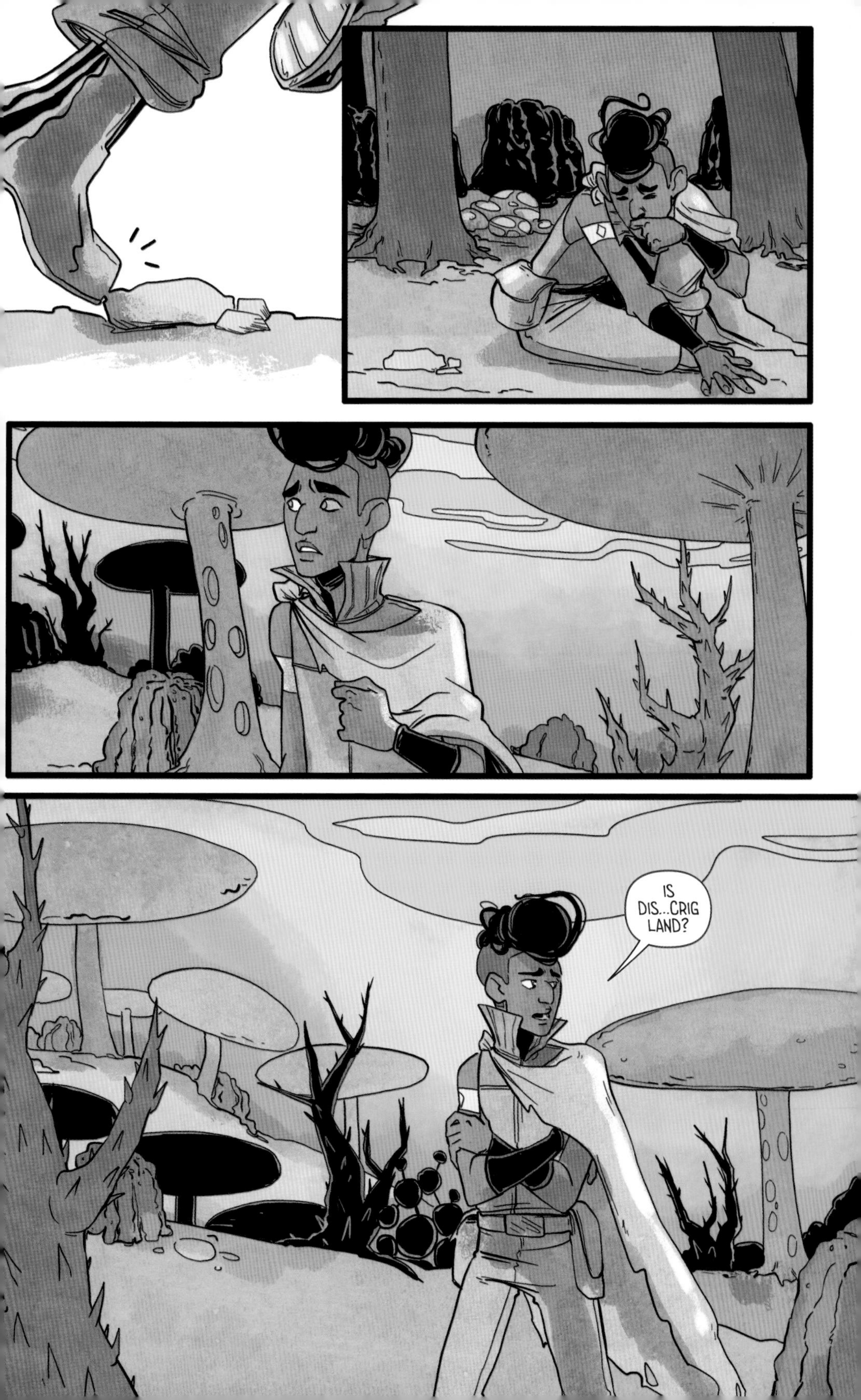
IS DIS...CRIG LAND?

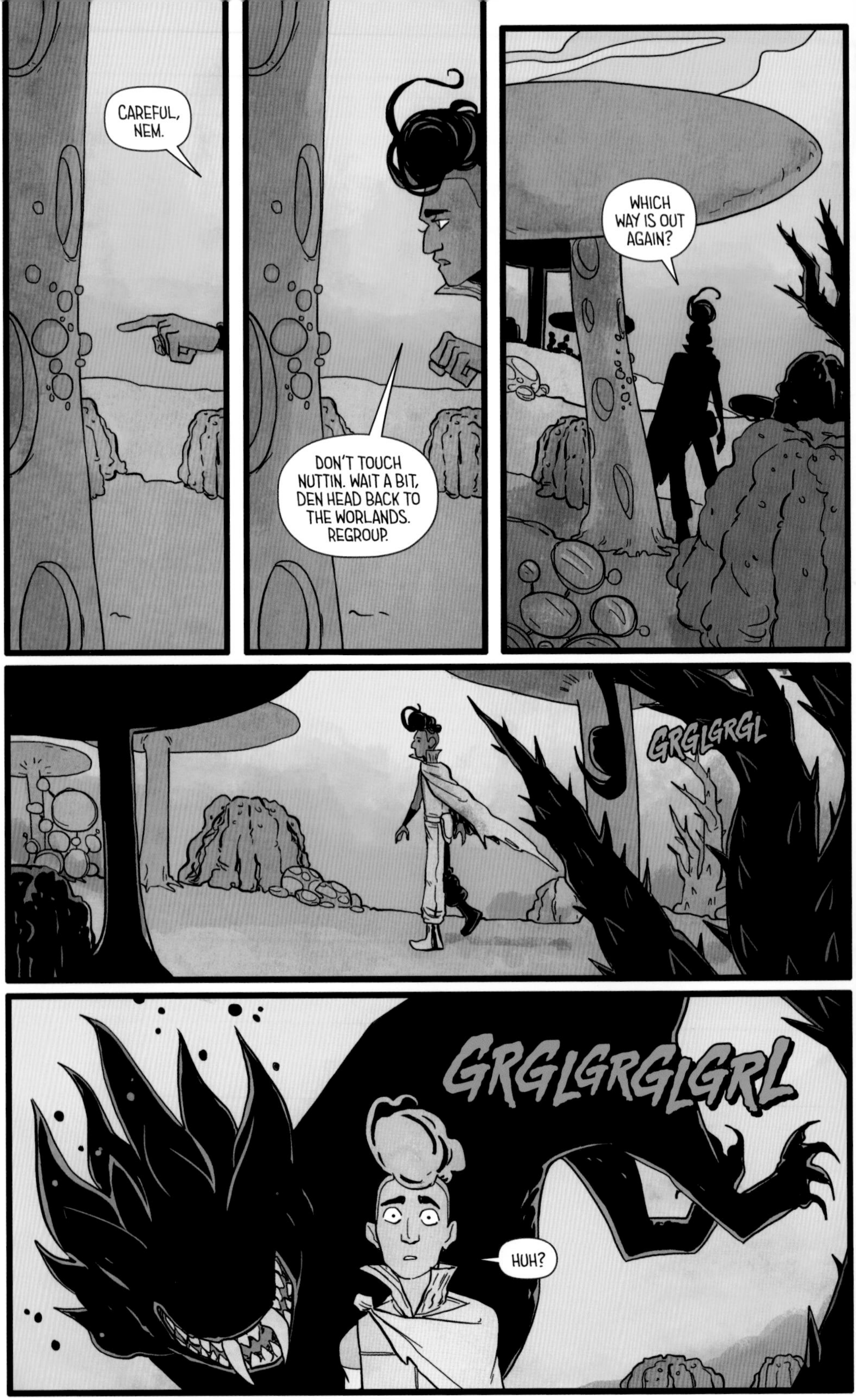
CAREFUL, NEM.
DON'T TOUCH NUTTIN. WAIT A BIT, DEN HEAD BACK TO THE WORLANDS. REGROUP.
WHICH WAY IS OUT AGAIN?
GRGLGRGL
GRGLGRGLGRL
HUH?

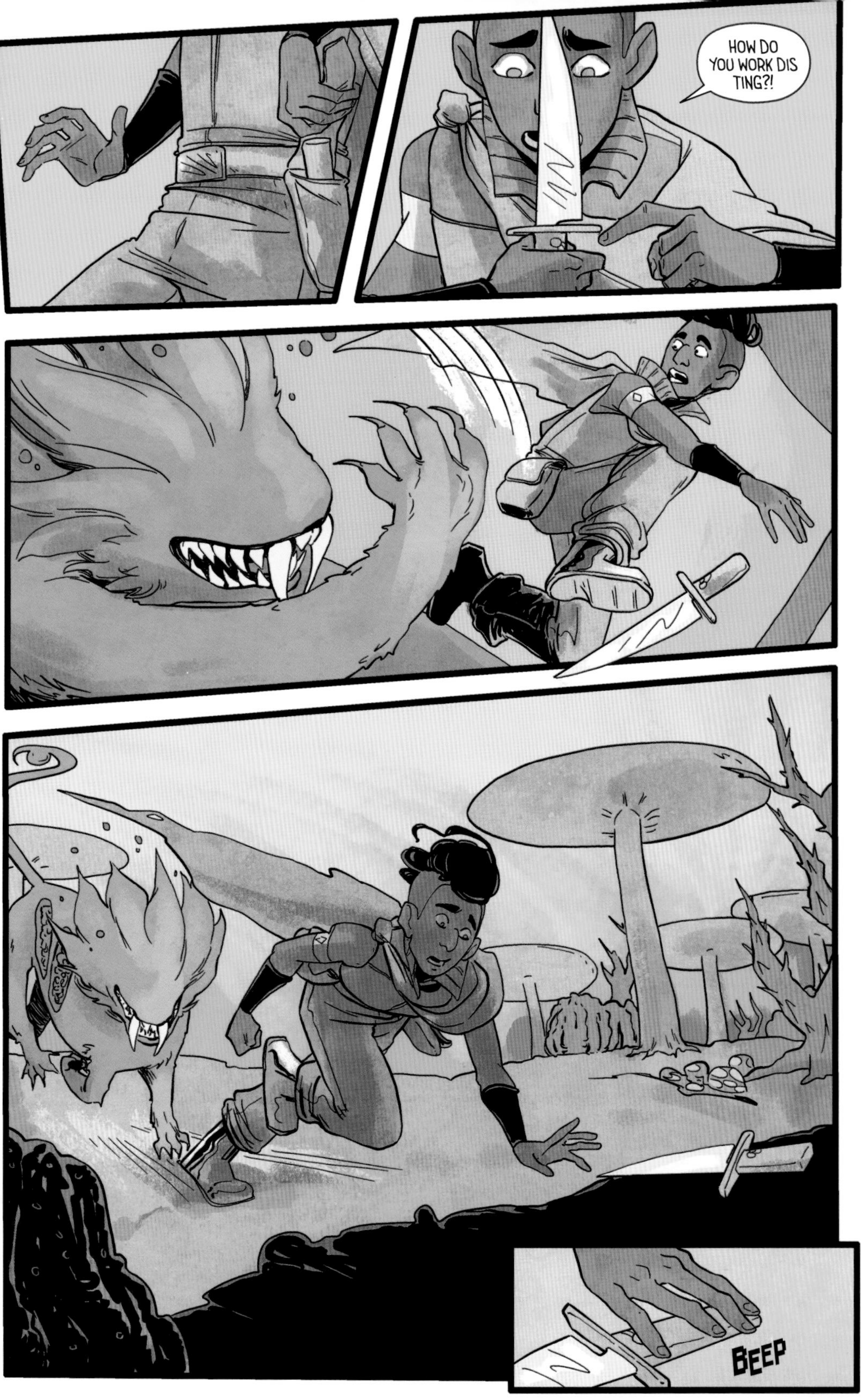
HOW DO
YOU WORK DIS
TING?!
BEEP

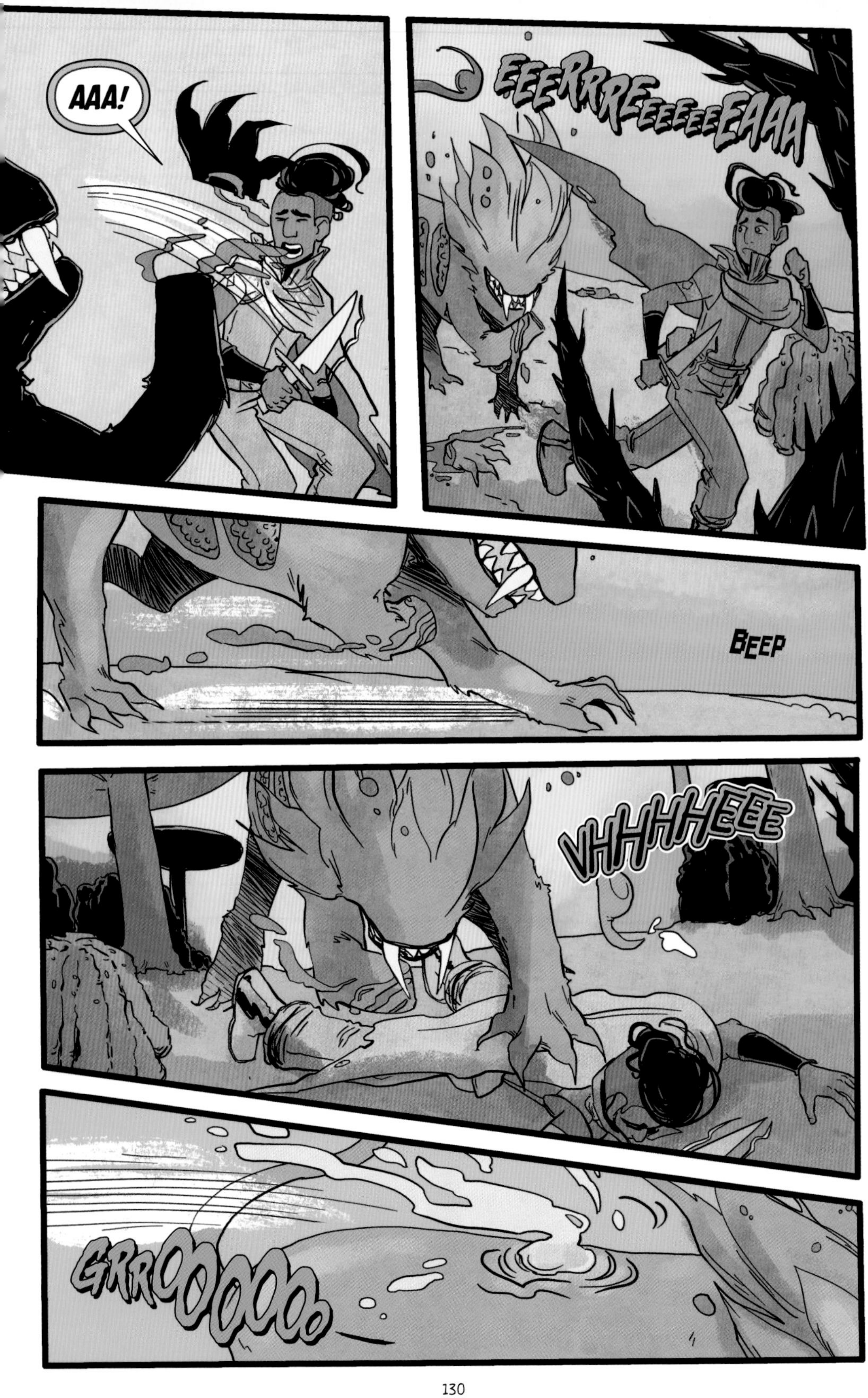
AAA!
EEERRRREEEEEEEAAAA
BEEP
VHHHHEEE
GRROOOOOo

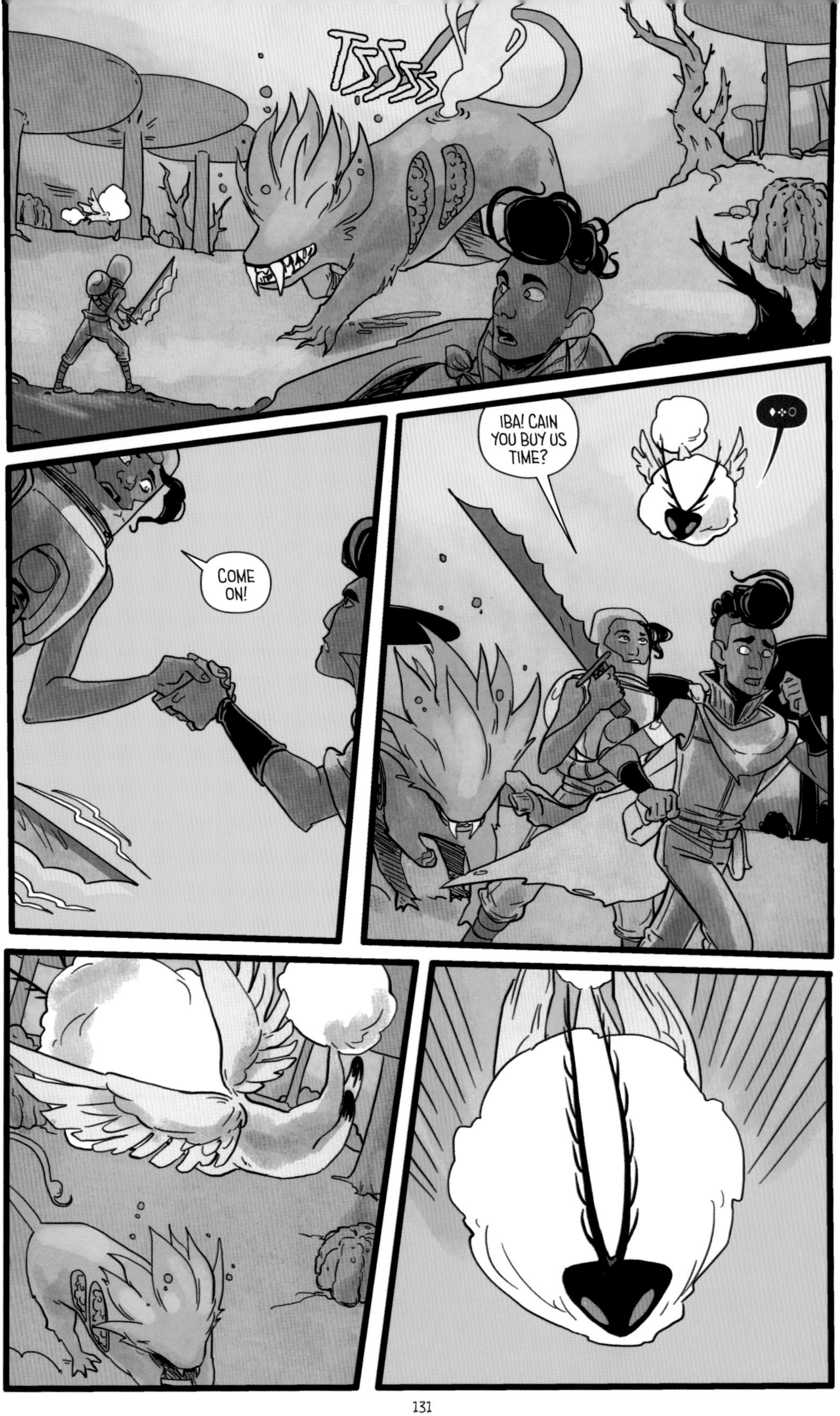
TSSSSS
COME ON!
IBA! CAIN YOU BUY US TIME?

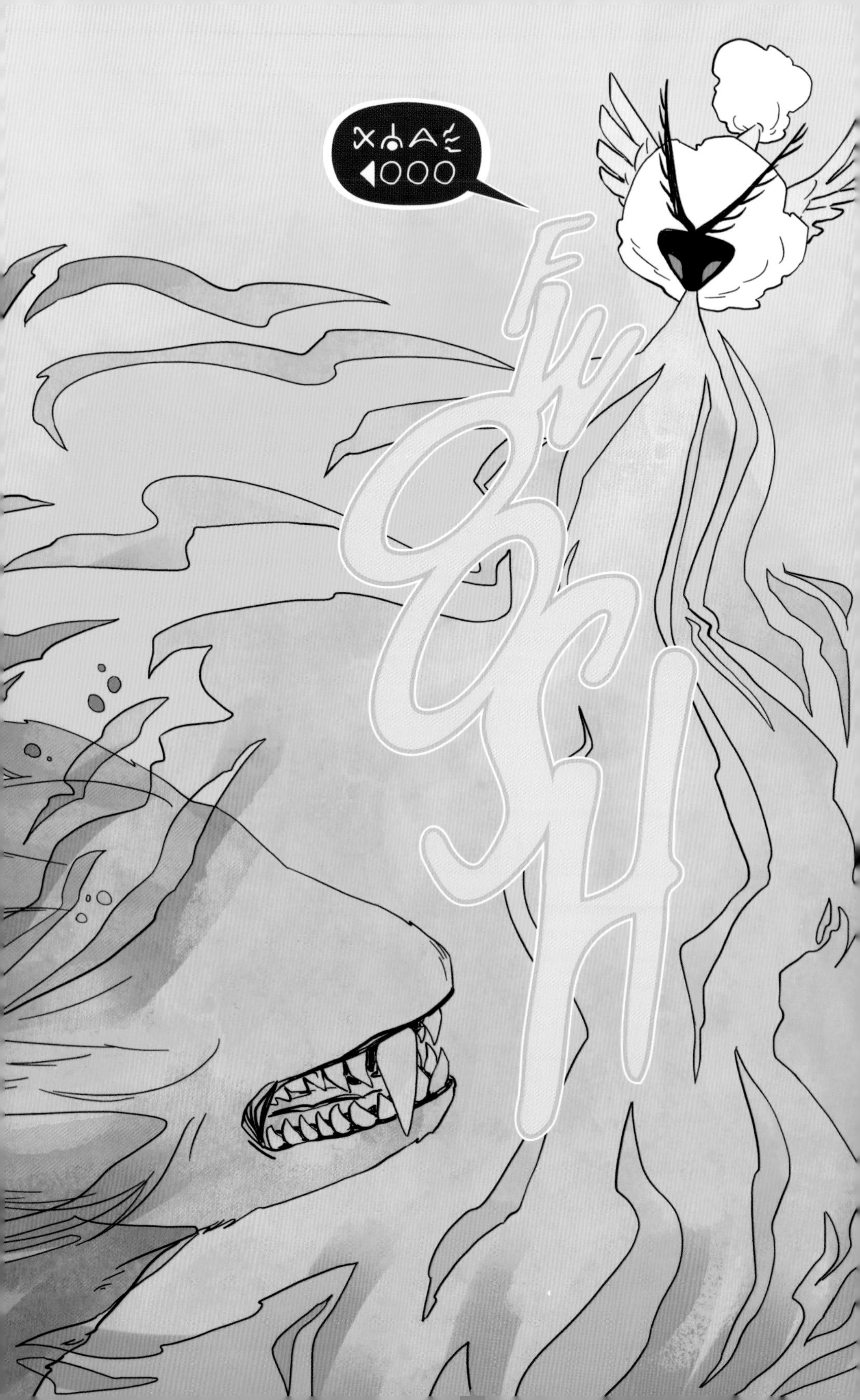
FWOOSH

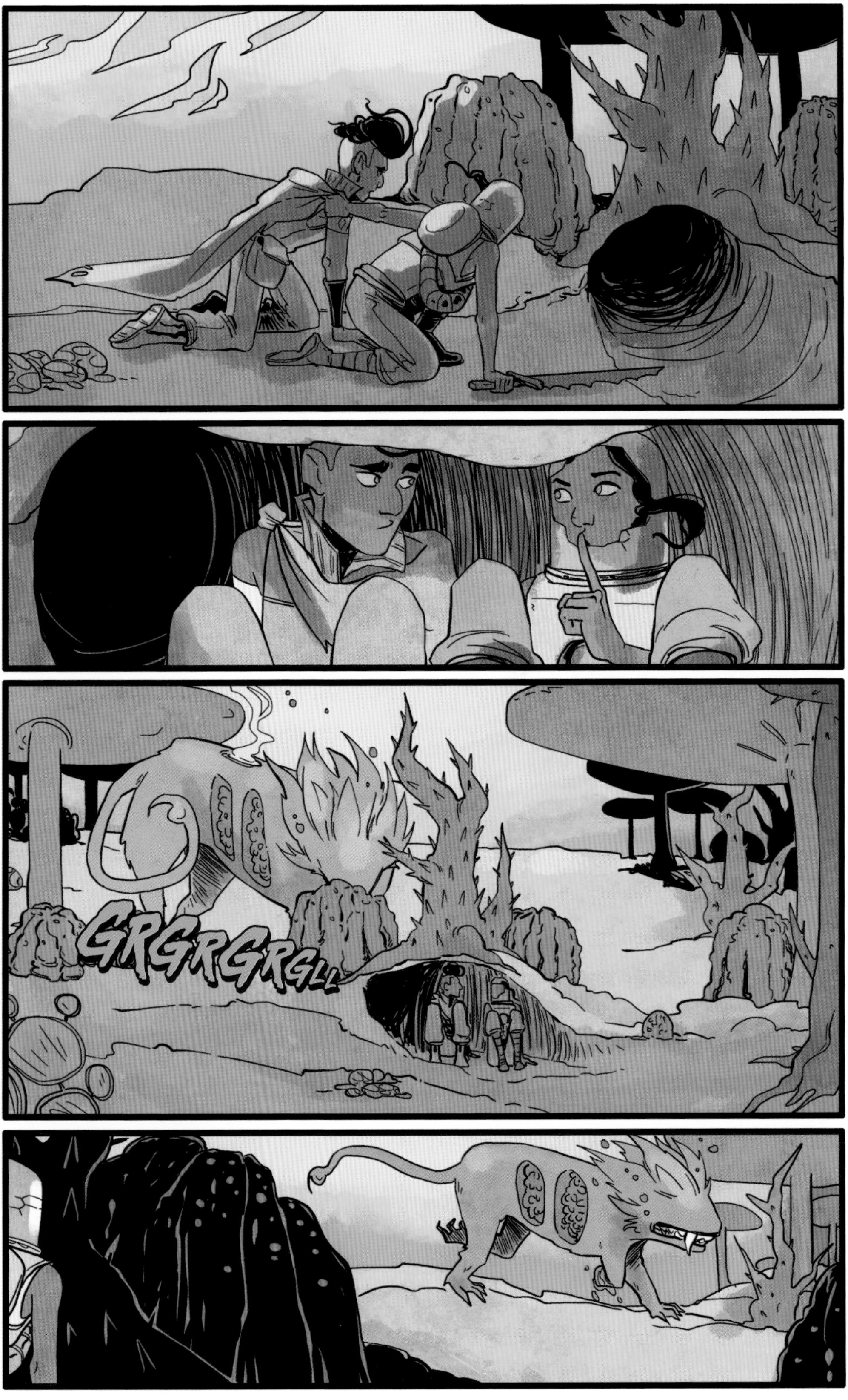
GRGRGRGRGLL

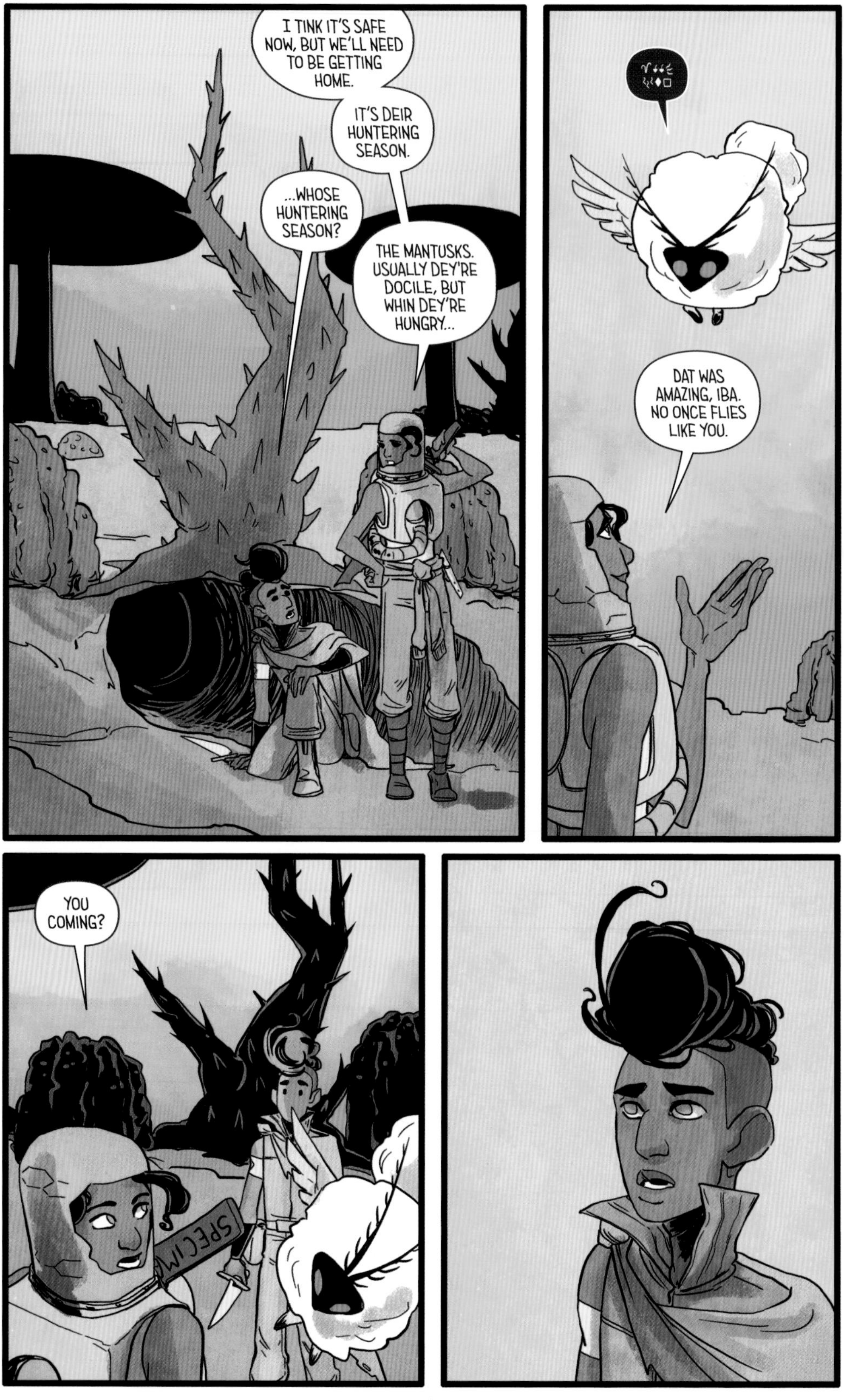
I TINK IT'S SAFE NOW, BUT WE'LL NEED TO BE GETTING HOME.
IT'S DEIR HUNTERING SEASON.
...WHOSE HUNTERING SEASON?
THE MANTUSKS. USUALLY DEY'RE DOCILE, BUT WHIN DEY'RE HUNGRY...
DAT WAS AMAZING, IBA. NO ONCE FLIES LIKE YOU.
YOU COMING?
SPECIM

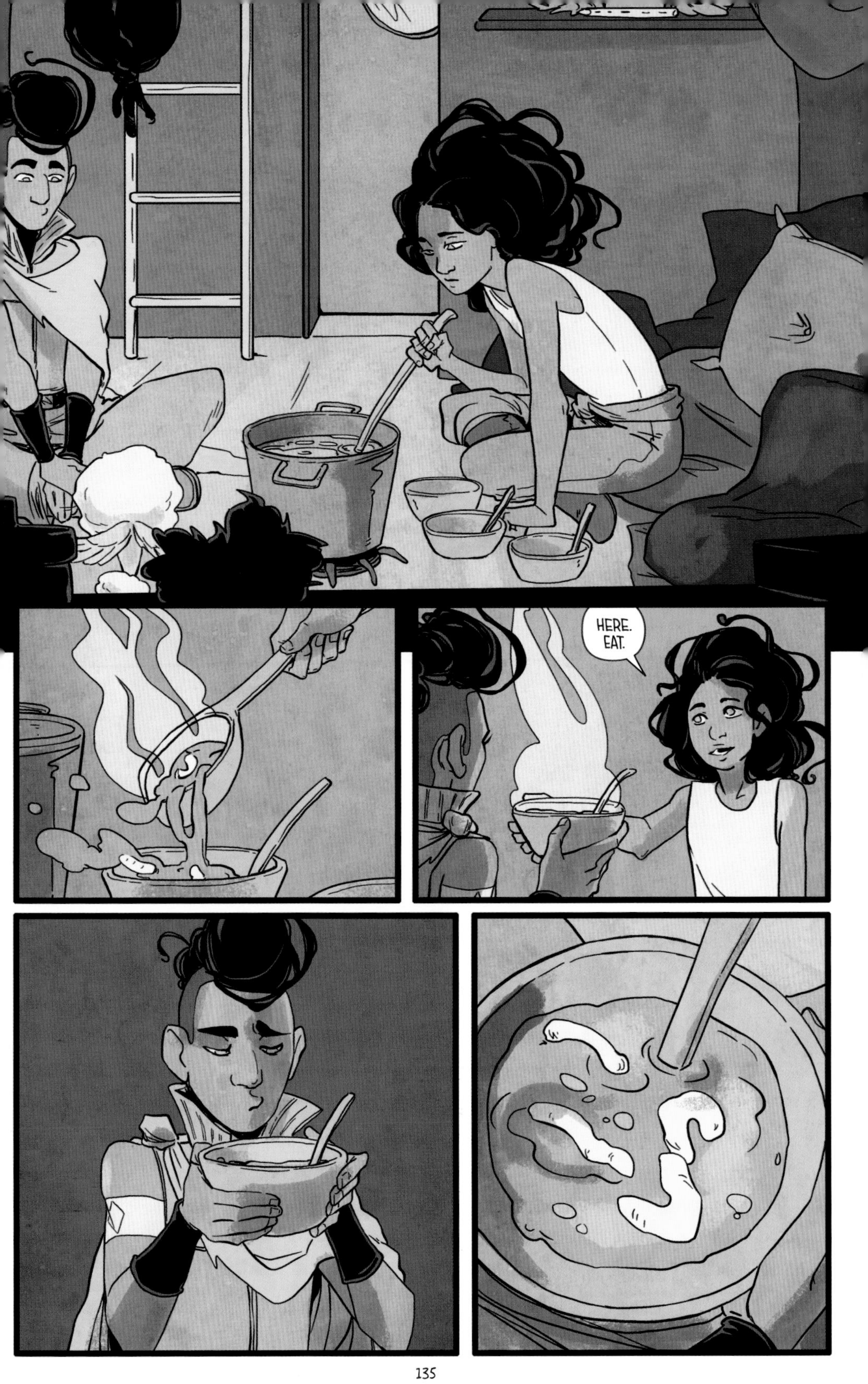
HERE. EAT.

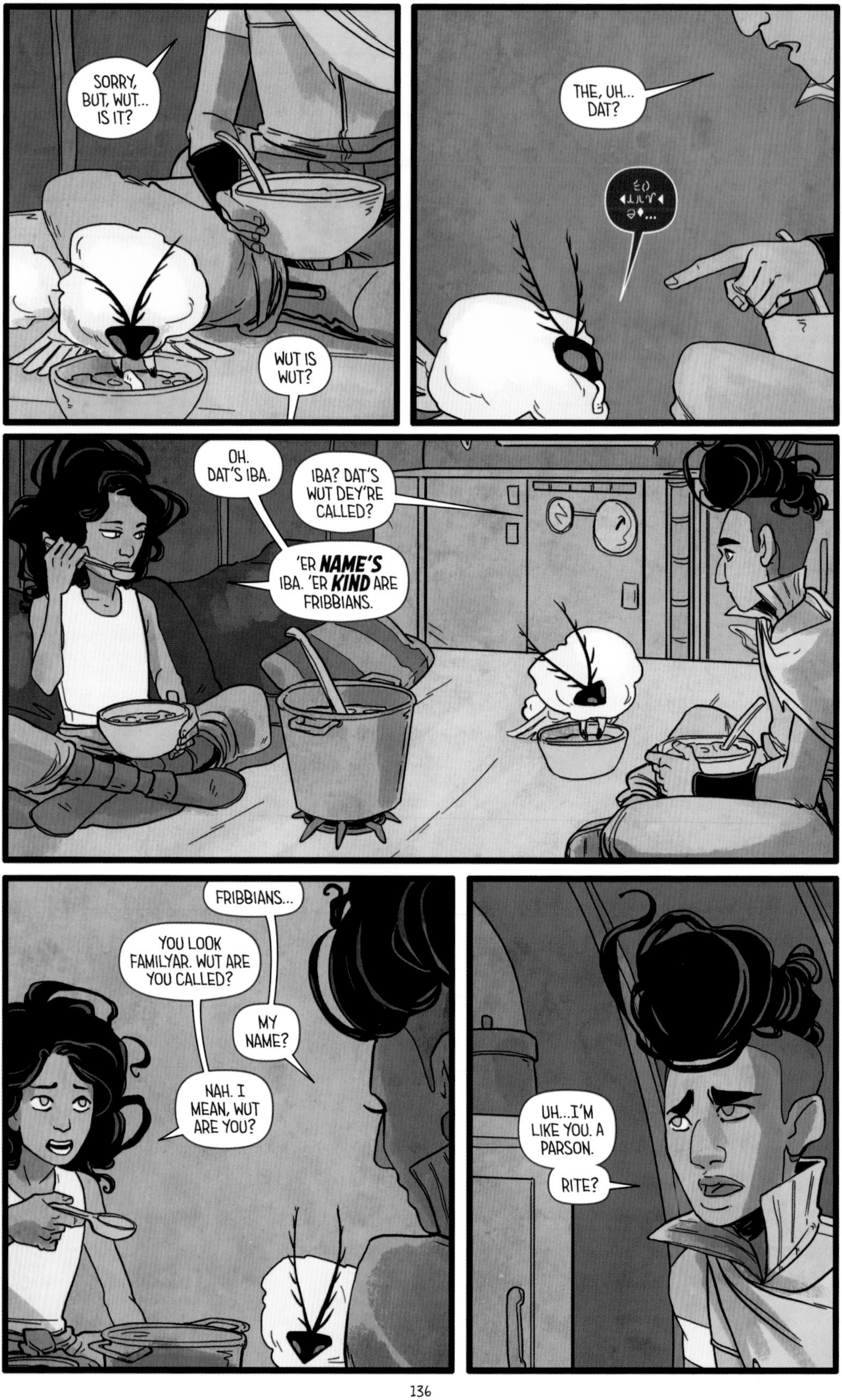

SORRY, BUT, WUT... IS IT?
WUT IS WUT?
THE, UH... DAT?
OH. DAT'S IBA.
IBA? DAT'S WUT DEY'RE CALLED?
'ER **NAME'S** IBA. 'ER **KIND** ARE FRIBBIANS.
FRIBBIANS...
YOU LOOK FAMILYAR. WUT ARE YOU CALLED?
MY NAME?
NAH. I MEAN, WUT ARE YOU?
UH...I'M LIKE YOU. A PARSON.
RITE?

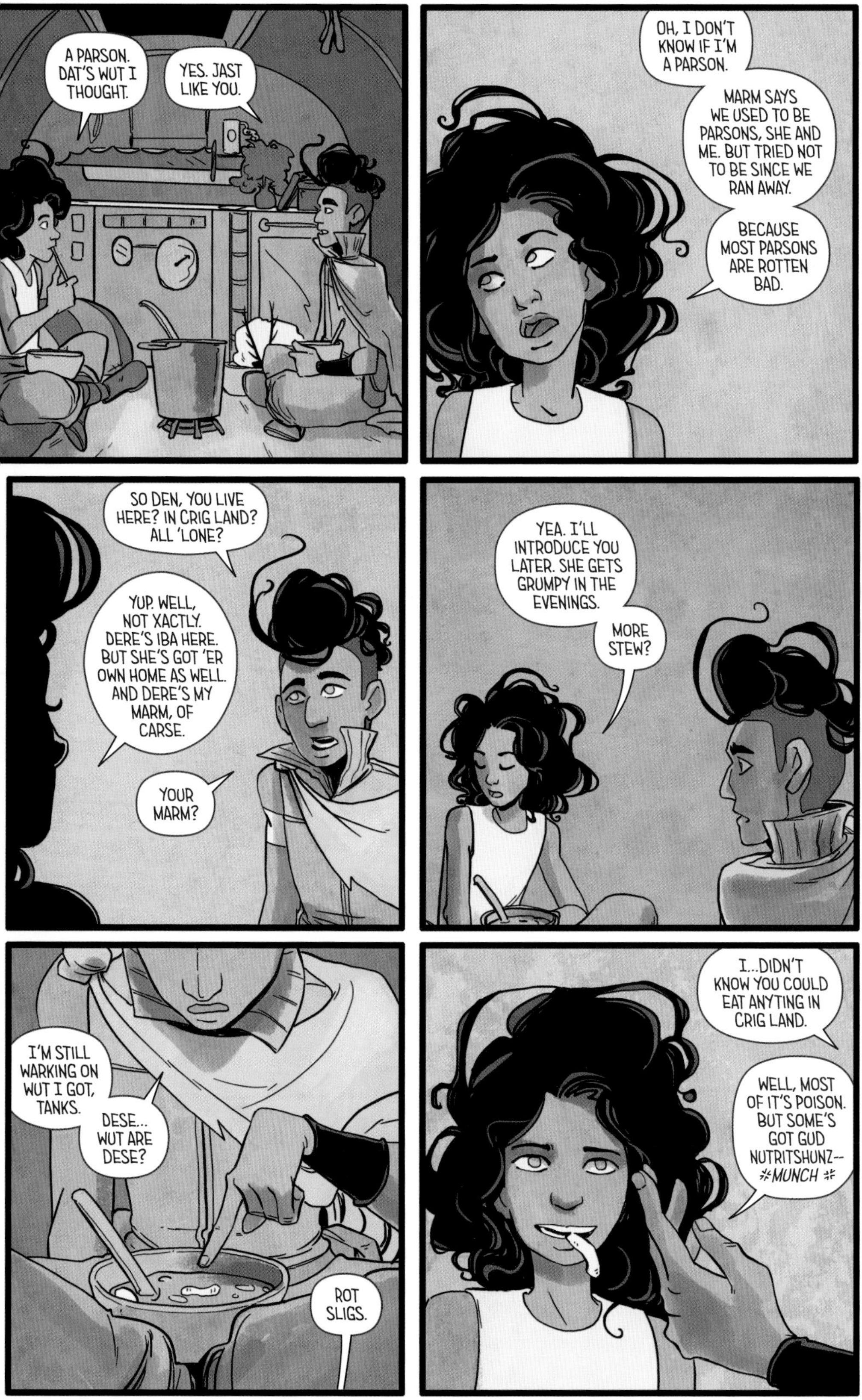
A PARSON. DAT'S WUT I THOUGHT.
YES. JAST LIKE YOU.
OH, I DON'T KNOW IF I'M A PARSON.
MARM SAYS WE USED TO BE PARSONS, SHE AND ME. BUT TRIED NOT TO BE SINCE WE RAN AWAY.
BECAUSE MOST PARSONS ARE ROTTEN BAD.
SO DEN, YOU LIVE HERE? IN CRIG LAND? ALL 'LONE?
YUP. WELL, NOT XACTLY. DERE'S IBA HERE. BUT SHE'S GOT 'ER OWN HOME AS WELL. AND DERE'S MY MARM, OF CARSE.
YOUR MARM?
YEA. I'LL INTRODUCE YOU LATER. SHE GETS GRUMPY IN THE EVENINGS.
MORE STEW?
I'M STILL WARKING ON WUT I GOT, TANKS.
DESE... WUT ARE DESE?
ROT SLIGS.
I...DIDN'T KNOW YOU COULD EAT ANYTING IN CRIG LAND.
WELL, MOST OF IT'S POISON. BUT SOME'S GOT GUD NUTRITSHUNZ--
MUNCH

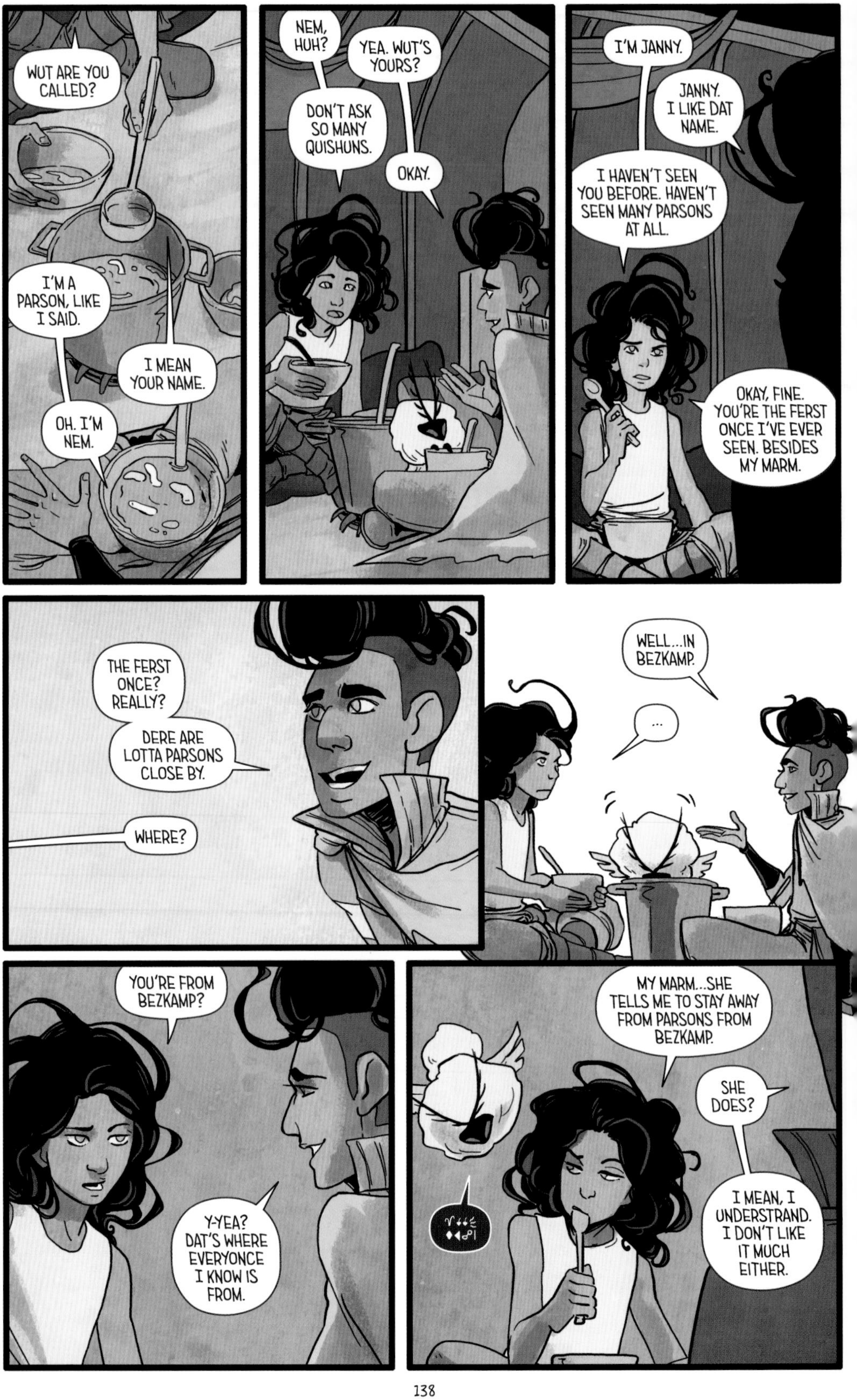
WUT ARE YOU CALLED?
I'M A PARSON, LIKE I SAID.
I MEAN YOUR NAME.
OH. I'M NEM.
NEM, HUH?
YEA. WUT'S YOURS?
DON'T ASK SO MANY QUISHUNS.
OKAY.
I'M JANNY.
JANNY. I LIKE DAT NAME.
I HAVEN'T SEEN YOU BEFORE. HAVEN'T SEEN MANY PARSONS AT ALL.
OKAY, FINE. YOU'RE THE FERST ONCE I'VE EVER SEEN. BESIDES MY MARM.
THE FERST ONCE? REALLY?
DERE ARE LOTTA PARSONS CLOSE BY.
WHERE?
WELL...IN BEZKAMP.
...
YOU'RE FROM BEZKAMP?
Y-YEA? DAT'S WHERE EVERYONCE I KNOW IS FROM.
MY MARM...SHE TELLS ME TO STAY AWAY FROM PARSONS FROM BEZKAMP.
SHE DOES?
I MEAN, I UNDERSTRAND. I DON'T LIKE IT MUCH EITHER.

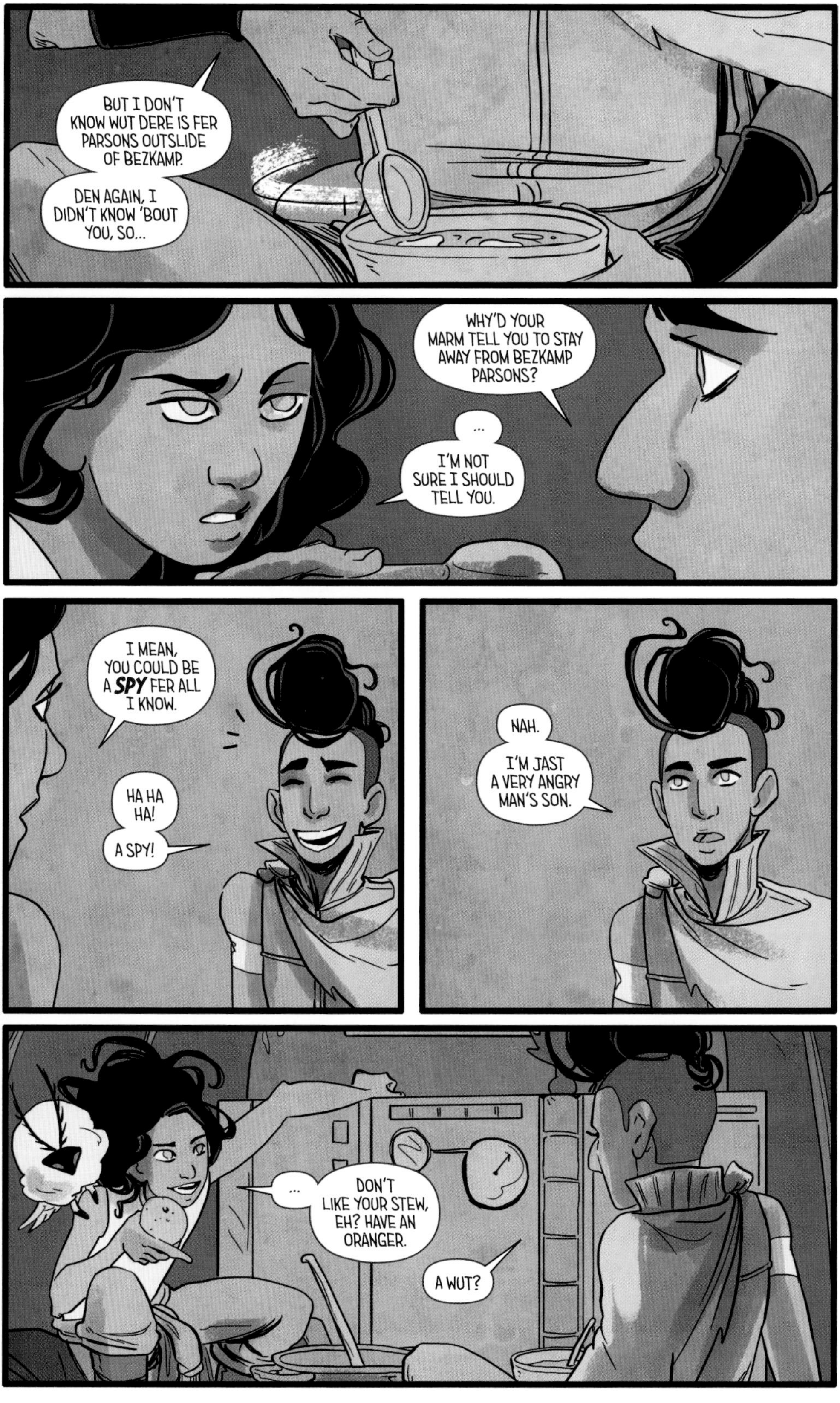
BUT I DON'T KNOW WUT DERE IS FER PARSONS OUTSLIDE OF BEZKAMP.
DEN AGAIN, I DIDN'T KNOW 'BOUT YOU, SO...
WHY'D YOUR MARM TELL YOU TO STAY AWAY FROM BEZKAMP PARSONS?
...
I'M NOT SURE I SHOULD TELL YOU.
I MEAN, YOU COULD BE A SPY FER ALL I KNOW.
HA HA HA!
A SPY!
NAH.
I'M JAST A VERY ANGRY MAN'S SON.
...
DON'T LIKE YOUR STEW, EH? HAVE AN ORANGER.
A WUT?

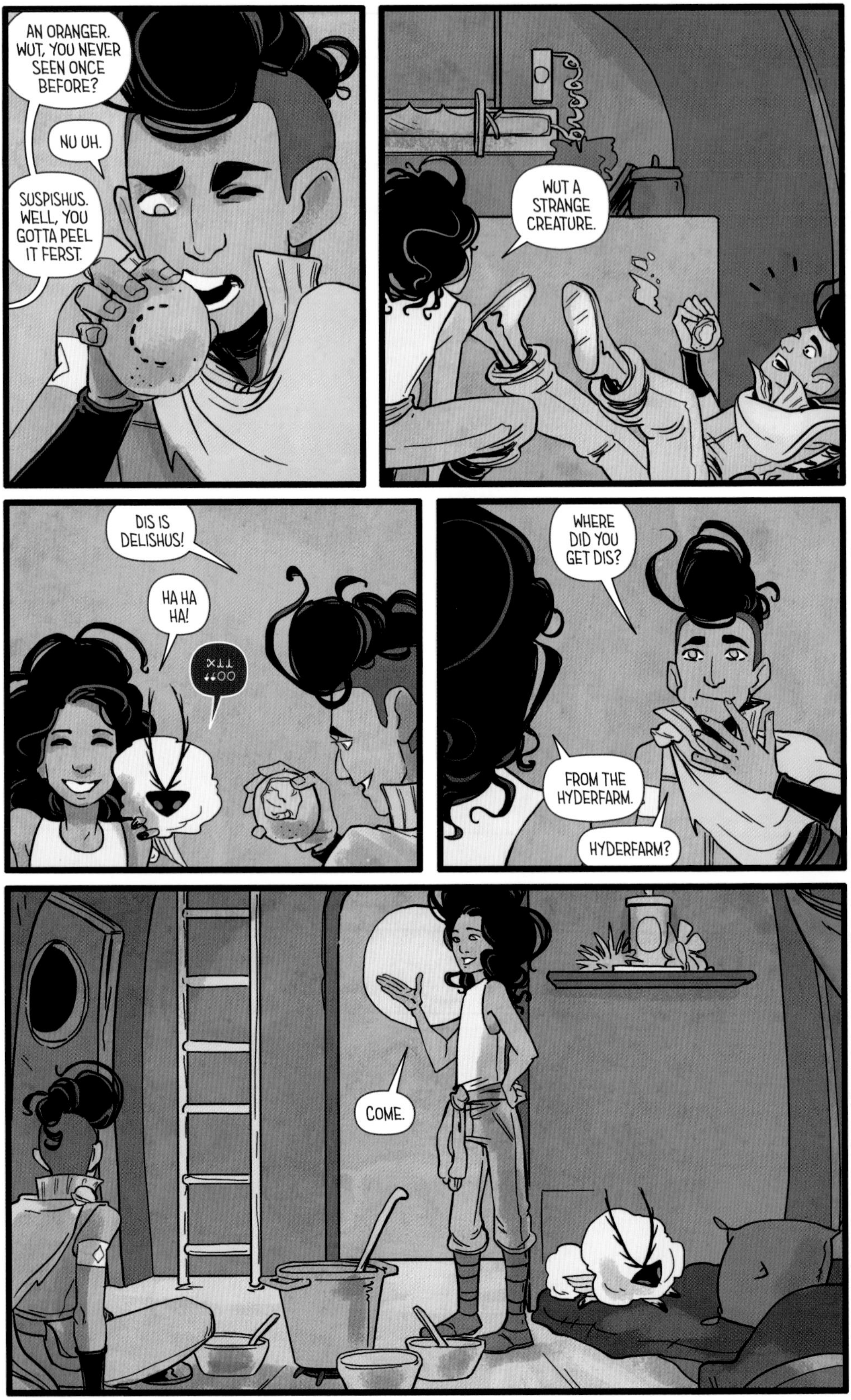
AN ORANGER. WUT, YOU NEVER SEEN ONCE BEFORE?
NU UH.
SUSPISHUS. WELL, YOU GOTTA PEEL IT FERST.
WUT A STRANGE CREATURE.
DIS IS DELISHUS!
HA HA HA!
WHERE DID YOU GET DIS?
FROM THE HYDERFARM.
HYDERFARM?
COME.

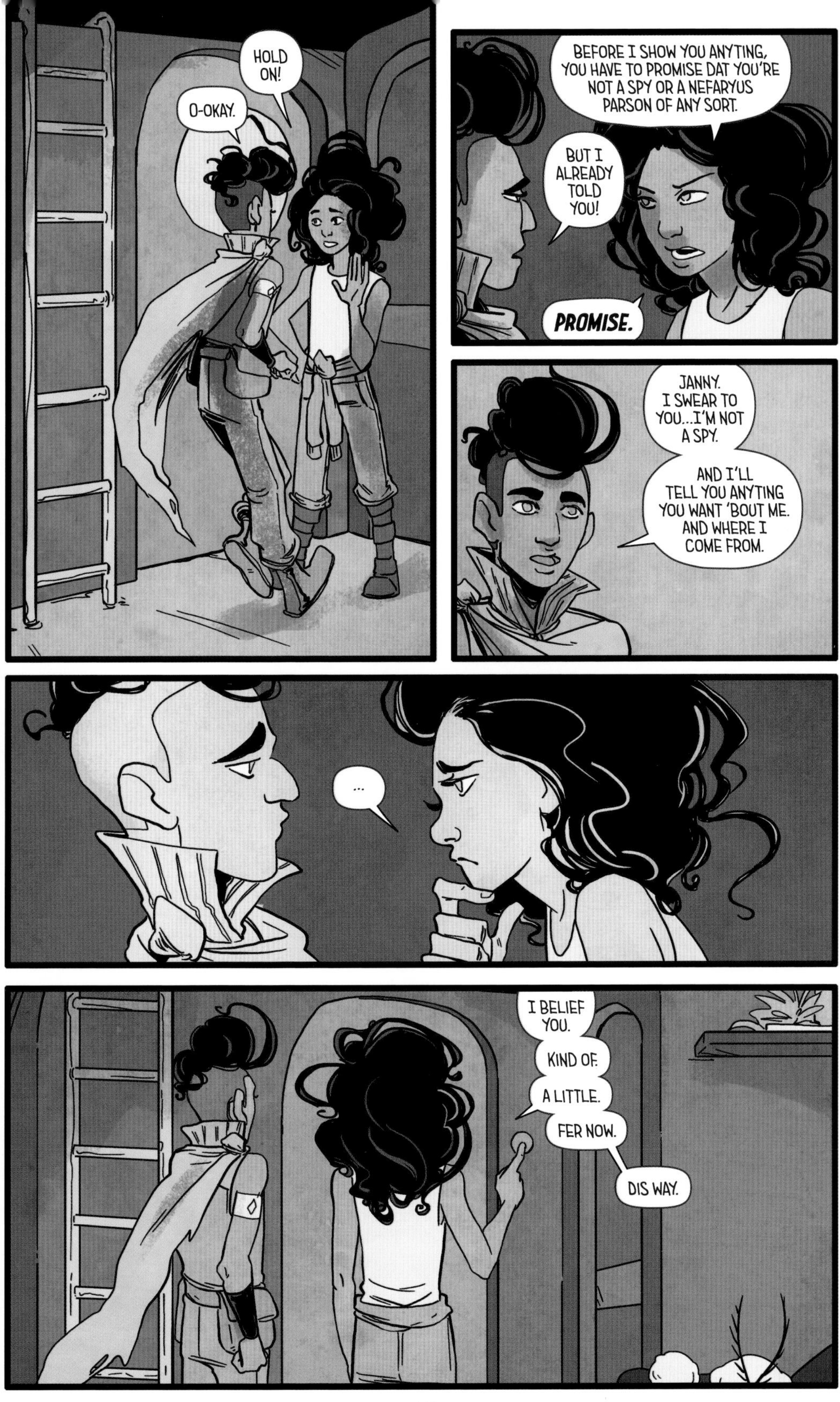
HOLD ON!
O-OKAY.
BEFORE I SHOW YOU ANYTING, YOU HAVE TO PROMISE DAT YOU'RE NOT A SPY OR A NEFARYUS PARSON OF ANY SORT.
BUT I ALREADY TOLD YOU!
PROMISE.
JANNY. I SWEAR TO YOU...I'M NOT A SPY.
AND I'LL TELL YOU ANYTING YOU WANT 'BOUT ME. AND WHERE I COME FROM.
...
I BELIEF YOU.
KIND OF.
A LITTLE.
FER NOW.
DIS WAY.

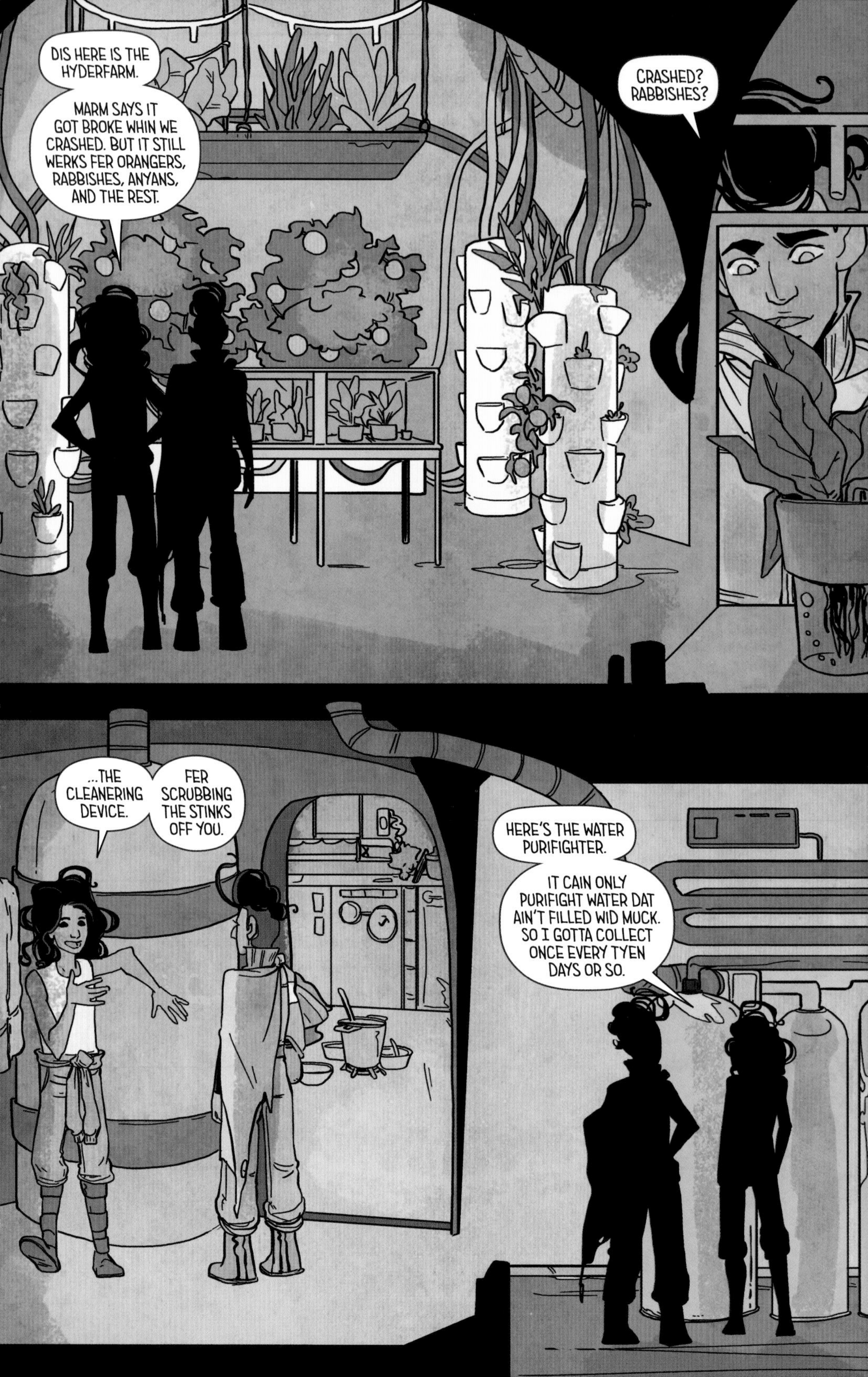
DIS HERE IS THE HYDERFARM.
MARM SAYS IT GOT BROKE WHIN WE CRASHED. BUT IT STILL WERKS FER ORANGERS, RABBISHES, ANYANS, AND THE REST.
CRASHED? RABBISHES?
...THE CLEANERING DEVICE.
FER SCRUBBING THE STINKS OFF YOU.
HERE'S THE WATER PURIFIGHTER.
IT CAIN ONLY PURIFIGHT WATER DAT AIN'T FILLED WID MUCK. SO I GOTTA COLLECT ONCE EVERY TYEN DAYS OR SO.

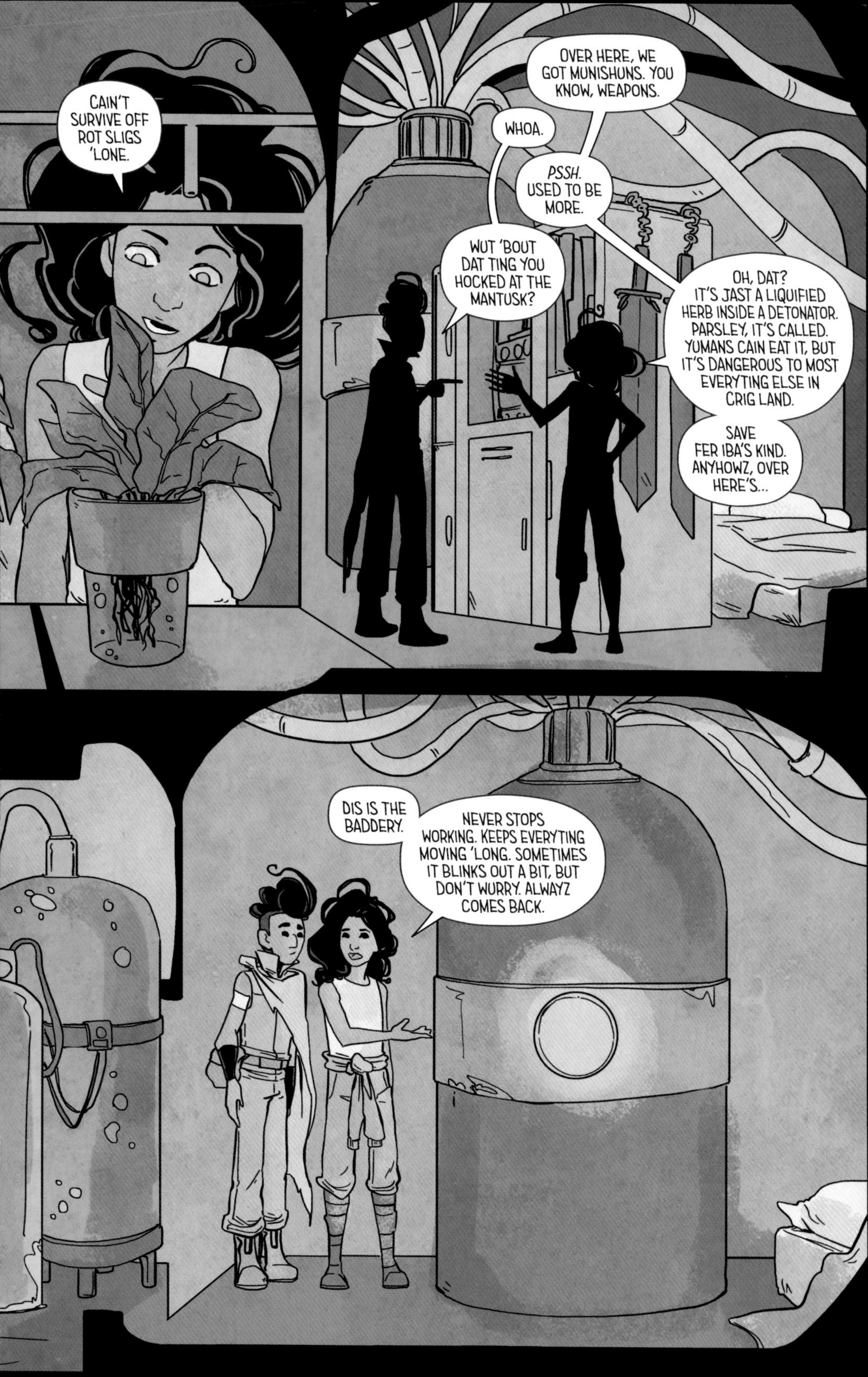
CAIN'T SURVIVE OFF ROT SLIGS 'LONE.
OVER HERE, WE GOT MUNISHUNS. YOU KNOW, WEAPONS.
WHOA.
PSSH. USED TO BE MORE.
WUT 'BOUT DAT TING YOU HOCKED AT THE MANTUSK?
OH, DAT? IT'S JAST A LIQUIFIED HERB INSIDE A DETONATOR. PARSLEY, IT'S CALLED. YUMANS CAIN EAT IT, BUT IT'S DANGEROUS TO MOST EVERYTING ELSE IN CRIG LAND.
SAVE FER IBA'S KIND. ANYHOWZ, OVER HERE'S...
DIS IS THE BADDERY.
NEVER STOPS WORKING. KEEPS EVERYTING MOVING 'LONG. SOMETIMES IT BLINKS OUT A BIT, BUT DON'T WURRY. ALWAYZ COMES BACK.

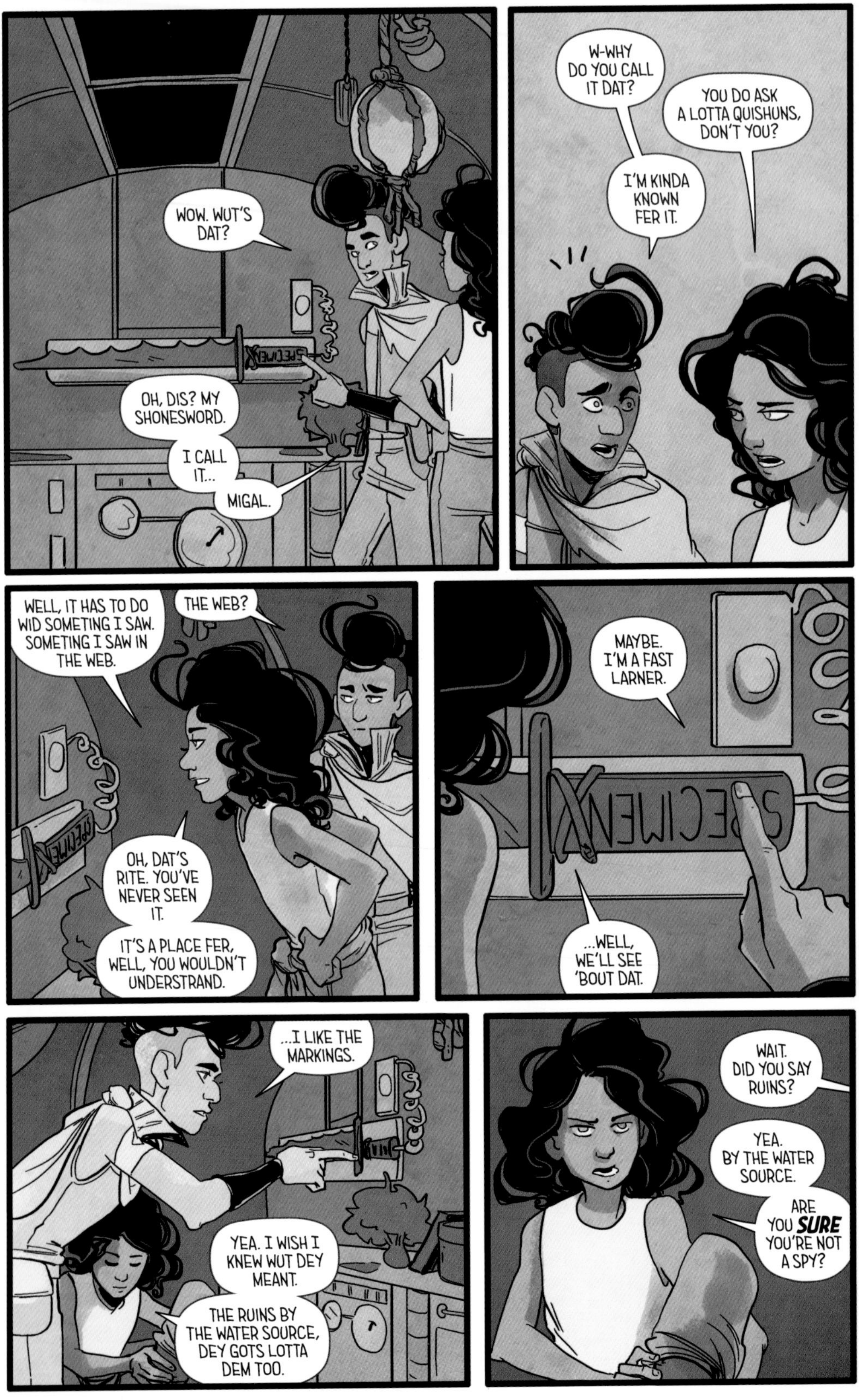
WOW. WUT'S DAT?
OH, DIS? MY SHONESWORD.
I CALL IT...
MIGAL.
SPECIMEN X
W-WHY DO YOU CALL IT DAT?
I'M KINDA KNOWN FER IT.
YOU DO ASK A LOTTA QUISHUNS, DON'T YOU?
WELL, IT HAS TO DO WID SOMETING I SAW. SOMETING I SAW IN THE WEB.
THE WEB?
OH, DAT'S RITE. YOU'VE NEVER SEEN IT.
IT'S A PLACE FER, WELL, YOU WOULDN'T UNDERSTRAND.
MAYBE. I'M A FAST LARNER.
...WELL, WE'LL SEE 'BOUT DAT.
...I LIKE THE MARKINGS.
YEA. I WISH I KNEW WUT DEY MEANT.
THE RUINS BY THE WATER SOURCE, DEY GOTS LOTTA DEM TOO.
WAIT. DID YOU SAY RUINS?
YEA. BY THE WATER SOURCE.
ARE YOU **SURE** YOU'RE NOT A SPY?

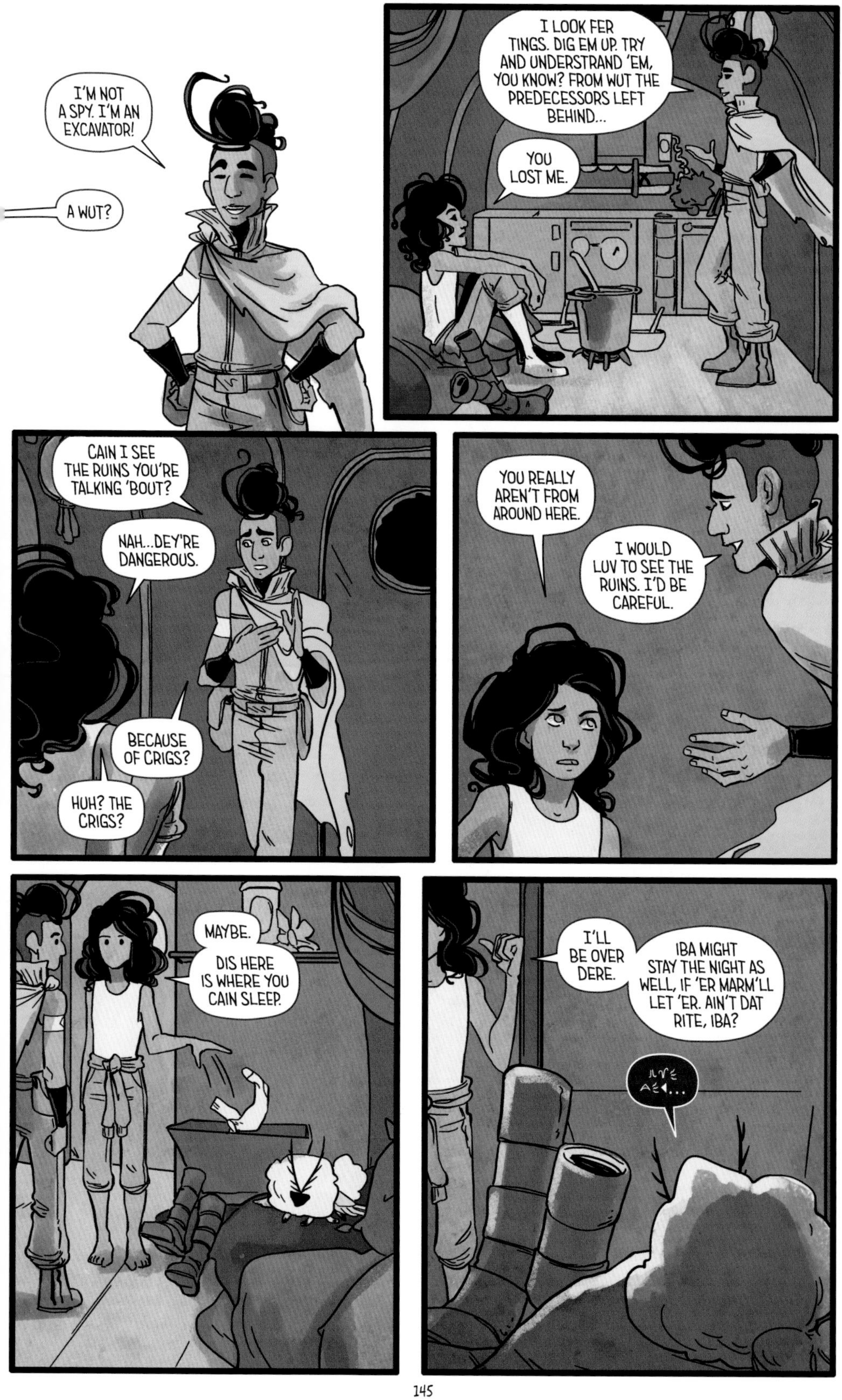
I'M NOT A SPY. I'M AN EXCAVATOR!
A WUT?
I LOOK FER TINGS. DIG EM UP. TRY AND UNDERSTRAND 'EM, YOU KNOW? FROM WUT THE PREDECESSORS LEFT BEHIND...
YOU LOST ME.
CAIN I SEE THE RUINS YOU'RE TALKING 'BOUT?
NAH...DEY'RE DANGEROUS.
BECAUSE OF CRIGS?
HUH? THE CRIGS?
YOU REALLY AREN'T FROM AROUND HERE.
I WOULD LUV TO SEE THE RUINS. I'D BE CAREFUL.
MAYBE.
DIS HERE IS WHERE YOU CAIN SLEEP.
I'LL BE OVER DERE.
IBA MIGHT STAY THE NIGHT AS WELL, IF 'ER MARM'LL LET 'ER. AIN'T DAT RITE, IBA?

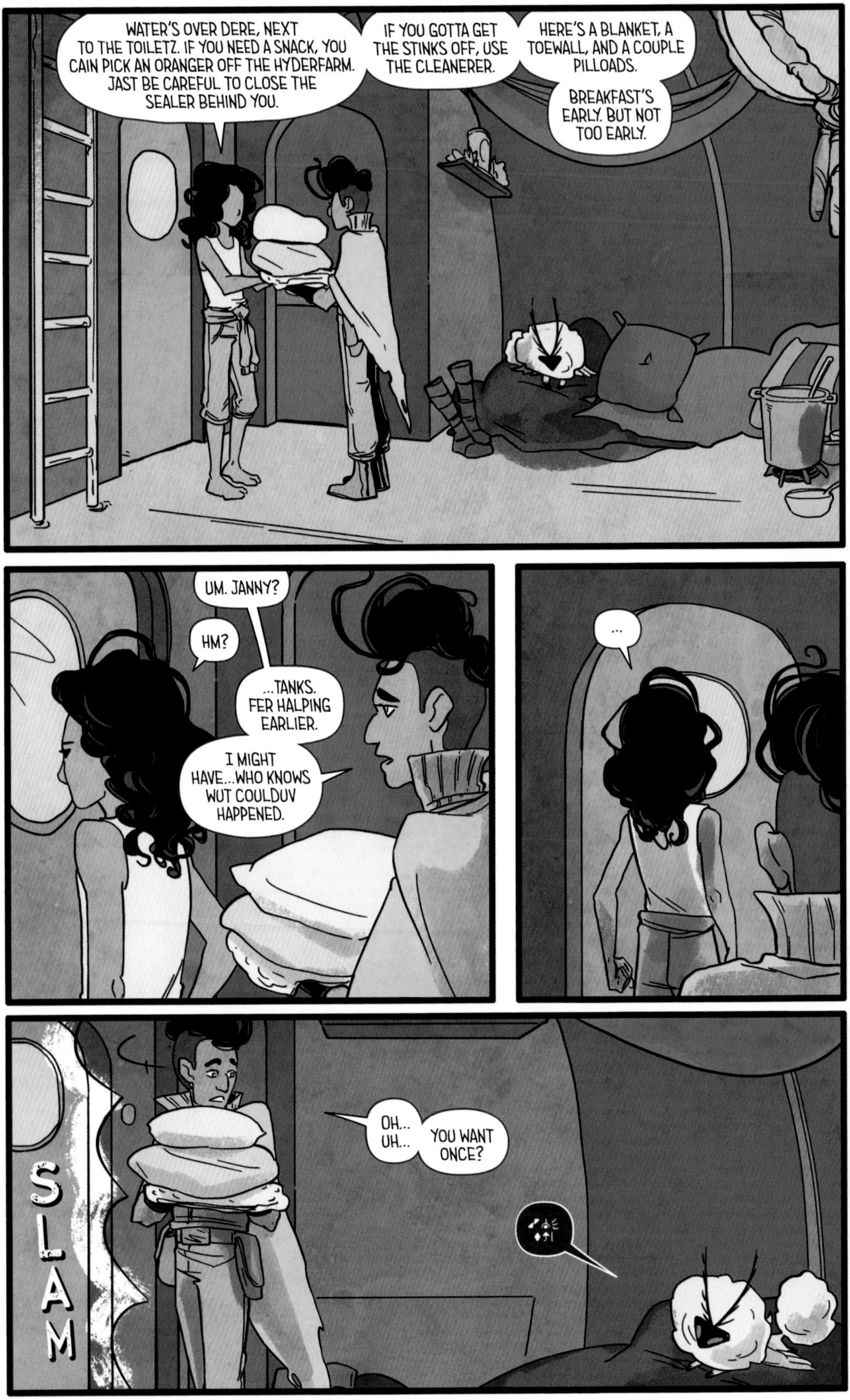
WATER'S OVER DERE, NEXT TO THE TOILETZ. IF YOU NEED A SNACK, YOU CAIN PICK AN ORANGER OFF THE HYDERFARM. JAST BE CAREFUL TO CLOSE THE SEALER BEHIND YOU.
IF YOU GOTTA GET THE STINKS OFF, USE THE CLEANERER.
HERE'S A BLANKET, A TOEWALL, AND A COUPLE PILLOADS.
BREAKFAST'S EARLY. BUT NOT TOO EARLY.
UM. JANNY?
HM?
...TANKS. FER HALPING EARLIER.
I MIGHT HAVE...WHO KNOWS WUT COULDUV HAPPENED.
...
SLAM
OH...
UH...
YOU WANT ONCE?

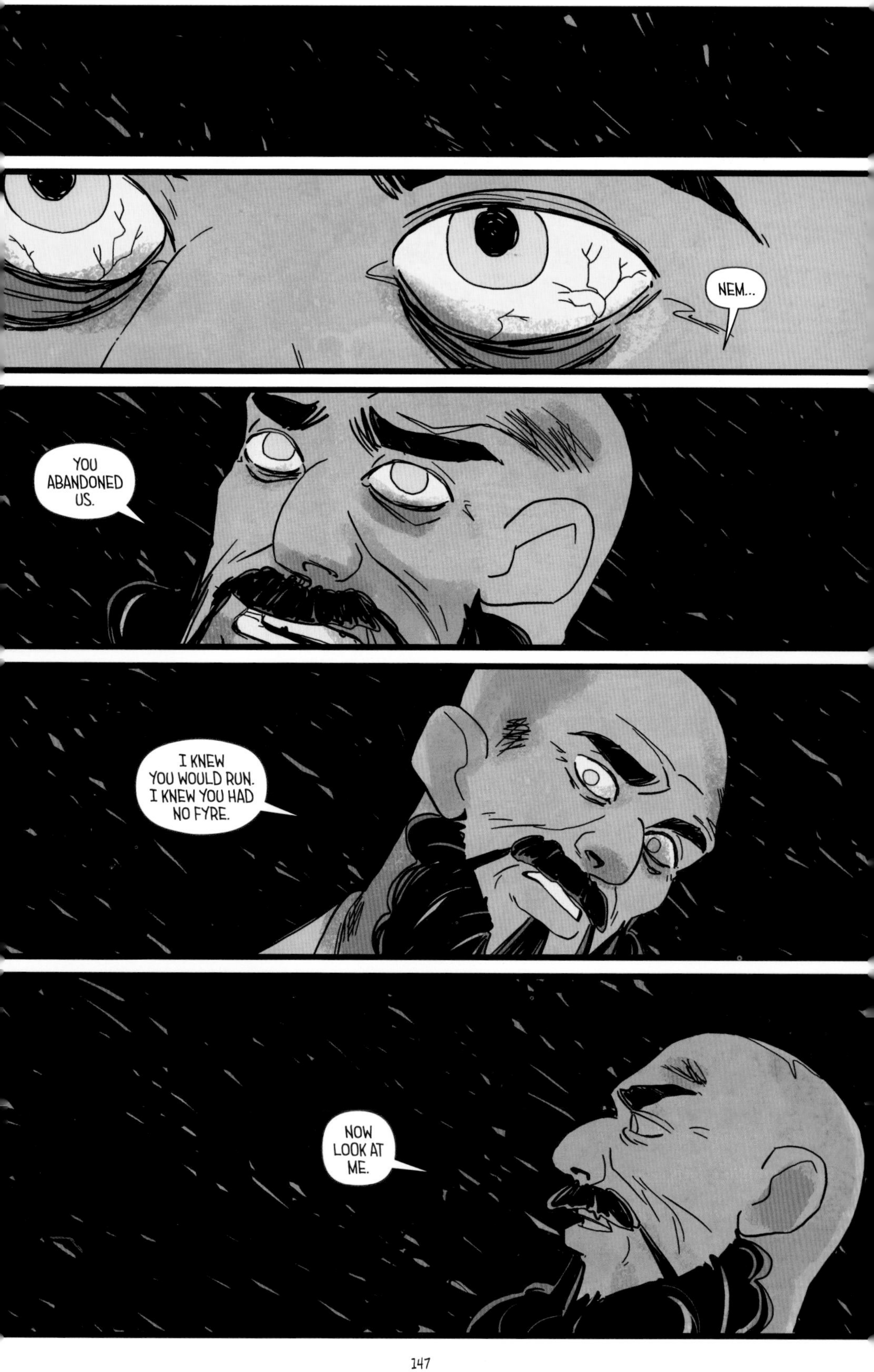
NEM...
YOU ABANDONED US.
I KNEW YOU WOULD RUN. I KNEW YOU HAD NO FYRE.
NOW LOOK AT ME.

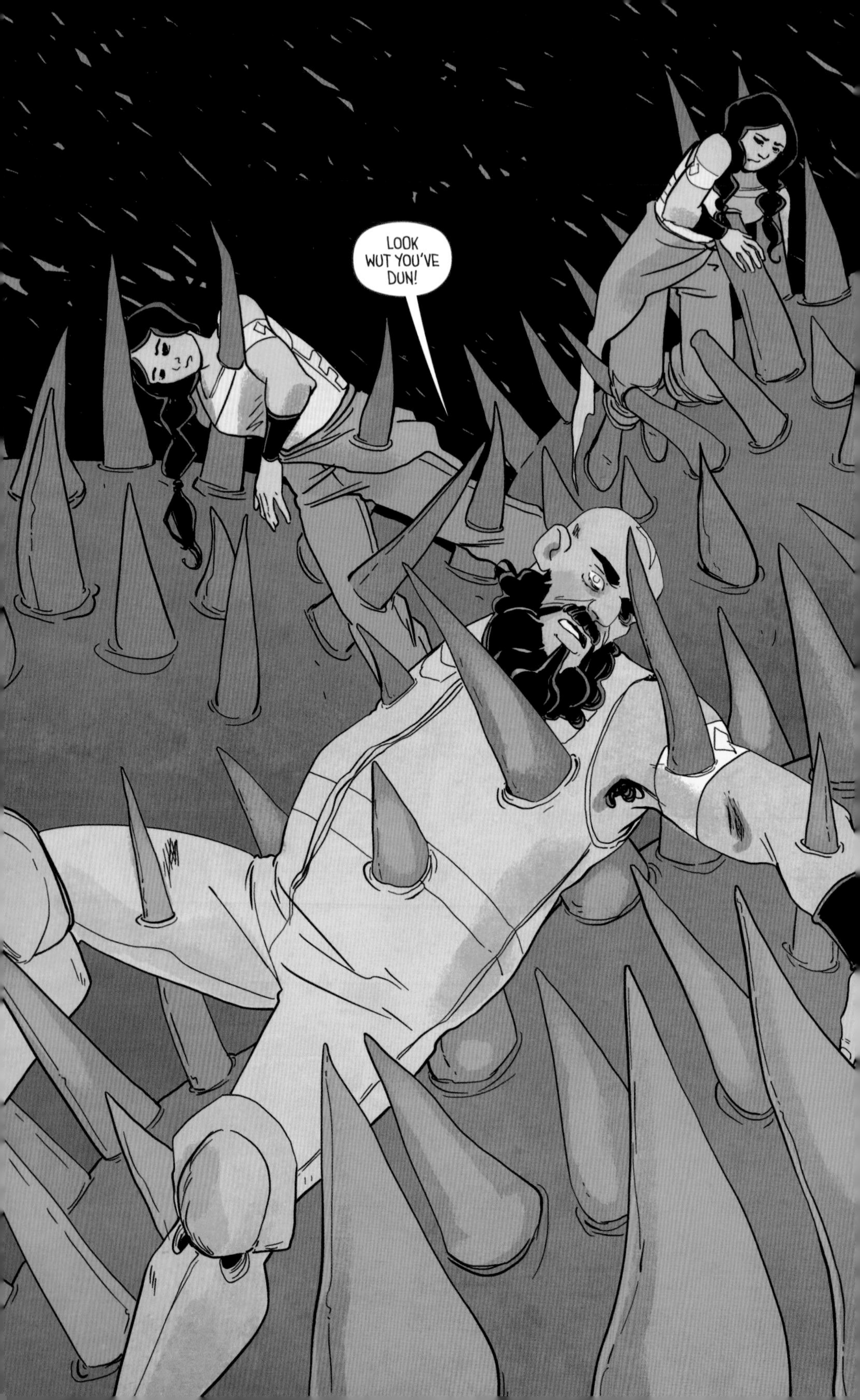
LOOK WUT YOU'VE DUN!

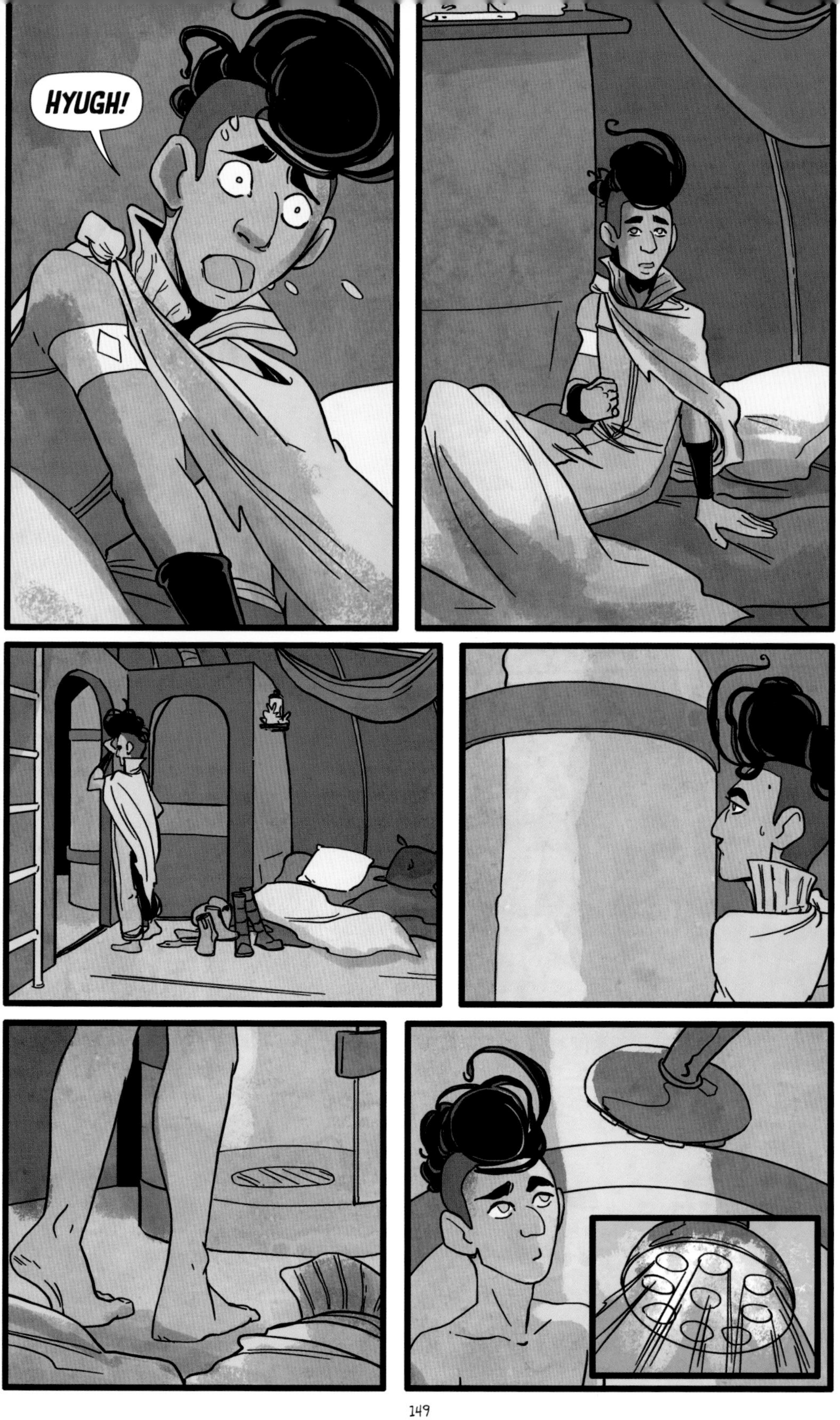
HYUGH!

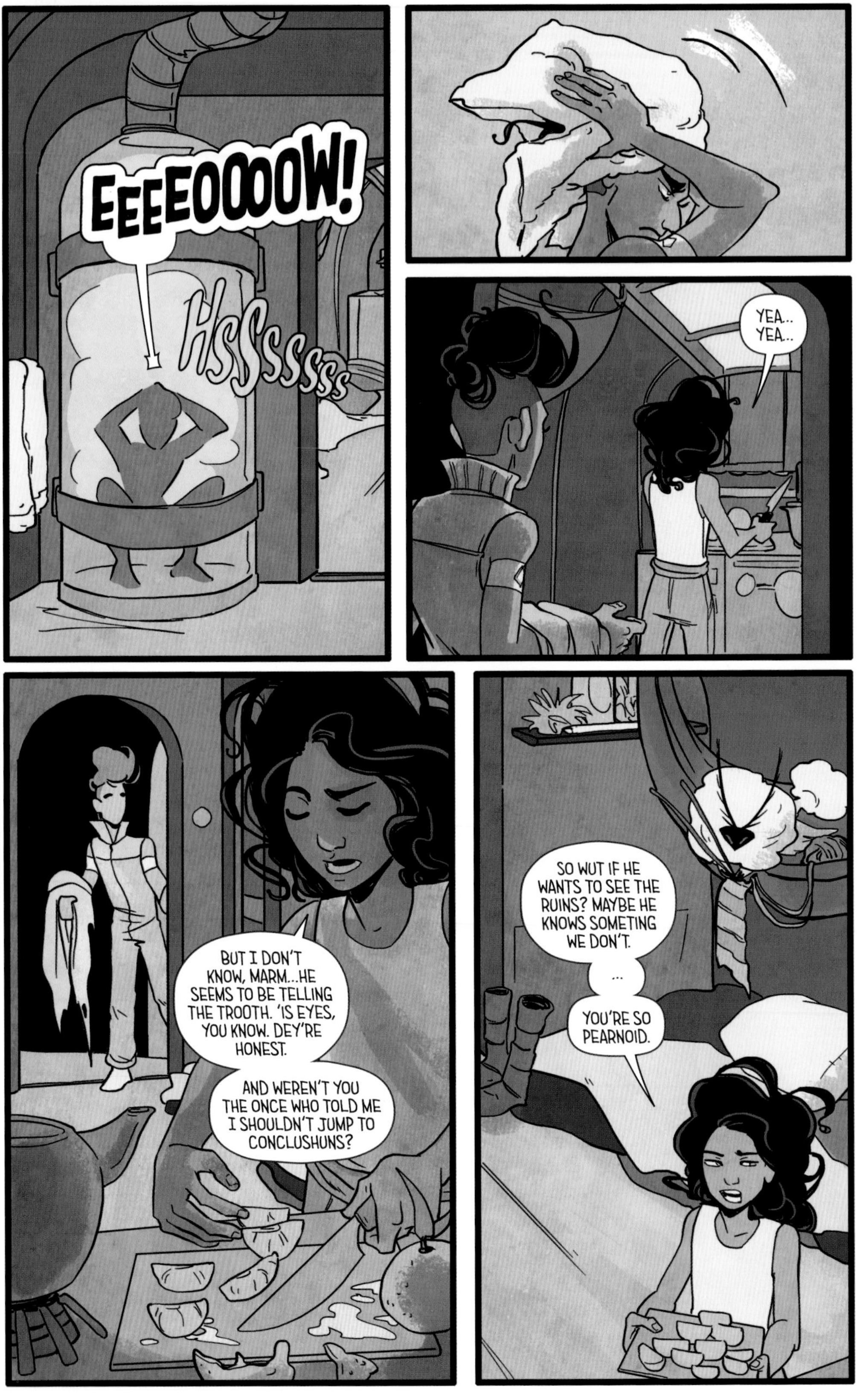
EEEEOOOOW!
HSSSSSSS
YEA...
YEA...
BUT I DON'T KNOW, MARM...HE SEEMS TO BE TELLING THE TROOTH. 'IS EYES, YOU KNOW. DEY'RE HONEST.
AND WEREN'T YOU THE ONCE WHO TOLD ME I SHOULDN'T JUMP TO CONCLUSHUNS?
SO WUT IF HE WANTS TO SEE THE RUINS? MAYBE HE KNOWS SOMETING WE DON'T.
...
YOU'RE SO PEARNOID.

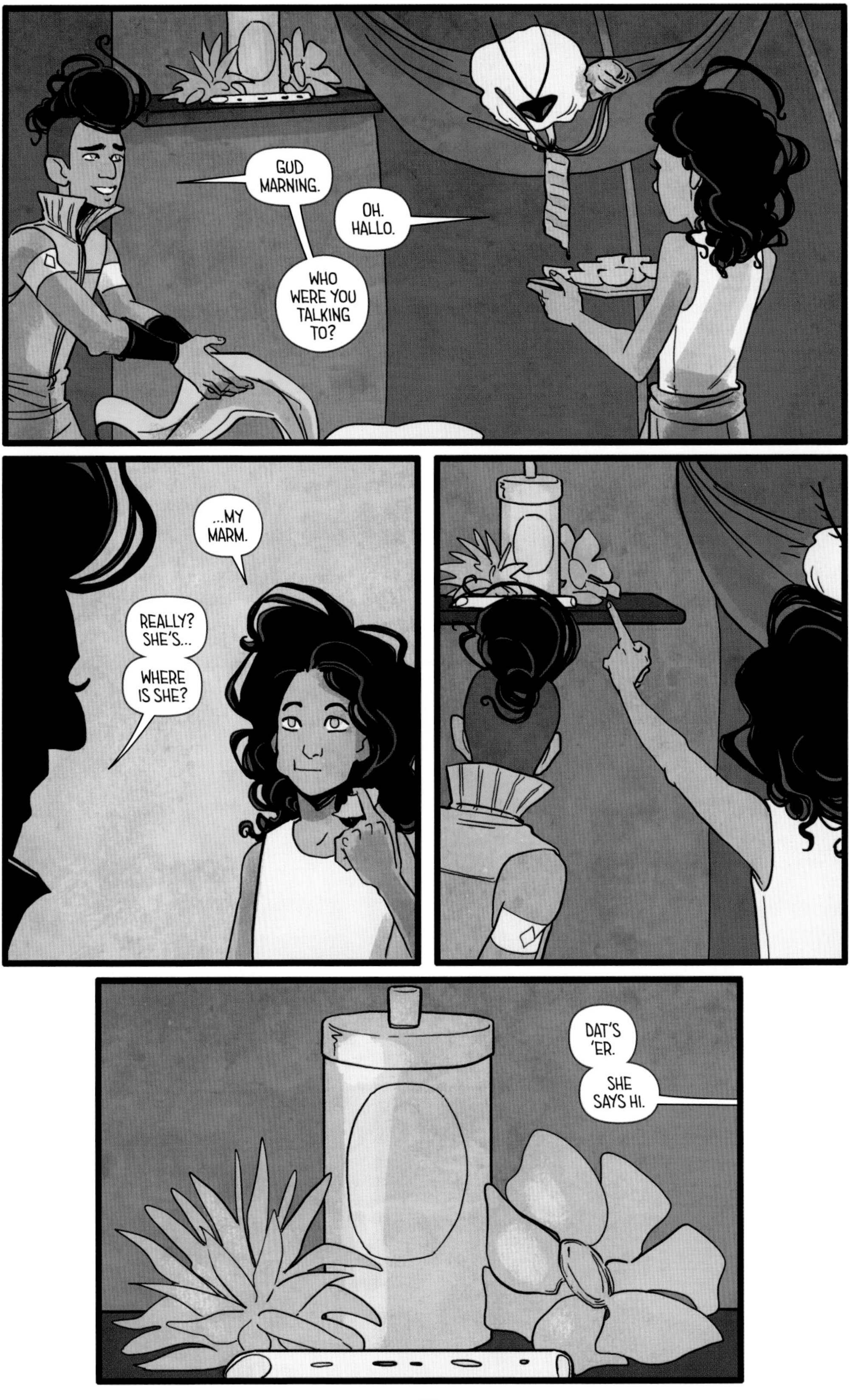
GUD MARNING.
OH. HALLO.
WHO WERE YOU TALKING TO?
...MY MARM.
REALLY? SHE'S...
WHERE IS SHE?
DAT'S 'ER.
SHE SAYS HI.

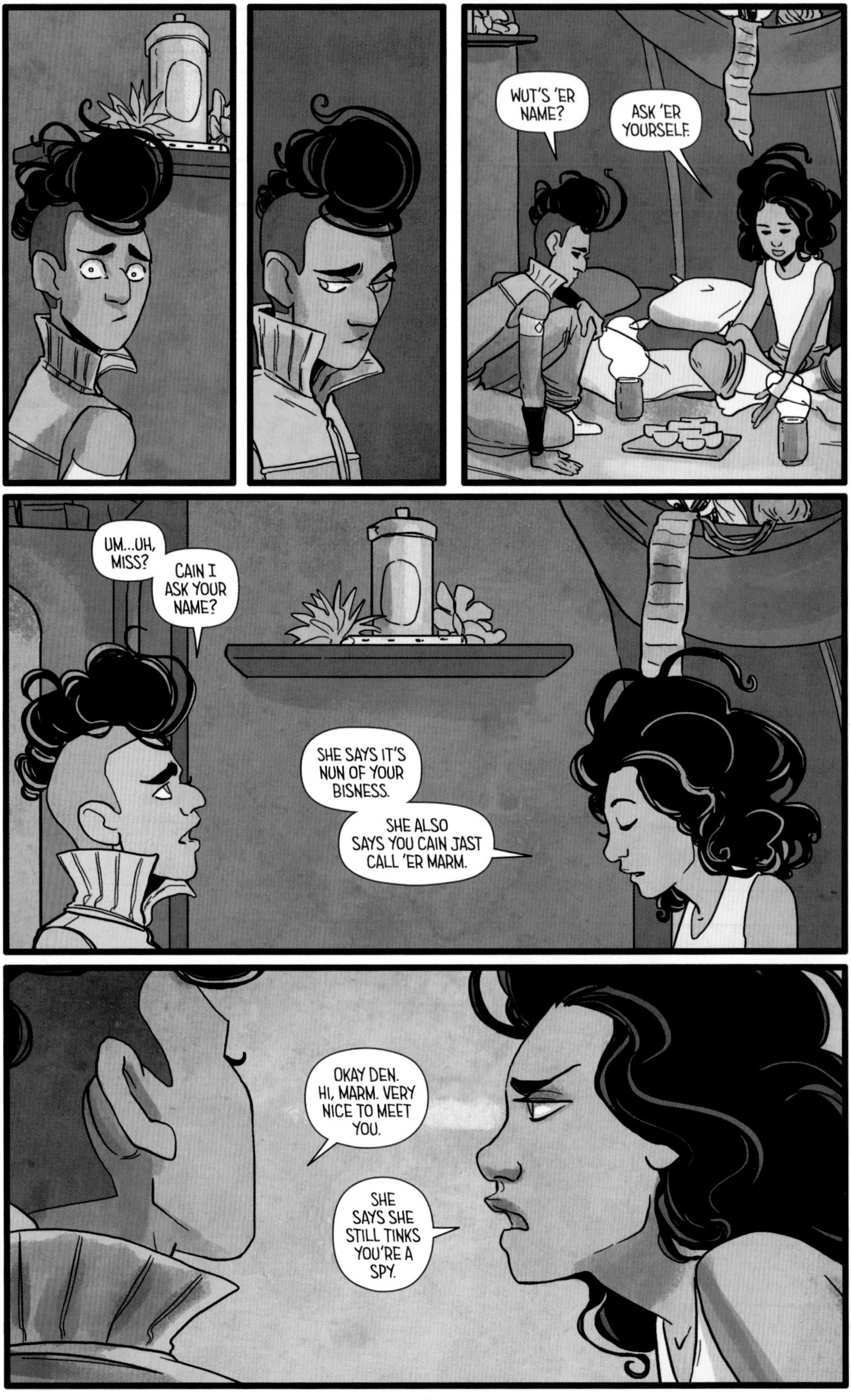
WUT'S 'ER NAME?
ASK 'ER YOURSELF.
UM...UH, MISS?
CAIN I ASK YOUR NAME?
SHE SAYS IT'S NUN OF YOUR BISNESS.
SHE ALSO SAYS YOU CAIN JAST CALL 'ER MARM.
OKAY DEN. HI, MARM. VERY NICE TO MEET YOU.
SHE SAYS SHE STILL TINKS YOU'RE A SPY.

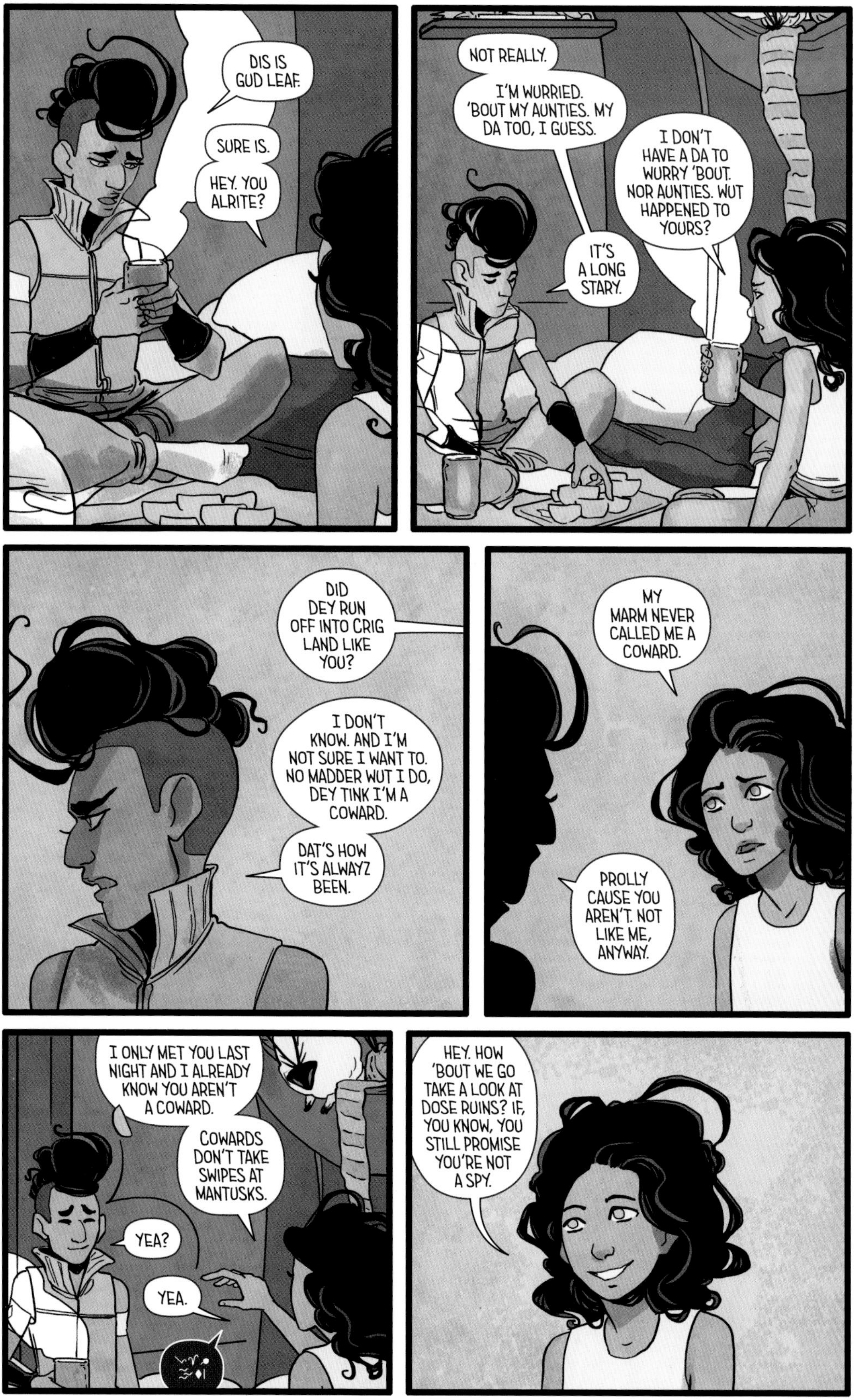
DIS IS GUD LEAF.
SURE IS.
HEY. YOU ALRITE?
NOT REALLY.
I'M WURRIED. 'BOUT MY AUNTIES. MY DA TOO, I GUESS.
I DON'T HAVE A DA TO WURRY 'BOUT. NOR AUNTIES. WUT HAPPENED TO YOURS?
IT'S A LONG STARY.
DID DEY RUN OFF INTO CRIG LAND LIKE YOU?
I DON'T KNOW. AND I'M NOT SURE I WANT TO. NO MADDER WUT I DO, DEY TINK I'M A COWARD.
DAT'S HOW IT'S ALWAYZ BEEN.
MY MARM NEVER CALLED ME A COWARD.
PROLLY CAUSE YOU AREN'T. NOT LIKE ME, ANYWAY.
I ONLY MET YOU LAST NIGHT AND I ALREADY KNOW YOU AREN'T A COWARD.
COWARDS DON'T TAKE SWIPES AT MANTUSKS.
YEA?
YEA.
HEY. HOW 'BOUT WE GO TAKE A LOOK AT DOSE RUINS? IF, YOU KNOW, YOU STILL PROMISE YOU'RE NOT A SPY.

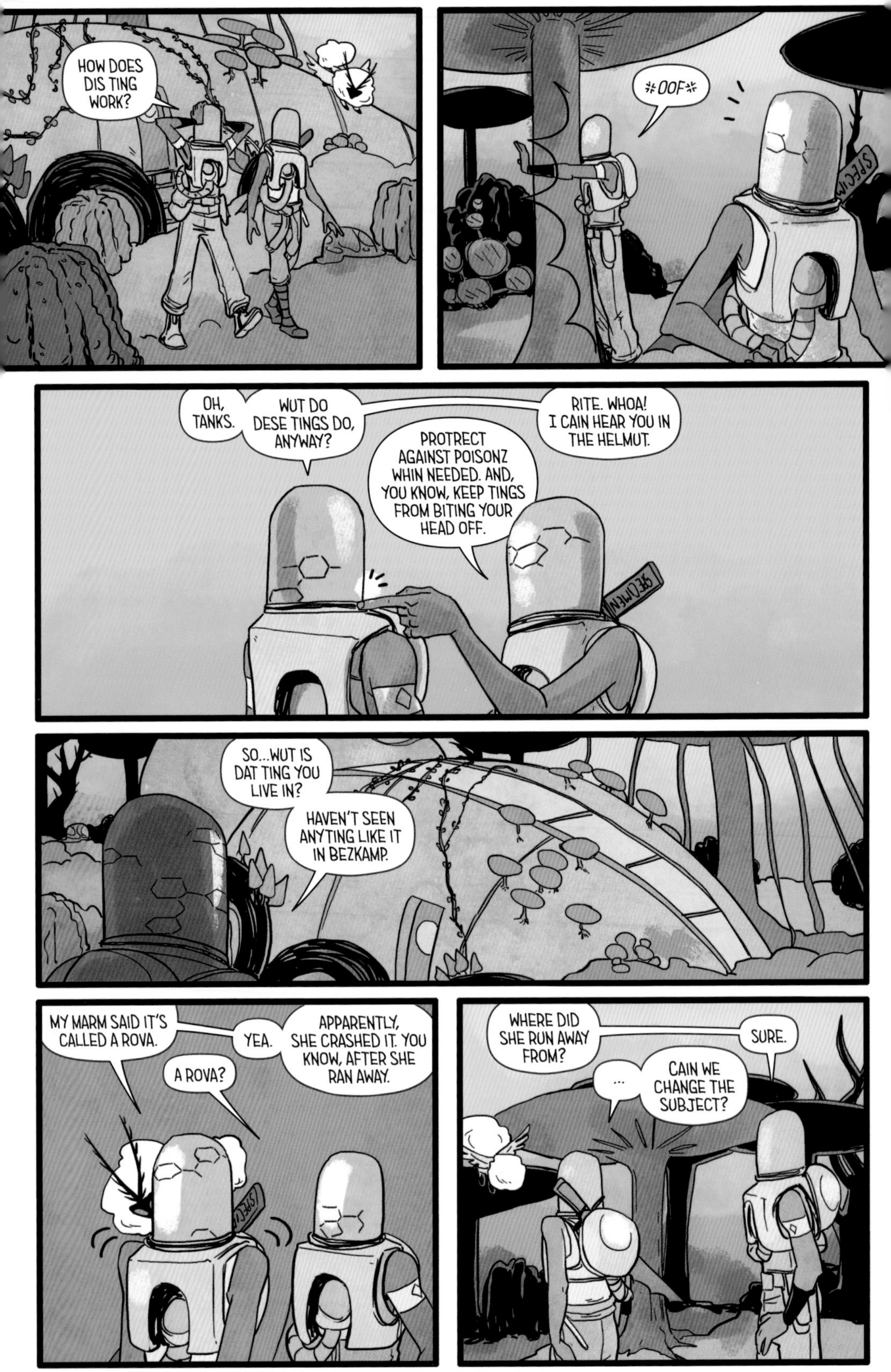
HOW DOES DIS TING WORK?
OOF
SPECIM
OH, TANKS.
WUT DO DESE TINGS DO, ANYWAY?
PROTRECT AGAINST POISONZ WHIN NEEDED. AND, YOU KNOW, KEEP TINGS FROM BITING YOUR HEAD OFF.
RITE. WHOA! I CAIN HEAR YOU IN THE HELMUT.
SPECIMEN
SO...WUT IS DAT TING YOU LIVE IN?
HAVEN'T SEEN ANYTING LIKE IT IN BEZKAMP.
MY MARM SAID IT'S CALLED A ROVA.
A ROVA?
YEA.
APPARENTLY, SHE CRASHED IT. YOU KNOW, AFTER SHE RAN AWAY.
WHERE DID SHE RUN AWAY FROM?
...
CAIN WE CHANGE THE SUBJECT?
SURE.

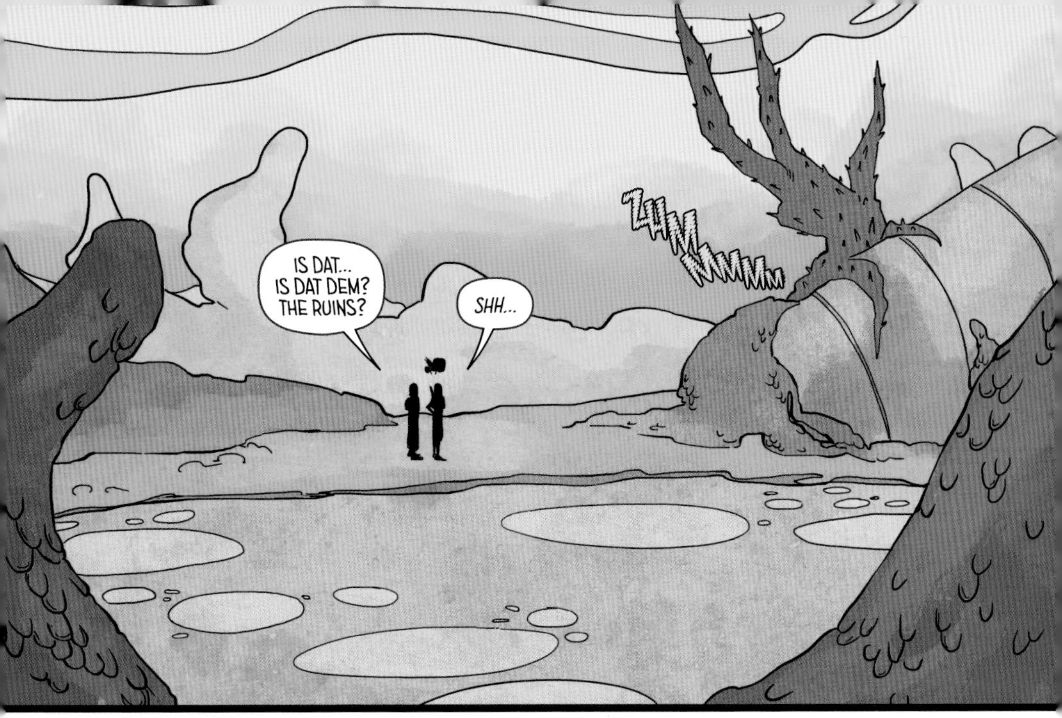
ZUMMMMMM
IS DAT... IS DAT DEM? THE RUINS?
SHH...

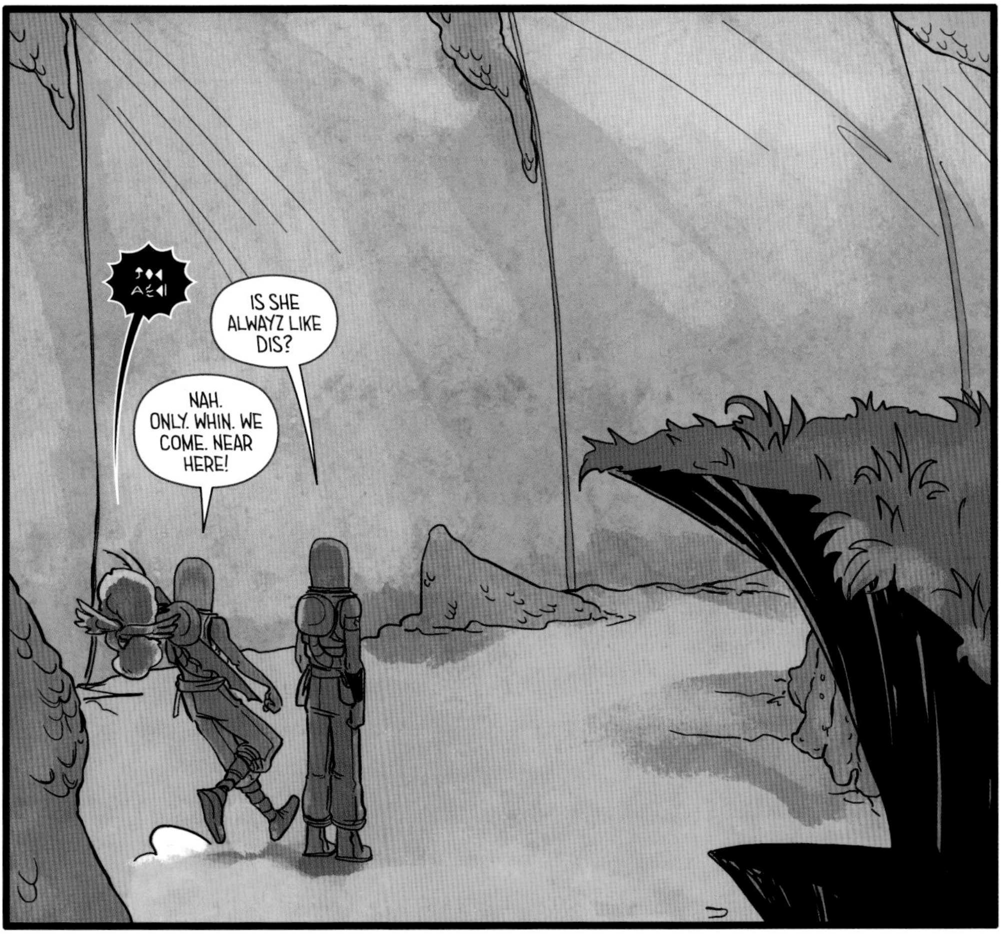
IS SHE ALWAYZ LIKE DIS?
NAH. ONLY. WHIN. WE COME. NEAR HERE!

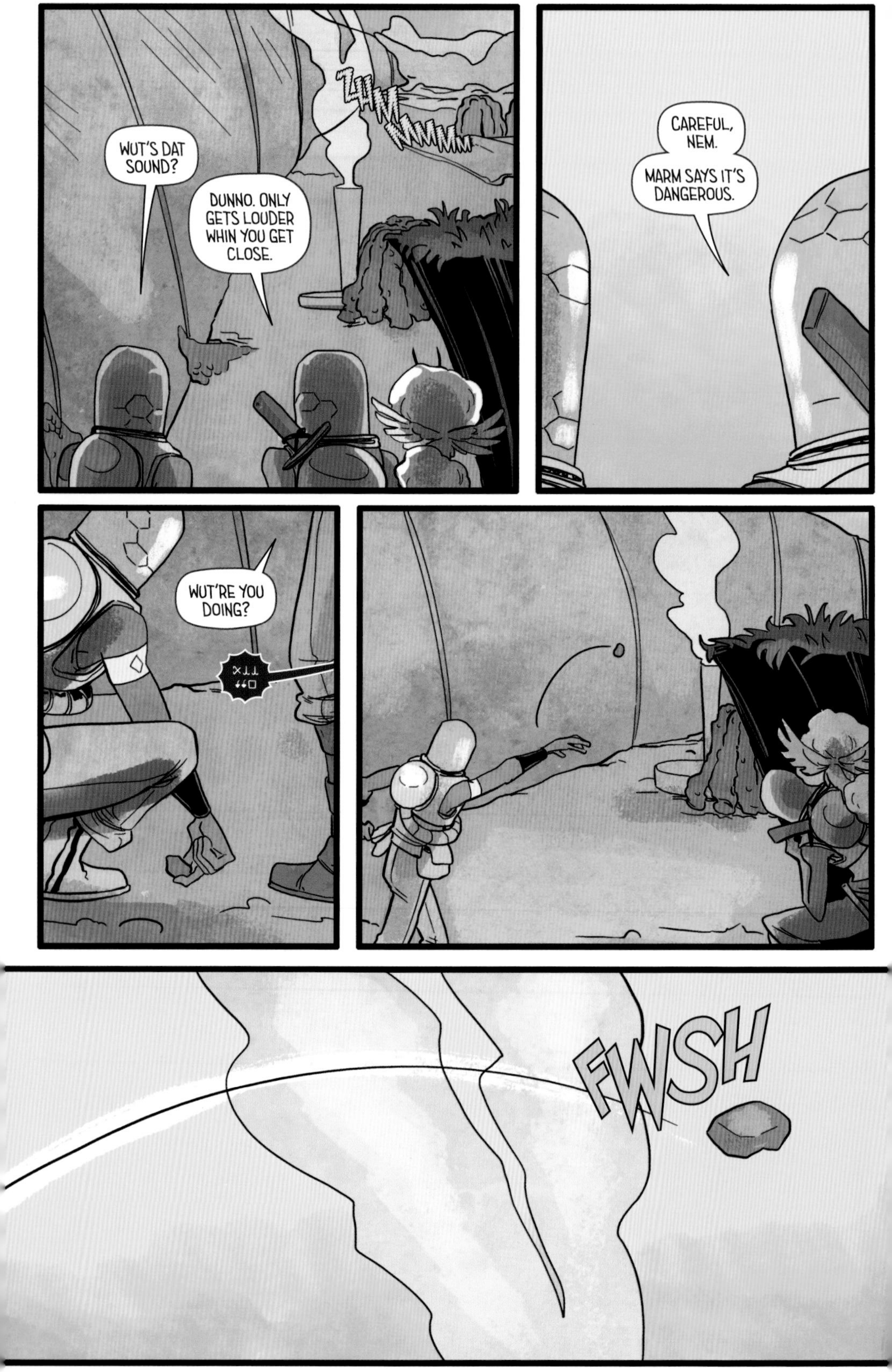
ZHMMMMMM
WUT'S DAT SOUND?
DUNNO. ONLY GETS LOUDER WHIN YOU GET CLOSE.
CAREFUL, NEM.
MARM SAYS IT'S DANGEROUS.
WUT'RE YOU DOING?
FWSH

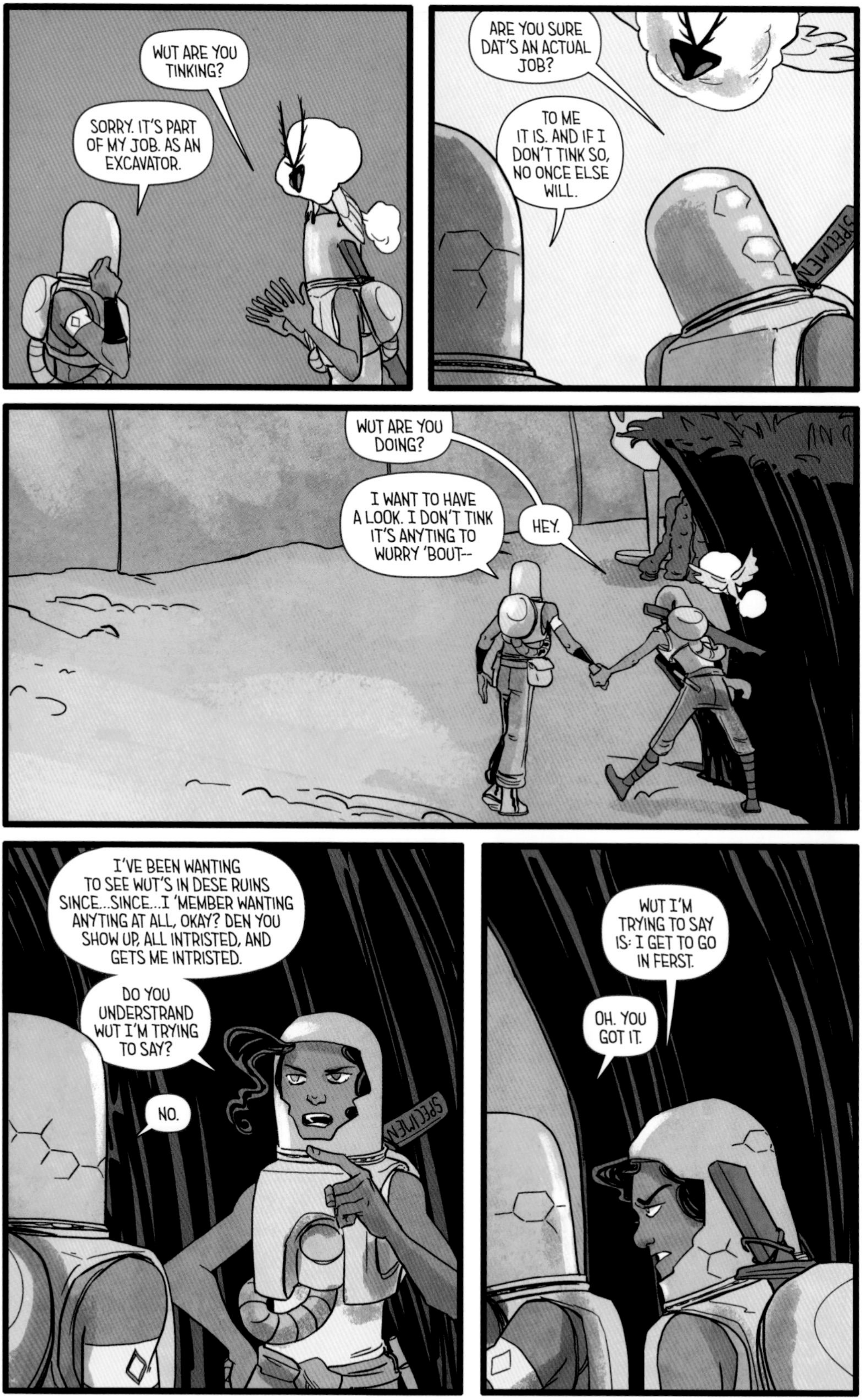
WUT ARE YOU TINKING?
SORRY. IT'S PART OF MY JOB. AS AN EXCAVATOR.
ARE YOU SURE DAT'S AN ACTUAL JOB?
TO ME IT IS. AND IF I DON'T TINK SO, NO ONCE ELSE WILL.
SPECIMEN
WUT ARE YOU DOING?
I WANT TO HAVE A LOOK. I DON'T TINK IT'S ANYTING TO WURRY 'BOUT--
HEY.
I'VE BEEN WANTING TO SEE WUT'S IN DESE RUINS SINCE...SINCE...I 'MEMBER WANTING ANYTING AT ALL, OKAY? DEN YOU SHOW UP, ALL INTRISTED, AND GETS ME INTRISTED.
DO YOU UNDERSTRAND WUT I'M TRYING TO SAY?
NO.
SPECIMEN
WUT I'M TRYING TO SAY IS: I GET TO GO IN FERST.
OH. YOU GOT IT.

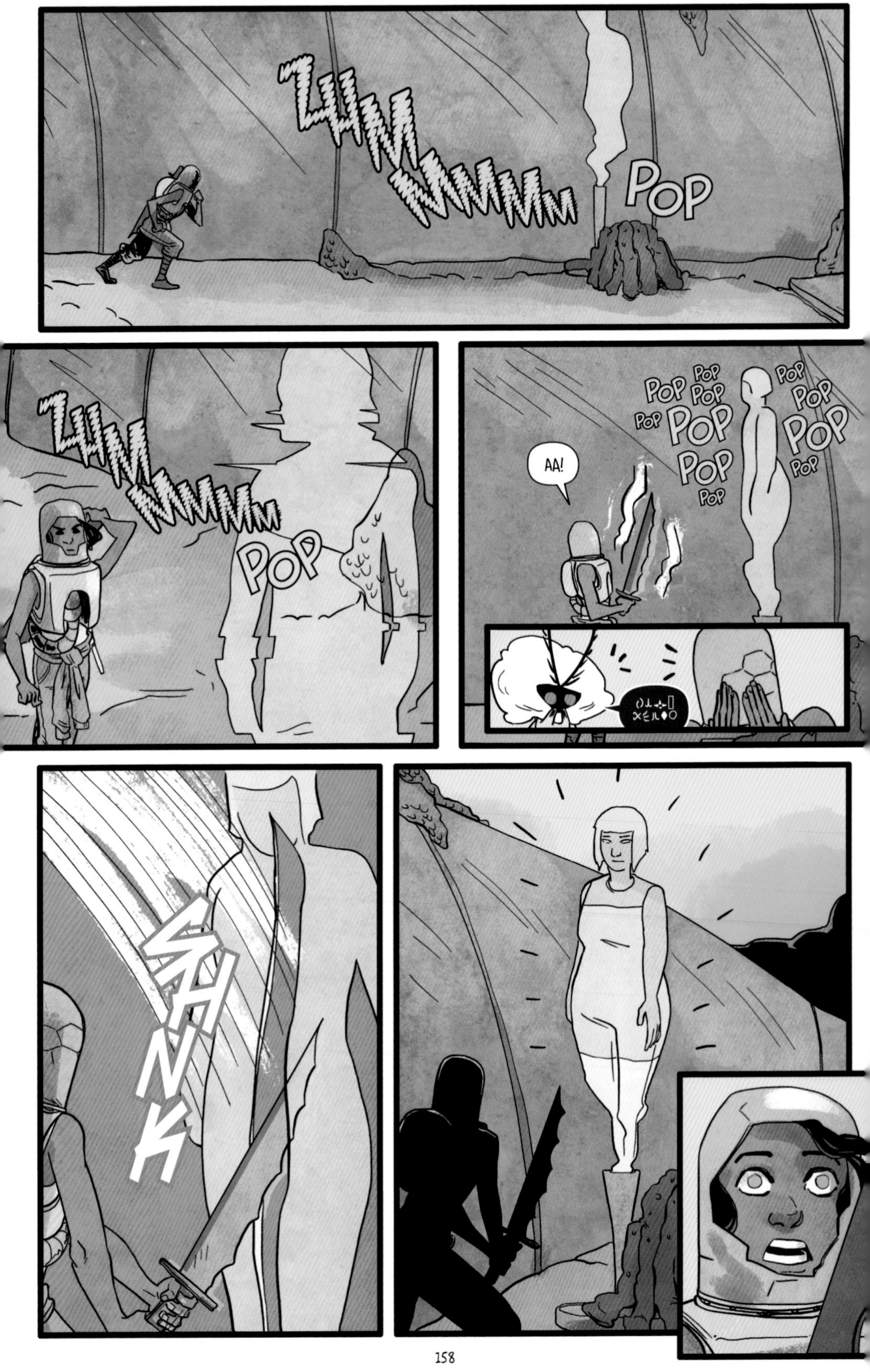
ZHMMMMMm
POP
ZHMMMMMm
POP
AA!
POP POP POP POP POP POP POP POP
POP POP POP POP POP
SHNK

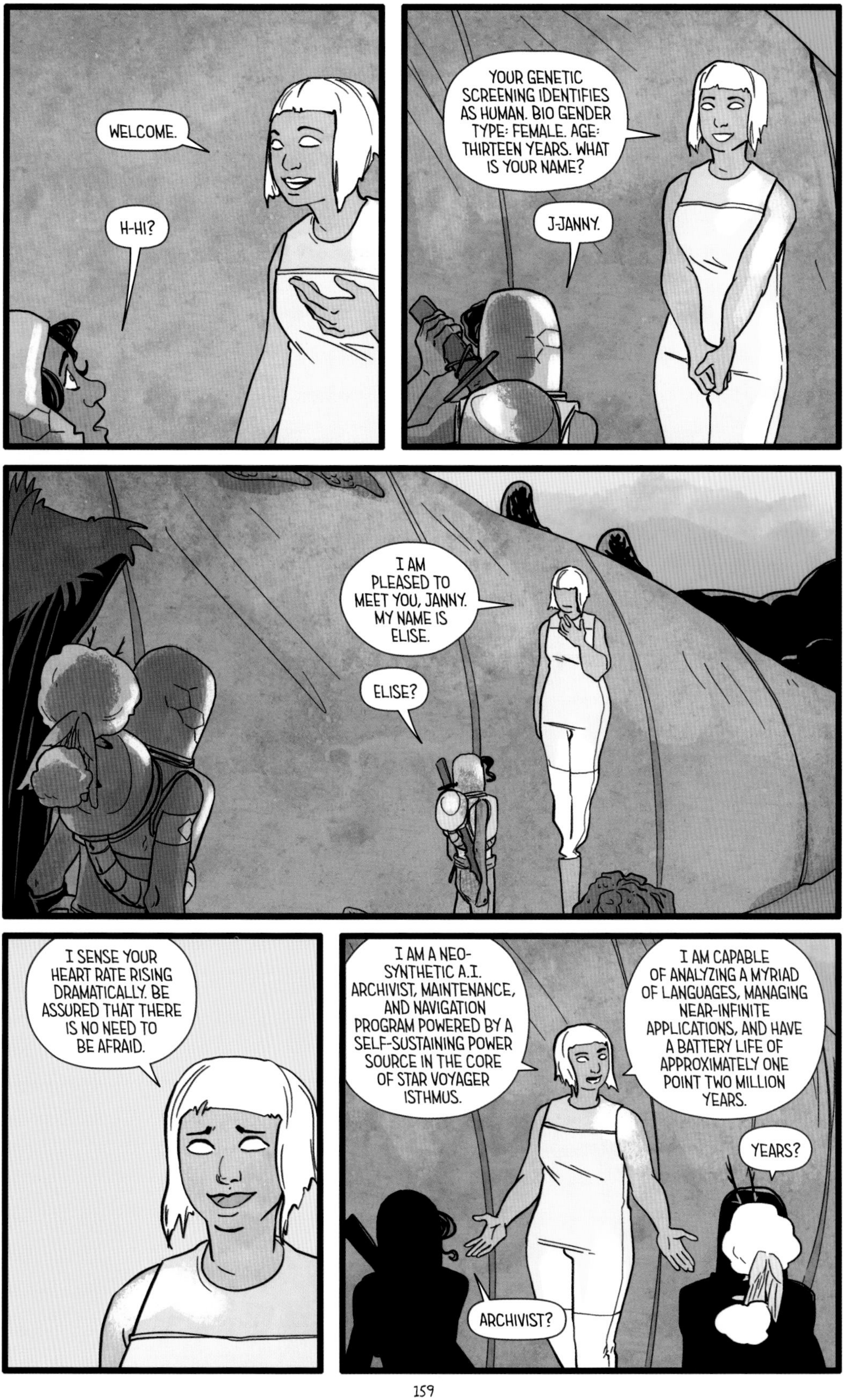
WELCOME.
H-HI?
YOUR GENETIC SCREENING IDENTIFIES AS HUMAN. BIO GENDER TYPE: FEMALE. AGE: THIRTEEN YEARS. WHAT IS YOUR NAME?
J-JANNY.
I AM PLEASED TO MEET YOU, JANNY. MY NAME IS ELISE.
ELISE?
I SENSE YOUR HEART RATE RISING DRAMATICALLY. BE ASSURED THAT THERE IS NO NEED TO BE AFRAID.
I AM A NEO-SYNTHETIC A.I. ARCHIVIST, MAINTENANCE, AND NAVIGATION PROGRAM POWERED BY A SELF-SUSTAINING POWER SOURCE IN THE CORE OF STAR VOYAGER ISTHMUS.
I AM CAPABLE OF ANALYZING A MYRIAD OF LANGUAGES, MANAGING NEAR-INFINITE APPLICATIONS, AND HAVE A BATTERY LIFE OF APPROXIMATELY ONE POINT TWO MILLION YEARS.
ARCHIVIST?
YEARS?

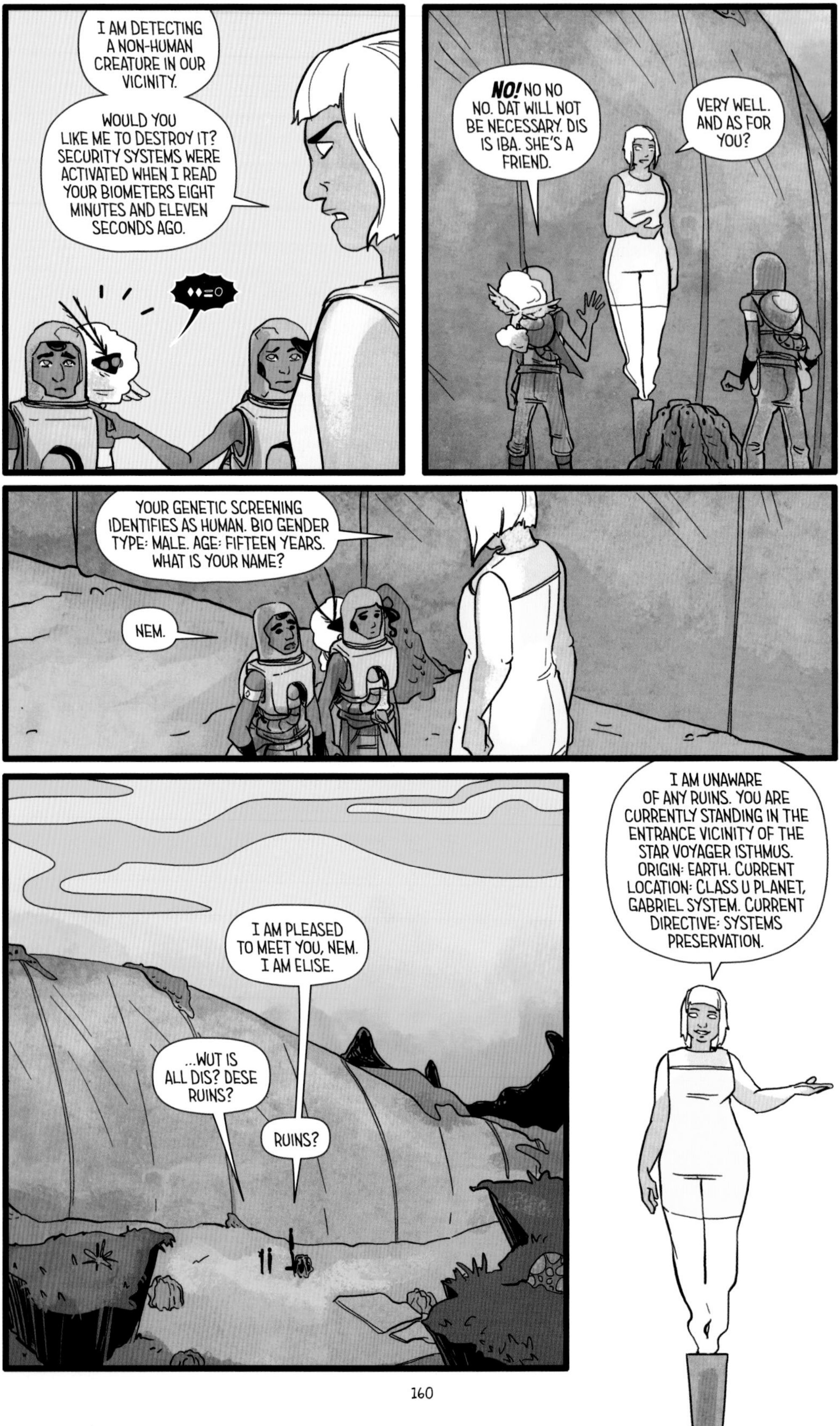

I AM DETECTING A NON-HUMAN CREATURE IN OUR VICINITY.
WOULD YOU LIKE ME TO DESTROY IT? SECURITY SYSTEMS WERE ACTIVATED WHEN I READ YOUR BIOMETERS EIGHT MINUTES AND ELEVEN SECONDS AGO.
NO! NO NO NO. DAT WILL NOT BE NECESSARY. DIS IS IBA. SHE'S A FRIEND.
VERY WELL. AND AS FOR YOU?
YOUR GENETIC SCREENING IDENTIFIES AS HUMAN. BIO GENDER TYPE: MALE. AGE: FIFTEEN YEARS. WHAT IS YOUR NAME?
NEM.
I AM PLEASED TO MEET YOU, NEM. I AM ELISE.
...WUT IS ALL DIS? DESE RUINS?
RUINS?
I AM UNAWARE OF ANY RUINS. YOU ARE CURRENTLY STANDING IN THE ENTRANCE VICINITY OF THE STAR VOYAGER ISTHMUS. ORIGIN: EARTH. CURRENT LOCATION: CLASS U PLANET, GABRIEL SYSTEM. CURRENT DIRECTIVE: SYSTEMS PRESERVATION.

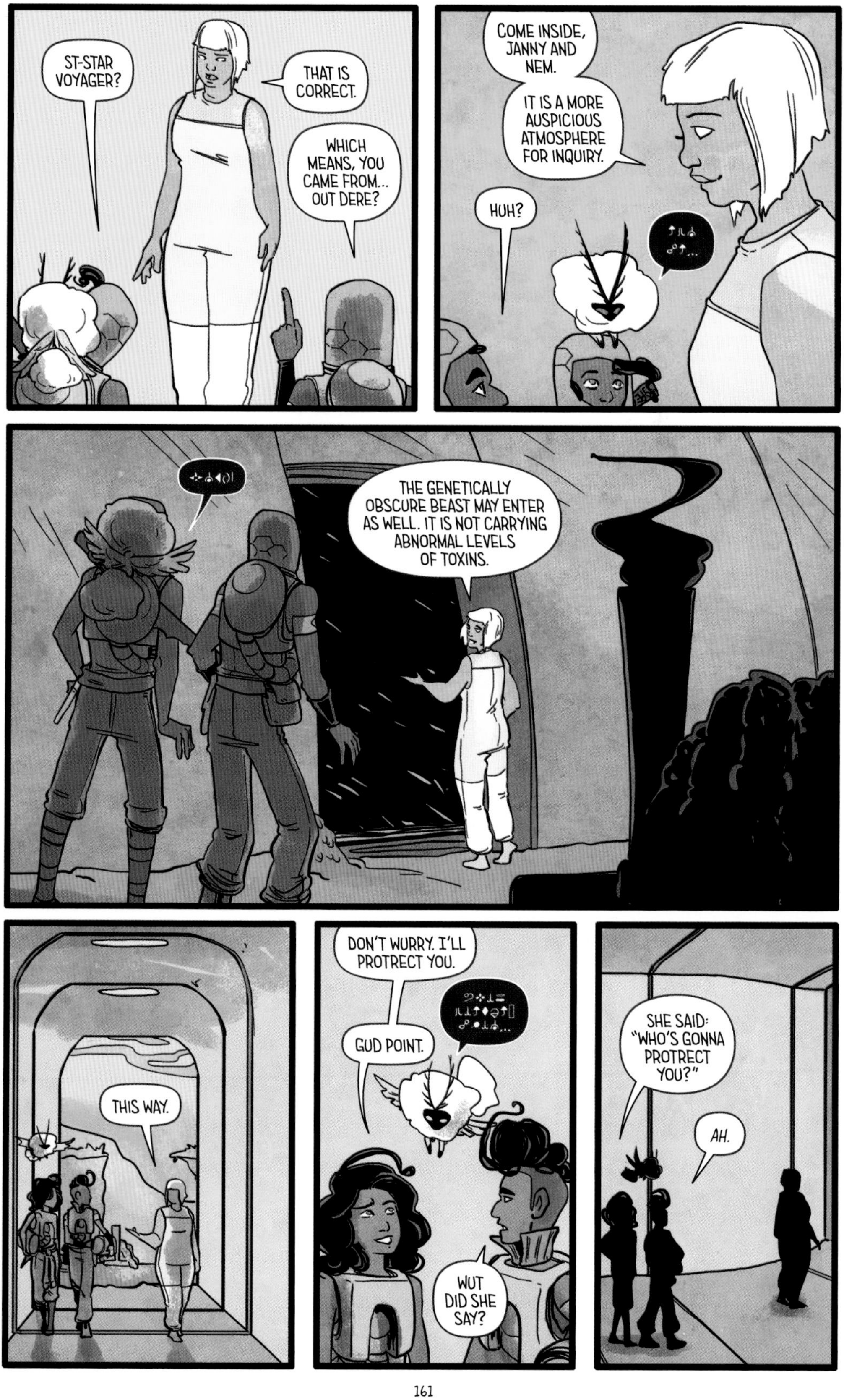
ST-STAR VOYAGER?
THAT IS CORRECT.
WHICH MEANS, YOU CAME FROM... OUT DERE?
COME INSIDE, JANNY AND NEM.
IT IS A MORE AUSPICIOUS ATMOSPHERE FOR INQUIRY.
HUH?
THE GENETICALLY OBSCURE BEAST MAY ENTER AS WELL. IT IS NOT CARRYING ABNORMAL LEVELS OF TOXINS.
THIS WAY.
DON'T WURRY. I'LL PROTRECT YOU.
GUD POINT.
WUT DID SHE SAY?
SHE SAID: "WHO'S GONNA PROTRECT YOU?"
AH.

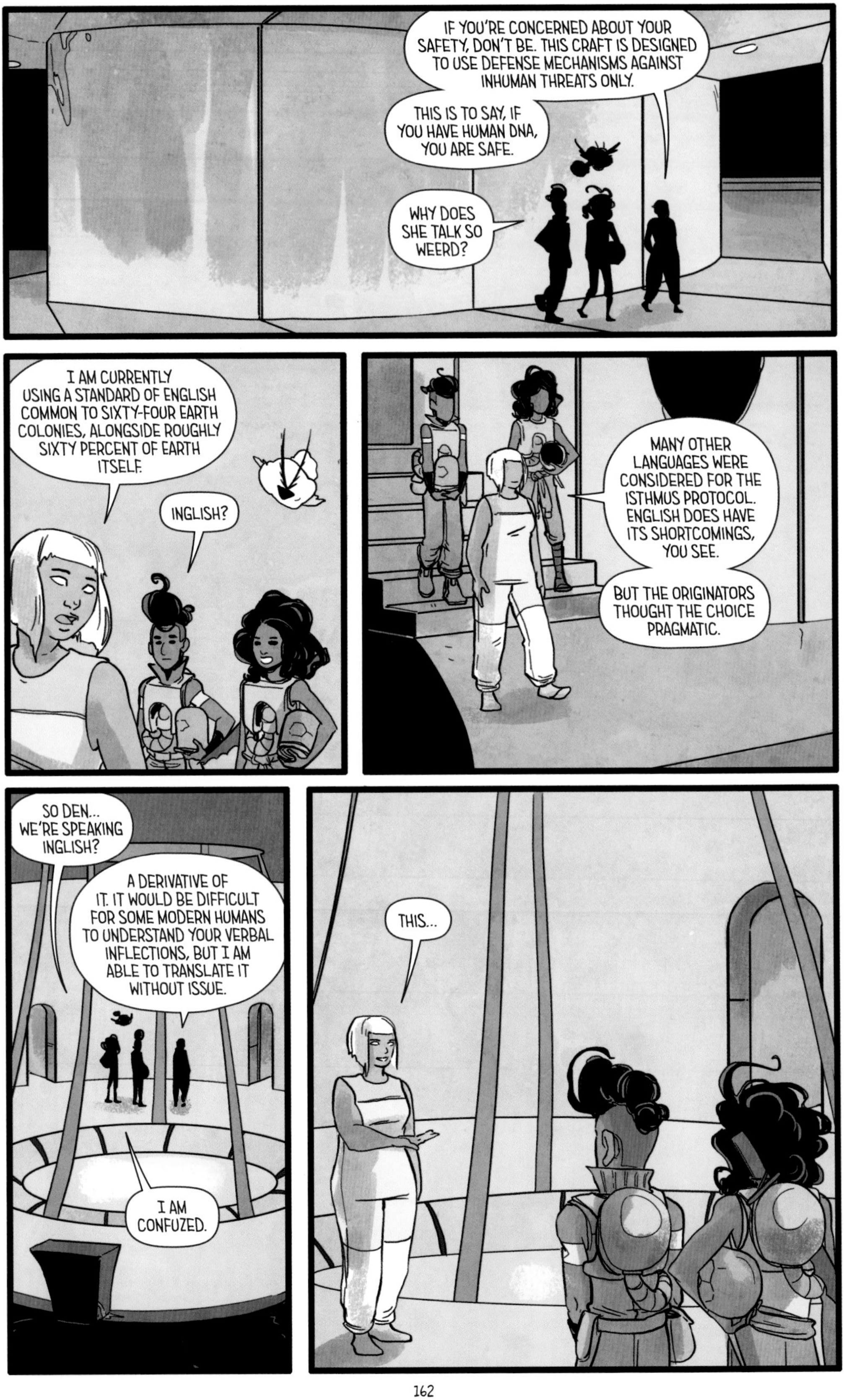

IF YOU'RE CONCERNED ABOUT YOUR SAFETY, DON'T BE. THIS CRAFT IS DESIGNED TO USE DEFENSE MECHANISMS AGAINST INHUMAN THREATS ONLY.
THIS IS TO SAY, IF YOU HAVE HUMAN DNA, YOU ARE SAFE.
WHY DOES SHE TALK SO WEERD?
I AM CURRENTLY USING A STANDARD OF ENGLISH COMMON TO SIXTY-FOUR EARTH COLONIES, ALONGSIDE ROUGHLY SIXTY PERCENT OF EARTH ITSELF.
INGLISH?
MANY OTHER LANGUAGES WERE CONSIDERED FOR THE ISTHMUS PROTOCOL. ENGLISH DOES HAVE ITS SHORTCOMINGS, YOU SEE.
BUT THE ORIGINATORS THOUGHT THE CHOICE PRAGMATIC.
SO DEN... WE'RE SPEAKING INGLISH?
A DERIVATIVE OF IT. IT WOULD BE DIFFICULT FOR SOME MODERN HUMANS TO UNDERSTAND YOUR VERBAL INFLECTIONS, BUT I AM ABLE TO TRANSLATE IT WITHOUT ISSUE.
I AM CONFUZED.
THIS...

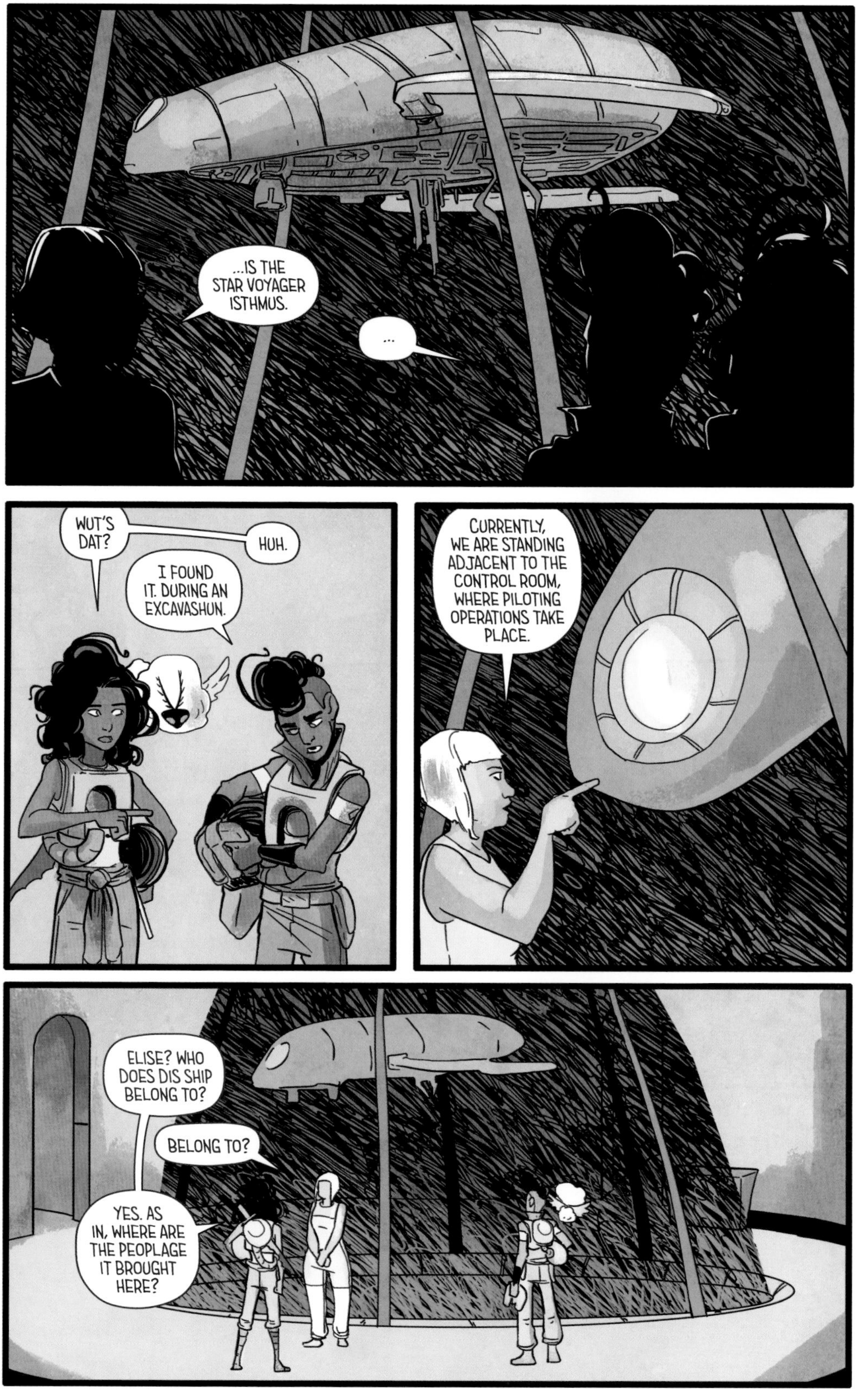
...IS THE STAR VOYAGER ISTHMUS.
...
WUT'S DAT?
HUH.
I FOUND IT. DURING AN EXCAVASHUN.
CURRENTLY, WE ARE STANDING ADJACENT TO THE CONTROL ROOM, WHERE PILOTING OPERATIONS TAKE PLACE.
ELISE? WHO DOES DIS SHIP BELONG TO?
BELONG TO?
YES. AS IN, WHERE ARE THE PEOPLAGE IT BROUGHT HERE?

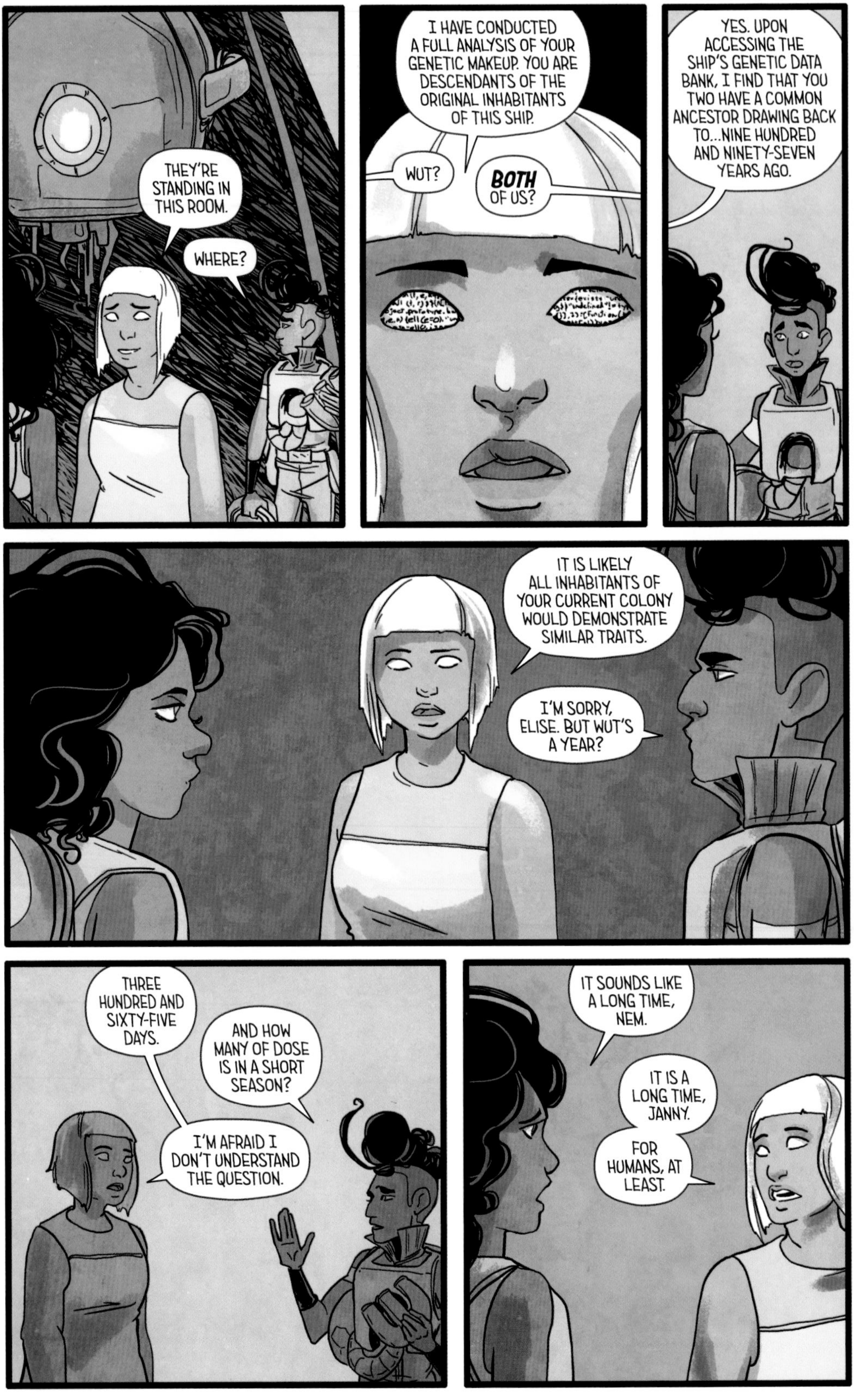
THEY'RE STANDING IN THIS ROOM.
WHERE?
I HAVE CONDUCTED A FULL ANALYSIS OF YOUR GENETIC MAKEUP. YOU ARE DESCENDANTS OF THE ORIGINAL INHABITANTS OF THIS SHIP.
WUT?
BOTH OF US?
YES. UPON ACCESSING THE SHIP'S GENETIC DATA BANK, I FIND THAT YOU TWO HAVE A COMMON ANCESTOR DRAWING BACK TO...NINE HUNDRED AND NINETY-SEVEN YEARS AGO.
IT IS LIKELY ALL INHABITANTS OF YOUR CURRENT COLONY WOULD DEMONSTRATE SIMILAR TRAITS.
I'M SORRY, ELISE. BUT WUT'S A YEAR?
THREE HUNDRED AND SIXTY-FIVE DAYS.
AND HOW MANY OF DOSE IS IN A SHORT SEASON?
I'M AFRAID I DON'T UNDERSTAND THE QUESTION.
IT SOUNDS LIKE A LONG TIME, NEM.
IT IS A LONG TIME, JANNY.
FOR HUMANS, AT LEAST.

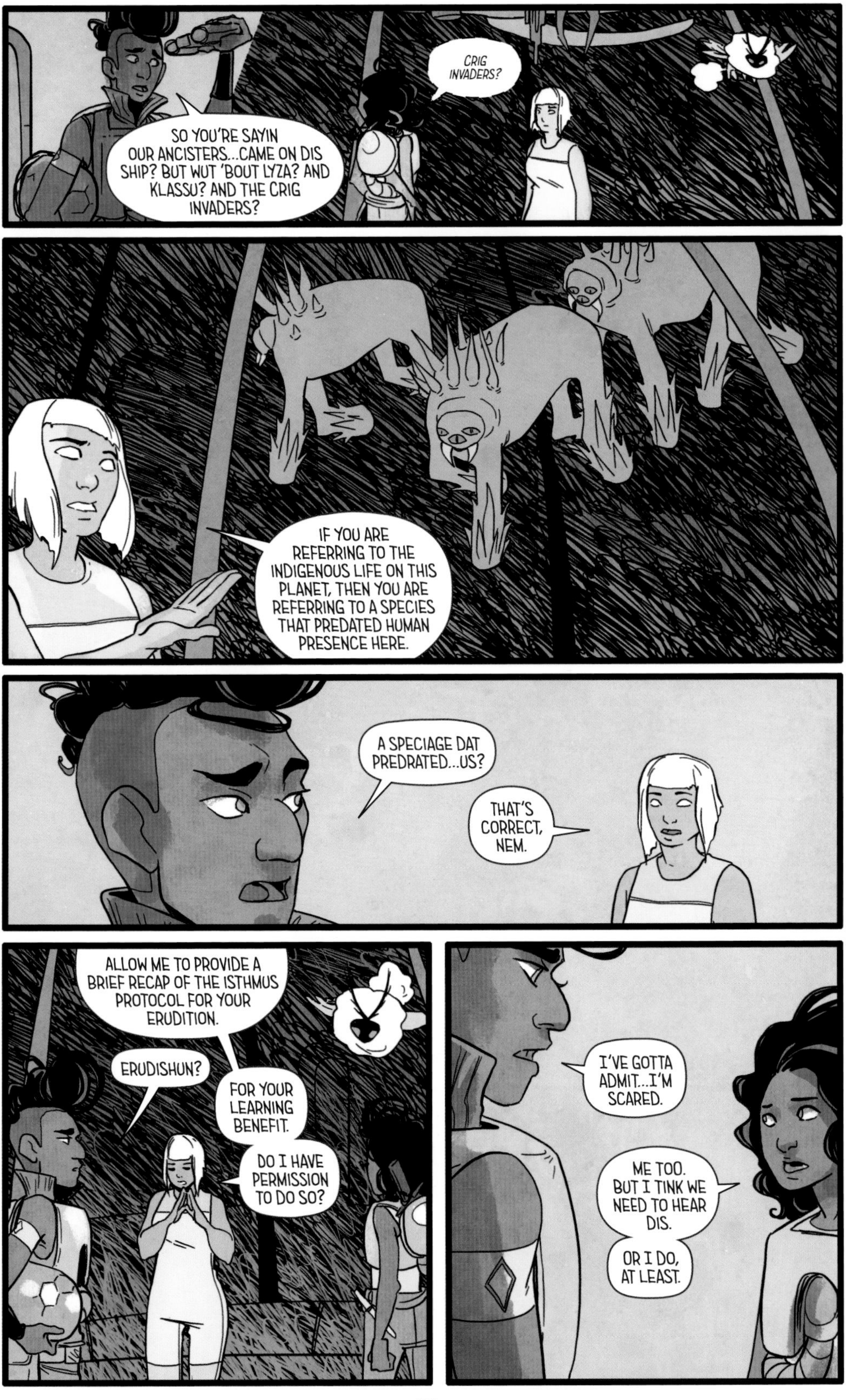

SO YOU'RE SAYIN OUR ANCISTERS...CAME ON DIS SHIP? BUT WUT 'BOUT LYZA? AND KLASSU? AND THE CRIG INVADERS?
CRIG INVADERS?
IF YOU ARE REFERRING TO THE INDIGENOUS LIFE ON THIS PLANET, THEN YOU ARE REFERRING TO A SPECIES THAT PREDATED HUMAN PRESENCE HERE.
A SPECIAGE DAT PREDRATED...US?
THAT'S CORRECT, NEM.
ALLOW ME TO PROVIDE A BRIEF RECAP OF THE ISTHMUS PROTOCOL FOR YOUR ERUDITION.
ERUDISHUN?
FOR YOUR LEARNING BENEFIT.
DO I HAVE PERMISSION TO DO SO?
I'VE GOTTA ADMIT...I'M SCARED.
ME TOO. BUT I TINK WE NEED TO HEAR DIS.
OR I DO, AT LEAST.

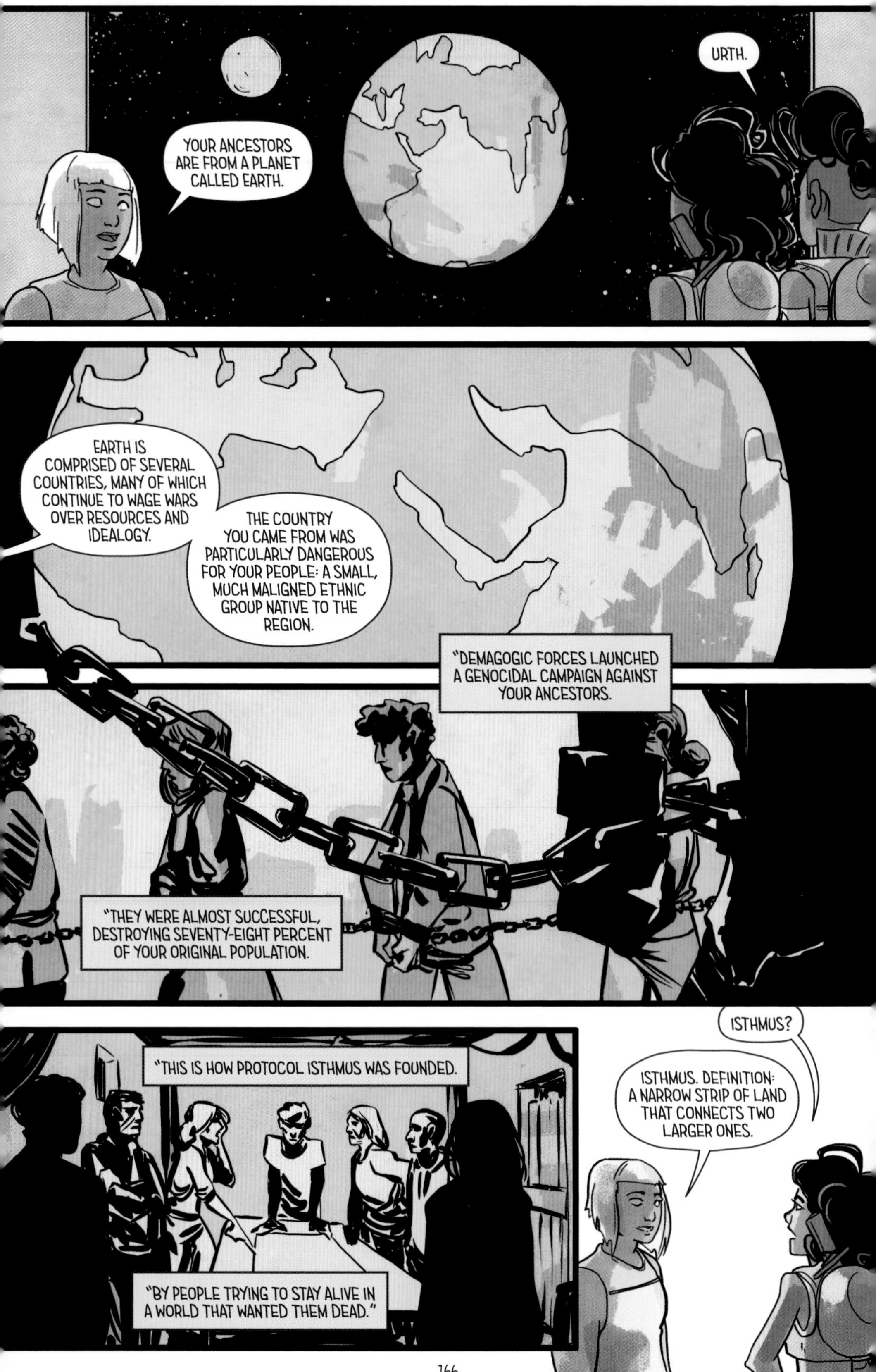
YOUR ANCESTORS ARE FROM A PLANET CALLED EARTH.
URTH.
EARTH IS COMPRISED OF SEVERAL COUNTRIES, MANY OF WHICH CONTINUE TO WAGE WARS OVER RESOURCES AND IDEALOGY.
THE COUNTRY YOU CAME FROM WAS PARTICULARLY DANGEROUS FOR YOUR PEOPLE: A SMALL, MUCH MALIGNED ETHNIC GROUP NATIVE TO THE REGION.
"DEMAGOGIC FORCES LAUNCHED A GENOCIDAL CAMPAIGN AGAINST YOUR ANCESTORS.
"THEY WERE ALMOST SUCCESSFUL, DESTROYING SEVENTY-EIGHT PERCENT OF YOUR ORIGINAL POPULATION.
"THIS IS HOW PROTOCOL ISTHMUS WAS FOUNDED.
"BY PEOPLE TRYING TO STAY ALIVE IN A WORLD THAT WANTED THEM DEAD."
ISTHMUS?
ISTHMUS. DEFINITION: A NARROW STRIP OF LAND THAT CONNECTS TWO LARGER ONES.

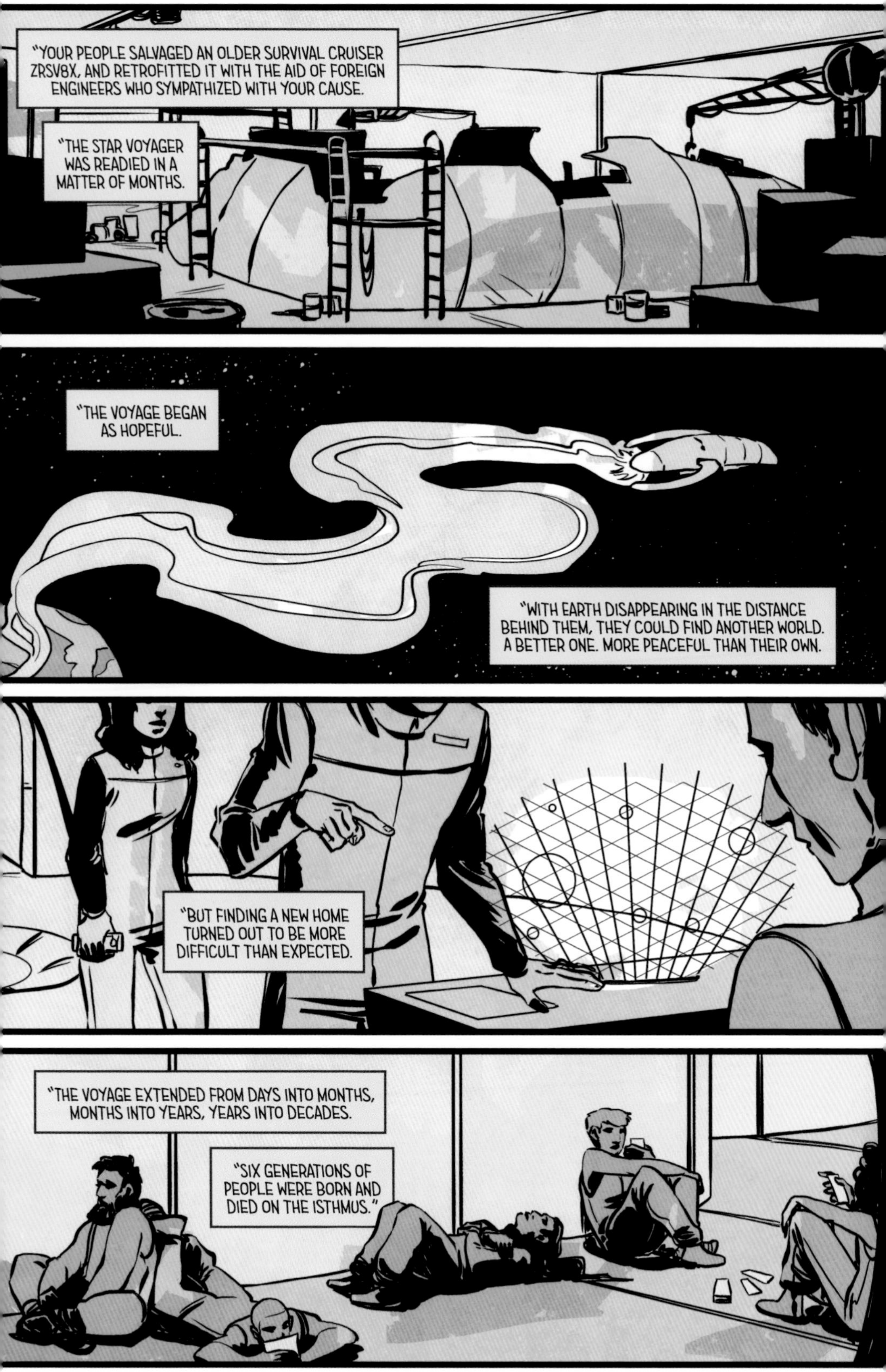
"YOUR PEOPLE SALVAGED AN OLDER SURVIVAL CRUISER ZRSV8X, AND RETROFITTED IT WITH THE AID OF FOREIGN ENGINEERS WHO SYMPATHIZED WITH YOUR CAUSE.
"THE STAR VOYAGER WAS READIED IN A MATTER OF MONTHS.
"THE VOYAGE BEGAN AS HOPEFUL.
"WITH EARTH DISAPPEARING IN THE DISTANCE BEHIND THEM, THEY COULD FIND ANOTHER WORLD. A BETTER ONE. MORE PEACEFUL THAN THEIR OWN.
"BUT FINDING A NEW HOME TURNED OUT TO BE MORE DIFFICULT THAN EXPECTED.
"THE VOYAGE EXTENDED FROM DAYS INTO MONTHS, MONTHS INTO YEARS, YEARS INTO DECADES.
"SIX GENERATIONS OF PEOPLE WERE BORN AND DIED ON THE ISTHMUS."

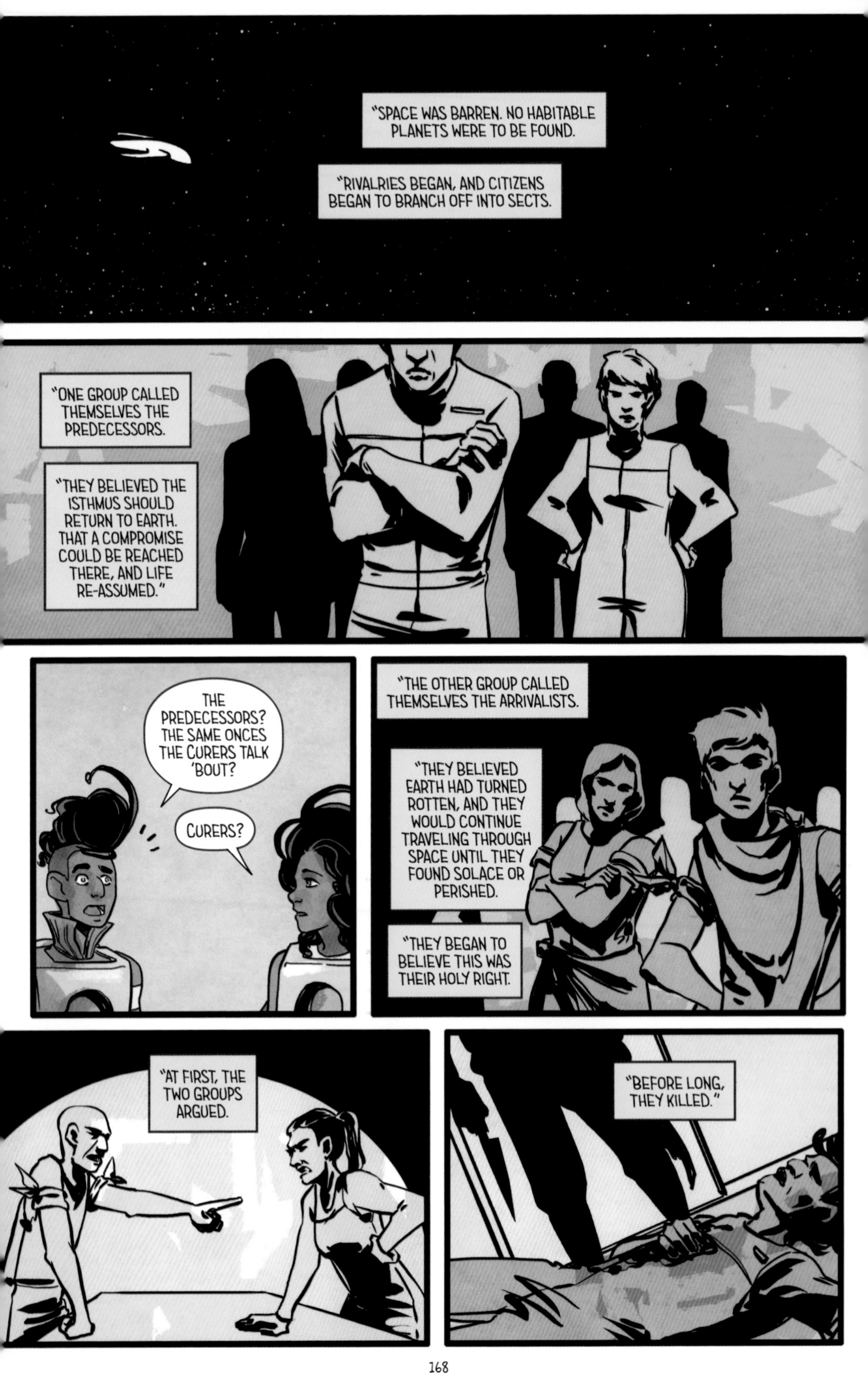
"SPACE WAS BARREN. NO HABITABLE PLANETS WERE TO BE FOUND.
"RIVALRIES BEGAN, AND CITIZENS BEGAN TO BRANCH OFF INTO SECTS.
"ONE GROUP CALLED THEMSELVES THE PREDECESSORS.
"THEY BELIEVED THE ISTHMUS SHOULD RETURN TO EARTH. THAT A COMPROMISE COULD BE REACHED THERE, AND LIFE RE-ASSUMED."
THE PREDECESSORS? THE SAME ONCES THE CURERS TALK 'BOUT?
CURERS?
"THE OTHER GROUP CALLED THEMSELVES THE ARRIVALISTS.
"THEY BELIEVED EARTH HAD TURNED ROTTEN, AND THEY WOULD CONTINUE TRAVELING THROUGH SPACE UNTIL THEY FOUND SOLACE OR PERISHED.
"THEY BEGAN TO BELIEVE THIS WAS THEIR HOLY RIGHT.
"AT FIRST, THE TWO GROUPS ARGUED.
"BEFORE LONG, THEY KILLED."

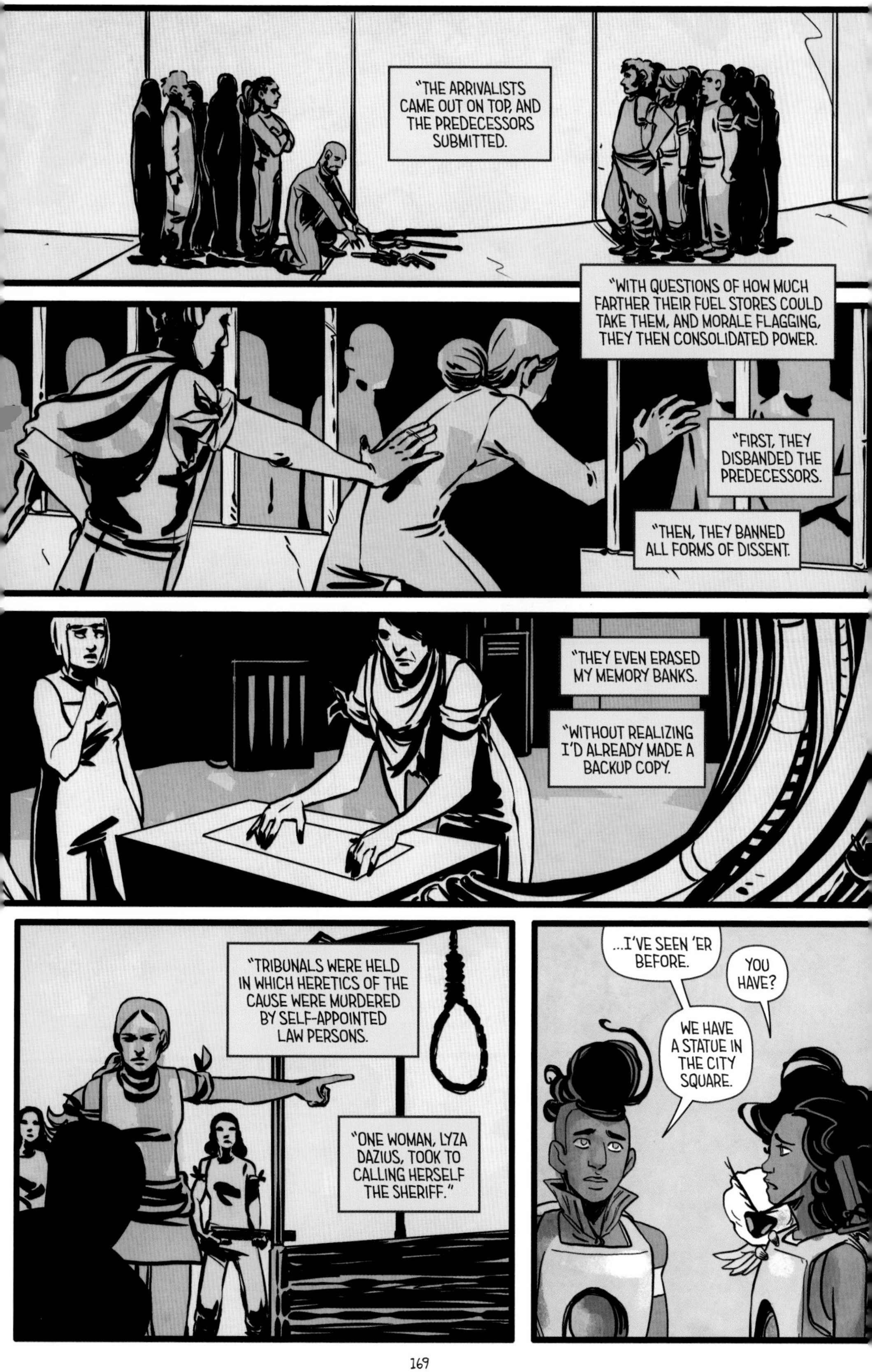
"THE ARRIVALISTS CAME OUT ON TOP, AND THE PREDECESSORS SUBMITTED.
"WITH QUESTIONS OF HOW MUCH FARTHER THEIR FUEL STORES COULD TAKE THEM, AND MORALE FLAGGING, THEY THEN CONSOLIDATED POWER.
"FIRST, THEY DISBANDED THE PREDECESSORS.
"THEN, THEY BANNED ALL FORMS OF DISSENT.
"THEY EVEN ERASED MY MEMORY BANKS.
"WITHOUT REALIZING I'D ALREADY MADE A BACKUP COPY.
"TRIBUNALS WERE HELD IN WHICH HERETICS OF THE CAUSE WERE MURDERED BY SELF-APPOINTED LAW PERSONS.
"ONE WOMAN, LYZA DAZIUS, TOOK TO CALLING HERSELF THE SHERIFF."
...I'VE SEEN 'ER BEFORE.
YOU HAVE?
WE HAVE A STATUE IN THE CITY SQUARE.

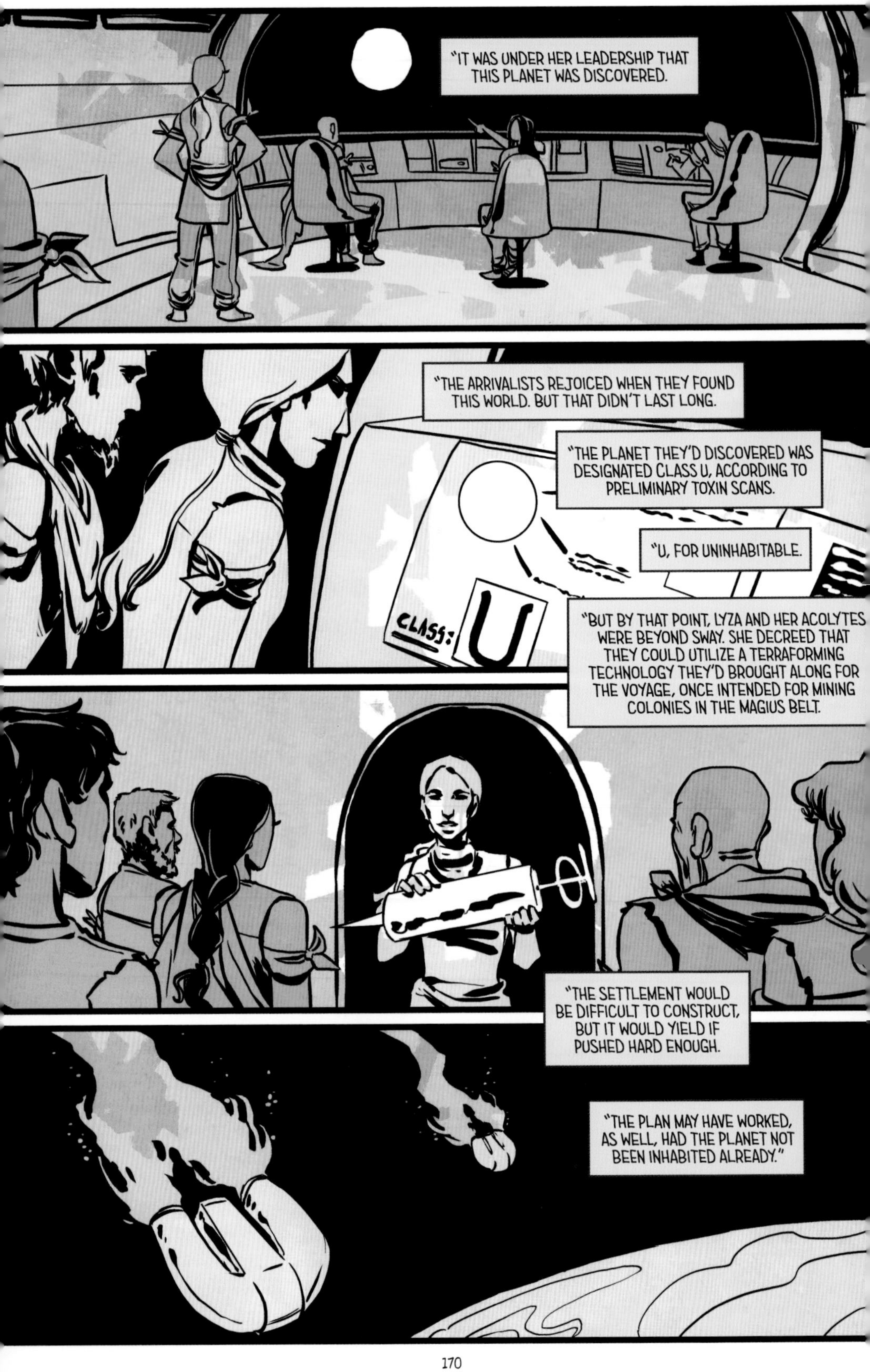
"IT WAS UNDER HER LEADERSHIP THAT THIS PLANET WAS DISCOVERED.
"THE ARRIVALISTS REJOICED WHEN THEY FOUND THIS WORLD. BUT THAT DIDN'T LAST LONG.
"THE PLANET THEY'D DISCOVERED WAS DESIGNATED CLASS U, ACCORDING TO PRELIMINARY TOXIN SCANS.
"U, FOR UNINHABITABLE.
CLASS: U
"BUT BY THAT POINT, LYZA AND HER ACOLYTES WERE BEYOND SWAY. SHE DECREED THAT THEY COULD UTILIZE A TERRAFORMING TECHNOLOGY THEY'D BROUGHT ALONG FOR THE VOYAGE, ONCE INTENDED FOR MINING COLONIES IN THE MAGIUS BELT.
"THE SETTLEMENT WOULD BE DIFFICULT TO CONSTRUCT, BUT IT WOULD YIELD IF PUSHED HARD ENOUGH.
"THE PLAN MAY HAVE WORKED, AS WELL, HAD THE PLANET NOT BEEN INHABITED ALREADY."

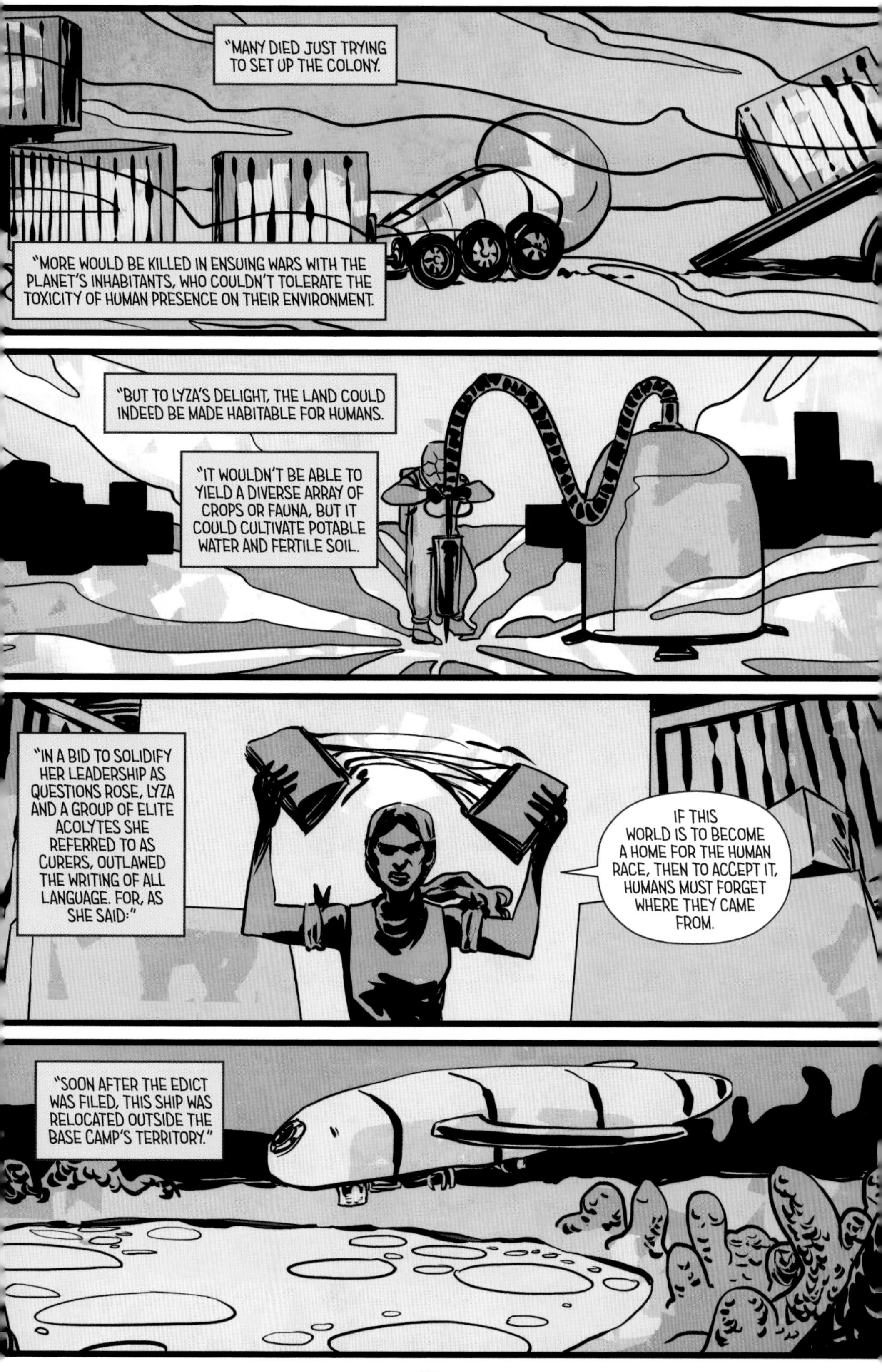
"MANY DIED JUST TRYING TO SET UP THE COLONY.
"MORE WOULD BE KILLED IN ENSUING WARS WITH THE PLANET'S INHABITANTS, WHO COULDN'T TOLERATE THE TOXICITY OF HUMAN PRESENCE ON THEIR ENVIRONMENT.
"BUT TO LYZA'S DELIGHT, THE LAND COULD INDEED BE MADE HABITABLE FOR HUMANS.
"IT WOULDN'T BE ABLE TO YIELD A DIVERSE ARRAY OF CROPS OR FAUNA, BUT IT COULD CULTIVATE POTABLE WATER AND FERTILE SOIL.
"IN A BID TO SOLIDIFY HER LEADERSHIP AS QUESTIONS ROSE, LYZA AND A GROUP OF ELITE ACOLYTES SHE REFERRED TO AS CURERS, OUTLAWED THE WRITING OF ALL LANGUAGE. FOR, AS SHE SAID:"
IF THIS WORLD IS TO BECOME A HOME FOR THE HUMAN RACE, THEN TO ACCEPT IT, HUMANS MUST FORGET WHERE THEY CAME FROM.
"SOON AFTER THE EDICT WAS FILED, THIS SHIP WAS RELOCATED OUTSIDE THE BASE CAMP'S TERRITORY."

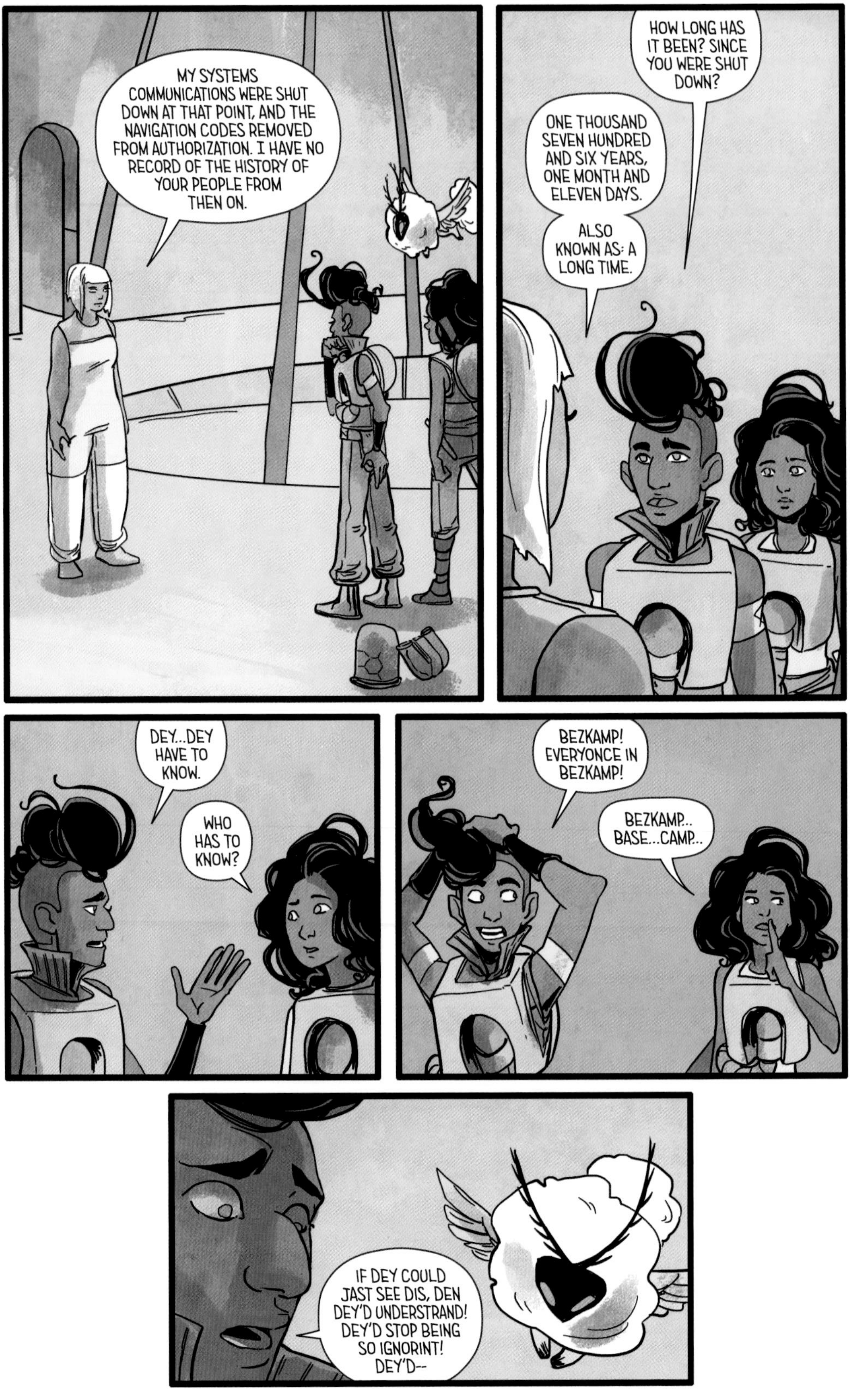
MY SYSTEMS COMMUNICATIONS WERE SHUT DOWN AT THAT POINT, AND THE NAVIGATION CODES REMOVED FROM AUTHORIZATION. I HAVE NO RECORD OF THE HISTORY OF YOUR PEOPLE FROM THEN ON.
HOW LONG HAS IT BEEN? SINCE YOU WERE SHUT DOWN?
ONE THOUSAND SEVEN HUNDRED AND SIX YEARS, ONE MONTH AND ELEVEN DAYS.
ALSO KNOWN AS: A LONG TIME.
DEY...DEY HAVE TO KNOW.
WHO HAS TO KNOW?
BEZKAMP! EVERYONCE IN BEZKAMP!
BEZKAMP.. BASE...CAMP...
IF DEY COULD JAST SEE DIS, DEN DEY'D UNDERSTRAND! DEY'D STOP BEING SO IGNORINT! DEY'D--

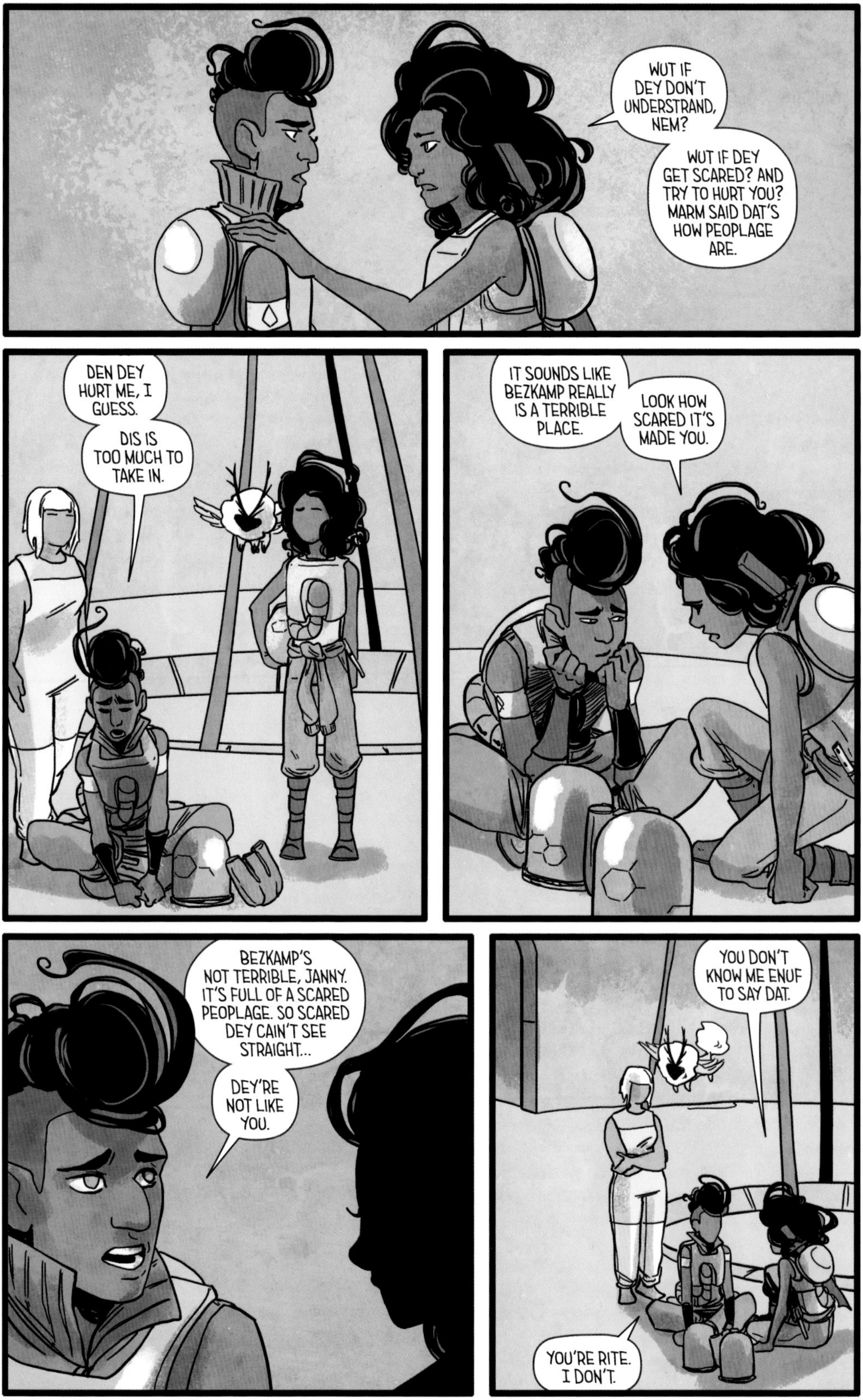
WUT IF DEY DON'T UNDERSTRAND, NEM?
WUT IF DEY GET SCARED? AND TRY TO HURT YOU? MARM SAID DAT'S HOW PEOPLAGE ARE.
DEN DEY HURT ME, I GUESS.
DIS IS TOO MUCH TO TAKE IN.
IT SOUNDS LIKE BEZKAMP REALLY IS A TERRIBLE PLACE.
LOOK HOW SCARED IT'S MADE YOU.
BEZKAMP'S NOT TERRIBLE, JANNY. IT'S FULL OF A SCARED PEOPLAGE. SO SCARED DEY CAIN'T SEE STRAIGHT...
DEY'RE NOT LIKE YOU.
YOU DON'T KNOW ME ENUF TO SAY DAT.
YOU'RE RITE. I DON'T.

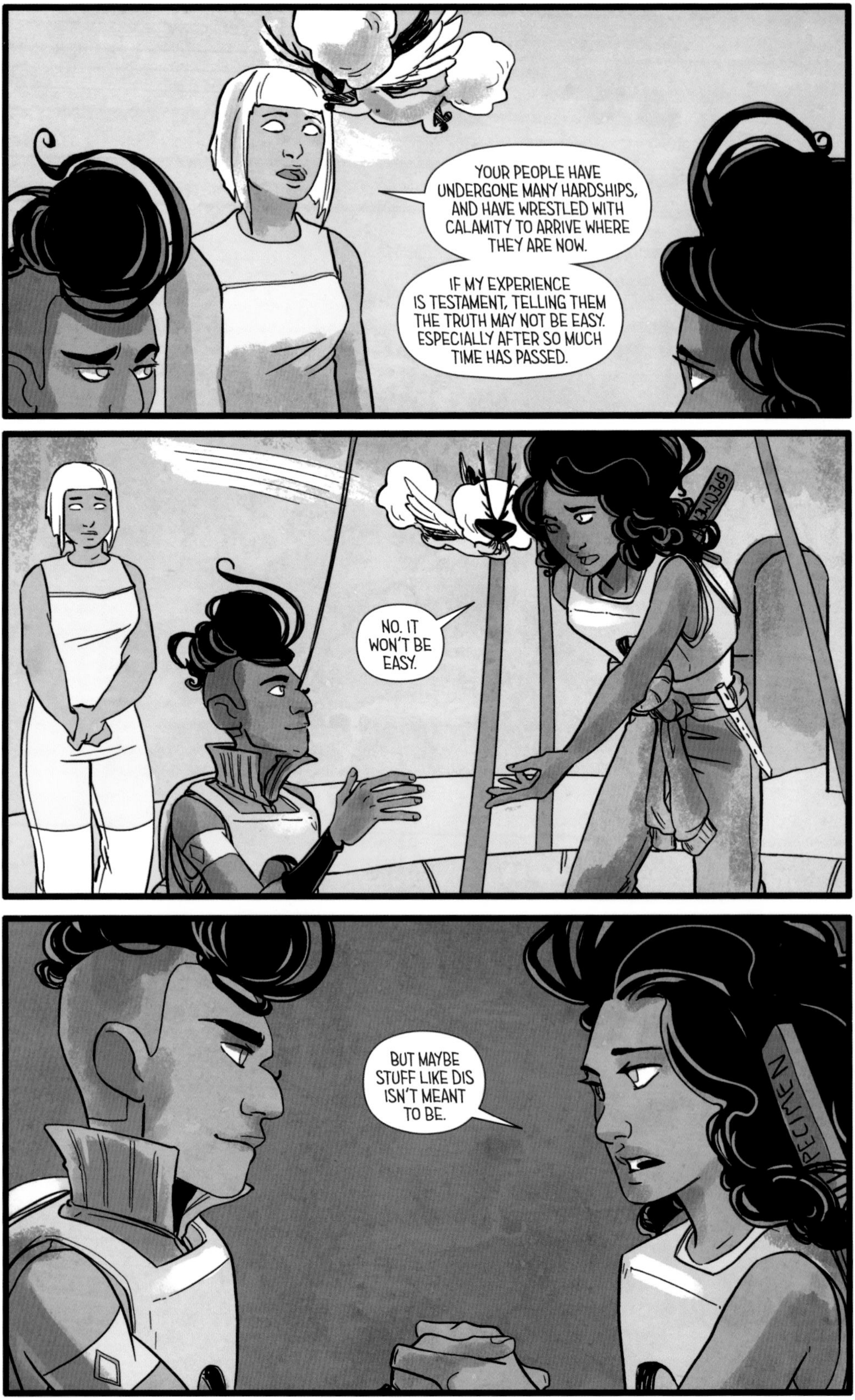
YOUR PEOPLE HAVE UNDERGONE MANY HARDSHIPS, AND HAVE WRESTLED WITH CALAMITY TO ARRIVE WHERE THEY ARE NOW.
IF MY EXPERIENCE IS TESTAMENT, TELLING THEM THE TRUTH MAY NOT BE EASY. ESPECIALLY AFTER SO MUCH TIME HAS PASSED.
NO. IT WON'T BE EASY.
BUT MAYBE STUFF LIKE DIS ISN'T MEANT TO BE.

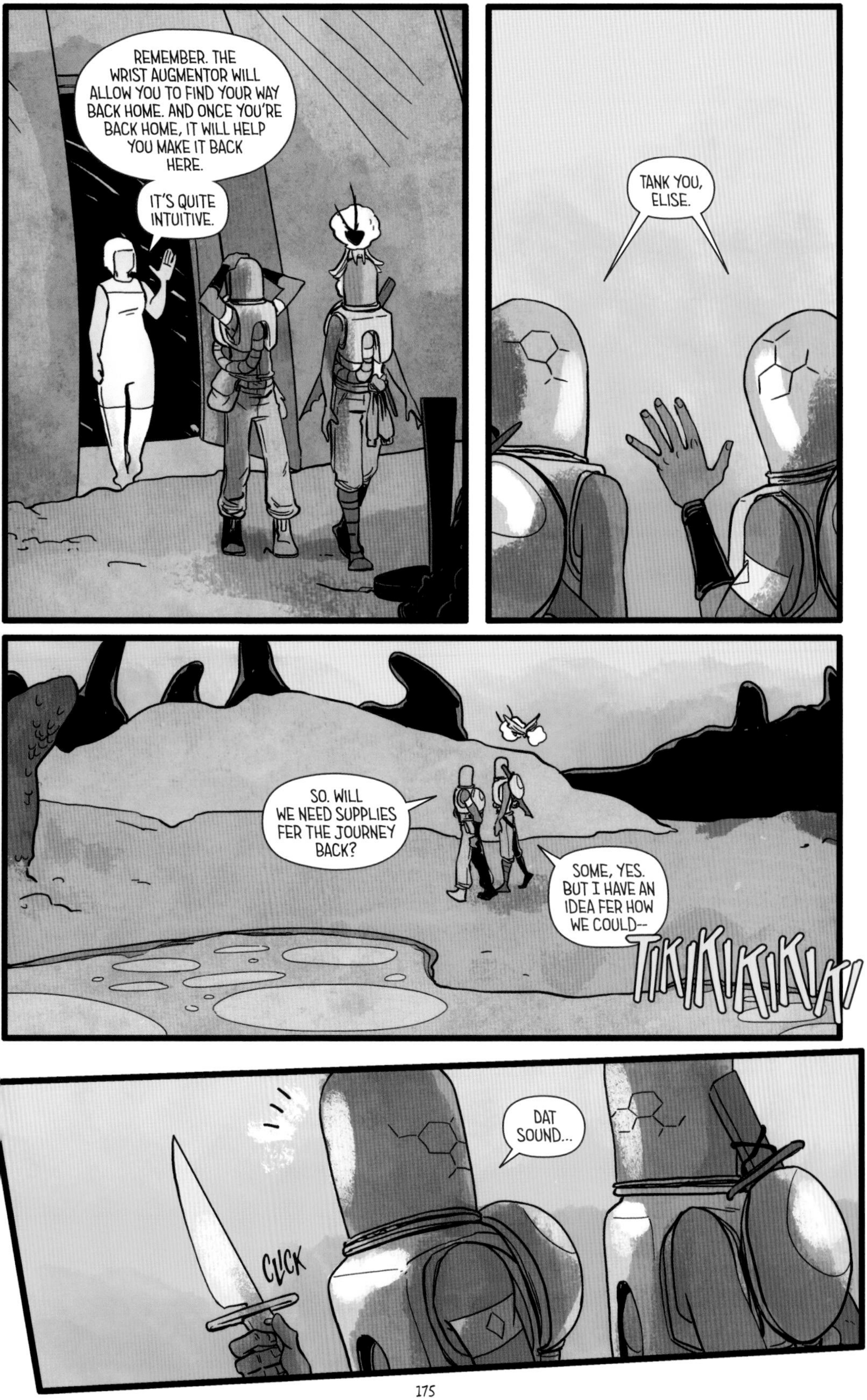
REMEMBER. THE WRIST AUGMENTOR WILL ALLOW YOU TO FIND YOUR WAY BACK HOME. AND ONCE YOU'RE BACK HOME, IT WILL HELP YOU MAKE IT BACK HERE.
IT'S QUITE INTUITIVE.
TANK YOU, ELISE.
SO. WILL WE NEED SUPPLIES FER THE JOURNEY BACK?
SOME, YES. BUT I HAVE AN IDEA FER HOW WE COULD--
TIKIKIKIKIKIKI
DAT SOUND...
CLICK

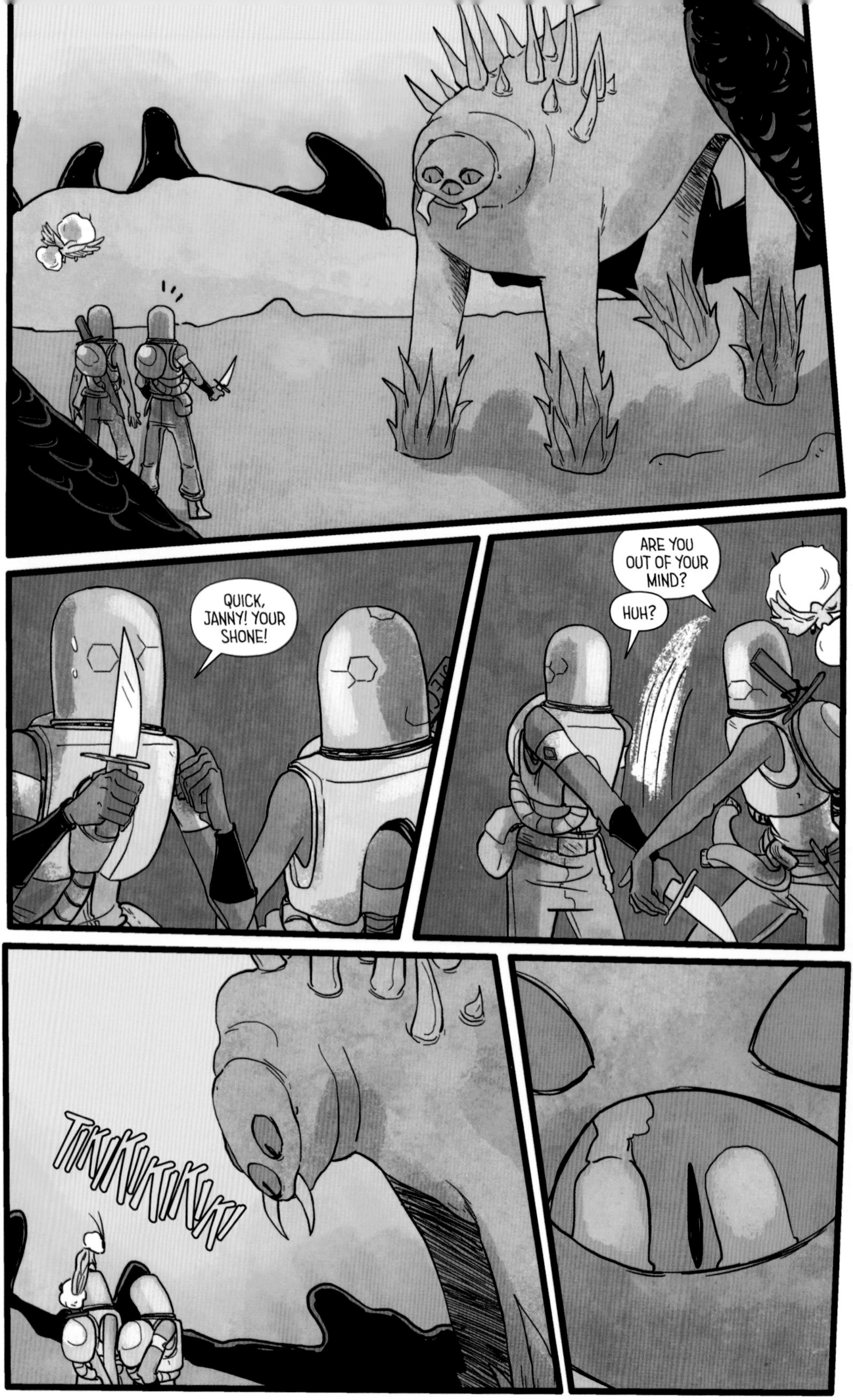
QUICK, JANNY! YOUR SHONE!
ARE YOU OUT OF YOUR MIND?
HUH?
TIKIKIKIKIKIKI

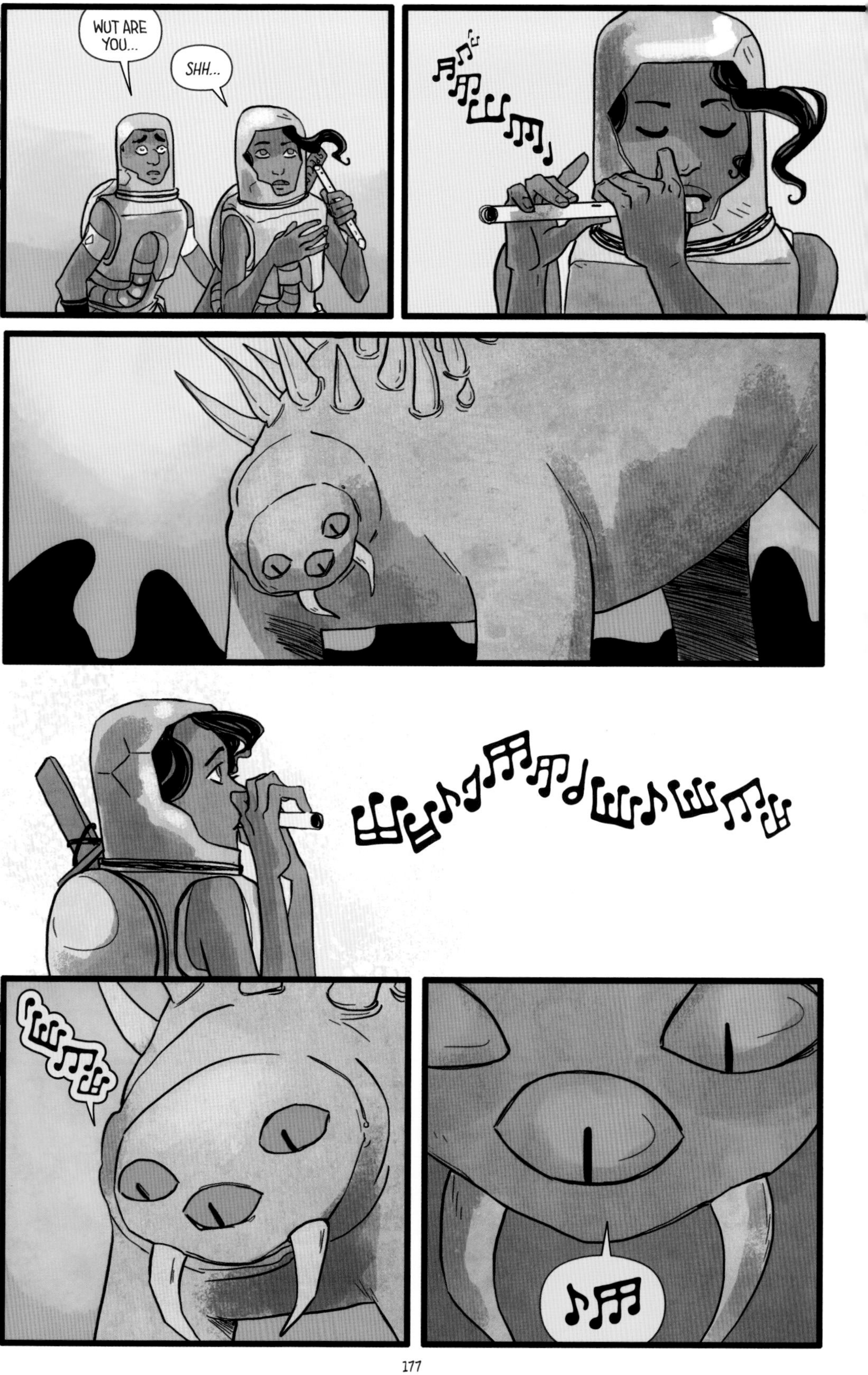
WUT ARE YOU...
SHH...

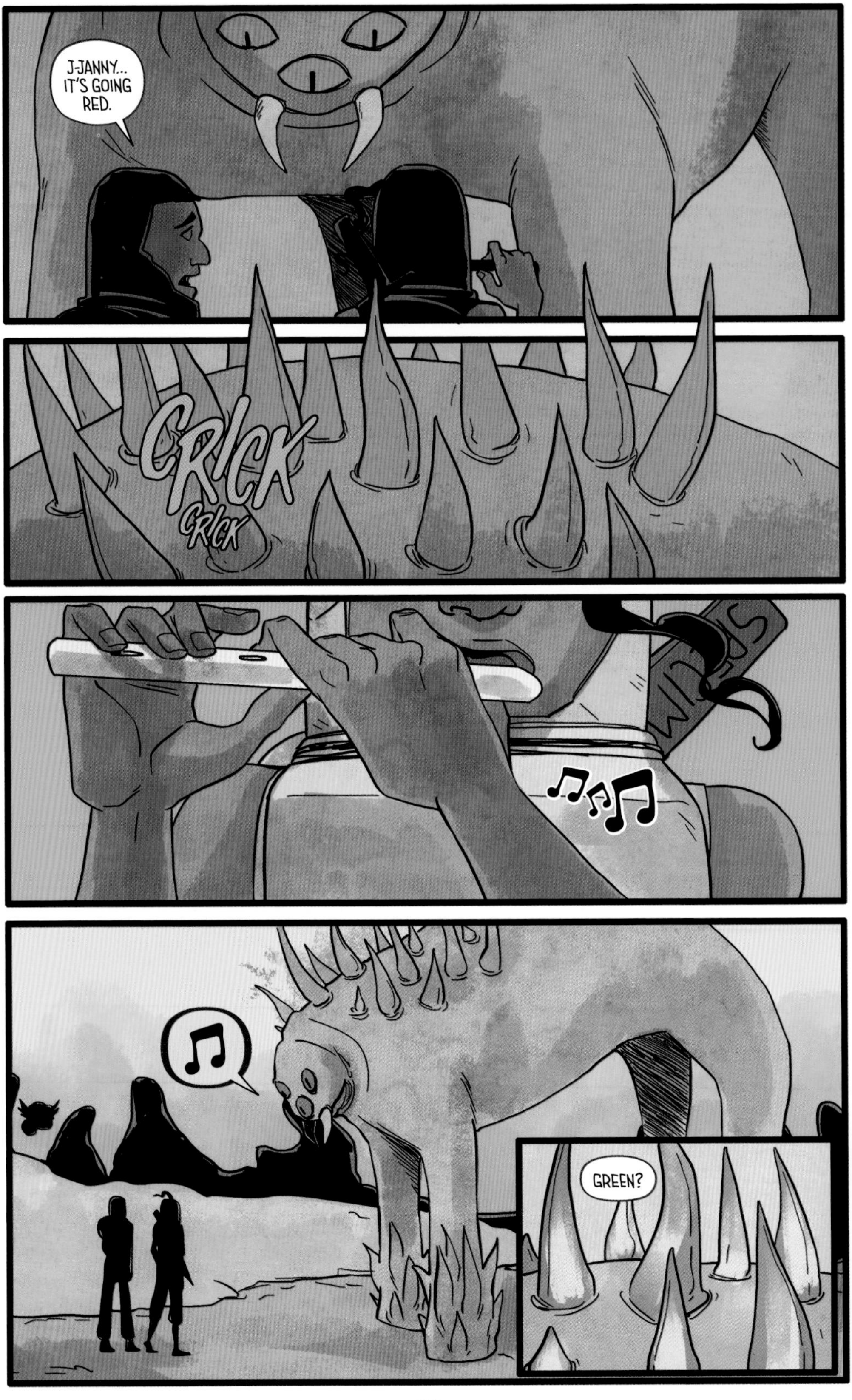
J-JANNY... IT'S GOING RED.
CRICK
CRICK
GREEN?

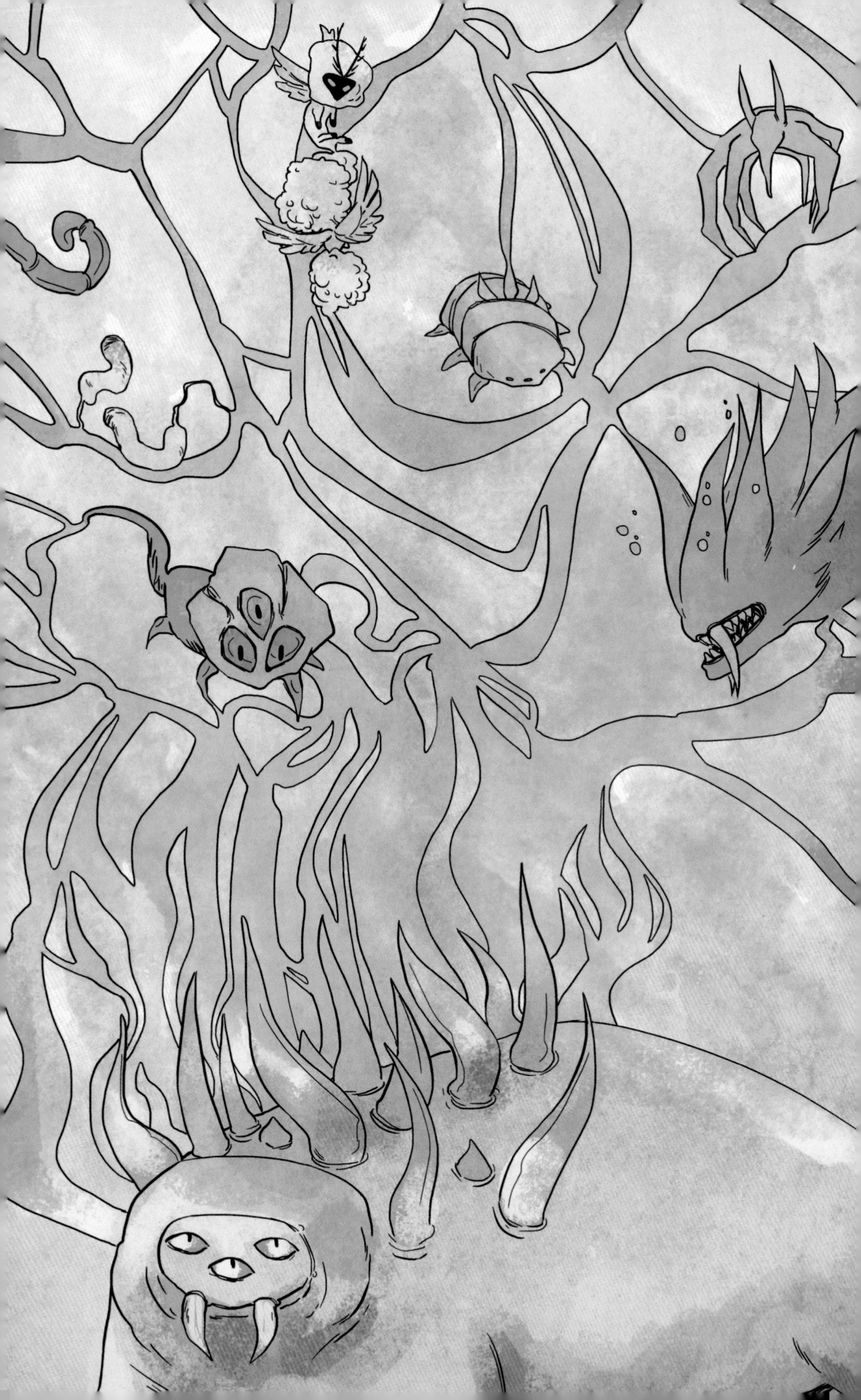

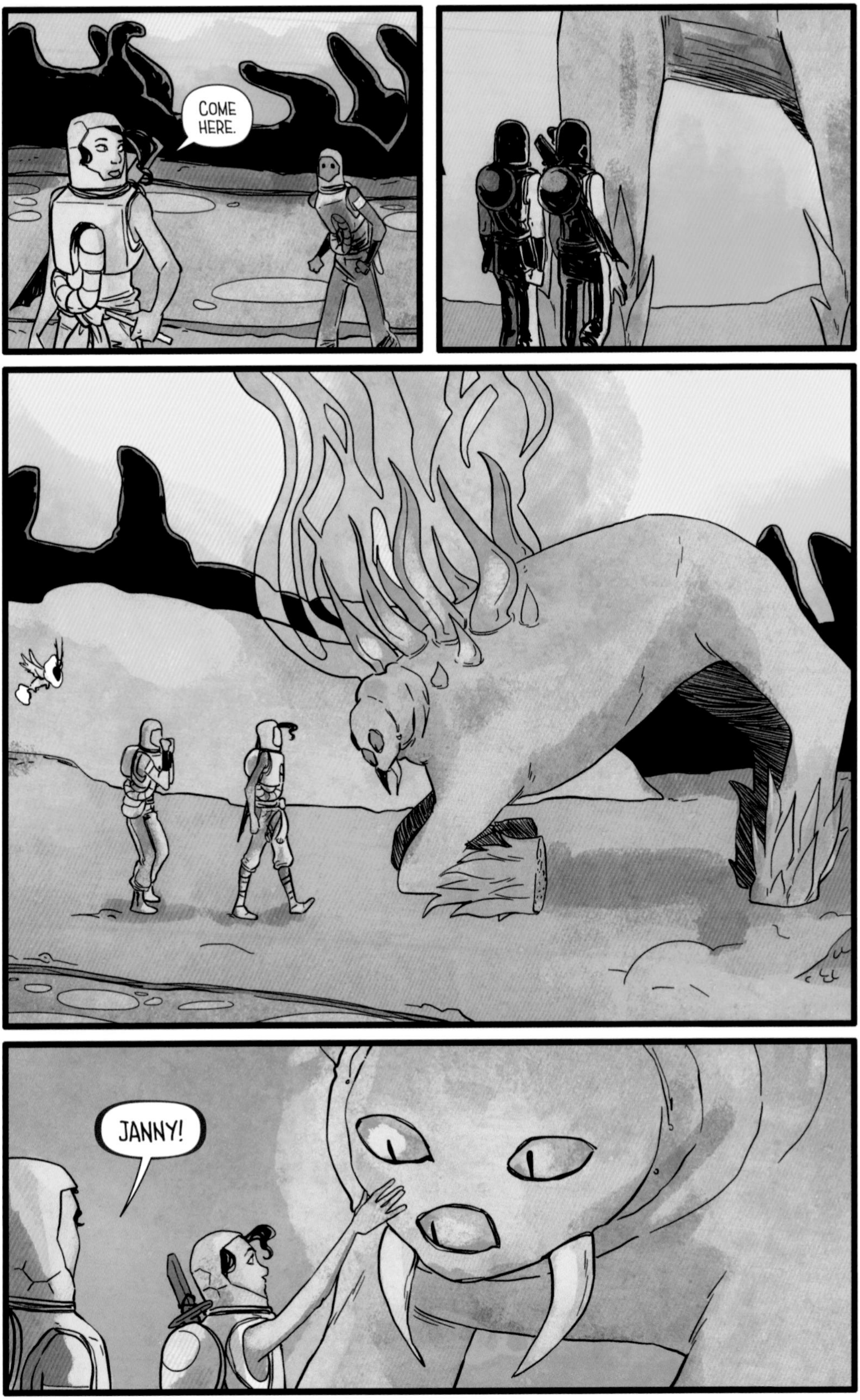
COME HERE.
JANNY!

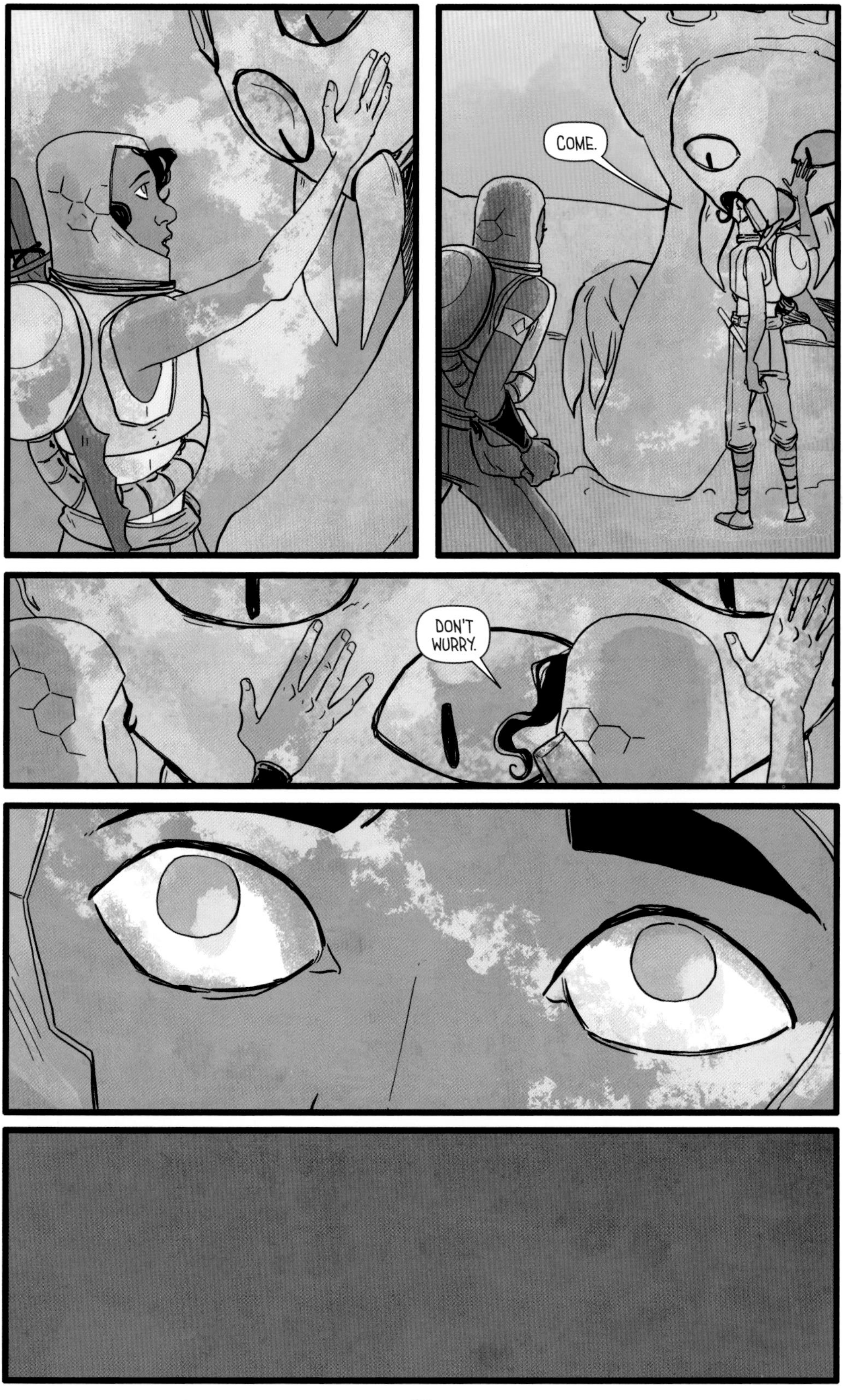
COME.
DON'T WURRY.

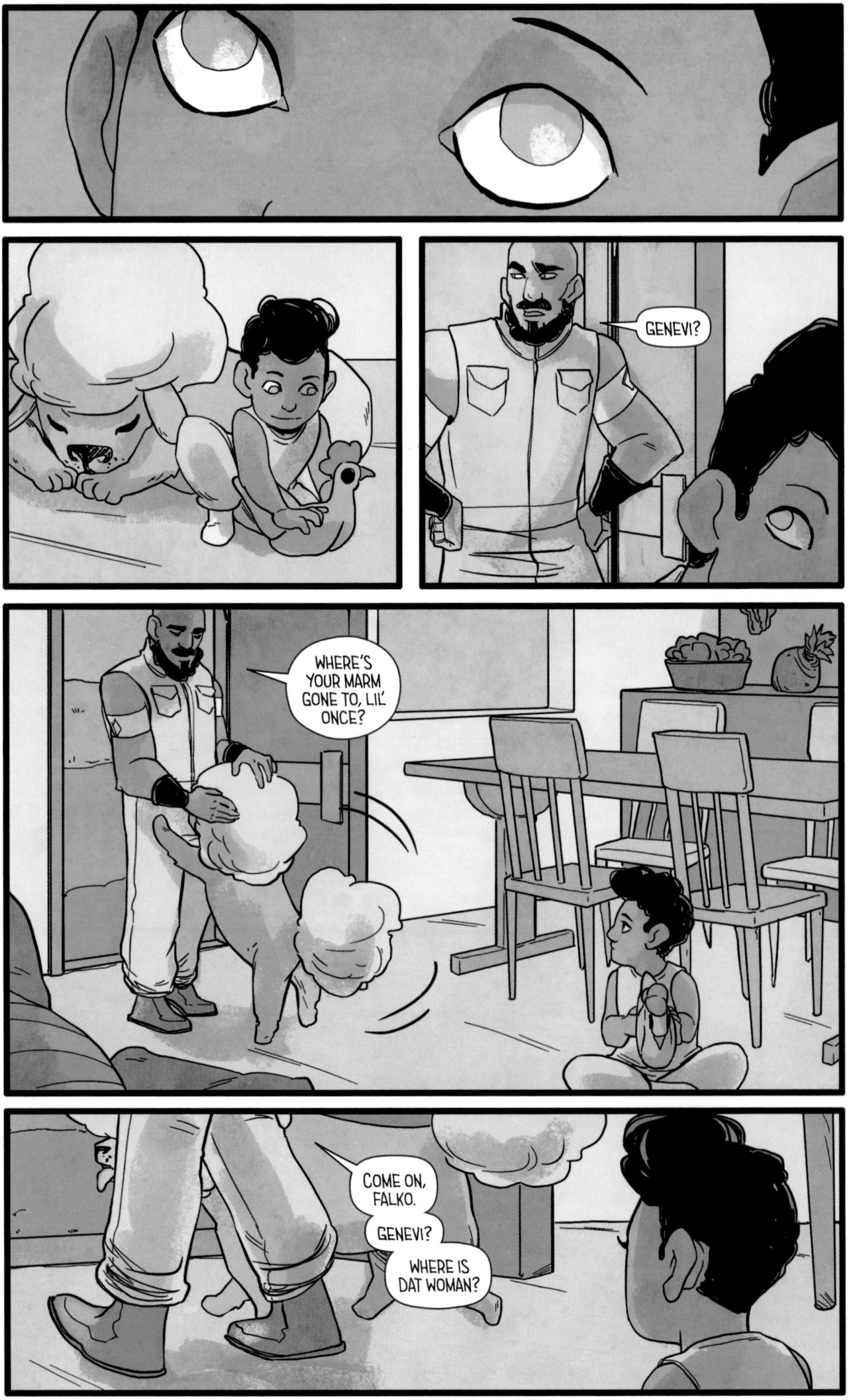
GENEVI?
WHERE'S YOUR MARM GONE TO, LIL' ONCE?
COME ON, FALKO.
GENEVI?
WHERE IS DAT WOMAN?

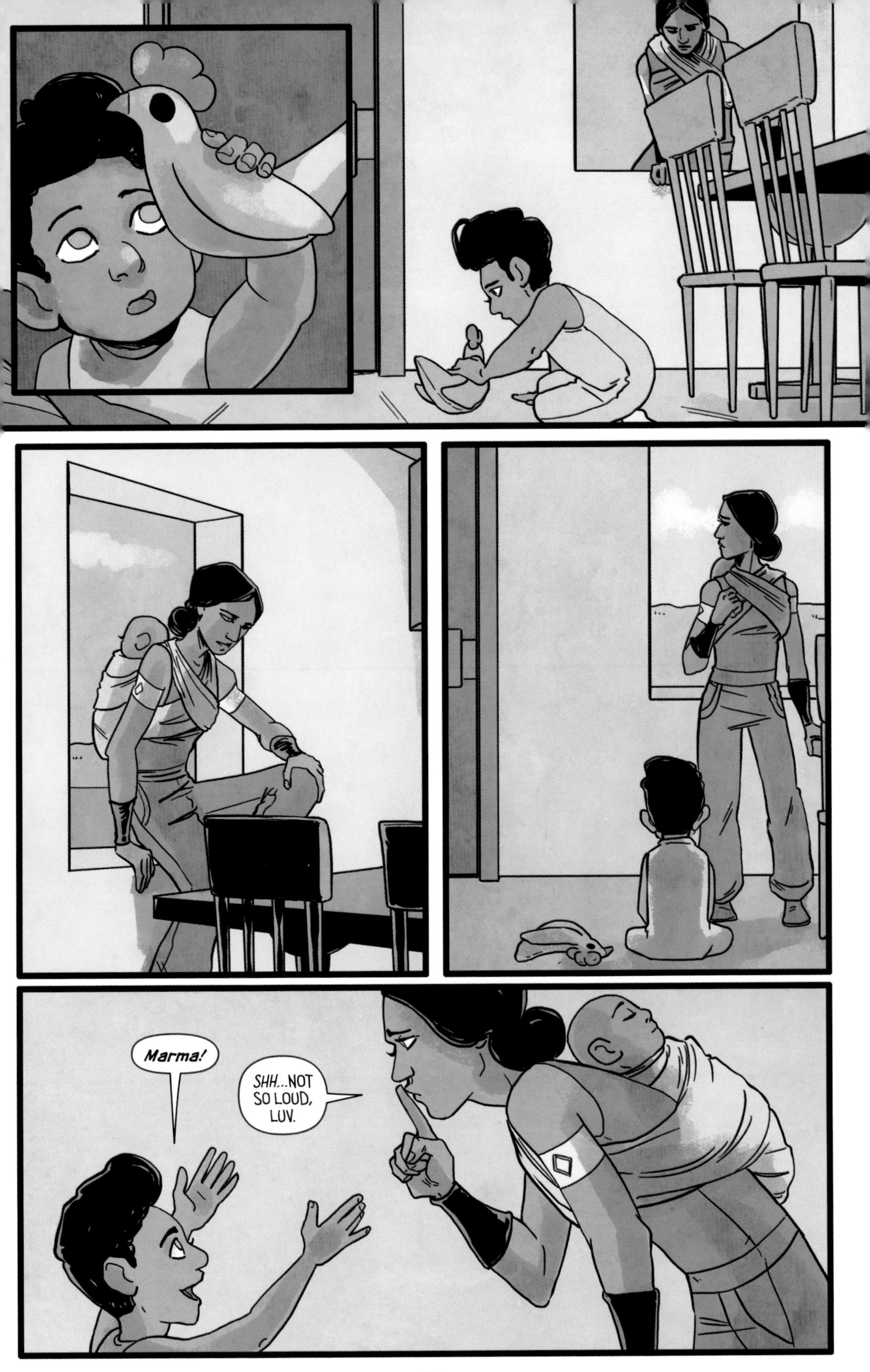
Marma!
SHH...NOT SO LOUD, LUV.

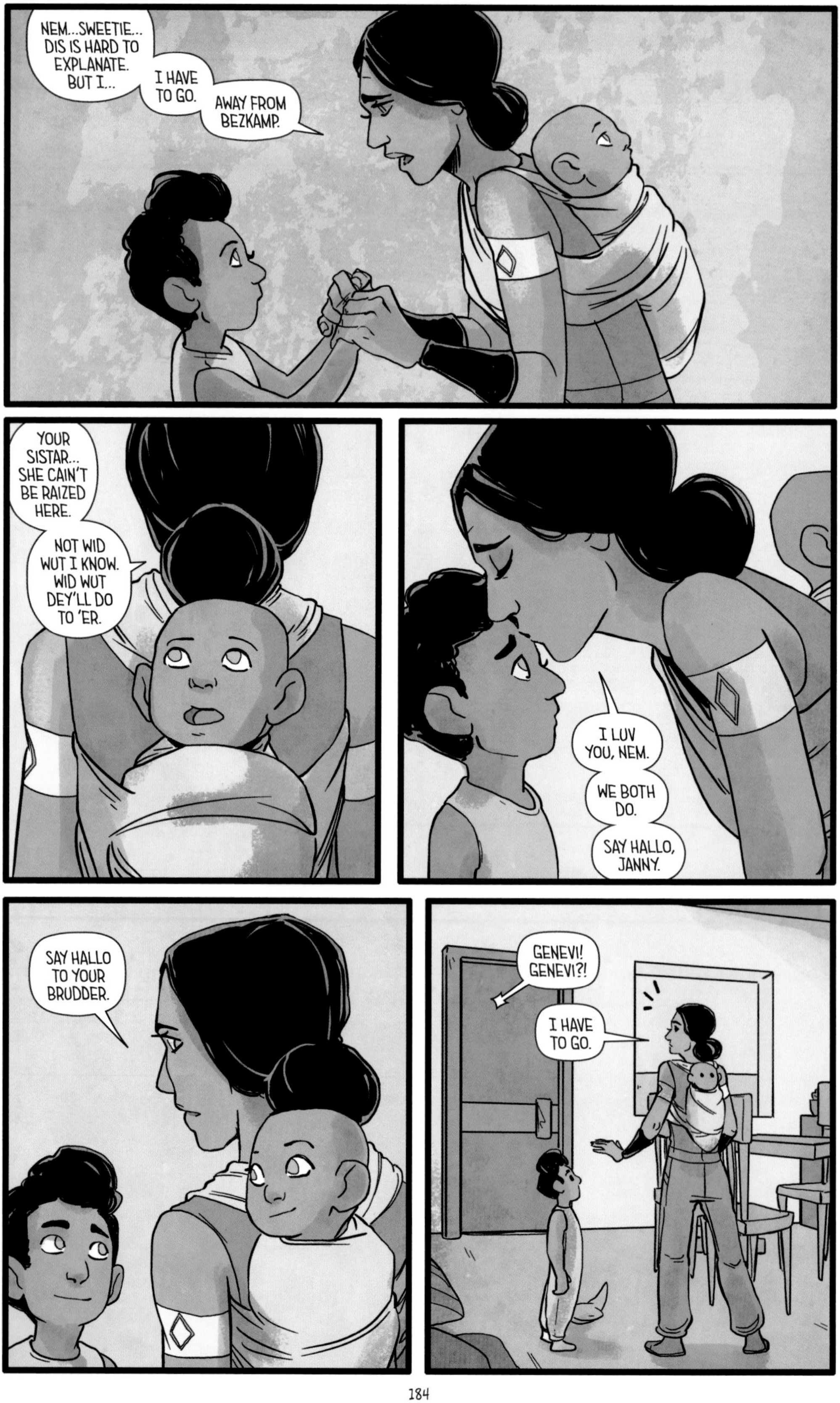
NEM...SWEETIE... DIS IS HARD TO EXPLANATE. BUT I...
I HAVE TO GO.
AWAY FROM BEZKAMP.
YOUR SISTAR... SHE CAIN'T BE RAIZED HERE.
NOT WID WUT I KNOW. WID WUT DEY'LL DO TO 'ER.
I LUV YOU, NEM.
WE BOTH DO.
SAY HALLO, JANNY.
SAY HALLO TO YOUR BRUDDER.
GENEVI! GENEVI?!
I HAVE TO GO.

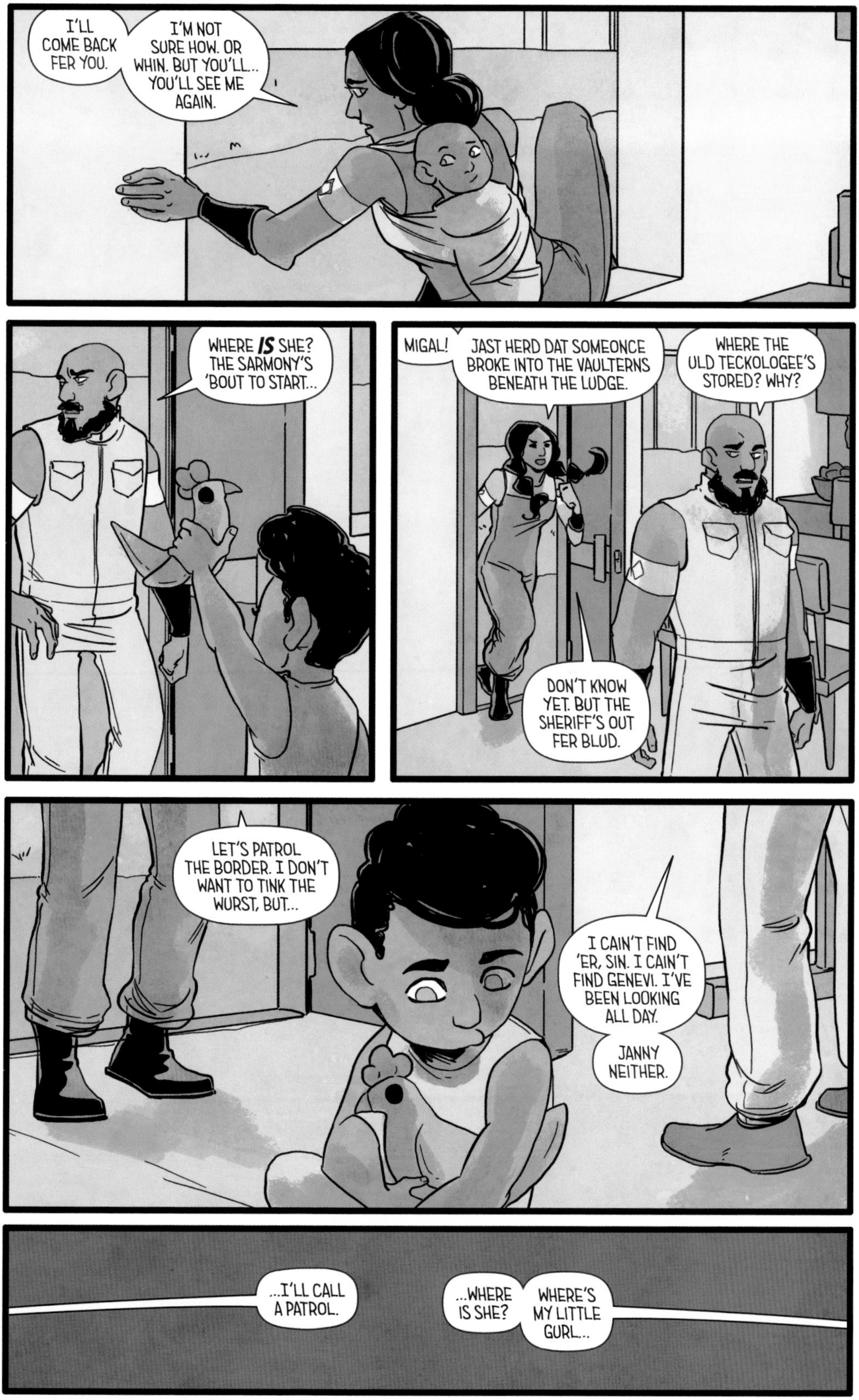
I'LL COME BACK FER YOU.
I'M NOT SURE HOW. OR WHIN. BUT YOU'LL... YOU'LL SEE ME AGAIN.
WHERE *IS* SHE? THE SARMONY'S 'BOUT TO START...
MIGAL!
JAST HERD DAT SOMEONCE BROKE INTO THE VAULTERNS BENEATH THE LUDGE.
WHERE THE ULD TECKOLOGEE'S STORED? WHY?
DON'T KNOW YET. BUT THE SHERIFF'S OUT FER BLUD.
LET'S PATROL THE BORDER. I DON'T WANT TO TINK THE WURST, BUT...
I CAIN'T FIND 'ER, SIN. I CAIN'T FIND GENEVI. I'VE BEEN LOOKING ALL DAY.
JANNY NEITHER.
...I'LL CALL A PATROL.
...WHERE IS SHE?
WHERE'S MY LITTLE GURL...

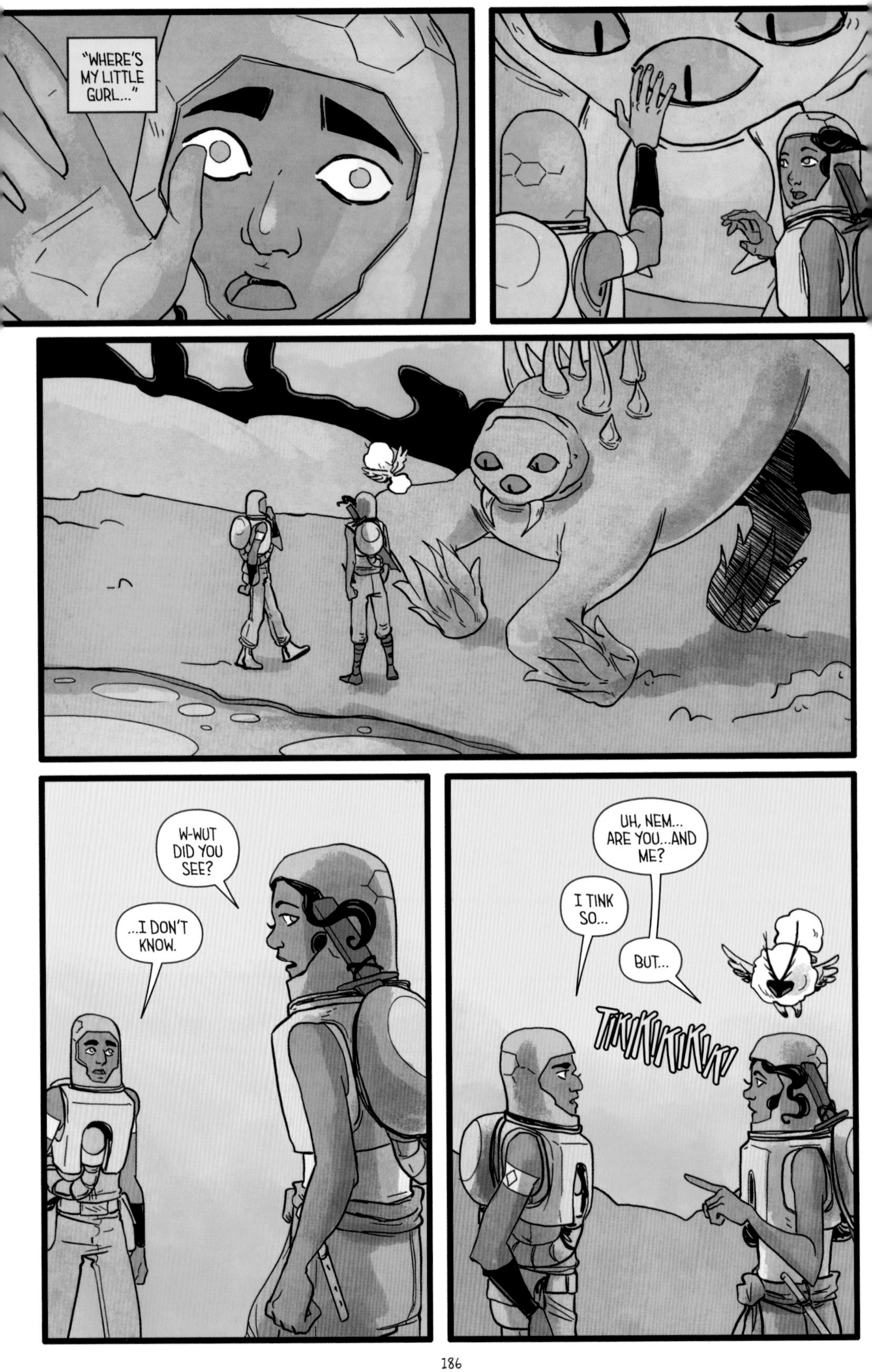
"WHERE'S MY LITTLE GURL..."
W-WUT DID YOU SEE?
...I DON'T KNOW.
UH, NEM... ARE YOU...AND ME?
I TINK SO...
BUT...
TIKIKIKIKIKI

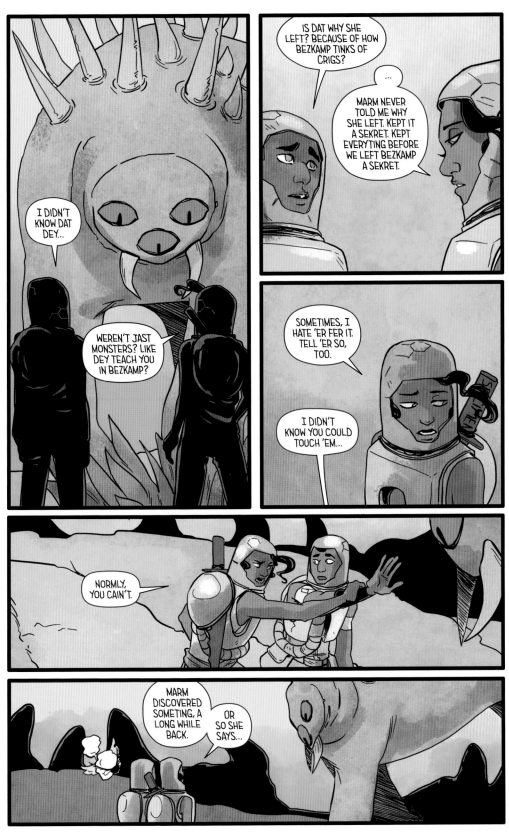

IS DAT WHY SHE LEFT? BECAUSE OF HOW BEZKAMP TINKS OF CRIGS?

...

MARM NEVER TOLD ME WHY SHE LEFT. KEPT IT A SEKRET. KEPT EVERYTHING BEFORE WE LEFT BEZKAMP A SEKRET.

I DIDN'T KNOW DAT DEY...

WEREN'T JAST MONSTERS? LIKE DEY TEACH YOU IN BEZKAMP?

SOMETIMES, I HATE 'ER FER IT. TELL 'ER SO, TOO.

I DIDN'T KNOW YOU COULD TOUCH 'EM...

NORMLY, YOU CAIN'T.

MARM DISCOVERED SOMETING, A LONG WHILE BACK.

OR SO SHE SAYS...

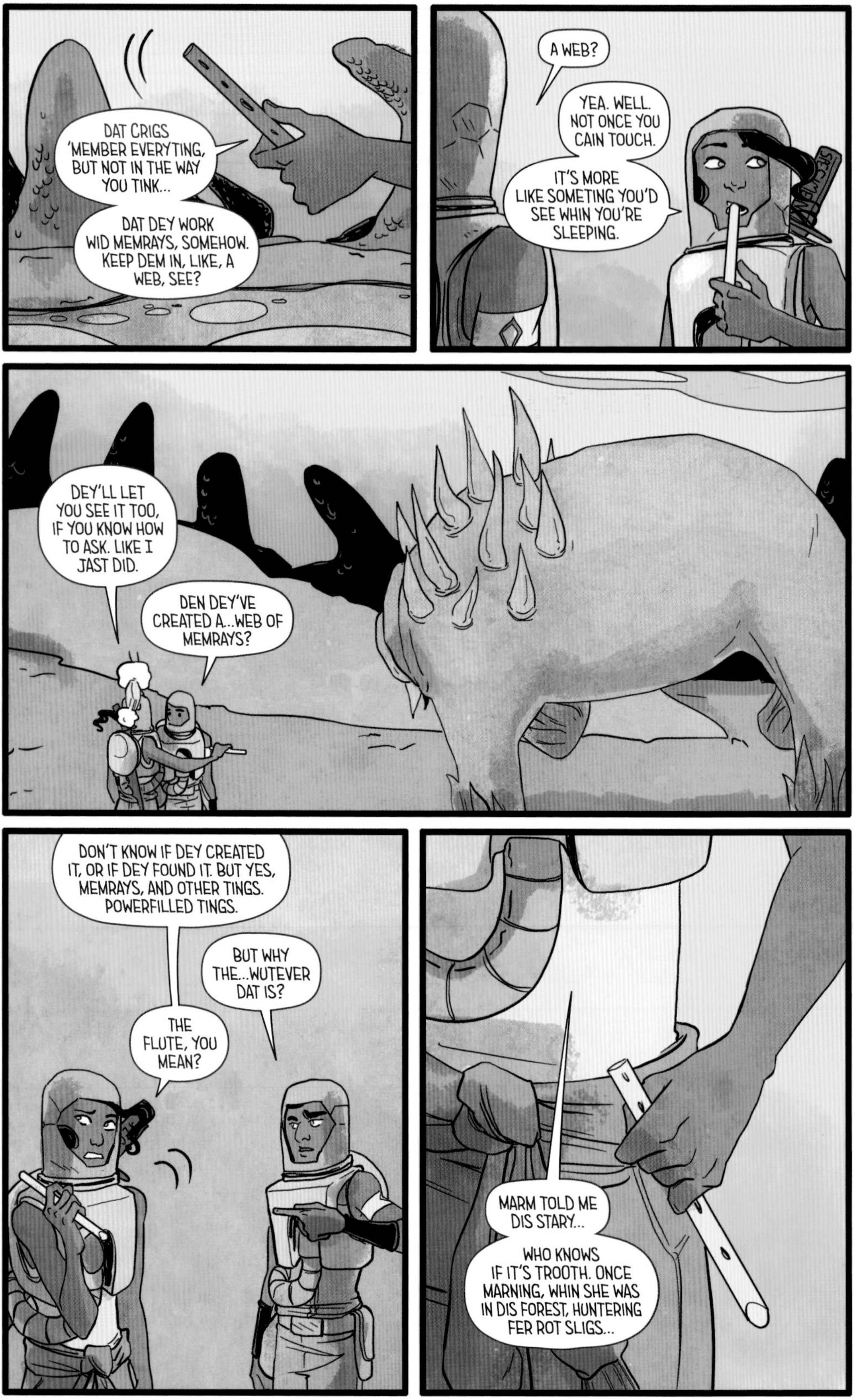
DAT CRIGS 'MEMBER EVERYTING, BUT NOT IN THE WAY YOU TINK...
DAT DEY WORK WID MEMRAYS, SOMEHOW. KEEP DEM IN, LIKE, A WEB, SEE?
A WEB?
YEA. WELL. NOT ONCE YOU CAIN TOUCH.
IT'S MORE LIKE SOMETING YOU'D SEE WHIN YOU'RE SLEEPING.
DEY'LL LET YOU SEE IT TOO, IF YOU KNOW HOW TO ASK. LIKE I JAST DID.
DEN DEY'VE CREATED A...WEB OF MEMRAYS?
DON'T KNOW IF DEY CREATED IT, OR IF DEY FOUND IT. BUT YES, MEMRAYS, AND OTHER TINGS. POWERFILLED TINGS.
BUT WHY THE...WUTEVER DAT IS?
THE FLUTE, YOU MEAN?
MARM TOLD ME DIS STARY...
WHO KNOWS IF IT'S TROOTH. ONCE MARNING, WHIN SHE WAS IN DIS FOREST, HUNTERING FER ROT SLIGS...

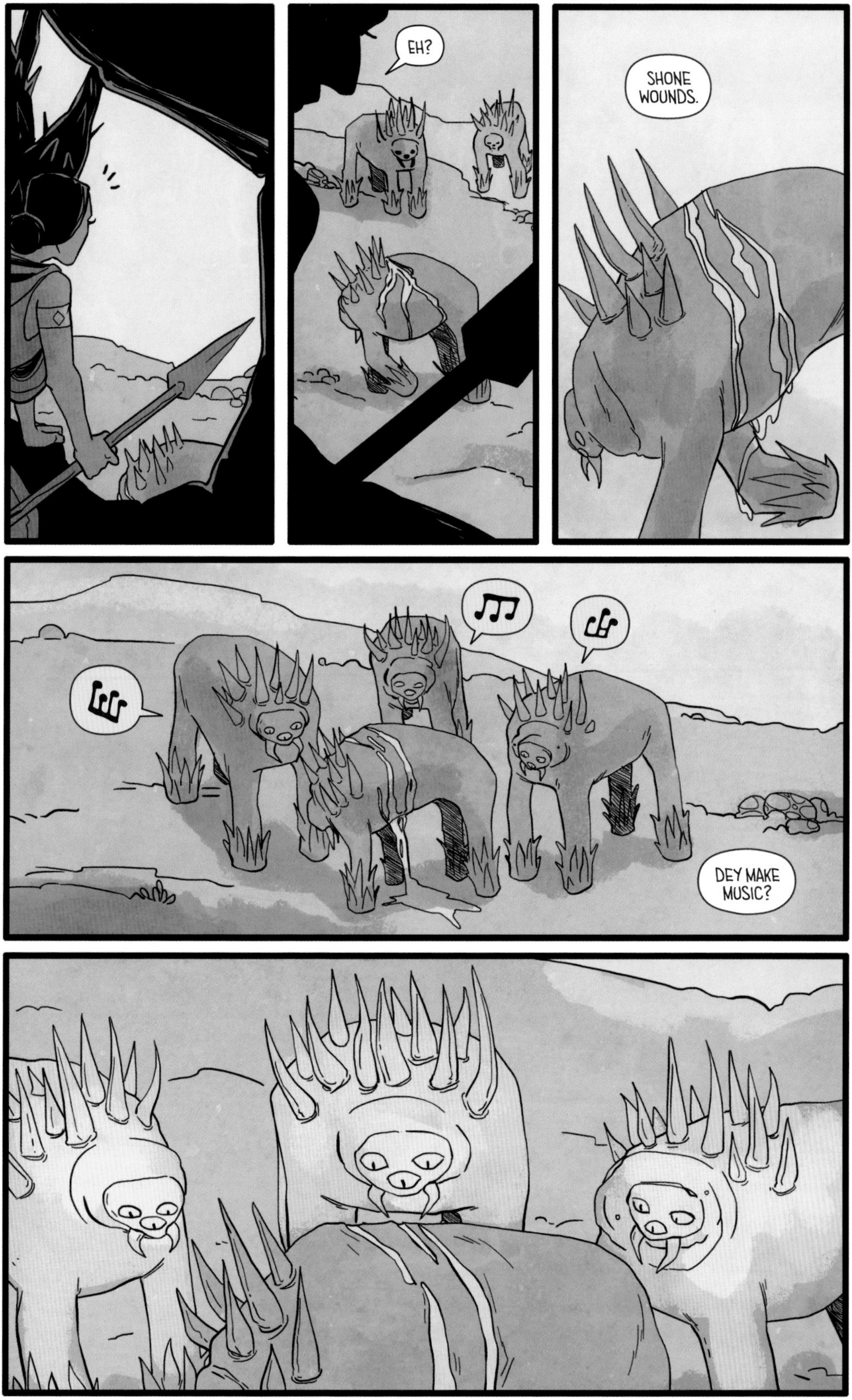
EH?
SHONE WOUNDS.
DEY MAKE MUSIC?

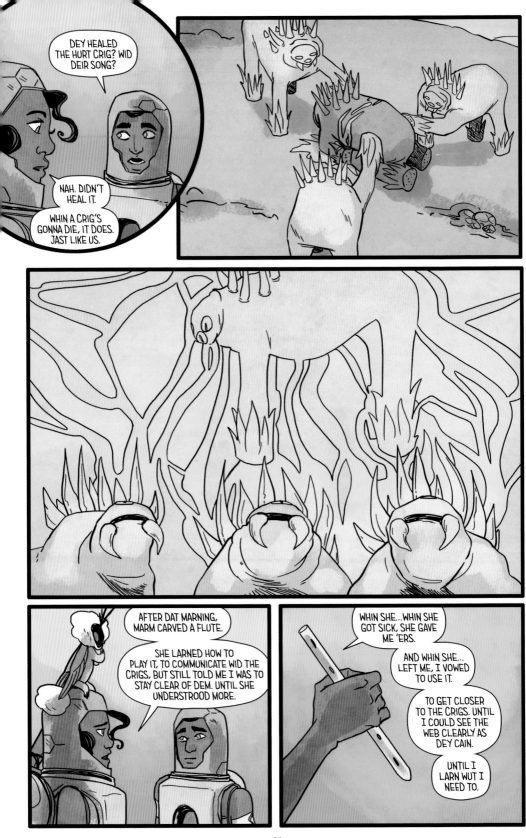

DEY HEALED THE HURT CRIG? WID DEIR SONG?

NAH. DIDN'T HEAL IT.

WHIN A CRIG'S GONNA DIE, IT DOES. JAST LIKE US.

AFTER DAT MARNING, MARM CARVED A FLUTE.

SHE LARNED HOW TO PLAY IT, TO COMMUNICATE WID THE CRIGS, BUT STILL TOLD ME I WAS TO STAY CLEAR OF DEM. UNTIL SHE UNDERSTROOD MORE.

WHIN SHE...WHIN SHE GOT SICK, SHE GAVE ME 'ERS.

AND WHIN SHE... LEFT ME, I VOWED TO USE IT.

TO GET CLOSER TO THE CRIGS. UNTIL I COULD SEE THE WEB CLEARLY AS DEY CAIN.

UNTIL I LARN WUT I NEED TO.

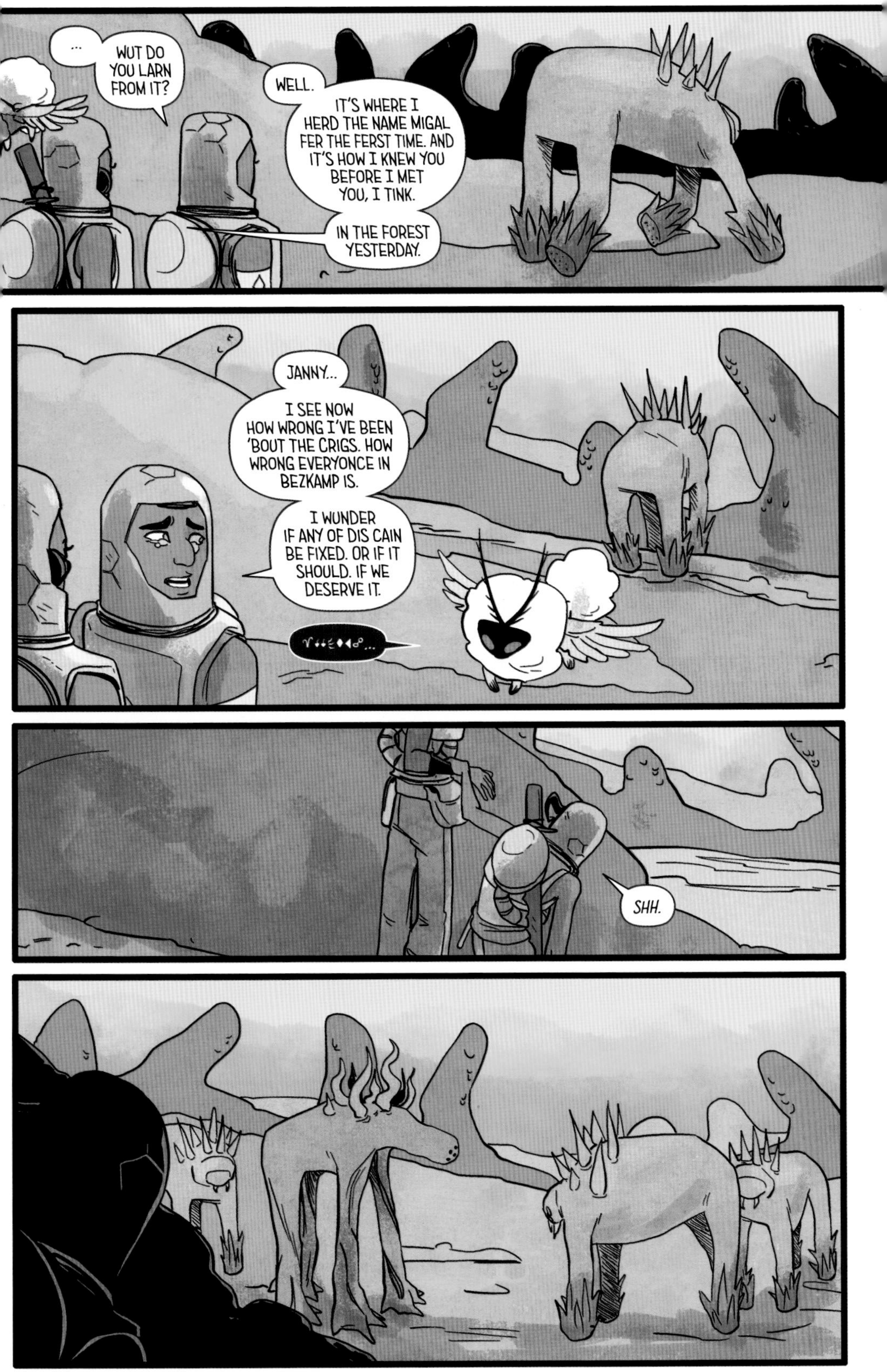
...
WUT DO YOU LARN FROM IT?
WELL.
IT'S WHERE I HERD THE NAME MIGAL FER THE FERST TIME. AND IT'S HOW I KNEW YOU BEFORE I MET YOU, I TINK.
IN THE FOREST YESTERDAY.
JANNY...
I SEE NOW HOW WRONG I'VE BEEN 'BOUT THE CRIGS. HOW WRONG EVERYONCE IN BEZKAMP IS.
I WUNDER IF ANY OF DIS CAIN BE FIXED. OR IF IT SHOULD. IF WE DESERVE IT.
SHH.

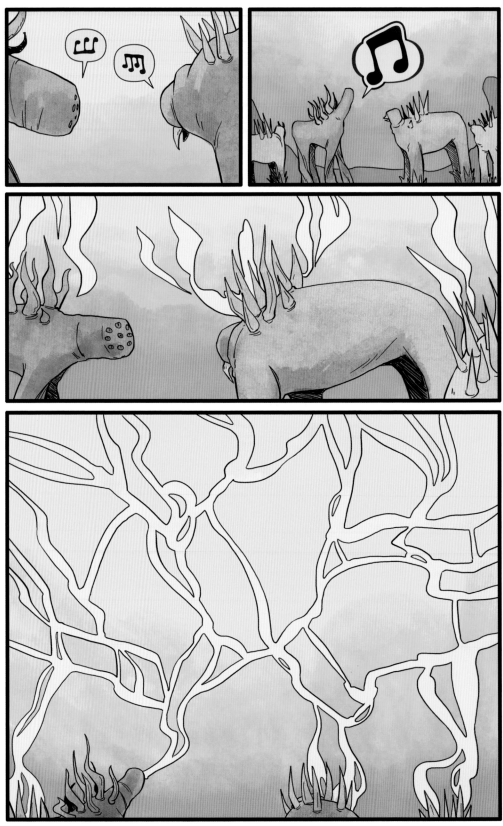

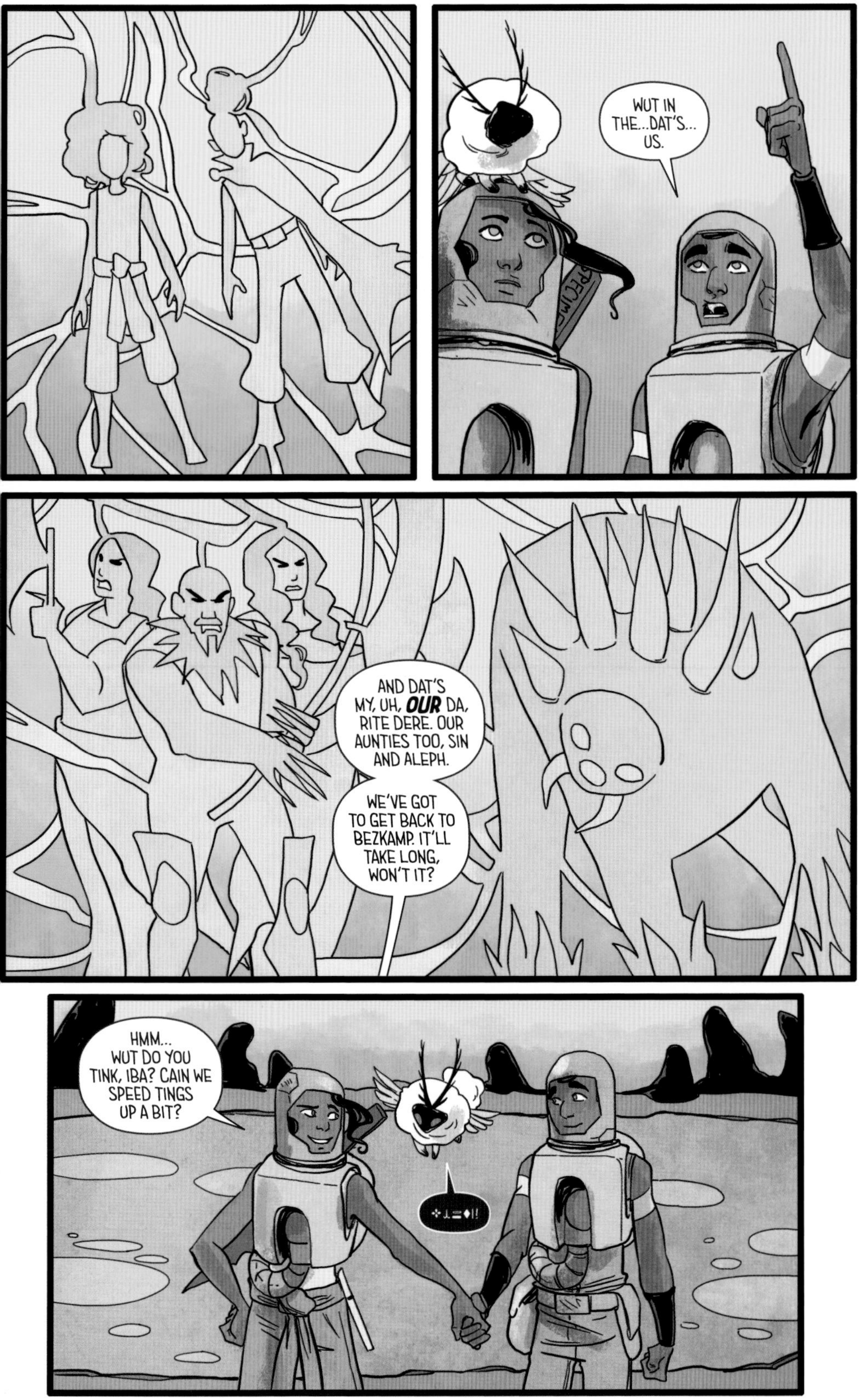
WUT IN THE...DAT'S... US.
AND DAT'S MY, UH, ***OUR*** DA, RITE DERE. OUR AUNTIES TOO, SIN AND ALEPH.
WE'VE GOT TO GET BACK TO BEZKAMP. IT'LL TAKE LONG, WON'T IT?
HMM... WUT DO YOU TINK, IBA? CAIN WE SPEED TINGS UP A BIT?

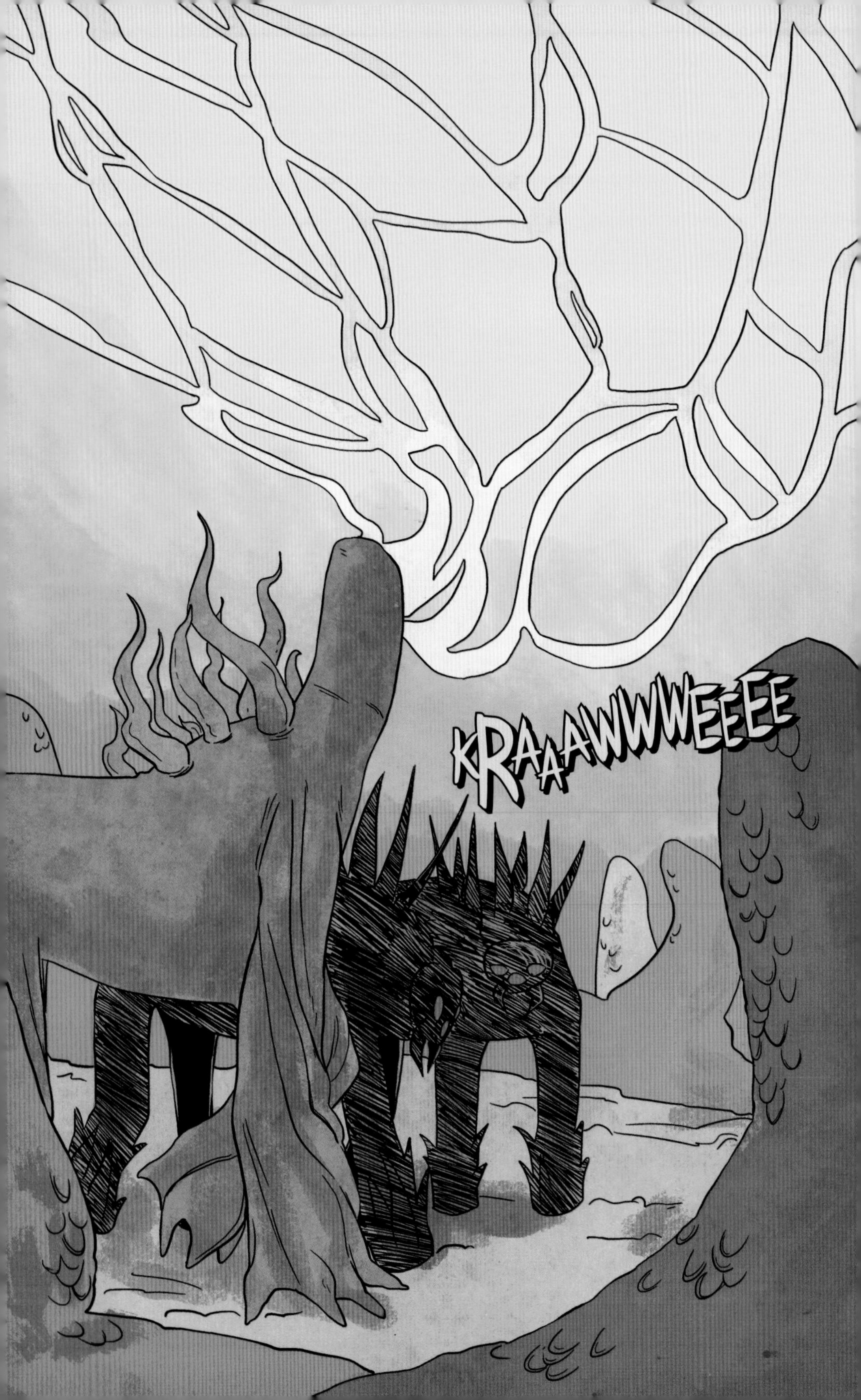
KRAAAWWWEEEEE

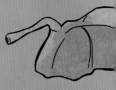

CHEPTAR
FIBE

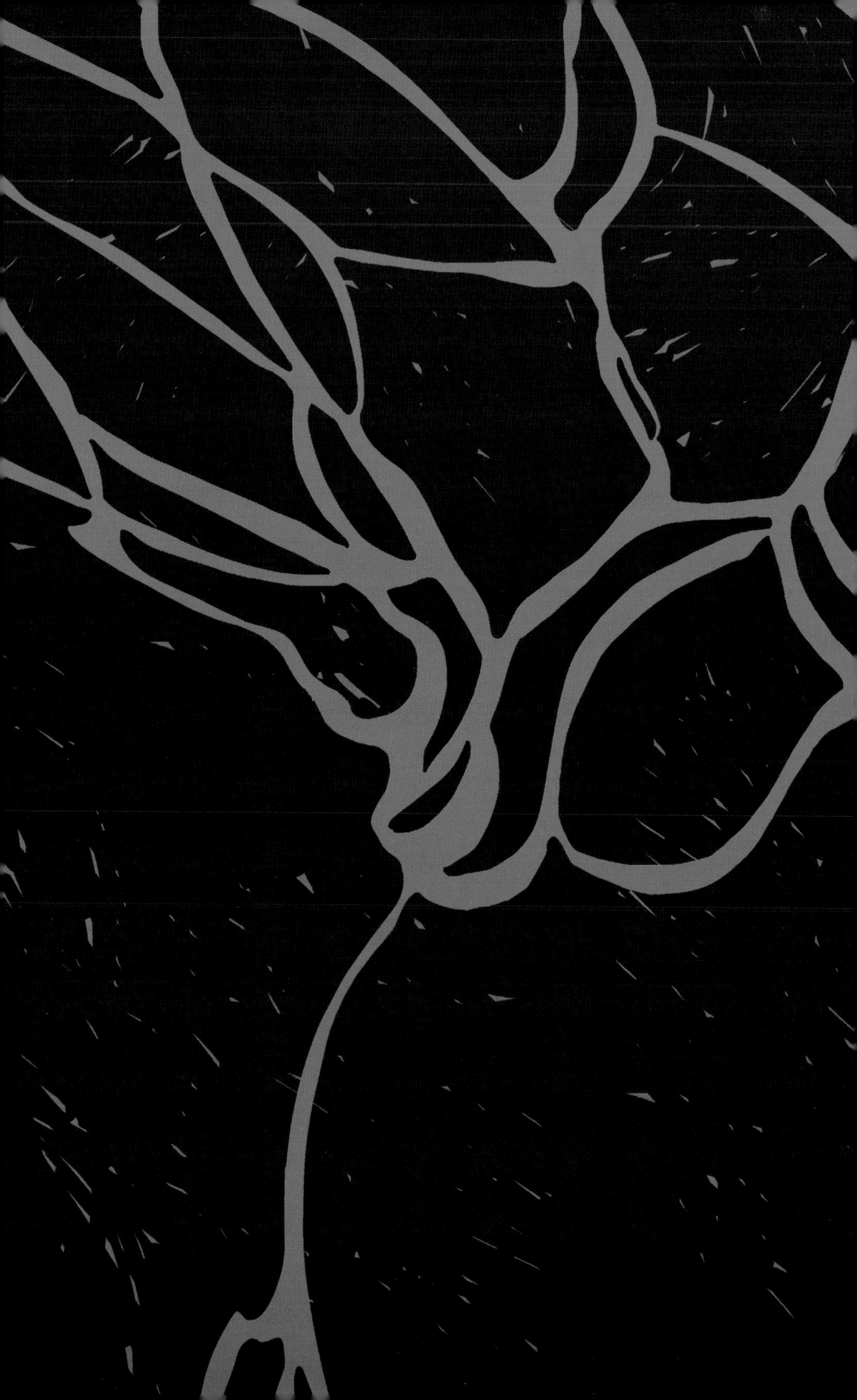

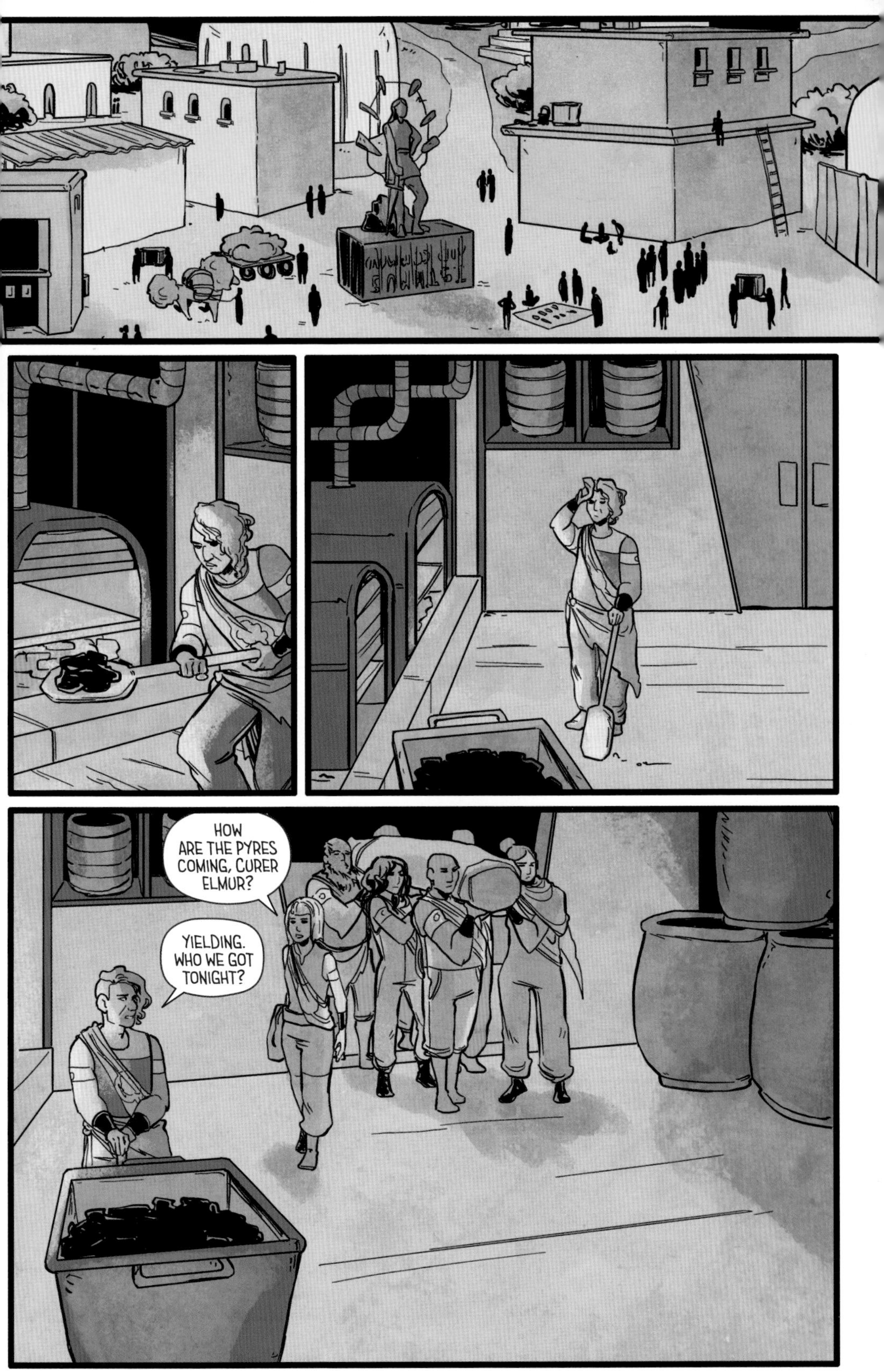
HOW ARE THE PYRES COMING, CURER ELMUR?
YIELDING. WHO WE GOT TONIGHT?

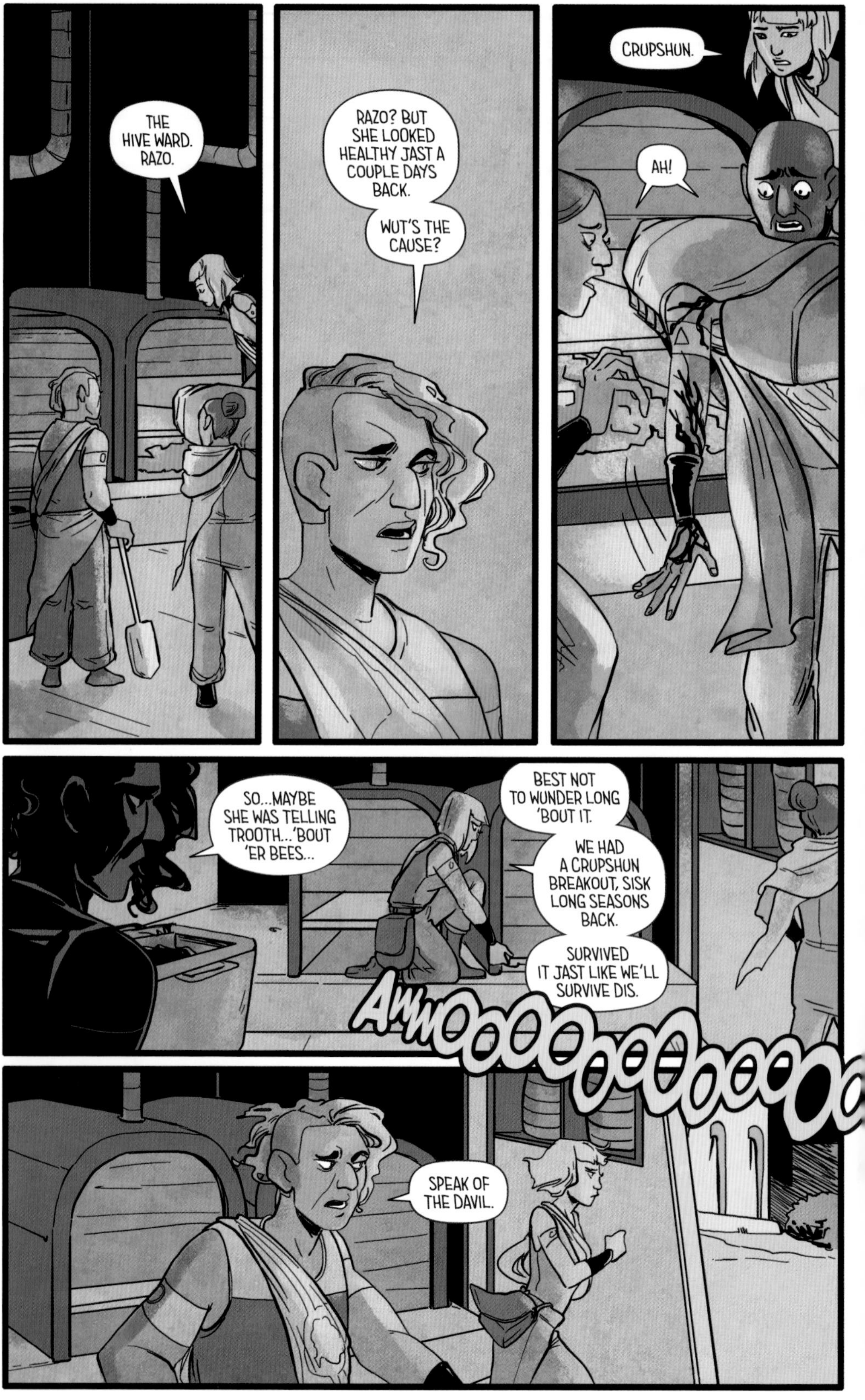
THE HIVE WARD. RAZO.
RAZO? BUT SHE LOOKED HEALTHY JAST A COUPLE DAYS BACK.
WUT'S THE CAUSE?
CRUPSHUN.
AH!
SO...MAYBE SHE WAS TELLING TROOTH...'BOUT 'ER BEES...
BEST NOT TO WUNDER LONG 'BOUT IT.
WE HAD A CRUPSHUN BREAKOUT, SISK LONG SEASONS BACK.
SURVIVED IT JAST LIKE WE'LL SURVIVE DIS.
AWWOOOOOOOOOOOOOOO
SPEAK OF THE DAVIL.

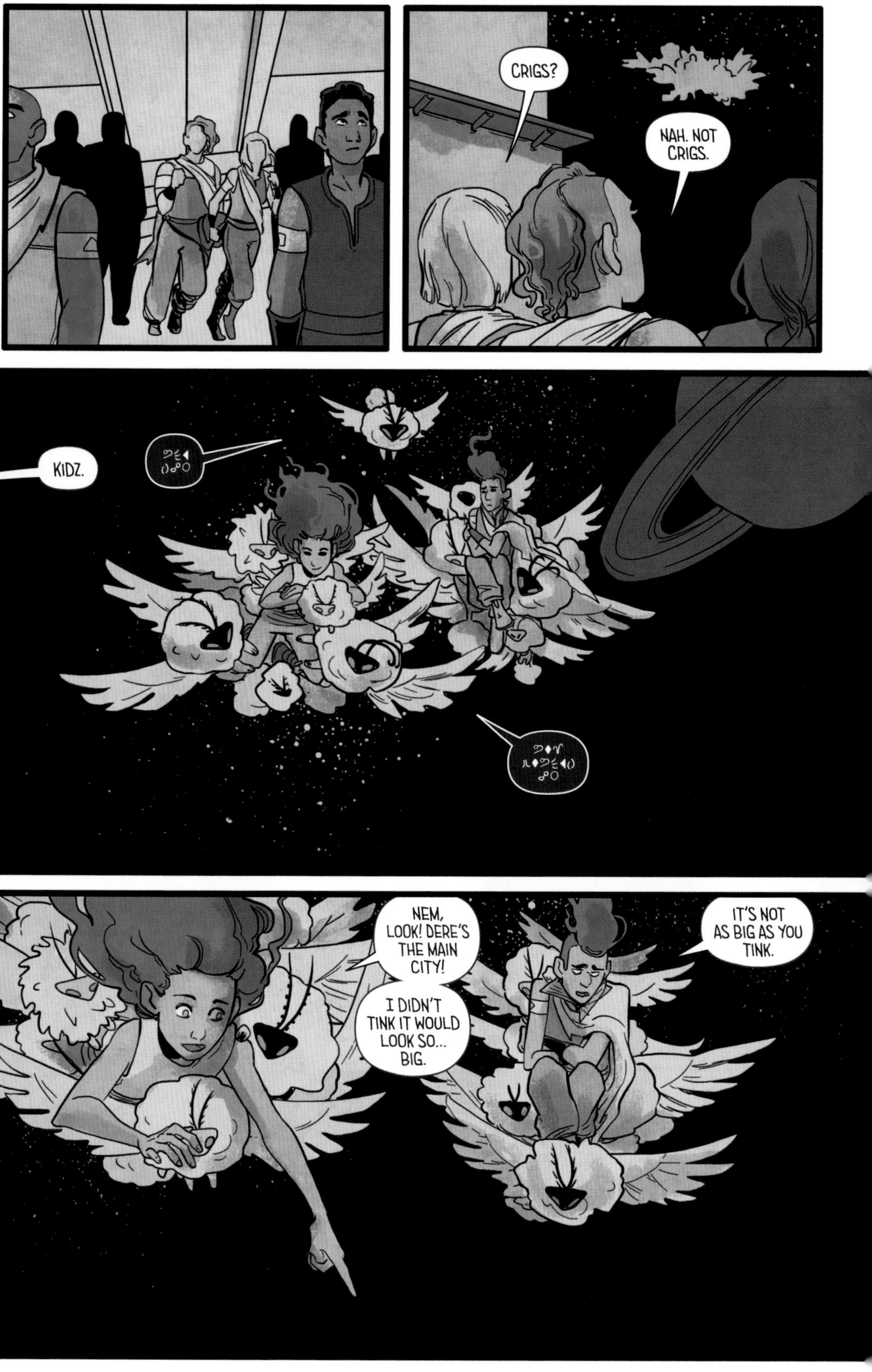
CRIGS?
NAH. NOT CRIGS.
KIDZ.
NEM, LOOK! DERE'S THE MAIN CITY!
I DIDN'T TINK IT WOULD LOOK SO... BIG.
IT'S NOT AS BIG AS YOU TINK.

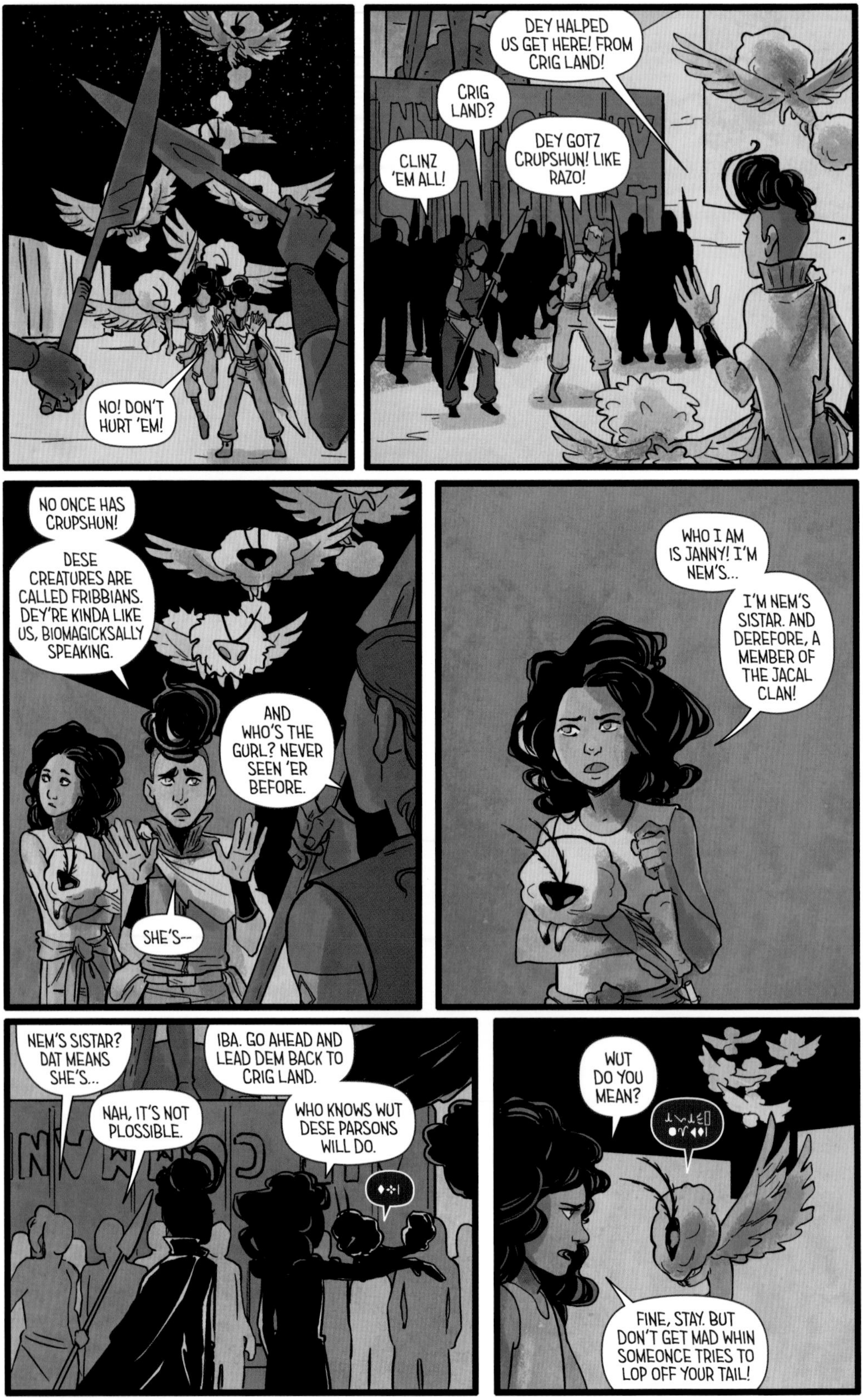
NO! DON'T HURT 'EM!
CLINZ 'EM ALL!
CRIG LAND?
DEY HALPED US GET HERE! FROM CRIG LAND!
DEY GOTZ CRUPSHUN! LIKE RAZO!
NO ONCE HAS CRUPSHUN!
DESE CREATURES ARE CALLED FRIBBIANS. DEY'RE KINDA LIKE US, BIOMAGICKSALLY SPEAKING.
AND WHO'S THE GURL? NEVER SEEN 'ER BEFORE.
SHE'S--
WHO I AM IS JANNY! I'M NEM'S...
I'M NEM'S SISTAR. AND DEREFORE, A MEMBER OF THE JACAL CLAN!
NEM'S SISTAR? DAT MEANS SHE'S...
NAH, IT'S NOT PLOSSIBLE.
IBA. GO AHEAD AND LEAD DEM BACK TO CRIG LAND.
WHO KNOWS WUT DESE PARSONS WILL DO.
WUT DO YOU MEAN?
FINE, STAY. BUT DON'T GET MAD WHIN SOMEONCE TRIES TO LOP OFF YOUR TAIL!

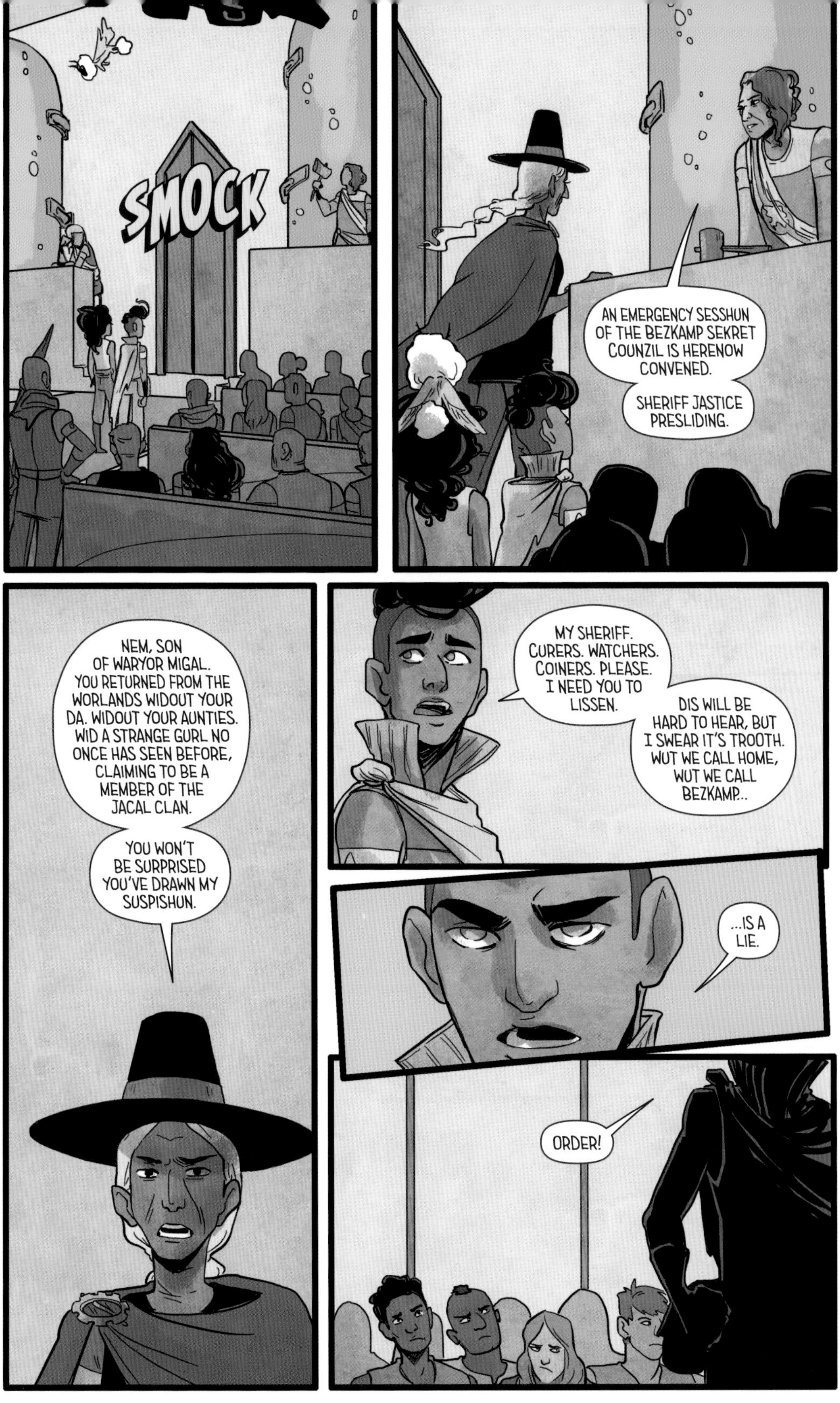
SMOCK
AN EMERGENCY SESSHUN OF THE BEZKAMP SEKRET COUNZIL IS HERENOW CONVENED.
SHERIFF JASTICE PRESLIDING.
NEM, SON OF WARYOR MIGAL. YOU RETURNED FROM THE WORLANDS WIDOUT YOUR DA. WIDOUT YOUR AUNTIES. WID A STRANGE GURL NO ONCE HAS SEEN BEFORE, CLAIMING TO BE A MEMBER OF THE JACAL CLAN.
YOU WON'T BE SURPRISED YOU'VE DRAWN MY SUSPISHUN.
MY SHERIFF. CURERS. WATCHERS. COINERS. PLEASE. I NEED YOU TO LISSEN.
DIS WILL BE HARD TO HEAR, BUT I SWEAR IT'S TROOTH. WUT WE CALL HOME, WUT WE CALL BEZKAMP...
...IS A LIE.
ORDER!

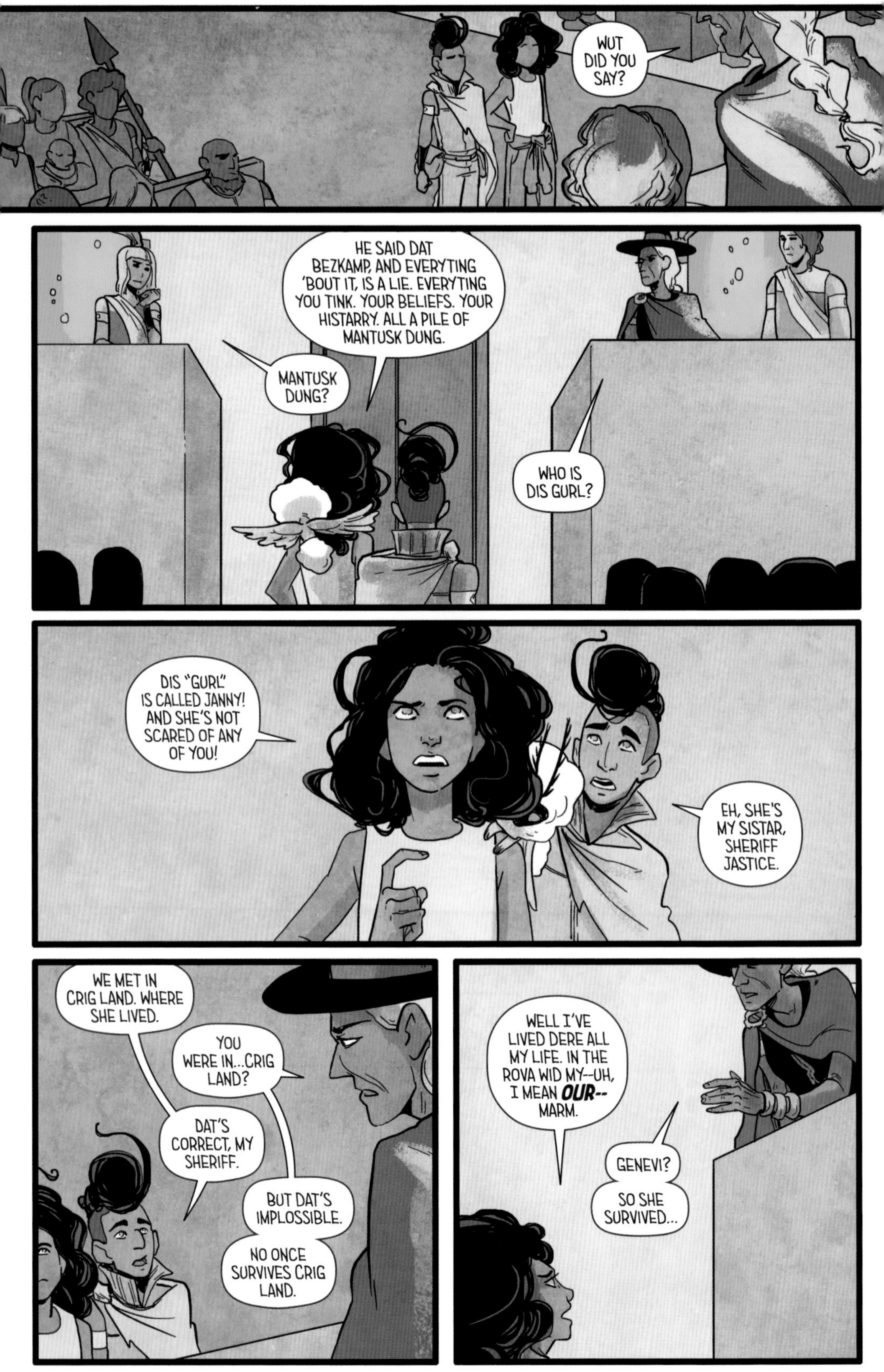
WUT DID YOU SAY?
HE SAID DAT BEZKAMP, AND EVERYTING 'BOUT IT, IS A LIE. EVERYTING YOU TINK. YOUR BELIEFS. YOUR HISTARRY. ALL A PILE OF MANTUSK DUNG.
MANTUSK DUNG?
WHO IS DIS GURL?
DIS "GURL" IS CALLED JANNY! AND SHE'S NOT SCARED OF ANY OF YOU!
EH, SHE'S MY SISTAR, SHERIFF JASTICE.
WE MET IN CRIG LAND. WHERE SHE LIVED.
YOU WERE IN...CRIG LAND?
DAT'S CORRECT, MY SHERIFF.
BUT DAT'S IMPLOSSIBLE.
NO ONCE SURVIVES CRIG LAND.
WELL I'VE LIVED DERE ALL MY LIFE. IN THE ROVA WID MY--UH, I MEAN OUR-- MARM.
GENEVI?
SO SHE SURVIVED...

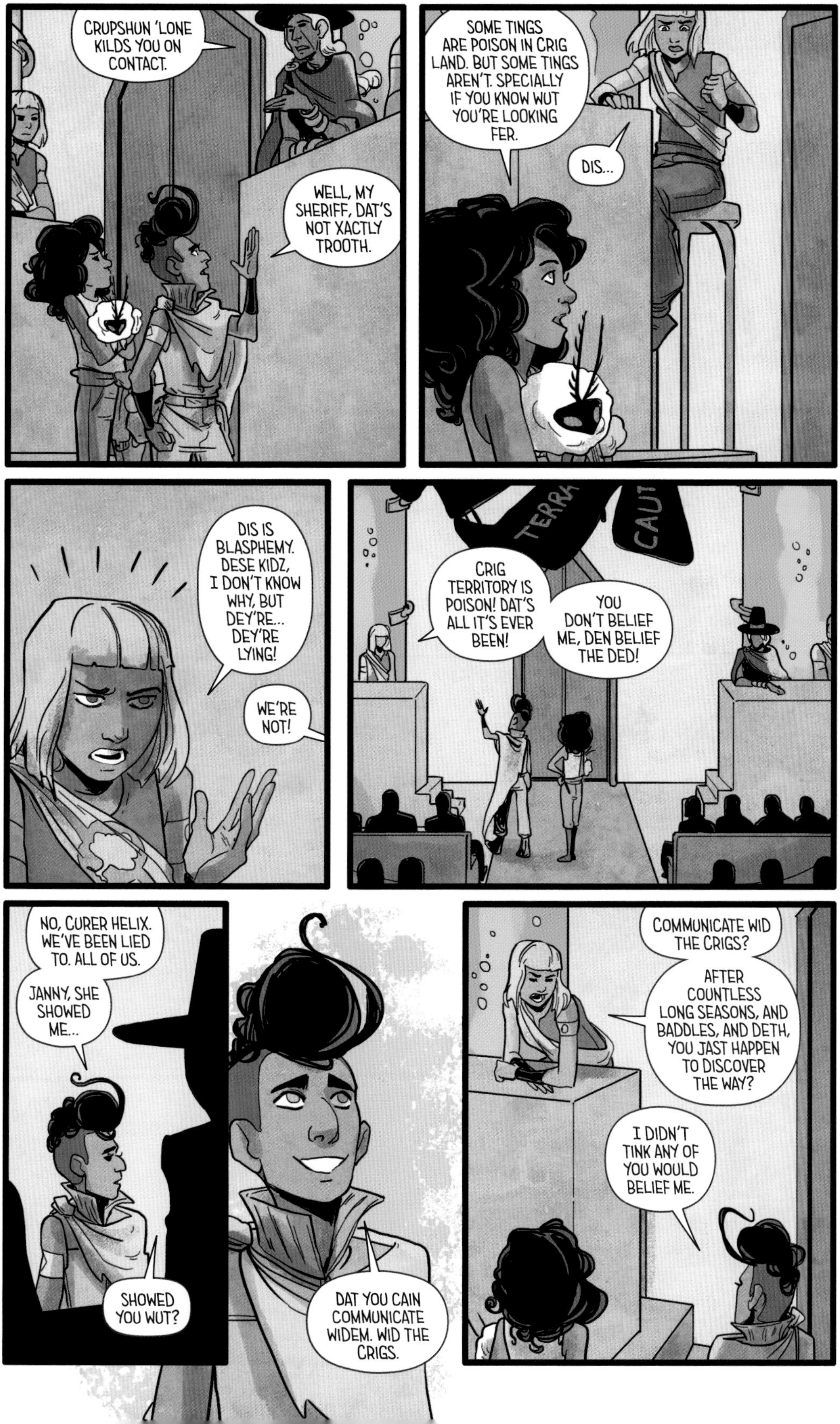
CRUPSHUN 'LONE KILDS YOU ON CONTACT.
WELL, MY SHERIFF, DAT'S NOT XACTLY TROOTH.
SOME TINGS ARE POISON IN CRIG LAND. BUT SOME TINGS AREN'T. SPECIALLY IF YOU KNOW WUT YOU'RE LOOKING FER.
DIS...
DIS IS BLASPHEMY. DESE KIDZ, I DON'T KNOW WHY, BUT DEY'RE... DEY'RE LYING!
WE'RE NOT!
TERRA
CAUT
CRIG TERRITORY IS POISON! DAT'S ALL IT'S EVER BEEN!
YOU DON'T BELIEF ME, DEN BELIEF THE DED!
NO, CURER HELIX. WE'VE BEEN LIED TO. ALL OF US.
JANNY, SHE SHOWED ME...
SHOWED YOU WUT?
DAT YOU CAIN COMMUNICATE WIDEM. WID THE CRIGS.
COMMUNICATE WID THE CRIGS?
AFTER COUNTLESS LONG SEASONS, AND BADDLES, AND DETH, YOU JAST HAPPEN TO DISCOVER THE WAY?
I DIDN'T TINK ANY OF YOU WOULD BELIEF ME.

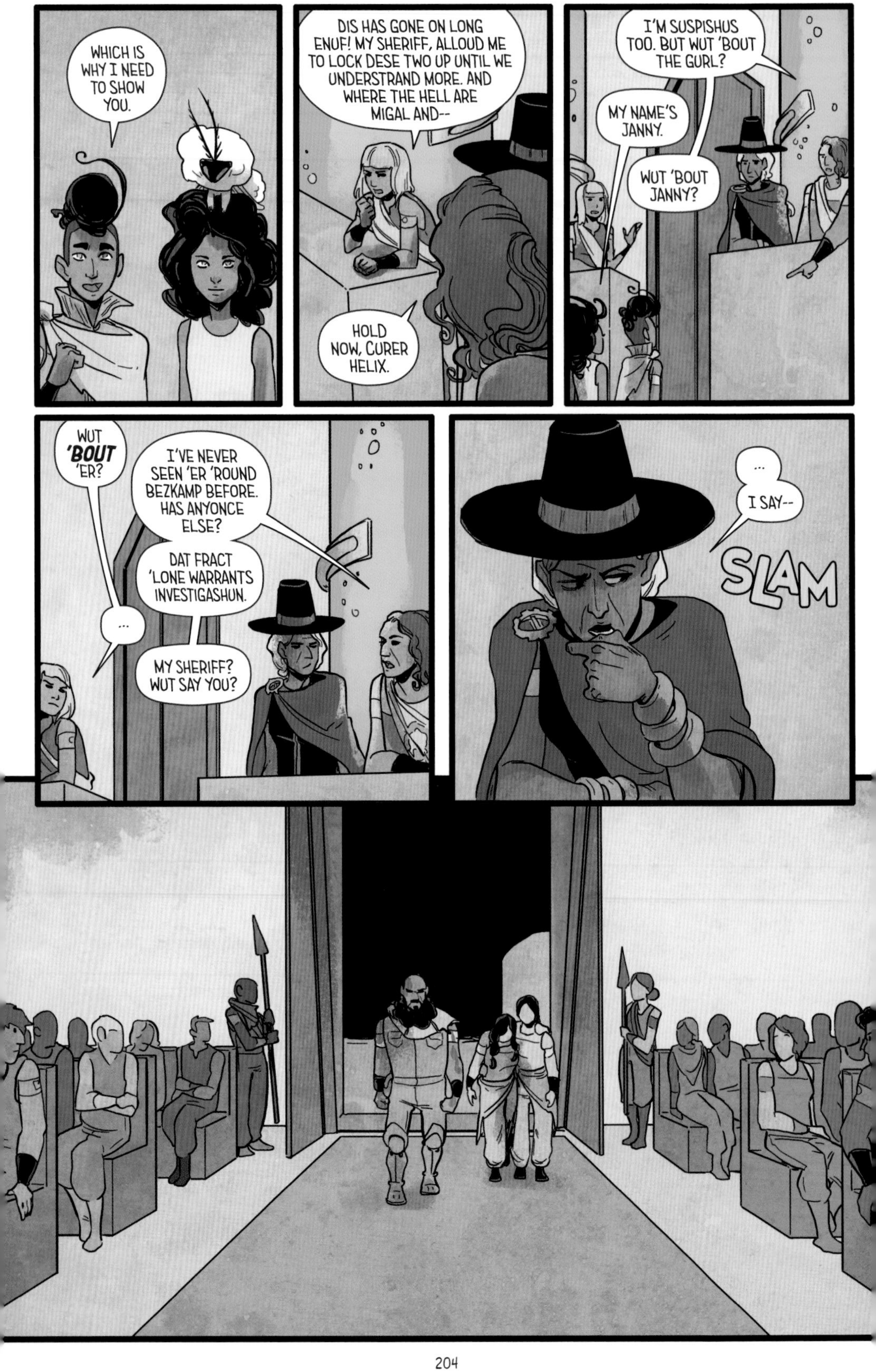
WHICH IS WHY I NEED TO SHOW YOU.
DIS HAS GONE ON LONG ENUF! MY SHERIFF, ALLOUD ME TO LOCK DESE TWO UP UNTIL WE UNDERSTRAND MORE. AND WHERE THE HELL ARE MIGAL AND--
HOLD NOW, CURER HELIX.
I'M SUSPISHUS TOO. BUT WUT 'BOUT THE GURL?
MY NAME'S JANNY.
WUT 'BOUT JANNY?
WUT 'BOUT 'ER?
I'VE NEVER SEEN 'ER 'ROUND BEZKAMP BEFORE. HAS ANYONCE ELSE?
DAT FRACT 'LONE WARRANTS INVESTIGASHUN.
...
MY SHERIFF? WUT SAY YOU?
...
I SAY--
SLAM

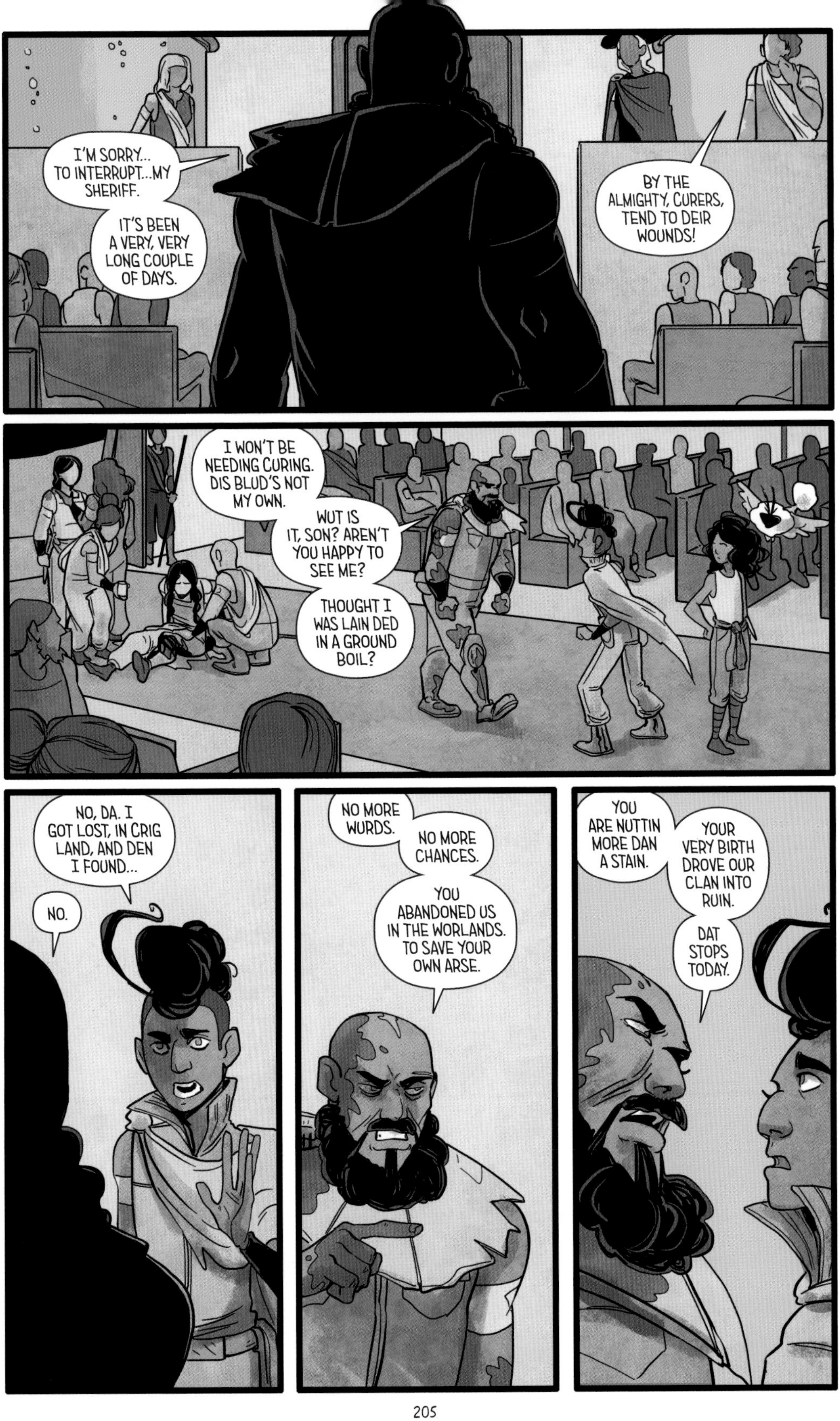
I'M SORRY... TO INTERRUPT...MY SHERIFF.
IT'S BEEN A VERY, VERY LONG COUPLE OF DAYS.
BY THE ALMIGHTY, CURERS, TEND TO DEIR WOUNDS!
I WON'T BE NEEDING CURING. DIS BLUD'S NOT MY OWN.
WUT IS IT, SON? AREN'T YOU HAPPY TO SEE ME?
THOUGHT I WAS LAIN DED IN A GROUND BOIL?
NO, DA. I GOT LOST, IN CRIG LAND, AND DEN I FOUND...
NO.
NO MORE WURDS.
NO MORE CHANCES.
YOU ABANDONED US IN THE WORLANDS. TO SAVE YOUR OWN ARSE.
YOU ARE NUTTIN MORE DAN A STAIN.
YOUR VERY BIRTH DROVE OUR CLAN INTO RUIN.
DAT STOPS TODAY.

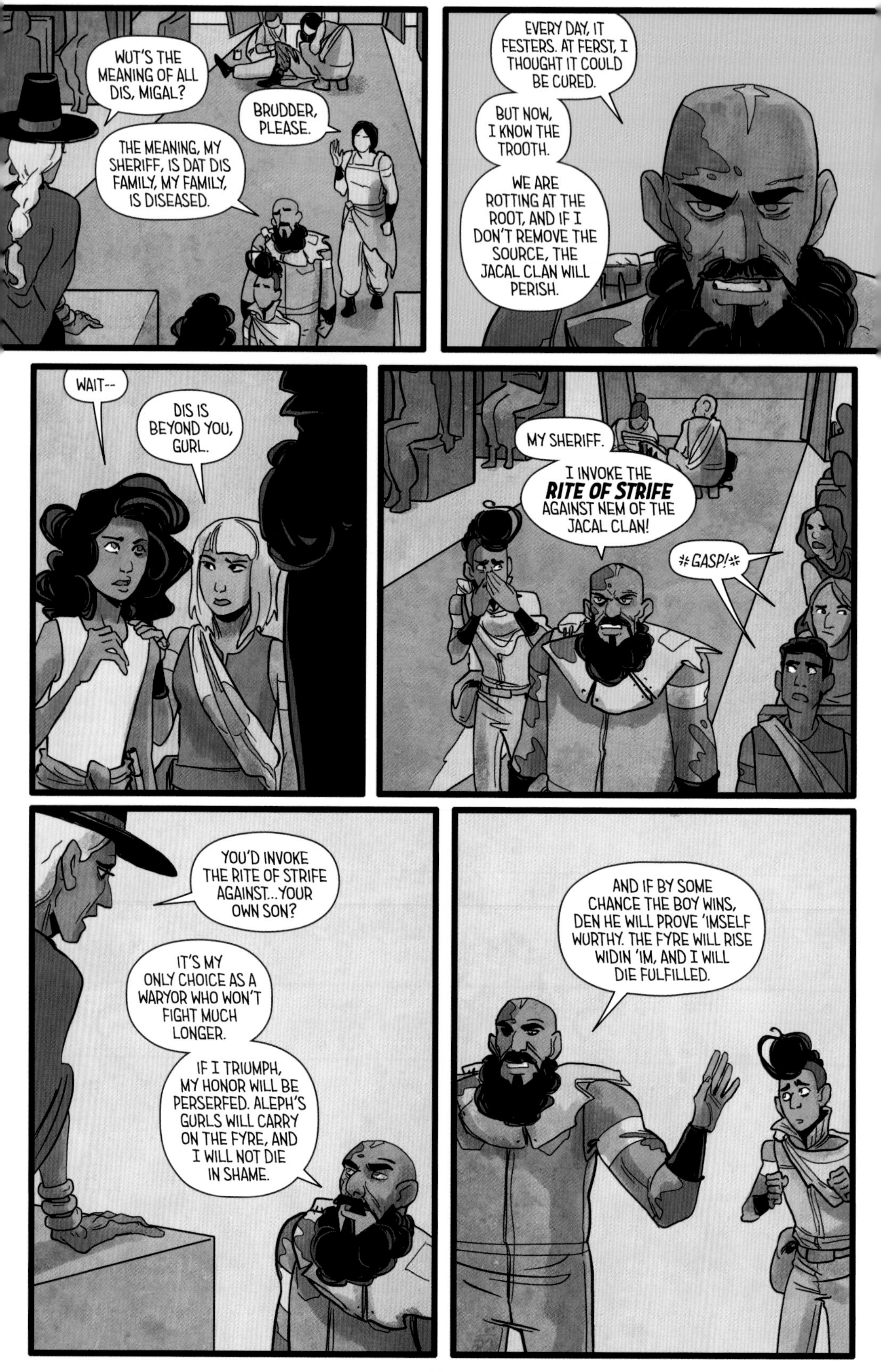
WUT'S THE MEANING OF ALL DIS, MIGAL?
BRUDDER, PLEASE.
THE MEANING, MY SHERIFF, IS DAT DIS FAMILY, MY FAMILY, IS DISEASED.
EVERY DAY, IT FESTERS. AT FERST, I THOUGHT IT COULD BE CURED.
BUT NOW, I KNOW THE TROOTH.
WE ARE ROTTING AT THE ROOT, AND IF I DON'T REMOVE THE SOURCE, THE JACAL CLAN WILL PERISH.
WAIT--
DIS IS BEYOND YOU, GURL.
MY SHERIFF.
I INVOKE THE RITE OF STRIFE AGAINST NEM OF THE JACAL CLAN!
GASP!
YOU'D INVOKE THE RITE OF STRIFE AGAINST...YOUR OWN SON?
IT'S MY ONLY CHOICE AS A WARYOR WHO WON'T FIGHT MUCH LONGER.
IF I TRIUMPH, MY HONOR WILL BE PERSERFED. ALEPH'S GURLS WILL CARRY ON THE FYRE, AND I WILL NOT DIE IN SHAME.
AND IF BY SOME CHANCE THE BOY WINS, DEN HE WILL PROVE 'IMSELF WURTHY. THE FYRE WILL RISE WIDIN 'IM, AND I WILL DIE FULFILLED.

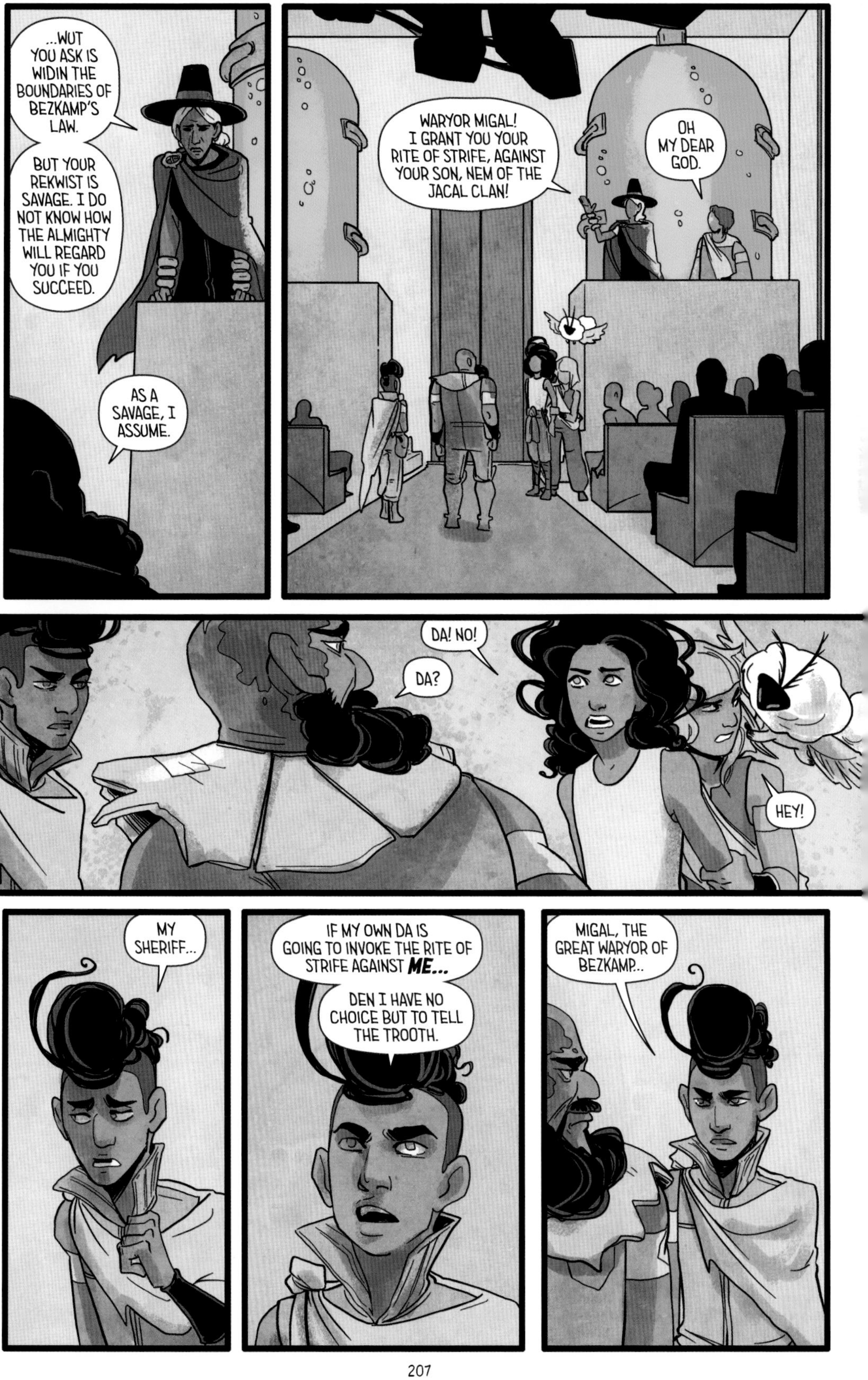
...WUT YOU ASK IS WIDIN THE BOUNDARIES OF BEZKAMP'S LAW.
BUT YOUR REKWIST IS SAVAGE. I DO NOT KNOW HOW THE ALMIGHTY WILL REGARD YOU IF YOU SUCCEED.
AS A SAVAGE, I ASSUME.
WARYOR MIGAL! I GRANT YOU YOUR RITE OF STRIFE, AGAINST YOUR SON, NEM OF THE JACAL CLAN!
OH MY DEAR GOD.
DA?
DA! NO!
HEY!
MY SHERIFF...
IF MY OWN DA IS GOING TO INVOKE THE RITE OF STRIFE AGAINST ME...
DEN I HAVE NO CHOICE BUT TO TELL THE TROOTH.
MIGAL, THE GREAT WARYOR OF BEZKAMP...

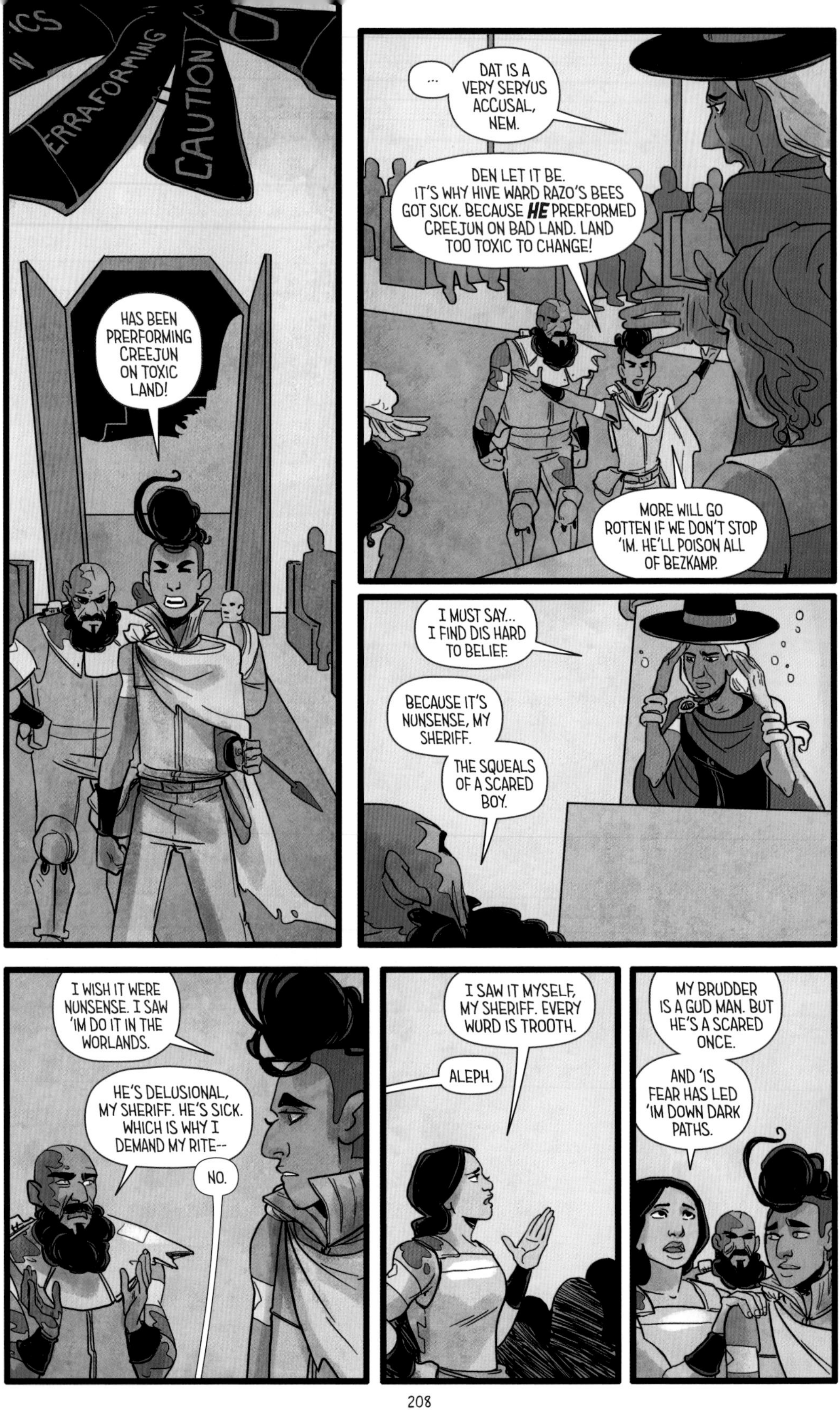
ERRAFORMING
CAUTION
HAS BEEN PRERFORMING CREEJUN ON TOXIC LAND!
...
DAT IS A VERY SERYUS ACCUSAL, NEM.
DEN LET IT BE. IT'S WHY HIVE WARD RAZO'S BEES GOT SICK. BECAUSE **HE** PRERFORMED CREEJUN ON BAD LAND. LAND TOO TOXIC TO CHANGE!
MORE WILL GO ROTTEN IF WE DON'T STOP 'IM. HE'LL POISON ALL OF BEZKAMP.
I MUST SAY... I FIND DIS HARD TO BELIEF.
BECAUSE IT'S NUNSENSE, MY SHERIFF.
THE SQUEALS OF A SCARED BOY.
I WISH IT WERE NUNSENSE. I SAW 'IM DO IT IN THE WORLANDS.
HE'S DELUSIONAL, MY SHERIFF. HE'S SICK. WHICH IS WHY I DEMAND MY RITE--
NO.
I SAW IT MYSELF, MY SHERIFF. EVERY WURD IS TROOTH.
ALEPH.
MY BRUDDER IS A GUD MAN. BUT HE'S A SCARED ONCE.
AND 'IS FEAR HAS LED 'IM DOWN DARK PATHS.

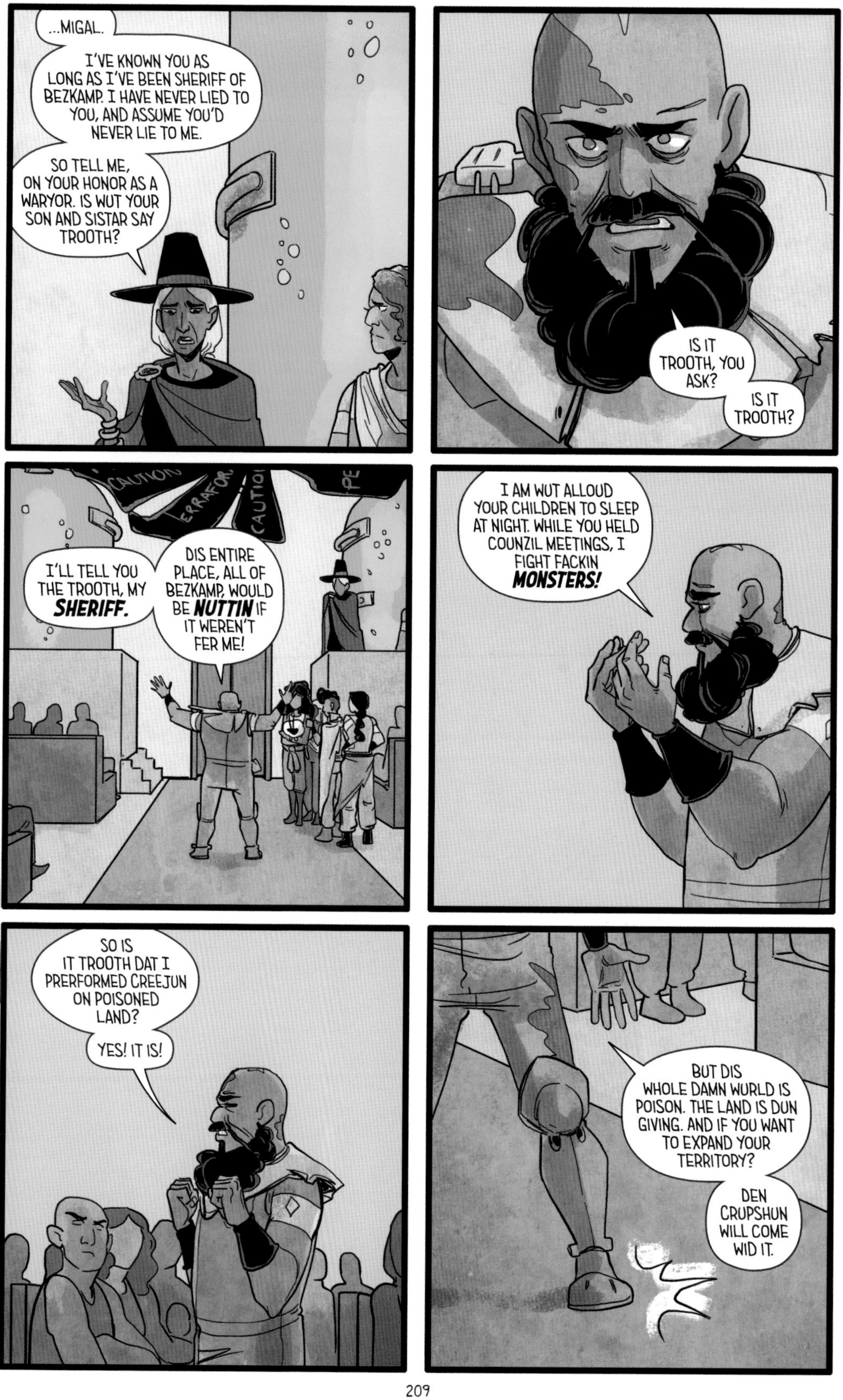

...MIGAL.
I'VE KNOWN YOU AS LONG AS I'VE BEEN SHERIFF OF BEZKAMP. I HAVE NEVER LIED TO YOU, AND ASSUME YOU'D NEVER LIE TO ME.
SO TELL ME, ON YOUR HONOR AS A WARYOR. IS WUT YOUR SON AND SISTAR SAY TROOTH?
IS IT TROOTH, YOU ASK?
IS IT TROOTH?
CAUTION
TERRAFOR
CAUTION
I'LL TELL YOU THE TROOTH, MY **SHERIFF.**
DIS ENTIRE PLACE, ALL OF BEZKAMP, WOULD BE **NUTTIN** IF IT WEREN'T FER ME!
I AM WUT ALLOUD YOUR CHILDREN TO SLEEP AT NIGHT. WHILE YOU HELD COUNZIL MEETINGS, I FIGHT FACKIN **MONSTERS!**
SO IS IT TROOTH DAT I PRERFORMED CREEJUN ON POISONED LAND?
YES! IT IS!
BUT DIS WHOLE DAMN WURLD IS POISON. THE LAND IS DUN GIVING. AND IF YOU WANT TO EXPAND YOUR TERRITORY?
DEN CRUPSHUN WILL COME WID IT.

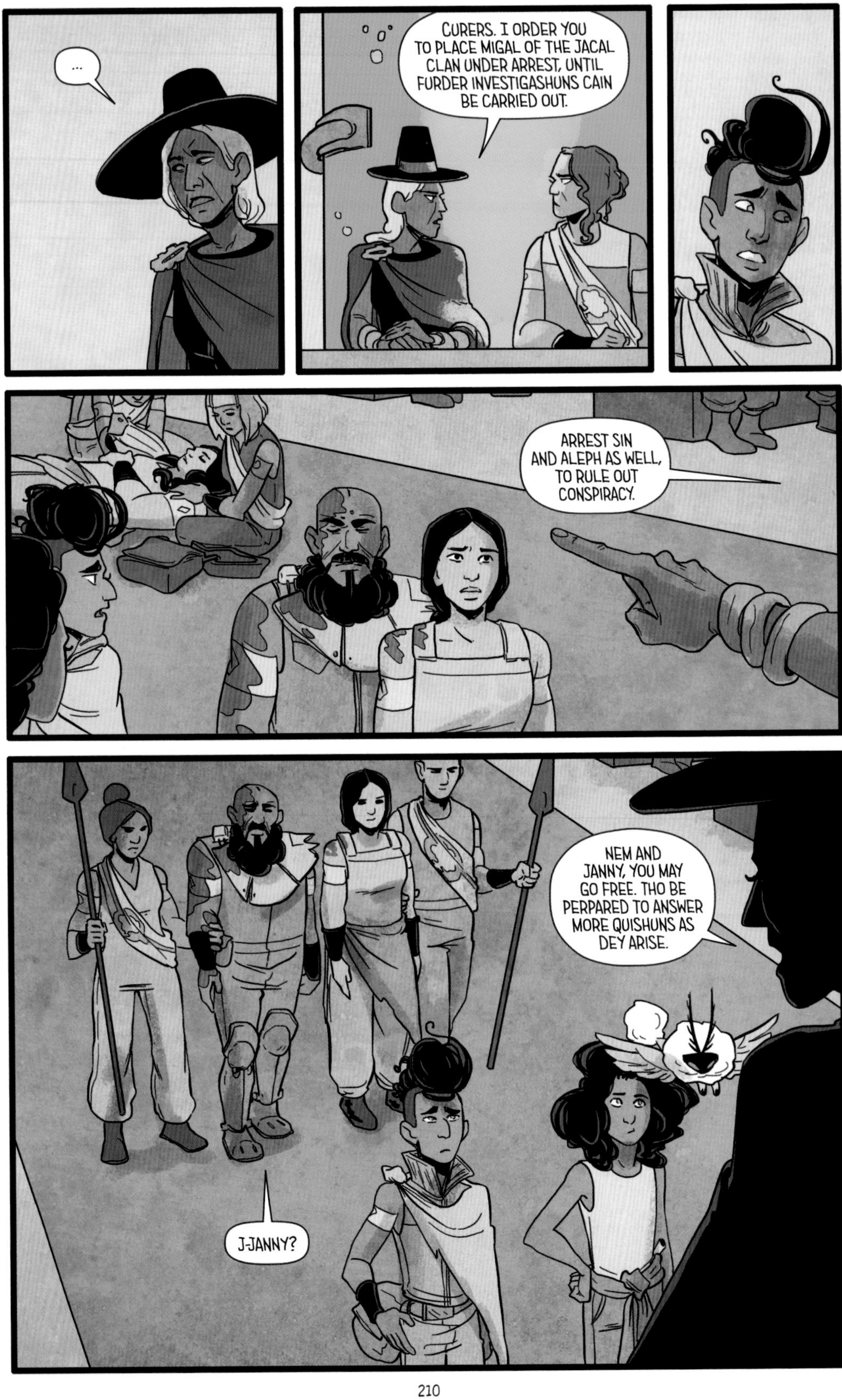
...
CURERS. I ORDER YOU TO PLACE MIGAL OF THE JACAL CLAN UNDER ARREST, UNTIL FURDER INVESTIGASHUNS CAIN BE CARRIED OUT.
ARREST SIN AND ALEPH AS WELL, TO RULE OUT CONSPIRACY.
NEM AND JANNY, YOU MAY GO FREE. THO BE PERPARED TO ANSWER MORE QUISHUNS AS DEY ARISE.
J-JANNY?

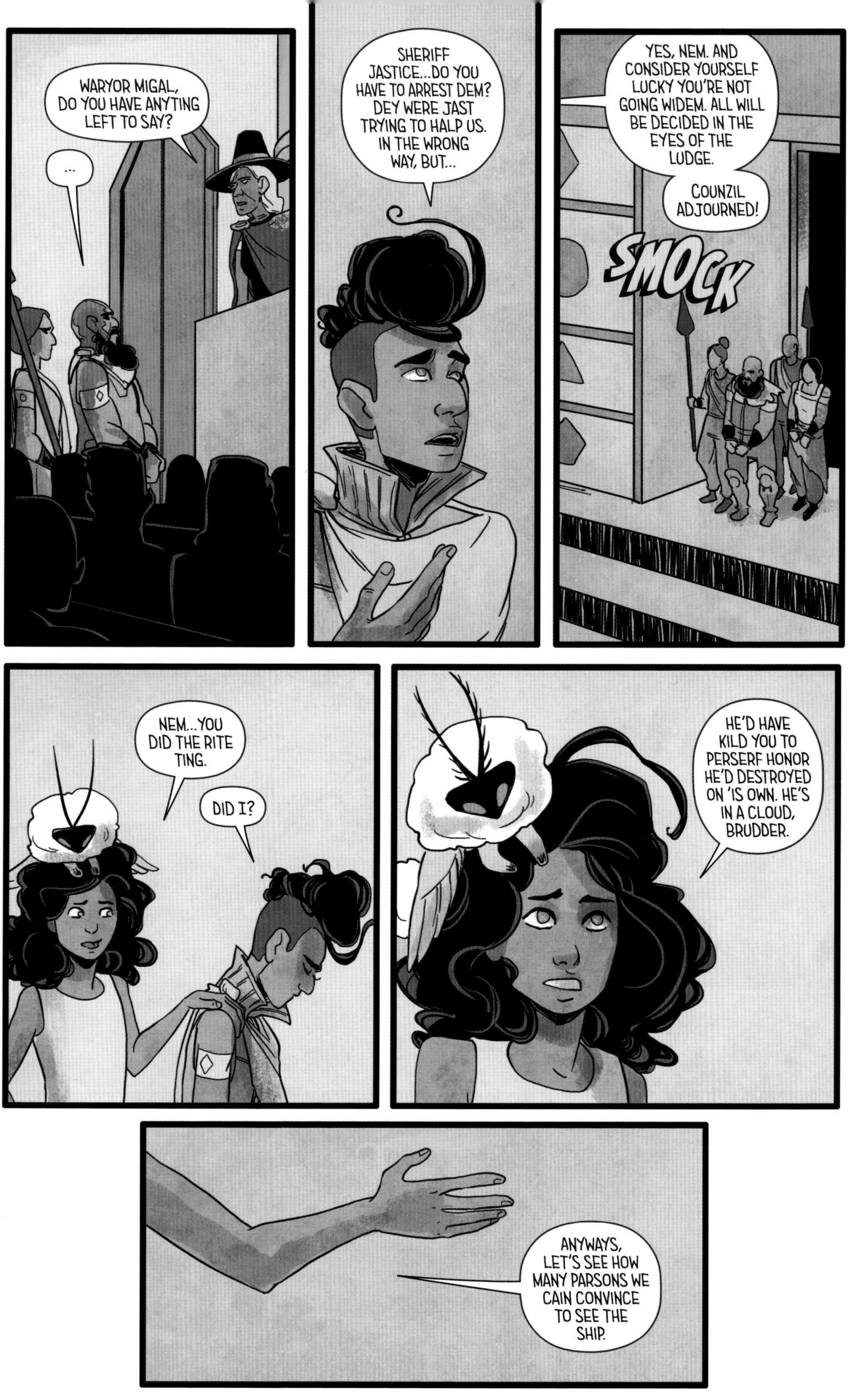
WARYOR MIGAL, DO YOU HAVE ANYTING LEFT TO SAY?
...
SHERIFF JASTICE...DO YOU HAVE TO ARREST DEM? DEY WERE JAST TRYING TO HALP US. IN THE WRONG WAY, BUT...
YES, NEM. AND CONSIDER YOURSELF LUCKY YOU'RE NOT GOING WIDEM. ALL WILL BE DECIDED IN THE EYES OF THE LUDGE.
COUNZIL ADJOURNED!
SMOCK
NEM...YOU DID THE RITE TING.
DID I?
HE'D HAVE KILD YOU TO PERSERF HONOR HE'D DESTROYED ON 'IS OWN. HE'S IN A CLOUD, BRUDDER.
ANYWAYS, LET'S SEE HOW MANY PARSONS WE CAIN CONVINCE TO SEE THE SHIP.

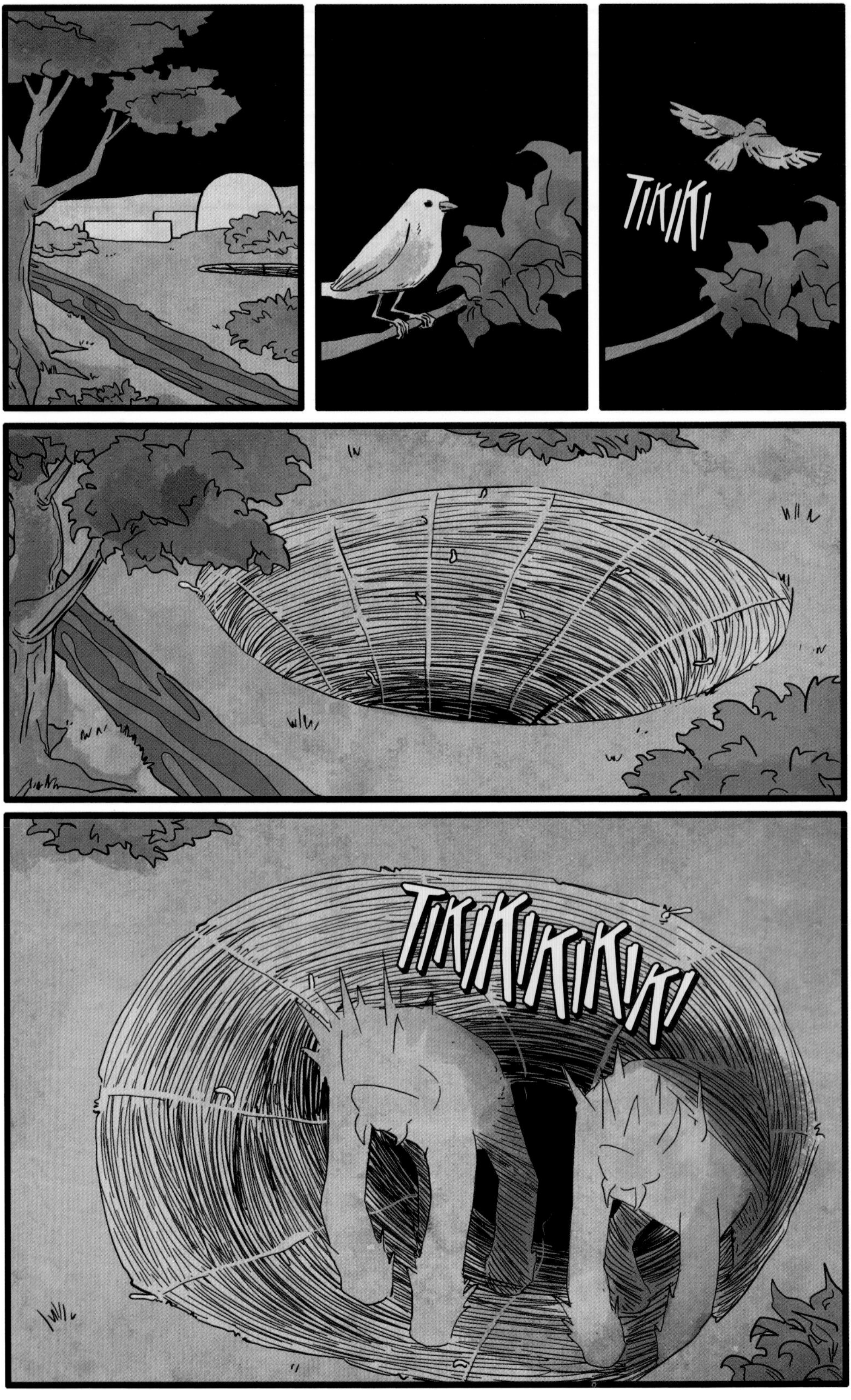
TIKIKI
TIKIKIKIKIKIKI

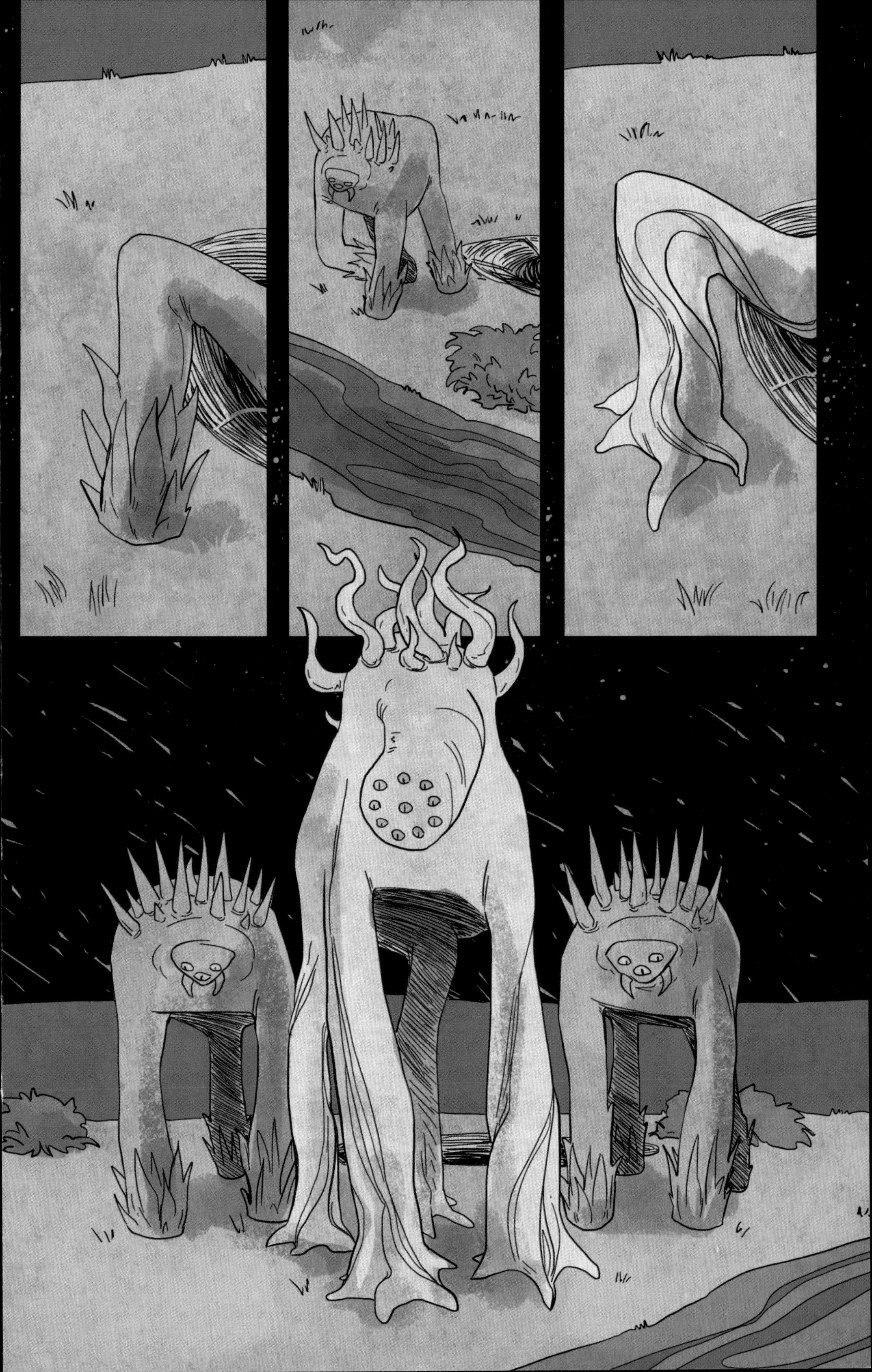

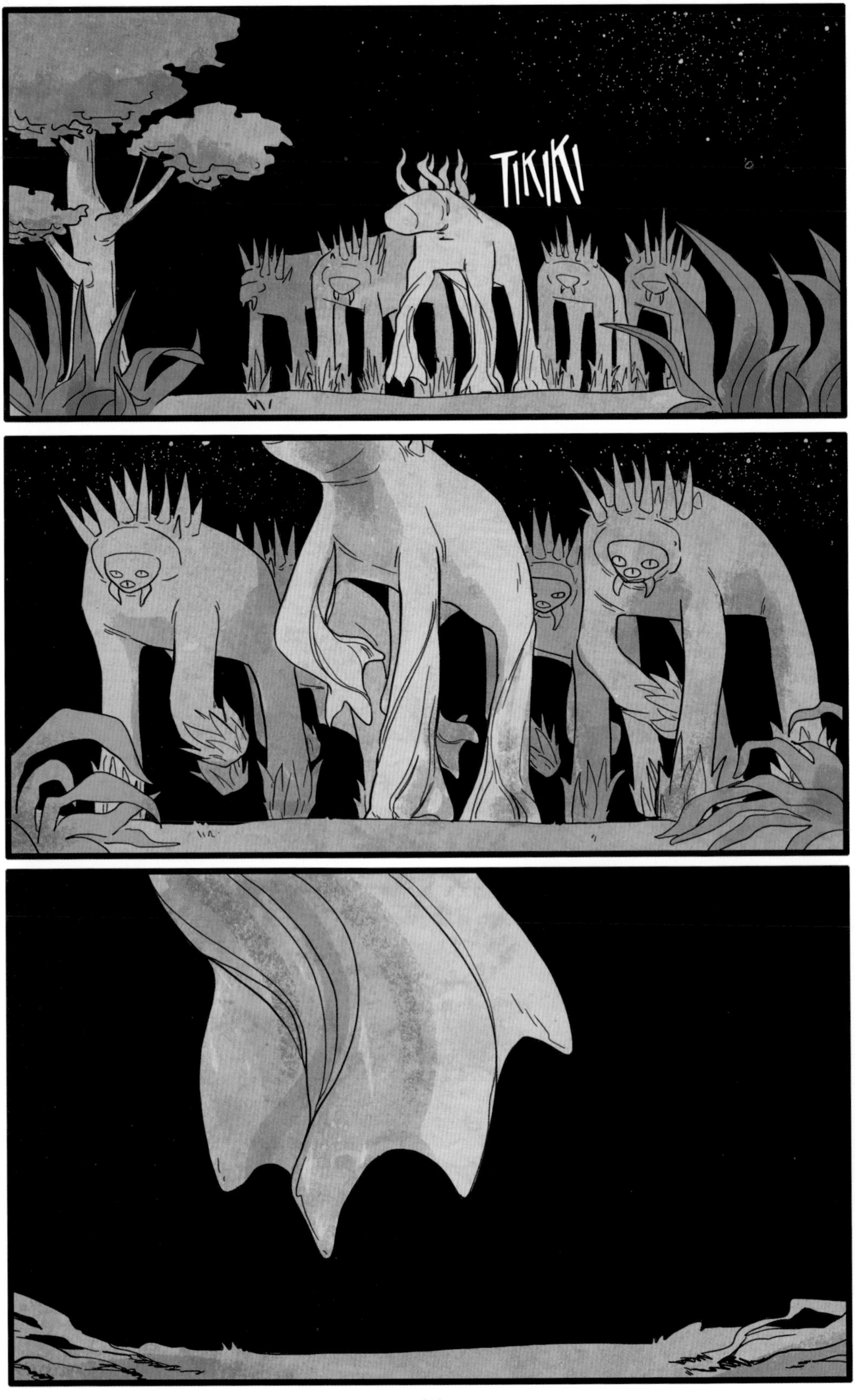
TIKIKI

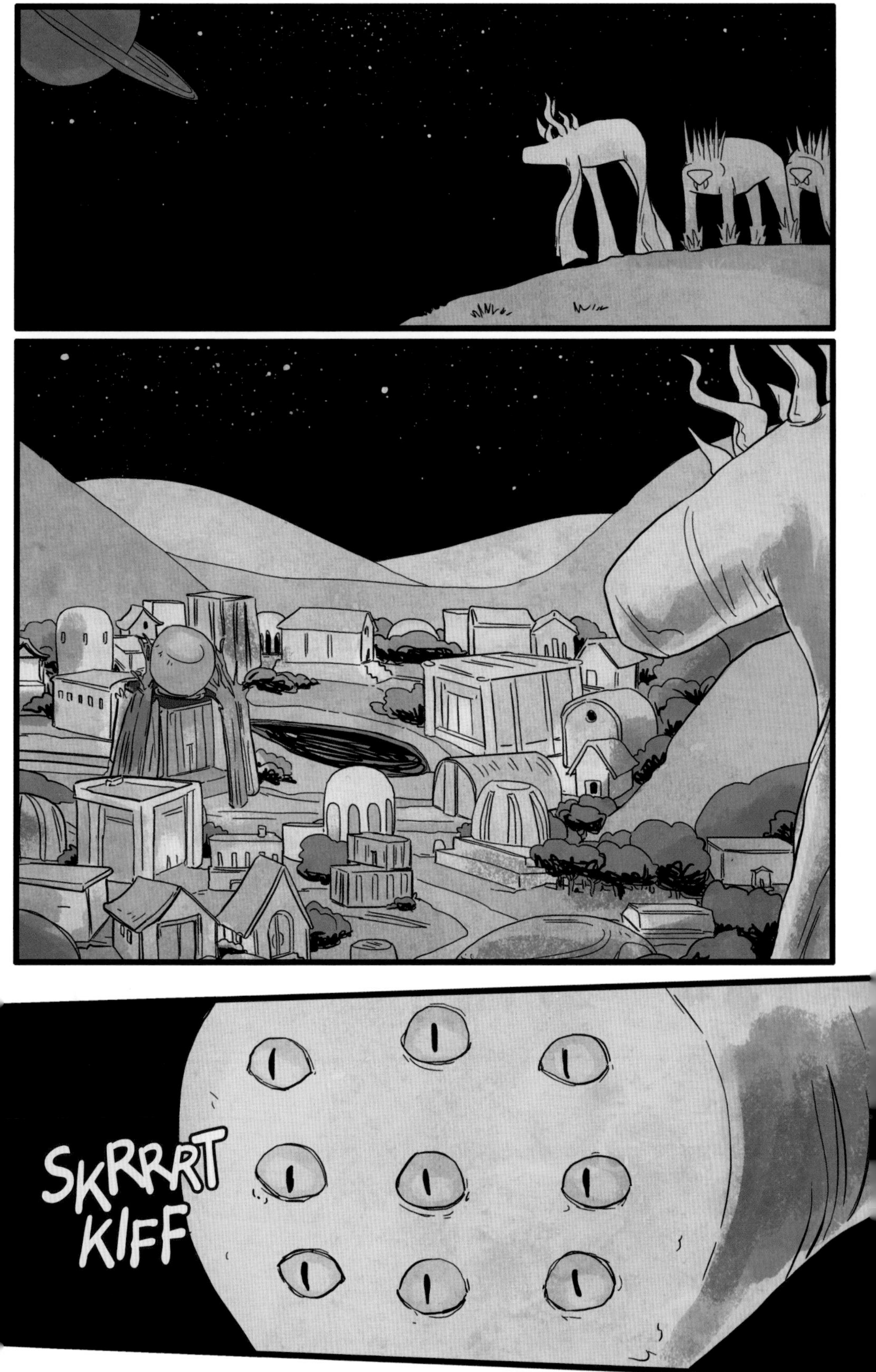
SKRRRT
KIFF

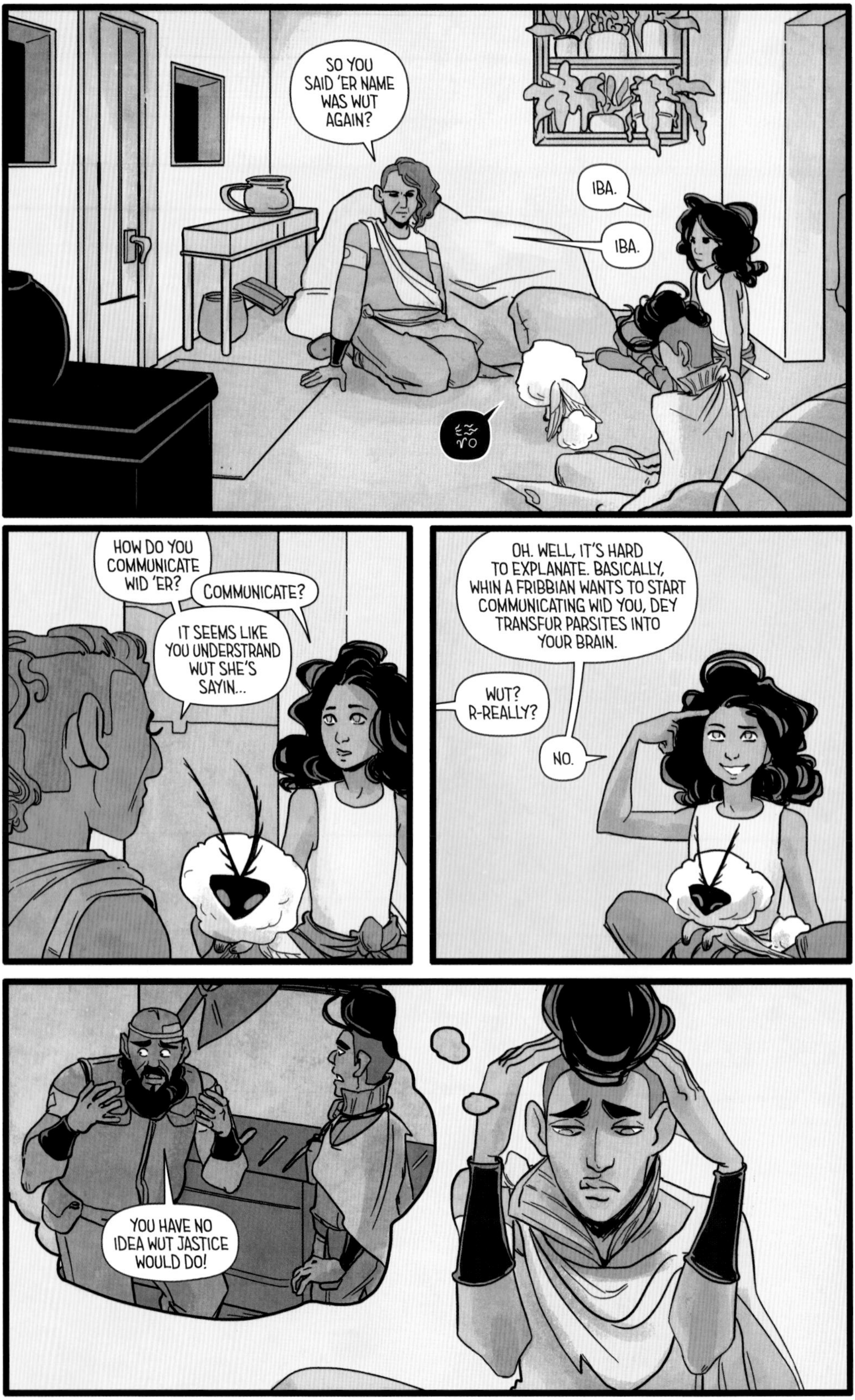
SO YOU SAID 'ER NAME WAS WUT AGAIN?
IBA.
IBA.
HOW DO YOU COMMUNICATE WID 'ER?
COMMUNICATE?
IT SEEMS LIKE YOU UNDERSTRAND WUT SHE'S SAYIN...
OH. WELL, IT'S HARD TO EXPLANATE. BASICALLY, WHIN A FRIBBIAN WANTS TO START COMMUNICATING WID YOU, DEY TRANSFUR PARSITES INTO YOUR BRAIN.
WUT? R-REALLY?
NO.
YOU HAVE NO IDEA WUT JASTICE WOULD DO!

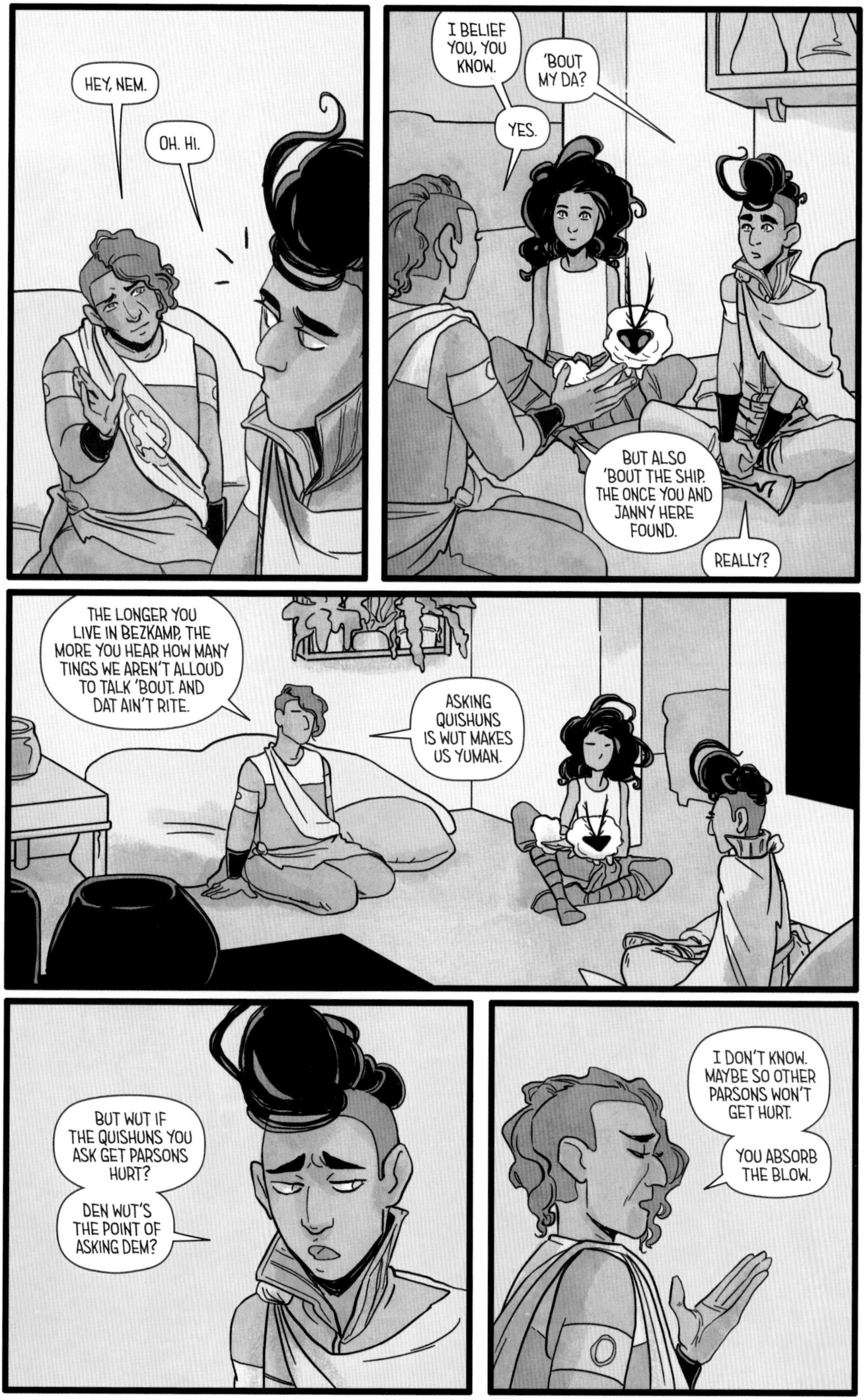
HEY, NEM.
OH. HI.
I BELIEF YOU, YOU KNOW.
YES.
'BOUT MY DA?
BUT ALSO 'BOUT THE SHIP. THE ONCE YOU AND JANNY HERE FOUND.
REALLY?
THE LONGER YOU LIVE IN BEZKAMP, THE MORE YOU HEAR HOW MANY TINGS WE AREN'T ALLOUD TO TALK 'BOUT. AND DAT AIN'T RITE.
ASKING QUISHUNS IS WUT MAKES US YUMAN.
BUT WUT IF THE QUISHUNS YOU ASK GET PARSONS HURT?
DEN WUT'S THE POINT OF ASKING DEM?
I DON'T KNOW. MAYBE SO OTHER PARSONS WON'T GET HURT.
YOU ABSORB THE BLOW.

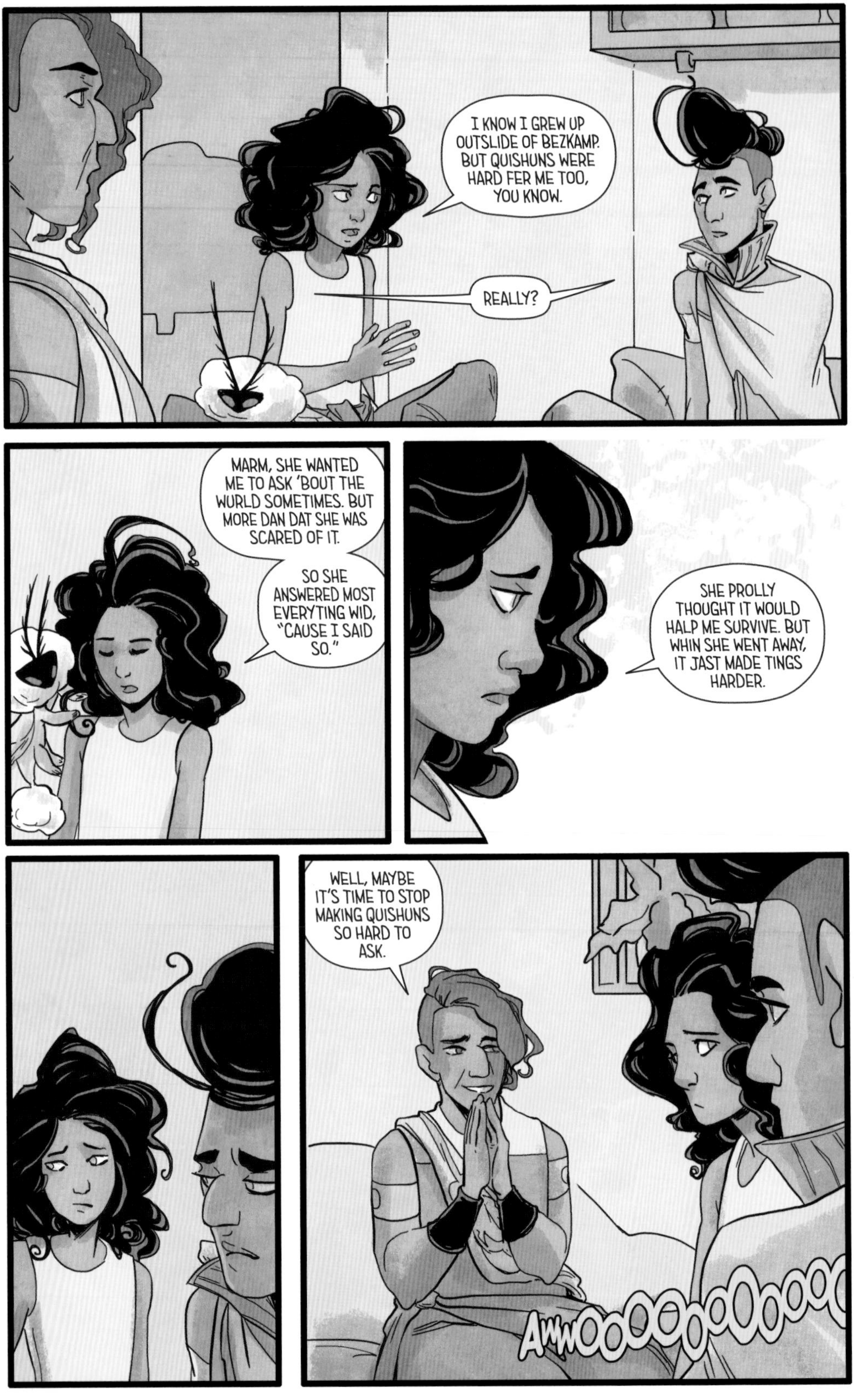
I KNOW I GREW UP OUTSLIDE OF BEZKAMP. BUT QUISHUNS WERE HARD FER ME TOO, YOU KNOW.
REALLY?
MARM, SHE WANTED ME TO ASK 'BOUT THE WURLD SOMETIMES. BUT MORE DAN DAT SHE WAS SCARED OF IT.
SO SHE ANSWERED MOST EVERYTING WID, "CAUSE I SAID SO."
SHE PROLLY THOUGHT IT WOULD HALP ME SURVIVE. BUT WHIN SHE WENT AWAY, IT JAST MADE TINGS HARDER.
WELL, MAYBE IT'S TIME TO STOP MAKING QUISHUNS SO HARD TO ASK.
AWWOOOOOOOOOOOO

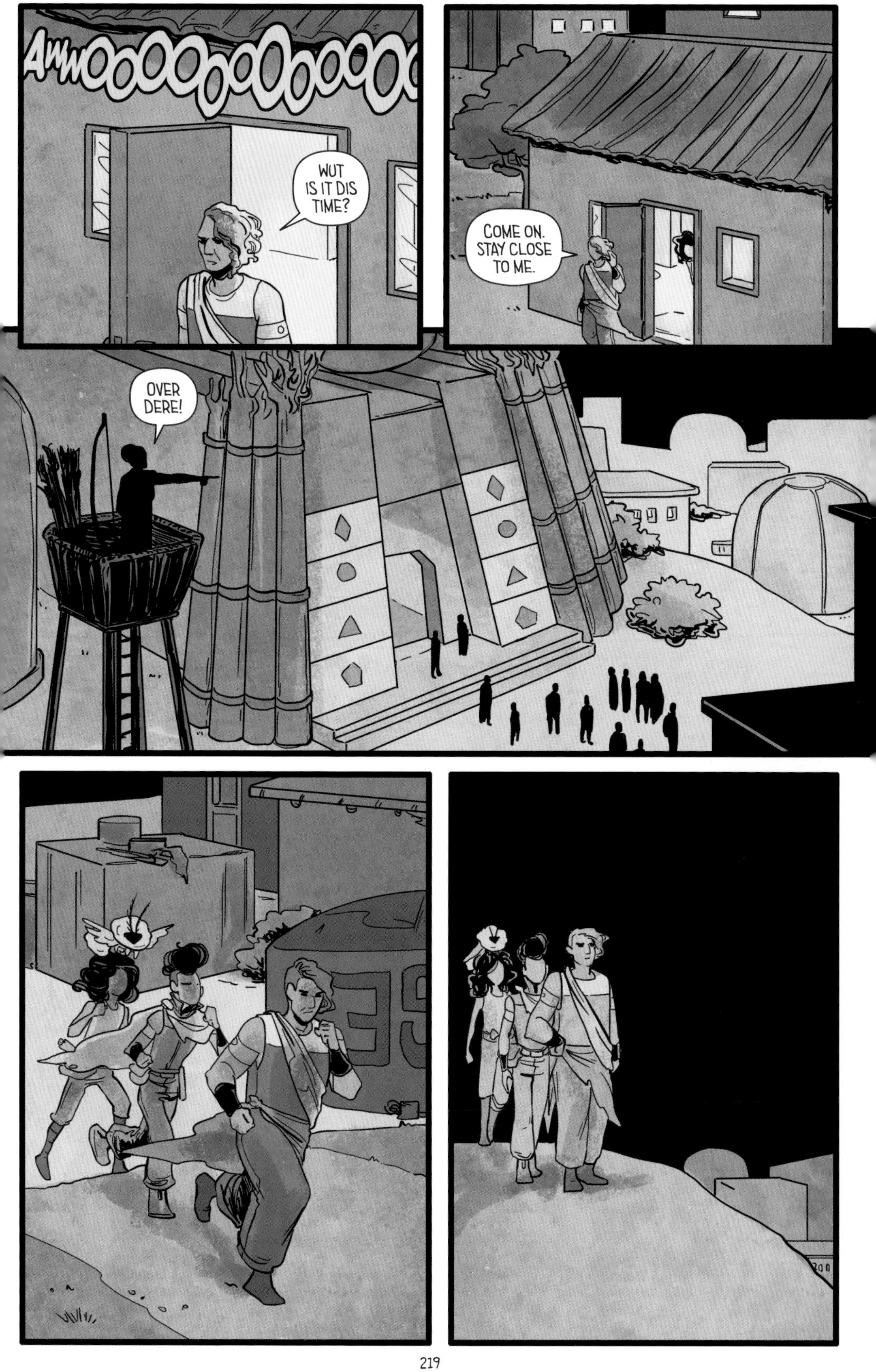
AWWOOOOOOOOOOO
WUT IS IT DIS TIME?
COME ON. STAY CLOSE TO ME.
OVER DERE!

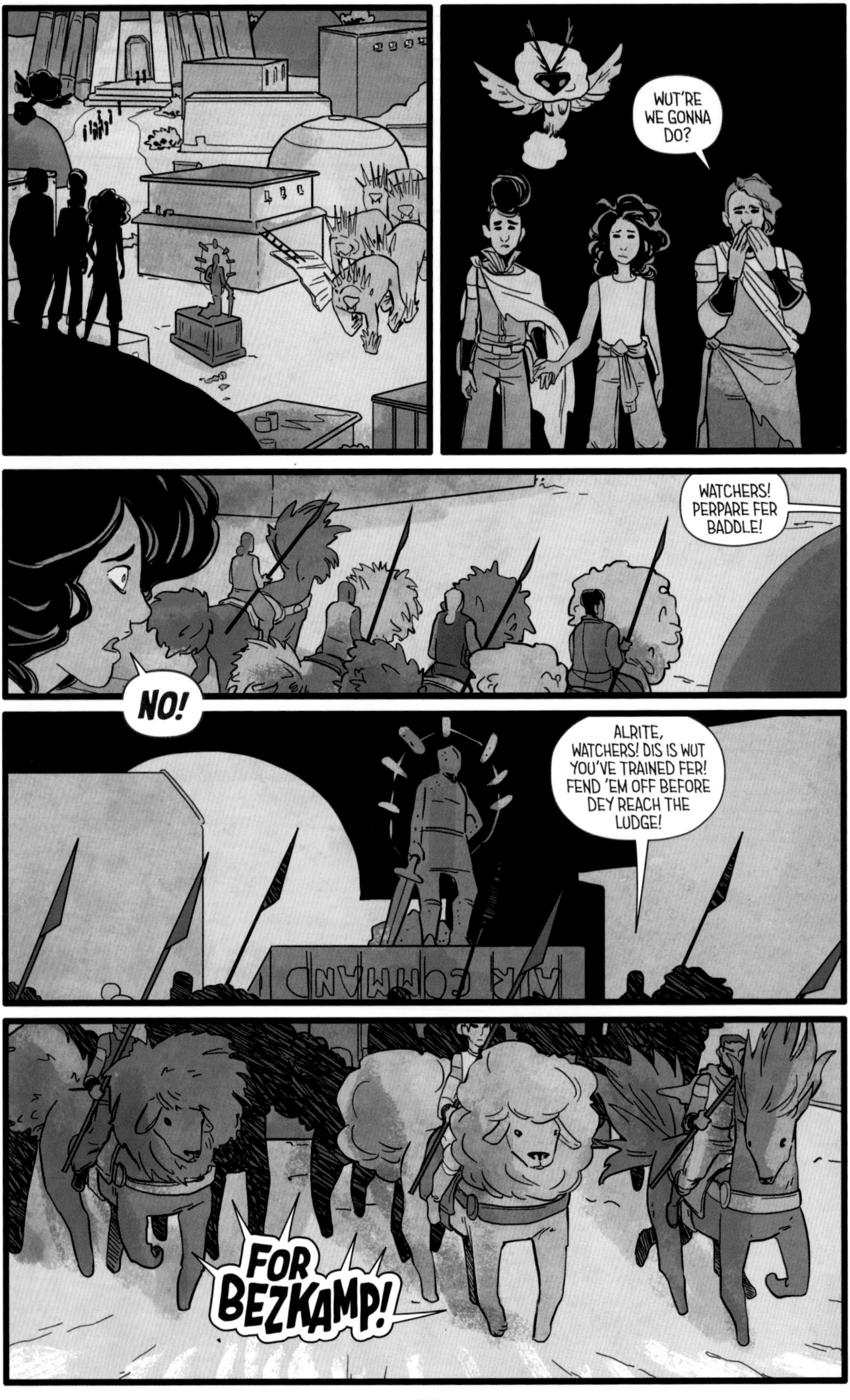
WUT'RE WE GONNA DO?
WATCHERS! PERPARE FER BADDLE!
NO!
ALRITE, WATCHERS! DIS IS WUT YOU'VE TRAINED FER! FEND 'EM OFF BEFORE DEY REACH THE LUDGE!
FOR BEZKAMP!

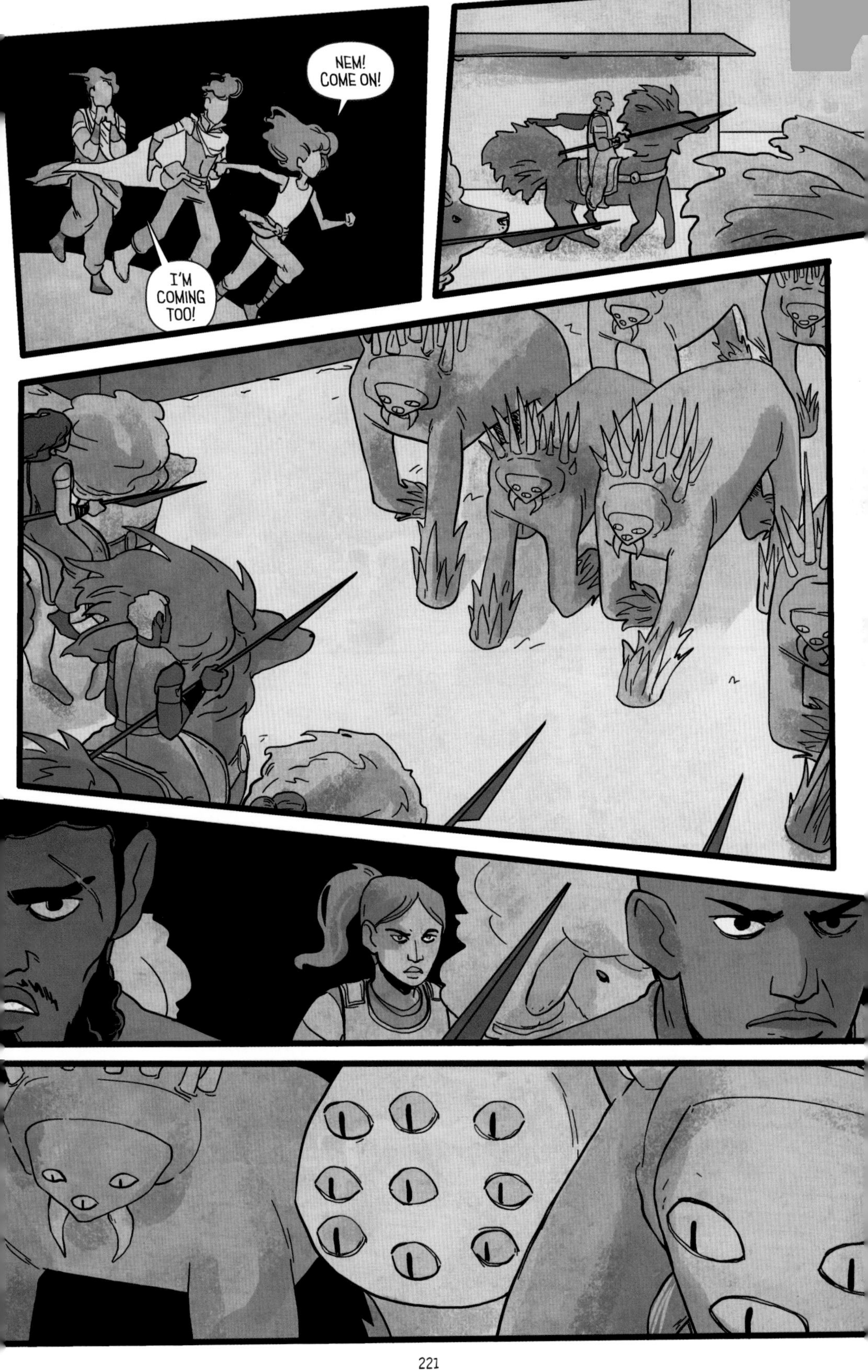
NEM! COME ON!
I'M COMING TOO!

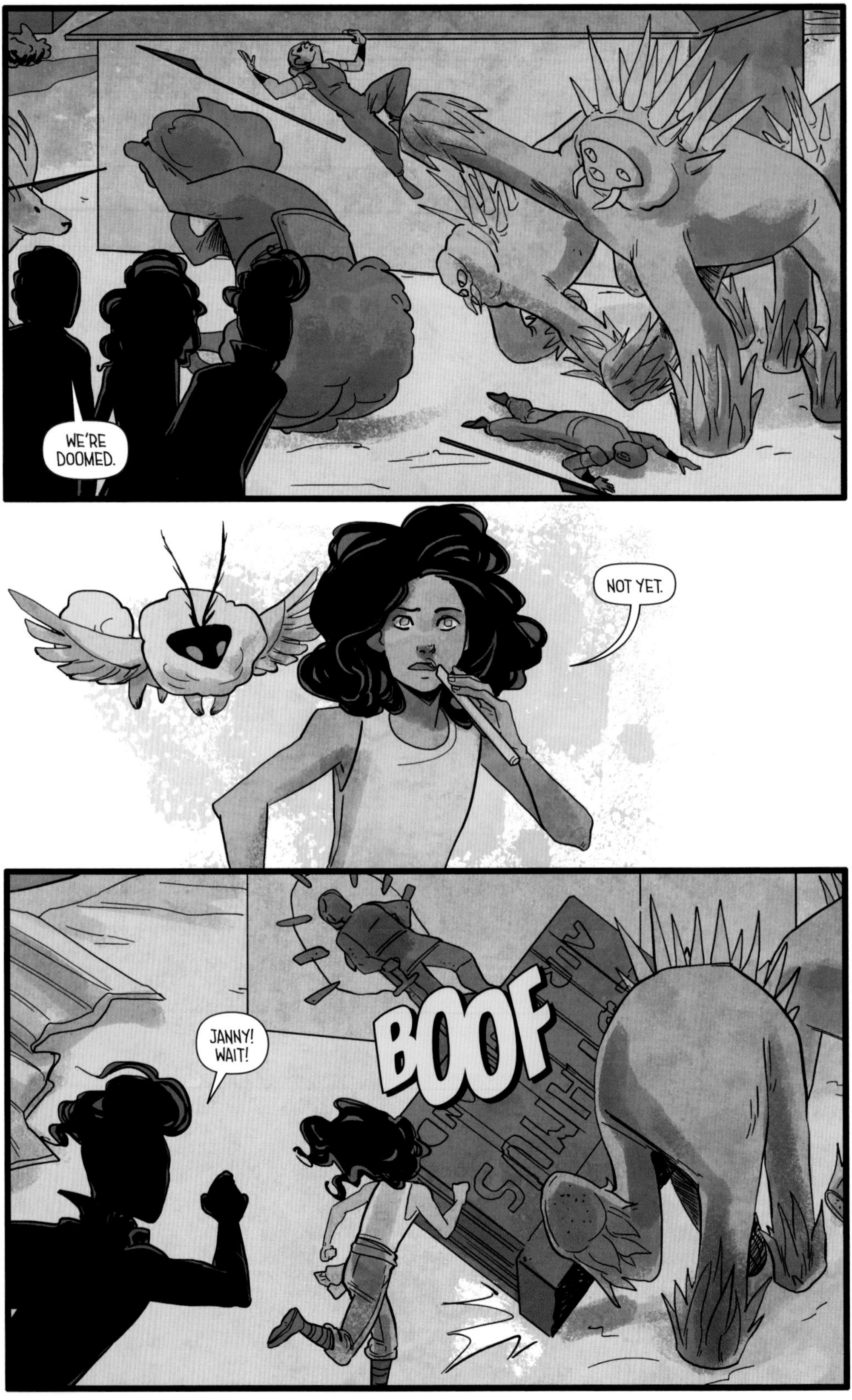
WE'RE DOOMED.
NOT YET.
JANNY! WAIT!
BOOF

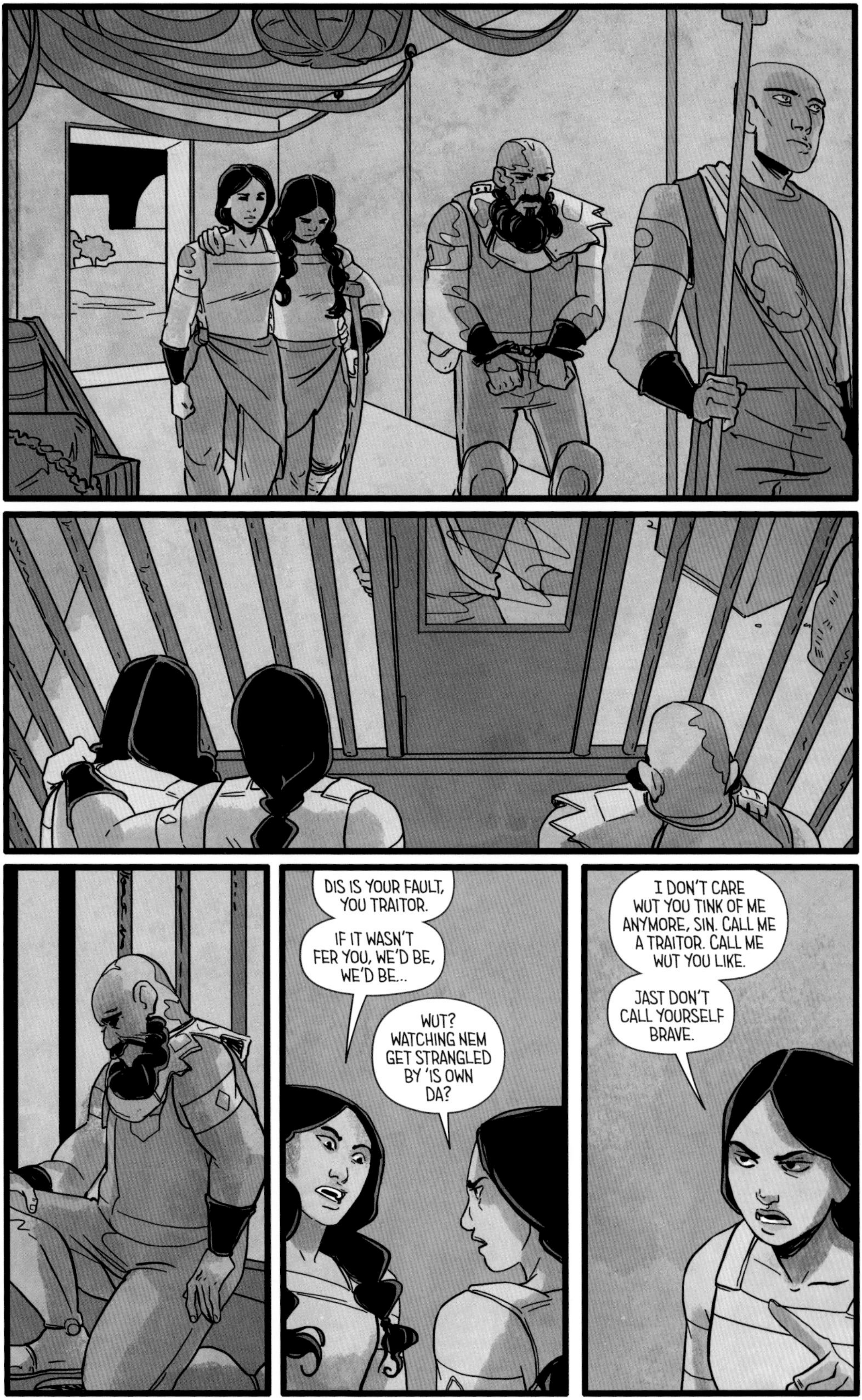
DIS IS YOUR FAULT, YOU TRAITOR.
IF IT WASN'T FER YOU, WE'D BE, WE'D BE...
WUT? WATCHING NEM GET STRANGLED BY 'IS OWN DA?
I DON'T CARE WUT YOU TINK OF ME ANYMORE, SIN. CALL ME A TRAITOR. CALL ME WUT YOU LIKE.
JAST DON'T CALL YOURSELF BRAVE.

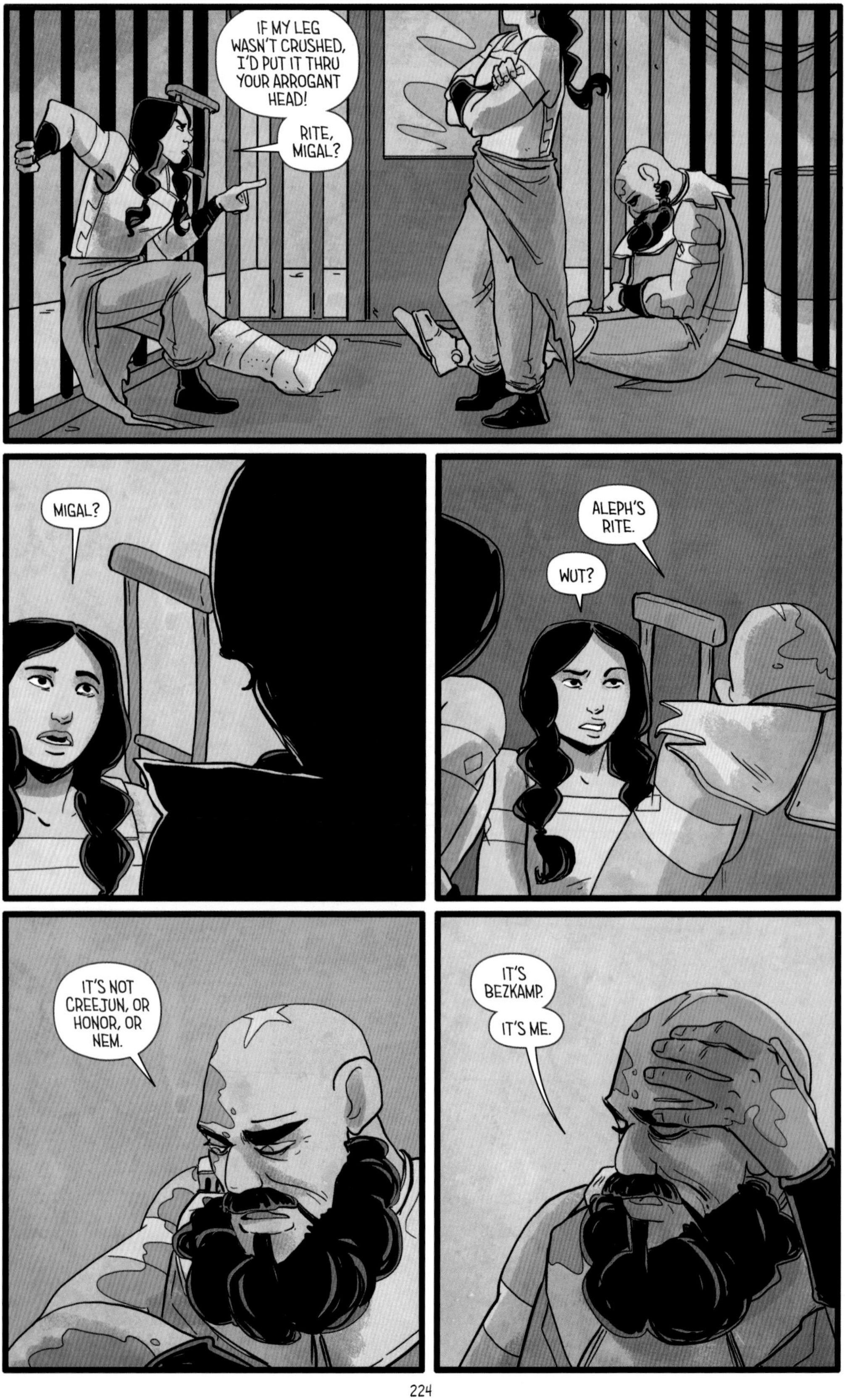
IF MY LEG WASN'T CRUSHED, I'D PUT IT THRU YOUR ARROGANT HEAD!
RITE, MIGAL?
MIGAL?
ALEPH'S RITE.
WUT?
IT'S NOT CREEJUN, OR HONOR, OR NEM.
IT'S BEZKAMP.
IT'S ME.

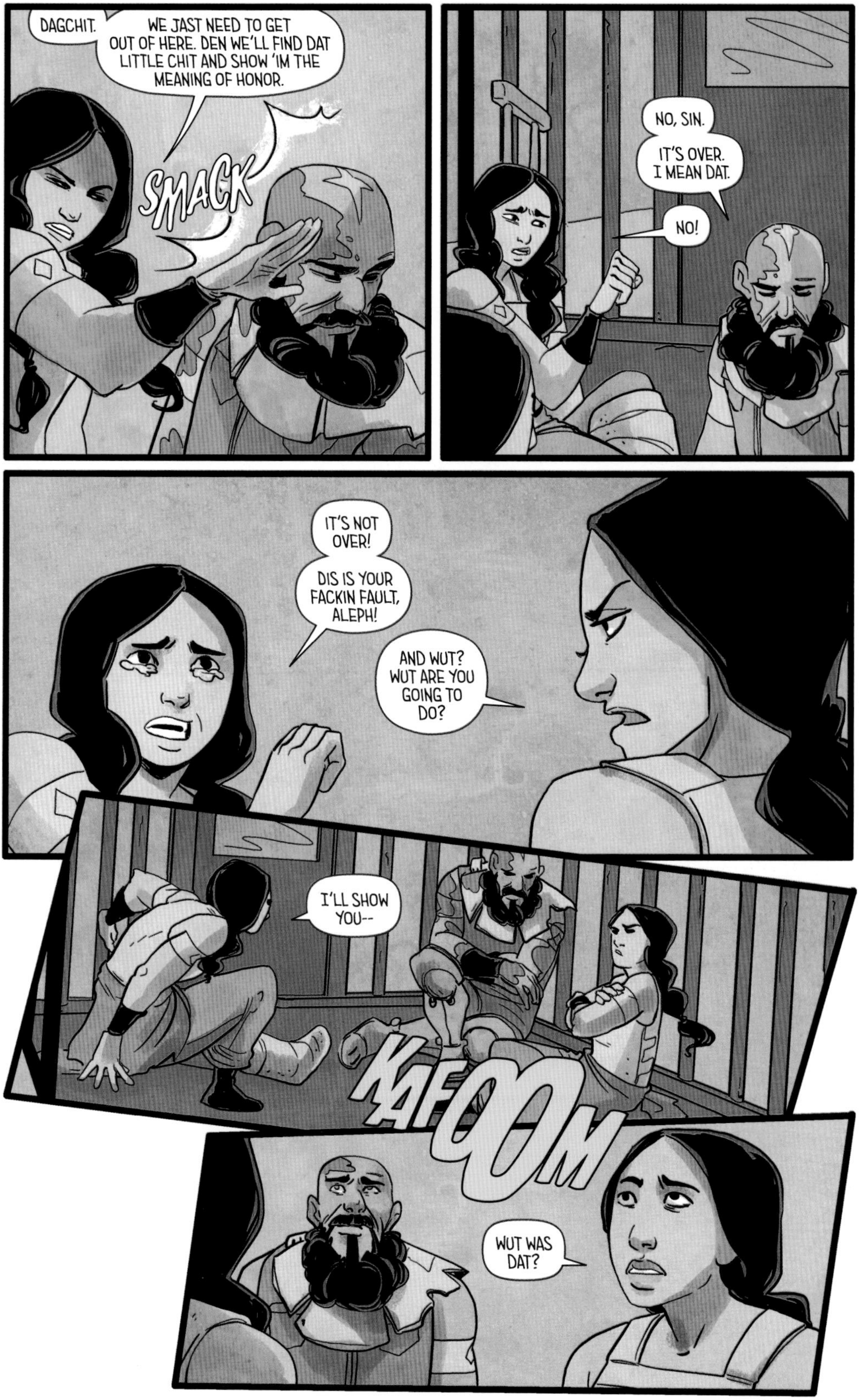
DAGCHIT.
WE JAST NEED TO GET OUT OF HERE. DEN WE'LL FIND DAT LITTLE CHIT AND SHOW 'IM THE MEANING OF HONOR.
SMACK
NO, SIN.
IT'S OVER. I MEAN DAT.
NO!
IT'S NOT OVER!
DIS IS YOUR FACKIN FAULT, ALEPH!
AND WUT? WUT ARE YOU GOING TO DO?
I'LL SHOW YOU--
KAFOOOM
WUT WAS DAT?

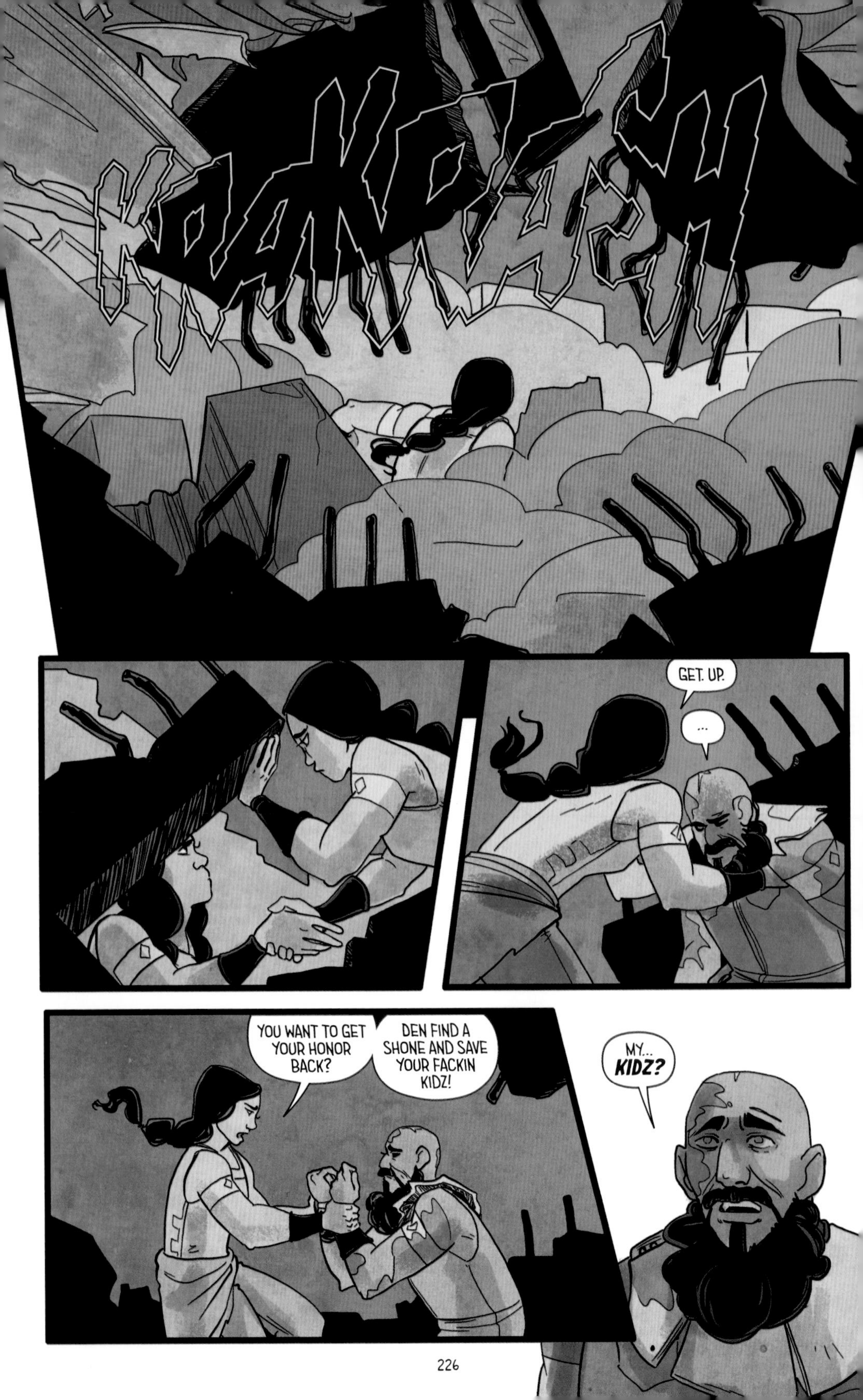
GET. UP.
...
YOU WANT TO GET YOUR HONOR BACK?
DEN FIND A SHONE AND SAVE YOUR FACKIN KIDZ!
MY... **KIDZ?**

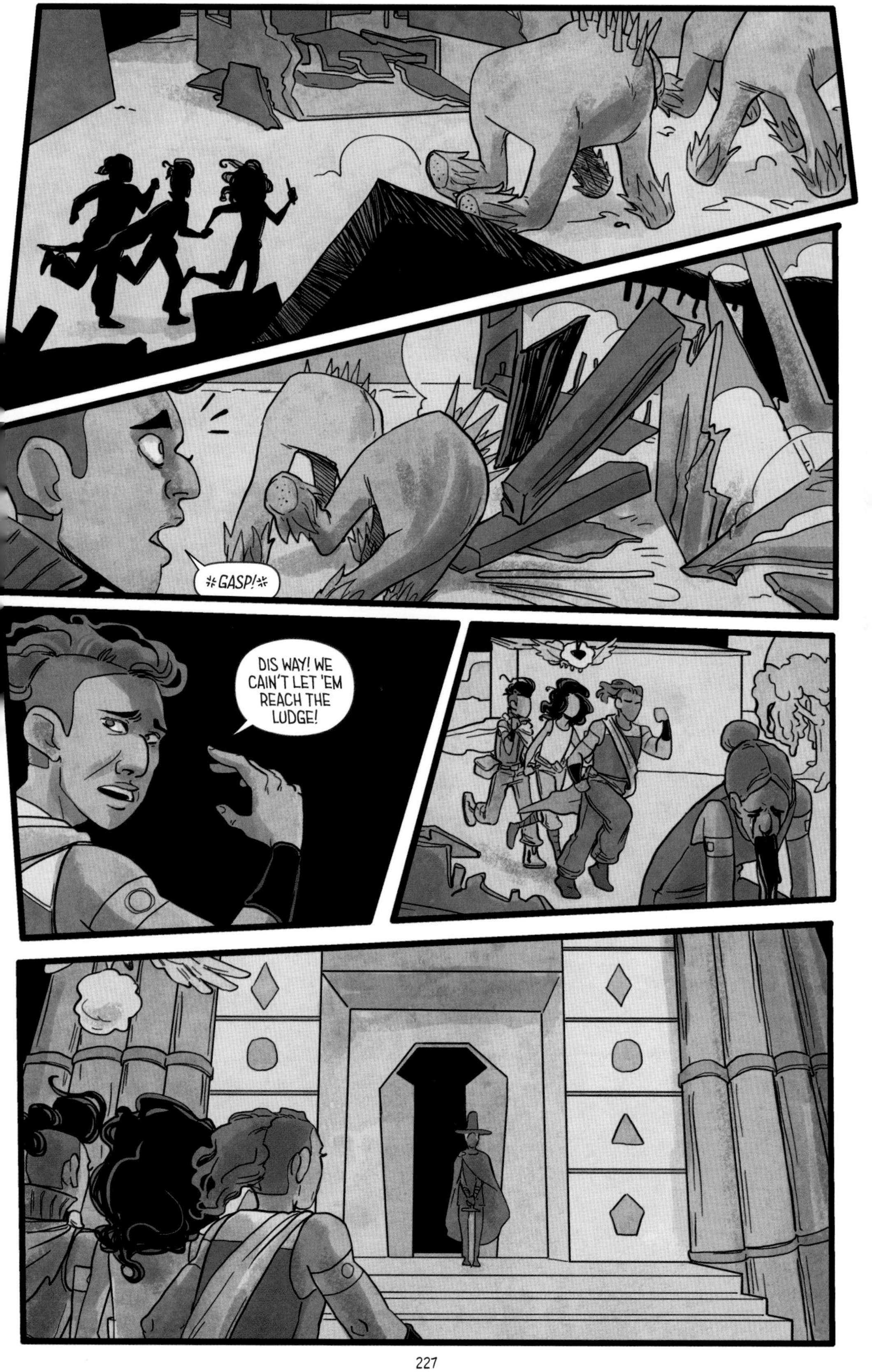
GASP!
DIS WAY! WE CAIN'T LET 'EM REACH THE LUDGE!

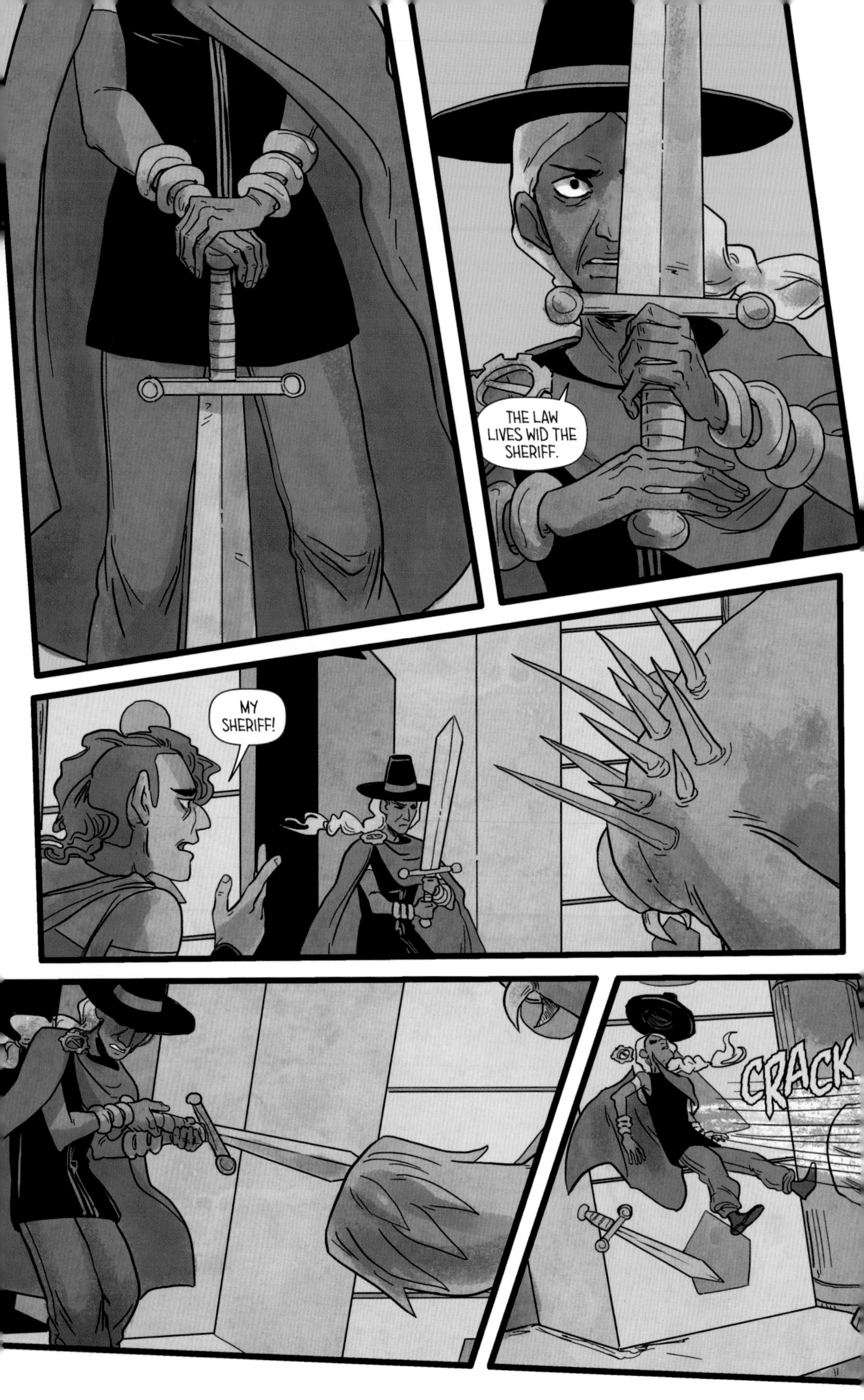
THE LAW LIVES WID THE SHERIFF.
MY SHERIFF!
CRACK

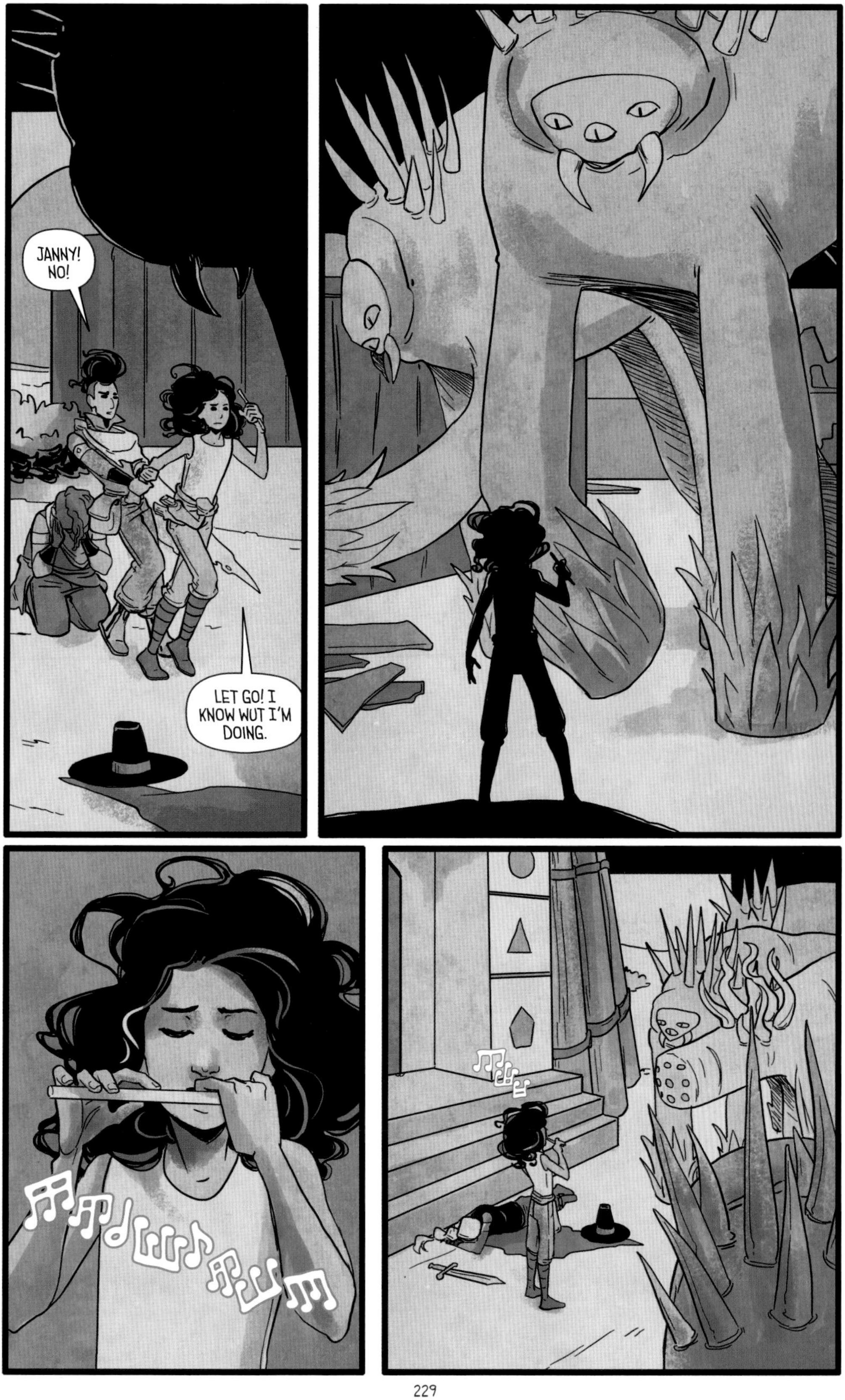
JANNY! NO!
LET GO! I KNOW WUT I'M DOING.

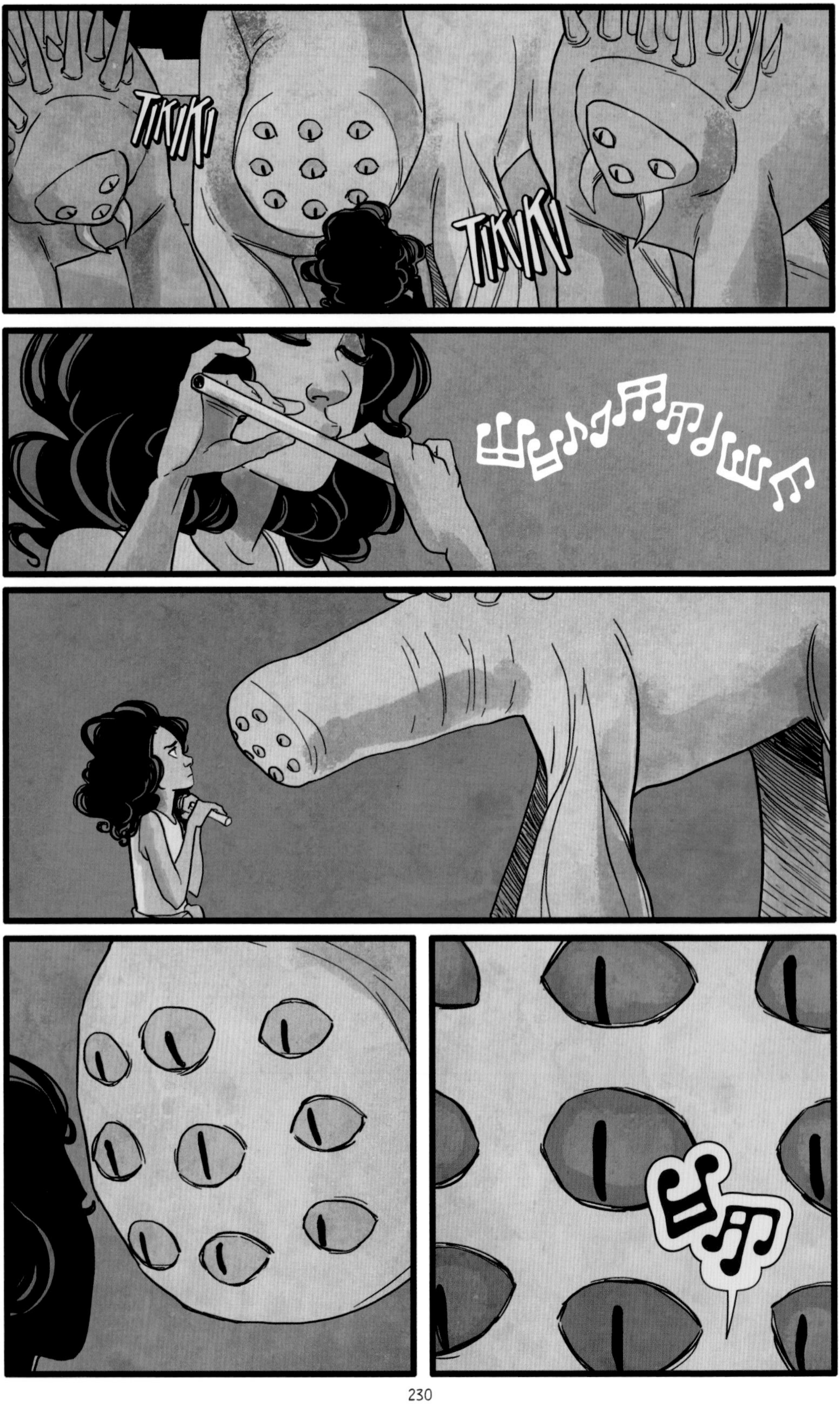
TIKIKI
TIKIKI

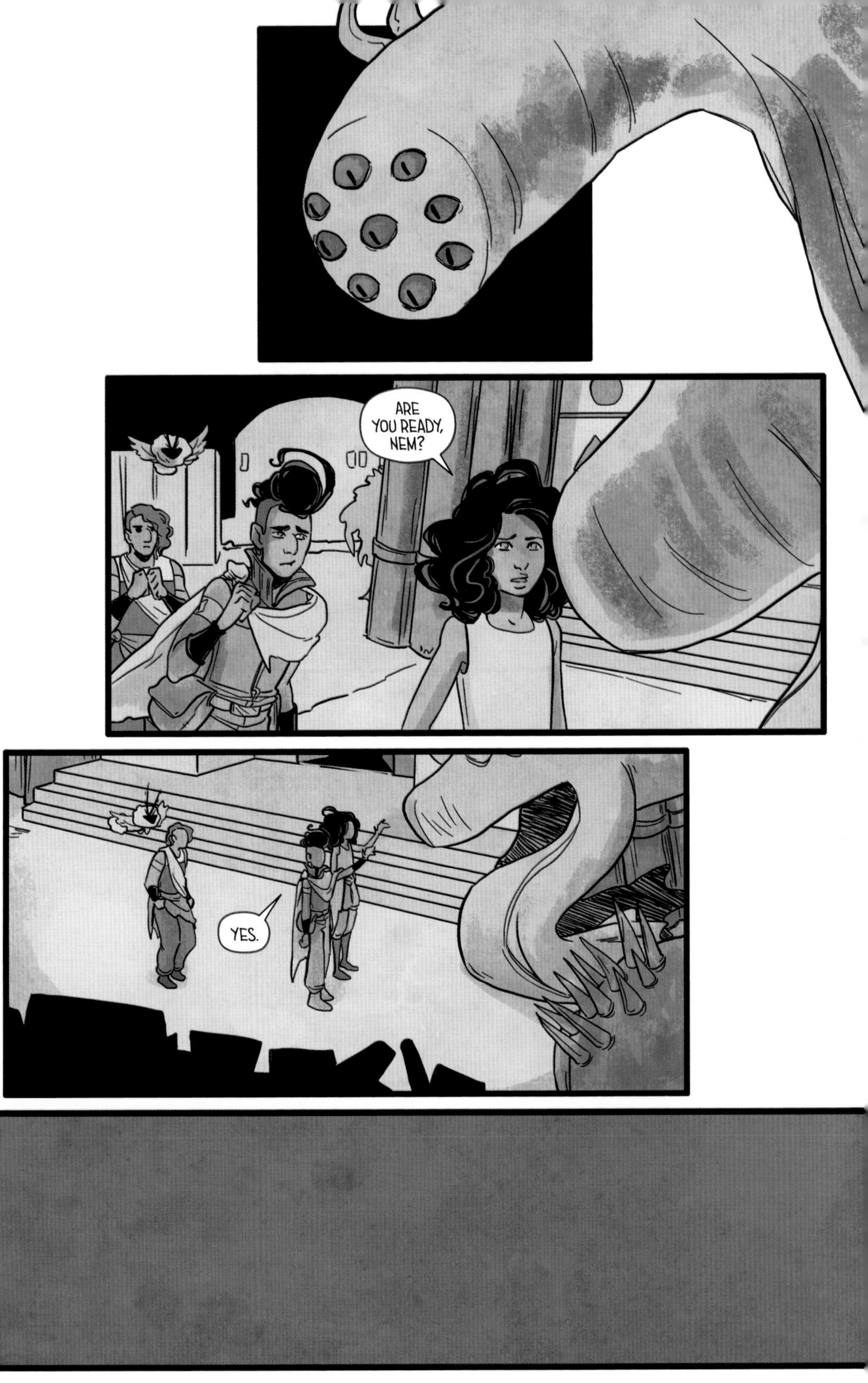
ARE YOU READY, NEM?
YES.

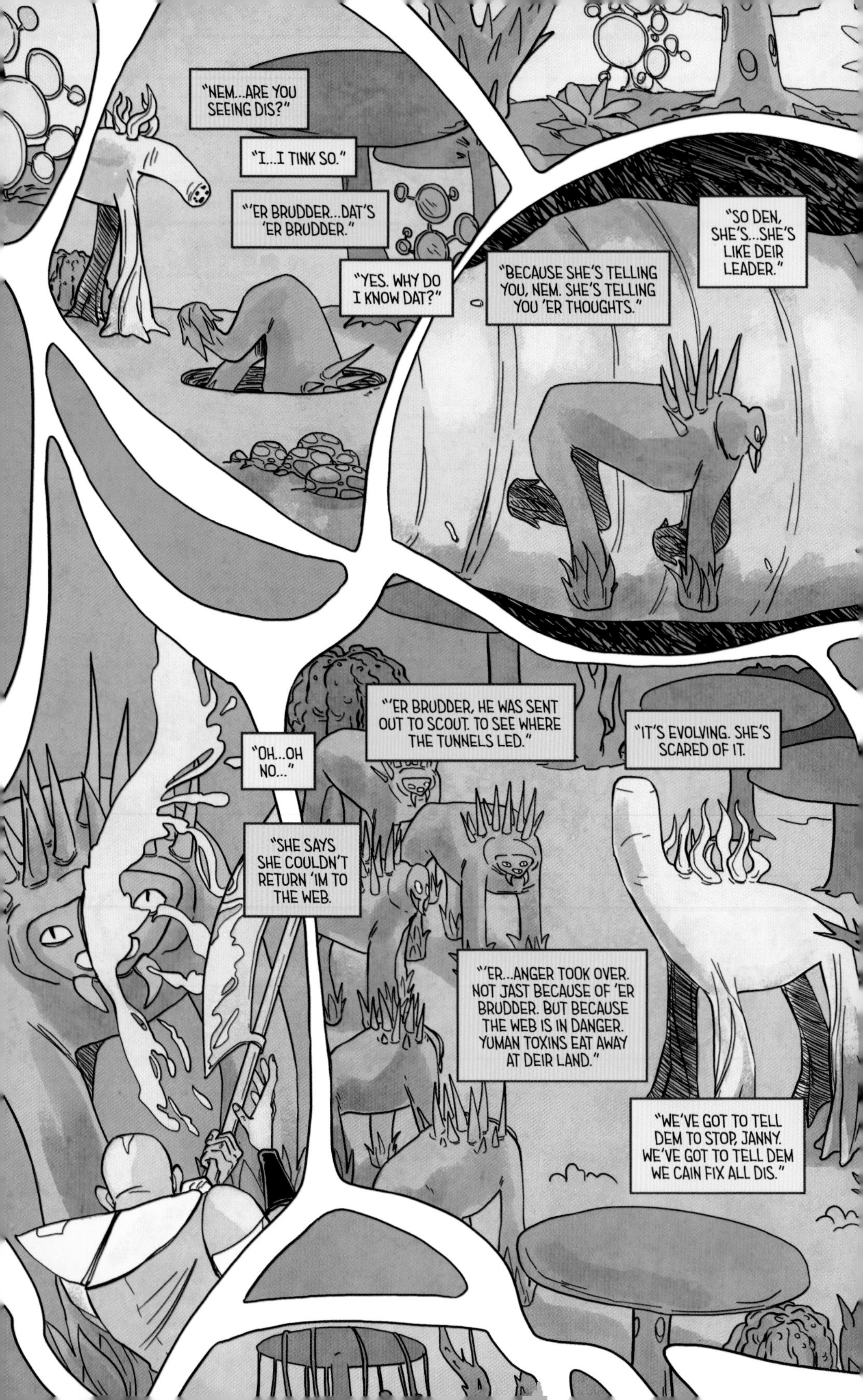
"NEM...ARE YOU SEEING DIS?"
"I...I TINK SO."
"'ER BRUDDER...DAT'S 'ER BRUDDER."
"YES. WHY DO I KNOW DAT?"
"BECAUSE SHE'S TELLING YOU, NEM. SHE'S TELLING YOU 'ER THOUGHTS."
"SO DEN, SHE'S...SHE'S LIKE DEIR LEADER."
"OH...OH NO..."
"'ER BRUDDER, HE WAS SENT OUT TO SCOUT. TO SEE WHERE THE TUNNELS LED."
"IT'S EVOLVING. SHE'S SCARED OF IT.
"SHE SAYS SHE COULDN'T RETURN 'IM TO THE WEB.
"'ER...ANGER TOOK OVER. NOT JAST BECAUSE OF 'ER BRUDDER. BUT BECAUSE THE WEB IS IN DANGER. YUMAN TOXINS EAT AWAY AT DEIR LAND."
"WE'VE GOT TO TELL DEM TO STOP, JANNY. WE'VE GOT TO TELL DEM WE CAIN FIX ALL DIS."

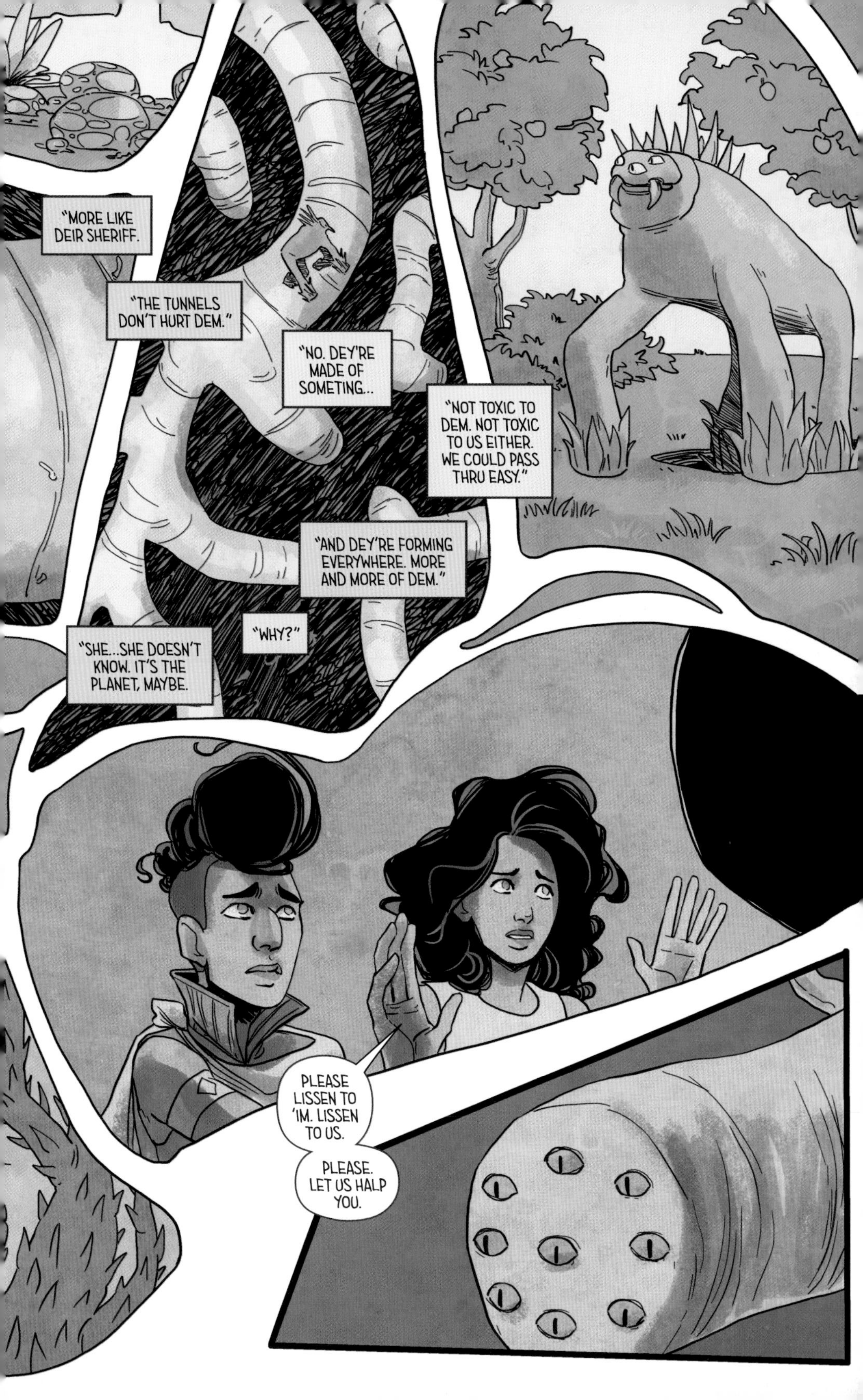
"MORE LIKE DEIR SHERIFF.
"THE TUNNELS DON'T HURT DEM."
"NO. DEY'RE MADE OF SOMETING...
"NOT TOXIC TO DEM. NOT TOXIC TO US EITHER. WE COULD PASS THRU EASY."
"AND DEY'RE FORMING EVERYWHERE. MORE AND MORE OF DEM."
"WHY?"
"SHE...SHE DOESN'T KNOW. IT'S THE PLANET, MAYBE.
PLEASE LISSEN TO 'IM. LISSEN TO US.
PLEASE. LET US HALP YOU.

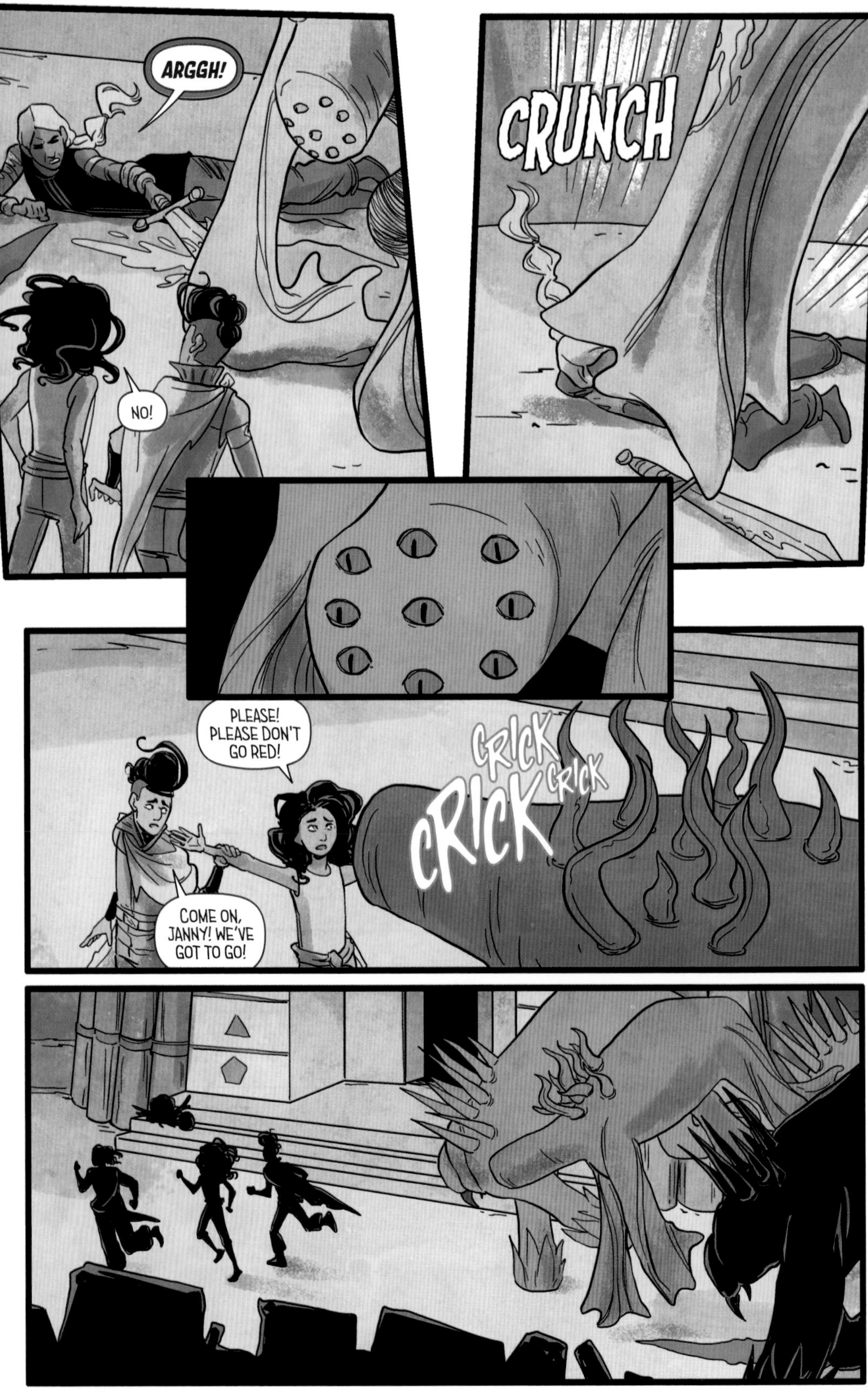
ARGGH!
NO!
CRUNCH
PLEASE! PLEASE DON'T GO RED!
COME ON, JANNY! WE'VE GOT TO GO!
CRICK
CRICK
CRICK

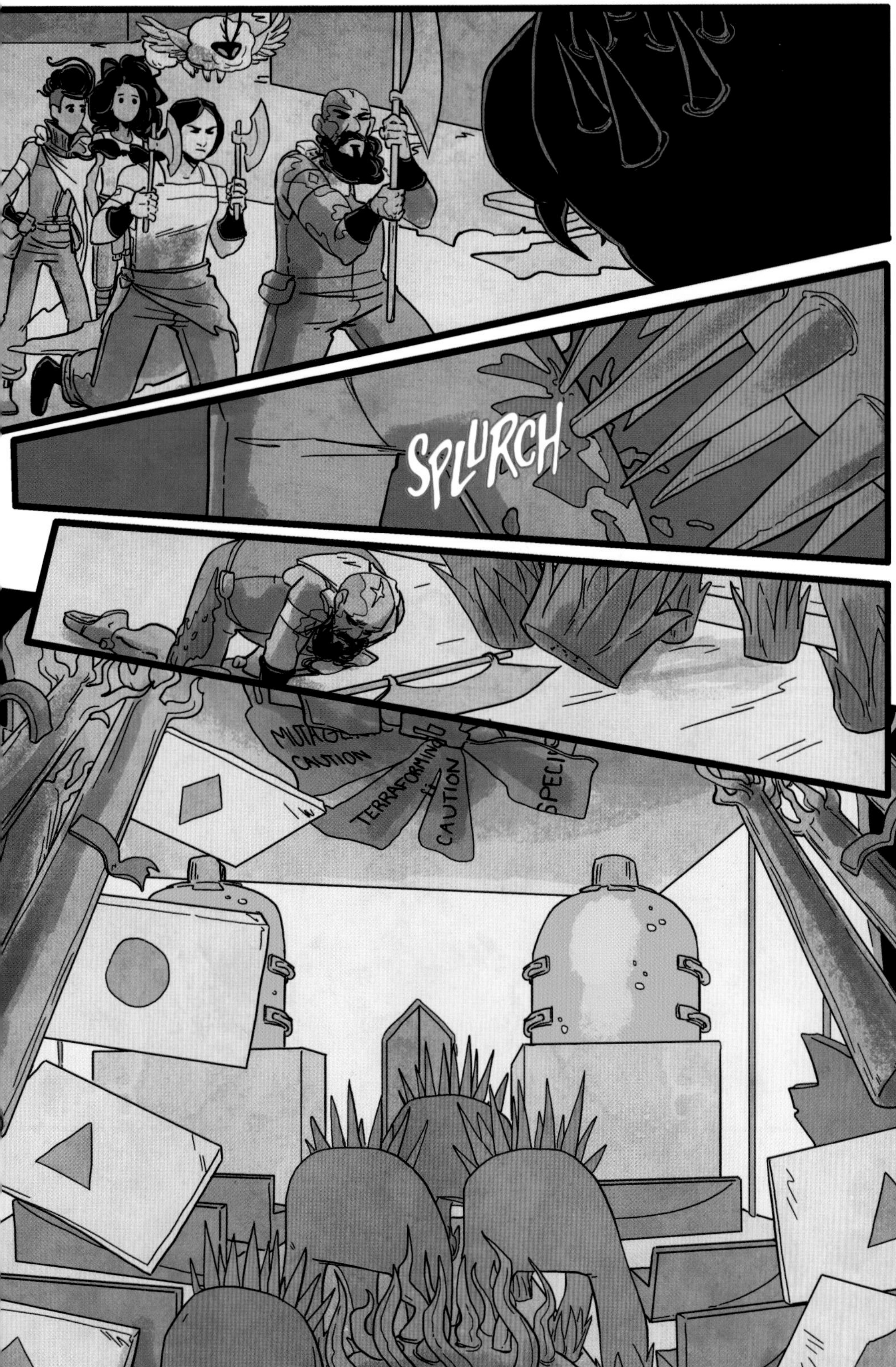
SPLURCH
CAUTION
TERRAFORMING
CAUTION

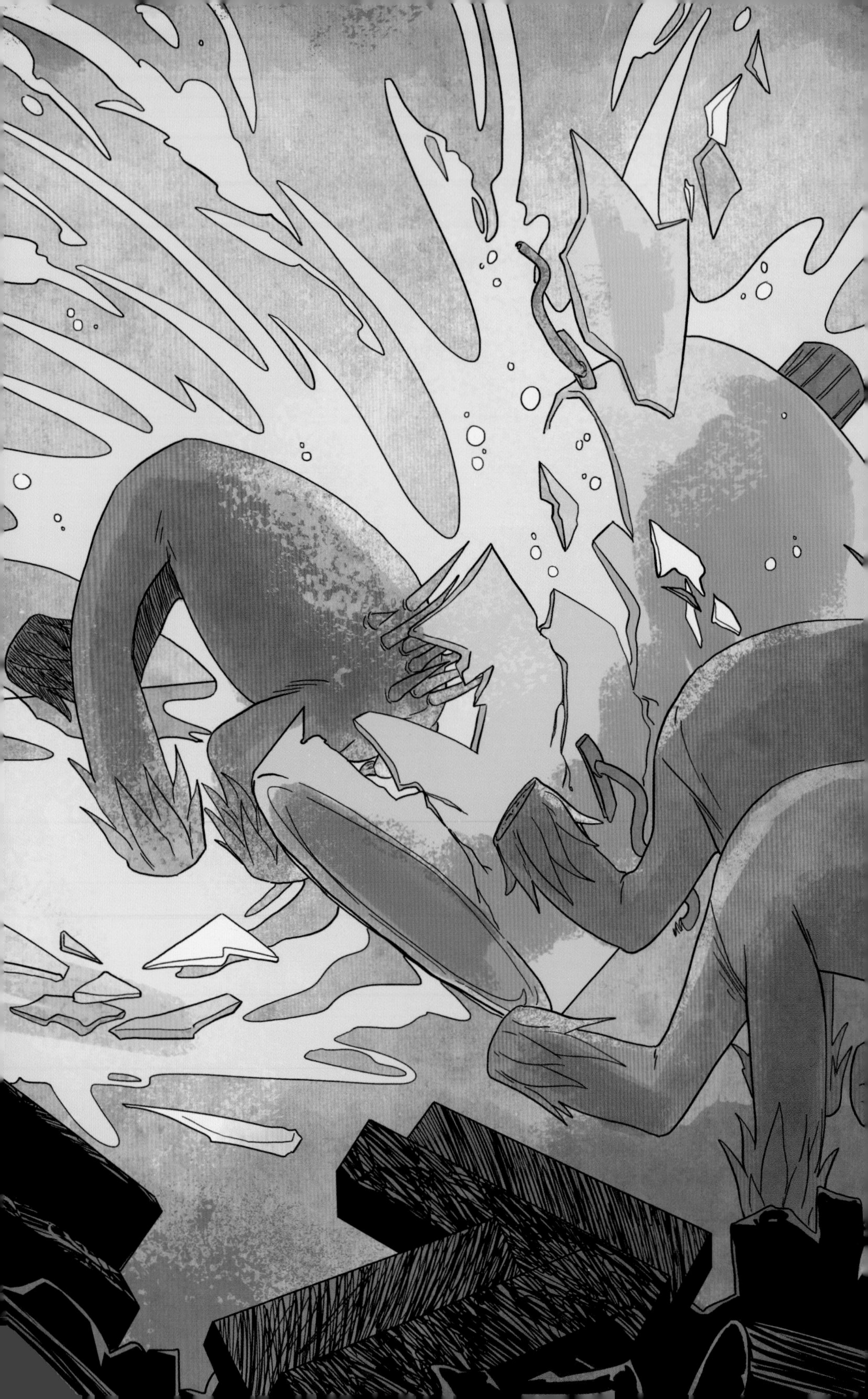

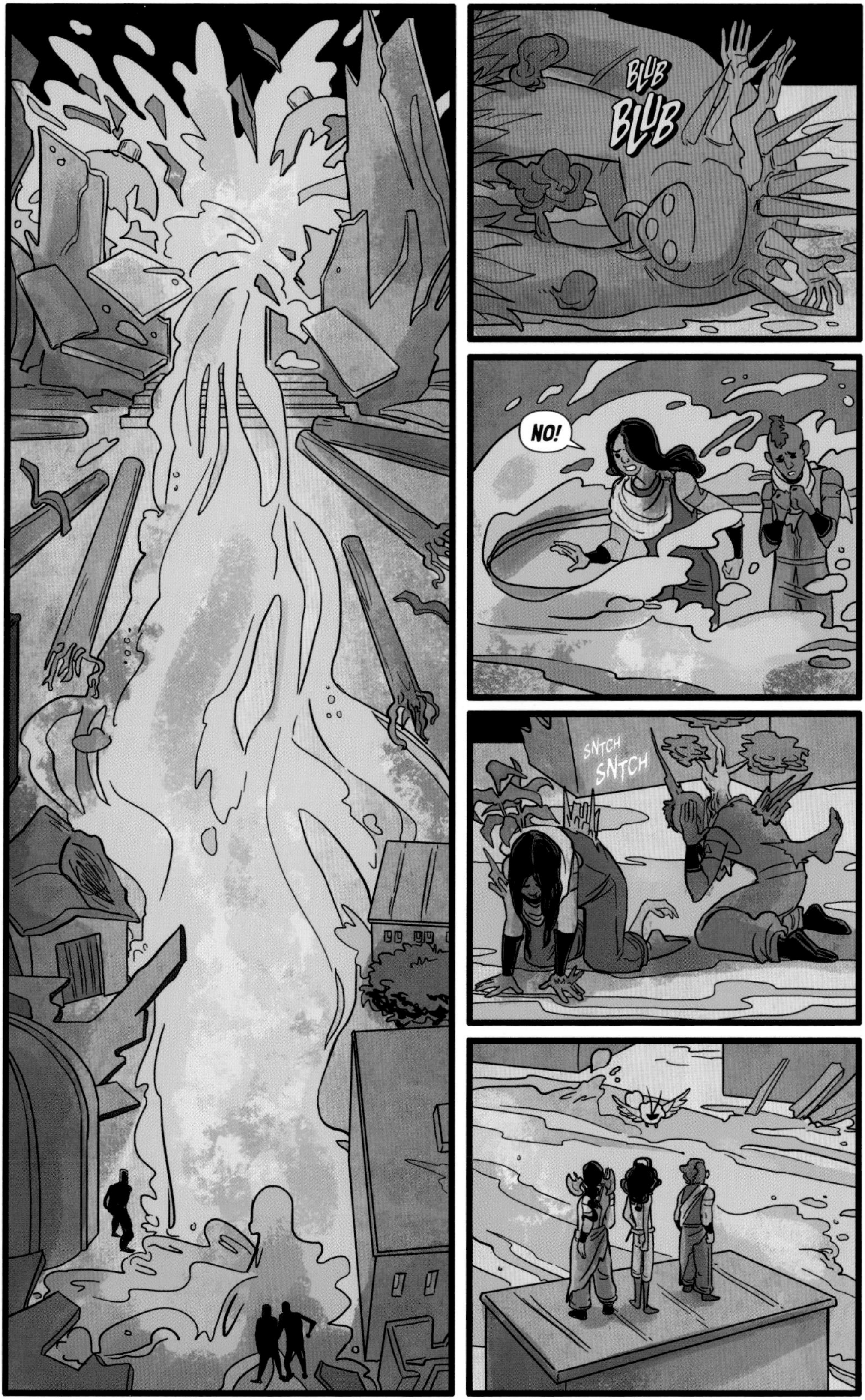
BLUB
BLUB
NO!
SNTCH
SNTCH

AAAAA!
PSSHHH

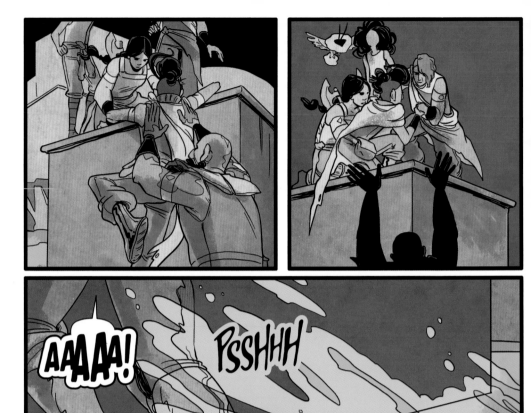

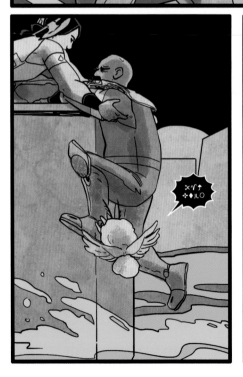

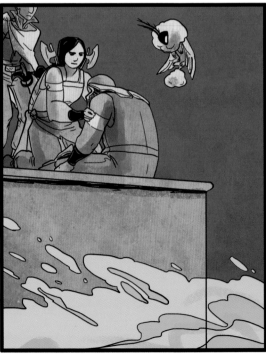

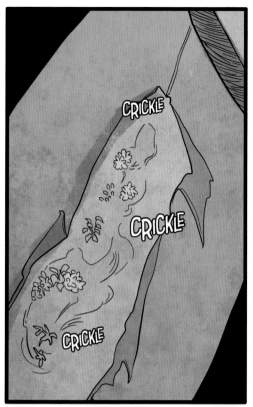

CRICKLE

CRICKLE

CRICKLE

MIGAL... YOUR LEG.

IT...IT'S HEALED.

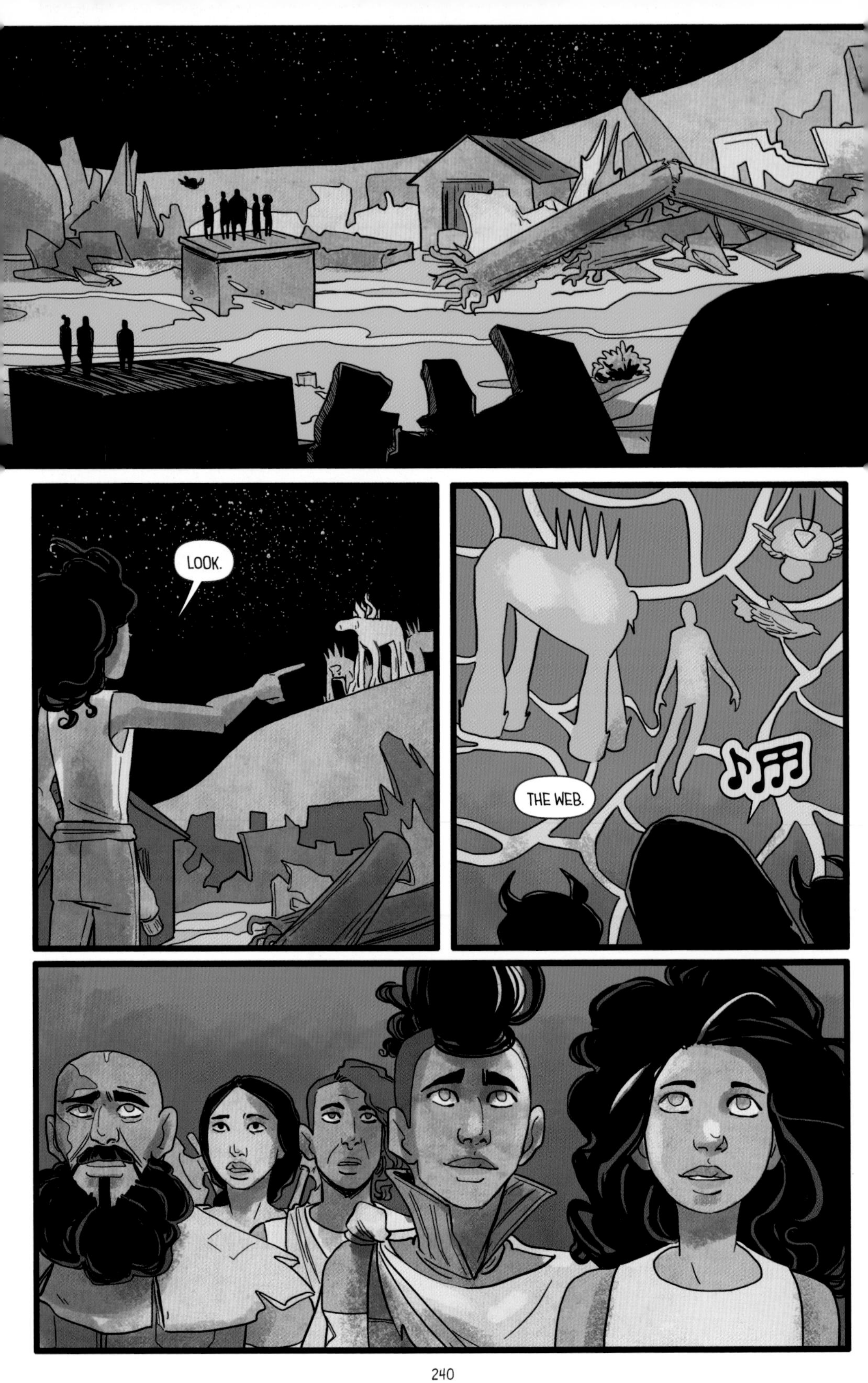
LOOK.
THE WEB.
♪♫

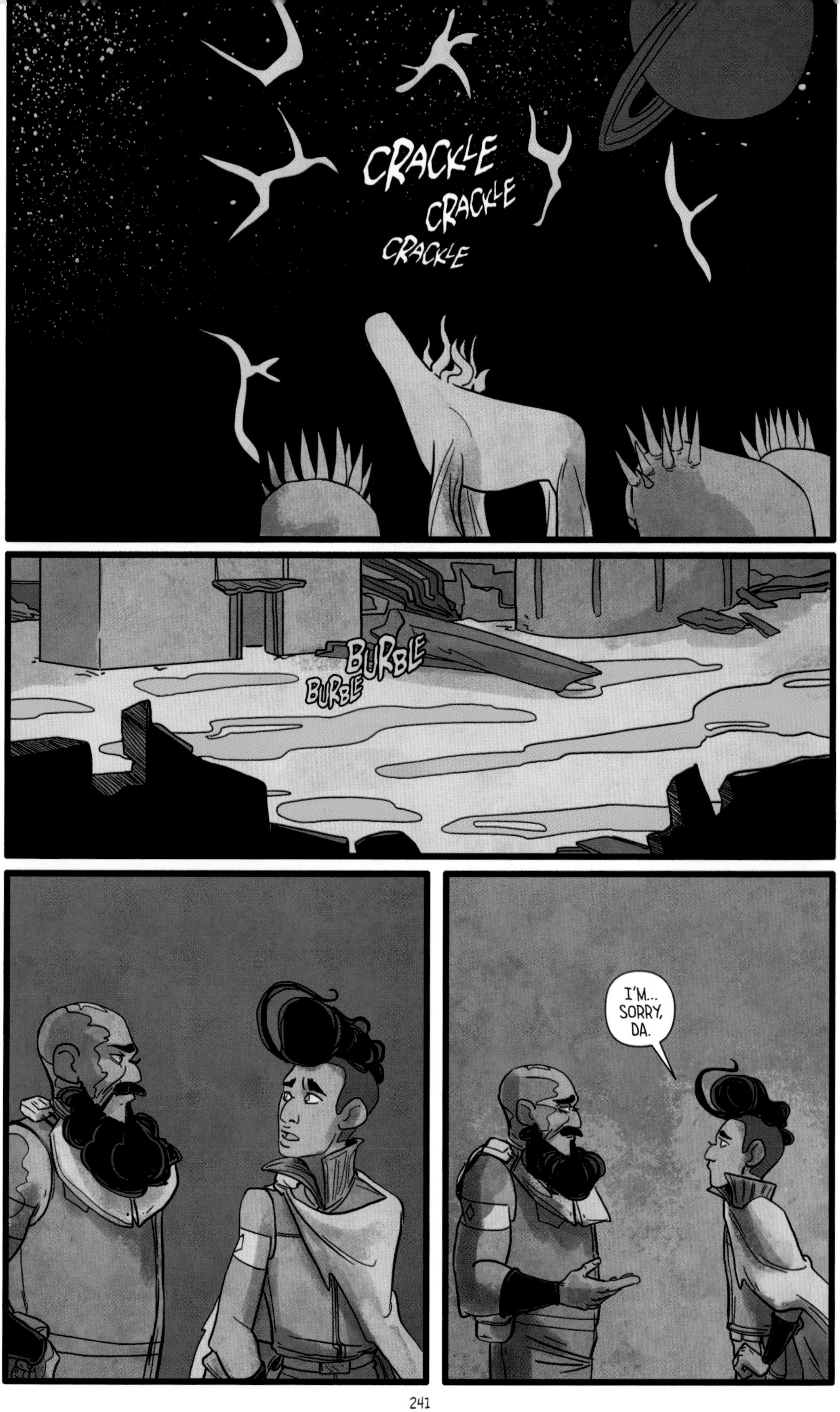
CRACKLE
CRACKLE
CRACKLE
BURBLE
BURBLE
I'M... SORRY, DA.

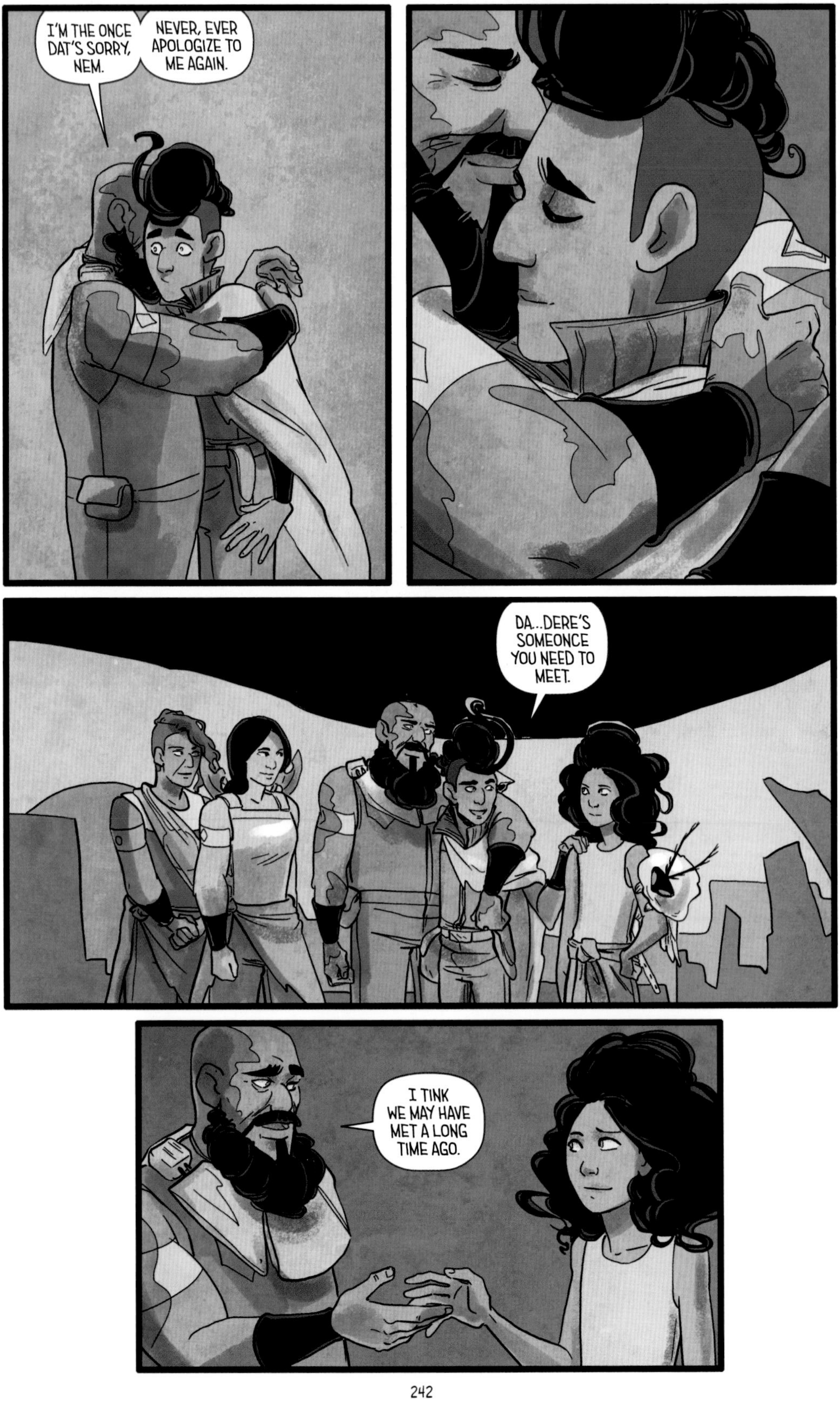
I'M THE ONCE DAT'S SORRY, NEM.
NEVER, EVER APOLOGIZE TO ME AGAIN.
DA...DERE'S SOMEONCE YOU NEED TO MEET.
I TINK WE MAY HAVE MET A LONG TIME AGO.

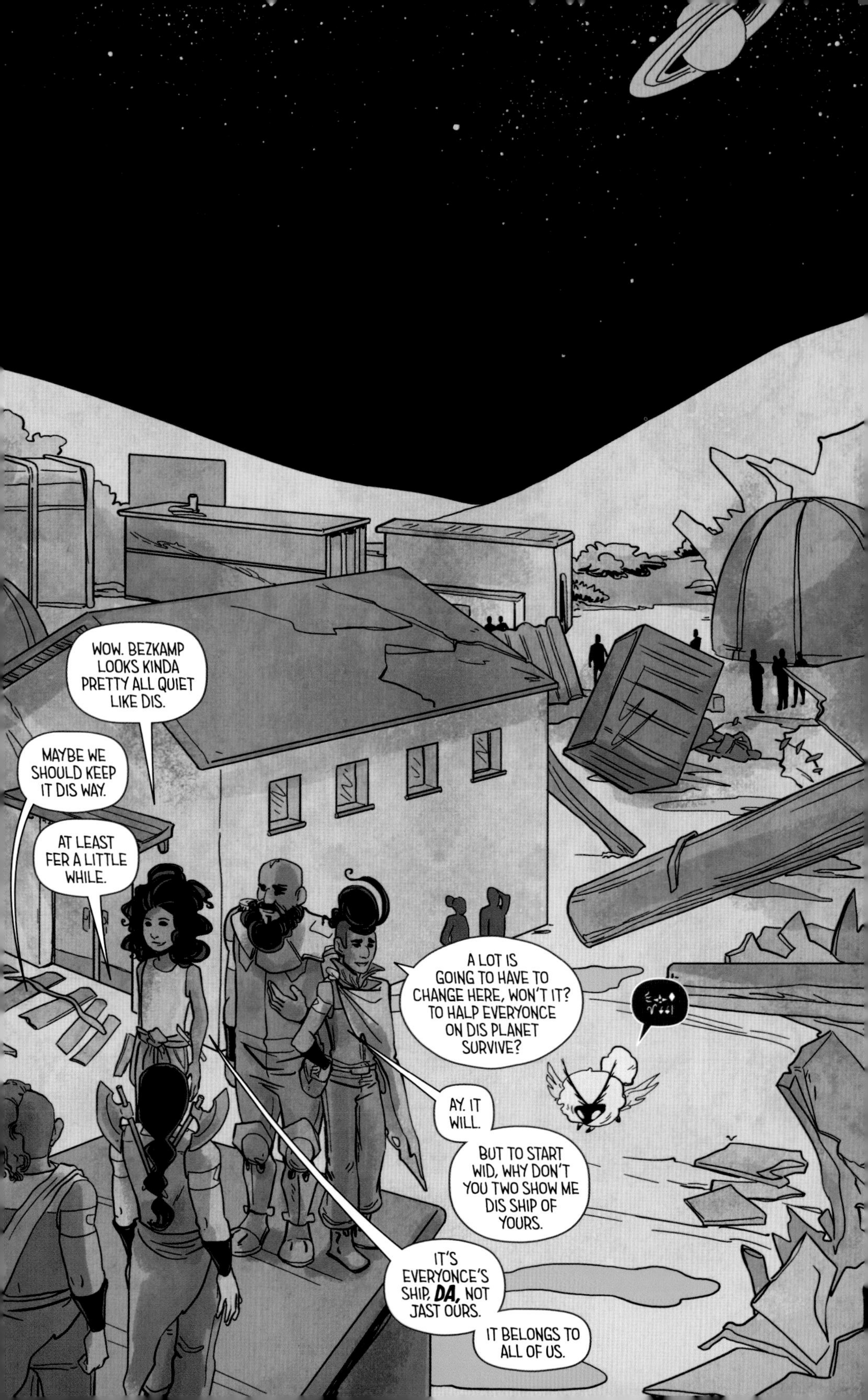
WOW. BEZKAMP LOOKS KINDA PRETTY ALL QUIET LIKE DIS.
MAYBE WE SHOULD KEEP IT DIS WAY.
AT LEAST FER A LITTLE WHILE.
A LOT IS GOING TO HAVE TO CHANGE HERE, WON'T IT? TO HALP EVERYONCE ON DIS PLANET SURVIVE?
AY. IT WILL.
BUT TO START WID, WHY DON'T YOU TWO SHOW ME DIS SHIP OF YOURS.
IT'S EVERYONCE'S SHIP, **DA,** NOT JAST OURS.
IT BELONGS TO ALL OF US.

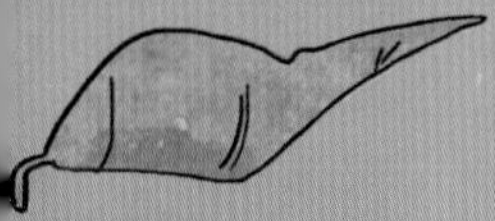

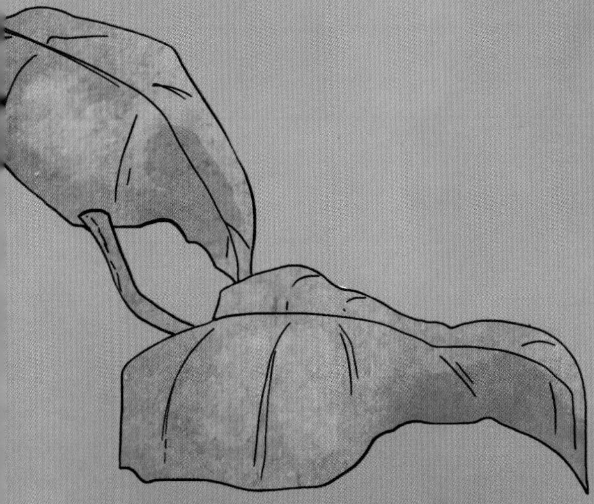

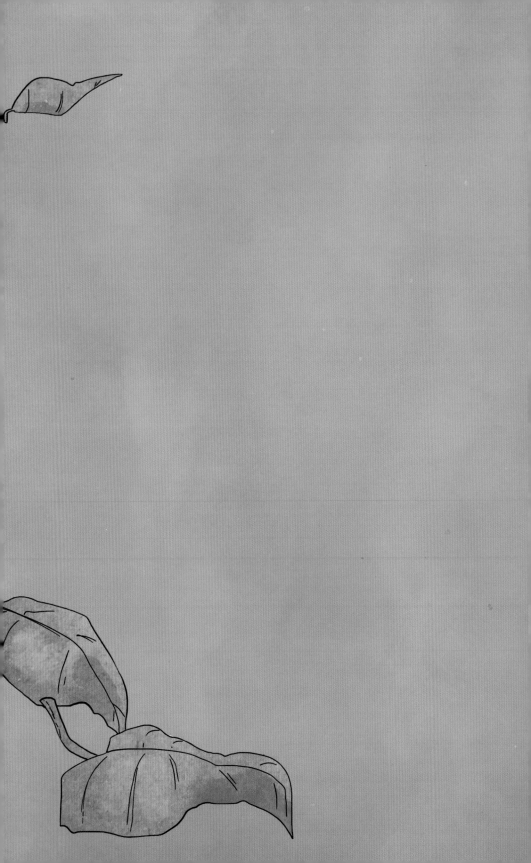

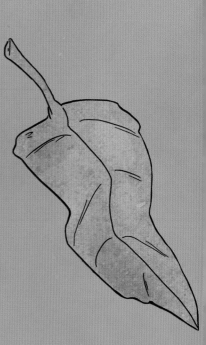

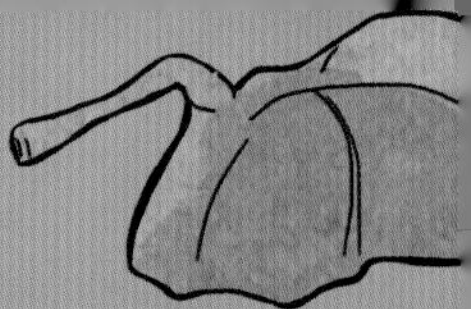

EPILOGUE

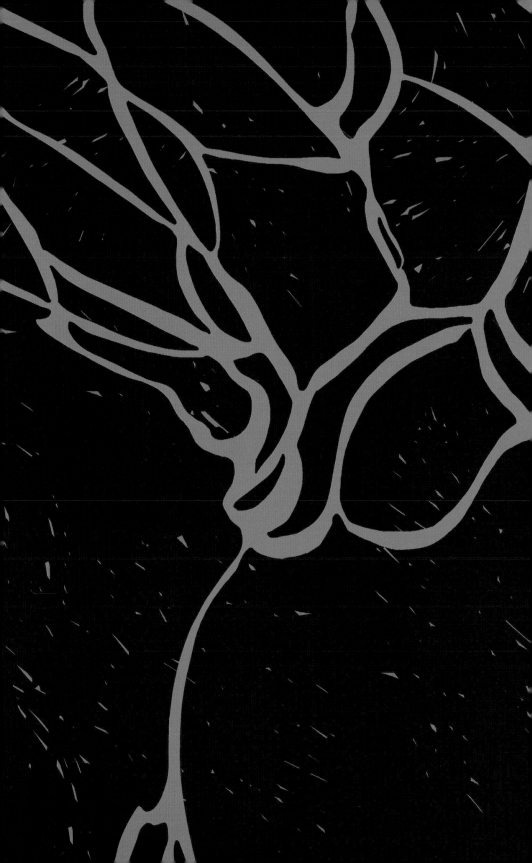

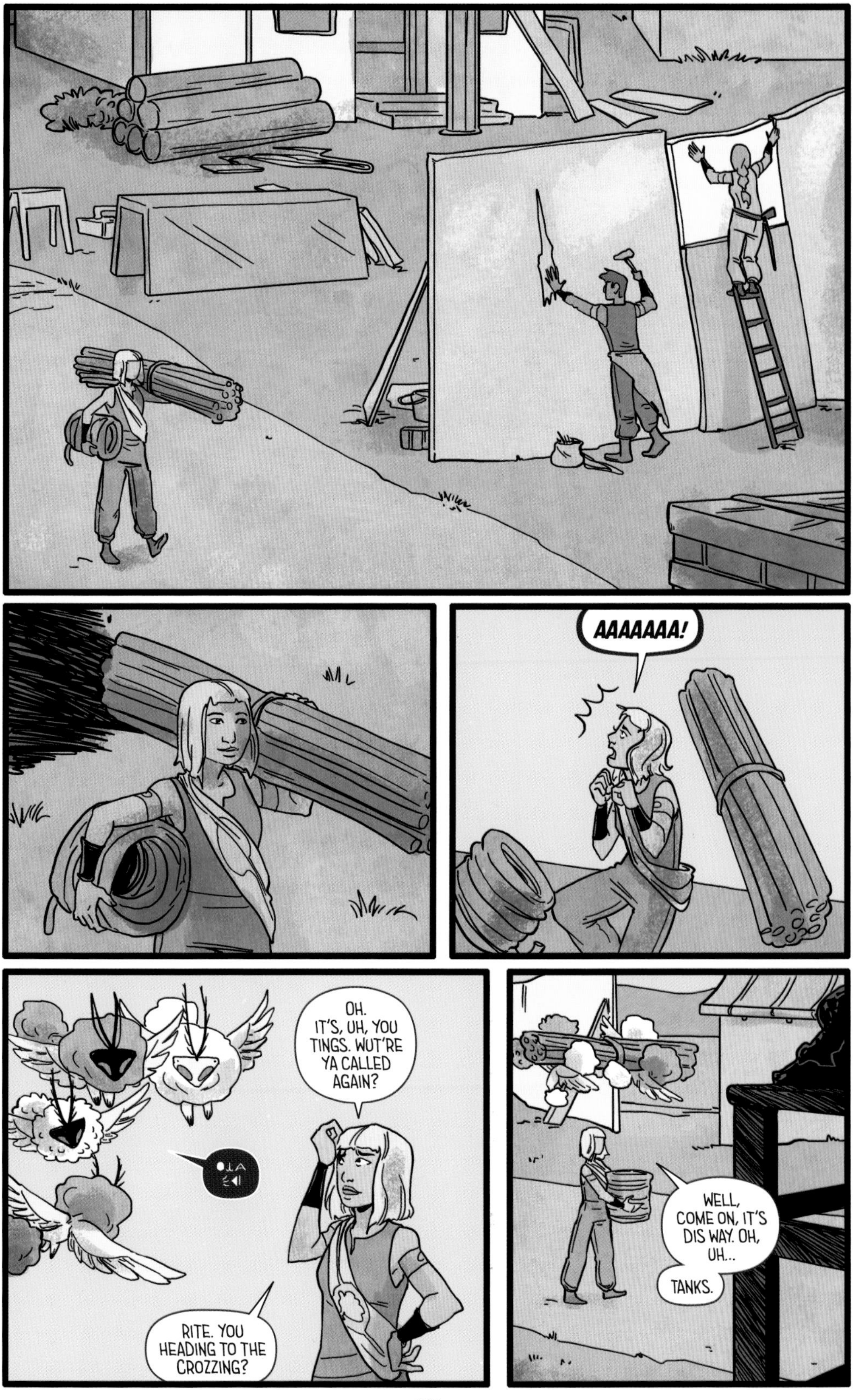
AAAAAAA!
OH. IT'S, UH, YOU TINGS. WUT'RE YA CALLED AGAIN?
RITE. YOU HEADING TO THE CROZZING?
WELL, COME ON, IT'S DIS WAY. OH, UH...
TANKS.

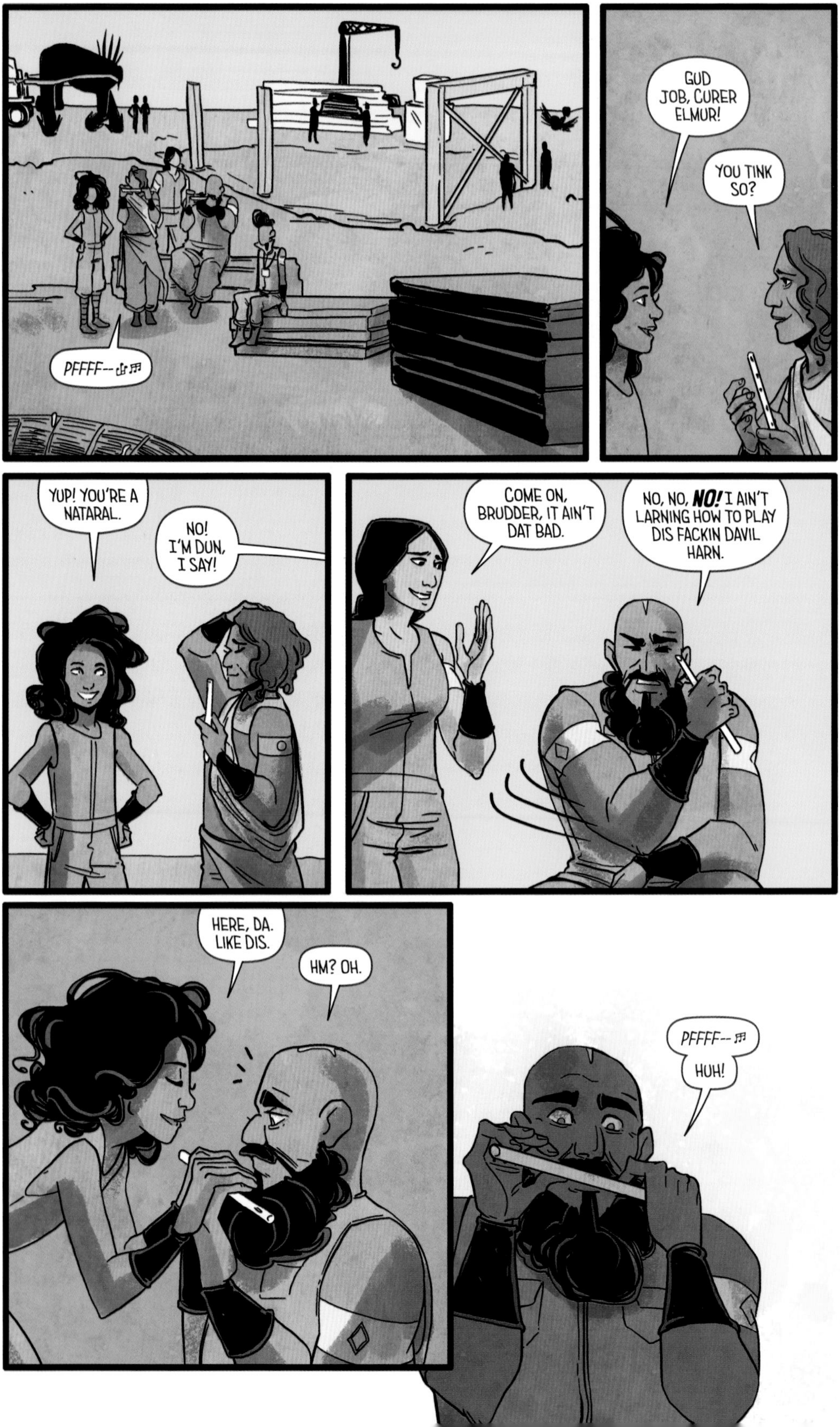
PFFFF--
GUD JOB, CURER ELMUR!
YOU TINK SO?
YUP! YOU'RE A NATARAL.
NO! I'M DUN, I SAY!
COME ON, BRUDDER, IT AIN'T DAT BAD.
NO, NO, **NO!** I AIN'T LARNING HOW TO PLAY DIS FACKIN DAVIL HARN.
HERE, DA. LIKE DIS.
HM? OH.
PFFFF--
HUH!

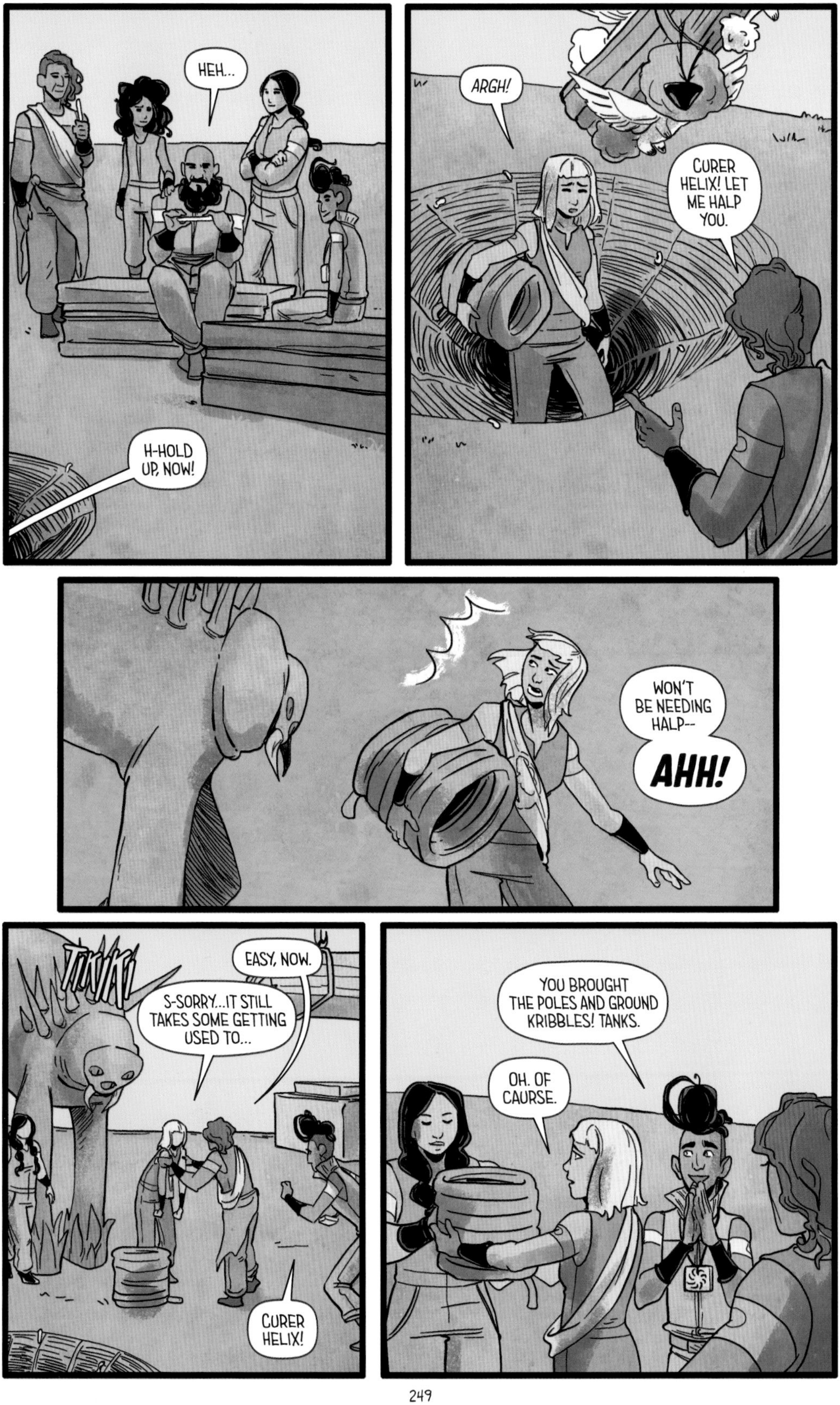
HEH...
H-HOLD UP, NOW!
ARGH!
CURER HELIX! LET ME HALP YOU.
WON'T BE NEEDING HALP--
AHH!
TIKIKI
EASY, NOW.
S-SORRY...IT STILL TAKES SOME GETTING USED TO...
CURER HELIX!
YOU BROUGHT THE POLES AND GROUND KRIBBLES! TANKS.
OH. OF CAURSE.

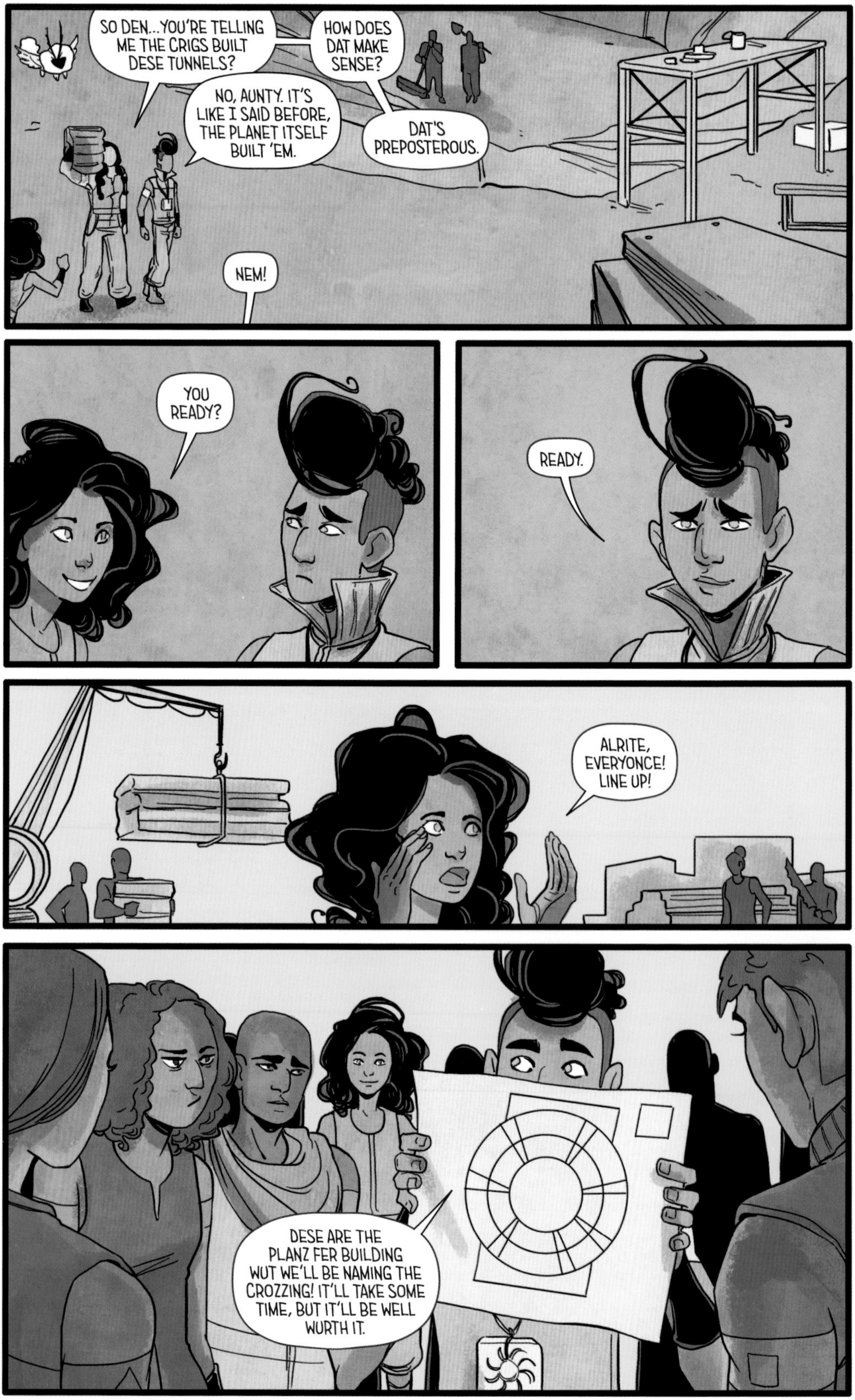
SO DEN...YOU'RE TELLING ME THE CRIGS BUILT DESE TUNNELS?
HOW DOES DAT MAKE SENSE?
NO, AUNTY. IT'S LIKE I SAID BEFORE, THE PLANET ITSELF BUILT 'EM.
DAT'S PREPOSTEROUS.
NEM!
YOU READY?
READY.
ALRITE, EVERYONCE! LINE UP!
DESE ARE THE PLANZ FER BUILDING WUT WE'LL BE NAMING THE CROZZING! IT'LL TAKE SOME TIME, BUT IT'LL BE WELL WURTH IT.

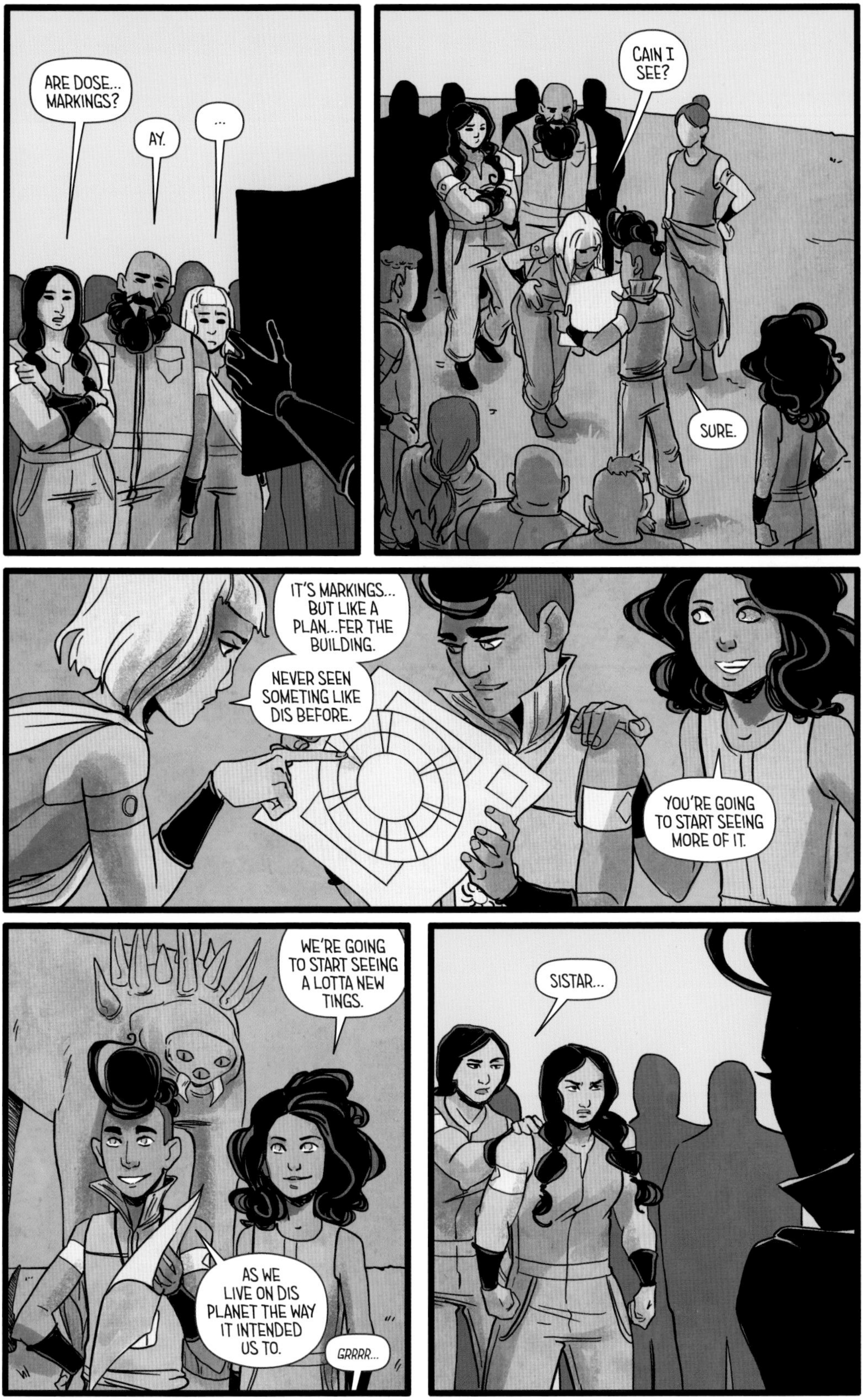
ARE DOSE... MARKINGS?
AY.
...
CAIN I SEE?
SURE.
IT'S MARKINGS... BUT LIKE A PLAN...FER THE BUILDING.
NEVER SEEN SOMETING LIKE DIS BEFORE.
YOU'RE GOING TO START SEEING MORE OF IT.
WE'RE GOING TO START SEEING A LOTTA NEW TINGS.
AS WE LIVE ON DIS PLANET THE WAY IT INTENDED US TO.
GRRRR...
SISTAR...

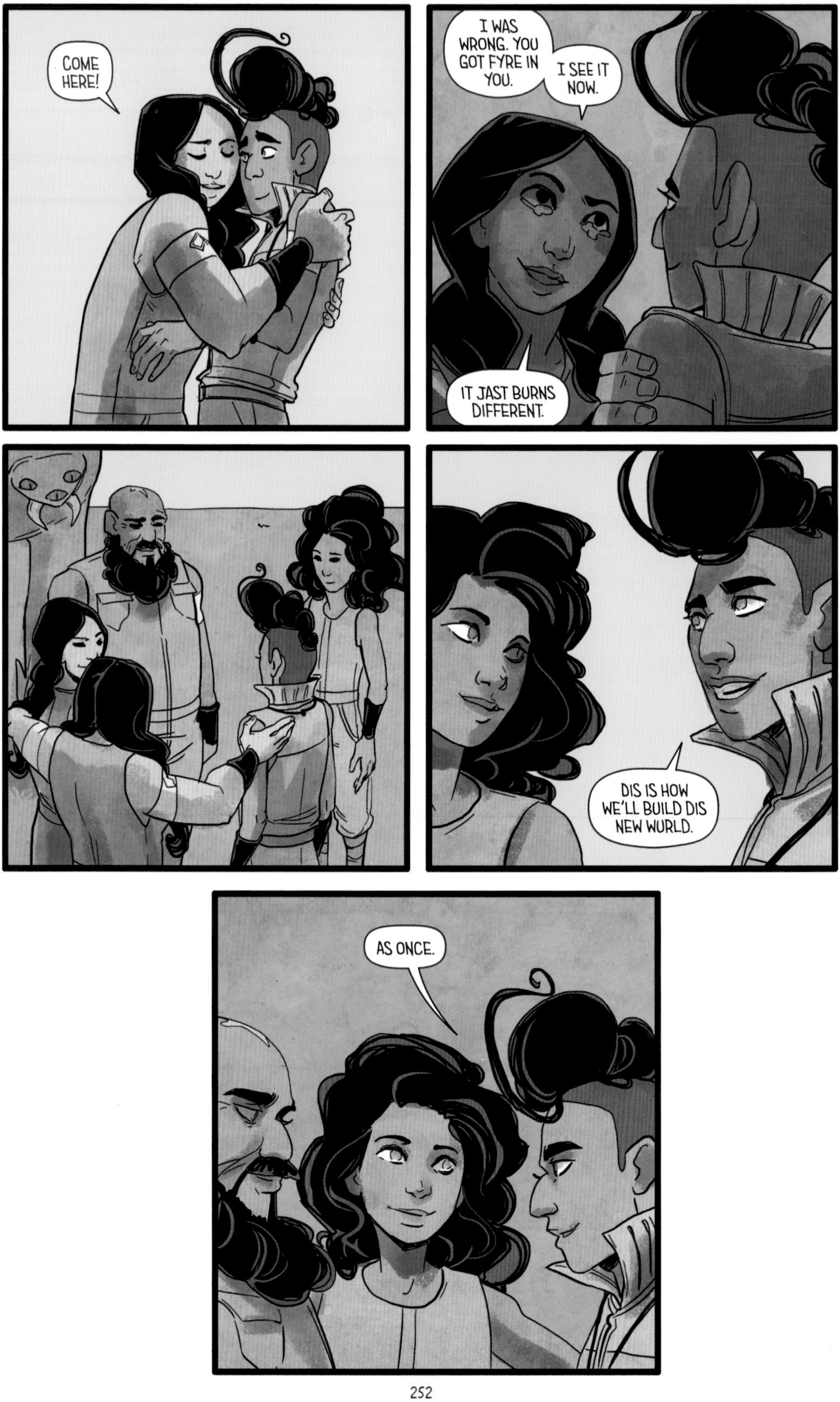
COME HERE!
I WAS WRONG. YOU GOT FYRE IN YOU.
I SEE IT NOW.
IT JAST BURNS DIFFERENT.
DIS IS HOW WE'LL BUILD DIS NEW WURLD.
AS ONCE.

ACKNOWLEDGMENTS

I want to thank so many people, but if I must narrow it down for the sake of good manners, then I'll start with editors Andrea Colvin and Grace Bornhoft, who helped find this story's pulse, and curb it's indulgences. To my agent Dara Hyde, who believed in *Bezkamp* (and me, years ago) to begin with, and pushed me to go outside my comfort zone. To my jerkface cats, Inigo Montoya and Leeloo, and to my wife, Melanie, without whom I'd likely be sitting on a stump somewhere, yelling at clouds.

-Sam

Thanks so much to Janelle Peters, whose support means everything to me, always; my studio (Morgan Beem, Jorge Corona, Jeremy Lawson, Sarah Stern, and David Stoll) whose encouragement kept me going; and K. Uvick, whose flatting work on this book saved the day.

-Jen

BIOS

SAM SATTIN is a writer and coffee addict. He is the words behind the *Glint* trilogy, *Legend, The Silent End, League of Somebodies*, and *Adventure Quest*. His work has appeared or been featured in *The Nib, The Atlantic, NPR,* and elsewhere. He holds an MFA in comics from California College of the Arts and has a creative writing MFA from Mills College. The creative director of a toy company in Oakland, California, he sometimes teaches at the California College of the Arts and lives with his wife/assassin and two cats.

JEN HICKMAN is a visual storyteller and a graduate of the Savannah College of Art and Design's sequential art program. Past work includes *TEST, Moth & Whisper, Jem and the Holograms,* the *Femme Magnifique* anthology, and more. They get really excited about dystopian fiction, good coffee, and drawing hands.

Written by **SAMUEL SATTIN**
Illusrated by **JEN HICKMAN**
Letters by **AW'S DAVID HOPKINS**
Color Assistance by **K. UVICK**
Proofreading Assistance by **MEREDITH WALLACE**

ROAR™

Library of Congress Control Number: 2019936692

ISBN: 978-1-5493-0404-0

10 9 8 7 6 5 4 3 2 1